PRAISE FOR THE POWERFUL STORYTELLING OF ANDREW M. GREELEY AND HIS MOST COMPELLING NOVEL EVER...

Rite of Spring

*   *   *

"Greeley's vivid imagination has spun a fine . . . gripping tale with a dollop of psychic phenomena, a dose of international terrorism and espionage and a potpourri of passion."

—United Press International

*   *   *

"He writes of love and passion, risks and pursuits, high adventure and the generosity of winning."

—*Pittsburgh Press*

*   *   *

"Plenty of energetic action . . . with an appealing spiritual dimension."

—*Irish America*

*   *   *

"Andrew M. Greeley is a fascinating novelist . . . with a rare, possibly unmatched, point of view."

—*Los Angeles Times*

*   *   *

more . . .

Rite of Spring

Andrew M. Greeley

WARNER BOOKS

A Warner Communications Company

For the Kenskis

Henry
Margaret
Kate
Carolyn
Erin Noele

WARNER BOOKS EDITION

Book design by H. Roberts
Maps by Heidi Hornaday

Warner Books, Inc.
666 Fifth Avenue
New York, N.Y. 10103

 A Warner Communications Company

Printed in the United States of America

This book was originally published in hardcover by Warner Books.
First Printed in Paperback: November, 1988

10 9 8 7 6 5 4 3 2 1

NOTE

Like all the men and women who live in the Time Between the Stars, Brendan Ryan is a creature of my imagination. The City and the Neighborhood and the Beach might be better places if the Ryan clan were God's creatures rather than mine. But, for weal or woe, they correspond to no one in what is loosely called the real world. Msgr. John Blackwood Ryan is like no known rector of Holy Name Cathedral.

Cindasoo, who will return later, God willing, speaks authentic AE (Appalachian English, a variant of American English) and is not intended to be a stereotype. In fact, she "talks funny" partly because it's fun, partly to protect herself, and partly because she is a covert Appalachian militant.

—AG

All things rising, all things sizing
Mary sees, sympathizing
With that world of good,
Nature's motherhood.
Their magnifying of each its kind
With delight calls to mind
How did she in her stored
Magnify the Lord.

—*Gerard Manley Hopkins*
"May Magnificat"

You have seen, Thomas, and have believed. Blessed are those who have not seen and yet believe.
—Gospel of the Second Sunday of Easter, Cycle A

Passion is but one manifestation of hope, the trickiest of God's games.
—*Msgr. John Blackwood Ryan*

one
A
MORNING
IN
SPRING

1

I wanted the woman, body and soul, as badly as I had ever wanted anything in all my life.

I had entered Dufficy's Irish Store on Michigan Avenue to buy a present for my daughter, Jean, a student at Stanford, who was going to Ireland for the summer.

The woman and I had exchanged a few words, a couple of quickly averted glances. I could hardly remember what she looked like when I stumbled out of the store.

Yet she was my destiny. I knew it. So, it seemed, did she.

The image of her body, pliant and happy under mine, hit me as I was leaving the store. I must have her. I, Brendan Ryan, the quietest of quiet men, had made up his mind.

I must have her. I would have her.

Soon.

Thus spring came violently to Michigan Avenue the last week in April, and with it the beginning of my fall from grace.

I leaned against the window of Stuart Brent's bookstore as exhausted as though I had run four miles. The gentle touch of a morning breeze against my face hinted at the caress of a woman's hand. The delicious lethargy that pervaded my body suggested that I had been enfolded in her embrace, her breasts pressed soothingly against my chest. My lightweight gray suit, prudently withdrawn from mothballs after I had heard the morning weather forecast on WFMT, was already wilted. My tailor-made broadcloth shirt was soaked with sweat.

What did she look like? I must remember. A smile, a soft voice with a touch of the brogue, a white dress, a delicate and tasteful scent . . . nothing more: the beginning, perhaps, of Brendan Ryan's foolish pursuit of the Holy Grail.

Should I return to Dufficy's Irish Store and look again? No, that would be a mistake. I must not be late for the discussion of my tangled financial and legal affairs with Nick and Eileen. Already they thought I was not serious enough about the litigation.

As other pedestrians brushed by, barely aware of my existence, and autos crowded noisily toward the Ohio Street access to the Outer Drive, I looked down at the neatly wrapped package in my hand—the elegant green and white paper emphasizing Dufficy's image as Irish indeed, but Michigan Avenue Irish. *Ruins of Medieval Ireland*, a present for my daughter Jean who hoped to go to Ireland in pursuit of her new career as a photographer—a career discovered a few months before in a first-quarter sophomore class at Stanford. The wrapping was wet from my perspiring fingers.

I tried to dry my hand on the sleeve of my jacket; it would go to the cleaners that night anyway. Jean hated me. Her suggestion that we have dinner before she returned to Palo Alto for exams was doubtless designed merely to extract money from me for the Irish trip, money that her mother wouldn't give her. Yet her interest in Ireland matched my own. She would not notice the sweat-smudged paper. Compulsively fastidious as always, I wanted the present to be perfect.

It was not that hot yet. High in the low eighties, said the announcer, as usual with the educated solemnity of a distinguished professor's inaugural address. It was no more than seventy at ten o'clock in the morning. I was sweating not from the heat, but from a sudden and furious outburst of sexual passion, totally unexpected and barely resisted.

I should be ashamed, I told myself resolutely. I should

summon the energy to detach myself from the window of Stuart Brent's—filled with colorful books about African art, I noted absently—and proceed with all deliberate speed to the prestigious offices of Minor Gray and Blatt, the firm to which Nick and Eileen and I all owed our legal allegiance.

I felt no shame or guilt. Rather, I was as exultant as a teen-age boy with a crush on a new girl in the neighborhood. I stepped toward the door of Dufficy's, proudly marked with a quote from Yeats, as though to establish that it did indeed belong on the Magnificent Mile, cheek by jowl with Stuart Brent's, at least as snobbish as the supercilious bookstore if not more so.

I had to know what she really looked like.

As I write these words, the face and figure are already fading from my memory. I try to recapture those first paralyzingly vivid impressions with the melancholy realization that I may well have created them myself, that Ciara had no existence other than in my imagination.

I do not think of myself as a passionate man. I am sure my friends and associates would agree with this judgment. There was relatively little sex in my marriage. Madonna, my former wife (if, in these days of lunch-counter ecclesiastical annulments, that is the proper term for her), claimed not to enjoy sex. After Jean's birth and several unsuccessful attempts to establish a pattern of normal sexual relations (whatever that term may mean), I found that I did not enjoy it much either. Our moments of passion were occasional, the occasion usually being when Madonna had had a few more drinks than she could manage and turned, if I may use the word, lewd. While these brief incidents were exceedingly pleasurable, I did not look forward to them with much eagerness. I assumed, since I felt no need to seek a lover or have recourse to prostitutes, that I was at the low end of the curve of sexual need.

In forty-two years of life I had made love to only one woman, both rarely and poorly. Therefore I was utterly unprepared on a warm day in April to step off Michigan Avenue and, surrounded by Aran Island sweaters and Waterford crystal, into a sexual encounter so peremptory that I would walk out a few moments later as soaking wet as though I had been jogging in a steam bath.

The interlude was brief, a minute or two at the most. A

book chosen, a few words exchanged, a package wrapped, a bill paid, a receipt neatly folded into my wallet. Yet I knew after my first glance at her shy smile behind the cash register that here was the woman for whom I had waited all my life.

My temptation, as violent as a spring morning with tornado warnings posted, was hardly to rape. Already I adored the woman. I would make her mine forever with only the most tender seductions.

As I said, a teenage crush.

Perhaps, I thought, as I paused in front of the words of Willy Yeats, I had already possessed her and been possessed by her. I could not positively say that we had not made love. I was aware that not even our hands had touched in the exchange of book and money, receipt and package. Yet something had passed between us that had never occurred in twenty years of marriage to Madonna.

The woman in the store, the woman in the white dress with the shy smile, felt the same temptation I did. She was as frightened of it as I was. And as vehemently attracted to me as I to her.

I turned away from Dufficy's and hurried down Michigan Avenue. I must not keep my patient law partners waiting.

Now I tease the roots of my memory, searching like a dentist for a tender nerve. Fertility was much on my mind that morning, not, as it were, in the front pages of my own internal daily newspaper, but on the back pages, in the feature section, in the part of my brain over which I glance very hastily when trying to order my agenda each morning. President Reagan was embarking for China. Chris Wallace had spoken on the *Today* program from Peking as I was eating breakfast (coffee and toast). Hart and Mondale were clubbing each other into the ground. The Cubs were, unaccountably and doubtless accidentally and transiently, in first place. I had to see Nick and Eileen about possible litigation to recover some of the money taken from me by John King Sullivan, my longtime friend and commodities broker. I had scheduled a luncheon appointment and a meeting after lunch with clients nervous about their tax shelters. Then I had to talk to two overzealous IRS agents who had doubts about a tax shelter for yet another client.

Only the last gave me much promise of pleasure. Although

I avoid competitive situations as often as I can, some kind of atavistic Celtic battle lust emerges when I protect my clients from the depredations of the Service—an enemy which, in my more candid moods, I admit is faced with a difficult if not impossible task and constrained by limitations and legislation which, if I were on their side, I would despise. Yet in battle with them, Brendan Herbert George Ryan becomes, however superficially, Finn MacCool, mythological Irish warrior hero.

Invulnerable and always victorious.

Then I would revert to Brendan Ryan, ineffectual father, for supper with Jean, an uncertain encounter with a young woman who seemed a total stranger.

The fertility subtext, however, was present on my agenda for that day in spring—to change back my metaphor. Eileen Kane was pregnant, as was Catherine Curran, Nick's wife—elderly pregnancies both. Eileen had quoted her shocked obstetrician with an aloof and disdainful smile. After some preliminary grumbling, which did not appear very sincere, the two women seemed exceptionally happy and swore that the current pregnancy, elderly or not, was the easiest yet.

My daughter, whom I would meet in a few hours, was marvelously nubile, herself a lure for male reproductive urges. I rejoiced and yet felt sad. Madonna had known I wanted more children desperately. But she had insisted that the demands of raising one child were more than enough and that, anyway, she would not endure the discomforts of pregnancy again merely because I was an only child and had a kinky need for a large family.

"Large families," she had said, "are dumb. Believe me, I know."

She was the second of seven, a quarreling, contentious clan whose factional boundaries seemed to change with the seasons.

I never discussed the matter with Jean—I never discussed anything with her—but I hoped that, an only child, too, she would want several children. Grandchildren might compensate for the family I had never had. I knew that these hopes were ridiculous. Jean would protect her children from me with contempt, just as Madonna had protected Jean from me.

All these reflections are noticed only in retrospect, as I try to sort out the puzzle of the woman who apparently never existed, a masturbatory fantasy, as the psychiatrist I consulted (once) insisted.

All I was aware of that morning was that with the abrupt coming of spring warmth to Chicago and the appearance of light spring dresses, the Magnificent Mile becomes a distracting showcase of breasts and thighs, bellies and buttocks, throats and ankles, emerging instantly and dramatically at about the same time and with the same life-renewing effect as crocuses and tulips.

This was a mostly academic observation in, to switch the metaphor again, the feature pages of my brain. I dabble in scholarship, perhaps because I should have been a professor instead of a lawyer. Madonna often called me a dilettante, and I suppose the charge is valid. "Jack of all trades and master of none," she would say with her usual fine touch for an original phrase. Evolutionary biology, in any event, is one of my fields of interest. The human body, I told myself that morning, is designed to produce reactions in the body of the opposite sex that lead to reproductive and quasi pair-bonding behavior. It is interesting, I observed, superciliously, I fear, that despite our sophistication these days about sex and fertility, the same processes are going on when spring appears that did millions of years ago.

I trust I establish sufficiently my pedantry. I was engaged, or so I thought at any rate, in an abstract consideration of academic theory. None of these womanly bodies, in a wide variety of appealing shapes and ages, were to be mine. They were data rather than prizes to be pursued. Although I was technically free to remarry, I could not imagine myself ever risking that relationship again. As a Catholic, old-fashioned about sexual morality if little else, it would be unthinkable for me to take a lover.

I was not, I would have said, a tumescent adolescent ogling every neat pair of legs on Michigan Avenue.

And so, in a discreet and expensive Irish export shop, I would be seized by the same kind of primal lust that doubtless beset my male ancestors hundreds of thousands of years ago. For a woman whose physical appearance I could barely remember five minutes later, when, spent and shaken, I turned away from Dufficy's and strode down Michigan Avenue with what I hoped was brisk common sense.

There is no fool, I told myself, citing another one of Madonna's insightful dicta, like an old fool.

Later, Blackie Ryan, Eileen's brother and my cousin, would bluntly correct the dictum: "There's no fool like the fool who thinks he has withdrawn from the human condition."

I imagine myself striding towards the Chicago River, a comic figure trying to escape from the human condition into which he has been unceremoniously deposited. Perhaps that absurd vaudeville character, a ridiculous little man with silver hair and a dimpled chin, is indeed me. Yet I knew him in another century and on the other side of the mountain.

Foolish adolescent horniness, I assured myself. You'd make a complete jackass of yourself if you went back to that store and drooled over her. Put the whole absurd incident out of your mind.

Even then, however, a part of me knew better. I would return and I would pursue, just as my imaginary ancestor had pursued a female who had attracted his attention at the entrance of his cave—or, perhaps more accurately, at the edge of a communal waterhole (presumably smaller than Lake Michigan)—long before we became human.

I confess that I had no doubt she wanted to be pursued, evidence enough to the psychiatrist of my masturbatory fantasies.

I insisted as I crossed the river on the Michigan Avenue Bridge, under a lacy blue sky and a gentle sun which turned the buildings along the river pastel, that I would not return to Dufficy's that afternoon. I would certainly not ask her if they carried any books by serious contemporary Irish photographers.

The first thing I did in my office, with Nick and Eileen listening, was to phone the IRS agents and postpone the appointment till the next morning.

I had toppled from the pedestal of grace.

2

Something happened between the bridge and Minor Gray and Blatt's corporate aerie on the LaSalle Street canyon that disconcerted me as it always does, but which at the time seemed to have no relationship to the as yet undefined woman in Dufficy's. Now that I must ponder the possibility that Ciara never existed save as a creature of my fantasy—and all the implications of that for my own sanity—the incident at Michigan and Wacker Drive takes on special importance.

You must understand that in addition to being the quietest of quiet men, I am strange in another way.

I see things and people that others don't see. I recognized this phenomenon early in childhood, when I would tell my parents or my playmates about people I had seen. Their shocked reaction quickly taught me to distinguish sharply between my "special" events and "ordinary" events.

The phenomena that happened long ago or will happen sometime in the future or are happening at some great distance now are easily recognizable as distinct from the phenomena that others can see. The best way I can describe them is to say that they are played on a videotape that seems to be either in front of or behind the tape of ordinary consciousness. I suspect that it was more difficult as a child to make the distinction, but I learned, under the pressure of circumstances, to recognize the difference quickly enough.

I don't ask you to believe that such events happen. I will be content for the purposes of this story if you accept as a given that I experience them as happening. Or think I do.

I normally turn left on Wacker and walk to Dearborn. Michigan Avenue is more aesthetically pleasing because of the lake and the park on the left. But one saves a few minutes of time, particularly if one makes the lights, by cutting across the Loop on the diagonal street. Ordinarily I keep to the river side of Wacker, both because I like the river and because I am wary of the southwest corner of Michigan and Wacker.

However, on that warm April morning, in another century and on the other side of the mountain, I had no time for foolish fantasies. The green light was an opportunity to be seized. So I grabbed it, perhaps to make up for the opportunity I had definitively ruled out a few blocks back.

As best I can remember my state of mind at the time, enough to testify to it in a court of law but hardly enough to convince a psychiatrist, I was not reflecting at all on the southwest corner as the site of Fort Dearborn, the massacre of whose garrison is marked by the first of the four stars in the Chicago flag (presumably to become five stars if Mayor Washington and Alderman Vrdolyak permit the 1992 World's Fair to occur).

As soon as I crossed the line of the fort's wall, marked by metal studs in the sidewalk, I walked into another century. I saw the garrison leave the fort and begin its fateful trek through the dunes toward the Vincennes Trail (on which I had walked many times as a boy). They would never reach the trail, and only a handful would escape from the ambush that waited at what we now unromantically call 18th Street.

As usual the half-breed scout "Captain" Billy Wells led the way, his face painted black in anticipation of the death that he knew waited for him.

How can I describe for someone who has not had such an experience (technically known as retrocognition) what it is like? The settlers and troops are not ethereal and ectoplasmic creatures. They are as real to me as are the summer-suited pedestrians purposefully rushing along Michigan Avenue with their important and expensive briefcases. I see their worried faces, hear the crying children, sense their fear. Yet the traffic on modern Michigan Avenue does not completely vanish; it fades into the background perhaps, yet it remains. For a few moments I feel that I have a choice between the two worlds, that if I warn them, the garrison and the settlers will not die.

I try to warn them. I choose with futile heroism to abandon 1984 for 1814. It doesn't work. The first Chicagoans fade away slowly, leaving me embarrassed and awkward, wondering if anyone else has seen them and then whether I have made a fool of myself.

So far, at any rate, no one seems to have noticed my hesitancy on the brink of another world. This interlude was rather brief. Only a few minutes, unlike the hour and a half in a previous experience.

On Michigan Avenue, who notices a man standing near the wall of a building, peering quizzically into the distance?

And into the past.

Need I say that, good lawyer and amateur scholar that I am, I have checked every detail—the clothes, the uniforms, the construction of the fort, the physical appearances of the people, even the weather? In most instances, I have all the details right. An occasional disagreement with the history books can be explained by the fact that the books are wrong.

Or that I have deliberately projected details into my vision to persuade myself that it's authentic and not a product of a vivid imagination in a man who had a taste for Chicago history as a child. In some sense it does not matter. Most people don't have such experiences, whether they be projection or retrocognition. I've had them all my life.

I am, you see—and I'd never admitted this to anyone before that morning in April—a psychic. Not before then, nor for some time afterward, in point of fact. Not the kind of freak who performs on the stage, mind you, or who finds criminals for the police. Rather, I am part of that five to ten percent of the population which has frequent and varied psychic experiences—extrasensory perception, clairvoyance, déjà vu, retrocognition, antecognition, communication from great distances. Even an occasional contact with the dead. Everything but out-of-body experiences.

When I was a kid, I thought everyone could see the people and the events I saw. My parents lovingly explained that it was all right to see make-believe people when you were very young, but grown-ups didn't talk about such things. Since then I've learned that maybe sixty percent of us have such experiences once in a while. And a few of us have them often. I did a considerable amount of reading about psychic phenomena in college and occasionally dig into the literature today. But, for the last twenty years, until I met—or perhaps created—Ciara, I did not pursue the subject seriously.

It was not, you see, all that important. It didn't cause any special problems in life and wasn't much of a help either. At best it was of minor interest. At worst it was a nuisance—

which was most of the time. I have no idea what causes it, although I'm amused when I run into an article by some scientific dogmatist explaining that the phenomenon can't possibly exist.

Do I pick up psychic energies that are lurking at what was in 1814 the mouth of the Chicago River? Or do I re-create the scene for myself out of my own forgotten memories of books I read when I was a little boy? Or both?

I don't think anyone knows, and I personally find Irish history and evolutionary biology and medieval common law (on which I've published a few articles and about which I contemplate a book) much more interesting fields and also more useful.

Most of the time what my psychic kink (call it that, if you want, for the lack of a better name) picks up makes no sense at all. I feel sorry for the performers who must fake a good deal of the time because the signals they receive from their audiences are so confusing. Sometimes it is dead wrong: my vivid images of a Sox World Series victory celebration turning into a race riot last autumn, for example. Other times it misses the point completely: long ago I learned that it was an unreliable guide for commodities investment. Occasionally it is both scary and accurate—a pleasant evening visit from an aunt of my mother's who had died in England that very day (a woman whom I'd never met and for whom I had no close feelings). Sometimes it is helpful—call my parents, who now live in Tucson, because they're worried about how I'm surviving the divorce trauma.

I would, however, have called them anyway.

All in all, until Ciara, being a psychic was of less importance in my life than being five feet eight inches tall and having silver-blue eyes which women from four to eighty-four find "cute."

My colleagues arrived in my office promptly at ten-thirty, Eileen a specialist in criminal litigation and Nick an expert in civil trials. We had been classmates though not close friends at St. Praxides grammar school. Eileen, who is married to Red Kane the columnist, is my cousin. Nick is married to her cousin on her mother's side, Catherine Collins, the artist who escaped from a prison camp in South America. When divorce and embezzlement threatened to wipe out much of my life, they came riding to the rescue, as the Ryan clan always does, whether I want to be rescued or not.

"We can probably recapture a quarter of a million for you." Nick tossed a sheaf of papers on my unadorned and uncluttered desk. "Net of expenses. King Sullivan has accounts all over the place."

Nick is a tall, broad-shouldered athlete who has never been close to being out of condition. His thin brown hair is always short and neatly combed, and behind thick black-rimmed glasses, his pale blue eyes watch with the patient mildness of an Indian hunter. Nick's carefully disciplined charismatic energies make him a natural leader; he's a member of the executive committee of the firm and will be managing partner someday unless he finally accepts a seat on the federal bench.

"But we won't pick up anything," Eileen's arresting green eyes considered me coolly, "unless we get a criminal conviction against King."

They both despised King Sullivan from our school days, but because I still considered him my friend, they carefully refrained from attacking him in my presence. He was an adversary to be studied clinically and objectively, not a son of a bitch to be denounced.

"How're you doing?" I asked, smiling at her.

"Great." Eileen relaxed and beamed happily. "Little Redmond here," she patted her stomach, "is kicking up more of a storm than all the others put together. And you're changing the subject."

Pregnancy mellowed Eileen Ryan Kane, but only a few minutes at a time.

"First things first," I said lightly, causing her to beam again. "And Catherine?"

"Great," Nick replied proudly. "Says she wants at least three more."

"Crazy woman," Eileen snorted, not in complete disagreement. Her voice suggests bells sweetly ringing in the distance, across fields of wheat or perhaps flower-strewn meadows—a recollection of her youthful flirtation with a musical comedy career.

I picked up the sheaf of notes Nick had given me. Impregnation was part of my fantasy in Duffcy's, an intensely pleasurable part. I would fill this woman's appealingly flat belly with my child. Is it normal for potency to enhance the pleasure of sex? I wondered. When a couple has determined to have a child, are their unions more rewarding? It had never been so with Madonna, not even at the beginning of marriage, when we both wanted her to conceive.

"The government will not go to trial unless they're sure of your cooperation." Nick removed his glasses and began to polish them. "That's final."

"Patsy and the kids," I began tentatively, knowing we were going down the same path again. King and Patsy, priding themselves on their Catholic traditionalism, had produced seven kids, the eldest of whom was a high school dropout and part of the Chicago punk rock scene. King was an alcoholic, probably incurable, and Patsy—dear, gloriously lovely Patsy—had been in private mental institutions twice, at least.

Had fertilization, in the name of publicly proclaimed religious principles, made their sex life any more rewarding? I doubted it.

"It's up to you," Eileen sighed, an Irishwoman's immemorial protest against the obstinate childishness of men. "He won't go to jail in any case. They'll plea-bargain for a *nolo contendere*. The trial will last five minutes. There's lots of money on both sides of the family."

She was wearing a royal blue maternity jumper and a print blouse with a bow. There were gray streaks in her dark hair, but her round, wholesome face was youthful and vital, and her figure, carefully disciplined like everything else in Eileen's life, seemed even more desirable in its blooming pregnancy, a defiant reassertion of the powers of life. I envied Red Kane and felt a brief, vivid stab of desire for her.

When we were certain that Madonna was pregnant, we suspended our meager sex life. That morning I pondered the ecstasy of making love to a pregnant woman. Indeed, the ecstasy of making forbidden love to my pregnant partner and friend.

I drove off the mind-bursting images of Eileen's full and naked body next to me in bed and tried to concentrate on my financial problems. The images did not leave easily. I was already caught up in my dangerous rite of spring.

While I make more than enough money as a tax lawyer,

since my law school days, I have invested in the commodities market, mostly for the fun of it. Economics is another one of my dilettante interests. A small investment in a futures contract was at first merely a way of testing my instincts that the experts were wrong about the business cycle and I was right.

"Gambling, pure and simple," Madonna had dismissed my little hobby. "Horse players die broke."

She did not object to spending my Board of Trade income, however; and while I'm broke, or nearly broke, at the moment, the reason is not that I've made bad guesses about the market.

I take long-term positions, rather than trading the daily swing of the market, and these days mostly in government bond contracts at the Board of Trade and T-bill contracts at the Merc. Basically, if you think the economy is going up, you buy contracts (go long), expecting that the interest rates will rise and your bonds will be worth more money. If on the other hand you think that the economy is going to slacken, you sell (short) and profit from the fact that you can meet your obligations with contracts that cost less than your sale price.

Taking a position, they tell me, requires the steel nerves of an experienced poker player. I don't have steel nerves and I don't play poker, but I am able to resist panic when the short-run trends go against my position and I have to use some of my capital to cover my margins. I make it a practice not to pay any attention to *Wall Street Journal* forecasts because I feel that by the time their reporters have information, it's already dated.

I've lost a fair amount of money because of confidence in my own economic judgment against that of the experts. But I've made a lot more than I've lost, which is all a commodities investor can expect.

I don't trade myself. I am totally unsuited by temperament and personality for the frantic rumble of the trading pit. I take my positions early in the year, September or October, call my brokers (until recent years at one of the big firms), tell them what to do, and sit back and wait for six months.

When King Sullivan's string of travel agencies folded, I transferred my accounts to his new commodities firm, set up by his father, who was a retired trader. While commodities trading is the last refuge of Chicago Irish with more money than sense, King was my friend, and I felt that it really didn't matter who called in my orders.

It turned out that it did matter. For several years King had been using my money to trade both ends. He would, for example, go short on my account and with the same funds buy on his own account. In a large firm with effective controls a broker couldn't do this without someone blowing the whistle on him. There was no one in John King Sullivan's office who could blow the whistle on him.

Last autumn I felt that the economy would soften in the spring, despite the election campaign, and that the smart long-term position was short. I also saw an opportunity to regain some of my capital, three-quarters of which had been consumed in the divorce settlement—a flat payment of two million dollars to Madonna and another million in a trust fund to guarantee to myself that I would not lack money for the alimony payments.

Nick and Eileen gritted their teeth over the settlement but did not argue.

King, desperate to cover his own losses, did not fill my orders. He simply used my money for his own short-term margins and lost it all—nearly a million dollars. I was the biggest of his victims but not the only one. The Feds finally caught up with him.

My friend Father Ron Crowley, who is a radical liberation theologian (although pastor of an affluent Lake Shore parish), tells me that I should practice the gospel injunction to forgive my debtors and that in any event commodities trading is a grievous sin of exploitation.

Nick Curran had different advice: "It's not just your money, Brendan; King has been taking people for years. You let him off this time and he'll be into a new scam next year."

Charitably, he did not say what he thought: John King Sullivan had always been a crook.

"I don't need the money," I said slowly, glancing out the window at the flowing tides of people on LaSalle Street. Ron was probably right: there was nothing of eternity in that frantic movement of humankind. "Rebuilding my capital was only a game. King and Patsy are friends."

King, Patsy, Ron, Madonna, and I had been friends since

the first grade. Nick was a loner until the Ryans, the "other" Ryans, picked him up in his teens. Eileen was always on the opposite side because even in the first grade Patsy and Madonna had detested the "other" Ryans. If this reaction bothered Eileen and her brothers and sisters, they managed to keep their dismay well hidden.

"Strange kind of friends," Nick began. "What have they—"

"Nick." Eileen's green eyes, normally ice cool, flashed a warning, mother superior admonishing a novice. "It's Brendan's choice."

All my life it had been my choice.

Yet, to finish Nick's question, what indeed had they ever done for me?

"I have precisely the capital I had in 1967, when I began to invest." I opened a drawer of my desk and pulled out a manila folder. "There are certain tax advantages to my situation . . ."

So it went, as always. I paid less attention to the conversation that morning because I was preoccupied by the woman in Dufficy's. Were her eyes green like Eileen's? I thought not, but I couldn't be sure.

And was she carrying my child, as Eileen was carrying Red Kane's? Of course not. That was imagination, like the Fort Dearborn garrison.

Do women enjoy being impregnated? If they want the child especially? It depends, I decided, reviewing the literature on evolutionary biology, on how many they already have and how a society values fertility.

What must sex have been like when men and women knew that if conception resulted, there was a one in six chance of a dead baby or a dead mother? Maybe they didn't comprehend the exact statistics, but they knew the reality well enough.

I shivered slightly.

"All right, Brendan?" Eileen asked anxiously. Once, briefly, we had been in love. It was still a tender memory between us.

"Sure, just shaken by how much can go wrong in human lives."

"If we could have seen the future in the first grade . . ." Nick said thoughtfully.

My mind drifted back to the woman in the store. Much younger than Eileen, but something like her. Did she want to be pregnant? Was I picking up her psychic vibes?

I try to ignore other people's emotional emanations. I am not a voyeur, and in any event the vibes are usually confusing. This was a different relationship, however.

Different relationship? I did not even know the woman's name or what she looked like.

At lunch one day, while we were waiting for Nick and Red and Catherine (I had been delicately pulled into these weekly family sessions after Madonna left me), Eileen had been grousing, more or less in good humor, about the difficulties of "elderly" pregnancy. It was, she assured me in her crispest courtroom style, all Red's fault.

"Don't you want the baby, Eileen?" I asked innocently.

"Oh, Brendan, you poor darling." She touched my hand affectionately. "Don't pay any attention to my blather. Certainly I want him. Do you think someone my age becomes pregnant by accident? My doctor says it's irrational. Who cares? Law is fun. Babies are more fun."

It was an argument that would not stand up on appeal, yet I knew what she meant. Some of the younger women attorneys in our office had tried to give Eileen a hard time: pregnancy after forty was a violation of her obligations to other women.

"Mind your own goddamned business," Eileen had replied, picking up her reading glasses and returning to the brief on which she was working.

I abandoned my efforts to sort out sex and fertility. It was spring, and I had no woman and was alienated from my only child. Like my ancestors for millions of years, I wanted a woman to fondle and impregnate and a child to bounce on my knee. I would find both in the cool, stylish darkness of Dufficy's. I stirred uneasily. Even if I couldn't remember her physical appearance, I had to have her.

"You're too good, Brendan," Eileen sighed again, and stood up. "Thank God we never let you in a courtroom."

"Some people are fighters and some are not." I shrugged my shoulders in apology.

"I'm not sure you're not a fighter." Nick closed his folder. "You haven't fought yet, that's all. Anyway, we're agreed that we'll make a decision next week? The U.S. Attorney will have to decide shortly thereafter whether to go to a grand jury.''

We were agreed.

I could see no connection that day between the woman in the store and King and Patsy Sullivan. Or Ron Crowley. As I say, a psychic ''gift'' is not all that much use.

If I had seen the link, I might not have gone back to Dufficy's.

No, that's not true. Nothing would have kept me away from her. I had to find out her name. I would have returned to Dufficy's before dinner with Jean no matter what I had known about the future. Even as Eileen was praising my goodness, I was picturing the woman's body submitting, willingly, to mine. The image of pleasure was so powerful, I had to dig my fingernails into the palms of my hands to control it.

Yet I was not sure I would remember her. If there were two young women in the store, would I know which one she was, this woman who was carrying/would someday carry/wanted to carry my child?

3

''Not to say photographs.'' She frowned thoughtfully. ''Not like your man Ansel Adams that died the other day, Lord have mercy on him. But we have picturebooks that are not just scenery, like this one.'' The frown changed to a shy smile as she hesitantly handed me the book. ''All the pictures were taken before 1900. . . .''

Admiration and tenderness had temporarily replaced lust. There had been no problem recognizing her. She was everything that my first impressions had suggested, the kind of woman I had dreamed about since I first comprehended that women and men spend their lives together and share their bodies with one another.

''I think my daughter will like that,'' I said, trying to

sound serious and self-controlled despite my pounding heart. "And if you have Jill Uris's books . . ."

She was a heroine from a nineteenth-century Irish novel, tall (at least five feet seven), graceful, so soft-spoken that I could barely hear her, with a classical figure, a pale complexion, which colored quickly, under long, jet black hair, a high, clear forehead, big gray eyes, which were alternately studious and impish, faint crow's-feet that suggested both laughter and wisdom, and an oval face with delicately sculpted features, suggesting sensitivity and intelligence. She was, I guessed, about thirty, perhaps a little older, and, incredibly, without a wedding ring.

"Has your daughter been a photographer for long?" she asked while scanning the shelves behind her.

"Only a few months." I realized how much I resented Jeannie. She was a spoiled little brat. I'd never been able to admit that to myself before. "She's just nineteen, searching for a career. This may not last the summer."

"Ah, but wouldn't it be wonderful if it did?" She found the books. "She might see more in Ireland than we do. Sure, wasn't Mrs. Uris a better photographer than himself a novelist?" she added, with what might have been a wink.

The best part of her was her smile; it started slowly, even hesitantly, like the sun debating whether to emerge at the end of a rainy day, and then exploded in merriment, almost always ending in an unself-conscious laugh, especially when the smile hinted at a slight reprimand for my lack of faith in my daughter. Unlike most Irish immigrants, even her teeth were unblemished.

"He had some of the history right, but he didn't understand the personality or character." I thumbed through Jill Uris's books without the faintest notion how Jeannie would react. "I'll take these two."

She knew, as women usually do, that I was carefully evaluating her. She was embarrassed, unwilling to look me in the eye save for a quick glance, but not at all offended.

"Have you been to Ireland often, Mr. Ryan?" she murmured with a sigh that would have put Eileen Ryan Kane to shame. Blushing again, as if her question were too bold, she laid the books on the counter and began to write up the bill with her left hand.

"I've never been there," I admitted. "My wife doesn't like to fly . . ." I wanted to kick myself for mentioning a wife, especially since by decision of the Metropolitan Matrimonial Tribunal of the Archdiocese of Chicago I did not and indeed had never had one. "How did you know my name?"

"Wasn't it yourself that was on television the other night, talking about the World's Fair?" She looked up at me, her face scarlet, and then quickly looked away, though not before that blinding smile had turned into another laugh. "And sounding so terribly learned about the wicked dances at the first two of them?"

"Little Egypt and Sally Rand." She watched Channel 11, our educational station and, unlike ninety-five percent of my fellow Chicagoans, knew I was on the executive committee for the 1992 fair. "I suppose you Irish wouldn't approve."

"And with our women going into battle stark naked in ancient times." She bent over her calculations.

"And your men with incurable breast fixations in the same days; didn't himself have to be soaked in water all night long after the women of Ulster challenged him naked to the waist at the gates of the city? And you have me at a disadvantage, Miss . . . ?"

She was flustered, as well she might be. Her own full breasts, pushing against the thin fabric of a simple white belted dress, were superb. I battled unsuccessfully with images of her among the women of Ulster and myself as Cuchulain.

"He heated enough bathwater for the whole of Ireland for two months. But those were the old days. And my name is Kelly. Ciara Kelly." She pronounced the name as "Keyra" with ever so slight an "a" sound between the "y" and the "r." "C-I-A-R-A. It comes to forty-two pounds . . ." She shook her black hair in dismay. "Forty-two dollars and twenty-five cents, Mr. Ryan."

"Wouldn't I be knowing how to spell Ciara?" I gave her my Visa card. "Is that a Dublin accent?"

Her voice sounded like the waves breaking against rocks, low, soft, and yet somehow powerful.

The gray eyes wandered back to my face as she made the imprint from my card and considered me speculatively. It was my turn to be embarrassed, to feel my face grow warm.

"A mixed-up accent, a bit of Dublin and a bit of the West."

She was not about to reveal too much to me. I noticed for the first time an ugly scar on the back of her right hand, curving up her forearm.

"Have you been in Chicago long?"

"Not to say long." She lowered her eyes modestly and slipped my purchase into a bag. No carefully wrapped package this time. "Thank you very much, Mr. Ryan. Do come again."

I was being dismissed, but without prejudice.

"That time you sounded almost English."

"Perish the thought." She laughed easily, the viola section of an orchestra. "More like Trinity College."

I walked to the door, I hoped with dignity and self-possession. Even in Ireland, how could someone so desirable have escaped marriage?

I turned in the doorway. "Do you like Chicago?" I asked, paying no attention to the disapproving stare of the older woman standing guard over the Waterford.

Ciara Kelly was grinning at me, not exactly wickedly, more in benign amusement, a gracious countess with a pet serf. "Wouldn't I have to be seeing a lot more of it to make an educated judgment?"

"And would you ever answer a question except by asking another?"

She shook her head, as though I were a silly little boy. "And wouldn't I be a bit daft if I told one of the lord mayor's commissioners for the World's Fair that I didn't love Chicago?"

I escaped quickly, knowing that I had lost the first encounter and not minding a bit.

Harold would be pleased to hear that someone thought he was a lord mayor.

Evaluate me, will you, silver-haired Yank? Take off my dress in your imagination, will you? Well, sure I don't mind all that much, so long as you're after knowing that when it comes to blarney I can talk rings around you.

Rain clouds had drifted in from the west, but Michigan Avenue was bathed for me in purest gold. She found me amusing if not attractive, interesting if not appealing. Pretty good for a start. I was acting like a fifteen-year-old with his first crush; so what?

4

The longer I waited for Jean, the more I resented her. She had always been her "mother's little girl." Even as a baby she would cry in my arms and Madonna would brusquely snatch her back, complaining that I didn't know anything about babies.

It was Madonna's unshakable conviction that I was incompetent at everything from circuit breakers to tennis. Indeed, when she told me that she wanted a divorce—the day Jean graduated from high school—one of the reasons she gave was my refusal to try to improve as a tennis doubles partner even though I knew how important tennis was to her.

Jean screamed at me that I had ruined her graduation day, a worse temper tantrum than those that had more or less constituted our relationship during her teen years. She was her mother's teenager; for me there was rage and silence.

Now, like her mother, she was keeping me waiting. She would sail into the quiet dignity of Les Nomades anywhere from half an hour to two hours late, insouciantly refusing to explain or apologize, and would sulk if I asked why she was late. I hoped that unlike the last time I took her to supper she would wear something more appropriate than jeans, Indian beads, and a cowboy shirt tied several inches above the belt.

Her tardiness gave me time to fantasize about the appealing mixture of shy modesty and leprechaun wit hinting at wickedness that was Ciara Kelly. I would have her, of that I was sure, but I was still too bemused to plan my campaign. Storybook romantic and principled feminist that I am, I forced myself to include in my flamboyantly bawdy fantasies the careful notation that she was a treasure, and must be treated as such. She would be seduced indeed, and with violent, consuming passion, but protected, reverenced, cherished.

There were also a few dark clouds of bafflement and potential disappointment lurking in the bright sky of my erotic imaginings. Why was she not married? I would have, needless to say, been terribly disappointed if she were, yet there was mystery here that could mean trouble. And why was an educated woman (had she not said Trinity College?) working in a shop, even one on Michigan Avenue? And whence the ugly white gash on her arm?

Those who are in love, I read somewhere, are only happy when they can torment themselves with doubts. I was certainly in love, for the first time in my life.

My reveries were ended by Jovan, hovering at my table. "Your very lovely daughter, Mr. Ryan."

I glanced at my watch. Only ten minutes late after all. Blackie Ryan would later insist, when I was driven to seek spiritual advice from him, that my problem is that I fit people into molds of my own making and cannot cope when they escape from the mold. At first glance I did not think that the chic young woman in the white suit and lavender blouse with a slender neck shawl and amethyst pendant and earrings was my daughter. Too neat, too well groomed, too effusive, brown hair too short, brown eyes too happy to see me.

"Daddy, Daddy, you look gorgeous." An enthusiastic hug and a whiff of inviting scent. "And so happy! Do you have a girlfriend? You should marry again, you know. You are too absolutely cute not to find yourself a woman. Presents for me?" Rapid tearing of paper. "How totally awesome! Those shots are really there!" She was more interested in the nineteenth century than in Jill Uris. "Those poor people. Not so long ago, either. Thank you soooo much!" A generous kiss. "Uhmm . . . Definitely you should have a gorgeous woman."

Jean was short and trim, in most ways a carbon copy of my mother, though Madonna rejected the comparison out of hand. (Indeed, Jean was kept away from my parents as much as possible. Their quiet reserve was not appropriate for their only granddaughter, who was trained from her birth for social success.) She was pretty rather than beautiful, neatly shaped rather than voluptuous, energetically sensuous rather than overtly sexy, yet with the hint that beneath the ever-shifting and often shallow enthusiasms lurked the tinder for intense sexual flames, waiting for the right man to ignite. Marc Chagall's Chloe.

That night she was a very lovely, if not quite fully formed young woman, even if I was too dumb to compliment her. Rather, I murmured somewhat pedantically that I doubted I was qualified for marriage, seated her at our table underneath the Art Deco poster of the Arc de Triomphe, and nodded slightly when she ordered a "tiny kir" and raised an eyebrow for my approval.

Now, I thought, comes the appeal for money. The change in persona from sullen teenager to fashionable and affectionate daughter is part of the strategy.

"Daddy." She leaned forward and whispered, as though telling me a state secret. "Caitlin Murphy broke a boy's arm!"

It was perhaps the last opening gambit I expected to hear from her. Caitlin was the doyenne of the third generation of Ryans, daughter of Eileen's older sister, Mary Kate, and Joe Murphy, both of them psychiatrists.

"How do you know Caitlin?"

"Oh, she saw some of my pictures in a student magazine." Jean waved her hand, dismissing the importance of the facts of the case. "And she's in the photography masters program at the Art Institute and she wrote me the nicest letter and isn't she the most beautiful woman and so we had lunch today and this boy made a pass at her and she broke his arm and isn't that too much?"

I would have to admit that Caitlin, a tall, ravishing honey blonde with the lithe grace of a gymnast, was breathtaking. She had apparently also inherited the family propensity for picking up strays. Jeannie had become a stray. Poor child, I could hear them say. I resented their patronization, though God knows I was more than dependent on Caitlin's Aunt Eileen and Cousin Nicholas.

"She broke his arm at lunch? Today?"

"No, silly, cute daddy." She grinned appreciatively at me. "In some bar on Rush Street or someplace. She told me about it at lunch. This boy made a pass and she said no, so he, like, pawed her, and she said if you do that again I'll break your arm. And so he did it again and so she, like, broke his arm. She's black belt in karate and isn't that too much?''

"Did she seem to enjoy it?" How proud her grandmother, Kate Collins, Ed Ryan's first wife, would be, Lord have mercy on her, as Ciara would have said, of such a zany descendant.

"Certainly not." She sipped daintily at her drink. "She's not a sadist or something like that. The boys at the Zoo and places like that won't paw her again, will they?"

"Not unless she wants them to."

My daughter rolled her eyes, a gesture I was sure she'd picked up from Caitlin at lunch. "When she wants a boy to paw her, he'll know all right, and Daddy, why don't we know the other Ryans better? I mean, I know Mom couldn't stand them and all, but were you ever close to them? They *are* relatives, aren't they?"

So we ate our turbot in wine and lemon sauce and drank our Meursault and talked not of the money I still thought she wanted, but of Caitlin's family.

She and Caitlin were not close relatives, only fourth cousins. Her great-great-grandfather, Michael Ryan, and Caitlin's great-great-grandfather, James Ryan, had come to Chicago after the Civil War. The brothers fell out over Irish nationalist politics, which were fierce in Chicago in those days, and the two families drifted apart. By the time of my father, another Michael Ryan, and Caitlin's mother's father, Ed Ryan, there was no memory of the reason for the fight and no hostility. We were the South Side Ryans and they were the North Side Ryans, and in the days before everyone had an automobile, distance made us strangers—distance and social class: their family had much more money.

Then, after the Second World War, Ed Ryan and his wife moved to the South Side, to St. Praxides, where my father had been raised and where he returned when he and my mother came back from England. So the kids of both families grew up in the same neighborhood, distant relatives but strangers. We were friendly but not friends. Ed and Kate and their brood were extroverts, outgoing and gregarious, doubtless like Caitlin, while my mother and father kept to themselves, partly because they were quiet people and partly because they loved each other so much.

Jean nodded wisely. "So now we're the North Side Ryans and they're the South Side Ryans."

"I guess. Can I tell you more about my mother and father? Maybe it will explain me."

She patted my hand affectionately. "I understand you, Daddy. But tell me about them. I must see them on the way back to Stanford at the end of summer. I look so much like Grandmother Ryan in her wedding picture."

Her mother, I thought, would be profoundly offended.

There was never a time I can remember when my parents were not deeply in love with each other. Even now, when I visit them in Tucson, an ambience of affection—physical affection—fills their house, despite the fact that they are in their middle sixties. After they came home from the war, in which they saved each other's lives and a lot of other lives, too, they existed only for each other and for me. My father's insurance business was successful enough, but he could have made much more money if he did not come home most days on the 1:20 Rock Island to be with us. They were always friendly to others, and my mother, who was English and a convert, went to Mass at St. Prax's every morning, but they were content to let the world drift by. They had their books, their son, and each other. After I grew up, Mom went to work at the agency, and you could see both of them walking hand in hand down Longwood Drive after the 1:20 pulled into the station. I suppose their narrow, indeed miraculous, escape during the war explained most of it. But they were quiet, uncompetitive people, and they produced a quiet, uncompetitive son.

Who was, I didn't tell her, nearly as unlucky in love as his parents were lucky. Perhaps because he wasn't competitive enough.

"How totally neat! You mean they, like, actually sleep together?" Her eyes glowed in approbation.

"They love each other more than they did when they were your age," I said, thinking that such love may produce children who are not quite suited for the world in which they have to live. Perhaps the arm-breaking Caitlin had had a more appropriate family experience. "So maybe that's why I grew up with kids like Ron Crowley and Patsy Walsh and John Sullivan as friends instead of the other Ryans.''

I did not mention her mother and did not say that, left to my own, I would probably have drifted towards my cousins.

"Ron Crowley." She wrinkled her nose. "Is he a bomb at St. Jarlath's!"

"Jean." I felt my anger rise, as it often did when Jean displayed adolescent omniscience. "He is one of the most admired priests in America."

"Not by the young people in the neighborhood, he isn't!" Her temper flared as it did every time I became pedantic in response to what I took to be childish ignorance.

I ordered my "parent" instincts to be silent.

"Father Ron?" I said in a tone that indicated astonishment but acceptance of her version of reality. By way of distraction I also signaled the waitress for our dessert order. "I thought he would be a wonderful pastor."

We both ordered white chocolate mousse. "Bad for my figure," she groaned.

"There never will be anything wrong with your figure," I said, patting her hand as she had done mine earlier and thinking of how leathery and emaciated Madonna looked since she had gone on her diet and exercise fad.

"Sweet daddy," she said, delight shining on her pixie face. "I know there won't be if I really do have Grandmother Ryan's genes. That's just something you're supposed to say."

Then we returned to Father Ron. Despite his record as a crusading missionary in South America, his brilliant work in the inner city of Chicago, and support for disarmament and economic justice, the word on the young adult circuit from St. Jarlath's—next to our home parish on the North Shore— was that he was "like, totally authoritarian, a real Nazi." He abolished the parish council, dismissed most of the staff, had a popular curate transferred, fired a seminary professor who said Mass on Sunday and had the reputation of being a fine preacher ("Too many people were calling to find out what Mass Father Cross was saying"), banished teenagers from the parish gym, let the young adult club fold, and insulted the congregation every Sunday because they spoiled their children.

I was appalled; big, handsome, gregarious Ron had become exactly what he hated most in pastors. One more of our group who had reached passionately for happiness and had found instead frustration and bitterness.

"It must be hard, Daddy," she made a face at the taste of Jovan's complimentary Serbian liqueur but didn't put it aside, "to see your friends fu . . . messing up their lives."

"You're a mind reader, Jeannie. I don't quite understand it. We were so happy when we were young."

She nodded solemnly, not understanding but sympathetic.

It had been a charming dinner with an interesting and intelligent young woman, my lucky day for fascinating females. Unfortunately, I blew it.

"Now, about the money you'll need for the trip to Ireland." I took out my checkbook.

Jean recoiled as though I had put a tarantula on Jovan's spotless white tablecloth.

"I don't need . . ." Her eyes filled with tears. "That's not why I wanted to have dinner. . . ."

My pen poised over the open book, I realized what a fool I was.

Jean jumped to her feet, pain turning to rage. "I don't want your money," she shouted. "You're a stupid asshole. Mom's right, you're a dried-up old bastard."

"Jean . . ." I tried to reason with her. Jovan had appeared from nowhere, horrified at the disturbance of the serene environment of his restaurant.

"And I don't want your presents either." She threw Jill Uris's book at me and, shaking with sobs, stormed out of the room. I noted dismally that her legs, moving rapidly under the slits in a tight skirt which hinted at nylon-sheathed young thighs and flanks, were trim and elegant. Anger and passion in my daughter, I thought abstractly, were closely linked.

Jovan's dismay turned to polite sympathy. He placed a hand on my shoulder, like a wise Trappist monk. "A mistake, eh, my friend? It is hard with beautiful daughters. It will not be forever, she loves you too much."

He had never met her before, but he saw what I had missed.

I went home to my apartment building, worked out with weights for twenty minutes, and then swam an hour in the pool. I was not thinking of a body that would be presentable for a young lover. I was thinking rather that without my daily exercise I would not sleep a wink.

I took a warm shower, wrapped myself in a clean terry-cloth robe, made a cup of apple cinnamon tea, and sat by the window looking at the mixture of stars and clouds hovering above the blackboard-smooth lake.

Ciara Kelly was, I warned myself, very likely my last chance. Without her I was indeed destined for the fate Jean predicted for me, a dried-up old bachelor who for all the example of his parents had never learned how to love.

5

The weather, the monsignor said as he began his fatally inaccurate prophecy about our class, was one more blessing on the most blessed class in the twenty-year history of the parish. Most of the thirty-five of us, he noted, had begun in the first grade together, only a few years after the war was over and before the parish had begun to expand.

"You are the last of the one-room classes, the high-water mark of the parish's early years. The beauty of this day and the beauty of the ceremony in our brand-new church are merely an overture for the great achievements that lie ahead of you."

Our grammar school graduation day in June of 1956 was as close to a perfect spring day as Chicago ever sees: shimmering sunlight, light breezes, crystal blue sky, temperature in the low eighties, little humidity.

The monsignor was guilty of a slightly mixed metaphor, but it suited the emotions of the day: proud parents, sniggering boys, crying girls. We pretended to be more interested in the round of parties after the sun went down and in King's plans for beer in the forest preserve. Yet in our hearts my group believed that the monsignor was right. We were indeed special, and we would in due course show the world how special.

How wrong we were.

It was a wonderful summer, not much rain and not too much heat. Or so it seems in my memory. The girls went wild about Elvis Presley, and we made fun of him, agreeing readily enough that he was indeed a "hound dog." We saw *Around the World in Eighty Days* and *The King and I* and tentatively kissed in the darkness of the theater (I confess that I didn't). We sang "Que Sera, Sera," though we didn't mean it, and "On the Street Where You Live" and "I Could Have Danced All Night" from *My Fair Lady*.

We played volleyball and basketball in the "courts" (the church parking lot); hung out in front of Lewis's drugstore until the owner or the police banished us; necked in the forest preserve (well, they did; I didn't) except on weekends when the blacks took it over for barbecue roasts; and drank beer in the schoolyard (well, I didn't) and threw the cans on the front lawn of the convent. We went on our class picnic to Potawatami Park and turned over the rowboats as soon as they were launched (despite the imprecations of the young priest). We bragged that we were not afraid of high school (though we were), pretended to know much more about sex than we did, passed around early copies of *Playboy* (to the girls' dismay—though they were not above peeking), promised that we would always be friends, and committed ourselves to filling the next year with fun, fun, and more fun.

Our biggest excitement that summer was breaking into people's homes, especially on weekends, when many of the parents were away at Long Beach or Grand Beach or other summer locales. I suspect that we were secretly envious, despite our protests that the Club (our local country club) was much more fun. (My parents didn't belong to the Club, needless to say; I cannot imagine a place that would have made them more uncomfortable. But I tagged along with the children of members.) Mostly we were content to rearrange furniture and kitchenware, enough to let the occupants know we'd been there.

King would select the victim, study the house, lay the plans. Ron would egg us on when our courage flagged. The girls would stand guard. I would climb up on Ron's shoulders and pry open the window. The reign of terror attracted considerable attention from the police, but we were never caught.

I vetoed an attack on the house of the "other" Ryans, contending that they were relatives and fearing that we might do more damage than break a few dishes or spill some cosmetics once we got inside—so great was the distaste of the others for the Ryan clan, especially for their mother, who, everyone said, was a Communist.

And I heeded my father's delicate warning one night over sherry (certainly we had a glass of sherry before dinner, doesn't everyone?).

"Well, I hope those young mischief-makers try Ned Ryan's old house while they're up at Grand Beach."

"Darling, what a terrible thing to say." My mother looked up from the decanter in utter dismay.

"It'll serve them right. The imps, I mean. Ned Ryan charged a Japanese battleship with a destroyer escort in the Philippine Sea and won. If he sets his mind to hunting down the punks, they'll end up in reform school."

"It would only serve them right," my mother agreed.

"Anyone else's house," my father put aside his copy of the *Chicago Daily News*, "and the parents will buy off the owners and the police. No one buys off Ned Ryan."

Mr. Ryan seemed such a mild man. I wasn't sure whether my father meant what he said. I'm still not sure. And I'm afraid even now to ask either him or Ned.

We didn't raid their house, despite my friends' protest that I was a creep. And we didn't stretch our luck with any more raids.

The golden days, we thought, would never end. Eighth grade graduation day, with its flashing light bulbs, maroon and white ribbons, diplomas in dark blue binders, girls tottering on unfamiliar high heels, sentimental mothers, and proud nuns, was a spectacular beginning to the song of our lives. Unfortunately the rest of the music did not live up to the overture. Our lives are like an unfinished symphony, a statue whose sculptor died after a promising beginning, an abandoned novel with a fascinating but flawed premise, a film which was never released despite exciting advance publicity.

We worked for tutoring programs in black and Hispanic parishes for two years before John Kennedy's Peace Corps and the volunteer enthusiasm of the early sixties. On two Sundays a month we went to the county infirmary at Oak Forest to visit the "old people" with the Vincent De Paul Society of the parish.

If you've ever been in wards filled with the indigent aged, you know how depressing they can be. The sights, sounds, smells—above all, smells—were as far from our comfortable upper crust of the middle-class life as were the lower circles of Dante's Inferno. The question was not whether you got sick at Oak Forest but how soon. Ron and I were ill in the first half hour.

"I don't ever want to be old," he said, as we vomited behind a tree on the grounds. "I want to die when I'm healthy and getting close to old age—forty or something like that."

In retrospect it was a strange prophecy. Psychic or not, I can't claim a premonition at the time.

The girls were much better at it. Patsy was a persistent missionary, plugging away at old men and women who had not gone to confession or received Communion for forty years. Madonna sang, danced, told stories, wrote letters, gossiped. You could see their eyes light up when she slipped into the world, a trim, self-confident blonde angel of lightness and cheer.

She organized, produced, and directed musical shows, with which we toured the wards at Christmastime. The old people wept when she left.

"I want to spend my life helping people like that, Brenny," she said to me in the T-bird as we drove home after one such musical review. "I'd be a nun, only I don't know that that would do much good. I mean, I want to make it so that people don't have to live that way."

"Hmm . . ." I said.

"No, that's not true." She frowned at a stoplight that dared to slow her progress. "I'd enter the order after high school if Daddy would let me."

We graduated from high school and forgot about Oak Forest.

"We peaked out when we were seventeen, Brenny," King

groaned as he made himself another drink on the day he admitted that he had misappropriated my money.

"I know." I looked up at him, hardly able to believe that this fat, balding, battered man, a wounded oversized bull, was the same person as my handsome, mischievous teenage friend. "Why did it all end so soon?"

He hesitated, then poured another jolt of J&B into the tumbler. "I'll be damned if I can figure it out."

No more can I.

We reached for the stars, or thought we did, and fell on our faces. We were failures, most of us tragic failures. By the Memorial Day weekend of 1984 our fates were sealed. Alcoholism, theft, divorce, insanity, sudden death—our promise was cut short even before it had a chance to wither.

I don't yet understand why. No one would have guessed when we graduated from grammar school in June of 1956 that we were doomed. Our group was hailed as the most promising class St. Praxides had ever produced. Madonna was voted the outstanding girl, Ron the outstanding boy. King was the class president, Patsy crowned the Blessed Mother in May. I had the highest average in the class. Ron captained the football team, King the basketball team, Madonna the volleyball team. The "other" Ryans were, for once, left out, not that they seemed to notice it.

Madonna Clifford, slender and blonde, even at fourteen was said to be a great beauty. Patsy Walsh, short, cute, vivacious, was the driving energy behind every party. Ron Crowley, big, strong, genial, placated worried parents and teachers. King Sullivan, clever, witty, resourceful, devised the games, the tricks, the surprises.

I tagged along, not a hanger-on exactly, but because they wanted me. I could never understand why and still can't, except that I was the brightest kid in the class. I didn't belong with the stars and often would rather not have been there. I guess I was the mascot, the pet, the even-tempered go-between who could mediate the quarrels.

The girls both went to the brand-new Mother McAuley High School on 103d Street, where Madonna was the outstanding senior, and then on to St. Mary's of Notre Dame. Ron and King enrolled at St. Ignatius, where Ron won the senior prize and surprised everyone by rejecting his football scholarship at Notre Dame and signing up for the seminary. King went to Notre Dame but was expelled during his sophomore year, when he was caught for the second time with beer in his room. Neither of the girls graduated from college.

I went to St. Rita's High School, which was closer to home, and then to Loyola to which I could commute. The others in the group objected vigorously, not understanding the great attractiveness of a home steeped in love, as was our little house on the hill overlooking the park and the Rock Island station at 93d and Glenwood Drive.

I was the only one who went into the service, despite the protests of my wife and her family. My family history left me no choice. Military intelligence of course. A year in the Pentagon in a group that warned of the dangers of involvement in Vietnam that hesitated between minimum force and maximum force. Then nine months in that country, mostly in Saigon, as part of a team that sent warnings to Washington about the tenacity of the Viet Cong. No one listened. I came home in 1966, two years after the Tonkin Gulf resolution, with a medal, the bars of a captain, and grave fear for our country.

The months in Vietnam were not a complete waste. For others the memory of the war might be a lifelong burden. For me one particular incident, the cause of my medal, stands as ambiguous evidence that my life may not be totally worthless. Everything else I've done in my forty-two years is devoid of generosity and courage. For a few hours in Vietnam I proved to myself that I was capable of both, if the necessity arose.

That's not very much, I suppose, but it's all I have.

I paid a price for that one shining moment, as the song from *Camelot*, which we sang in the summer of 1960, put it. The year overseas ruined our marriage. Madonna, who did not mind the prospect of moving to McLean, Virginia, as an officer's wife, soon found that she would not be rubbing shoulders with senators and ambassadors at Washington cocktail parties. She quickly came to hate our tiny, furnished apartment. She took our new daughter home to mother with great relief. Comparing what her father could provide in the way of comfort with what I could provide—her family had moved to the North Shore to escape the "niggers," as her mother bluntly put it—she probably felt that it was a mistake to have ever married me. She was able to contain her enthusiasm for me on return. She was never an antiwar activist, but my bars and my medal did not impress her. It was always, "your goddamn war."

I had thought about an academic career, perhaps in economics or history, but I realized that, on a professor's salary, I could never support her in the style she would demand. So I went to work for my father and struggled through four years of night school at DePaul. I clerked at Minor Gray and Blatt, was hired as an associate the day I graduated, and then became a partner after two years (at the same time in 1972 that Eileen Ryan Kane also became a partner, when she left government work and the firm decided it needed competent women immediately). These were not inconsiderable achievements. But Madonna was unimpressed. Her father was a distinguished, outspoken, and thick-skulled surgeon. I could never be as good at anything as he was at everything.

Patsy and King already had two children and were expecting a third, King had been wiped out twice on the Board of Trade and had cracked up his Mercedes in a drunken accident on the Dan Ryan, Patsy had spent some time in the psychiatric ward at Little Company of Mary, Ron was leading the post–Vatican Council agitation against an old-fashioned seminary rector, and my wife, despite considerable literary and administrative talents, was content with attending women's charity luncheons (with her mother) up and down the North Shore.

We peaked out, in retrospect, shortly after our high school graduation, between the time Ron left for the seminary and the girls quit college—Patsy to marry King after he had been thrown out of Notre Dame and Madonna because she hated the nuns, the other students, and everything else about St. Mary's.

There were excuses. King's father was a successful trader all right, but he was drunk every afternoon and a heavy-handed authoritarian. His mother was so ineffectual as to be practically nonexistent. Mr. and Mrs. Walsh separated when Patsy was in college because he was not sufficiently successful at the practice of law to support her social ambitions. Mac Crowley was a jock who never grew up. Dr. Melvin Clifford was an insufferable boor (as my mother remarked in a rare moment of exasperated uncharitableness), and his wife one of the most mindless women I've ever known.

"It seems to me," my father began mildly as we dug into carne seca chimichangas at El Charro, Tucson's famous Sonoran restaurant (underneath a picture of someone who looked like Pancho Villa), "that the difference between my generation and yours is that we were perhaps too eager to assume responsibility for our behavior and you are perhaps too eager to reject such responsibility."

"Rather," my mother agreed with equal mildness.

"A good point," I agreed, realizing how often I justified my weakness in dealing with conflict in my marriage by arguing that I grew up in a family where there was almost no conflict.

"On the whole," he played with his wine margarita, "I think our fault was the less serious. It is better to exaggerate personal responsibility than to deny it."

"How does it seem with Jean's generation?" my mother asked, pining as always to know her granddaughter better.

"I'm not sure," I admitted. "Yet it does seem to me that with your greater responsibility there is less guilt. And with our lesser responsibility there is more guilt. Madonna, poor woman, has been running from guilt all her life. That's why she has to blame me."

"How sad," my mother murmured softly.

Yet we were not sad as children. At least we did not seem sad. As I remember my youth, it was very happy. If the rest of the group was unhappy, they were good at hiding it.

The five of us had good times together as far back into the early years of grammar school as I can remember—the two couples always together and Brendan Ryan as the unobtrusive fifth wheel. It was expected that Ron and Madonna, the most attractive and the best-looking of the class, would be paired. I loved Patsy, or so I thought, from the first day of the first grade, mostly, I suspect, because we were the shortest persons in the class and hence partners in every orderly "rank" the nuns established. Sadly for me, it seemed then, all her considerable affective energies were directed at King Sullivan. Their marriage, as he mumbled incoherently at the wedding banquet, fulfilled a romance that had begun at the Club even before they had entered St. Praxides.

That was right before he collapsed in a drunken stupor.

When it was necessary in the teen years for me to have a date, Patsy and Madonna (never, *never* Donna, by the way) chose one for me, normally a pleasant and presentable girl who offered them no competition and showed proper gratitude for being permitted into our group, even on a temporary basis.

Only once did I kick over the traces. I was never quite forgiven. It was one item on the agenda of my offenses when Madonna ordered me out of the house twenty-two years later.

It was senior prom time. Kate Ryan's death, though not a surprise, had shattered the whole family, especially Eileen, whom my mother had observed was the most fragile of all of them.

"Will Eileen Ryan be going to the senior prom?" she asked me at supper one night. For all her diligent efforts, she could never quite understand the arrangements of American secondary education. I explained that there were many senior proms, one for each high school, and that maybe Eileen would find a boy to take her to her own prom but that I doubted any boy would invite her to his prom.

"Most extraordinary," she murmured. "She's such a beautiful child."

"What the boy is saying, Jocelyn," my father wiped his mouth carefully with a napkin, "is that she is so self-possessed and so intelligent that she scares boys her own age. It is not unusual at that age in life in our country. Eileen will survive."

"You do think she is lovely, don't you, Brendan?" My mother filled my wineglass (civilized living in her house dictated one, possibly two glasses of "claret" with the evening meal).

"I hadn't noticed."

In retrospect my father was quite right. Eileen was more than most of us her age, male or female, could handle. So we reacted, as adolescents do, by pretending that we were unaware of her existence.

"Who are you going to take to your prom?" My mother did not give up easily.

"I don't know. Patsy and Madonna will find someone, then we'll triple at the McAuley prom."

"Can't you find someone by yourself?"

"I suppose."

That was the end of the conversation, save for a knowing wink from my father.

I called the "other" Ryans' number later in the evening. Eileen answered.

"Waiting on the phone, Cousin, for a cousin to call who needs a prom date?"

"Your prom or mine, Cousin?" One of the few unguarded remarks that I have ever heard cross her lips.

I took a deep breath, fearing the rage of my friends. "Both, I hope."

Silence. Then, "Oh, Brendan . . ."

"Is it a deal?"

"It's a deal."

The group was furious. They would not have to tolerate her at the St. Rita's prom because none of them was going, or the St. Ignatius prom because I would not be going to that. The McAuley dance was the sticking point.

"I will not be seen in public with that creep!" Madonna stormed.

"She's so stuck up," Patsy protested.

"A wet blanket on any party," King agreed.

None of this was true, but my friends believed it, I daresay, at the moment more strongly than they believed in the existence of God.

"Guess you'll have to find someone else to double with," Ron said. "You really should have asked us, Brenny."

"No one in the whole school will double with such a drip." Madonna's thin, pretty face crinkled in derision.

I didn't defend my cousin or my decision. I merely stuck by it.

To my surprise, Eileen was the toast of the St. Rita's prom. Her long brown hair, flashing green eyes, and matching strapless green gown (for which little artificial boning was required) stopped traffic on the dance floor. There was much joking about our names being the same.

"She's my mother," I explained to one of the wide-eyed Augustinian priests.

"Actually, we're secretly married," she said in a stage whisper.

I brushed her lips when we arrived at the door of her house shortly before 5:00 A.M.

"I'll never forget this, Cousin," she said fiercely. "Never."

"I'm sure I won't either."

Somehow it had been arranged that my crowd from St. Rita's and their dates would journey the next day to the Ryan house at Grand Beach. Mary Kate, Eileen's older sister, was in charge. The rain poured down all day, so we spent our time singing. Eileen, who had "taken" voice for as long as I could remember, led us from the piano, tirelessly banishing the temptation to boredom. After a while, as we stuffed ourselves with an apparently limitless supply of food, no one noticed the rain.

"What a dame!" one of my classmates said to me. "She even knows the second stanzas of songs."

The McAuley prom was not so pleasant. Patsy and Madonna, with the cruelty at which adolescent women can be so skilled, did everything they could to make Eileen feel unwanted and unnoticed. I consoled myself with the copout that she seemed unaware of their rudeness. Now I suspect that she had too much class to acknowledge it.

The boys who had been constrained to come to the prom noticed her all right, especially since I had absolutely forbidden her to replace the green dress with another.

The drinking party at the Cellar (on the lower level of Wacker Drive) which followed the dance was organized by a committee of parents who, in flagrant disregard of the laws of the sovereign state of Illinois, as I would later realize, argued that kids would drink on prom night and that it was better that the drinking be supervised.

Eileen and I left the party and walked silently, hand in hand, to watch the sun come up over the lake. This time she kissed me, and, if the truth be told, with considerably more vigor than I had dared to attempt.

"You're wonderful, Brendan." The green eyes glistened. "I love you."

I didn't know quite what to say. So I took her hand and we walked back to the Cellar to collect my tipsy friends.

The other two girls attacked her bitterly to me the moment we came through the door—in tones just loud enough so Eileen could hear them as she departed for a visit to the women's room.

"Did she let you fool around with her?" Patsy, her face contorted to an ugly sneer, began the attack.

"There's a lot of her to fool around with," Madonna blew cigarette smoke at me, "if you like fat women."

"I can't believe she'd wear that gross dress."

"She must have put the makeup on with a shovel."

"How can you stand such a disgusting girl?"

"She's cheap, everyone knows that."

"You ought to be ashamed of yourself, Brenny, making us sit at the same table with her."

Eileen did not seem to hear them. Later, on the dance floor, she made only one comment. "There's only one reason why you should be friends with those people, Brendan." She crinkled her nose thoughtfully. "And I don't think it's a good reason."

"What's that?"

"They need you."

"Need me?" I looked into her deep, magic green eyes.

"Without you they'd fall apart. And they know it."

"I don't know what you mean."

"Poor Brendan." She tightened her grip on my hand. "You think they're doing you a favor. It's the other way around. They'll fall apart eventually anyway."

A prophecy?

Maybe not. She might merely have seen what was obvious to everyone but me. I'm still not sure.

There was no senior summer romance between us. The Ryans decamped for Grand Beach in mid-June. My friends still thought the lake shore was "boring" and that the Club was the only place to spend the summer. We cheered for the Kennedy nomination, shivered at *Psycho* (the boys whistled at Janet Leigh), danced the Twist, made fun of Chubby Checker, avoided *La Dolce Vita* because the Church "condemned" it (not that we would have understood Fellini anyway), sang "Never on Sunday" and "Tom Dooley," and watched *Maverick* reruns.

No one kept me away from Grand Beach, however. I could

have gone there if I had wanted to. I could have dated Eileen at Loyola during our college years, since neither of us went away to school. But then, with Ron in the seminary, it was more or less understood that I would marry Madonna.

Years later, when Eileen joined our law firm and I was promoted to a partnership, we continued to keep our distance, friendly but not friends, understanding perhaps that there were energies between us that were not quite under full control.

"That trollop," Madonna stormed when she learned that Eileen was a full partner (information that reduced to zero the importance of my partnership). "Red Kane married her because he had to. Where there's smoke there's always fire. I won't have anything to do with her."

I sensed that some of the time her marriage with the columnist, one of the nicest men in Chicago for my money, was not happy. All the more reason to keep my distance. When she and Nick Curran took charge of me during the divorce, Nick was the leader and Eileen lagged behind uncertainly. Then, last fall, when she was trying the Hurricane Houston case, something changed between her and Red. "It was mostly my fault," she whispered to me one day after lunch in early January. "We wasted twenty years and made it only by the skin of our teeth. I'm not going to waste another twenty minutes."

Have I always been half in love with my cousin (distant enough so the relationship would not have been an "impediment"—as the Church called such things in the days when it worried about marriage and divorce)? I suppose. But I would have done less well than Red Kane in responding to her. Of that I am sure.

Or perhaps, after all, not so sure.

More to the point, was Ciara Kelly a psychic clone of Eileen? Different color hair and eyes, different personality, similar figures perhaps, but Ciara was taller. Same kind of woman?

No doubt about it.

On those warm prom nights in 1960, awkward, overdressed, nervous, feeling slightly ridiculous, under an enormous obligation to have a "good time" that we'd never forget, my friends dismissed Eileen Ryan as "out of it." I didn't agree, but I wasn't sure enough of my own tastes and judgments to disagree either.

Yet she made it and none of us did—professional success and personal happiness. The latter only recently and only by the skin of her teeth, as she insisted.

None of the rest of us even came close.

6

"Jesus and Mary be with this store," I said to Ciara Kelly as I closed the door quickly to keep out the wind gusts and the pounding rain.

The Cubs were still in first place, even if spring had departed.

"Jesus and Mary and Patrick be with those who shop in it," she replied, her brogue this morning more West of Ireland than Trinity College. "It's yourself who knows the customs and not ever visiting there, for which God forgive you. And did your daughter like your present?"

Her hair was swept back and done up in a knot on her head. Even in low heels she was as tall as I. She wore gray slacks and a white blouse and a gray sleeveless sweater, clean and neat but hardly chic. No makeup or jewelry, something I had not noticed the day before. Her neck, a lovely ivory arch, was as pale as the blouse. No sun for a long time. Had Ciara been a nun? That would explain a lot.

"She loved them at first." I was caught off guard by the question. I had not come to talk about Jean.

"At first?" Her gray eyes looked up from the package she was wrapping. "And then?"

You could not fool those gray eyes for long; in their depths was a shrewd horse trader at the county fair.

"We had a fight. My fault. She didn't take the books. I was stupid."

"Fathers are that way with nineteen-year-old daughters.

You can give it to her tonight. Nineteen-year-old daughters forgive easily, especially when you say you're sorry." The storm-banishing smile again. "You do tell her you're sorry when it's your fault, don't you, Brendan Ryan?"

"I won't see her tonight. We don't live together." I was stumbling for an explanation. "My wife and I are separated. An annulment, actually."

"That's a shame." She finished the ribbon on one package and began folding an Aran skirt into a green and white box. "You could mail it to her then with a card—there's a nice selection of Georgian Dublin cards over there. Fill one out and we'll mail it for you. No extra charge. . . . Course, if you want a refund," she peeked at me, her face crimson, embarrassed because of her boldness with a customer, "we'll be happy to do that too. I shouldn't be blathering away with my big Irish mouth . . ."

"Not at all, that's an excellent idea. I really didn't come in about the books. I just happen to have them in my briefcase . . ."

"Or there's some color pictures of sailboats off the West of Ireland . . ."

"Lovely." I glanced at them. Dories in the rain and a stiff wind. Tricky and dangerous. "Better not. I don't think Jean approves of my passion for sailing." Her mother surely doesn't, I added to myself.

"Do you sail now?" Her shyness disappeared. "What kind of a boat do you use? I did some of it in a boat just like this one when I was a wee one."

For a second or two she was a reckless hoyden, a tomboy sailing in the teeth of a gale. Her face glowed in a happy memory.

"A little bigger, I'm afraid. A thirty-foot Peterson."

"Jesus, Mary, and Joseph! A battleship!"

"Not quite," I said, noting to myself that I had now one more trick to play in my seduction game. And one more reason to be fond of her.

I chose a picture of Trinity College and wrote, "Sorry. Give me another chance. I love you, Dad," on the card and wondered how to deal with Ciara Kelly's ability to steer me away from my plans for seduction. I was new to the game, and I had selected an elusive Irish woman as my target.

I desperately wanted to take her in my arms and cry on her shapely shoulders for the youth that my friends and I had lost so easily and for which I had mourned the whole sleepless night long.

Instead I gave her the card and the books.

"Shouldn't you put the card in the envelope?" She held it gingerly.

"I should indeed, but why don't you look at it, since you know so much about young women, and tell me whether it's right."

Tears formed in her wonderful eyes. A weeper, like any good Irishwoman.

"If it's not she doesn't deserve you." Ciara took the books shyly from me and began another package. "And I'm sure she does."

I probe at my memories of that rainy morning when tornadoes were sweeping the land. Was the painting on the wall that day, the painting from Keenan's keep that would become so important a few weeks later, when I was searching for the will o' the wisp that had been Ciara Kelly? I can't say whether it was or not. My eyes were too busy studying her face and admiring her body to notice anything else. There was, even then, an electric current of hot sexuality leaping back and forth between us, like lightning dancing on Lake Michigan during a storm.

"Solti's doing the *Rite of Spring* tomorrow night," I said, plunging into my real reason for returning a third time to Dufficy's Irish Store.

"By himself, is it? Would you write your daughter's address on this label, please."

I wrote out her Stanford address. "With a bit of assistance from the Chicago Symphony. It's easier that way."

"Heaven knows we'd need some kind of sacrifice to bring spring to Chicago." She noted with a faintly raised eyebrow the California address. "And the poor girl dancing herself to death."

"Probably only figuratively. She'd be revived later as part of the rebirth ceremony."

"Ah, in Celtic lands surely. Nobody makes an Irishwoman dance until she dies. But does your man Stravinsky know that?"

The label was pasted on the package, and she stood ready to dismiss me again.

"Our springs are very short in Chicago." I took a deep breath. Now it starts. "So I thought maybe you'd help me help Sir Georg put us on the right track again. Dinner beforehand?"

She froze. It was as if I had injected a serum into her veins that turned a vital and interesting woman into a stone statue. She bowed her head and wrapped her arms around herself as though to keep out the winter cold.

"I couldn't do that, Mr. Ryan, sir. I'm sorry. I just couldn't. It's nice of you to ask me. I'm sorry if my blather deceived you."

"I'm sorry if I've been offensive." I felt my face turn to fire. "I didn't mean—"

"You haven't been offensive at all, Mr. Ryan. Not at all." Her voice cracked as though she might sob. "I appreciate the invitation. I just can't accept it. Please."

"No problem." Dauntless lover that I am, I began to look for the quickest possible way out. "Thank you for the help with the books."

"You're welcome, sir." Chin on her chest, shoulders sagging, the ice statue melting away, the snow woman disappearing in the slush. "I'm sorry."

The odd thing, I thought to myself, as I hurried down Michigan Avenue, is that I'm sure she wants to go. She likes me. She feels the same attraction I do. It pleases her too. What the hell happened? How did I blow it this time?

When I reached the sanctuary of my office, there were two phone messages, one from Patsy Sullivan, the other from Father Ron Crowley. It could not be a coincidence, I thought. I'm going to be subjected to more pressure to let King Sullivan off the hook.

I felt guilty that I had not wrestled with the ethical and human complexities of the issue in the last twenty-four hours. I had wasted too much time fantasizing about a woman who was frightened by a perfectly proper and perfectly courteous invitation to dinner and a concert.

I returned the calls. They both wanted to talk to me. Wouldn't take long. No, Patsy didn't have time for lunch. She had to be back to their home on Glenwood Drive when the "kiddies" came home from school. With the neighborhood like it is now, she didn't want them coming into an empty house.

Her presence in the house had not stopped her eldest son from buying drugs from the black kids of whom she was afraid. That was unfair and unjust, I told myself.

Ten o'clock tomorrow morning? Fine.

No, Ron didn't have time for dinner and a concert. Too much work in the parish. No, I don't expect you to drive up to this madhouse. What about a drink? Sherlock's Home? Tearing down the building? Really? A pity. Someone should demonstrate. Top of the Hancock? Fine.

Sometime between now and then I'd have to work out my position. I was caught between two sets of friends. Old friends and new friends. I'd have to decide which twosome to hurt—Nick and Eileen or Patsy and Ron.

Then it dawned on me that Nick and Eileen would not be hurt at all. Or angry or disappointed. I wasn't quite sure what to make of that insight.

And I didn't think at all about Ciara Kelly.

Until I fell asleep. She took full possession of my dreams. Pushy Irish bitch.

The next morning there was an envelope on my desk. "Delivered by hand to our switchboard, first thing this morning," my secretary remarked. "By a young woman . . ."

Mrs. Magner has worked for me since I came to the firm. Having successfully married off her own children, she now found me a new and interesting challenge.

The handwriting on the card, a photo of the black marble bust of James Joyce that American Express had erected in St. Stephen's Green on his centenary, was astonishingly cramped, not what I would have expected from such a gracious woman as Ciara Kelly. I had no trouble reading it, however:

"Picture me as looking as sad as himself. And him with the excuse of bad eyes and me only the excuse of cold feet. I'm sorry. Ciara."

I looked up Dufficy's number, wanting to protect my romance from Mrs. Magner's well-meaning interest. If I had asked her to call and she had spoken to Ciara, my present uncertainty would dissolve.

Maybe I designed matters so it wouldn't dissolve.

"Dufficy's," said the low, rich, raspberries and cream voice that I instantly recognized.

"Ciara Kelly? Brendan Ryan."

"Is it now?"

"Do you know where Orchestra Hall is?"

"Isn't that the place where the symphony orchestra plays?"

"Woman, if you keep answering questions with a question, you might get a good spanking."

I couldn't believe that in my anxiety I had said something so dumb.

Her response was immediate. "Ah, wouldn't that be an interesting erotic experience now. But, so's not to push my luck, Brendan Ryan, and not really deserving a second chance, yes, I know where it is."

"There's a club on the top floor . . ."

"The Cliff Dwellers, is it, the one that just admitted women members?" She was giggling at me.

"Would you be wanting to know whether it's the Cliff Dwellers? Well, it is, woman, and if you want to get anything to eat before the concert you'd better be there at six."

"Could I meet you downstairs in the lobby?" Shy and plaintive now. "I promise. No more questions."

"The food isn't spectacular, but I made an appointment for late in the afternoon . . ."

"Serves me right enough. I'll eat everything that's put before me, like me mother taught me."

"See you then . . ."

"You're a desperate man, Brendan Ryan."

"What does that mean?"

"It's a compliment." She hung up before I could ask for more of an explanation.

Thus did I fall from grace.

Or maybe, I don't know, fall into grace.

two
ADORATION
OF THE
EARTH

7

"Do you realize what your revenge will do?" Patsy leaned forward, her fingers twisted together in agonized prayer, perhaps to the Sorrowful Mother, for whom she had had a great devotion as a little girl. "Not to King or to me but to the kiddies? Do you want to get back at us so badly that you'd destroy their future?"

We were sitting across from one another, on two of the easy chairs I had arranged around the Sheraton table in my office—for relaxed conversations with clients worried about the IRS.

None of us had aged more dramatically than Patsy. All that remained of the cute little tyke, the child from a Walt Disney film, whom I began adoring the first day of the first grade, were the glowing brown eyes, and now the glow was from pain, not from enthusiasm. She wore jeans, a sweatshirt, and a Windbreaker, looking in our prestigious law offices like she might be a welfare mother or a battered wife. In a way she was both, I suppose. Her figure was as well-shaped as a sack of potatoes, her face puffy and spent, her hair disorderly, her shoes scuffed. Everything about her said, "I am a martyr for my kiddies. I devote so much of my life to them that I have no time to take care of myself.''

Patsy always needed a cause. Now she had one that was inexhaustible. She needed to sacrifice herself for others, and the "kiddies" were the unchallengeable others.

"I don't want revenge, Patsy," I said wearily.

Women at forty, Catherine Curran—who was approaching that turning point—had insisted vigorously at lunch a couple of months back, don't have to fall apart, not unless they want to. Certainly not, Eileen had agreed, and they want to usually because of a need to deny their sexuality.

"Is a million dollars worth the lives of five children?" She rummaged through her old and littered purse, found a partially used tissue, and dabbed at her eyes. "Do you hate us that much?"

Almost as though I had committed the crime by permitting her husband to steal my money.

Why had she married King? In 1962 that's what a woman did when she left college, especially if your closest friend was "practically engaged" and there was a boy who wanted to marry you. If Jean were dating someone like King, I imagine it would occur to me that he was not a very good marital prospect. In those days, however, I agreed with my contemporaries that King was bright, lots of fun, with sleek, dark Tyrone Power good looks, and a surefire success. All he needed was to find a woman who would make him settle down and straighten out.

Marriage was just the thing for John King Sullivan. Surely his parents thought so. Patsy would finish the molding of the man that they had begun. Patsy's parents also were enthused about the marriage, even though both bride and groom were just twenty. They were, I think, more impressed by the wealth of King's father than they were by King's evident alcohol addiction. In any meaning the word may have, he was an alcoholic by his twentieth birthday, despite the implicit conspiracy in the neighborhood to pretend that he was not.

Madonna told me many years later that Patsy lost her nerve a few weeks before the wedding and went over to the rectory to call it off. Incredibly, the priest she talked to (not the curate of our teens, who once remarked that a sign of a successful parish was the number of canceled weddings every year) persuaded her to give King the second chance for which he pleaded. That night King solemnly swore that he would stop drinking the day after their wedding. Poor Patsy believed him. Maybe King believed himself.

"I'm not going to try to regain any of the money, Patsy," I said, arriving at my decision as I talked to her. "I've told my attorney . . ."

"That hateful Nick Curran, he's always envied King. . . ." She twisted the tissue in her restless fingers.

I could not imagine anything further from the truth.

"I've told them that we will drop all civil action. The money doesn't make any difference to me."

"You'll still talk to the grand jury." The glow in her eyes was accusing and contemptuous.

I shifted uncomfortably in my chair and played with the sailboat model from the table. "I'm an officer of the court, Patsy. I don't want to talk to the grand jury. If the United States Attorney asks me to, however, I don't see how as a lawyer and a citizen I can refuse."

"You've always been one for high principles, haven't you?" she snapped bitterly. "Do you know what a trial will do to my kiddies?"

I thought to myself that it probably wouldn't make their lives much worse.

"There won't be a trial, Pat. There'll be a plea bargain and King will be placed on probation."

"With a courtroom scene and more headlines and it will be all your fault."

Patsy had acquired at least one skill in twenty-two years of marriage: now she knew how to hate.

Could she have "shaped up" King as everyone had confidently predicted she would at the wedding banquet at the Martinique on 95th Street—the best site her parents could afford?

A pretty, intelligent bride seems to have all the cards on her wedding day. If she'd said postpone the wedding for a year and prove to me you can stay sober, maybe he would have shaped up. Or if after marriage she had been willing to play her ace—stop drinking or I'll leave you—King might have changed.

Yet who is to say that King had the strength of character to respond to such demands? There was room for only one strong person in the family in which he was reared—his father. The difference between him and my wife, I tell myself now, is that Madonna might have been able to learn the self-discipline necessary for maturity if she had the motivation. King didn't even have the raw material from which character can be built.

I am in no position to be critical of Patsy. I did little to help Madonna—and she would have denied that any change was necessary in her character. Indeed, her version of our marriage was that after twenty years of trying to make a man out of me, she gave it up as a bad job.

What do you do to "shape up" a spouse? Neither Patsy nor I had learned the answer to that question. I knew I had failed Madonna, though I didn't know how. Did Patsy feel that she had failed King? Was her dedication to the kiddies a form of expiation?

"I'd walk out on the whole lot of them," Madonna told me contemptuously. "I wouldn't sacrifice myself for a drunken husband and a pack of brats."

Sure enough. Madonna decided not to sacrifice herself for me or for one child.

"It will be very quiet," I tried to reassure her. "Don Roscoe only wants publicity when he looks good."

When he goes after black basketball stars like Hurricane Houston or politicians, not when he goes after commodities brokers whose families have been major contributors to the Republican party for decades.

"Maddie is right about you." She leapt out of her chair and stormed towards the office door. "You have no balls. I hope you enjoy your yacht. Think of my kiddies while you're out there, and what you're doing to the man who was your best friend all your life."

I groaned softly to myself and walked down to Eileen's office. She was studying a law journal.

Eileen's office is sufficiently like the others in our fortress at Jackson and LaSalle so that you will know she is indeed a member of the firm, and sufficiently different so that you will know she is a woman member of the firm. The carpet is beige, the desk walnut, the law journals somberly imposing. But light blue and yellow sunbursts by Catherine Curran decorate either wall, and the chairs and couch are covered in the same color fabric—whether the sunbursts or the chairs came first is a question she refuses to answer. In addition to the sunbursts two miniature woodcuts of womanly nudes in dawn colors hang on the wall opposite her desk; since you can't see the models' faces, you don't know whether one might be Eileen—and she won't tell you. (I've been afraid to study them too closely, but, knowing a little of her sometimes unusual sense of humor, I wouldn't be surprised if she were both models.) The prints are delicate and far from obscene. But the model has a lovely body, and it is hard not to turn around and stare at them.

She denies that it is psychological warfare.

"No reading glasses?" I asked her, ignoring the nudes as I did habitually.

"Contacts. Part of the new deal with Red." She was wearing a seersucker maternity dress and looking fresh and self-contained, a woman for whom pregnancy was an honor, not a burden.

"His idea?"

"Course not," she grinned. "Did I see Patsy Sullivan rush by my door? Poor Brendan."

"I've made a decision, Eileen. No civil suits. I'll testify before the grand jury under subpoena."

"Fine." Why had I expected her to be critical? "I hope that satisfied her?"

"No, it didn't."

"Poor Brendan. I suppose you're being blamed for harming the kiddies?"

"Yep."

"Poor kiddies. I worry about her. She's a manic-depressive, you know. Probably in a manic state now."

"Can't they treat that with drugs these days?" I sank into one of her chairs and poured myself a cup of her always warm chamomile tea.

"My sister, Mary Kate the Shrink, says such people can be treated if they will take their pills every day. But at the high and the low point of the cycle they often won't take the pills."

"Poor Patsy."

"Poor everyone."

Several hours later I was sitting in the sleek bar at the top of the John Hancock Center, brooding over the changing colors of the lake far below and listening to the well-bred late-afternoon hum of executives with well-padded expense accounts and well-padded expensive women. I was drinking soda water, and the pastor of St. Jarlath's, Father Ron Crowley, was already on his third vodka martini. I might have matched him with my usual serious drink, John Jameson's straight up, but I was having supper shortly with Ciara Kelly and I'd need to have my wits about me for that.

"How come you're not drinking?" Ron gestured expansively.

"I'm going to the concert this evening."

"You don't have a date, do you?" He laughed crudely. "Some nice, comfortable, matronly widow? No, certainly not. You always were a loser with women, weren't you, Bren? Like you are with everything else."

"Course not." I laughed with him. No, not a comfortable widow at all.

The sun was slipping behind the high-rises, turning Lake Michigan into a golden plate, sparkling as though someone had carelessly scattered several handfuls of gems on it.

Ron looked like a colonel in British India who had eaten too much mutton, drunk too much claret, and gambled too much money at late-night games in the officers' club. His face was permanently flushed, his long and unkempt blond hair was laced untidily with a dirty gray, his eyes were bloodshot, his fingers trembled when they were not wrapped around the martini glass, his black clerical shirt, stuffed with stomach, hung out over his belt. The dashing young clerical radical of a few years ago looked fifteen years older than he actually was.

I remembered very clearly the night he told us he was going to be a priest. He had left early for Notre Dame because his athletic scholarship required him to be there for freshman football practice.

It was at dusk in mid-August of 1960 that he drove up to the park at 100th Street in his VW convertible. The park was kind of an oversize drugstore corner, where you smoked and waited for your friends and checked out the girls and tried to find out where everyone was going and drank beer and made out after dark.

Ron climbed out of the car, the perfectly conditioned college linebacker, thigh muscles bulging against his white bermuda shorts, arm and chest muscles bulging against his green Notre Dame T-shirt.

"Back from football practice?" Madonna asked uneasily. "You didn't get cut?"

"I quit." He leaned over the side of her T-bird convertible (the new one with the automatic hardtop cover) and spoke with the same quiet self-confidence that had made him captain of the team and outstanding senior at St. Ignatius. "Madonna, guys, I'm going to the seminary. I've always known that I was meant to be a priest. I can't keep running from God. I hope you don't mind."

We embraced him, shook his hand, congratulated him. In those days in the Neighborhood, there was no greater calling than the priesthood. Even if it broke your heart, as it did break the hearts of both Madonna and King, you still celebrated when one of your friends announced that he had a "vocation."

Later that night, King admitted his skepticism to me over the beginnings of his second six-pack: "He won't last. He found out in the practices at N.D. that he'll never be the all-American his father was. So he chickened. He thinks he can surpass the old man by being the one thing the old man never was."

My unvoiced doubts pertained to women. Ron in those days was breathtakingly handsome. Despite Madonna's vigilant eye, young women threw themselves at him with dizzy recklessness. Ron was not immune to them either. He dressed at the leading edge of fashion, the first one of our generation to show up at Sunday Mass in a charcoal gray suit with a pink shirt (yellow the following week). Women of every age adored him. While he never exceeded the line that Madonna had drawn as the limit of their sexual playfulness, he confided often to King and me that there were others who were not nearly so strict.

Maybe, I said to myself, it's either celibacy or polygamy for Ron. Monogamy would be too difficult.

Perhaps King was right about Ron's motivation—it was a

surprisingly sophisticated insight for him. But he was wrong in his prediction: Ron did stay in the seminary, sweated out the terrible turbulence of the Church in the sixties, and was ordained just after I came home from Vietnam. His charm and energy and zeal made him a marked man, and the era made him a radical. He volunteered for the inner city, fought with his pastor, whom he charged with racism even though the man had been in "black work" for twenty-five years, volunteered for Latin America, came back as an advocate of Hispanics and the "Third World," was assigned to the Peace and Justice Office of the diocese, labored mightily at the "Call to Action" conference in 1976 (an attempted coup of lower-level bureaucrats—claiming to be the "people"— against their bishops), and became a champion of "liberation." There was not a militant cause, not a protest meeting, not a crusade in which he was not prominent.

He wore himself out, running down his enormous physical energy, and took off six months for a sabbatical to "pray and reflect." In fact he used the time to learn the dynamics of "community organization" and returned, sounding like a Marxist, to take on the Cook County Regular Democratic organization. He endorsed Jane Byrne for mayor and helped her in the primary, which no one thought she was going to win until the snows came. She dumped him, as eventually she dumped everyone, before the general election. Then he went to work for the American Civil Liberties Union and gave that up when he found that he would never comprehend the dynamics of Jewish family infighting, which constitute the politics of that organization.

No one denied his sincerity, energy, or dedication, even when they disagreed with the goals of his most recent crusade. Many priests who would not think of walking on a picket line admired his integrity and courage. Cardinal Cronin, who must have found Ron's simple analyses maddening, nonetheless visited him when he was in the county jail. ("You're a goddamn fool, Ron," the cardinal was quoted as shouting at him, "but you're my goddamn fool.")

"I mean it, Brenny." He frowned heavily to indicate that it was him talking and not merely the vodka. "It's natural that men should dominate women. We always have. It's structured into the nature of things. They're weaker and we're stronger. Okay, the world is slightly civilized now and we have to pretend that everyone is equal, but deep down they want to be dominated. This feminism business is only a transient thing. You can't say that in public or there'd be hell to pay. But it's true. Anyway, they want to be dominated. It's in their nature. Find yourself a well-built widow and push her around a little. She'll love it.''

Was this really the Catholic peace activist of a year ago? The militant civil rights and antiwar protester of the seventies? The "Third World" enthusiast so often celebrated in the pages of the *National Catholic Reporter*? Had the pastorate of a rich suburban parish completely transformed him, or was Ron a burned-out case?

"Doesn't that legitimate rape and sexual harassment?" I asked dubiously.

He quaffed half his martini at a single swallow. "No woman," he licked his lips, "is ever raped who doesn't want to be raped. You can't say that these days without offending the nutty nun feminists, but that's the way it is.''

We had been discussing his problems in the parish, which, according to him, were the result of the necessity of tightening up after a "hyperpermissive" predecessor had let all authority collapse. "You can have only one boss, Brendan, you know that." The nuns who taught in his school, objecting to the "clear lines of responsibility" that he had laid down, were leaving. Good riddance to them. They would be replaced by nuns from Italy, who knew their place and would work for a lot less. Teach sound doctrine too. Would the well-educated and affluent parishioners of St. Jarlath's complain about grammar school teachers who could barely talk English and who had not attended American colleges? Too bad. Let them send their kids to the public schools.

"The trouble in your marriage, Brendan," he continued magisterially, "is that you were too soft on Madonna. If you had socked her in the chops a couple of times a year, everything would have been fine. She wanted that, you know, and you didn't have the guts to give it to her. Never treat a woman as an equal. They don't want it. They enjoy a good beating now and then. A belt on the mouth when she made one of her dumb comments would have been good for Madonna.''

"She felt that candor was part of her appeal." Maybe he was right, but I was not the one to belt any woman on the mouth.

"Candor? Is that what you call it?" He reached for a handful of popcorn. "She'll be a crude loudmouth like her father until someone pounds it out of her."

I could still hardly believe what I was hearing. When Madonna walked out on me, Ron had rushed to console me, mostly by telling me how much Madonna had suffered through the years of the marriage. Her decision, he assured me, was much harder on her than it was on me, but it was a sign of maturity and self-possession. Now he was telling me that I should have belted her as often as necessary (which for the last several years might have been almost every day).

The 95th Bar darkened rapidly. A fast-moving line of clouds was racing in from the western suburbs, blotting out the sun. The lake turned amber, then purple, and then a threatening greenish black. I would have to hurry to Orchestra Hall if my carefully selected light gray suit and color-coordinated tie were not to be soaked before I had a chance to impress the woman.

"Now, about King . . . No, I have to drive back. . . . Well, one more won't hurt. . . . What about you? . . . No, you don't have a date tonight, do you. . . . Sorry, only kidding. Anyway, about King. Do you understand how fragile he is now? The biopsies were negative, but the tests scared the daylights out of him. He knows it's time to settle down finally, if only for Patsy and the kids. He goes to AA every night and is really into it. He's pulling himself together, Brenny, and this time, with a little bit of luck, he's going to make it. Is your money so important that you want to endanger what might be his last chance?"

"I don't want the money back," I began.

"You do too." He dismissed my plea with a wave of his martini glass. "All you ever wanted was to be rich. And you've never forgiven him because Patsy loved him instead of you."

"I'm not bringing any civil actions." Perhaps, Ciara Kelly or not, I should order a Jameson's. "I will only testify before the grand jury if I am subpoenaed; there's no question of a trial; all Don Roscoe wants is a plea bargain to boost his conviction percentage. If you want to get King off the hook, talk to Roscoe.''

''What will happen,'' he sat straight up in his chair like he was an appellate judge, ''if you refuse to testify under subpoena?''

''I might be held in contempt of court and sent to jail.''

''How likely is that?'' he asked airily, as though it were unthinkable.

Did it finally come to that? Did friendship require that I run the risk of going to jail for a friend who had betrayed me? Was I willing to risk it? I suppose so, but I was no longer sure that King was my friend or ever had been.

Moreover, there was no danger of his being sent to prison.

''With Don Roscoe you can't tell. He has reason to want to get even with our firm.''

''The American legal system is totally corrupt.'' He drained the martini glass. ''It would not be sinful to disregard it.''

So there was some radicalism still left—when the authority belonged to someone else.

''Far from perfect, but the best we have,'' I replied firmly.

''So you wouldn't go to jail to protect your friend? Wouldn't Jesus be willing to do that?''

''I'm not Jesus.''

''You claim to be a follower of his, don't you?''

The group had decided that I was the criminal, not King, and that I should run the risk of jail in his place. It was a belief that approached lunacy. Yet all four of them now believed it absolutely. (I was sure that Madonna had cast her vote for conviction with the others.) The matter was so obvious to them that its self-evident truth was beyond discussion. I was to be the fall guy again.

No way. I had other things in my life now. Like Ciara Kelly. My Holy Grail.

''I've made my decision, Ron. It stands.'' The first time in my life since dating Eileen for the prom that I had stood up to them.

''God have mercy on you, Brendan.'' He shoved his empty glass out of the way, stood up heavily, and strode away from me with a briskness which was supposed to convey that I was not even worthy of contempt.

The effect was spoiled somewhat by the uncertainty of his weaving step and the trouble he had finding the elevators.

So I had at last broken with the group. It had taken long enough, heaven knows. I was astonished by the deterioration in Ron. I felt sorry for them. But I was not going down the same drain as they. Let the dead bury their dead; I bravely cited scripture to myself.

No one had told me about any biopsies for King. Friends indeed.

As I paid the bill, I glanced out at the now dark and somber lake and saw, or thought I saw, tombstones. Doom for me and my friends? Psychic nonsense. Maybe for them. But not for me.

I had a date, and my heart sang with joy.

A date with Ciara Kelly.

She was waiting for me in the lobby of Orchestra Hall. Ignoring the raindrops that were starting to fall, little wet mosquitoes stinging at my, I hoped, low-key sexy suit, I paused to admire her, to enjoy my desire for her, and to probe the quick but powerful sensation that she was carrying my son. . . . No, not my son, my child, gender unspecified.

She was wearing a tailored pinstripe white dress with a thick gray belt, emphasizing her slim waist, and gray buttons on the bodice, emphasizing her glorious torso. Her hair was still piled on top of her head, and her throat, framed in the V neck of the dress and adorned by a slender gold Celtic cross, was like the ivory in a Book of Kells print. There was a touch of makeup at her lips but no jewelry besides the cross. Elegance achieved at very modest cost.

I permitted myself to fantasize briefly about slowly removing her clothes. I had seen only two women naked in my life. She would be much more spectacular than either.

In none of these longings, images, and fantasies did issues of religion or morality arise. Having broken with my group, it seemed that I had almost abandoned the careful and precise sexual principles of my Catholic childhood. The only norm that mattered now was the command to make Ciara Kelly my woman.

I pushed open the door and entered the lobby. Her face lit up when she saw me. I had to strain to hear her soft words.

"Ah, Brendan Ryan, don't you look dapper now? Sure, a person would think you were dining with some grand lady. . . ."

"I am."

"You're not supposed to say things like that." She flushed and turned away. "And myself such a shy Irish biddy that I'm afraid to ride up to that Cliff Dwellers place by myself."

"I'll be proud to walk in with you. Every head will turn."

"Go 'long with you now." A gentle poke at my arm.

As we rode up the elevator in faintly embarrassed silence, I realized again that ours was a mutual attraction. She was as powerfully attracted to me as I was to her. Unaccountably, the woman liked me. She was as ill at ease with her agitated emotions as I was with mine. We were both reckless gamblers, throwing caution to the winds for perhaps the first time in our lives.

I tried to imagine practicing Ron Crowley's strategy on her. Maybe Ron was right. Maybe Madonna needed more pushing around. It wouldn't work for five seconds with Ciara Kelly. She did not wear an armor of solid muscle as did Eileen Kane. On the contrary, she was if anything soft as well as pale; in a few years she would need to worry about exercise should she want to keep her figure. Yet she was a big, strong woman. Belt her in the mouth and she'd belt you back. Hard.

I laughed at the absurdity without thinking that she would hear me.

"I amuse you, do I, Mr. Ryan?" She cocked a contentious eyebrow as we left the elevator.

"I spoke with a man this afternoon, who advocated keeping women in line by belting them in the mouth."

"And you considered the advisability of that policy in the present instance." She preceded me up the stairs to the top floor of the building, the "Attic" as the club was called in its early years, after it was founded by a group of Chicago architects, most of whose names are now legendary. She turned her head back to keep an eye on me. "And decided that it would not work at all."

"A man could get hurt." The rear view of her, which I had not previously considered in such elaborate detail, was in its own way as interesting as the front view, a set of complementary geometric curves that demanded careful study and exploration.

"He could indeed." She stopped at the door of the club, fascinated yet hesitant, a little girl entering a new school. "This is a grand place!"

"More like an English club, I am told, than are many of the English clubs."

"None of them have that grand lake out there, smiling at us like a mother with her child. And no watercolor paintings of sailboats either." She glanced around the paneled walls of the crowded room. " 'Tis a fine place to be taking a woman to dinner, and herself a coward when you asked her."

"Have you sailed recently?" I took her arm and guided her through the tables to our place in the corner near the book rack.

"Not in years. I'm terrible out of condition, to tell the truth."

"Would you like to sail on the *Brigid* with me on Sunday?" I pulled out the chair for her. It was a question that in my campaign strategy was not programmed until tomorrow.

She watched me very seriously as I sat down across from her, considering her answer carefully. "I'd like that, Brendan Ryan." She nodded solemnly. "I'd like that very much." A quick grin banished the seriousness. "Sure I'll be so dreadful clumsy for want of practice that you'll throw me over the side."

You're as much in love, woman, as I am. I agree. Hang the consequences.

"Against such a chilly possibility, would you like a drink now to warm you up?"

She glanced around the room with mock slyness. "I don't suppose that such a terrible grand place would have a wee drop of John Jameson's?"

"On the rocks?"

She looked at me in mock horror. "Do I seem altogether uncivilized?"

"Only altogether lovely." I felt my face grow warm. Hers turned crimson to match.

We toasted each other with the tiny shot glasses. "Slainte, Brendan Ryan."

"Slainte, Ciara Kelly."

I don't remember much of the dinner conversation. Her voice was so soft that I had to lean close to hear her words. She had, it seemed, four different dialects—thick West of Ireland, Dublin literate, British Isles educated, and plain old American with softer consonants and richer "a" sounds than you would hear from a Chicago native. She moved among them unself-consciously, depending on how vulnerable she felt. The dense brogue, sometimes almost untranslatable, correlated with a flushed face and the deep Irish sigh that suggests to those not familiar with it the advent of a serious asthma attack.

I learned that she was thirty-four years old, a few more years of life behind her than I had thought. She offered nothing more about her background, and, despite my nervous curiosity, I resolved not to ask.

Yet I wondered again that night why a woman of obvious intelligence and education would be working as a sales clerk for a salary which, judging by her inexpensive clothes, could not amount to much. A tiny cancer of suspicion gnawed at the back of my brain: she knows you're wealthy.

We had a second drink, rather to my surprise. "Would you be wanting another?"

"Well, to prepare for all the dancing, I suppose I should." Much like I suppose I should really say the Stations of the Cross after the Rosary—a moral and religious obligation.

Since it was Solti's last week before he returned to his other jobs in Europe, the Cliff Dwellers was filled, but I recognized none of my friends. Moreover, when we were shown to our seats in the hall, none of the regulars around me seemed to be there. At the end of the season, tickets are often exchanged or given away. Somehow I was relieved. I didn't want to have to explain Ciara Kelly just yet. In days to come I avoided restaurants where I was known or might be recognized, telling myself that it was not yet time to display her.

And perhaps, from what I know now, because she was not there to display.

We paused again at the door of the concert hall while Ciara drank in the great ivory and red room.

"Like it?"

"It's too nice for someone such as me," she whispered, as if she were in church.

"Go along with you, woman. The best is none too good for you."

"Listen to him, will you?"

Safely in our place, halfway back on the main floor center, she studiously consumed the program notes.

"Do you come often to the concerts, Brendan Ryan?"

"Not too often the last couple of years. I have season tickets, but my wife lost interest in classical music and I didn't like coming alone."

Sir Georg appeared to the usual enthusiastic applause and was greeted with a whispered "Darlin' man" from my companion.

She sat straight upright as he raised his baton and leaned forward tensely to catch every note of music, every nuance of direction. The Beethoven overture caused her to clench her fists and smile. Stravinsky's masterpiece seemed to take possession of her soul.

After the first few bars, she clutched my hand frantically, as if I were to keep her from joining the priestess in her mad dance, which was to bring the fertility of spring alive again. Stravinsky's wild, frenzied rush of spring vitality appeared to be pouring into her body and flowing out of it.

Well, Brendan, you've found yourself an odd one.

When Solti finished, with a military snap of his baton and a polished imperial bow to the orchestra, then wheeled to face the cheering audience, she crumpled like a used tissue; her damp hand slipped out of mine; and she looked at me out of the corner of one watery gray eye.

"Haven't I been making a terrible fool out of myself now?" The West of Ireland brogue was so thick that at first I thought she was speaking in Gaelic.

"I think you reacted just the way Sir Georg and old Igor wanted you to react."

We stood with the rest of the crowd and yelled for half a dozen more bows from conductor and orchestra.

I suggested that we stretch our legs in the lobby, and Ciara, still pale and limp from the music, gratefully agreed.

Solid sheets of rain were pounding the pavement of Michigan Avenue, and the lions on the Art Institute across the street were intermittently illuminated by blue phosphorescent flashes of lightning. Thunder rumbled almost immediately after the lightning; the storm was above us and moving out over the lake.

"It'll be over before we leave; it's not one of your Irish all-day rains."

She nodded, still in the grip of Stravinsky's manic dance.

I glanced around the lobby, an Irish politician casing the house at a wake. No one I knew.

Except Madonna. And in tow a certain notorious Chicago gossip columnist, surely alcoholic and rumored homosexual, who specialized in mean and picky hatchet jobs. I turned away, hoping she would not notice me.

No such luck. In a few moments Madonna jabbed my arm. "I knew you'd find a girlfriend." In the same tone as if she'd said she knew I was going to take up cocaine. "Aren't you going to introduce us?"

Her diets, health food, and jogging had made her not thin, but emaciated. Once a lovely, slender woman with intense sex appeal, she had become a scrawny bird of prey with sharp, hawkish features caked in powdery beige makeup; brittle, strawlike hair, and the bent-forward-from-the-shoulder posture of a praying mantis.

I was embarrassed, angry, and yet heartbroken for her. In the name of looking younger than her age, she had made herself look older. As Ron had destroyed his physical attractiveness with neglect, Madonna had destroyed hers with excessive care.

I made the introductions with as much aplomb as I could muster under the circumstances. I presented Madonna as "Madonna Clifford," the name she used in her North Shore art gallery advertisements.

So there would be no mistake, she quickly added, "Although we were married for almost twenty years, he's ashamed to admit it."

"Oh." Ciara was ashen.

"Did you like the Stravinsky, Madonna?" I tried to sound pleasant.

"Stravinsky, havinsky." She dismissed my small talk as the kind of ineffectual dodge she had come to expect from me. "You're welcome to him, my dear. Maybe you can make a man out of him. I couldn't. You've got your work cut out for you." And then, turning to me, "Kind of young, isn't she, Brendan? I figured you'd go for someone fat all right, but much older. See you around, my dears."

She bounced away, trying unsuccessfully to create the ambience of the witty, frothy woman about town.

I was wishing that one of the thunderbolts would strike me and carry me off, perhaps to Alpha Centauri.

"I'm sorry, Brendan," Ciara said quietly. The first time she hadn't added my last name.

"Why should you be sorry?" I snapped irritably.

"Because you've been unfairly hurt."

"Thanks, Ciara," I relented. "Madonna has always prided herself on her candor."

"That's what it's called, is it now?"

"She hasn't always been that way." I rose to my presumed wife's defense. "She was once a sweet and lovely girl. Life has not been good to her."

"Poor woman." Followed by the prolonged asthmatic sigh. "Still, I can see why you sought the annulment." Her various brogues were replaced by plain American.

"It was her idea, not mine." We joined the crowds walking back into the auditorium for the rest of the concert.

"Really?" Ciara was startled. "Ah, but it's none of my business now, is it?"

I had no answer for her. During the Mozart concerto, however—early Mozart and light and happy—it was my turn to capture her hand and hold it. There was not the faintest hint of resistance.

Maybe if I had known what would happen to Madonna and had heard Ron's advice years earlier, I thought, I would have listened to him. No, there had to be a better way. She had failed me, surely. But I had failed her too. If Ciara Kelly was thinking I was a bad risk or doubting my masculinity because I didn't walk away from such witchery, she might very well be correct in her judgments.

The storm had indeed passed over, leaving in its wake the rich, earthy, fertile smell of spring. The last of my senses had been captured by my new woman.

"You're going sailing with me on Sunday." I ticked it off on my fingers.

" 'Tis true."

"And we're going back to Orchestra Hall on Saturday for a whole evening of Mozart." Another finger ticked.

"Ah, are we now?"

"Aren't we now?"

"Who's answering with questions this time? . . . All right, don't hit me. . . . We are."

"So what are we doing tomorrow night?"

"Well . . ." She seemed to be searching for an excuse.

"Well . . ." I persisted.

"I see in the papers that this place called The Body Politic is doing Brian Friel's *Volunteers*. You know, the *Freedom of the City* man."

"And *Philadelphia Here I Come* and *Translations*, which they did last year."

"Well . . ." Her face took on an expression of leprechaun craftiness.

"Well . . ."

"Well, would you ever think we might see that?"

"I think it might be arranged."

She clapped her hands with innocent enthusiasm. "I'd enjoy it ever so much. . . . And there I go, sounding English. Ever so much indeed!"

She lived at Chestnut Place, a modestly priced red brick rental skyscraper. There was no invitation up to her room. I would have been astonished if there had been.

"Thank you very much, Brendan Ryan." She extended her hand to me. " 'Twas a glorious evening." She smiled gentle approval of me and everything I stood for. "You're a desperate man altogether."

"Thank you, Ciara Kelly, for making it glorious." I held her hand and kissed her forehead. "I'll see you tomorrow."

She slipped away quickly so I wouldn't see her face. I was sure, however, she was crying.

As I finish writing these words, I briefly think to myself that Madonna met her. She can confirm that Ciara Kelly really existed.

Then I realize how foolish and futile such a thought is.

9

"I do not intend to waste the rest of my life," Madonna's face was warped in anger and hatred, a harpy swooping down on its prey, "enhancing your public image by pretending to be nothing more than a good wife and mother."

We were perhaps two hours into Madonna's announcement, after Jean's graduation party, that she wanted a divorce. There was not much discussion, only bombardment. Madonna was now a middle-aged Barbie doll, not unattractive certainly, but with a petulant frown permanently frozen into the lines of her face.

"I thought you were happy in the wife and mother role," I said wearily, now hoping that the nightmare would soon end and I could quietly leave. She had carved out the role for herself, or so it had seemed to me.

"How could any woman be happy," her lips twisted into a contemptuous sneer, "married to a man without balls? Do you realize how lousy a lover you are, Brendan? You're as useless in bed as you are on the tennis courts. I've taken lovers ever since you went away to your goddamn war. I have a right to sexual fulfillment. And, while I'm at it, I had my tubes tied after Jean. So there never was a chance for the stupid son you wanted."

I didn't altogether believe her. I'm still not sure whether she was telling the truth or merely tormenting me.

In the previous exchange I had been denounced as a "patriarchal chauvinist" because I wouldn't let her pursue her own career—despite the fact that I was the one who raised the career question in the early years of marriage until she finally told me she never wanted to hear the word again. A "patriarchal chauvinist without balls"? Perhaps somewhat contradictory, but anger, not logic, was Madonna's agenda.

I was overwhelmed by her attack. Yet I could not take it seriously because I suspected that it had all been carefully practiced in the Femtherapy group of which she was a member. The script was being acted out now, not with me as the relevant audience, but the group to which she would report triumphantly the next day. I was nothing more than a witness at the dress rehearsal. They would swarm around, hug and kiss her, and celebrate her freedom.

And they would congratulate her on forcing me to listen to "every last word."

I was sad because I had loved her deeply once, or thought I did, and because I had thought that someday, somehow, our marriage would "work out." I was resigned because I knew that there was now no saving the relationship; Madonna might have second thoughts later, when she came down off her emotional high and when she lost interest in the Femtherapy group, but she was much too proud ever to admit a mistake. And, finally, I was relieved; I would no longer have to bear her noisy contempt.

So I recited my lines in the script with little enthusiasm. Should we not try again? She was sick of trying with me; it was a waste of her precious time. Maybe we ought to go into family therapy? I was the one who needed the therapy, not her. Perhaps we might talk to a priest? She had talked to Father Ron, and he said it was about time that she drew the line. And so on.

Eventually it was over—at the end a screaming and crying session with Jean in which she sided with her mother—and I was out in the mild spring night. Alone and guilty because I did not feel more pain.

I ought not to be thinking that I was well rid of her. The tempting thought, however, would not go away.

As I look over these pages I am painfully aware that my initial intention to be fair and objective about Madonna has only been paid lip service. I must be at pains to explain that she was not a ranting monster. She was a lonely, frightened, angry woman. I was a convenient target for her loneliness, fear, and anger; and a fair target, too, because I did nothing to protect her from those devastating emotions. Indeed, I hardly recognized them in the early years of our marriage. Her mother and father might have been more appropriate targets—they were the ones who treated Madonna as a mirror to reflect their own glory from the moment of her conception. She was never able to see Lourdes and Melvin Clifford as her enemies. On the contrary, they were always her loyal allies in the long battle against, as she saw it, the real problem: her inept and inadequate husband.

How does a husband become adequate in a conflict with a wife filled with unperceived self-contempt? And how does a father prevent such self-contempt from being transmitted to his daughter? For Melissa Jean was designed to reflect Madonna's glory in the same way Madonna reflected Lourdes's glory. What else does one do with a daughter?

Yet I did fail Madonna. She came to marriage seeking value as a person, though she would not have said that. She did not find it. For that I am to blame.

I never did court her or propose to her in the conventional sense. I had been her number-two beau through the high school years, to be called on without apology when Ron was unavailable. She cried on my shoulder, not his. And she sought my advice when she was uneasy because of his roving eye.

Since two beaus were required for each "deb" (the word was never used), I was her second escort at the first Presentation Ball, a Catholic cotillion set up in opposition to the Passavant Cotillion. It seemed to Ron and me that it was a dreary and pompous affair, justified by frequent references to the "Mrs. Frank J. Lewis Milk Fund" for whose purposes it was alleged to be directed. Madonna accepted readily enough our contempt for the heavy solemnities and at the same time accepted her mother's ecstatic protestations that the day Madonna was accepted for the Ball was the happiest day in her life.

We were buddies and friends, a more relaxed relationship than lovers. "I don't know what I'd do without you, Brendan," she said after a long and tearful session about rumors that Ron was weary of her.

"You'll never have to do without me," I said manfully.

I can't say that I was in love with her in those days. I wasn't in love with anyone in the sense of being emotionally preoccupied with them, except for Eileen during the prom weeks. My group was a locus of commitment rather than a source of satisfaction.

Not being able to write to Ron at the seminary, she poured out letters from school to me, long, witty, painful letters. She was homesick, the other girls were snobs and immoral besides, the teachers were drips, the rules were outrageous, the nuns were pathetically old-fashioned. I suppose the truth was that at St. Mary's she was merely another freshman and not the center of everyone else's existence.

Gradually, when it became reasonably certain that Ron would stay in the seminary, we became lovers, not, heaven save us as good Catholics in those days, that we went to bed together. Our exchanges of affection became more passionate—making out, necking, petting, as such activities were called in those days. I enjoyed such interludes enormously, more, I confess, than much of the sex that took place between us after marriage. At first I was the initiator, a young male animal on the prowl. Then gradually Madonna became the aggressor. Her lips were warm and demanding, her body firm and eager, the line beyond which we could not go increasingly flexible and porous. She was hungry for as much love as I could give. And then some.

We confessed our sins on Saturday so we could receive Communion on Sunday, dutifully promised the priest we'd stay away from the occasion of sin, and fell from grace in a final frenzy of affection as she boarded the South Shore at 111th Street for her return to her hated college.

So it came to be taken for granted that we would marry. While I did not formally propose and was taken aback when Lourdes Clifford began to discuss the size of the wedding party at dinner in September of 1962 (Madonna, having kept her promise of two years of college, was now free to work in her father's office, and we were celebrating her "joining the team"), the picture of life with Madonna was so attractive that I saw no reason to object. My only stubbornness was that we would not be married till I graduated and that I had a military obligation.

No one seemed to mind. Only many years later did I come to understand that in the Clifford house, the wedding as a festive celebration was what mattered, not the physical or personal relationship that came after.

My parents and I were swept, unprotestingly, aside as Lourdes and Madonna planned the production—twenty-six in the wedding party, a bouquet of roses affixed to every pew, seventeen priests, including five monsignors, in the sanctuary, trumpets and violins in the choir loft, a papal blessing to be announced by the pastor, bridesmaids in pink, groomsmen in pink-tinged summer formals, over a thousand guests at the South Shore Country Club, a wedding not to be forgotten.

Heavily girdled and smelling of a mixture of strong gin and stronger Chanel, Lourdes charged through the preparations, wedding protocol book in one hand, checkbook in the other, with a martyred weariness that said someone had to assume responsibility lest both families be humiliated by gaucherie.

It was hard to tell who was the audience for which the spectacular was being staged. To whom was it necessary to prove that the Cliffords were paragons of taste, sensibility, and etiquette? To listen to Lourdes and her flustered, harried daughter, one would have thought that the jury was the whole city of Chicago, all of whose citizens were watching with a jaundiced eye for the slightest breach of propriety or the faintest hint that cost was an important consideration.

In fact, the audience was the wives of the Neighborhood and of Dr. Clifford's colleagues, who had already decided from advance reports that the Clifford/Ryan nuptials would be a tastelessly extravagant binge and came seeking only evidence for this prejudice. They were not disappointed.

Time forces charity upon me. The nouveau riche are nouveau because they have just made their money and they are not altogether sure they will keep it. When Mel Clifford was growing up in the 1930s and struggling through medical school while he worked a largely mythical sanitary district job, the family did not have a bathtub or a shower in their apartment in Bridgeport. They used the single old-fashioned tub in his grandparents' flat on the first floor. The doctor's mother and father never moved away from that building. One of the first things Mel did when he came home from the war, wounded on Guam (according to a rumor, by falling out of a jeep), was to buy a totally new plumbing installation for the building.

We were the children of the professional generation that started late because of the Depression and the War and then in a few short years became richer than they had dreamed possible at places like Guam, where it did not seem they would live till morning. Their displays of wealth (and most were not as egregious as the Cliffords') were meant for themselves more than for others, as proof that finally after decades of trying, the Irish had become respectable.

It took another generation to realize that respectability wasn't worth the candle.

We who were their children presented them with a dilemma. On the one hand, spectacles like the Presentation Ball and Madonna's wedding demonstrated to the whole world that the Irish now had a bathtub in every dwelling unit and more besides. On the other, there was the gnawing worry that, not having been forged in the crucible of the Depression, we would not understand suffering and not have the strength of character that had been necessary for our parents' climb to affluence and success.

No one dared to say publicly what my father said privately one night to Ned Ryan on one of those rare occasions when the "other" Ryans supped at our house:

"Not many of these folks can admit that they lucked out because they happened to be the right age in the right time and place."

"Not luck but pluck." Kate Ryan grinned over her sherry glass.

"Not Catholics but Calvinists," Ned sighed. "Well, it's a lot easier to admit that your parents were lucky."

I suppose, finally, the "other" Ryans (who were not invited to our wedding; neither Lourdes nor Madonna would hear of it) were the ultimate target of our production. We would show those rich Irish who had a generation head start on us that we were as good as they were and that we were catching up with them.

Unfortunately for the satisfaction of my in-laws, the "other" Ryans didn't know there was a race.

There was nothing in the protocol books that prohibited the Shannon Rovers Irish Warpipes band from escorting us into church, or green, white, and orange ice cream representing the Irish tricolor in addition to the wedding cake for dessert, or the Notre Dame victory march as the bride and groom progressed to the head table at the reception. Nor did the books prevent Notre Dame motifs in the dining hall decorations—banners, flags, seals, pennants, even though I had gone to Loyola and Madonna had quit St. Mary's in disgust without finishing her exams at the end of the sophomore year.

Nor did the books dictate that the Cliffords ought not to leak the week before to everyone who would listen that the cost of the wedding was in excess of $20,000.

My bride was a frazzléd emotional disaster area the last weeks of our courtship. Like her mother, she suggested by her frantic behavior that it was necessitated by my family's lack of concern for what "people will say."

We saw little of each other in those final weeks; Madonna was so angry at my irresponsibility that she would not speak to me at the rehearsal and the rehearsal dinner.

Did I have any second thoughts during these frenzied preparations? No more, I suppose, than most young men would under similar circumstances. I enjoyed wonderful fantasies of Madonna in bed, fantasies in which my partner was completely different from the pale, chain-smoking young woman whose mother had driven her to daily attacks of nausea. I consoled myself with the bridegroom's usual self-deception that after marriage I would not have to share my wife with her mother. I considered with grave face and little thought my father's delicate question of whether this was what I really wanted. Eileen was already married to Red Kane, hastily enough to cause uplifted eyebrows among Madonna's friends. What else or who else might I have wanted?

I knelt in the rear corner of St. Praxides for Eileen's wedding. Redmond Kane did not look eight years older than Eileen. He was handsome, attentive, and hopelessly in love with her.

I mentioned my secret presence to Eileen a few weeks ago at lunch.

"Oh, there was nothing wrong with Red. The problem was always me. For twenty years. I'm making it up to him now, poor man."

"Does he accept that scenario?"

Her gemlike green eyes softened. "He thinks it the other way around, poor misguided soul." She chuckled. "It makes for interesting times . . . and elderly pregnancies."

With Eileen married, there seemed no reason not to proceed to the altar with Madonna. Perhaps I was trapped by a series of decisions I had previously made—or more precisely refused to make. The point is that if I was trapped, I wanted to be trapped. Or more accurately did not want not to be trapped.

The Church was no help. The parish priests, having decided long before the day of our monstrosity that they lacked the conviction and the stamina to resist nouveau riche brides and mothers, did their best to avoid Lourdes and Madonna whenever they saw them bearing down on the rectory with tight lips and fevered eyes.

We attended a pre-Cana conference, by way of marriage preparation, at which a priest preached abstract theology, a doctor spoke of technical sex, and a married couple reported with cloying sweetness how much fun it was to have children. Madonna wrote out lists of things to do, and I delighted in convoluted images of Madonna undressing. We hurriedly filled out the ecclesiastical forms in the rectory the night of the rehearsal, having dragged a curate away from his Young Christian Students meeting with insincere apologies and the excuse that there had been no other time for these formalities. He was barely civil to us as we assured him separately and together that we were entering marriage freely, that we understood its nature and purpose, that we had never been married before, that we intended to have children, and that we would not practice birth control.

Madonna was still not speaking to me. Hence she could only sigh noisily when it developed I had not brought my baptismal certificate, which had been mailed from England. I promised to produce it before the ceremony in the morning. The priest was so upset with us, doubtless with reason since the rectory had been inundated with Clifford family phone calls for the last several days, that I could see a flickering temptation in his ice blue eyes to threaten to call the whole affair off if I forgot the certificate again.

He resisted the temptation, fearing, I suspect, that Lourdes would storm the Vatican palace itself.

And I thought that if I could be sure the wedding would be canceled I'd lose the proof of my baptism.

The marriage was a spectacular success for everyone but Lourdes who would barely speak to me all day, and refused to dance with me, because my military guard of honor did not clash their swords at the proper time. My bride, now soft and submissive, and I danced to the music of *Hello, Dolly!* and *Fiddler on the Roof*, interrupted periodically by Dr. Clifford's insistence on the Notre Dame Victory March.

Patsy was unable to be matron of honor because she was too far along in her second pregnancy (in three years of marriage). Ron was forbidden by seminary rules to participate in the wedding party. He assisted at the altar, handsome and virile among the collection of rather decrepit lap-dog clergy that Dr. Clifford had assembled to represent the Church's approval of the occasion.

King was the best man, strained and puffy in his tight-fitting summer formal. He had been wiped out at the Board of Trade and was setting himself up with his father's money in a big auto dealership in Joliet.

"No problem," he assured me, using his favorite expression, "no problem at all. This way Patsy and the brats will be only twenty minutes away from work. Maybe when the brats are older I'll go back to the Exchange. Exciting place. Can't beat it for action."

Something had changed in King nonetheless. His eyes danced with cheerful mischief as they always had; but behind them there now seemed to lurk a hint of doubt or fear or perhaps resignation, a tiny but insidious worm. Despite my wedding day happiness, I began to worry about him.

"Was it rough down there?" Madonna's brother asked.

"No problem at all." He waved his hands as if performing a magic rite over his lost capital. "A piece of cake." He snatched another glass of champagne from a passing tray.

We were married, then, with what the Cliffords were certain would pass for high good taste in the neighborhood at that time, and with no preparation for either the sex or the conflict of married life.

The wedding night was a disaster. My bride, who had been

so ready and even eager to give me most of her body, was quite incapable of giving me all of it. My dreams of a naked and aroused woman were quickly destroyed by Madonna's timorous—and faintly nasty—prudery.

Our honeymoon, on a damp and misty Maine island (Madonna's hitherto unsuspected fear of flying scrubbed our planned trip to Ireland, though officially that was blamed on my military obligations), was not much better. Sexual release was granted me, but no sense of manly mastery. Madonna seemed sexy, but in the actual physical union of our bodies, she went no further than toleration. Even then there was the implication that it was somehow my fault. Our sex life was foredoomed to failure because by definition I was an inadequate male lover.

The affectionate foreplay that was the barely tolerable preparation for marriage permitted us by the Church (and then only if we confessed it) was banished from our life. Now it was supposed to lead to intercourse, and Madonna didn't want much intercourse. Only in bed and only at night with the lights out. And only as an obligation that could be quickly fulfilled. Otherwise no "fooling around." Good Catholic wife that she was, she would not run the risk that we might have complete fulfillment in an improper manner.

Occasionally there was more than sexual release—mostly when Madonna had had several drinks. On such nights, one during our honeymoon, the pleasure between us was so overwhelming as to threaten to tear apart my sanity. Madonna was capable of ecstasy and in the midst of it capable of piercing cries of satisfaction and fulfillment. Deep within the St. Mary's of Notre Dame prudish matron there was a brazen, bawdy, lascivious woman, inaccessible, unfortunately, when she was sober. She would not discuss such interludes the next morning and indeed resolutely refused to discuss sex with me at all.

"Your mind is obsessed with dirt, Brendan," she would say, dismissing my plea that we ought to talk to someone about our marriage or at least talk to each other. "I'm not going to entertain you or some voyeuristic shrink talking about my sex life. There's nothing wrong with our marriage."

There was a lot wrong, however. I see now that we were

out of "sync" from the engagement announcement on. Madonna wanted to be married, I wanted a wife and lover. We never had a chance to straighten it out. Years ago I blamed her family and the Church for our woeful lack of preparation. Now I realize that few Catholics of my generation stumbled into marriage with any notion of what they were doing. The family and the Church cooperated in the conspiracy to keep us ignorant, but they were only part of a larger conspiracy which hid both the conflict and frustration and also the possible pleasures and rewards of married life from the young.

It was sink or swim on your own.

We never learned to swim.

Can a husband jolly a passionate but prudish wife into being a good partner in bed? Now I would say "yes, surely" to that question. But then I didn't know how. Or perhaps I did and lacked the courage to face the devastating barrage of ridicule which flattened my hesitant attempts at mastery.

"Who ever told you that you were a great lover? Come on, don't play around with me; get it over with."

Madonna was soon suffering from the coming of Jean. I was busy with my Pentagon duties. In long and tearful phone conversations with her mother, she blamed me for her exile in Arlington—previously my service commitments were pertinent only because they made possible a military wedding. Lourdes was convinced that if I were willing, Dr. Clifford had enough influence to have me reassigned to Chicago.

God help me, I was willing. Dr. Clifford's clout, however, was weak. I was blamed for the failure of the transfer to materialize. If I really wanted it, it was darkly hinted, I could get it. "Daddy" couldn't do it all himself.

By the time I left for Vietnam, we were both relieved to be rid of each other.

When I came home, shaken by a sexual experience that revealed other possibilities, nothing had changed. We settled down to separate lives, marked by occasional excruciatingly pleasurable encounters and long periods of silence. I lost myself in work and school and later in the law, my boat ("Dirty little thing!" Madonna sneered contemptuously), and my various intellectual hobbies. Madonna devoted herself to punctilious housekeeping; the education of Melissa Jean (who became "Jean" by her own stubborn decision when she

went to high school; "Everyone is Melissa," she said trucu-
lently, "except the Jennifers and the Micheles." "It was
your father's idea," her mother replied, dismissing the issue
with little regard for the truth); to elaborate social obligations
in which I was only a necessary symbolic presence, as I had
been at the wedding, and to occasional bursts of short-lived
enthusiasms—art, charity, health foods, and finally watered-
down feminism.

I think she marched once or twice in protest against "your
goddamned war," and more recently in some of Father Ron's
antinuclear demonstrations, but she was not part of the radicalism of the late sixties and early seventies. Her enthusiasms
rarely tended toward political or social relevancies. Indeed,
while we were at the upper end of the sixties generation, neither of us was ever really part of it. I was too busy with work
and school. Madonna was too busy with her social life (on
the North Shore, since it was unthinkable that we not live
close to her mother and father; when I came home from the
war the house had already been picked out) and with making
Jean the perfect daughter. History, like married love, passed
us by.

I told myself it would change when I graduated from law
school or when I became a partner or when Jean went away to
college.

We watched the events of our generation as spectators, the
way most of my age group participated, I would imagine.
The Free Speech Movement at Berkeley, Selma, Martin
Luther King, the assassinations, the Conrad Hilton riot, the
Beatles, the Rolling Stones, Woodstock, Altamont, *Hair*,
Kent State, the marches on Washington, burning draft cards,
acid, pot, protests, Watergate, Jesse Jackson swinging from
the banners at Miami Beach, McGovern a thousand percent
behind his vice-presidential nominee, Chappaquiddick,
Abbie Hoffman, priests and nuns marrying and turning
Marxist, the Berrigans, English Mass, the birth control
encyclical—all were things to be read about in the *New York
Times* or to listen to as described by Walter Cronkite.

We felt the Big Chill a decade before its icy fingers
touched most of our generation.

Some of my contemporaries were involved in the struggles
of the late sixties. Nick and Eileen, both U.S. Attorneys,

were gassed in front of the Hilton. Catherine Collins left her religious community, married a priest (temporarily), and was tortured in a prison in South America. Red Kane, Eileen's husband, covered every important event from King's "I Have a Dream" speech to the Tet offensive in Saigon (in which his brother was killed and he barely escaped death). I realized that history was passing me by. I was content to let that happen. Perhaps if my marriage had been happier, I would not have cut myself off from the world beyond my Indian paths. Or maybe I am the sort of man who lives in the midst of history and fails to recognize it because he finds the past more stimulating than the present.

I have my regrets. I also have my memories of a couple of days in Vietnam in the spring of 1966 that still hallow my life. My most treasured recollections of the sixties and early seventies are not of frustrated dreams and failed idealism, but of adventure, sharp, quick, terrifying. And ambiguously successful.

At Jean's graduation Mass, I felt maudlin. From 1960 to 1982 is a short time, yet the length of a generation more or less. What did I have to show for my generation? A few shining hours in war with a tragic after effect, a couple of million dollars, a sailboat, a handful of close friends, a lot of useless knowledge, a wife who does not love me and perhaps never did, and a daughter who does not know me very well and does not like the little she does know. At the end of the day I would lose the last two.

Yet the night before Jean's graduation we had a spectacular sexual encounter, this time both of us cold sober. Madonna was seductive, audacious, irresistible. And I prolonged her pleasure till she screamed for release. We huddled in each other's arms afterward as we had when we were teenagers necking in the forest preserve.

I thought we had turned an important corner. The next day she ordered me out of the house.

I still cannot comprehend what that night of love meant in her scenario—if it meant anything.

And she seduced me one night during the divorce proceedings. She had berated me for my failures in her lawyer's office. Then we waited in hostile silence for the elevator in the lobby, each pretending that the other did not exist. As soon as the door of the elevator had closed on us, however, she whispered, "I'm sorry for being a bitch, Brendan. Can I buy you supper?"

Yes, she could. And caress me lewdly during the meal. And strip for me like a reckless tart in the hotel room afterward. And smother me with affection and love.

Her exercise and dieting had at that time honed her body to perfection and not yet turned her into a possible anorexic. She was a luscious sexual prize. Or maybe I was the prize.

As I sank into a deep and complacent sleep, I was sure the marriage had been salvaged. The next morning she said that we were going ahead with the divorce. "A romp in the hay doesn't mean a thing."

I have often suspected that I probably could have had more of those per year after the divorce than I had before. As mistress and lover, Madonna and I would have been a great pair. Maybe I should have settled for that.

I console myself with the thought that I lost her to her family, that I was doomed to lose any conflict with Lourdes and Melvin (both of whom enthusiastically endorsed the breakup of our marriage). I suppose that such an excuse has some validity. Clearly I lost the fight with them. Whether I had to lose it is another matter.

Just as clearly I lost the feeble battle I waged for Jean. Her debut in the Presentation Ball the year before last was a replication of her mother's debut at the first ball in 1960. "The happiest day of my life," Madonna said in unconscious parody of her own mother. And when I foolishly attempted to moderate the size of our "Pres Ball" party, mother and daughter turned on me with the same vengeful fury with which Lourdes and Madonna had dismissed my hesitant question in 1964, "Does the wedding party have to be so big?"

"You want to take every joy out of my life, don't you?" Madonna hissed.

"You're such a nerd," Jean ranted, as she plunged into tearful hysteria.

I read over these pages and say that I am still unfair. Madonna was sensitive, fragile, intelligent, enthusiastic, gifted. I failed her, even if I'm not quite able to put my finger on precisely the nature of the failure. Our circumstances were, perhaps, not the most conducive to a happy marriage. Yet who does enter marriage without the odds being heavily against happiness? Many overcome the odds. We didn't. I don't want to exculpate Madonna. She didn't give me much help, God knows. But I don't want to exculpate myself either.

Msgr. Blackie Ryan, when I finally spoke to him after the dreadful occurrences I am about to relate, disagreed. "You will not permit yourself the humility," he shook his head disconsolately, "of conceding that perhaps it was all beyond your powers."

"I blew it," I responded. "With the right man, Madonna could have made it."

"What would he have done?"

"I don't know." I buried my face in my hands. She had been so sweet in my arms in the summer of 1963, just before Kennedy had been killed.

"Precisely."

"I can't forgive myself," I sobbed.

"You'd better start trying," the monsignor warned ominously.

10

Our lips touched tentatively, two wary forest animals not yet sure they trusted each other. Then the kiss became firmer, warmer, more demanding as passion melted our suspicion and fear. I took her in my arms, and after a moment of hesitation, her arms encircled me.

She moved back her head. "You're a terrible man, Brendan Ryan, kissing a poor woman in front of her apartment building where the whole world can see."

Before I could reply, her mouth returned to mine, she now more the attacker than I. We slipped into a languorous swamp of pleasure, soothing, relaxed, reassuring. Why fight it? Indeed, what was there to fight?

My program for seducing Ciara Kelly was ahead of schedule. I was not so sure, however, that her program for seducing me was one minute off its schedule.

Was now the right time?

I had slept little the night of the *Rite of Spring* concert; Madonna haunted me; what right did I have, after such a disastrous failure with one woman, to pursue another? Would I fail with Ciara as I had with my wife? When I finally drifted into sleep, I had made up my mind: no more women and particularly no more Ciara Kelly.

The next morning the sun came up over the lake with a burst of spring enthusiasm, the sky was radiantly blue, Grant Park was more lushly green after the rain, and a light lace was beginning to appear on the trees on Michigan Avenue.

Ciara Kelly was back on my agenda. Definitely.

That night we ate scallops creole and drank Jesuitengarten wine at Jackie's on Lincoln, where no one knows me. I explained how the commodities futures market worked; she listened intently and asked a few intelligent questions about "leveraged purchases."

"It's a gambler you are, Brendan Ryan." She winked at me over her white wine. "In the biggest casino in all the world."

"I don't even play poker." I found myself blushing at her cool, appraising gaze. "I'm not a competitive man. I don't even race my boat."

"Don't you now? Sure, that was the great fun of it for me. I guess I'm a competitive woman, though I've never thought about it. What else is it then, if not gambling?"

A woman had never stared at me so frankly before, stripping me psychologically and examining me with the detachment of a lab technician considering an interesting and not unattractive but rather odd species of bug. I was embarrassed, uneasy, and flattered.

"I'm matching wits with the economics experts." I sipped my wine very deliberately, keeping my cool at all costs, if you take my meaning.

"Sure." She laughed delightedly—the bug pleased her. "But you're not a competitive man."

I choked on the wine, tried to explain, and gave it up in the face of her continued laughter.

"You're not trying to understand, Ciara Kelly."

" 'Tis more fun to misunderstand, Brendan Ryan. Here, have some more Jesuit wine. You're so red in the face I think you need it."

We went across the street to watch Brian Friel's condemned IRA men excavate Wood Quay in Dublin. We did not hold hands. Ciara was silent and withdrawn after the play and pleaded to be taken right home. Nonetheless, she did not object when my lips brushed against hers at the end of the night.

The next day, Saturday, even more wondrously springtime, we wandered through the massive Chicago International Art Expo at Navy Pier. I was uneasy that my love might not be interested in art and thus lose some of the perfection I had found in her. She enjoyed it, however, even more than I did, reveling in the delirious panorama of shapes and colors under the white steel girders of the old pier. The Expo itself, Ciara averred, was a work of art—"late surrealism," she decided.

She turned up her nose at the new German Expressionists; marveled at a million-dollar Picasso; examined with intelligent skepticism the Russian Reconstructionists; laughed at the twenty-eight-foot sculpture of used shopping carts at the end of the pier; admired the city skyline ("not Georgian, but nice"); prowled the prestige galleries under the pier rotunda; tickled little babies, speaking to them in French or German where appropriate; and chose as her favorites two local artists, James Winn, an Illinois prairie painter in the Frumpkin and Struve exhibition, and Michael Casey, creator of Chicago neighborhood scenes in the Anne Reilly alcove.

"This is your country, isn't it?" She studied an Illinois field in January. "And a nice country, too, for all that."

"Have you been in it long?" I asked, hunting cautiously for information.

"Not to say long." She turned to a painting of an industrial park.

In the Reilly exhibition she stood transfixed before a haunting oil of a neighborhood street corner—church, tavern, and undertakers—shaking her head slowly as though she understood what Mickey Casey (whose mother was Ed Ryan's sister) was saying.

"Former police superintendent," I said. "Sort of a relative of mine. His mother was a Ryan. The gallery owner is his wife."

Neither Anne nor Mike was there. If they had been I would have steered my prize away without an introduction.

"Poor wee man sees it all," she said mysteriously. "The bitter and the sweet and the mixture, if you take my meaning."

I didn't quite.

"Poor wee man" was one of her favorite expressions. It was used for me at least once an hour. It conveyed in mixtures appropriate to the context admiration, affection, sympathy, pity, and, I think, prayer for the grace of a happy death.

We also glanced at the sunbursts and female nudes of Catherine Curran in the Reilly alcove. "Ah, erotic beauty without exploitation. Sure, the poor woman is good, isn't she?"

"She's done a book about Catholicism and the human body. A reformed Enthusiast, or maybe just a disciplined one. Had a big argument with Cardinal Sean Cronin at the Archdiocesan Art Commission's last public meeting. The cardinal said he wouldn't try to debate a woman who loved God more than anyone else he knew."

"A grand man your cardinal. I've read her book. How old is she now?"

"Turning forty and pregnant."

"Bless her heart." The asthmatic sigh—yearning to be pregnant herself. But she was, wasn't she? With my child.

"Started painting nudes as a kid transforming *Playboy* centerfolds. She'd certainly want to paint you if she ever met you."

Ciara blushed to the roots of her hair and down to her neckline. "I wouldn't want to be hanging naked in this great drafty hall, now would I? I suppose she's another relative?"

"Kate Ryan's niece, God be good to her."

"You Ryans are everywhere."

When we escaped the mile of art—biggest expo in the world, I told her proudly—I was asked would I ever take her to the beach. She would never dare go by herself. "That nice Oak Street place."

Before I could offer to walk her back to her apartment, she arranged that we would meet at Oak and Michigan in fifteen minutes. She appeared promptly, wearing slacks and a T-shirt over her swimsuit, which proved to be a uselessly modest navy blue maillot. I tried not to gape too obviously.

I was permitted to rub liberal amounts of Hawaiian tan cream on her back, a task of mind-bending pleasure. "This sun is not good for Irish skin at all, at all," I was informed. I was also permitted to buy her a hot dog and a Coke. "Only small ones, mind you."

After she had consumed two of both, and large ones at that, she announced her intention to take a wee swim in my lake.

"You can't, Ciara," I protested. "The water temperature isn't much over fifty."

"Sure." She wrapped a towel around her neck. "It's warm by Irish standards." She loped across the beach, a playful forest antelope, hardly pausing when she hit the cold, deep blue water and dived into the first small wave. She surfaced with a powerful crawl kick and swam out twenty yards or so, then returned, uttering not a single cry against the cold.

Still, she was shivering as she raced back to where I was waiting. She wrapped the blanket around her and discarded the wet towel.

"Ah, you can't beat it," she announced through clattering teeth. " 'Tis the most refreshing thing in the world."

"A good cure for concupiscence, I imagine."

"We don't have any of that in Ireland. And speaking of that, Brendan Ryan, you're staring at me like I wasn't wearing any clothes at all, at all."

"Sorry," I mumbled, feeling my face burn.

"Ah, don't be sorry." She jabbed my arm with an icy finger. "A woman is flattered when a man she wants to look at her that way looks at her that way, if you take my meaning." She was seized by a fit of laughter.

I wasn't sure that I did. "Does that mean I can go on looking?"

"In moderate amounts, as the priest used to say in secondary school." Yet another fit of laughter.

She didn't say what priest or which secondary school. Anyway, I went on looking. And imagining and fantasizing and daydreaming.

"We have a book of modern Irish art at the store," she told me as we left the beach in a golden haze of sunlight. "Some of them are quite talented, you know. Sure, none of the Dublin galleries could afford a place at your grand Chicago Expo. And your modern Irish artists having just one thing on their minds . . ."

"I take your meaning, woman. But I thought that you didn't have any of that in Ireland."

"We had it once and then it went out of fashion." She poked my arm again. " 'Tis coming back in again, or so I'm told."

Yet she was too shy to go to the beach by herself.

That night we listened to Solti conduct Mozart's no. 25 and no. 40, and to Peter Frankl play the Piano Concerto in A. We held hands by mutual and implicit consent. Afterwards, as we walked down Michigan Avenue and then ate a late supper in a Szechuan restaurant, Ciara bubbled like fresh champagne.

Winter returned on Sunday—gray sky, cold, twenty-knot winds, surly lake. Montrose Harbor was virtually deserted. Indeed, only a few hardy sailors had put their boats in the water, so dubious was the city about whether spring would ever come. Ciara, in jeans, a sweatshirt, and a thick dark blue Windbreaker, considered the *Brigid* carefully, touching the gleaming wood hull, feeling the polished teak fittings, sliding the neatly arranged sheets through her fingers, and pronounced *Brigid* a "proper" boat.

She also observed, so softly that I had to ask her to repeat it, that she imagined I had spent more time and energy on the *Brigid* than I had on my wife.

She did not seem daunted by the small-craft warnings and the threat of rain showers. I was not about to call it quits in the presence of a foreigner, and a woman at that. So we prepared the rigging of the *Brigid* and, using our twelve-horsepower auxiliary, steered out into the restless gray lake.

Ciara watched me carefully, and when I nodded, she clambered deftly to the cabin roof and hauled up the mainsail. She didn't wait for my instructions to raise the jib.

It was the kind of weather for which my poor old *Brigid* was made. Sensing that she was in skilled hands, she dug her nose into a wave and skimmed southward on a broad reach with the offshore wind pushing us toward Jackson Park and the University of Chicago.

Ciara stood next to the mast, one hand on the neatly fastened jib sheet, the other in her Windbreaker pocket, her jet-black hair tense in the wind like geese flying south in autumn, her face exultant, her shoulders thrown back defiantly— Grace O'Malley, the pirate queen of old.

She saw me admiring her again, flushed, and shouted, "Not a bad wee lake you have here."

"Not quite Galway Bay," I shouted back, "but it will do."

She shrugged, not committing herself to whether she had actually sailed on Galway Bay.

A good sailor she certainly was, the best crewperson I had had on the *Brigid* for many years, better even than Ron Crowley. We turned around at the Jackson Park point, after I had shown her in the binoculars the captured German submarine next to the Museum of Science and Industry, and began our run back. The wind had risen, rain was falling steadily, and we were bouncing on following seas. We donned oilskins and pulled up the hoods. Ciara, protesting how much she was out of condition, scampered gracefully about the boat, ready for but not anticipating my commands. So exhilarating was the run and so easy was it to work with Ciara, that I almost forgot my desire for her.

"You're daft, Brendan Ryan," she yelled happily when we finally turned into the entrance of Montrose Harbor and she began to wrap the sails—neatly and carefully, I noticed (and without any complaints of the sort that usually mark the final phases of a sailing venture). "Taking a poor woman out on this crazy lake in the rain."

"You're daft for coming with me, and yourself an experienced sailor."

"You're talking like me." She flushed and smiled as I helped her off the cabin roof, all too briefly holding her solid waist muscles in my hands. " 'Tis a bad influence I am."

We ate ham and roast beef sandwiches in the cabin and drank Beaulieu cabernet sauvignon (George Latour special reserve), which caused her to lick her lips appreciatively, took a brief nap—fully clothed and in opposite bunks—and then departed in my Mercedes (about which she made no comment) for the late afternoon Mass at Holy Name Cathedral. We knelt in the corner at the back so our sailing clothes would not cause too much shock to the devout parishioners.

"A nice wee priest," she said as we left. "And himself a good preacher too. I'd never heard the story about the Caravaggio painting with the risen Jesus as a teenager at Emmaus. Would you be thinking, Brendan Ryan, that's what Heaven is going to be like? All of us as teenagers? Were you happy as a teenager?"

"Yes, very happy. And you?"

"No." She jammed her hands into her Windbreaker pockets. "Not a bit . . . who is that nice wee priest?"

"Monsignor John Blackwood Ryan, rector of the cathedral, alter ego to Cardinal Cronin, and allegedly the brightest priest in the archdiocese."

"Such a harmless seeming wee man. Sure, you'd want to pat him on the head and take him home to his mother."

"So inoffensive that you wouldn't even notice him on an elevator, right?"

"One of the 'other' Ryans, is he?"

I had talked about myself, my family, my neighborhood, my life, incessantly through the weekend. Ciara Kelly had been told all there was to know about Brendan Herbert George Ryan, all except my adventure on that hot tropical day on a nameless tributary of the Mekong. Only after much more intimacy would I risk myself in that story, which no one had ever heard before.

And I, for my part, had learned a lot about her.

She said the Rosary every day and considered herself a loyal and devout Catholic, but she refused to take "them" (said with a slightly contemptuous jerk of her head in the general direction of Rome) seriously when they made rules, particularly about sex. "Poor dear men mean well," she observed, "but, sure, they don't know what they're talking about, do they now?"

She seemed to own only a few dresses, some blouses and slacks, and virtually no jewelry. Her makeup, even for dinner and concerts, was at most perfunctory—not that she needed much.

Only now that I have lost her, I note with astonishment that Ciara Kelly seemed incapable of complaint. Never once did I hear her complain about anything.

She was fluent in English and French and also, she assured me, in Irish. "Kind of half my first language." My name, I was told, meant " 'little king.' Brendan the Little King. Not," she said with a shy, wicked grin, "meaning anything pejorative by the expression, mind you." Then, realizing she might have hurt my feelings, "It refers to geography and not stature."

"I'm not sensitive about being five foot eight and three-eighths inches tall, Ciara," I said lightly. Well, not too sensitive.

"Well, you shouldn't be, with that darling silver hair and those wondrous silver eyes."

"I think it's my turn to blush."

"Good enough for you."

She did not smoke and, despite the two Jameson's at the Cliff Dwellers, drank very little. Her strongest language was "bloody hell." She was fiercely Irish nationalist. "The Brits don't belong on our island. And it's one island, not two." The fighting would stop finally, she insisted, when London made up its mind that it had to stop.

Yet she was also passionately pacifist. The terrorists in the North were "psychopathic killers"; the Dublin government, pathetic politicians devoid of integrity and courage; the English, unspeakable imperialists who would not abandon their belief in the inferiority of the Irish.

These convictions were stated in a tense whisper and accompanied by small, sharp hand gestures and fire sparks in her big gray eyes. Like most Irish political positions, hers did not seem totally consistent. My Ciara was a different woman when she talked about Northern Ireland—tense, abstracted, almost haunted. So I did not press her for clarification.

She seemed detached from material possessions. She praised the *Brigid* and ran an approving hand over the exterior of my Benz. Yet she moved in expensive restaurants as though she were untouched by them and immune to their supercilious atmosphere. She kidded me about my fashionable suits and recreational clothes. "Sure, that man looks like a page in *Esquire*. Or maybe like a male model in a page of *Vogue*."

"With a female model in tow."

She responded with one of her many laughs, explosive, not exactly raucous, uninhibited yet somehow melodious, a waterfall crashing through melting ice. "That'll be the day."

I gave her no presents, God forgive me; and she didn't seem interested in them anyway—though I'm sure she would have accepted them, poor wee woman. Never once did I hear the expression "I want" on her lips. She wanted me all right; and she knew I was wealthy. If that made any difference at all to her, it was counted against me.

"You wear those fancy clothes," she said, pointing a finger at the clothes I wore on the *Brigid*, "to make women think you're sexy." The charge was what Kate Ryan called "half fun and full earnest."

"Do they do the job?" I helped her into the cockpit.

"Like a lily needs gold leaf." She kissed me. "Still, I suppose they don't do any harm."

She had strong opinions on other matters, too, but these were articulated with intelligence and modesty, and she seemed capable of changing them when faced with a good argument. Her artistic tastes, I discovered at the Art Expo, were eclectic and sound, though perhaps modestly conservative. She thought an Italian sculptor, one of my favorites, "probably needs a good therapist, poor man." But when I explained and defended his work, she reconsidered his exhibit and admitted, "Well, I might change my mind about him, but not just yet."

She possessed enormous physical energy and a fierce appetite for food after exertion, whether walking the floor of Navy Pier or sailing on the lake. She promised that she would start exercising again soon, lest "all this Yank food turn me into a fat West of Ireland cow." She did not respond to my suggestion, innocent enough, that she might want to swim in the pool in my building.

She could nap at the wink of an eye—in my car between Chestnut Place and the harbor, in the boat after lunch, on the way to the cathedral—and then awaken fully on instant notice and be ready for action and fun. When challenged or excited, she was always good-humored and frequently exultant.

Her hair hinted at her disposition. When it was tied back, she was serious, intellectual, responsible. When it hung loose and flowed behind her in the breeze, she was impish, reckless, a little zany. When it was piled on her head, she was preoccupied by a strain of dark melancholy about her that was a little daunting.

"Pay me no mind, Brendan. I'm in one of my mauve moods. It'll go away. It always has. It's not your fault."

"Whose fault is it?"

"That's a long story with which I won't bore you." Said in a tone so positive and an accent so American that one knew one damn well better not push.

She would not tell me about herself. I learned from being with her that I was pursuing a passionate, lively, intelligent, and beautiful, if faintly haunted, woman. But I found out nothing about her family, her background, her life story, the reason she was living in Chicago and working for what must have been very little money at Dufficy's Irish Store.

Tactfully, or so it seemed to me, I did not ask questions about these matters; and she volunteered nothing. I suppose I should have been wary. Most of us, even the shy and the modest, are willing to talk about our families. Ciara's silence on the subject was mysterious and perhaps threatening. I wanted her so badly that I didn't care. That she was an admirable and brilliant woman seemed to be enough. The past didn't matter.

Not till it came back to haunt us.

What did I want from her? It should be obvious—sex. I wanted her naked before me. I wanted her in bed with me. I wanted to caress and fondle and squeeze and kiss her most intimate secrets. I wanted to be inside of her, shouting with triumphant male pride at my conquest. I wanted to hold her, sleeping peacefully and contentedly, in my arms. And I wanted all these pleasures not just once but scores, hundreds of times in as many different places and in as many different positions as time and ingenuity and self-control would permit.

Adolescent? I admit it. However, it was spring and I was hungry for a woman and falling in love with this woman. At least I thought I was falling in love. I told myself that she was a mystery it would take a lifetime of pleasure to solve and that my horniness differed from that of an adolescent in that I was more concerned about her happiness than a teenager would be about the happiness of a girl he wanted to screw.

I was pursuing my Holy Grail, seeking not only love but happiness, my elixir of youth, my leprechaun's gold at the end of the rainbow, or wherever else this woman leprechaun had hidden it. Later, after I lost her, I told Blackie Ryan that it was too much to expect that a woman could be all of these things.

"It seems to me that is what they are for." He rolled his nearsighted eyes. "So I am told at any rate. In the absence of a grail to pursue, life becomes tedious."

I didn't want a grail, only a woman in bed with me. Or so I thought.

Yet I wanted to make Ciara Kelly happy. I also wanted to screw her. Were not the two compatible? Why worry about it?

Because I worry about everything, that's why.

I wanted to fill her, impregnate her, fertilize her, bring my child to life inside her—even as I knew that before we had made love she was already carrying my child.

That was absurd psychic drivel that I still could not drive out of my head. I cannot expel that conviction even now, when I understand how impossible it is.

I was not, mind you, merely seeking a wild sexual fling, though I certainly wanted that too. I wanted a woman and a child, a family, a community. I might intend to use Ciara Kelly, always respecting her, I told myself, but I surely would not use her and discard her. Marriage? Well, why not? But no rush about that. The Roman Catholic Church had been no aid to me before, during, or after my first marriage, which it had in its wisdom recently decreed was null and void from the beginning. I did not want it mucking around in my sexual relationship with this new woman.

The Church was not totally responsible for the disaster between me and Madonna, but it was not innocent of blame either. I would not sit in an uncomfortable chair in a stuffy parish hall with Ciara beside me giggling uncontrollably and listen to the inanities of another stupid pre-Cana conference. I would not try to stifle yawns of boredom in a rectory office while an overeducated young priest or an undereducated older nun prated about the theology of matrimony. I would not fill out forms, hunt down certificates, make promises, wait for the appropriate delays, touch all the canonical bases, fulfill all the ecclesiastical requirements, merely to permit the Roman Church to bless my union with Ciara. If it wanted to be involved in my love for her, it could damn well do so on my terms and not on its own.

What would happen if I stormed into the cathedral rectory and delivered this ultimatum to Blackie Ryan, the beloved "Punk" of his siblings?

I could imagine.

He would mumble incoherently, shuffle absentmindedly out of the office, return a few minutes later with a somehow camouflaged bottle of Jameson's, and pour a stiff one for the three of us.

The goddamn Roman Catholic Church would own me again.

I pondered the scene with some satisfaction. He would toast our health and future together and quote, in the original, some Gaelic poet, to Ciara's delight.

Oh, yes, that's what my cousin Blackwood would do. It was no creepy, problematic psychic revelation. It was a certainty. Like the rising of the sun in the morning.

And it could wait until I was good and ready.

Or so I thought, as Ciara's lips reluctantly detached themselves from mine and her arms gradually released me. She did not, however, try to evade my embrace, but rather leaned her head, wearily and submissively, against my chest.

"The man tries to seduce me with a storm on a lake," she giggled, burrowing against me.

"Who's seducing whom?" I released her, swatted her rump lightly, and guided her through the door of the Chestnut Place. "I'll talk to you tomorrow."

She nodded dully, her eyes, heavy with both sleep and desire, resolutely refusing to acknowledge the presence of the doorman, and ducked around the obelisklike object that the architect had deposited in the middle of the lobby.

"We're probably the tenth couple he's seen make out tonight," I whispered into her ear as the elevator door opened.

"Would the other nine have been as good as we were, do you think?"

It was cold, not cool, on State Street—not much above the middle forties—and a persistent drizzle stung at my cheek. It did not matter. I was walking on the outer fringes of the garden of paradise.

I might have pressed for love tonight. She would not have refused. We were both tired and it was late. Tomorrow would be better. I would be a thoughtful and considerate lover.

As I walked down the Chestnut Street ravine, by the old Quigley Seminary (a gaunt gray imitation of the Sainte-Chapelle in Paris) where Ron had gone to school for a year; across from Crickets, in the old-fashioned red-brick Whitehall Hotel, where I must take her to eat as soon as our romance was public; past the 111 Chestnut building, where Jane Byrne was licking her wounds and awaiting a chance to throw another monkey wrench into Chicago politics, I started to have doubts.

It had been too easy. I had known her for less than a week. I had no facts about her background or her past. We had had four dates and a day on a boat. There had to be something wrong. Lovely and gifted women like Ciara are spoken for. They do not appear at the whim of a lonely, unhappy man and surrender after minimal effort.

I should rethink the whole matter. Find out more about her. Call my friend the consul general of Ireland. What did he know of a certain Ciara Kelly?

From the window in my own building, I looked down the quaint little ravine of Chestnut Street, with the bright lights of the Margarita Mexican restaurant creating mysterious shadows on the canyon walls. Somewhere in that wave-shaped red and beige brick building—not only late Harry Weese, but decadent Harry Weese—my true love would be sleeping.

Tomorrow night I could be sleeping with her. She was mine for the asking.

I didn't even know her apartment number. Or whether it might be on the other side of the building. Or her phone number. I knew practically nothing except that I wanted her and she seemed to want me.

I would wait a few days, however. For appearances' sake. So I would not seem too lustful.

And so I could find out more about her. Who, for example, was Ciara Kelly really?

All excellent intentions.

11

The next morning I had a thousand reasons for hesitation. It was too soon. I hardly knew her. She would not tell me anything about her origins. I was acting like an old fool. Or worse, like a teenage old fool. I had failed once in love. I would look ridiculous trying to make love to a woman almost ten years younger than I was. Vanity of vanity, as the man in scriptures says, and all is vanity.

I placed a call to the Irish consulate about Jean's trip. Might I ask if he knew anything about Ciara Kelly? Only a cad would do that. Well, a man who was worried about an Irish mystery might too. Well, I wouldn't do it regardless.

My virtue was unnecessary. The consul general was not in. Would I talk to the vice-consul? I thought not. Would you have him call Brendan Ryan? Of course, Mr. Ryan.

Then Jean phoned from Stanford. She was sorry she'd behaved like a little brat at dinner and was grateful that I'd sent her the books in the mail. What was this Dufficy's Irish Store anyway? I'll have to take you there when you come home. Kind of interesting. When I return from Ireland, do you think I could work for a couple of weeks? Yes, Daddy, *work!* I know it sounds strange coming from the spoiled brat of the Western world. Where? Could you find me a job at the Board of Trade? A runner or something like that? Well, I think maybe I might make a good trader. Don't laugh, Daddy, it's not funny. Well, I guess it is. Oh, I could be a photographer and a trader, too. They stop working early, don't they?

You really think I might be good at it? And you'll talk to your friends? Out of sight!

Speaking of coming home, might she stop in Tucson on

the way to visit Grandmother and Grandfather Ryan? Did I think they'd mind? Would I call and ask them? She didn't want to intrude.

"Would I get in trouble again, Jeannie, if I asked about airfare?"

"You'll never get in trouble again, Daddy," a sunny laugh, "when you offer me money. I have enough for the trip, but if you want to, like, reimburse me when I come home, that would be groovy."

"Groovy?"

"Old word that's come back. Would you please call Grandmother and Grandfather?"

"Immediately. I'll call you back."

My parents were astonished but delighted. Should we repaint the guest bedroom? my mother wondered.

"Don't be ridiculous, Mom. She means that she'll show up tomorrow. Lay in a new bottle of sherry and make a reservation at El Charro."

"Actually, we're rather seriously into margaritas," she admitted. "I'm afraid I've gone native."

Only in a very proper, very thoughtful, and very English way. Ah, the burden of empire.

What was going on inside Jean's pretty little head? The Board and my parents. Two mystery women to worry about.

What would Jean think of Ciara? Another reason to hesitate. If they didn't like each other, I would be caught in dangerous cross pressures.

"Mrs. Kane is here with a gentleman," my secretary informed me.

The gentleman was a process server with a summons bidding me to prepare myself to testify for a grand jury currently in session in the United States Federal Court, District of Northern Illinois, on or about June 1. Eileen must have left word at the switchboard to head him off so that she could be present when it was served. She seated herself comfortably in one of my easy chairs.

I thanked the gentleman for the document and poured Eileen her herbal tea. Another mystery woman. Not mine to worry about.

"You're looking quite content with yourself this morning,

Brendan.'' She peered at me intently, green eyes magnified now by unifocal contact lenses. "Good sail yesterday?"

"Excellent. You and Red must come with me some Sunday. We could sail over to Grand Beach."

"On his stomach? And what if he likes it? You know his enthusiasms." She continued to examine my face. "You're not in love, are you, Brendan? You look so happy. And this subpoena doesn't seem to bother you at all."

"I'm not in love," I lied, mentally cursing perceptive women. "I'll start worrying about this," I tossed the document at her, "when you tell me to. Are you sure about the plea bargain?"

"As far as I know," she rose thoughtfully from the chair and placed the empty teacup neatly on its rack, "there are some rumors on the street that King Sullivan is up to some new kinkiness. If he gets caught between now and his trial in another caper, he'll do time in Lexington."

For which, I thought, I would be blamed.

I called Jean back and told her that her grandparents would be delighted.

"Will they mind if I ask about the war?"

"No. They're not great storytellers like our cousins, but they're not embarrassed by their heroism."

"Really. Caitlin says her grandfather now thinks he sank the whole Japanese navy."

Ah. The Ryan granddaughters were swapping World War II stories. No harm in that, as far as I could see. No worry required on that count.

The pool in my building was closed on Monday evenings. I decided at lunchtime to walk over to the Chicago Athletic Club, the last of the men's athletic clubs on Michigan Avenue, for my daily swim. Virtue is to be found in exercise. Basketball as an antidote for horniness, as we learned on our high school retreats.

I would not go so far as to experiment with Lake Michigan as a remedy for concupiscence.

Coming out of the showers I encountered King Sullivan, a towel wrapped around his ample but diminishing stomach. His once lean and distinguished face now looked like that of a consumptive cherub. One would never have imagined from his cheer that he had stolen a million dollars from me.

"Hey, Brenny, great! You're as trim as ever. I'll catch up to you soon." He patted his stomach. "Notice how much I've lost? Not a drop of the sauce for two months. No problem. Did you get one of those subpoena things? Don't worry about it. All taken care of. Just go in and tell them the truth. No problem."

"I heard you were in the hospital for some tests."

He dismissed the biopsies with a wave of his pudgy paw. "No problem. Routine checkup. Everything is fine. You know how Ron and Patsy are. Worry about everything. Hey, let's get together for some golf this summer. What 'ya say?"

I agreed that it would be a great idea.

Did he know that his wife and his pastor had both pleaded with me to try to duck the grand jury appearance? He might and he might not. But it wouldn't matter. No problem.

Nevertheless, the little worm of worry that always lurked behind King's cheerfully dancing eyes seemed to have grown bigger. Was the grand jury responsible, or the biopsies?

I felt depressed as I walked back to my office. Spring does not come to Chicago with any delicacy or decency. It rather tumbles toward maturity with the heedless speed of a fourteen-year-old boy racing toward manhood. Dandelions erupt overnight, leaves smash out of the delicate buds of trees, acrid smells—the last rottenness of winter, perhaps—fill the humid and oppressive air. Heavy clouds roll in without warning, seeming to push down on the land to slow, if it be possible, the pell-mell rush of spring. Life is purchased only at a heavy price.

God in heaven, what prices Patsy and King had paid! What kind of price would I have to pay for Ciara Kelly? It would not, I thought, as I considered the return message from the consul general, be worth it. I crumpled the pink slip and tossed it into the wastebasket. I had an afternoon of appointments.

The last of the appointments was canceled. So I pondered the problem of trading in futures on the Standard & Poor's Stock Index or the Chicago Board Options Exchange. Last month there had been some fiddling with the April call option, either a sophisticated new game of arbitrage between New York and Chicago or, more likely, a subtle new form of crookedness.

As I jotted numbers on a piece of paper, I realized that there was an even more subtle kind of dishonesty that no one had discovered yet. Trading on stock index futures was a new brand of gambling, and many of the possibilities for kinkiness remained to be discovered.

I played a couple of games with my PC XT on past option calls. Sure enough, I could have cleared a quarter of a million without being caught. This time.

I flipped the papers into the same wastebasket that contained the consul general's return call. For fifteen years I had been devising cleverly dishonest ways to beat the commodities market. It was an amusing game. I had not the guts to play it for real. I'd make my money within the law or not at all. And enjoy my secure self-esteem and virtuous self-righteousness.

I turned off my PC XT and looked at my Casio watch. Five forty-five. It was safe to walk across the Loop and down Michigan Avenue to my apartment. Dufficy's Irish Store was closed.

As a punishment for my sins, I was caught in a wild thunderstorm and soaked to the skin. Every cab in the Loop was occupied. So, bedraggled, disheartened, and feeling very old, I trudged home, convinced that spring was a trick to blind us to the inevitability of the passing of time and the coming of death.

I crossed to the east side of the Magnificent Mile and did not even look across the street at Dufficy's Irish Store. That, too, was a trick.

I showered, donned a clean terry cloth robe, cooked some frozen asparagus in the microwave for supper, and sat down at my manuscript about jury selection in medieval England.

Out over the dark lake there were flashes of light, another weird psychic phenomenon with which I had long since learned to live. As far as I could understand them they were auras of future dangers. But since they rarely had any content, there was no way to avoid the danger of which they warned. So I mostly ignored them.

Ciara Kelly was at least one danger I had escaped in the nick of time.

12

The next morning I stood across the street from Dufficy's Irish Store with what I'm sure was a smirk of amused self-confidence. I had made a fool out of myself, but at least I was wise enough to stop before my folly became a public fact at which all might laugh.

The storm had wiped away the smell of dirty and heavy air. A light east wind blew off the lake, and the sky was crystalline, the air sparkling and clean. The skyline of Chicago glowed with three-dimensional clarity, a photographic art magazine day.

I was caught again in the rite of spring, still pursuing the Holy Grail.

I would look into the shop for just a minute. Say hello to her. No reason to be rude. Oh, no. No reason at all.

I hesitated at the curb, ducked through the traffic, and decided on the east side of Michigan Avenue that I would drink a cup of tea at the Marriott before venturing into Ireland. I even took two steps in the direction of the hotel.

My feet betrayed me. I found myself inside the shop gaping at Ciara Kelly. More precisely I was gaping at her wondrous breasts.

"You were going to show me that book of modern Irish artists," I said, forcing my eyes to concentrate on hers.

"Was I now?" She was wearing a red and white candy-striped shirtdress that seemed to float around her like a morning breeze. Her hair hung loose, a sign of a giddy, girlish mood. New dress, inexpensive but attractive. Bought for me? A little angry at me? Ah, well, what did it matter?

She found the book on a counter and opened it for my inspection. I stood next to her as she turned the pages.

"One thing on their mind, indeed," I said lightly.

"This is Jim Fitzpatrick, a wee red-haired man. Does wonderful posters of mythic heroines." I noticed for the first time how long and elegant were her fingers. Did she play the piano, or perhaps the violin?

"I know his work. This one looks like you."

"Too skinny by half—the goddess, that is."

"I don't agree." My fingers touching hers.

"You didn't call yesterday, Brendan Ryan." So soft I had to guess at the words.

"I lost my nerve."

Short laugh. "A good thing. I lost mine too."

We were in each other's arms, laughing at our joint idiocy, lovers who have escaped a minor quarrel without even quarreling. Then our laughter transformed itself to fierce hunger. Our lips, our bodies, our total selves pressed against each other in an implacable demand for unity.

"Oh, God, you're a desperate man, Brendan Ryan," she murmured, and then sought my lips again.

Every part of her body that touched mine, breasts, belly, thighs, said surrender. So easy a conquest. Not clear who the conqueror is. Doesn't matter.

I pushed the dress back off her shoulders. Boldly my hand seized a lace-protected breast. My lips moved across her chest, my teeth nibbling her smooth, warm flesh.

With considerable difficulty she pushed me away. "Not in the shop, Brendan . . ." A small chuckle. "Mind you, it's an interesting idea . . ."

Reluctantly, my breath coming in compulsive gasps, I permitted her to escape from my arms. "After work?"

She nodded, rearranging her clothes with clumsy and trembling fingers, shy and embarrassed now.

"Your apartment or mine?"

"Yours."

I kissed her again. Once more the dance of passion swept through us. She pushed me away.

" 'Tis a terrible hungry man you are; you'd not let a poor honest working woman," she was laughing happily, "earn her poor honest living. Get along with you to your plush law office and spend the day in dirty and obscene thoughts."

"If you're in them, they can't be dirty."

"Go along with your nonsense."

At the door I steadied myself for reentry into the sunlight of Michigan Avenue and reality.

"Brendan Ryan."

"Ciara Kelly?"

"I love you."

The cliché did not even stick in my throat. "Not half as much as I love you."

I struggled through a heavy day of appointments, most of them designed to keep the IRS raiders at bay. When I wasn't fighting off distracting and intensely perverse images of Ciara, I was praying for tax simplification—even if it did put me out of business.

I forgot that it was the day of my weekly lunch with the Kanes and Currans at the Chicago Club, a generous but barely disguised custom that began two weeks after Madonna threw me out of the house. Nick had to come to the office to drag me away.

Catherine Curran, always a clown, despite her sufferings in Costaguana, started in on me as soon as we were seated at our table. "Brenny's in love, guys," she announced brightly, her brown eyes dancing impishly. "What's she like, Brenny? Will she pose for me?"

Catherine, like Eileen, was bursting with life. In a pink sundress with a short white jacket, she looked like a personification of healthy spring. What would it be like, my corrupted imagination wondered, to be in bed with two pregnant women, two of the favorites from your harem? Did Catherine and Eileen realize they created such fantasies in the imaginations of some men? Maybe most men?

I was sure that they would be delighted if they did know. However, it was not my job, Heaven save us all, to inform them.

"What makes you think she's the sort of model you like?" Her husband took her hand. "And why would he introduce her to us, anyhow?"

My new group, more protective, less demanding than the old, but still determined to push their way into my life. Not yet.

"I'll make no comment," I said airily.

"You don't have to when you order a Jameson's for lunch," Red Kane said. "Pay no attention to them, Brendan. All Irishwomen are matchmakers."

"I won't make any decisions about matches till we meet

her." Eileen's green eyes glinted. "Which had better be soon, counselor, do you understand?"

I took refuge in another "No comment."

I assumed, however, that the next week or the week after she would be the sixth at our lunch table. In the warmth of my friends' affection and concern, and in the vitality of the two women in pastel maternity dresses, content and complacent with their carrying of life, I slipped deeper into the lifegiving and life-absorbing rhythms of the spring ritual. I would soon drink from the Holy Grail. Lunching with them and making love with Ciara were part of the same prodigal, renewing ritual.

Catherine would definitely want to paint her.

Later, when I thought my sanity was slipping from my fingers, I asked my friends if they remembered the luncheon banter. They did indeed. "I was sure that you were going to spend the night with a woman, and a good woman at that, in both senses of the word," Eileen said. "She was real enough to you that day, Brendan. I can't imagine her not being real."

Yet there was then not the slightest evidence that she had ever existed.

She was real enough when I took her arm outside the Irish Store at 5:30, her hair unaccountably bound up. Serious business ahead of us. We walked silently down Michigan Avenue, oblivious of the rest of the world, expectant, nervous, eager, uneasy. Above us the sky had become ominous, dusty pink and soiled lemon, soiled bedsheets, with rapidly scudding low clouds.

"Tornado warnings are out," I remarked.

"Ah, is that what you Yanks call it?" Nervous snigger.

My arm around her waist, solid, substantial, unquestionably real and of this earth, it seemed, we rode up in the parking lot elevator to avoid contact with the doormen and neighbors.

"I hope you're calm and confident, Brendan Ryan," she murmured tensely, "because I'm scared half out of my mind."

"Not to say scared." I patted her rear end, also notably solid, affectionately. "Don't worry. It's not like Olympic gymnastics. Little men won't hold up cards with numbers on them when we're finished."

Our embrace began halfway down the corridor to my apartment. The fires of the spring rite burn not only for the very young. Inside the door we did not even try for the bedroom. The beige couch in the parlor seemed comfortable enough. I began to unbind her hair, the first step in making her my own.

The bedding of Ciara Kelly was an odd, if satisfying, experience. She was not exactly a virgin, it seemed, but with little sexual experience—even less than I—and much sexual fear and ambiguity. Her courage failed her almost at once.

I had pushed away the top of her dress and was caressing her still-covered breasts, as gently as my frenzied state would permit. Her arms draped with the dress, she put her knotted hands in my way, as though she were praying to me. "Please, Brendan."

Outside my window the thunderstorm had begun. Jagged flashes of lightning clawed at the gloomy sky, thick curtains of rain dashed across the city, obscuring whole neighborhoods as they hurried toward the skyline and the lake.

"The woman has the right," I clenched my teeth, withdrew my aching fingers, and quoted the columnist Ellen Goodman, "has the right to say 'yes' and then change it to 'no.' But the woman had better make up her mind."

" 'Tis a terrible thing for a woman to have to take off her clothes." Her face was contorted in misery, her body tense and withdrawn. "And in broad daylight too."

I eased the dress off her arms and returned my fingers, feather light, to her breasts.

"I'll not make love, woman, to someone as beautiful as you in the dark. Seeing you naked is part of the game."

She glanced at the window and the city stretching beyond. "Anybody could look in."

"At this height, only God."

"Could we wait till later?" She sighed with pleasure as my fingers found the flesh of her breasts. I took firm possession of them.

"It's now or not at all," I said, astonished at my own fierceness. I kissed her chin. "Yes or no?"

"I don't know, Brendan, I don't know. Oh . . ." She drew in her breath sharply as my fingers very carefully toyed with her breasts, staking a claim on them but not yet claiming to possess them. "Don't . . ."

"Yes or no, woman?" I demanded, my fondling becoming more imperative. Her heart was pounding wildly. Under the lace I found a slowly ripening nipple.

She closed her eyes and gritted her teeth. "The woman," she spoke through tight lips, "wants a good loving from you the worst way in the world. She's terrified out of her empty mind. And ashamed like she was a First Communion girl naked in church. Stupid Irish prude."

"I'm not accepting excuses." My fingers went to the front hook of her bra. Her hand intercepted mine.

She took a deep breath, eyes still shut. Then a slow grin. "The woman gives Molly Bloom's answer and serves notice that any later retraction should be treated as null and void." Her eyes opened, gray fields soft with love. "Clear enough statement to justify your actions, counselor?"

She undid the hook herself.

Has not every man dreamed of what I had—a license to sweep away reluctances and resistances? "You're enjoying every second of this, aren't you?" she complained.

"I sure am. And so are you, woman."

She was and she wasn't. Our lovemaking was a mixture of comedy, struggle, and passion. With comedy and passion slowly overwhelming the struggle.

"We must have music," she announced abruptly. "Let me go, you monster rapist. This is not an excuse."

I had all my clothes off, and Ciara was clad only in her panties—plain, unadorned cotton. She was utterly delicious. Vulnerable but glorious. There was no need for music.

But music we were going to have. She pulled a cassette out of her purse, fiddled with my stereo, and popped in the tape.

"The *Rite of Spring*?"

"Not Solti's, but at the moment it doesn't seem to matter."

"You want to make love to Stravinsky?" I reached for the elastic on her panties. She tried to dodge me.

" 'Tis better than Ravel altogether," she sniggered. "If you take my meaning. Now get on with your evil designs."

So we continued with a background of Igor Stravinsky and

tornado-force winds shaking the windows and forcing the steel girders in the building to moan and groan with agony.

The music was a burst of bravado, a gesture of wild Irish flair. She was still frightened. What were the terrible demons that haunted her? I wondered as our union progressed—half wrestling match and half athletic coupling. It did not matter. My task was to overcome the demons and admire her courage for daring to try.

Finally, as the orchestra's music swelled to the mad crescendo of the sacrificial dance, I lost the remnants of my self-control and claimed her completely. My brain was clogged with an insane image of her body swelling with the shape of my child within. Spring, fertility, love, life all rushing together to create unbearable pleasure. Ciara by then was able to reply, an aroused, passionate woman as out of control as I. Our own rite of spring was accomplished. We drained the Holy Grail together.

We did not even notice when the music stopped.

13

"The great fat Irish cow gave you a hard time on your ride," she said bitterly.

We were lying on the floor of my living room, underneath the Picasso print, sweaty and exhausted.

"You're not fat," I said, truthfully enough. Naked, Ciara was slender to the point of thinness. The fullness of her body came from bones and shape, not from weight.

"God, I'm sorry." She was weeping bitterly. "And yourself such a wonderful lover too."

To tell the truth, as she would have said, I thought I was a pretty wonderful lover, too, especially for the little practice I'd had through the years. I had captured the woman and, to judge by her sighs and moans and then sharp shrieks of pleasure, she had enjoyed the experience.

"You weren't all that bad yourself, once you got started."
I patted her approvingly.

She was not ready for consolation. "I'll make it up to you,
Brendan," she promised grimly. "I swear I will. Oh, my
darling, darling Little King Brendan." She attacked me with
kisses, manic, tearful, adoring kisses. "Poor, dear, wonderful man."

Then she went into Irish endearments, whose tender affection needed no translation.

"You'll be the death of me, woman," I murmured. "Give
me a chance to breathe."

"Only one breath," she said, leaning over me, marvelous
breasts against my chest, her face intent on making me
happy.

"Come on." I struggled away and took her hand. "We do
have a bed in this house."

Dutifully she followed me into the bedroom and waited till
I drew the blinds and climbed into bed. Then she slipped in
beside me and resumed her Gaelic endearments and her determined kissing.

"A man doesn't have a chance to get his second wind with
you, Ciara Kelly," I protested, insincerely and not altogether
accurately.

Much later, she awoke me to say she should go back to her
apartment. It was almost midnight.

"Is that necessary?" I yawned.

"It is," she said positively.

So I dressed and escorted my babbling lover through the
Chestnut Street ravine and kissed her, positively but briefly,
before turning her over to the sleepy doorman.

"I'll see you tomorrow?" she asked dubiously.

"Damn well better believe it."

The demons were scurrying around the fringes of the canyon on my return walk. I ignored them.

So began my love affair with Ciara Kelly, a passionate and
sometimes inhibited woman, who made love to Stravinsky
and adored me more than I possibly deserved.

Just the kind of woman I would create for myself if I were
the hero in a novel I was writing. Presumably no mortal
woman would think of making love with the *Rite of Spring*
roaring ecstatically in the background; no mortal woman

would have ivory thighs and generous hips and swelling breasts like hers, not really. Or if there were such a beautiful woman, why would she fall in love with me?

So Ciara Kelly, fact or fiction, is gone. If she does actually exist somewhere in the world, I'll never find her, never pin her unpredictably unresponsive body to my bed again.

So be it. At least for a time I knew her and loved her.

For the next two weeks she was the only reality in my life. I went through the motions of practicing law and watching the S&P Index call options at the CBOE. I ate the weekly meal with the Kanes and the Currans, and merely smiled wisely when the two women demanded more information about "her."

"Will we like her, Brenny?" Catherine demanded.

I merely laughed. They damn well better like her. How could they not?

I talked on the phone with both my parents and Jean about her pilgrimage to Tucson, which had apparently been a huge success.

"Such an intelligent and self-possessed young woman," my mother said, as though she could not believe it. "One would almost think she were English."

"Awesomely neat," was Jean's terse judgment. "Isn't it exciting that they're writing their memoirs?"

Which was news to me. And indeed exciting. But not as exciting as Ciara Kelly.

While it lasted, life with Ciara was delightfully erratic. She was a West of Ireland faerie spirit, a manic, half-pagan, partly savage lover, whose intermittent loss of nerve was balanced with a brazen, comic eroticism of which most men fantasize but which, after some years and some experience, they come not to expect in their women. You almost didn't notice that while she was giving you herself unreservedly, she was telling you nothing about herself. Gift, but no self-revelation. I was too bemused, too sotted with desire to care.

We were lovers for only a couple of weeks. We made love, however, more often than Madonna and I had in the last decade of our marriage—sometimes, especially at the beginning, serious, almost somber love; other times, particularly during our last days together, we were comic lovers. I told myself that she would wear me out, but I managed to hang on to the roller coaster I had set in motion, often just barely.

One night, after I had walked home with her to her apartment building, I tried to make a written accounting of the woman. I threw away the balance sheet after an hour of work. As I remember, however, I saw her as naive and sophisticated, innocent and earthy, transparent and mysterious, terrified and trusting, fun-loving and deadly serious.

You get the idea—I was in love. Looking back at those weeks, however, and taking into account both my adolescent fixation on her and the mystery of her departure, I nonetheless still feel that she was a puzzle, a riddle, an enigma.

I tossed my balance sheet, "In re: Ciara Kelly," into the wastebasket because I loved her too much to care about the bafflements. Anyway, everything seemed to fit together in perfect harmony, logical and psychological, when I was with her.

There were times when she was an elegant, gracious lady, a woman of the world, a Parisian countess; and other times, by her own description, a bitchy Irish prude; yet other times, a madcap, erotic imp. Like piloting a boat in heavy seas, one learned to ride with the waves.

There were yet other times when she would be so inexplicably angry at me after love that she would lie on the opposite side of the bed rigid and silent like a kidnapped slave girl who had been forced to submit against her will. Then I would awake not a quarter of an hour later to find her clinging to me desperately, as though she were afraid I would slip away. Her favorite position seemed to be huddled in my arms like a frightened child seeking protection.

She was irresistibly affectionate. "Trouble with you, Brendan Ryan," she told me as she hovered, bare-breasted, over me, long black hair brushing my chest, caressing my face with delicate fingers, "is that you're a great, powerful lover and marvelous good at all the prior activities too, but you're almost worthless at accepting mild affection. Well . . ." watching me with eyes so filled with admiration as to make me want to weep, ". . . if you continue to be involved with me, you're going to have to learn to sop up affection when I offer it. Now hold still while I sing to you till you're ready to be loved again."

She sang what sounded like a Gaelic lullaby, but then all Irish songs sound like lullabies.

"Translate it for me?" I begged.

"Sure, I will not. The words are too gross altogether."

At first I found it hard to submit to such, it seemed to me, time-wasting nonsense. I learned quickly enough to enjoy it. Time stopped, the world stood still. I would let her minister to me forever.

I drove her out to the Neighborhood, through the curved streets and the wooded hills of that magic community, the highest elevation in Cook County, a little bit of woodland still surviving in our prairie city. I showed her Glenwood Drive, the Maze, the Courts of St. Praxides, Louis's drugstore. Perhaps she would not see them all as magic like I did.

"It's a great, powerful place altogether," she said thoughtfully.

"Great, powerful" (her alternative to "Great, fucking" she told me once) was best translated as "fine," but with many nuances, not all of them non-ironic, depending on the context.

For the first time, however, the Neighborhood made me sad. It was no longer the paradise garden of my youth and adolescence, but the origin of so many blighted dreams and frustrated hopes, the starting point of so many senseless pilgrimages, the beginning place of so many messed-up lives, the locale of so many ghosts that emerged not only on Halloween but every day of the year.

She sensed my melancholy as we stopped for a few moments in front of the stained-glass window of St. Prax's—depicting that saint with a great, powerful ax (Prax's Ax, to one and all) setting forth to chop the wood from which the Bethlehem manger would be built. (Or was it a boat for St. Christopher? It was always a matter of debate among the nuns.)

"Ah, my poor Little King Brendan." She drew my head to her bosom. " 'Tis a terrible heavy sadness that weighs on you here. The magic doesn't have to stay sour, you know. Some dreams do come true after all."

It was a remarkable reading of my mood. I was perilously close to tears. I vowed to myself that eventually Ciara Kelly and I would move back here and begin life again. I almost stopped at the "other" Ryans' house on Longwood to introduce her to Ned and Helen, his second wife. And then we could have gone next door to the lovely Eileen's sister, Mary Kate Murphy, the Freudian analyst, and her husband, Joe Murphy, the Jungian from Boston.

I drove by the Ryan compound without stopping. Save that pleasure for later. That afternoon I took her for a Wendella cruise on the Chicago River and along the shore of the lake, managing to get slightly seasick, as I usually do when I'm not at the helm of a sailboat but wallowing, even ever so slightly, between waves. I overcame my nausea by concentrating on Ciara's comparison of Chicago from the lake with the strand at Inch on Dingle Bay—"The two places in the world closest to Heaven," she shouted wildly over the wind. "Sure, the trip would be shorter than from anywhere. I think I want to die either at Inch or on one of these boats. Faith, it would be a hop, skip, and a jump to Heaven."

"We'll visit Inch someday."

"And make love on the beach." We were the only customers on the boat, and the crew too far away to hear. "Do you think it would be difficult? Would sand be a problem?"

It was a problem to be discussed seriously and responsibly. No joking around about screwing in the anteroom of Heaven.

"Not if you had a big enough blanket."

"You're daft, man." She hugged me. "Altogether daft."

She had learned my moods quickly. And also my fantasies, as she demonstrated the next day when we were on the *Brigid*, sailing north with an east wind on a fluffy day with ice cream cone clouds.

" 'Tis said that some American women strip to the waist on boats when they are far enough offshore," she announced suddenly.

"Doesn't happen in Ireland, I guess?"

"Not with the Irish male's great, terrible breast fixation. I don't suppose it's ever happened on this boat."

I could hardly believe my ears. The night before she had protected herself from my gaze with a sheet held underneath her chin while she lectured me again about the politics of Northern Ireland, not a word of which I understood.

"Not to my knowledge."

"Not even your wife?"

There were occasional questions about Madonna, shrewd, cautious probings of my marriage. She was trying to calculate, I guess, what went wrong. Fine. When you find out, tell me.

"Madonna rarely came on the boat. She didn't approve of nakedness."

"Poor woman," she said, pulling the sweatshirt over her head.

It was not a sight with which I was totally unfamiliar. A bedroom is one thing, however. A thirty-foot boat at flank speed is something else. I lost control of the tiller, and *Brigid*, jealous perhaps of a rival lover, heeled dizzily.

"Tend to your steering," she shouted, hands defiantly on her hips. "The scenery is meant to be admired not pawed . . . for the moment."

"Admirable it is," I gasped, bringing the boat back into line. "And delightful too."

"I want to delight you," she exulted, arms stretched triumphantly over her head. "I want you to be able to think of nothing else but me. I want to drive you out of your mind with desire. Now mind what you're doing with the poor boat."

She could not keep her distance for long. Within a quarter of an hour she was snuggled in my arms in the stern. "Trouble with bare tits on a day like this is that it's cold."

"There are a number of approved and recommended ways of keeping warm."

We made love leisurely in the cabin, anchored not in the harbor but behind the Navy Pier breakwater, with the skyline watching, I imagined, in surprised amusement. Ciara avowed that boat cabins were the best place in the world for loving, though I was sure she'd never had the experience before.

I didn't bring her to the weekly lunch with my new group. Our relationship was still too private, I told myself, too new, too fragile. Moreover, she had told me nothing about herself, despite my increasingly obvious hints that I wanted to know more about who she was and where she came from.

Sometimes she would weep in my arms, protesting that her tears were from "too much happiness altogether." There was happiness in the tears, all right, but something else, too, that I did not quite understand and was not sure I liked—a kind of frightened hopelessness, as if she were sure that it would all have to end.

Could she, I wondered, have a husband somewhere else? It didn't seem likely. Even an unhappy marriage would have involved more sexual initiation than she seemed to have received.

I persuaded her that she might swim in the little-used pool in my building. She carried her swimsuit from the Irish Store.

"You'll not wear that terrible ugly swimsuit in my pool," I insisted, giving her the almost weightless little Lord & Taylor plastic bag I had been carrying.

She removed the floral print bikini (relatively modest, all things considered) with feigned dismay. "Ah, one of the great, powerful, immoral things the bishops are after warning us about." She inspected the size and colored. "Bloody hell! You've been measuring me, Brendan Ryan. Shame on you."

"Put it on, woman," I ordered.

"I'll do no such thing." She faded into the bathroom and emerged a minute or two later, awkward and uncertain. "Ah, there's too much of me and not enough of it."

"That's the general idea." I put my arms around her. "It's a grand suit altogether."

"Stop talking like me," she sniffed. "And keep your hands to yourself, man. We can't make love and swim both."

"Why not?" I demanded, my hand already underneath the bikini.

"Swim first." She drew in her breath and her head tilted as the pleasure chemicals rushed into her blood.

"No way. The nice thing about this design is that it comes off so easily."

When we finally made it to the pool, she swam for forty-five minutes with a relaxed, confident kick that effortlessly ate up the laps.

"Well, at least the wicked thing stays on in the water. . . . Keep away from me, Brendan Ryan. Not in the pool we don't."

Riding the elevator back to my apartment, still gasping for breath, she observed, "It's a terrible thing for a woman to let herself get so badly out of condition. I've fallen apart altogether. Sure, I won't be able to work tomorrow. Lucky we did the loving beforehand."

"Did we now?"

"Stop talking like me!" She poked me, hard. "Brendan, not in the elevator."

So I waited till we were back in the apartment. Then I waited till she had showered to clean the chlorine from her hair. Showers had become part of routine. "Loving isn't dirty, but I am," she asserted. "And they'll be private showers for the moment, do you take my meaning?"

I admitted that I did.

After she emerged from the shower, hair limp and loose, wrapped in a yellow towel, I agreed that we both needed a glass of Jameson's to warm us up, though I was more than warm enough.

We frolicked with one another, made love, and napped. I awoke to find my naked woman standing by the bed with the Jameson's bottle and two clean tumblers. "Another drop won't do us any harm," she informed me.

So we lay under the rumpled sheets in the darkness of my bedroom, the smell of shampoo still on her, and watched the lights of the jets dotting the night sky like fireflies on the approaches to O'Hare and drank our Jameson's—straight up, naturally—settled and self-satisfied companions in passion.

"You were in the war, Brendan?" she asked suddenly.

"I was, before it really was a war. I came home in 1966."

"Did you shoot at anyone?"

"Yes."

"Kill them?"

What a strange line of questions. Why did she want to know?

"I suppose so. I didn't stop to make sure."

"How do you feel about it?"

"Sorry if anyone is dead. Glad that I'm still alive and the others I was protecting."

"It was self-defense, was it?"

"You better believe it. Protecting the innocent even."

She was quiet in the darkness next to me.

"Do you talk about it much?"

"Not ever, not to anyone. Except my father and mother, who were in the Second World War."

"Your mother?"

"Both."

"Do you want to talk to me about it?"

I did indeed want to talk about it, to tell Ciara Kelly about a different Brendan Ryan from the one she knew. And the third woman in my life. Yes, I wanted to tell Ciara Kelly about her too. Regardless of what she thought of me after the story was finished.

"Very much. May I put my arm around you while I talk?"

"After I fill your glass again."

14

Red lights flashed around the house as our boat, the advance party for Operation Dakota, slowed down and turned toward the riverbank.

"Did you see any red lights, Corporal?" I said to the kid who was driving the launch.

"No, sir," he said. "They don't have traffic lights up in this part of the country, sir."

"I am well aware of that, Corporal."

"Yes, sir."

The lights were my own internal warning signals, my erratic psychic sense foretelling, accurately if imprecisely, the dangers that were to come. The psychiatrist I would see after the disappearance of Ciara Kelly and the other springtime disasters was perfectly prepared to admit that I had hallucinated her. But he brusquely denied the existence of psychic powers and extrasensory phenomena.

"Dere iss no such ding as ESP," he assured me dogmatically. "Iss a scientific impossibility."

"A scientific impossibility," Blackie Ryan would comment yet later, "that affects three-fifths of the people in the country. The good doctor would have voted for the conviction of Galileo."

On that hot, humid night in up-country Vietnam during the spring of 1966, I knew little about ESP, but enough to realize that the warning lights were not required to tell me that it was a stupid mission.

Then I saw Guy and Marie Tho on the veranda of their bamboo house, built on stilts so that part of it extended over the river, and forgot about dangers. Marie was the sort of woman who without even trying makes you forget everything else in the world.

The official histories of the war mention our mission, but in cautious and obscure words. I suppose that it is still cloaked in security wraps to protect any of the survivors who may still be working in Vietnam—for the CIA. Who else?

Or maybe the secrecy is to protect the geniuses who devised the project, some of whom went on to become very important members of the military establishment.

So I will be properly judicious in my description.

Someone had a very bright idea about intelligence gathering in the months after the 1966 election, when, as we knew in Nam but as the American people did not yet know, there would be an enormous buildup of American military power.

The idea did not have a chance to work. Worse, by sending small American teams into that particular part of the country, it was likely to provoke Viet Cong reaction, causing considerable risk to the team members and the native personnel.

In any case, I was the second in command of one of the teams, chosen not because of any talents of my own, but because they thought they needed someone who was Catholic and spoke French. (My mother had taught me French when I was a kid by talking to me in that language for half an hour every day.) I also suspect that the man I replaced had the kind of clout that Dr. Clifford thought he had. My predecessor was on his way back to the Pentagon, and I was dragged from my analysis desk in Saigon and converted from a chair-bound officer to a command officer.

Under a major who was an old OSS hand and now in the final stages of dementia.

Marie Tho made me forget about him too. She was about thirty then, the mother of four children, including a lovely baby daughter, perhaps four months old, named Emily. I was six years younger, over a year and a half away from my wife, and suddenly aware, in the presence of that slender, elegant woman with high, conical breasts, deftly curving hips, trimly sculpted legs, and exquisite face, how deep and powerful were my unacknowledged sexual hungers.

The Thos were educated Catholics from the North, members of the mandarin class that had been civil servants for the French empire, like President Diem, whom Cabot Lodge seems to have had murdered. They and their community had migrated to the South after Dien Bien Phu and established a rubber and rice plantation in this remote upriver jungle district. Hard working and industrious, more Chinese than Tonkinese, it seemed, they had prospered and now faced with stoic resignation another migration, another new beginning.

They had agreed enthusiastically to help "the Americans," believing that we might protect their community, their church, their priest.

Soon they would learn better.

"Lieutenant Ryan? So nice to have you. You will be welcome to stay here in our house. We will be honored if you take your meals with my family. May I present my wife, Marie?"

Her almond eyes locked with mine. She moved her head slightly, disconcerted, as I was, by the electricity between us. "Welcome, Lieutenant Ryan," she murmured, lowering her eyes.

Guy Tho was a handsome little man with silvering hair at his temples, a smooth blend of French and Asian intellectual. We became instant friends and spent many long hours discussing Napoleonic and Anglo-Saxon law and Thomistic philosophy on his veranda as the radio crackled next to us. I'm sure that in those days he found me a naive young cub. Yet he was unfailingly courteous and respectful, treating me like a learned senior colleague.

There was little to do but talk and make sure the daily patrols poked through the thick, steamy, sweet-smelling jungle beyond the plantation perimeter. It was an exercise we performed because sending out patrols was what armies did and not because we had any hope of finding the Viet Cong before they decided to sweep down from the mountains in the distance and wipe us out.

I had come to Vietnam with the "pay any price" idealistic faith of the Kennedy years, though in my case it was always a soft-spoken and slightly skeptical faith. "Wars are won," my father had told me long before, "by the side that makes fewer mistakes. Pray not for good leaders but for leaders who are less stupid than the leaders of the other side."

Six months in Vietnam had convinced me that the other side would have to be monumentally stupid to be worse than us. We were, I thought then and still think, the good guys. Read any newspaper account of the current situation in Vietnam and learn that poverty, corruption, and tyranny are at least as bad if not worse than they were when our side was running Saigon. There was hope in those days, and there is no hope now.

Regardless of who was good and who was bad, who was the lie and who was the half-truth, it was clear that Program Policy Budgeting System, Robert McNamara's contribution to military theory, could not be transferred from Ford Motor Company and Pentagon management to fighting a war against a tenacious Asian enemy.

I'm not sure today whether we could have won if we'd done it right. Nor do I know what doing it right would have meant. But I was certain as I sat on the Thos' veranda, ogling Marie, arguing philosophy with Guy, and worrying about my lunatic CO, that we were going down the path to sure defeat.

My Kennedy idealism faded quickly in Vietnam. Pragmatic American enthusiasm was not subtle enough, perhaps not cynical enough, to cope with the twisted and historically rooted complexities of Southeast Asia. We had blundered in with our "can do" spirit, our massive technology, and our Harvard Business School management techniques, and were in the process of making a bad situation worse, expanding the size of the sinkhole with our every move. Southeast Asia would have been better off if we had not become involved.

Later I would make the same decision, not without some ambiguity, about my involvement with the Thos and would go home reluctant to leave my observer's position on the banks of the river of the human condition. Ordinarily, it seemed to me, you only made things worse when you became involved, whether as a nation or as a person. Even when you had behaved bravely. Perhaps especially when you had behaved bravely.

The junior officers in my team, most of them ROTC-trained like me, in the air-conditioned basements in Saigon, poring over data sheets on their cheap metal desks, were unanimous in this viewpoint about the war. Which is why we were sent home to be replaced by more brilliant analysts, West Point careerists who understood that you told superiors what they wanted to hear instead of what they ought to know.

The war would soon be in the hands of the professionals, men like my CO, though not as berserk, who were skilled at the bureaucratic game of getting their "ticket punched" with a Vietnam tour and incompetent at fighting the kind of war in which we were engaged. Probably any other kind of war too.

Not many of them went as far toward the deep end as my CO, who would take his machete in hand each morning, sling an M 16 over his shoulders, and stride out into the jungle to "kill me some Charlies." One of our noncoms told me that the major chopped the tops off bamboo plants and fired his automatic weapon into rice paddies.

We could tell when he was coming back; the sound of gunfire in the distance meant that Major Schilling was mowing down imaginary Charlies.

"How will we know the difference," the noncom asked, "when the VC really attacks?"

"We hope it's after the major comes in."

I realized that we were the forward outpost, the first one that the VC would attack should they decide to come down from the mountains and clear us out of the province as an object lesson to the local people and to exiled Catholics from the North that they would only make matters worse for themselves by cooperating with the Americans.

Our unit, two officers and a dozen enlisted men, would have to sound the alarm for the other stations. Thus, for all practical purposes, the fate of a hundred or so Americans and about the same number of Vietnamese Catholics depended on a CO who later might easily have made the cast of *Apocalypse Now*. If he should be out with his machete and his M 16 shooting up imaginary Charlies when the real ones showed, I'd be in charge.

I reviewed the tactics courses I'd had in ROTC at Loyola and concluded that if the VC came down the river—which would be what I would do if I were in their position—the only proper response would be what we euphemistically called "redeployment": getting the hell out of there as quickly as we could.

When my supercharged imagination was not preoccupied with fantasies about Marie's charms, I tried to figure how I could, as an inexperienced first lieutenant, give the orders for a redeployment and how we could fend off the VC while we were waiting for the cavalry to come riding over the hills.

Our operation should have been called Little Bighorn.

I studied the tactical layout of our situation almost as intently as I studied the relationship between Guy and Marie. He was older than she, perhaps in his middle forties, although the childlike faces of the Vietnamese made it hard to guess age. There was obvious affection between them, but, it seemed, not much passion. Guy was a dry and pedantic if charming man. Marie was devout and pious—she made the sign of the cross whenever she passed one of the many statues in their house—but also deeply sensuous. Moreover, she seemed more fatalistic than her husband, certain that the atrocities which had wiped out the other members of her family would eventually claim her too.

"I do not care," she said one night, bouncing the infant Emily on her knee, "if they bury me up to my head in the sand and permit the ants to destroy me as they did my little sister. I hope that this one," she poked a finger at the happily gurgling little girl, "somehow survives and escapes to America."

Her husband gently but firmly reprimanded her for lack of faith.

We spoke rarely to each other, implicitly agreeing that the energies that raced back and forth between us were dangerous.

One afternoon I was poking around in the river ponds, downriver from their house. I didn't permit myself to realize that I was looking for Marie.

I found her, as I thought I would, bathing in one of the pools, playing in the water with the delighted Emily.

"You shouldn't be here, ma'am." I tried not to look at her olive skin, long black hair, and small, high breasts—a delicate Asian water deity. "If there's an attack, you'd be in serious danger."

She held Emily close to her body, a symbolic protection of modesty. "I will die, then, with my little girl."

"Guy would say that was lack of faith."

"Faith did not save my parents or my sisters."

"I think you'd better permit me to accompany you back to the house, ma'am."

She shrugged her delicate little shoulders. "Am I permitted to dress?"

"Certainly, ma'am."

"Then you will hold the *enfant*?" She passed the smiling child—she always seemed to smile—to me, revealing, as she stepped out of the pool and onto the rock at the edge of the pond, her full womanly beauty.

An innocent movement for a Vietnamese? A tease? A natural gesture? An invitation?

Probably all four in some complex mixture. I turned away and played with the delighted Emily while she dressed. We walked back to the house in silence, my own embarrassed, hers, as far as I could tell, perfectly self-possessed.

I told myself that if I were a little more certain of her invitation, neither the commandment against adultery nor the obligations of hospitality would have stopped me. Looking back, there was no reason to doubt the invitation. I was too well indoctrinated in virtue, or perhaps too inhibited, to respond. Later I would love her too much to exploit her weakness.

We were visited one afternoon by a brigadier general, a lean, dour, hard-bitten man, who viewed our post with an expression of distaste that indicated either a bad ulcer or horror at the lunacy of Operation Dakota.

He ate lunch with the Thos, the major, and myself. The major, perfectly sober in the presence of the brass, raved about the opportunities for "killing Charlies" in our zone.

As he was boarding his helicopter, in a clearing I had ordered in the rubber plantation about twenty yards behind the house, he sent the major back for a map case that had been left in the house.

"What do you think, son?"

It took me several seconds before I realized he was talking to me. ROTC officer that I was, I spoke the truth. "It should be called Operation Little Bighorn, sir."

"Humph . . . Are there evacuation plans?"

"None that I know of, sir. And, if there were . . ."

"The major would not activate them, right?"

"Yes, sir."

He thought for a moment.

"When I get back to HQ, I'll create such a plan. Helicopters. We will call it . . . let me see, Red Baron. I'll inform the major." He glared at me significantly. "You will know the code too."

"We'll remove the Vietnamese personnel?" I was thinking of Marie. And Emily. No anthill for that cheerful little girl, if I could help it.

"Negative," snapped the general. "We cannot assume responsibility for them."

"With respect, sir . . ."

"Yes?" he barked irritably.

"If we do not take care of them," the answer sprang to my lips without thought, "we will confirm the enemy propaganda that it is not safe to trust Americans."

He thought about it. "Right," he spat out finally. "Good thought, son. We'll get them out too. . . . You from the Academy?" He glanced at my hand to see if I was wearing a West Point class ring.

"Loyola University in Chicago, sir."

"More like you," he grumbled, "and we might win this war."

"Yes, sir."

The major never told me about Red Baron, but the next day I began building a small perimeter around the house and the landing pad: foxholes, barricades, fire points. The major was too busy on his hunt through the plantation for Charlies to notice.

Marie emerged from the house late in the afternoon with the grinning Emily in her arms.

"I would respectfully submit, ma'am," I could on occasion sound like I was a West Point grad, "that it is unwise to return to that pool."

"For me or you, *mon capitaine*?" She smiled enigmatically.

"For both of us, ma'am." I managed to force the words through my tight throat. "In different ways, perhaps."

She laughed softly and slipped down the path, her slim hips swaying under her tight-fitting dress with slit sides, like a young tree in a strong breeze. That's the way they walk all the time, I told myself.

In addition to constructing a perimeter from which we could be evacuated, I began to explore upriver in our small launch, assuming that the VC would strike at dusk, when it would be difficult for our air support to be called in.

For a week nothing happened, then another week. Marie and I did not speak. Guy and I discussed Jacques Maritain and Etienne Gilson, French Catholic philosophers. The radio crackled every day. The mid afternoon rain became heavier, the sun hotter. I counted the days until my return to my wife and daughter. Only another month. My men—they were mine now—swam in the river. The major continued to shoot up the plantation. Emily continued to laugh.

Then another week.

And three days into a fourth week.

My sergeant and I were returning in the boat, a little earlier in the afternoon than usual. Half a mile upriver from the Thos' house, an automatic weapon opened up on us—like a string of firecrackers on the Fourth of July, with phosphorescent flashes dashing over our heads.

I pushed the throttle full forward and raced away while the jungle behind us exploded with noise and fire and bursting white lights.

The VC made mistakes, too, almost as many as we did. If someone had not been trigger-happy that day, all of us would have been dead in a few hours.

I ran the boat into the landing beneath the veranda of the Tho house at full speed, calmly ordered my men into position, and warned Guy to prepare his family and dependents for evacuation. The world went into slow motion, frame after frame passing before my eyes, so that I had plenty of time to see what was happening and make my decisions.

Much later I read an article by John Brodie, quarterback for the San Francisco 49ers, and apparently also a psychic, in which he described the same phenomenon occurring during (some but not all) pass plays. He could see the defensive patterns developing like a frame-by-frame slow-motion film and "check off" his pass at the last fraction of a second to select a secondary receiver who was in the clear.

Obviously, I thought in my slow motion, that kind of firepower meant a major attack. I turned on the radio transceiver and reported, "Red Baron. I repeat, this is Operation Dakota. Red Baron. Red Baron."

The major appeared on the veranda and tried to take the transceiver away from me.

"We're going to have a feast of Charlies tonight," he ranted.

None of the men was watching. I coolly slugged him with the butt of my M 16.

"Corporal," I ordered a man who came rushing up the steps, "the major seems to be a casualty. Remove him to the perimeter."

"Dakota, we acknowledge," the transceiver crackled. "Red Baron. Your lucky day. The air force has some ordinance in the area."

In later days in Vietnam, coordination between ground and air was often disastrously bad. It was indeed our lucky day—or so it seemed at first. The other side had blown its cool; then F104s tore the VC's sampans to pieces before they could turn the big bend in the river and descend on us.

The enemy was swatting a pesky fly with a howitzer.

See, General, I was right. The Catholics are important to them.

It was sixty miles to our base. If the choppers were on their way at once, we would need only half an hour. Ignoring the screams of the Vietnamese, which I couldn't understand anyway, I formed my tiny command into its defensive perimeter and waited for the enemy.

They came almost at once, not from the river but through the neatly ordered lanes of the rubber plantation, a score or so of little men in black pajamas, appearing like make-believe ghosts in the fading light, firing automatic weapons, throwing grenades, and screaming like lunatics. If we had not been prepared, we would have fled in panic and been cut down.

As it was, we were prepared and they were the ones who were cut down. I squeezed the trigger of my M 16. Oddly enough it worked. I had won the marksmanship prize in my

ROTC company. And in man-to-man combat too. I'd sworn to myself that I would never use either skill to kill.

They crumpled like rag dolls at the edge of the rubber trees. What did they think in their last seconds of life? Were they dying for Karl Marx, for a socialist Vietnam? Or because their commanders would kill them if they did not charge?

A handful of them raced back down the lanes, firing wildly at us.

"Hold your fire," I ordered, realizing for the first time that I had never ordered my men to open fire. I must have started to shoot and then they joined me.

"We slaughtered them, sir," yelled the sergeant triumphantly.

"Yeah," I said, feeling no enthusiasm for what had happened. "They'll be back."

They were back indeed. In fifteen minutes, I suppose, though it seemed like a couple of eternities. They were more cautious this time, hiding behind the trees and firing at us intermittently. Testing our defenses and carrying off their dead.

If they'd been any good at their work, they would have discovered that our defenses were pretty weak. Their commander would wait till dark—dusk was already thick around us—and wipe us out.

Then we heard the sound of choppers, huge khaki dragonflies hovering protectively above us.

Two of them settled quickly onto the landing area. No fire from the enemy. Surprised and uncertain, perhaps.

"One more craft coming," an officer on the lead chopper shouted.

I ordered the civilians onto the first chopper and the still unconscious major and the Thos onto the second.

"Marie!" Guy screamed at me, his face twisted in anguish. "She is not here."

"I'll find her," I replied, still cool and confident. "You get out of here with the others. We'll be in the last chopper."

"She is my wife!" he pleaded, tears streaming down his grief-stricken face.

"I'm in charge," I said, surely the most foolish words I've uttered in my whole life. "I'll bring her out. Now get on that helicopter. That's an order."

I must have sounded terribly military. He did as he was told.

There were six men left besides me when the two giant dragonflies lifted off the ground and disappeared quickly down the river.

"Give us five minutes, Sergeant," I said quietly. "If I'm not back by then, leave without me."

He hesitated.

"That's an order."

"Yes, sir."

I never told Madonna about that act of madness. A husband and a father recklessly playing hero for a provocative Asian woman.

In any case, it was more than ten minutes before the third chopper arrived. By that time the VC had brought up their mortars and were zeroing in on the landing area.

Stumbling over roots in the twilight, I rushed through the underbrush toward the pool, not reflecting until I was almost there that if Marie had not returned to the perimeter behind her house, the reason was that the VC had already captured her.

I crawled the last twenty yards through the brush and peered cautiously at the dusk-shrouded pond. They had her, all right, and if they had not been so busy at their work, they would have heard me.

She was tied naked to a tree with a knife at her belly. Two of the men were peasants in black pajamas, indistinguishable from any rubber plantation worker. The third, the man with the knife, was dressed in white shorts and shirt, an officer or a cadre. It was not rape they had in mind. Not yet. They wanted information. Why were the Americans ready?

One of the other men pulled a small wailing object out of the water. What could it be?

Emily.

I thought of Melissa Jean back home in Chicago, calmly switched my weapon to manual fire, lined up the man with the knife in my sights, and with now the slowest of slow motion put a bullet in the back of his head, smashing it like a grapefruit. Then, with what seemed like infinite leisure, I shifted my gunsight to the man who had been dunking the poor little girl and killed him. Emily fell back into the water.

The third man turned in my direction and raised his AK-47. Much too late. I had blown his head away before he was able to aim.

These were the first of the enemy I was certain I had killed. The only emotion I felt was fury at what they were doing to Emily.

I heard, as if from a great distance, the sound of an incoming chopper and the muffled flumps of mortar rounds. I ran around the pond, snatched the fiercely protesting Emily out of the pool, cut the rope binding Marie to the tree, and ordered her to stop vomiting and follow me.

She obeyed.

We reached the perimeter just as the chopper disappeared above the trees. Mortar rounds were exploding all around us, sending up little balls of silver smoke and dirt.

A naked woman with a trickle of blood running down her belly, a hysterical little girl, and a now thoroughly frightened first lieutenant, who knew with total certainty that soon he would die.

I had saved Marie's life. Now she saved mine.

"We must go down the river in a sampan," she said softly. "Come with me."

The mortars stopped as abruptly as they had begun. I imagined the enemy creeping through the trees for their final attack. "Come with me," she repeated.

My terror ebbed. I followed her into the house.

Quickly she found black coolie pajamas and broad hats for the two of us. "You must wear the hat over your face," she said. "You are short enough to be a Vietnamese." She jammed food and a wad of money into two baskets, presented me with the somewhat placated Emily, and led the way to the boat dock beneath the house. We boarded a sampan, perhaps fourteen feet long, with a small cabin in the front. She skillfully poled us out of the dock and into mid-river. We turned once in the current and then began to drift almost casually downstream.

The mortars resumed fire. Marie's house erupted in a cloud of incandescent smoke and then burst into flame. She did not even look back.

During the voyage down the river, a bizarre mixture of terror and quiet restfulness, Marie was the pilot and the commanding officer who steered us through the swift currents and the slow, and poled us away from the tangled jungle at the banks when we drifted too close. She decided when we would paddle way into shore and hide till dark. She gave the instructions on handling the boat. She talked in the local dialect to the uneasy and suspicious people we encountered. She slipped into a village one night to buy fruit.

Her orders were always given as a polite request, as if she were asking me for a favor. She spoke and acted as though she were devoid of emotions. "It would perhaps be useful, *mon capitaine*, if you remained very close to me when we pass that sampan, so that they will look at my face and not yours."

You bet, honey.

VC patrols roamed the area, making sure that there were no Americans left and collecting taxes (tribute) from the peasants. We hid in a small stream for two days, waiting till she learned from the natives that it was safe to travel downriver again.

Every sound in the jungle made me reach for my M 16. Finally, Marie told me somewhat impatiently that she'd let me know when it was needed.

We slept during the day, huddling in the stifling heat under the bamboo cover that was our cabin, pressed close together in what was even in those circumstances a delightfully sensuous embrace. Emily, merry little child, created no fuss as long as her mother's breasts were available when she was hungry.

Only once did Marie show emotion. I woke late one afternoon, soaked in sweat and with a terrible headache, to hear her crying softly.

She was worried about Guy and the other children. I assured her that they were safe and held her in my arms while she cried herself back to sleep. Whatever hesitancies there had been in my love for her disappeared. In a twinkling, love became adoration.

Later that night, after she had nursed her daughter, half asleep, I reached for a breast. She smiled benignly and guided my lips to first one nipple, then the other. Her milk was sweet and warm, her body firm and restful, her eyes, just visible in the moonlight reflected on the water, were soft and big with pleasure.

I did not ask her to nurse me again.

Six days after we had fled, we were picked up by an armed patrol that stumbled on us without warning just as we had paddled ashore at dawn.

I shoved my weapon into the wide sleeves of my pajamas while they pulled Marie out of the boat and knocked her to her knees. They wore American-made uniforms and carried M 1s. Government provincial troops who, from the point of view of the peasants, were as much a threat as the VC.

They pushed me in the direction of their lieutenant, who had already pulled back the shoulder of Marie's black jacket and was admiring his prize. I buried the muzzle of my weapon into his belly and told him, in the GI language he would understand, that he was one step away from being a dead motherfucker.

They apologized profusely, doubtless expecting to be executed, and led us to the nearest American outfit, a marine patrol. The gyrenes were impressed by how tough I looked, and even more impressed by Marie. They took us back to the headquarters of Operation Little Bighorn.

"You didn't make love to her?" Ciara asked, her eyes staring off in the distance, seeing something that was far away.

"I could have. Easily. She didn't desire me the way she'd done the first day at the pool. Yet she would have given herself to me for the asking. Out of gratitude and affection. I adored the woman. She was so brave, so smart, so good. We told each other our life stories while we floated down the river under the stars. I have never had a closer friend. I wanted her more than I have wanted anyone till I met you. Somehow it didn't seem right. Now I wonder. Maybe drinking her milk was as bad. I've never had pleasure quite like it. Typical male fantasy, I suppose."

"Sure, you have no monopoly on it." Ciara jabbed my ribs playfully. "We're nursed and weaned, too, you know."

"I don't even want to think about the kinky fantasies that makes possible."

"You do too." She kissed me reassuringly. "There's nothing wrong with fantasies."

"Do you think I was a coward because I didn't make love to her?"

She rested her head on my chest. "Ah, sure, you did the right thing altogether. Still, I wouldn't have thought less of you if you'd made love to the poor woman. And herself wanting it, too, I suppose. You're a great, powerful hero you are, Brendan Ryan, and a noble one at that."

"I'm not so sure," I said. "When we finally reached the base we learned that the second chopper had been hit by enemy fire and crash-landed at the base. The major, Guy, and two of the kids had been killed. I got a medal."

"Glory be to God." I felt her tears on my chest. "Still you did the right thing, Brendan."

"Did I? If I had not ordered Guy out, he might have lived. If I had ordered them to wait for us, the VC might not have hit them. We mucked up going into that place, and I mucked up getting out."

"You can't torment yourself that way," she insisted.

"I should have locked the woman in the house. Or warned her husband to keep her away from the pond." I went on remorselessly with accusations I had never spoken to anyone before. "I wanted to keep open the possibility of going back there and making love . . ."

"Hush," she ordered weakly. I hushed.

"They're all dead now?" she asked, stroking my cheek gently.

I watched the lights of a jet gliding through the darkness toward O'Hare. It was easy to fly a plane. You follow the instructions and it takes off and lands. You program the automatic pilot and the plane goes where it is told. Not so easy to pilot your life. "Oddly enough, no. No thanks to me. I couldn't deal with her grief, so I went back to my basement in Saigon after I kissed her and Emily good-bye. She married an American navy commander six months later. Somehow he managed to extricate her whole community, priest included, and ship them to America."

"A bad man?"

"No, a hell of a nice guy. Marie didn't choose her first husband. She was smart enough to make the right choice the second time around. A good Catholic like she is, kind of conservative but flexible and pleasant. He retired as a rear admiral. They live in San Diego now. She owns a string of Chinese restaurants—high-class places.''

"You see them, then?"

"Occasionally. When I'm on the West Coast. Not too often. It wouldn't be safe. I love her. I always will."

"She loves him?"

"Very much."

"Does she still love you?"

"Yes. In a way."

Ciara kissed me gently. "Terrible question. Lucky Brendan. If you had made love to her, she wouldn't dare still love you."

I'd never thought of it that way. "Perhaps."

"No perhaps about it."

"Oddly enough, it turns out now that the Holy Roman Church has decided that Madonna and I were never married. It would not have been adultery to make love to Marie. I could have brought her home as my wife."

"It wouldn't have worked out and you know it." Her lips roamed about my face. "Besides, then you wouldn't have noticed me in the Irish Store."

"There's that." I held her tightly. "You've been worth waiting for, Ciara Kelly. . . ."

"Go 'long with you." Gently she pushed me away, but the kisses continued. "And the wee lass?"

"Emily?"

"And who else would I mean?" She stopped kissing me to indicate her response to such a stupid question.

"That's kind of strange. She's at Stanford. Valedictorian in her class at some Catholic school in San Diego. Very lovely kid. Completely American."

"And she and your daughter are good friends?"

I swatted her lovely rump in mock displeasure. "You're an incurable romantic, woman. I don't think she and Jeannie know each other."

"You didn't tell your daughter?" Ciara turned on the bed lamp so she could examine me in angry disbelief. "What kind of a 'quare crayture' are you, Brendan Ryan?" Her accent was West of Ireland again, a mixture of shock and incredulity. "What are you afraid of?"

"Messing in people's lives," I said. "And messing them up."

She stared at me, considering me again as if I were some newly discovered and baffling form of animal life. Will she kiss me again, I wondered, or reach for her panties and bra and ask me to take her back to Chestnut Place?

Irishwoman that she was, she did both.

And invited me to have supper there on Sunday night, after sailing.

I had been judged and found not guilty by reason of insanity, and then committed to tender care to see if my sanity might be restored.

It had not been a bad night after all.

15

"There'll be no sailing today." Ciara pointed at the limp mainsail. "Ah, well, there's an ancient Irish adage to cover the situation." She giggled. "In fact there's an ancient Irish adage to cover every situation."

She jumped into the cockpit, agile and graceful in white shorts and red sweater, inexpensive recent additions to her meager wardrobe.

We drifted lazily five hundred yards offshore. The skyline was wrapped in tissue paper haze under a bright sun. An occasional ripple in the water, changing its color from dark blue to dark green, was the only sign of a breeze. For a sailor, a disappointing day. Summer doesn't last long; every weekend is precious.

"What's the old Irish wisdom?"

She furrowed her lovely forehead. "Let me think now. Ah, it goes something like this: A bad day for sailing is a good day for loving."

"Let me drop the anchor first."

Our bodies were becoming familiar with each other and

loving it. Ciara was telling me none of the secrets of her life—a mysteriousness that made her all the more desirable. But she hid nothing of her growing sexual passion.

With some embarrassment I would undress first. Embarrassment and also, to admit the truth, a growing masculine vanity that my woman was so quickly turned on by my body. It was supposed to be the other way around, but there was nothing wrong, I told myself to drive away my initial shame, with it happening both ways.

I had just finished Leo Steinberg's wonderful book about the sexuality of Christ in Renaissance art. He noted that in a few paintings of the Resurrection the risen Lord is depicted in a state of sexual arousal to symbolize power and vitality. I didn't know whether this was blasphemous, but it was surely true that to be sexually aroused in the presence of Ciara made me feel more powerful than I ever had before in my life. Power over her? Rather, knowing that my sexual arousal had the power to arouse her and that I could satisfy her desire and make her content, complacent, happy. Knowledge which, in its turn, increased my own arousal so that my body seemed to be charged with tremendous electrical energy.

The most delicate of all the phases came next. Ciara would be temporarily caught in a conflict between her own hungers and the residue of her prudishness and fears. She would clench her fists, not in anger, but in a determined effort to restrain them from resistance to being disrobed. Once her clothes were off she was a wanton, but the process of being stripped was both painful and pleasurable for her. Perhaps painfully pleasurable would be a better way to put it. When I slipped away her panties, it was as if she'd crossed the line between scrupulosity and bawdiness and was free to go on to more forthright, not to say brazen, pleasures.

That morning on the *Brigid* she resisted more than usual, perhaps because her businesslike underwear had been replaced by bits of mostly transparent lace—the result, doubtless, of the same frugal shopping expedition that had produced the shorts and sweater.

"Dear God in Heaven, Brendan Ryan," she sighed as I finished my undressing task, "I don't know why you tolerate me, I really don't. I'm such a great, powerful puritan about all this."

"Tell you the truth, I rather enjoy it."

"I'm sure you do. Fantasy that you're raping the poor captive . . . terrible Viking carrying off a nun. . . . Oh, Brendan, don't stop."

So it went. That morning lovemaking was particularly good. I was learning that more rewarding than to pleasure yourself with a woman was to pleasure her so that her body was shaken by deep and cataclysmic joy, ecstasy that subtly addicted her body to yours.

I needed Ciara like I had needed no one before in my life. She needed me even more.

That time, as was often the case, at the very height of my satisfaction, I saw her body growing large with my child.

Which, as I told myself while I stroked her reassuringly afterward, is what the rite of spring is all about.

"Should we abandon this craft for the sun and sand of Montrose Beach?" I asked her sleepily.

" 'Tis a wonderful fine place, save for one thing." She pronounced the word "ting," deliberately, I suspected, manifesting the Irish "th" problem. (There's no "h" sound in their language. Ciara did it because she knew it was one more aspect of her that turned me on.)

"And that is?"

"Sure, we can't make love there, can we?"

"You're insatiable, woman."

"You have no one to blame but yourself for that, Brendan Ryan. And yourself such a gorgeous man." Her lips began to explore my face, my chest, my body. "Well, one more time and then the beach. Have to save something for tonight."

"It may take a while . . ." I protested.

"Not at all, at all."

I tried at such times not to be shocked by the discovery that I was a sex object being used, however lovingly, by a woman for her own pleasure. "Hold still, Brendan." She shook her head, sending her long black hair tumbling behind her shoulders. "I'm not finished with you yet, at all, at all. . . . Saints preserve me, Brendan, I love you so much, every last wonderful bit of you." Sweat poured from her body and dripped on me as she did breathtaking things to me and moaned ecstatically in pursuit of her own delirium.

"You terrible, wanton thing," I groaned.

"Terrible altogether," she sighed in return, and then, as her body arched backward in convulsive spasms, she cried out in pure animal joy. Again and again and again.

Orgiastic sex with a vengeance, yet somehow innocent and graceful. Her hunger for me was simple, uncomplicated, childlike; and her happiness afterward reminded me of a little child at the Christmas tree. Brendan Ryan, great seducer of the Western world, became a present Santa Claus had brought to a wide-eyed little girl—a girl who studied the reactions of her new toy very carefully indeed, so she would know exactly how it worked.

You're going to have to be good to keep up with this one, Brendan Ryan. You've transformed a spring breeze into a hurricane.

Later, I turned on the auxiliary motor and pointed the bow toward the harbor. Ciara lolled in the cabin, contentedly naked.

"Haven't you forgot one important thing, Captain Brendan Ryan?"

"What would that be?"

"Isn't my swimsuit at my apartment?"

More questions in response to questions. Deliberate now, at least half the time.

"'It's not, not at all, at all. Look in the cabinet."

"Glory be to God," she exclaimed. "Do you want me to appear on the beach worse than naked?" As if to protest the very thought, she pulled a blanket around her body and hugged herself to fend off both immodesty and cold.

"Not quite."

"Sure, it's Montrose Beach, not the Copacabana. And I'm not one of your Brazilians. I won't wear it."

"You will, woman. Now put it on and stop arguing with me. If there's one ting I can't stand 'tis an argumentative woman."

She slammed the cabin door shut with a derisive bang. A few minutes later she emerged in a white outfit that indeed would have done very well in Rio.

"I don't know, Brendan." She was still glowing from sexual pleasure but awkward and uncertain.

"I do."

"You'd just be wanting to show off your prize, wouldn't you?"

"Would I now?"

"You would indeed. Well . . . are you sure?"

"Quite sure."

"All right." She agreed half dubiously and half happily, and pulled on her sweater and shorts. "The nuns at my school would be horrified."

"What school?"

"My school in Ireland."

Still the woman of mystery.

As we were leaving the *Brigid*, she carrying the lunch basket, I returned to the cabin and stuffed her bra and panties into my Windbreaker pocket.

"Give them back to me, you terrible man," she demanded, face flaming.

"I can't have such things lying around my boat. Sure, it would shock the occasional priest that uses it."

"You're teasing me."

"I am. But if you're good, as hard as that is for a woman from the West of Ireland, I'll give them back at the end of the day."

"It's a word that can have many meanings, isn't it now?"

I shoved her rear end off the boat, and she swung a strong arm in my direction.

Montrose Harbor is created by a hooklike landfill that pushes out into the lake. Its point separates from the shore by the fifty yards or so of harbor mouth that is further narrowed by two concrete breakwaters. It is a snug little harbor surrounded by beach and sloping green lawns. Ciara found a spot on the lawn near the outer breakwater that reminded her of Ireland despite the Chicago skyline which loomed directly to the south of us. I spread our blanket and we set up camp.

It was an idyllic day. Ciara swam for half an hour, pronouncing the lake much warmer, and attracted attention, as she walked back to our blanket, both for her hardiness and for her well-displayed beauty.

"They're all staring at me," she whispered.

"Because you're glowing so brightly."

"It's from the waters of the lake."

"Certainly it is."

We covered each other with suntan lotion and lay on the blanket holding hands while the perspiration rolled off our bodies. It was uncomfortably humid, but that suited the dissolute, desert-island mood we were both in—lethargic, languorous, complacent, deeply and abidingly satisfied with our love.

"All we need is a troop of hula dancers."

"Would you listen to him now? One woman isn't enough for him?" She poked my ribs, gently enough.

"Hey, I didn't specify only women dancers!"

"Sorry." She giggled and kissed my shoulder. "I'm not much good at mind reading."

We ate lunch and drove back to my apartment, where we showered (independently still), cleaned the dishes from our picnic ("I'll not be having you think I'm one of your sloppy Irish housewives"), and strolled down Michigan Avenue, people-watching and noise-listening—auto horns, lovers' conversation, chattering kids, crying babies, reproving mothers. She must have packed spare lingerie in her bag, because she made no attempt to recapture my prizes. At Superior Street she protested that she was "destroyed" from all her "exertions" and didn't have "a hope" of walking another block. We returned to the little square around the water tower and relaxed on a bench. I was dispatched to buy ice cream cones, even though it would do terrible "tings" to her figure. "I won't be wearing that terrible indaycent bikini for long, at all, at all, if you keep making me eat your American ice cream," she claimed, capturing a large glob of chocolate that had escaped to the corner of her lips. "Then you'll lose interest in me altogether."

"I will indeed."

She was too busy with the cone to poke me.

We were even fellow chocolate freaks.

Ciara inspected every baby and small child who passed, flirting with the little boys, playing with the little girls, and complimenting the mothers of both with outrageous blarney in her thickest West of Ireland accent.

She should have children of her own. She would soon. That's what spring is all about.

I returned to our bench with the popcorn she had requested. "I've always thought that this little square was kind of like something you might see in Paris."

"Paris, is it?" She glanced around the square. "Sure, 'tis easy to see you haven't been to Paris."

"Not as good?" I stuffed some popcorn in my mouth.

"Not as good, is it? Glory be to God, Brendan Ryan. What little square in Paris would have something as wonderful as that?" She gestured admiringly toward the soaring John Hancock Center. "Or that?" She pointed at the Olympia Center, known to everyone in Chicago as the Needless Markup Center because of the presence of Neiman-Marcus in the building. "Paris doesn't have any quaint little squares with cute nineteenth-century water towers and Skidmore Owings and Merrill prizewinners for a backdrop. It's a wondrous meadow in the high mountains."

"With the Chestnut Street ravine feeding into it . . . You sound as though you like Chicago."

"It's a great, powerful city. And beautiful besides."

"And yourself planning to stay here, is it?"

She jabbed at my arm with her popcorn box. "Stop talking the way I do. One of us is enough. Maybe too much."

End of discussion.

We ate supper at Jerome's on North Clark, after I had persuaded her that she did not need to dress for it. "Your legs will earn us a good table in their outdoor café," I insisted.

The maître d' was a woman, but she sized up Ciara admiringly and did indeed give us a corner table, at which we could eat and from which we could continue to people-watch. If I observed a young woman for what Ciara deemed was an inappropriately long period, she would reprimand me, "half fun and full earnest."

"Love with one woman," I sighed, mocking her sigh, "makes you notice all women."

"It's not the noticing I mind." She was polishing off an artichoke in lemon butter with great relish. "It's the devouring of them. You might at least leave the poor tings their clothes. Anyway, you should do it like I do," she winked mischievously, "with more taste and discretion."

We ate Alaskan rockfish and drank a bottle of sauvignon blanc. Ciara insisted on chocolate mousse for dessert and a "wee drop" of Baileys Irish Cream. Three glasses of Baileys later she was delightfully giddy.

"It's been a grand day altogether, Brendan Ryan. No one will ever say you're not good to your women."

A lot of people had said it, but I wasn't about to argue.

It was eleven o'clock when I finally dragged her away from several conversations with other patrons of the restaurant. "I didn't embarrass you, did I?" she asked anxiously.

"You couldn't possibly embarrass me, Ciara Kelly. Every man in that place envied me." I guided her to the door of my car. "Take you back to your apartment?"

"Have you lost your ardor altogether?"

I found an empty parking lot and demonstrated, with few preliminaries and considerable vigor, that I had not.

"Have you ever done it that way before?" she asked me when we were done.

"I've never had a woman who drove me to it before, Ciara Kelly."

She giggled in satisfaction and snatched her bra and panties from the pocket of my Windbreaker.

"Not that I mind," she giggled again, "but I don't have all that large a supply, if you take my meaning."

Looking back on that incident, if I had kept her undergarments, I might have had some evidence. But then, perhaps you can't have evidence of someone who doesn't really exist, not, at least, in the same time and space that you do.

At Chestnut Place she insisted that it was not necessary for me to get out of the car, which meant that she didn't want me to. We were still protecting the poor doorman from scandal.

"See you tomorrow night." She turned away. Then she turned back to the car, eyes filled with tears. "Dear God, I love you, Brendan Ryan," she said in her thickest brogue and softest whisper. "I know I'm fluthered, but it doesn't matter. I'm out of my mind with love for you."

"Isn't it risky to tell a man that?"

She kissed me with enough tenderness to break my heart. "I don't care at all, at all." Then she ran to the door, leaving me with visions of a life in which every day would be as blissful—and as unpredictable—as that day.

There was no question of Ciara sailing with me on Sunday. I was invited to her apartment for supper, and the supper had to be well prepared. "When you're after a meal," she proclaimed, "you should be doing it right!"

I sensed, or perhaps only hoped, that our relationship would change that Sunday. Perhaps I would be invited not only into her apartment but into her life.

I sailed in the morning, worked on my manuscript in the afternoon, and set forth down the Chestnut Street ravine at five o'clock, carrying two bottles of Baileys and two dozen roses. The doorman rang apartment 960, and I was shown the way to the elevator.

"You're on time." Ciara glowered at me from the doorway, a saucepan in her hand. "You were supposed to be late."

For a moment I was quite speechless. Ciara had designed the night to make more explicit the gift of herself she had promised. She had even gift-wrapped herself. She was dressed in a lilac nylon and lace lingerie arrangement that would have stopped any man cold. More of the J.C. Penney's shopping expedition I thought, and instantly reprimanded my snobbishness. She was dazzling regardless of how little money it took to make her dazzling. Her hair was burnished and lustrous, black lava on new-fallen snow; her face carefully made up; red stones, rubies, I thought, on her ears and at her neck—the family jewels, doubtless, or all that remained of them. Her body radiated an enticing scent. Her gray eyes were both easing and inviting.

She knew she was devastating and was embarrassed, for the record anyway.

"Well, what are you standing there staring at?" she demanded, the corners of her mouth struggling unsuccessfully against a grin. "Are you going to come in and give me those gorgeous roses, or are you going to stand there and stare?"

"Can I come in and stare?"

"You're a terrible man altogether, Brendan Ryan." She brushed my cheek with a quick kiss.

"Jesus and Mary be with this house," I said as I entered.

"Jesus and Mary and Patrick be with you," she replied promptly. "And there's a wee jar of the creature on the coffee table for you while I'm finishing the stew."

Her studio apartment, weirdly shaped like a bent corkscrew, was like a hotel room—utterly devoid of the slightest imprint of her personality. No photographs or drawings, only a handful of paperback books, some in French; a tiny transistor radio; a black-and-white portable TV; the simplest and most inexpensive furniture, drapes, and bedspread; functional beige walls and carpet. The occupant, you sensed, had only touched down for a few hours and then would be on her way.

"You get a nice view of Washington Square Park, the Newbury Library, and the Montgomery Ward building out the window." She sailed back in from her tiny kitchen, amid the rustle of fabric, with a plate of hors d'oeuvres concocted from cheese and ham. "Don't eat too much of them or you'll spoil your supper."

How to reconcile the flair and energy of the occupant with her bland dwelling place? I felt vaguely uneasy. While she was in the kitchen, I quickly wrote down her phone number and slipped it into my pocket.

"Woman of the house?"

"What would you be wanting?"

"You."

"I'm cooking your dinner, you idjit."

"Come have a wee jar with me."

"I can't do two things at once," she exploded in a burst of temper.

"Cool it, woman!" I shouted in return. "Or I'll come out there and take the back of my hand to you."

Silence. Then a shamefaced Ciara, mixing spoon in hand, appeared at the kitchen door. "I'm sorry, Brendan darling. When I was a little girl, I swore I'd never do that to a guest. It was good of you to call me on it. Just a second and I'll be with you."

In only a few seconds she was seated on the chair across from me on the sofa—the only furniture in the room besides the bed. She took a deep breath and relaxed. "An Irish fishwife, and I'm not even a wife. Slainte to you anyway, Brendan Ryan, failte and slainte."

"Slainte to you, too, woman of the house." I toasted her gravely.

"I'm sorry I was so rude." She put down the drink, Jameson's, and made a face. "I know a happy hostess is better than an efficient one. Damn it, I want to be both."

"You look wonderful."

She stirred uneasily. "I'm not sure that I'll ever be any good at this seduction business. I feel . . ." she waved her hands awkwardly ". . . silly."

"It's my impression that women enjoy dressing that way. What do you call it?"

"A teddy and a wrap coat . . . and a garter belt too." Averted head and blush.

"Even more than we men enjoy them dressing that way."

She considered me very carefully. "You're a very clever man about women, Brendan Ryan. And yourself not having much experience with them. Remind me to be careful with you. Anyway, you're right save for the first attempt, when the woman feels clumsy and silly."

"You don't look silly. Maybe you'd relax if you sit next to me and let me kiss you. It's not a proper way to come into the house, not kissing the woman of the house."

"You'll never get your supper," she warned.

"Only a kiss for now."

It was, however, a very intense kiss, driving down into the depths of her soul. Her jaw sagged, her eyes blurred, her head rested against my chest.

"Ah, you'll be the destruction of me altogether. Truly if you want to eat, I'd better go back to the kitchen."

She was, in addition to everything else, a good cook— Caesar salad, prosciutto and melon, a California white, and, true to her promise, lamb stew, indeed the most skillfully seasoned lamb stew I'd ever eaten, accompanied by Beaulieu cabernet sauvignon, George Latour special reserve.

Poor woman shouldn't spend her few dollars on expensive wine.

All by candlelight and WFMT music and witty conversation—in which nothing at all was said about her past.

I helped her clear the table, a gesture that caused a flicker of amusement in her astonishing gray eyes.

"Sherry trifle for dessert, and cappuccino," she announced.

"Ciara Kelly for dessert."

"Brendan . . . no . . . I've worked hard on the sherry trifle. You Yanks don't know how to make it. Oh, God . . . no . . . *Brendan*!"

"Two desserts."

"Sherry trifle first . . ."

"No." This time her clothes, such as they were, came off first.

She giggled merrily as my fingers fumbled with slippery fabrics and unfamiliar fastenings. "Sure, you're tickling me, you clumsy oaf."

I wasn't, but I liked the suggestion. A new kick. She shrieked in outrage, but she liked it too. Our sex was turning away from serious passion and in the direction of play. It was even better that way.

It was also prolonged and sensitive and deeply rewarding. We both knew we had crossed the mountain range. It was no longer an affair, not as far as our bodies were concerned. Whatever we might think in our heads, our loins had already decided: Ciara and I were now one flesh. For keeps.

Then we ate the sherry trifle, drank the cappuccino, and sipped our "wee jar" of Baileys. In fact, I ate two helpings of the sherry trifle and admitted that, indeed, we Yanks did not know how to make it.

"I'm thinking you liked it better than you liked me," she protested.

"Do I have to choose?"

"Course not." She had put back on what might, I suppose, be called the robe of her ensemble—not that it made much difference in the scenery. As we drank the Baileys, she seemed abstracted, far away. Perhaps drifting further away.

I would marry her. That was that. The sooner the better. So questions must be asked.

"Who are you, Ciara Kelly?"

She jumped up from the sofa, startled and angry.

"Not who you think I am, Brendan Ryan." The brogue was now almost undetectable. "I'm not the charming Irish innocent you've created in your fantasy, not the sweet superannuated virgin whom you've seduced and intend now to redeem."

"Huh?"

"Get out of here!" she screamed at me. "I never want to see you again!"

"What did I say?" I stood up, prepared to leave.

"It's not what you said, it's who you are—a smug, self-important little bourgeois hypocrite."

I sat back down on the sofa. "I'm not leaving here till I receive an explanation."

"You can stay all night. I won't say another word to you." She flounced into the bathroom and returned in an aged and tattered bathrobe.

"At least you didn't put your hair in curlers."

A small smile, quickly repressed.

"You don't mind if I get myself mildly fluthered on your Irish Cream?"

"It's yours, you brought it."

"You already broke your word that you wouldn't say another word."

She closed her eyes. Her face became a mask of pain, as though someone were squeezing the life out of her.

"All right." She opened her eyes and crumpled into the corner of her chair. "You have a right to know."

She had graduated from secondary school at the age of sixteen, highest honors in her class and a university scholarship. Not that they would collect any money for it. Her father was a prominent lawyer, wealthy by Irish standards, and well known. He was a stern man, harsh and demanding of his children and narrow in his views. Ciara was to be a nurse and that was that.

She thought she might want to be a nurse, as a matter of fact, but she resented that she was being given no choice. Of all the children, she was the only one with the nerve to tangle with her father.

Either nursing, he said, or you go to work as a shop girl.

So she defied them all and signed up for a year of volunteer service as a nurse's aide with an Irish missionary community that maintained a hospital in the Congo. Her father could hardly refuse her permission to go to Africa. Ireland was heavily involved in the U.N. peace keeping mission in the Congo. It was a matter of national pride. Nor could he stand in the way of a possible religious vocation for his daughter. After all, one of his principal charities was a hospital administered by nuns, and he had praised their work publicly as a sign of stability in a foolishly changing Church.

He warned her, however, that she was a rash and disrespectful young woman and that God would punish her terribly for her imprudence. Which indeed He did.

Africa fascinated and overwhelmed her. She was appalled by the poverty and sickness, charmed by the patients at the hospital, exhausted by the heat and the string of tropical illnesses which were part of acclimating, intrigued by the nuns' courage and cheerfulness, and repelled by the rigidity of their community rule. Their hospital was near Lubumbashi (formerly Elizabethville), far away from the region of Katanga where the violence had been and where the Irish troops had died. The nuns insisted there was no danger in their part of the country, and so she wrote dutifully every week to her mother. There were no replies because her father had forbidden the rest of the family to write to her.

Then there were rumors of a rebellion at the other end of the province—a group of unpaid soldiers (the central government at Kinshasha had plenty of money but did not seem to be very skillful at paying its troops in the outlands) who had drifted across the border into the former French Congo, which had gone Marxist. The Russians paid them, equipped them with guns and munitions, and sent them back as "patriotic socialist revolutionaries." The troops called themselves Simbas—lions.

"They won't come here," Mother Superior said confidently. "Even if they do, they won't hurt us. The African people love us."

The Simbas came early one morning, crazed with drink and drugs (also furnished by the Russians). They bayoneted all the men patients, and the women too, after they'd raped them. They gathered the nuns and the nurses in the courtyard and amused themselves with them till daylight, and then killed them, as slowly and painfully as possible. Some survived, screaming, until the end of the day, when the Simbas finally blew their brains out with automatic weapons.

They spared Ciara and two black girls who were nurse's aides because they were young and pretty and could offer amusement for several days. Ciara lost track of the number of times she was raped and degraded. After the first day she prayed for death.

The Simbas, who seemed to have a plentiful supply of drugs and drink, often threatened them with death, pointed the guns at their heads or their bellies or their sex organs, and pulled the triggers. They found it greatly amusing when the young women screamed in anguish and then discovered that the guns were not loaded this time.

Then one morning they cut off the breasts of the two black girls and stuck bayonets up their wombs until they bled to death, laughing crazily all the while. The sergeant in charge of the execution swaggered to the post to which Ciara was tied, drained a bottle of liquor, smashed it against a tree, and raised it to her face. She prayed that she would die quickly.

There was a short burst of automatic weapon fire and blood poured out of the sergeant's stomach as he tottered and fell. Paratroopers from the French Foreign Legion had arrived. About the same time they saved most of the foreigners at Lubumbashi. Ciara, or what was left of her, was the only one they saved at the mission station. The Simbas, too drunk to fight, quickly surrendered.

When the Legionnaires saw what had happened to the patients and the nuns and the nurses, they executed all the Simbas, most of them with machine gun bullets fired into the groin. At the end of the day, Ciara, hysterical with fear and humiliation, was the only living being left from the hospital and invading force.

Sure, the Africans loved them. Many of the people whom the nuns had healed shouted with glee as they were tortured and killed. The Legionnaires killed many of them too. One can't blame all Africans, not even all of those in the mission area. Who does not do what they think the men with the guns want them to do? Yet every time she sees a black man, she remembers the Simbas and is afraid. She's ashamed of her reaction. It's not fair. She goes out of her way to be friendly. But she can't forget the Simbas. Or the man in whose badly cut arm she had put stitches only a few days before. He laughed enthusiastically and taunted her in broken English as she was raped.

She was only turned seventeen. She knew nothing at all about sex.

The Simbas were no worse than most men in conquering armies. Most Americans don't know what happened in Stuttgart in 1945 when the American army captured the city. Men have raped women for the whole history of the race because they are stronger and have the weapons. What are the statistics in America? A third of the women in the country have been raped, most of them by men who had some kind of power over them—husbands, lovers, fathers, brothers, uncles, friends. What right did she have to be immune from the ordinary lot of womankind? Rape doesn't happen in civilized countries? What country is civilized? And how thin is the line separating civilizations from barbarism? The world will be civilized only when women are safe from the men with the weapons and from the relatives who have power over them.

She came home a heroine. A survivor of martyrdom. No one was supposed to know what had happened to her. Everyone did, naturally. It was just not discussed in the Ireland of the late 1960s. Her father told her it served her right for her disobedience and pride. She cursed him and said she would never set foot in his house. She went to see him when he was dying, and he refused to see her.

I filled both our glasses when her story ended. My stomach was knotted, my throat tight with fury, my hands clenched. I had to be careful of what I said.

"So what?"

My words stirred her out of her reverie. "What do you mean, so what?"

"I don't mean so what about your pain or so what about the memories that torment you. I mean, so what about us?"

"No man wants a woman who has been soiled that way."

"Now who's the male chauvinist?"

"It's true."

"It's not true. I grieve with you, Ciara. I admire you even more for the strength it took you to bounce back . . ."

"I haven't bounced back." She drew her old green robe more tightly around her.

"Bullshit. As I was saying, I grieve for you. I will suffer with you. I admire you for your guts. I'll help you fight off the fears when they return. I'll not let you use this to put me off."

"Get the hell out of here," she screeched hysterically.

"You said that before. Drink your Baileys."

"You want to make me fluthered so you can rape me like they did."

"You're too smart to say something dumb like that, Ciara. The whole point of this crazy dialogue is you want to know whether a man can make effective love to you after he knows what the Simbas did to your poor young body. It's a fair question. I propose to answer it for you."

So far so good, Brendan Ryan. Nick and Eileen would be astonished at how good you are in court.

"You can't make me."

"I'm not trying to make you do anything, Ciara Kelly. You've challenged me and I intend to respond to your challenge."

"I won't fight you off," she said with infinite sadness. "Do whatever you want to do. I won't enjoy a second of it. That's all over for me."

Which was absolute nonsense. As the two of us proved in rather short order.

Then there were many tearful apologies.

"I didn't know I was testing you, Brendan darlin'," she said, sniffling in a tissue. "I mean I suppose I was doing that, but I didn't mean to. You poor dear man, what a terrible thing to have happen the first night you visit a woman's apartment. Sure, you should walk out and never come back again."

I held her close and stroked her thick black hair. "I didn't and I won't, I hope that's clear enough."

"I'll make up even worse stories if you love me the same way after them." The woman leprechaun was never too far away, not even at the most painful moments.

"I'll always love you, Ciara Kelly. I don't like the tests, but you're entitled to as many as you want."

"There'll be no more of that." She sat up straight and pounded her bed—onto which we had moved earlier in the process. "I'm yours, Brendan, my dearest," she bent over me and kissed me, her breasts firm against my chest, "for as long as you want me, any time you want me, any way you want me, any place you want . . ." the inevitable laughter, "even in your car parks, oops, parking lots."

I felt, poor fool that I was, that I had won. No longer a loser, Ron Crowley, but a winner.

"That's a gift, woman, that I'll not be refusing." She lay in my arms, quiet, passive, a pure gift. Her gray eyes were solemn and liquid. I kissed both of them and laid her back in bed.

"Completely yours," she whispered softly.

I covered her with the sheet and thin blanket. "You need a good night's sleep."

"The house is a terrible mess," she protested. "I can't have you leaving thinking I'm a slob."

"I'll clean up."

"A holy martyr," she sighed peacefully.

It was no great task to dispose of the remains of a dinner for two, especially since the wine and Baileys bottles were quite empty. I turned on the dishwasher, scrubbed the pots and pans, cleaned off the sink and the stove, polished the glasses while the dishwasher hummed happily in the background.

Ciara and I had both been activists, I reflected as I put the glasses in her small but fastidiously neat cabinet. Not quite like the protesters of our generation—and we did overlap the activist generation, one of us at either end of it—but young people who were firmly convinced that we could make a difference. I would be an intelligence officer in Vietnam, as my father had been in Europe, and help make Southeast Asia safe for democracy. She would follow in the wake of fifteen centuries of brave Irish missionaries and heal and convert the pagans of Africa. We both had failed. We both had come to understand after painful losses—much more painful for her than for me—the futility of trying to solve the twisted problems of humankind and rebuild the world with such poor tools as generosity and enthusiasm. We had, perhaps necessarily, withdrawn into our narrow private lives. Now we had each other. Could it be that with each other some of the old generosity might be reborn? We would be more cautious. No more Congo or Vietnam, but carefully thought out enthusiasm and rationally controlled generosity. With frequent sips of the Holy Grail of our springtime passion for each other.

Looking back, I realize how much of an idjit, to use her word, I revealed myself to be in such reflections. Men in love never think very clearly.

"Sure, you'd make a grand wife," she said as I turned off the kitchen light and crept into the parlor.

"Go to sleep, woman." I kissed her gently. She watched me with a smile that I can only call adoring. "No more talk."

"Yes, Brendan."

I tucked her in and kissed her again. "Pleasant dreams."

"I love you, Brendan."

I suppose I rode down the elevator. I was so happy, however, I'm sure I could have floated to the ground.

There were uncertainties, but only sounding in the recesses of my brain like a bell tolling at a great distance. She had told me nothing about the sixteen years since she'd come home from Zaire. How had she managed to climb out of her tragic suffering and become the mature woman she was?

And what was a woman who could read modern French novels doing working as a sales clerk?

Those issues were minor, I assured myself. We'd clear them up in the next few days.

The Chestnut Street ravine was crawling that night with demons and shades, warnings and threats, dangers and dooms. I paid them no attention. Psychic manifestations were unimportant when compared with the woman whom I now planned to marry.

I showered in my apartment and sat for a few moments staring out at the lake, savoring my joy. Ciara Kelly was mine.

What enormous willpower it must have required for her to recover from the terrible traumas of the Congo, and to risk a love affair with me, and to make of herself a trusting and generous gift. Ah, my Ciara, you're a woman with a heroine's strong will.

And stubbornness.

Still, I'm pretty good at coping with you when you're stubborn.

I saw a jetliner catch fire in the sky, streak across it like a meteor, and plunge into the lake. Then another liner followed it. Shaken, I turned on WBBM, the news station, and listened for fifteen minutes. No report of any plane accidents.

Another psychic kink. I tried to dismiss it, but couldn't quite banish the picture of the flaming light slicing across the sky. A death symbol, perhaps.

I concentrated on Ciara's slow and magic smile, and the image of the fire disappeared.

I would probably have to tell her about the peculiar psychic things that happened to me. Unlike Madonna, she would notice them.

I slept peacefully and well, and awakened at five, still blissful. The night before at her apartment had not been a dream. Indeed, I *had* won Ciara. I went back to sleep and did not wake till nine o'clock. So besotted with love that I had not set the alarm. I shaved quickly, swallowed half a cup of tea while I was dressing, did not bother to turn on the radio or glance at the paper for the morning news, and dashed for a cab so that I wouldn't be too late for my 9:30 appointment.

It was a quarter to ten when I jumped out of the cab at 211 West Jackson and rushed for the elevator.

On the third floor I nodded briefly at the receptionist. Oddly enough, she screamed. What was the matter with her? I wondered, as I rushed down the beige-carpeted corridor to my office. Heart attack? Maybe I ought to go back and check.

Someone else must have heard her.

My secretary was not at her station, which was unusual. And my client was not in the office. Strange. He was a compulsively punctual man. Had he left already? That would not be like him.

I pulled his folder out of my file drawer.

"My God . . . !"

It was Eileen. She and Nick were standing at the door, pale and stricken. Like they'd seen a ghost.

"You're dead, Brendan," she said in a weird, choked voice.

"Blown up early this morning," Nick agreed.

three
THE
DANCE
OF
SACRIFICE

16

"I don't care what was on the radio," I said with elaborate casualness as I poured out two cups of hot water and put the herbal tea bags in them. "I am not dead. I am very much alive. I was not blown up last night. As in the case of Mark Twain, reports of my death are greatly exaggerated."

"God . . ." Eileen breathed softly. "But who? . . ."

Nick shook his head, as though trying to clear away mental cobwebs. "What made you think I was dead?" I asked amiably, relaxing in my judge's chair.

"Your boat blew up last night."

The tips of Nick's fingers touched his forehead as though he were desperately trying to recapture his sanity.

"The cops are all over." Eileen frowned deeply.

"The *Brigid*?" Now I was shocked and incredulous.

"Two people on it," Eileen said.

"A man and a woman," Nick continued.

"The man was tentatively identified as you. Who else would be on your boat?"

I felt like I was watching a late-night TV movie, one that was running in the wrong direction.

"I don't understand . . ."

"What the fuck are you doing here alive?" At the door of the office stood a tall, lean, bald man in a gray suit with angry darting eyes.

"Lieutenant Samuel Norton of Homicide." Eileen waved a casual hand. "Like most cops he thinks that obscene language establishes his masculinity."

"Where the fuck have you been?" The lieutenant's voice was thin and piercing.

"The rotund spear carrier behind him," Eileen continued dispassionately, "is Sergeant O'Connor. It's not clear whether he can talk."

"I said where the fuck have you been?" Norton was paying no attention at all to Eileen.

"Either you keep a civil tongue in your head, Lieutenant," her green eyes sparkled dangerously, "or my client will have nothing to say to you."

The lieutenant turned menacingly toward her. "What do you mean 'client'?" he snarled.

Nick Curran eased out of his chair and stood toe to toe with the lieutenant. "What does a lawyer normally mean by the word 'client,' Lieutenant? And how tall was the male deceased who was removed from the boat early this morning?"

"Over six feet," Lieutenant Norton said grudgingly.

"As you can see, Lieutenant, Mr. Ryan is no taller than Sergeant O'Connor, a little over five foot eight. That's the first stupid mistake for the Chicago Police Department. Why did you tell the press that you suspected the body was Mr. Ryan's without making the obvious inquiry about his height?"

"We're checking dental X rays." The lieutenant backed off from his eyeball-to-eyeball confrontation with Nick. Just as well, for if his violent temper had caused him to lay a hand on Eileen, Nick would have broken his back. And Sergeant O'Connor's, too, for good measure.

"You can forget about Mr. Ryan's dental X rays," Nick said easily. "I think we can assure you they won't match the teeth of the deceased."

"Where were you at midnight?" The lieutenant turned abruptly on me, the veins in his forehead standing out like mountain ridges on a topographic map.

"In my apartment."

"What time did you go into the apartment?" He sounded like a prosecuting attorney closing in on a victim.

"Red? Eileen." Eileen was speaking into my telephone. "We have a resurrection on our hands. He's alive and well and looking fit. God knows who was in the boat. We have a cop from Homicide with a foul mouth here in the office. Name of Norton. You know him? Huh? Well, spread the word to the press that Brendan Ryan is alive and the homicide officers of the Chicago Police Department neglected to call his apartment on the off chance that he might not have been the body on the boat, a body which, by the way, is several inches taller than Mr. Ryan. Got it? Thanks. Love you."

"You bitch." He hissed at her.

"Get out of here." Nick stepped toward Norton, who backed up another step.

"Nicholas!" Eileen said imperiously. "We have witnesses, and we'll take it up in due course with Internal Investigations in the police department. For the moment I would suggest that Mr. Ryan answer the lieutenant's questions."

"I returned to my apartment about eleven-thirty." I still felt like I was watching a late-night movie, but now that I was somehow inside the television screen. "I chatted briefly with Charlie, the doorman, went up to my apartment, and promptly went to bed. I overslept and came in to the office late without listening to the radio or television this morning."

"Had you been on your sailboat at all yesterday?"

"In the morning and early afternoon, till about two o'clock."

"And what were your actions after that?"

"Just to establish the ground rules, Lieutenant," Eileen drummed her fingers on my desk, "my client, who may very well have been the target of a murder attempt, does not have to answer any of your questions. He's answering them now out of a spirit of cooperation, which is more than your attitude merits. Don't push us."

"I worked in my apartment till about five in the afternoon on a manuscript." The words flowed automatically. "And then I had supper at the apartment of a friend. . . ."

The lieutenant was about to ask the name of the friend, so I answered his question before he asked it.

"Her name is Ciara Kelly. She lives at the Chestnut Place, apartment 960, and she works at Dufficy's Irish Store on Michigan Avenue."

"We'll check into all of this," Norton snarled. "You better be telling the truth. Come on, O'Connor."

The two men left our office, a storm system receding.

"Charming man," Nick observed lightly.

"I'm confused." I felt like I was coming out of anesthetic after an operation. "Will someone please tell me what the hell is going on."

"The *Brigid* was seen leaving Montrose Harbor a little after 11:30 last night." Nick was ticking facts off on his fingertips. "As you know, there aren't many boats in Montrose or any of the other harbors yet, but somebody with a berth near yours recognized the *Brigid* going out and assumed you were on it. There wasn't much of a breeze so the boat was under auxiliary power, even after it left the harbor entrance. The other sailors said that it was perhaps a hundred fifty or two hundred yards beyond the harbor mouth when there was a flash, like an explosion in the cabin, and then the ship was engulfed in flames. Luckily, I suppose, the Coast Guard cutter was coming down the shore at just that time, having picked up two kids whose fourteen-foot Boston Whaler had run out of gas early in the evening. They used their fire equipment on the flames and managed to get a line aboard. Then they towed the craft into the breakwater and secured it there while they extinguished the fire. Otherwise the water from their equipment probably would have sunk it. They pumped out the hull and found two bodies in the cabin, both 'scantily clad,' to use their words. Somebody on the police force called Mickey Casey, and he called Ed Ryan, who got me out of bed at about six this morning. I went over to the morgue." He hesitated briefly. "It wasn't very pleasant, even for a scene in the morgue. The bodies were burned completely beyond recognition. I was too dumb to think about height. . . ."

"The Coast Guard," Eileen continued remorselessly, "thinks that there was arson involved, though they're not quite ready to say that to the press yet."

"Arson?" I was clutching for rationality as a drowning man clutches at a life jacket that has been thrown to him.

"Perhaps," she filled her cup with hot water and immersed a new tea bag in it, "some kind of radio-controlled mechanism. If the Coast Guard cutter hadn't been on the spot, the *Brigid* would have burned to the waterline and sunk. By the time the divers would have had a chance to look at it, there might not have been any evidence. Maybe no bodies either."

"But who were they?" I exclaimed. The incredible enormity of what had happened was finally beginning to affect me. "Who would have taken the *Brigid* out?"

"They were running it from the cabin, apparently." Nick was staring out the window but seeing none of the traffic on LaSalle Street below him. "The people in the harbor saw the lights on in the cabin, and that's where the bodies were found. You lock your cabin, I suppose?"

"Of course."

"Who has a key to it?"

"No one!"

"I hate to have to say this, Brendan," Eileen rose and stood behind my judge's chair, her hand on my shoulder. "Perhaps you could phone your friend Miss Ciara Kelly and see . . ."

"And see if she's still alive," I said hollowly.

From memory I punched out the number of Dufficy's Irish Store. "This is a recorded announcement . . ." A sweet and melodious Irish voice, but not Ciara's. "Dufficy's Irish Store is closed today. We'll be open tomorrow from nine o'clock in the morning until five-thirty at night. If you have an important message for us, please leave your name and phone number and the message after you hear the sound of the beep."

"The store she works at is closed." I was trembling like a mainsail luffing in a heavy breeze.

"Her apartment." Eileen's hand tightened on my shoulder.

I fumbled with my wallet, groped for the slip of paper on which I had written her phone number the night before, tried to punch the number, and could not make contact between my fingers and the buttons on the phone. "Here," I gave the number to Eileen, "you do it."

Nick pushed the buttons and gave me the phone. At the

other end there was no answer. I let it ring twenty, thirty times, still no answer. Ice cold, I put the phone back in its cradle.

"No answer," I said unnecessarily.

"Is Jean home from Stanford yet?" Eileen asked suddenly.

"Oh, God," I moaned. "And Madonna too . . ."

"Their number?" Nick asked crisply and punched it in as I gave it to him. The line was busy.

"Dear God in heaven, poor Jeannie will be out of her mind with worry and grief."

"Red will have the word out on the news stations in a few more minutes," Eileen said reassuringly, her fingers still digging into my shoulder. "You're still alive, Brendan. That's what matters. That's our starting point. Everything else is going to be all right."

Nick rang the Lake Forest number again. "What do we do now?" I groaned.

"We first of all try to learn who those poor people were and figure out why the boat caught fire and who, if anyone, was responsible for it. But before any of that . . ." She released my shoulder and opened the top-secret liquor cabinet in my credenza and removed an almost full bottle of Jameson's. "All three of us need some of this."

"The line's ringing." Nick jammed the phone into my hand.

"Jean Ryan," said the tearful and woebegone voice at the other end.

"Thank God, Jeannie. It's your father. I'm alive. I wasn't on the boat. We don't know who the people were. I didn't have the radio on this morning. No one called the apartment. I found out only when I arrived here at the office a few minutes ago. I'm alive, Jeannie. It's all right. It's all right!"

I listened to her convulsive sobbing and sipped from a very large shot of Jameson's that Eileen had poured for me. I gave Jeannie plenty of time to regain control.

"I was so afraid that I had lost you, Daddy." It sounded like the croak of an old woman. "After I'd only just found you. I'm so glad. . . ."

I felt the sting of tears in my own eyes. At first, embarrassed, I tried to stop them and then I realized that with my friends Nick and Eileen that was not necessary.

"We have lots of time to become good friends, Jean. Lots of time. Everything's going to be all right. I'm terribly sorry that you had to suffer all the unnecessary worry. Stay there at the house. I'll be up in an hour or an hour and a half." I glanced at Eileen for approval and she nodded. "Have one of your friends come over. Don't go outside and don't say anything to reporters. Hang up on them if they call you."

We spoke for a few more moments, promising that we'd spend a lot of time together in the next few weeks, and then I hung up, feeling that I was beginning to take charge of the bedlam in which I had suddenly found myself.

Ciara. Oh, God!

I punched the number of Dufficy's Irish Store. The same recorded message. Then her apartment. Nothing.

"Maybe Brendan and I could drive up to Lake Forest." Nick was thoughtfully polishing his thick horn-rimmed glasses. "We might stop at Montrose Harbor and take a look. The fire department arson investigator and the Coast Guard might be able to tell us something. Eileen, you could make a few phone calls so that our friend Norton doesn't silence them."

"A good idea. Get Brendan the hell out of the office and away from the working press. I'll let my husband, the distinguished national columnist who doesn't have to work for a living, be our spokesperson. He'll love it."

Eileen reached for the phone but it rang before she could lift it. "Brendan Ryan's office. . . . Oh, sure, honey, your dad's right here."

"Daddy." Solemn, somber, horrified. "Mother isn't here."

"What! Oh, my God, no!"

"I got home from Tucson yesterday and there was a note for me saying that she had a headache and was going to bed early and I would see her this morning. You know how late she sleeps when she takes those sleeping pills of hers. I . . . I . . . I didn't want to wake her when the news came over the radio. I mean, I didn't know how to tell her. Then when I talked to you and found you were still alive, I went down to her room to give her the good news. . . . And Daddy, she wasn't there. It looked like her bed hadn't been slept in."

"Nick Curran and I will be right up, Jeannie. We're leaving this minute."

I was immobilized, paralyzed, frozen.

"Brendan . . ." Nick shook me vigorously. "Brendan, what is it?"

"Madonna. She's not at the house, hasn't been there since yesterday afternoon."

For what seemed like half of eternity, my office was as quiet as a mausoleum. Then Eileen picked up the phone. "Yes? Oh, Mike . . ."

"Mike Casey?" Nick asked. Eileen nodded.

"I'm sorry we didn't call you, but it's been crazy here in Brendan's office. You've heard the good news? It may take me a long time, Michael, to forgive you for not getting rid of that so-and-so, Norton, when you were acting superintendent. . . .

"I know, but it's going to be unpleasant enough as it is. Anyway, I don't want to call him with this information, because God knows what he'll do with it. But talk to some of your friends in the department and tell them they should begin to compare the woman's dental work with the X rays of Madonna Clifford Ryan, the estranged wife of Brendan Ryan. The same dentist, Brendan?" She glanced at me and I nodded. "She hasn't been home since yesterday afternoon. As far as we know, she didn't have a key to the boat." An eye cocked in my direction for support. "And she didn't like sailing, but she's definitely missing. I'll be at my office here at Minor Gray and Blatt. Nick and Brendan are driving up to Lake Forest to protect poor Jeannie from the vultures. Stay in touch."

Nick made a quick call to Catherine that heralded my resurrection. Before we left the office I tried Ciara Kelly's apartment again. Still no answer.

On the way up the drive I said to Nick, "Turn off at Chicago. She lives at Chestnut Place."

Nick maneuvered over to Chestnut and stopped in front of Ciara's apartment building. I dashed in the door.

"Is Ms. Kelly in?" I breathlessly asked the doorman.

"Who, sir?" He looked puzzled.

"Ms. Ciara Kelly." I gave him the apartment number.

"I think that apartment is vacant, sir. Just a minute." He

thumbed through a worn sheaf of pages, reached the end, and thumbed through it again. "Yes, sir, it's vacant."

An icy chill raced through my body. I was dead and Ciara didn't have an apartment in this building?

"I must have the number wrong then. Ms. Kelly's apartment."

"I don't think we have a Ms. Kelly, sir." He started to thumb through the sheets of paper again.

"Let me look." I yanked the pages away from him.

There was a Kafer and a Kennelly, but no Kelly.

"Thank you," I mumbled. "Sorry to have disturbed you."

"Find her?" Nick watched me anxiously as I jumped into the seat next to him.

"She doesn't live here, Nick." I shut my eyes, confused, exhausted. "Apparently has never lived here. I think I'm going mad."

"Nonsense," he said confidently. "It's a very bad day, but tomorrow will be different."

Had my hyperactive psychic sense created her out of my own frustrated sexual longings?

Was such a thing possible?

Maybe.

17

The *Brigid* was a scorched and twisted wreck, her remnants being probed and tormented by fire department and Coast Guard technicians.

"A clumsy job," said the new fire lieutenant, huddling in his black jacket against the blustery east wind that was beating against us off the gray and dangerous lake.

Eight-foot waves, I mentally noted, not that it made any difference.

"It's so damned easy to convert ordinary walkie-talkie

mechanisms to radio-controlled bomb detonators. Every two-bit crook thinks he's a frigging mechanic.''

"Definitely arson?'' Nick asked.

The young man looked up from the hulk of the *Brigid*. "Don't quote me,'' he said cautiously, "but hell yes. A detonator that kicked off a tin of gasoline underneath the bed blew the two of them in an instant. No wonder their bodies were so fried.''

I turned away from the boat and into the fresh slashing of the wind, lest I become sick and perhaps even collapse on the spot. Dear God in Heaven, no!

"Not all that bad an idea,'' the fireman went on thoughtfully. "If the frigging Coast Guard,'' he jerked his head contemptuously toward a petty officer who was poking around in what had once been the *Brigid*'s bow, "hadn't come along when they did—the first time the frigging feds have ever been around when anyone needs them—we might never have found any of this stuff.''

"Any hope of tracing the equipment?''

"Nah. Buy it in any Radio Shack store in town.''

I was numb, dazed, incoherent, a zombie going through motions, a principal lead in a tragedy, who had forgotten his lines. What to do about the *Brigid*? She was insured. Not that insurance could restore anyone's life. Rebuild the boat? With all the memories that were attached? An unlucky boat on which death had occurred? Who would ever want to sail it? I wanted to shout out horrible curses at the murderers who had destroyed my beloved *Brigid*. *Brigid*, however, was only a thirty-one-foot sailboat. Who were the humans who died with her? And who were the fiends who sent them to God's judgment seat while they were making love on the same bunk on which Ciara and I had made love a few hours before?

Was Ciara one of the victims? Or Madonna? Or someone else? When would the terrible uncertainty end?

Jean's eyes had been dry and her face composed when we arrived in Lake Forest. The young priest from the parish, two of her girlfriends, and a handsome, wiry black Irishman were in attendance, fierce guardians ready to repel any invaders. Without makeup, dressed in a simple skirt and blouse, Jean looked thirteen instead of nineteen.

"It was her, Daddy," she said, her hands folded quietly in her lap. "I know it was."

"We can't be sure, Jeannie." I put my arm around her. "Your mother hated sailing. Don't forget that."

"I don't care." She squeezed my hand tightly. "I *know* it was her. Oh, Daddy, how terrible!"

The slim young man, perhaps a year or two older than Jean, had been introduced to me only as "Tim." He had shaken hands with me briskly and flashed a beautiful set of gleaming white teeth in an appropriately brief smile of acknowledgment. I noticed that he and Nick seemed to know each other, then I realized that it was Tim Murphy, Mary Kate Ryan Murphy's second son. Mary Kate and her daughter Caitlin had wasted not a moment in calling out the reserves.

It was decided that, accompanied by her entourage, Jean would go to the Cliffords' house to be waiting for them when they returned later in the day from their medical convention in San Diego.

"They'll need me there to help when they find out," she said dully.

The police department, Eileen had told them in a hurried phone call, already had collected the X rays and the charts from our dentist. It would be some time before they could make a certain identification, but in a few hours we would learn, unofficially and off the record, the truth.

I hugged Jeannie fiercely, and she hugged me back with equal fierceness. "Take good care of her," I said to the priest and to Tim Murphy. "Don't let anyone hurt her."

With those two determined young men as her escort, I doubted anyone would try. In the back of my head, however, there was a terrible fear: If it is Madonna, Jeannie will blame me.

Before Nick and I left the house to drive to Montrose Harbor and then back to the offices, I tried Ciara's number again. Still no answer.

Madonna or Ciara? I didn't want it to be either, but if I had to choose, it would not be a difficult decision.

"What do you think, Brendan?" Nick was wiping raindrops off his glasses as we stared at the ruined boat. "Damned good thing you weren't in the boat, eh?"

"A bad thing for them. A good thing for me."

"I wonder if you were the target?" He put his glasses back on and eased me away from the breakwater and toward the parking lot and his maroon Chevrolet Celebrity (no Porsche or Benz or BMW for Nicholas B. Curran). "Did the arsonist want to kill you or the people who were actually killed?"

I was thunderstruck. "It never occurred to me that I might be a target. I thought Eileen said that to fend off Sam Norton! Who would want to kill me?"

"King Sullivan?"

"That's absurd, Nick." I paused and looked back along the breakwater towards the ruins of the *Brigid*. It would have to be a new boat, perhaps custom-made, to have some of the *Brigid*'s characteristics. "King wouldn't be capable of something like that, and besides, he's set with a plea bargain, isn't he?"

"I know." Nick again took my arm and drew me away from the breakwater and the scorched hulk of the *Brigid*. "My point is that we're not sure yet who either the real or the intended victims are."

If Ciara wasn't the woman on the boat, then where was she? And how might she have been involved in the explosion off the entrance to Montrose Harbor?

I was still too dazed and too shocked to put my anxieties and questions and doubts in any sensible order, but I did know in the pit of my stomach that I had lost Ciara.

At the Minor Gray and Blatt switchboard we were told, in tones that admitted of no possible dissent, that we were to go at once to Mrs. Kane's office. Eileen was sitting behind her desk, pale, preoccupied, thoughtful. At the coffee table was a young black associate of the firm, Art Savage, who looked like a college football linebacker, which was precisely what he had been at Iowa State.

"Art is joining the team on this case." Eileen spoke like an archduchess who has made decisions that are not to be discussed. "In addition to his talents at litigation he demonstrated in the Hurricane Houston case, he will restrain Lieutenant Norton, should such restraints be required. Is that clear, Nicholas?"

"Yes, ma'am." Nick flopped into an empty chair and grinned. "Anything you say, ma'am."

"It's because I'm bigger and stronger and faster and better than you are." Art laughed, a pleasant young man who simply hadn't been mean enough to make it in pro football.

"Younger, at any rate," Nick agreed ruefully.

Eileen poured me the ceremonial cup of apple cinnamon tea. "No word on tentative identifications yet." She settled wearily into her chair. "Now about Ciara Kelly, Brendan."

"Yes?"

"We've been trying to find her, as you can imagine." Her voice was carefully neutral. She fiddled with a photograph of a Minnesota winter scene done by her son, John Patrick. "But we were able to reach Martha Dougherty, the owner of the Irish store next to Stuart Brent's. Apparently they proclaim holidays more or less to suit their convenience. She tells me that no one named Ciara Kelly works for them or has ever worked for them."

"What!" I was as astonished as I had been in the morning, when I heard about the explosion on the *Brigid*. "But that's impossible . . ."

"We spoke with the management at Chestnut Place. They have no record of anyone named Ciara Kelly ever living in the building. Moreover, apartment 970 has been unoccupied for the last three months."

It had seemed the night before—was it only the night before?—that the apartment was barely lived in. "I was there with her last night, Eileen," I said, burying my head in my hands. Good God in Heaven, was I losing my sanity too?

"We called the number you gave us, and it's not in service."

"But it was in service when I rang this morning . . ."

I reached for the phone and punched out Ciara's number. I heard the annoying musical beep and then the computerized voice telling me, "The number you have dialed is not in service. Please check your directory . . ."

I punched the number again and smashed the phone down in its cradle as soon as I heard the beep. "I know the phone rang this morning."

"Perhaps you were ringing the wrong number, Brendan." Her green eyes were sad and sympathetic. "The telephone company tells us that the line has not been in service for the last year. Do you have any other leads that we might follow?"

"She was an immigrant," I blurted desperately. "She told me she had a green card. I'm sure the Irish consul general knew about her. . . ."

"Art." She turned to the young associate. "Would you call the consul general and check it out? Also, see if there's someone in the building who has a good contact over at the INS and determine whether they have, indeed, issued a green card in anyone's name that is even remotely like Ciara Kelly."

"Yes, ma'am." Art bounded out of his chair like he was blitzing the Illinois quarterback.

"I don't understand, Eileen." I heard my own voice quavering. "I've dated her for the last two weeks. She was as real as you and Nick are. I . . . I was in love with her. . . ."

"It's a strange one, Brendan." She nodded sympathetically. "I don't doubt you for a moment, but it would certainly be a big help if we could find her or figure out what's happening. Norton's undoubtedly making the same investigations and he will create a big fuss about an alleged alibi that doesn't exist."

"Am I a murder suspect," I shouted, "merely because my boat exploded and I had the good fortune not to be on it?"

"Not a real murder suspect," Nick said soothingly. "Rather, a newspaper suspect for an ambitious, angry, and not-terribly-bright police lieutenant. We're not pleading before a jury now, we're pleading before the people who read newspaper headlines and listen to ten-second clips on the five o'clock news."

"We'll beat 'em, Brendan. Don't worry."

The phone next to her elbow rang, interrupting her encouragement.

There was something wrong with the narrative I had just heard, a piece that didn't fit, an element of information that didn't make sense. I reached for it in the dark basements of my brain and it slipped away from me. Until the Memorial Day weekend I continued to encounter it, flitting across my path like a bat at sunset.

Finally Blackie Ryan caught the elusive piece of the puzzle, as obvious once one saw it in daylight as it was obscure before it was seen.

"Mrs. Kane . . . Yes, yes. Put him through. This is Eileen, Michael. Any news?"

What little color there was left in Eileen's face drained away. Her eyes closed, her jaw tightened. "There's not likely to be a mistake about it, is there? . . . No. Surely, we'll be ready for them. Thanks much for calling. Give my best to Annie."

"Madonna . . ." I said in a hoarse whisper.

"That was Mike Casey." Eileen's eyes were still closed. "Even a retired deputy superintendent can have powerful connections in the police department. They have a tentative identification based on dental X rays." She opened her eyes and sighed deeply. "I'm terribly sorry, Brendan, terribly, terribly sorry. They won't have a confirmation on it till tomorrow sometime, but Mike says there's no chance of them being wrong."

She opened her eyes and regarded me with infinite sadness. "Sam Norton is on his way over here. He doesn't have anything but nasty innuendos. Let me call the tune and give short legal answers to whatever questions he asks. Grief comes later? All right?"

I nodded dumbly. Love for Madonna had ended long ago, and yet I once had loved her, or thought I loved her with great tenderness and affection. I remembered the tall, slender blonde fourteen-year-old spiking a volleyball and shouting her team to victory. Dear God in Heaven, please. Please what? Just please!

"Nicholas," she said softly. "Go find Art. He will intimidate our friend Norton into something resembling civilized behavior."

Sam Norton, accompanied by Sergeant O'Connor and another policeman who was never identified, arrived at the office doorway at the same time as Nick and Art Savage. Norton glared balefully at the young associate and did not introduce the third policeman, and Eileen countered by not introducing Art.

"Your wife was murdered on that boat, Mr."—he said the word with disdain—"Ryan. Do you realize that?"

"Do sit down, Lieutenant Norton." Eileen gestured towards a chair. "What you mean is that Mrs. Ryan was killed in the explosion on the boat, at least if the tentative identification is correct. You have no conclusive evidence yet that there was a murder."

"There goddamn well was a fucking murder." The lieutenant exploded, as he sat tentatively on the very edge of the chair. The two cops stood silently behind him.

"Savage," Eileen tapped her blotter thoughtfully with a pen, "would you be so good as to take notes of this conversation so that we have appropriate evidence when we lodge our protest with the Professional Practices Board. Now," she said, leaning forward, pointing the handle of a letter opener at Norton, "let's be clear about what's happening here, Lieutenant. There is a strong reason to believe that Mr. Ryan's wife died in an explosion on his yacht, off Montrose Harbor early this morning. You have come here, as I understand it, to ask Mr. Ryan some informal questions. At this point, you are not even certain that a crime has been committed, and you're in no position to make formal charges. My client will be happy to cooperate in responding to your question, subject to my decision as to whether the question is appropriate. I reserve the right to terminate the interview, should you become abusive. Is that clear?"

"Did your wife have a key to the boat?" Norton flipped open a large spiral notebook.

"Don't answer that, Brendan." Eileen's eyes blazed as she half rose from her desk. "Are my conditions clear, Lieutenant Norton? Answer me or we will adjourn this meeting now!"

"Yeah, they're clear." The lieutenant sneered at her.

Art Savage was on his feet, and halfway across the room.

"Sit down, Savage," Eileen ordered him. "Your job, for the moment, is to take notes. You may answer the question, Brendan."

"To the best of my knowledge, my wife . . ." My voice faltered. "My late wife did not have a key to the cabin of the *Brigid*. She was not interested in sailing."

"Then how did she get on the boat?" he asked contemptuously.

"I have no idea."

"You and your wife were divorced, weren't you?" He made it sound like divorce was a crime.

"That is correct," I said, trying to remain cool and keep my temper.

"Then you have an ecclesiastical annulment," he continued, as though that were even worse a crime. It dawned on me, in a fleeting irrelevancy, that Sam Norton, like everyone else in the room with the exception of Arthur Savage, was a Catholic.

"And there was a very large divorce settlement?"

I glanced at Eileen, and she nodded imperceptibly. "Approximately two million dollars, Lieutenant. It's a matter of public record."

"And that divorce settlement was not final yet, is that not correct?"

"I had not thought of that, Lieutenant." By desperate effort I kept my voice even. "I once loved my wife very much. I have fond memories of our marriage. I have not thought about the divorce settlement."

"That two million dollars reverts to you, does it not?"

"Lieutenant," Nick Curran interjected, "you haven't come over here to inquire about the fine points of divorce law, have you?"

"And the trust fund you've set up to guarantee the alimony payment for your wife and daughter, that reverts to you, too, doesn't it?"

Eileen hesitated, but flickered an eyelash of instruction in my direction. "It does."

"And you recently lost a large sum of money in commodities speculation, didn't you?"

"The matter is pending before a grand jury." Nick's fists were clenched, his thin face fiery red. "In point of fact, the money was removed from Mr. Ryan's account by his broker."

"Regardless." The lieutenant smiled cheerfully. "Within the last few months, Mr. Ryan, isn't it true that you've lost a million dollars, and this morning you got three million dollars back?"

"I would not accept that formulation," I said, now strangely bold and self-possessed again.

"Your formulation may not matter," the lieutenant said

triumphantly. "You needed the money and you profited from your wife's death. Wouldn't you agree that you had excellent motive for blowing up that sailboat this morning?"

"You can't get away with a question like that, Lieutenant, and you know it."

Art Savage was on his feet again, looking rather frighteningly like Mean Joe Green.

"Sit down, Savage," Eileen barked.

"What's the matter with you, man?" Norton spat out. "I'm not black, but I wouldn't let that white bitch call me a savage."

Art grinned beatifically. For the first time I knew what Eileen's game was. " 'Cause that's my name, Lieutenant Norton. Arthur Savage."

"You must remember him, Lieutenant," said the unintroduced cop. "He was a linebacker for the Cincinnati Bengals."

"Only for the exhibition season." Art slipped back into his chair, almost gently.

"Any more questions?" Eileen said with ice in her voice, knowing that she didn't even have to mention a formal complaint to the Professional Practices Board.

"Yeah," the lieutenant bellowed angrily. "Where is this Kelly woman that you dreamed up as an alibi? We haven't been able to find any trace of her."

"That will be quite enough, Lieutenant." Eileen rose majestically. "We have no proof yet that a crime has been committed. The client is not charged with or even suspected of a crime. He does not need an alibi. The whereabouts of Ms. Kelly are not at the present time relevant."

"He damned well is going to need an alibi soon," Norton snapped, and stormed out of the office, his two henchmen in tow, the unintroduced one grinning openly behind his boss's back.

"Nice mousetrap, Eileen," I said wearily. "That may slow him down a bit."

"Rather the opposite, I think," she said, sinking back into her chair and looking now every day of her forty-three years. "It's enough to get him off the case over the long haul, but for the next few days we're going to have to put up with him. . . ." She drew large circles on her desk blotter as she pondered intently. "Brendan, you wouldn't have any objection to a lie detector test, would you?"

I was sinking deeper into a nightmare swamp. My wife was dead, my love had vanished, and now I was, for all practical purposes, a murder suspect. "Not if you think it advisable. Let me say for the record, by the way, that I didn't kill Madonna or whoever was with her on the boat last night."

My three colleagues laughed in nervous unison. "We're sorry, Mr. Ryan," Art Savage said. "The thought that you might have simply would never have occurred to any of us."

"There's no way to avoid it," Eileen continued thoughtfully. "The newspaper headlines tomorrow morning will say, 'Police question lawyer about wife's death in boat blast.' The only way we can undercut that even a little is by announcing that you have volunteered to take a police-supervised lie detector test. Are you willing to do that?"

"Certainly."

"Good. Arthur"—and she smiled at the young man with maternal affection—"by the way, you were wonderful. Just magnificent . . . When little Redmond here," she patted her stomach, "shows up, you're going to take over all my cases. Your histrionics are better than mine will ever be. Anyway, get on the horn to the state's attorney's office, talk to the first assistant, and find out whom they're going to assign to the case. Tell the assistant and tell the prosecutor that a police officer was here in the office making wild and unfounded accusations against Mr. Ryan and that, to clear the air, we are formally offering to take a lie detector test."

"Yes, ma'am." Art Savage bolted enthusiastically from the office.

"Will they go along do you think?" I asked.

"Rich," Nick said, meaning Richard M. Daley, the state's attorney, the son of the later mayor whom everyone on LaSalle Street called by his first name (except Ned Ryan, who always called him "Mr. Daley" because he had called the late mayor "Dick"), "will think about it overnight, cautious, careful man that he is, and then insist that our offer be accepted. He's not going to permit the state's attorney's office to become a tail for Sam Norton's kite."

Eileen picked up the ringing phone. She listened patiently, glowing with pride and affection. "Redmond Peter Kane," she said firmly, "you are fifty-three, going on fifty-four years old, you have three going on four children." She patted little Redmond. "You are a distinguished, internationally syndicated Pulitzer Prize–winning columnist. You absolutely will *not* punch anyone in the mouth! Besides, if there's any reprisals necessary, I can take care of myself. Thanks for the offer anyway. Should I ever need that kind of help, you'll be the first to know about it!" Her smile was broad and happy now. "Bye-bye, darling."

When she'd hung up, I staggered to my feet, feeling like a zombie, a man at the most only half comprehending, slowly weakening in my struggle to break out of a nightmare.

"Where are you going, Brendan?" Eileen asked gently.

"Back to the apartment, I guess." I turned around, not altogether sure where the door to her office was. "Jeannie is taking care of Madonna's family. My parents are staying in Tucson. I need a good night's sleep. I suppose we have to make the funeral arrangements tomorrow. The wake will be the next day and then the funeral. Somehow I've got to get through those days and then do your lie detector test."

"Will you make the funeral arrangements?" Nick asked, standing at my side as though he were a guardian angel still in charge of me.

"I don't suppose so. Jean and the Cliffords will probably take care of things. I don't imagine the Cliffords will want me interfering."

"Are you sure you don't want to go home with one of us?" Eileen was standing on the other side of me. Two guardian angels now, shepherding me toward the elevator.

"No, I think it best to be alone for a while. . . . I'm terribly grateful to the two of you for your help. . . . I have no right to friends like—"

"Nonsense," Nick said crisply. "It's our privilege being able to stand by you."

"You're a good man, Brendan," Eileen added. "You deserve better than what's happened to you today."

"I don't deserve friends like you." I was getting sentimental, maudlin; that had to stop.

"You never have understood, have you, Brenny?" Eileen asked. "You never understood why people like you."

"Mrs. Kane, your brother's on the telephone," her secretary said as we moved into the corridor.

Eileen took the call at the secretary's desk. "Punk? Thanks for calling. Pretty shook up . . . but doing well, all things considered. What?" Again the color drained from Eileen's face. She leaned against the secretary's desk, badly shaken. "You can't be serious. . . . Oh, my God . . ." Her jaw sagged, and again her eyes closed. Nick jumped to her side, steadying her. "Yes, yes. Certainly. I'll put him on. . . ." She looked up at me. "It's my brother Blackie, Brendan; he'd like to talk to you."

I took the phone from her trembling hand, wondering what new disaster had happened. It really didn't matter. The swamp in which I was caught couldn't become worse. "Good afternoon, Monsignor. This is Brendan Ryan."

"My deepest sympathies, Brendan." A vague, ineffectual, but unquestionably sincere voice. "You deserve better."

"That's what your sister said," I replied listlessly.

"I very much regret having to make this call. . . . Cardinal Cronin asked me to do it, however. The published reports say that you have no recollection that anyone else besides yourself had a key to the *Brigid*. . . ."

"Yes, that's correct. Madonna didn't like to sail."

"But surely Father Ron Crowley had a key, didn't he? As I recall, he sailed with you several times each summer?"

"Oh, no," I gasped.

"You see," Monsignor Blackie Ryan said apologetically, "the associate pastor at St. Jarls called the cardinal an hour ago. No one has seen Father Crowley since late yesterday afternoon, when he left the rectory in sports clothes, dressed, as a matter of fact, as though he planned to spend some time on Lake Michigan."

18

Melvin Clifford's fists beat ineffectually against my chest, like those of a child pounding playground equipment in a temper tantrum. "Murdered our daughter," he screeched, as the flashbulbs popped around us. "You ruined her life, you ruined her marriage, and then you killed her!"

Behind him Lourdes Clifford screeched hysterically while Joan, their dumpy, tublike unmarried daughter, tried to console her, despite her own convulsive sobbing. Damien Clifford, squat, balding, and, as always, frantic, struggled to pull his father off me.

"Get away from him, Daddy. He'll try to kill you too!"

A long time ago Clifford had been my height but had seemed taller because of the ramrod-stiff military posture that he had affected ever since his service with the First Army in the Second World War. Now that he was shriveled and withered and old, a fragile leaf just fallen from a tree, he seemed several inches shorter and had to reach up to try and pound my face. I raised an arm in gentle self-defense.

"You should be castrated," he screamed, sounding like a martinet on temporary release from a home for terminally ill, retired military officers. Damien—Damie to all who knew him—finally pulled his father away. Damie had never been good enough for anything. He had failed at two American medical schools and finally had barely made it through a Mexican university. Haplessly determined to be a great surgeon like his father, he was bounced from his surgical residency after six months of blundering. Now he earned his living by working the night shift in the emergency room in a fading inner-city hospital. Neither he nor Joannie would ever have to worry about money, however; arrogant, domineering, inflexible, Mel Clifford had been fortunate in his choice of investment advisers. The fact that his investment man had been a colonel in the war prevented Mel from meddling in his work the way he had destructively meddled in the lives of his children.

Having dragged his father off me, Damie renewed the assault on his own initiative. "Castrating you would be too good for you, you murdering bastard," he yelled, flailing at my stomach as more flashes exploded all around him.

I pushed him away but he returned to the battle. I was still among the living dead, a zombie, living off crackers and Jameson's. Dr. Clifford was an old man who had lost his beloved daughter. I could hardly hit him back. Damie was what Jean would call a nerd. I cocked my fist with a blessed sense of relief. Finally, I could strike out against those who were assaulting me.

Mike Casey, former deputy superintendent of police, looking like a well-dressed Basil Rathbone, intervened quietly. "Please, Dr. Clifford, this only makes things worse."

Damie Clifford was quite prepared to make things worse, but he was incapable of resisting Mike Casey's iron grip on his shoulders. He permitted himself to be led away and ushered with his parents into the undertaker's office.

The reporters turned on me. "Do you have any reply to Dr. Clifford's charge?"

"Have you really agreed to a lie detector test?"

"Who do think killed your wife and Father Crowley?"

"Do you think it's good taste for you to come to the funeral?"

"Is it true that you knew Father Crowley in the first grade?"

"Do you agree that Father Crowley's murder was political assassination?"

Mike threaded his way through the reporters, quietly and effectively. "Mr. Ryan doesn't have any comment, fellows."

Somehow it had been arranged that Mike would take charge of me through the wake and funeral. A lawyer, a retired deputy superintendent of police, and a painter, he had married a few months earlier Anne Reilly, a glamorous art dealer who was listed last year as one of the ten most beautiful women in Chicago. Anne and Mike had been grammar school sweethearts. Her marriage, like mine, had been annulled, but for me there was no grammar school sweetheart because I had already married a grammar school sweetheart, whose body was in the closed casket at the front of Sheean's funeral parlor.

Casey was the son of Ed Ryan's late sister, an extremely effective cop and the author of two scholarly monographs on police work. The Ryan family, having made a collective decision to take care of me, apparently had assigned Mike to watch over me. Still staggering through a world in which a nightmare of dreams and reality had blended, I offered no objections.

The newspaper headlines were shattering:

DR. CALLS EX-SON-IN-LAW KILLER!
SUSPECT IN PRIEST MURDER CASE TO TAKE LIE TEST
CARDINAL PERMITS MASS FOR PRIEST, WOMAN FRIEND
POLICE 'NEAR SOLUTION' IN DOUBLE MURDER CASE
LAWYER SEEKS 'MYSTERY WOMAN' FOR ALIBI

The Caseys had picked me up in mid morning and driven me to the funeral home in Highland Park from which the casket containing Ron Crowley's body was to be brought to St. Jarlath's for the parish wake. It had been arranged that we could visit the casket privately before the procession to the church. I would be spared the press while paying my last respects to the man who was, I suppose, the closest friend I ever had. Cardinal Cronin, Mike Casey told me, had authorized Church funerals for Ron and Madonna with the terse announcement "We leave the final judgment to God." The cardinal had "no comment whatsoever" on published reports that Father Crowley and Mrs. Ryan were "scantily clad" when fire swept the *Brigid*.

"Apparently the apostolic delegate," Mike shrugged his shoulders, implying that the apostolic delegate was about as important as a Chicago alderman who was not also a ward committeeman, "or I guess they call them papal nuncio now, raised hell with Cronin. I hear the cardinal told him to 'stuff it.' "

The three of us now stood quietly in front of the bronze casket in the empty funeral parlor, all that remained of Ron Crowley. Images raced through my clouded mind, like a freight train roaring past on a foggy night: Ron hitting a home run in a softball game when we were ten years old—scoring at home by sliding under the catcher's tag; Ron scoring a winning touchdown for St. Ignatius in a Catholic football game; Ron and Madonna making out in the back of the car at the McAuley High School prom; Ron informing us that he was quitting Notre Dame to enter the seminary; Ron's moving and brilliant talk at his first Mass banquet at the Martinique on a scorching hot June Sunday; Ron at an anti-war protest march in the early seventies; Ron, haggard and bearded, brought home from South America against his will because of failing health; Ron, flushed and overweight, the last time we met. Dear God, I prayed, please try to understand him. Ron did not choose to be a hero. We all cast him in that role, his family, his friends, his teachers, his admirers. He tried hard. He wanted to be a good priest. Forgive him whatever sins he committed. Grant him peace somewhere else that he was never able to find here.

I was distracted while I was praying by the thought that, if I were to judge by Jean's report, the people of St. Jarlath's would not greatly grieve for their new pastor. For them he had not been a hero at all. Perhaps, after a life of struggling to be an all-American, the Reverend Ron Crowley had wearied of the game.

Curiously enough, however, in death he had achieved what had escaped him in life: all the newspaper stories had described him as a "consensus high school all-American" and said that he had given up certain "all-American status" and "probable success as a pro" to become a priest.

And some Catholic left-wing groups condemned his death as "political murder" and "a CIA assassination." These groups (most of whose members seemed to be intense and angry nuns, if one was to judge by their TV appearances) contended that Father Ron Crowley was a martyr, liquidated on orders of the Reagan administration because of his bitter opposition to the United States' involvement in El Salvador and other Central American countries. Father Crowley was, they said in tones that admitted of no disagreement, "a hero of the people and a saint whom we will not forget."

As best I could remember, Ron had not been involved in a demonstration or a march for the last eighteen months, since shortly after his appointment to St. Jarlath's. Either the Catholic radicals did not know of the transformation that occurred after he was assigned to St. Jarlath's or they didn't care about it. "They're more interested in TV exposure for themselves," Mike Casey had said tersely, "than they are in mourning Father Crowley."

We left Ron's wake in somber silence and went on to the funeral home in Lake Forest, where, because of unhappy chance, I arrived at the same time as my in-laws, or ex-in-laws, as the newspapers called them.

By unspoken consent, the Cliffords stood at the left of the casket to receive sympathies of mourners first, and I at the right of the casket to shake hands with anybody who was willing to be seen speaking to a murder suspect. Jean arrived with a grim-visaged Tim Murphy in resolute attendance. She stood in front of the casket, a bit to the left side, and hence somewhat closer to her grandparents than to her father. She smiled wanly at me from a distance but did not draw close enough for us to talk. My brief adult friendship with my daughter, I concluded, was yet another casualty of the explosion on the *Brigid*. How could it be otherwise, after she had spent a couple of days with the angry and hate-filled Cliffords?

Irish wakes are usually complex mixtures of grief and joy, of mourning and defiance of death, but something about the multiple tragedy of this particular wake seemed to suppress the Celtic propensity for defiance and joy. The line of mourners passed by the ornate, gray-tinged casket in heavy, stricken silence, their faces betraying bafflement and horror at the possibility of murder, suicide, revenge, adultery, sacrilege. Condolences were whispered in undertones that could hardly be heard. There were no noisy gatherings at the back of the parlor or in the lobby of the funeral home. Mourners were in a hurry to escape this wake, where the contaminating touch of evil seemed to linger.

Madonna, I thought, would not very much like this wake. Indeed, if she were alive, she would certainly not come to it.

The only ones who seemed inclined to keep alive ancient and pre-Christian traditions of wake-as-festival were the Ryan clan. They turned out en masse. A quick consensus had doubtless been reached in a series of phone calls. Madonna had never liked any of them and they were scarcely good friends with the Clifford family, but fourth cousin or not, Brendan Ryan was still "family." He might need support at the wake, though to tell the truth, he was well rid of the woman; so the Ryans would be there, paying perfunctory respect to the Cliffords, hugging and kissing Jean, who was being squired by one of their own, and lingering with me, to demonstrate that they thought the hint of murder allegations in the press was ridiculous. Their handshakes were firm and brisk, their hugs tender and reassuring, their words of sympathy brief and poignant. Only the Ryans brought me close to tears during my wife's wake.

A strange, quixotic bunch, a throwback, perhaps, to more ancient Irish days of loyalty. The Ryans had family problems like all families; at various times many of their marriages were in jeopardy (including her own, according to Eileen's brief hints). They knew, as do all families, the meaning of suffering, tragedy, and premature death. But unlike most of the South Side Irish of our generation, the Ryans did not approach life with cautious prudence. They did not minimize the risks or hedge the bets or play the conservative percentages. They did more than meet life halfway—they charged into it aggressively, embracing every possibility, every challenge, every opportunity that came anywhere near them. As my mother had once remarked long ago, "They're a bit much, but they're never dull."

Eileen seemed to have lost all the aura of tough, aggressive defense counsel that she radiated at the offices of Minor Gray and Blatt. With her big, genial husband's arm around her, she was an attractive, pregnant matron, a sensitive and vulnerable wife and mother, mourning a woman who was, perhaps, not a close friend, but nonetheless someone she'd known most of her life and with whom she had skipped rope almost every day in the pigtail years. Her eyes were red and her face stained with tears when she rose from a kneeler and embraced me. "I'm so sorry for you, Brendan," she murmured through her tears. "Sorry for you, sorry for Madonna, sorry for Jean, sorry for everyone."

"It'll be all right, Eileen." I held her in one arm and shook hands with her handsome husband with the other. "Nice of you to come, Red. I really appreciate it."

"We Ryans have to stick together." Red's affable face

broke into a broad grin. "And God knows you've been nice enough to the woman down in the office."

"The woman's not a bad lawyer." I felt myself grinning in reply.

"Not a great lawyer," he said, "a good one. A very good one, but not what you'd call great."

"Ah." I found the brogue coming on me, too, and thought fleetingly of Ciara Kelly and how she would like Red Kane. "Not to say great. Sure, and hardly the kind that would win the Pulitzer Prize if they gave it for briefs."

"I take your meaning."

"You're both male chauvinists, that's what you are—genetically bred into Irish males, I guess. You're not really all that much to blame."

So, for a few moments, the pall lifted and I could think of Ciara Kelly and at least hope that I would see her again.

"The lie detector test is tomorrow at eleven?" I released the Kanes from my embrace.

"Right. I noticed our friend Sam Norton and his henchmen loitering around the door." Eileen jerked her head in their direction. "Doubtless waiting for you to break down and confess. He doesn't want the test at all. He claims he has enough of a case for an arrest and an indictment and that a lie detector test would be a waste of time."

"Does he?" I said, feeling the kind of fear in my stomach that I had not known since Vietnam.

Eileen shook her head impatiently. "He wants to position himself so that if the murders aren't solved, he won't be blamed. Rich Daley wouldn't hear of any other steps until a lie detector test is over.

"You have to understand," Eileen continued, her husband's big strong arm holding her close, "you're the only one they know who would have a motivation. But they have no evidence to link you to what happened and, as a matter of fact, no certainty about who was the target. If it was a professional contract, and it looks like either a contract or a terrorist caper, they probably never will find out who did it. Norton wants to be able to blame it on someone.

"I don't think he'll try anything here, with Mike Casey around." Eileen squeezed my arm as she and her husband prepared to make room for Mary Kate and Joe Murphy,

Tim's parents. "Mike still intimidates cops, even though he's retired. Besides, politics change and Mike may well be back in power in another couple of years, a thought scary enough to make Norton think before he opens his mouth."

"I still can't believe it all," I said. "I keep trying to focus, to think intelligently about it all. It is as though somebody threw a circuit breaker in a part of my brain that does the thinking."

"Don't worry, Brenny." She departed with a dazzling smile of reassurance. "Until things get better for you, your friends will do all the thinking that needs to be done."

Friends? Why should anyone like me have such good friends? How would I ever be able to repay them?

By a quarter to ten, the flow of mourners had diminished and the Cliffords stalked out with the dudgeon of a jury that has just delivered a murder verdict. Jean said something to Tim Murphy and then walked across the room and stood next to me.

"After living with those people for two days, I can almost sympathize with her." She embraced me and rested her head against my chest. "'Oh, Daddy, they are such terrible people!'"

So I had not lost my adult daughter/friend after all.

"You have to understand their past." I stroked her short, fine brown hair. "The transition from Depression to prosperity was a lot tougher than people realize."

"You're always making excuses for other people, Daddy." She sighed. "Face it: Mom was a bitch on wheels. She cared about you only because you made her life-style possible. And she cared about me because, as long as I was the perfect Barbie doll little girl, people praised her. I think she brought me into the world principally so I could be in the Pres Ball. When that was over, as far as she was concerned, I didn't exist!"

"That's too harsh, honey." I tilted her head up so I could look at her tear stained face and study her sad eyes. "Your mother had a very hard life. You've only had to put up with your grandparents for two days; they dominated every breath she took for forty-two years."

"She wanted it that way," Jean replied bitterly. "And if

she'd lived long enough, she would have ruined my life the way they ruined hers."

"She's dead now, Jeannie," I pleaded. "Please forgive her."

"She would never forgive you or me, never!" Jeannie argued stubbornly.

"You know better than that, kid."

"I'm sorry, Daddy." She pulled a tissue out of her purse. The black suit she was wearing, I thought, was utterly appropriate for a Barbie doll mourner. "I forgive her; I hope she's happy; I hope she finds the happiness that she missed out on here on earth. It still makes me mad that you have to suffer so much."

I thought to myself that if I didn't deserve friends like the Ryan family, I didn't deserve either a daughter like Jean, who suddenly and unaccountably had become fiercely loyal to me, almost as though I had borrowed her temporarily from the "other" Ryans.

"Timmy seems to be a very nice boy." I took her arm and walked toward the door of the funeral parlor, where that handsome young black Irishman waited for her.

"He's all right." She blew her nose and reached for another tissue.

"Just another boy, or someone special?" I asked lightly.

"*Well*," she considered thoughtfully, "he's not *really* just another boy, but he's not someone special yet either."

"Your friend Caitlin has lent him to you on approval?"

She laughed in spite of herself. "Daddy, you're so funny!"

I kissed Jeannie, shook hands with Tim, and bid them good night. Back in the room with the casket, I saw a priest standing unobtrusively at one end of it. He was short, pudgy, and wore an ill-fitting clerical suit that may very well never have been pressed. He was staring grimly at the casket, his nearsighted eyes blinking rapidly behind thick, rimless glasses; indeed, so innocuous that you would hardly notice him, so apparently a cipher that he could drift into the funeral parlor and not be seen, rather like a contemporary Father Brown.

But there was anger in his eyes, and fury in his knotted fists. I thought of Chesterton's Father Brown, and then thought of a line from another one of Chesterton's works, which seemed much more appropriate for Monsignor John Blackwood Ryan: "It is Richard, it is Raymond, it is Godfrey in the Gate!"

At what was he angry? The Cliffords and the whole post–World War II new-rich suburban Irish culture that had ruined so many lives and about whose responsibility, I was quite sure, Monsignor Ryan had not the slightest doubt. But also, I suspect, angry at all the evil energies and forces in the world that keep us from being the kind of creatures God wants us to be.

"Thank you very much for coming, Monsignor," I said, standing behind him.

He looked around, startled, and seemed at first neither to recognize me nor to realize who I was. "Brendan Herbert George Ryan," he said. "Never underestimate the immensity of God's mercy or the lunatic passion of His love."

"I'm sure that's true, Monsignor; but I still don't understand why God does something like this."

There is considerable debate in the Ryan family as to where Blackie received his middle name. Some argue that he is named after an Irish revolutionary chieftain of the 1700s named Blackwood, who was allegedly one of the leaders of the "Whiteboys," a remote ancestor of the IRA; others in the family, thinking that "Blackwood the Whiteboy" was a mischievous family joke, argue that Kate Collins Ryan had made a blackwood convention in bridge the night her son John was conceived.

"The youngest first-grader in Holy Name Cathedral doesn't call me Monsignor," he began, his eyes blinking rapidly. "And I don't accept that God is responsible for the tragedy of Ron Crowley and Madonna Clifford. He wanted their stories to be very different, and He was unable to write them the way He wanted. I reject all other explanations."

"But what does that do to God's omnipotence?"

"Omnipotence be damned!" As he talked, Blackie Ryan was exploring his pockets, apparently searching for his car keys. "Anytime the necessities of Greek philosophy force us into a position that is at odds with the scriptural self-revelation of God, I say reject Greek philosophy. But we have raised generation upon generation of Roman Catholics to believe, not because of the scriptures, but because of Greek philosophy, that everything that happens in the world is directly attributable to God. That, it seems to me, is patent nonsense."

"You mean that there are some evil things that God would like to prevent but can't?" I could no more focus on philosophical discussion than I could on the urgent task of organizing my thoughts and my life.

"Precisely. God is the great improviser, the great player-by-ear. When bad things happen, or we do bad things to one another, He simply adjusts His game plan and achieves His goals by an alternative path. Humans are responsible for the death of your wife and your friend. God isn't."

"Oh," I said, wondering if all priests of his generation so abruptly dismissed Aristotle. "That's Whitehead, isn't it?"

"Didn't Professor Whitehead himself say that his philosophy was the first one to be directly inspired by scriptures? . . . At any rate," he finally discovered the car keys in the pocket of his trousers and switched them to the pocket of his coat, "I searched our parish census files for a record of Ciara Kelly. I'm afraid I didn't find her."

"I'm beginning to wonder whether she's a figment of my imagination."

"Oh?" He peered at my face intently, as though he were trying to recall who I was. "I can't imagine anyone, Brendan, anyone less likely to create an imaginary woman. No, Ciara Kelly lives, and she is the most interesting part of this whole mystery."

"I was in love with her, Monsig . . . er, I mean Blackie."

"All the more reason for finding her. . . . You'll excuse me, but I must return to the cathedral. My Lord Cronin will need someone to listen to his tale of the doings over at St. Jarlath's."

"A madhouse?"

"To put the matter mildly." Blackie rolled his eyes. "The grief of the parishioners was underwhelming, to say the least, and their outrage over the pickets protesting political murder has already notably surpassed their grief at the loss of a pastor none of them liked. My Lord Cronin quite properly bemoans the harm done to the diocese and to the Church and to the priesthood by this unseemly mess."

"Ron was not well." I was defending a priest to another priest, the same way I defended Madonna to her daughter.

"Indeed, yes." The priest began to search for his car keys again. "He had promised my Lord Cronin to seek psychiatric help and then repeatedly reneged on the promise. A bad choice, if I may say so."

"Do you think that what happened to Madonna and Ron was something they chose? Were they responsible for it? Will they be punished like they were responsible?"

"Ours is a God of love, not justice, Brendan Ryan, a fact for which we should all be profoundly grateful. I will do neither Ron nor Madonna the discredit of suggesting they were not, in some fashion, morally responsible. I also refuse to believe God did not and does not love them." He shrugged his shoulders helplessly. "On some later occasion the two of us can challenge the Great Improviser and suggest that in these particular circumstances His improvisations were not all that impressive. Sometime after all of this settles down, you must come see me."

"To talk about the Great Improviser?"

"Of course not. To talk about Ciara Kelly. What else?"

It is hard not to like Blackie Ryan, and even harder to disagree with his theology when he begins to talk about it. But I did not want to seek counsel from him now or ever about the mystery of Ciara Kelly.

The Caseys were waiting for me in the parking lot. Sam Norton, Mike informed me, had long since departed. "I think I make him kind of nervous."

They drove me back down the lake shore to the apartment. I watched the passing Chicago skyline, glittering and peaceful in the gentle warmth of the starlit spring night, and felt myself drifting away from my problems and achieving a sense of serene unity with the quiet stability of the city at night.

Only after my shower, as I sat in the usual terry cloth robe, sipping my final Jameson's of the day and watching the reflection of the stars on the lake, did I remember Blackie Ryan's conviction that somewhere there was a Ciara Kelly whom I had to find.

I had found her once, I could find her again.

But look at what the result of finding her had been. Might

not another search for Ciara Kelly produce even greater disasters?

Suddenly I had an inspiration. The floral-patterned bikini that Ciara wore in the pool—it was always neatly folded and placed in a bathroom cabinet. It should still be there.

Despite the numbing effect of the Jameson's, I jumped out of my chair and ran to the bathroom and threw open the cabinet. The place where her swimsuit had been was empty, but the towels that had been piled on that place were still stacked on a higher shelf. Ciara Kelly's bikini was not in my apartment, but there was a hint that it might have been there once. Perhaps that hint would be a starting point for the search that Blackie Ryan had demanded.

19

"Please answer yes to this question: Are you a woman?"

"Yes," I responded, knowing that they wanted to test my reactions to a lie. "I am a woman."

"You were born in 1942, is that correct?" The woman's voice whined like that of a perpetually angry schoolteacher, perhaps a nun who was unhappy in her religious order.

"Yes, I was."

"How many traffic citations have you had in the last three years?"

"None."

"Have you ever been arrested and charged with speeding?"

"Yes, I have."

"When?"

"About twelve years ago, I believe." My head felt like someone was working a jackhammer on it. I still could not focus on the murder of my wife and best friend. Was he really my best friend? Had he ever been? The circuit breakers in my brain were flipping back and forth as the woman police sergeant, who was the lie detector technician, mixed routine questions with questions about the murder.

"Did you yourself install the incendiary device in your yacht?"

"No, ma'am, I did not."

"Did you pay someone else to do so?"

"No, I did not."

"Did you love your wife?"

"That's a tough one." I hesitated. "I was very angry about the divorce. I still cared for her. I suppose I experienced a sense of relief, however, after the marriage was over."

"Are you happy that she's dead?"

"No, I am not."

"Do you have any idea who killed her or Father Crowley?"

"No, I do not."

"You say you met Ciara Kelly in Dufficy's Irish Store?"

"That's right."

"You became very friendly with her?"

"Yes, I did."

"You claim you were with her the night of the explosion on your yacht."

"Yes, but I believe I had left her apartment before the time of the explosion."

"Were you intimate with her?"

"Yes."

"How often?"

"I didn't count."

"Did you ever cheat on your wife?"

"No."

We were in a windowless room in the police headquarters at 11th and State. I sat at a table strapped to a machine that measured the reaction of my body to questions and answers. One technician was monitoring the machine while the other, the woman sergeant, was asking the questions, a mixture of those given her by Sam Norton and approved by Deputy Superintendent Cosmo Gambino and routine questions that enabled them to monitor the responses of my body when I had no reason to lie. Behind me, watching the output, were Norton, Gambino, a young prosecutor from Rich Daley's office named Joe Urbanik, Eileen Kane, looking pale and exhausted, and Mike Casey. Gambino obviously disliked and feared Casey.

"You don't work for the police department anymore," he said ungraciously. "You've got no right to come in here."

"Ah, Cosmo." Mike's frosty blue eyes glinted cheerfully. "As unperceptive as ever. I am a practicing attorney, am duly certified by the Illinois Bar Association. Mr. Ryan is a client of mine, and if you try to exclude me, I'll have to drag your ass over to superior court and have a judge put an injunction on you. Nothing would make me happier."

"I'm not so sure about that," Gambino grunted pugnaciously. "If I say you can't come in here, then you can't come in here."

"Don't be an asshole, Gambino." Joe Urbanik was no more than twenty-five years old, perhaps only a year out of law school, and arguably the toughest person in the room. "If you try to exclude Mr. Ryan's attorney, the state's attorney's office will withdraw from this whole procedure. We'll tell the press why. Do you want to call Mr. Daley or should I call him? Or are you going to wise up and realize the Supreme Court interprets the Constitution and you don't?"

Gambino muttered incoherently but raised no more objections to Mike Casey's presence.

"Was your wife unfaithful to you?"

"I did not think so until the time of the divorce. She claimed then that she had been unfaithful. I'm not sure that I believed her."

"Did you know that she was having an affair with Father Ron Crowley?"

"I did not know that, and to this day I do not know it."

"You have how many children?"

"One."

"A daughter?"

"Yes, Melissa Jean by name, usually called Jean."

"Where does she attend school?"

"Leland Stanford Junior Memorial University."

Not even a trace of laughter in the droning female voice.

"Was Father Ron Crowley really your closest friend?"

"I had thought of him as such for many years. I suppose in the last few years we drifted apart."

"Did you suspect that he was having a love affair with your wife?"

"I did not suspect that, and I do not now know it to be a fact."

"Did you murder your wife and Father Crowley?"

"No, I did not."

"Did you arrange for their murder?"

"No, I did not."

"Do you know who is responsible for their deaths?"

"I do not."

"You still insist you were with Ciara Kelly at the time of the explosion?"

"No, I was not with her at the time of the explosion. I was with her before the explosion. At the time of the explosion, I was in my apartment."

"Did you purchase the remote control materials from which the incendiary device in your yacht was made?"

"I did not."

"Do you know who did purchase them?"

"I have no idea."

"Do you think Ciara Kelly was involved in the murder of Mrs. Ryan and Father Crowley?"

"It's a possibility, I suppose." And one that had occurred to me a couple of times, but which seemed madly improbable. But then, Ciara's disappearance also seemed madly improbable. "I have no reason to think so, however."

And so the questioning continued for two and a half hours. I wondered how a body that was as weary, as heartsick, and as physically ill as mine could possibly give the sorts of signals to the polygraph from which the technicians would be able to make any sense. I felt like a character in a Franz Kafka novel, or perhaps an inhabitant of purgatory, destined to spend all but a few moments of eternity answering the same questions.

Finally, however, the sergeant said, "That will be all, Mr. Ryan. Thank you very much."

With businesslike efficiency she removed the tentacles of the machine from my arm and shoulder and wrist and chest. Her pale and not unpretty face was an expressionless mask. "Would you step into the next room please. Your attorneys will join you shortly."

Eileen, I thought, looked relieved as I walked unsteadily into the next room, and Mike Casey managed a quick, covert, thumbs-up sign. However, it was half an hour later before they did join me, both of them looking angry. "We're all right," Mike said. "Let's get the hell out of this place before I vomit."

We hurried down the corridor and into the elevator, Mike acknowledging with a curt nod the friendly greetings from his former staff members. There wasn't much doubt whom they wanted as superintendent of police. And there was also, I thought, not much doubt that Mike Casey was happy he'd made the transition from being a cop to being a lawyer and that he would not make the return pilgrimage.

The sky above State Street was overcast, rain threatening again, the temperature near ninety, a debilitating, oppressive Chicago summer day, even though it was still the month of May.

"I never thought I'd be so happy to get out of that place," Mike said grimly. "What assholes, you should excuse the expression, Eileen."

"My sentiments precisely," she said through tight lips. "Oh, it's all right, Brendan. You came through with flying colors. Sam Norton tried to intimidate that poor young woman into saying that the test was 'inconclusive.' She wasn't buying it. At first Gambino tried to lean on her too . . ."

"A cheap trick from a deputy superintendent, if I ever saw one. I wanted to tear those three stars off his uniform," Mike Casey said bitterly.

So finally Gambino agreed to make the usual announcement that there was nothing in the test to implicate Mr. Ryan in the crime, and to add that the investigation would continue and that no one had been cleared of suspicion.

"That dumps the ball in Rich Daley's court," Mike concluded. "Norton will press for an arrest and an indictment. Some people over there at the state's attorney's office will say 'Hey, we might get lucky with a judge and jury and get a conviction no matter how thin the evidence is.' There will be a big fight over it. Rich will sit and listen. They'll adjourn without a decision."

"That may be, Brendan," Eileen concluded, as she

opened the door of the Volvo, "where things are going to remain."

"I don't understand," I murmured. "I thought I passed the lie detector test."

An elderly cop, whose job it was to preside over the parking lot, came up to shake Mike Casey's hand. The brusqueness Mike had displayed with police staff members inside the building vanished. He chatted amiably with the cop and offered to bet him five dollars that the Cubs would finish higher than the White Sox.

"My five bucks against one of your paintings, Mickey," the old Irishman said with a laugh.

"You'd have to be dealing with my new wife on that one, and she's a sharp trader, she is." Mike poked him in the ribs. "See you soon, Marty."

In the car Eileen explained the situation in which I was trapped. "Let me continue Mike's scenario: there'll be another meeting over there at the end of the day. You're the only suspect they have, Brendan, and you're obviously not a very good suspect. Gambino will hedge; Norton will urge an arrest and an indictment. Some of them will repeat their point from previous discussions: with the right judge and the right jury and some bad mistakes by Eileen Kane, your defense attorney, they might possibly be able to get a conviction. The more cautious people from the state's attorney's staff will say 'Who the hell are you trying to kid? It's a rotten case, and even if she's a nursing mother, Eileen Kane isn't going to blow one that easily.' Rich Daley still won't say much. He'll take the lie detector output home with him, and tomorrow morning there'll be a cautious announcement from the state's attorney's office that there's no reason to seek a grand jury indictment at the present time. As far as they're concerned that's the end of it for you."

"The cops," Mike went on, "will have more pressure on them than the state's attorney's office because of the media. So the police department will say that the investigation is continuing, that there are a number of suspects, and that you can no longer be considered the principal suspect. And that's the way it'll be, maybe indefinitely. Norton will try to strong-arm some of the people from Montrose Harbor into saying that they saw you fooling around the boat. He'll have his stooges poke around radio supply stores to see if they can find out where the equipment for the incendiary device was purchased. They'll lean on a few of their softer mob stool pigeons to learn what the word on the street is about the contract. But Norton won't spend much time on it because he'll figure there isn't a payoff in pursuing it.''

"So that's the way it will be, Brenny." Eileen stared straight ahead. "The murder will remain unsolved, and the cloud of suspicion over you will never dissolve completely. Oh, sure, you passed the lie detector test and people will remember that. Your friends will be convinced you're innocent, but still you'll be three million dollars richer and people will whisper about that.''

"You're even more cynical than I am, Eileen," Mickey Casey said with a thin laugh as he stretched his long legs in the back of the Volvo.

Eileen turned right at Roosevelt Road and edged over toward Michigan Avenue.

"Even though I'm a lawyer, I guess I'm kind of naive. Where does justice fit in all of this?"

"Justice," Eileen exclaimed impatiently, braking just in time to obey a red light. "No point in violating traffic laws so close to 11th and State. Justice mostly doesn't figure. The police department and the prosecutors are both worried about the unsolved crime rate, their conviction percentages, the negative reaction to a rich man escaping indictment, and their media images. Justice only computes after all the other factors are taken into account.''

"Then why don't they go for an indictment? That would be a lot of good publicity for them, wouldn't it?"

"Not if a judge directed a not-guilty verdict. Besides, we lucked out in one important respect: the state's attorney is a decent man. Of the whole crowd that's going to be involved, Rich Daley is the only one for whom justice is the decisive issue. He'll study the lie detector output carefully and conclude that you didn't kill your wife and Father Crowley, and that it would be unjust to seek an indictment.''

"Maybe Joe Urbanik too," Mike Casey remarked.

"Maybe, maybe not."

We stopped at Monroe Street, between the Art Institute and Orchestra Hall; young women in sundresses were streaming by in both directions on Michigan Avenue. I thought of Solti's *Rite of Spring* and wondered again about Ciara Kelly.

"So the system works, if it works at all, because there's an occasional decent man in a decision-making position?"

"And each year," Mike Casey said sadly, "there seem to be fewer such men around."

"One thing would make Rich hesitate." The light changed and Eileen eased the car forward. "Norton made a big point about your responses concerning Ciara Kelly."

"Was I lying then?" All the circuit breakers in my brain were suddenly in the on position, and for a moment I was thinking clearly again.

"No," Mike said. "The machines showed that you were telling the truth. Norton argues that there obviously is no such person as Ciara Kelly and that proves you are such a sophisticated liar that you were able to fool the machine. Stephansky, the woman who conducted the test, stood right up to him and said the only correct conclusion was that you believe she does exist. Norton didn't like that at all, and he's going to continue to chew at the Ciara Kelly element. Unless I completely misunderstand our state's attorney, it will worry him a little, too, but not enough to change his mind."

The circuit breakers in my head began to flip on and off randomly again. "Not a very bright picture you paint for me, is it?"

"It'll get better," Mike Casey said. "It'll take time though."

"And your friends will stand by you," Eileen agreed. "Speaking of which, I suppose you've forgotten that this is the day for the Ryan family lunch. Anne and Mike are going to join us. We'll take a vote later to see whether they get permanent invitations. Me, I'm afraid it will turn into a discussion of art between Mike and Cathy Curran."

"Let me have a rain check," I pleaded. "Next week will be fine. Today I just want to return to my apartment and sleep for about eighteen hours."

"Sure," Eileen said. "But don't think we're going to forget about you. Next week, you'd better be there."

"You know, it's funny," I said, sounding rather wistful. "I had sort of intended to bring Ciara to the lunch today."

Both my friends were silent. So they, too, were dubious

about the existence of a Ciara Kelly. I could hardly blame them.

They dropped me off at my apartment building, her green eyes and his blue eyes both soft with affection and concern. I didn't deserve friends like that. I didn't want friends like that. I wanted to be alone, forever if possible.

20

I became a vegetable, existing but barely living, absorbing nourishment but refusing to think, continuing with life, surviving from day to day but avoiding any plans for tomorrow or the next day or the day after.

Vegetables don't indulge in self-pity and I did. It became the dominant, indeed the exclusive emotion in my life: Brendan Ryan as victim, as outcast, as martyr, betrayed by his wife, by his friends, by his community, by his lover. I felt no grief over the loss of Madonna and Ron, no pain for Jeannie, who had lost her mother, no compassion for the battered remnants of the Crowley and Clifford families, not even any concern for Ciara, for which God forgive me. I stayed away from the office, unplugged the telephone in the apartment, ignored messages from Nick and Eileen, avoided the Caseys, whose gallery was just down the street from my apartment, and declined a weekend invitation to Grand Beach. I did not make my bed or clean the apartment, and survived on fruit, crackers, and half a bottle of Jameson's a day, nursing my grudge against the cosmos because, innocent and honest man that I was, I would be forever tainted with the suspicion that I had murdered my wife and my closest friend.

The house in Lake Forest was empty now. The Cliffords had gone back to Florida, Jean had been carried off to Grand Beach by Mary Kate and Caitlin Murphy, and Madonna was dead. I realized that I had to do something about it. I certainly did not want to move back, yet Jean would need to have some kind of home for her vacations from Stanford. My apartment was hardly big enough for the two of us, and I could not expect her to stay at Grand Beach all summer long, however much such an arrangement might delight young Tim Murphy.

Although I had declined the Grand Beach invitation, I envied Jean her opportunity to go there, not so much wanting to deprive her of it but rather wanting to feel sorry for myself because I had never been permitted summer resort excitement when I was her age. My parents much preferred to put a pool in their backyard in Chicago, and while the "other" Ryans would have been delighted to share with me the sand and water and sun of Grand Beach, my group abominated the place and I accepted their decision. It seemed, as I tried to drown myself in the pathos of self-pity, that I had spent my whole life accepting the decisions the group had made for me. Now there was a new group, Nick Curran, Eileen Kane, Mike Casey, and their spouses, who were ready to replace the old and deprive me again of my free will.

God damn it, I would not permit that to happen!

Nick Curran sent a hand-delivered message to my apartment, reminding me of my grand jury subpoena on Monday morning of the next week. I plugged in the phone, called Nick, pretended that I was self-possessed and cheerful, and assured him that I would be there to talk to the grand jury. "Just give me till the end of this week, Nick," I said, trying to sound refreshed and businesslike, "and I'll be back at the office as good as new."

"I'm glad to hear that." He sounded dubious. "You won't be up at Grand Beach this weekend?"

"Give me another week," I pleaded.

It was already 5:30 in the afternoon—how had the day slipped away? In fact, what day was it?

I poured myself a glassful of Jameson's, ate an orange, cut myself some cheddar cheese, finished my supper with cheese, crackers, and Irish whiskey. Another furious late-afternoon thunderstorm—it seemed to have been the pattern the last few weeks—lashed against my apartment building. It reminded me of the night that Ciara and I had first made love.

Ciara? I had not thought about her for several days. She

was gone from my life, never to return. It was probably just as well.

The phone rang. Damn, I forgot to pull the plug. Well, let it ring. Perhaps it's something important. Nothing much could be important. Perhaps it was another disaster in my life. That I didn't want.

Nonetheless, forty-two years of a responsible life compelled me to pick up the phone. "It's Mary Kate Murphy, Brenny. There's nothing to worry about. Jean is fine. I thought I had better call you and tell you that we had a bit of an accident here this afternoon."

All the circuits in my brain were suddenly activated. Terror had sent a flow of energy into me that overrode all the disconnected circuit breakers. "My God, Mary Kate, what happened?"

"Jeannie's been taking long walks these days, getting her head screwed back on, she tells us. She was going down a hill over in Michiana—you know the one, Dogwood and Ridge—it fills up with water every time it rains."

"I'm afraid I don't . . ."

"Anyway." Mary Kate doubtless assumed everyone in the world was well-informed about the roads in Grand Beach and Michiana. "A car went out of control at the top of the hill, skidded down toward her. Fortunately your daughter is a good athlete; she dived off the road and the car missed her. She picked up some scratches and bruises and bumped her head a little, so we put her in St. Anthony's Hospital for the night. Joe and Timmy are with her. . . ." Mary Kate laughed. "So if she needs any Jungian psychotherapy, my husband will be glad to oblige."

My body sagged against the couch in my parlor. "Thank God everything's all right. . . . What about the driver of the car?"

"He didn't stay around, kind of hit and run, except that he didn't hit anyone. We reported it to the Michigan state police, but he'll be pretty hard to find. All Jeannie remembers is that it was a black car. She was too scared to remember the license number."

"Well, I'm glad she's all right." The circuit breakers flipped off, and I prepared to hang up the phone. "Thanks for calling me."

"She's in room 314 at St. Anthony's Hospital—that's area code 219-472-3600."

The clear implication was that if I didn't call Jeannie I would have to answer to Mary Kate Murphy and probably the entire Ryan clan, even unto the third and fourth generations.

"Thanks a million, Mary Kate. I'll call her right away."

"You'll be up here with us for the Memorial Day weekend."

"Is that an order?"

"It's an imperial rescript."

Dr. Mary Kate Murphy never denied that she was the empress of all the Ryans, even third and fourth cousins.

I called Jeannie at St. Anthony's Hospital. She sounded woozy and distracted but was delighted to hear from me. "I'm surprised the driver of the car didn't come back to help you," I said after she had assured me in five different ways that she was feeling "fine."

"Oh, he did back up, fast too, then another car came around the corner and he took off. I'm sorry I didn't notice the license numbers."

"You'll be up there all week?"

"Uh huh—they'll probably let me out of the hospital tomorrow after they do a few more tests, and I'll stay here for the weekend. Then I'll come into Chicago and stay at Connie's house and drive up with you next Friday afternoon."

"It's been decided that we're driving up on Friday afternoon, has it?" I managed to laugh. "Dr. Murphy doesn't take no for an answer?"

"No way, Daddy; we're going to stay with the Currans, and I will help Aunt Catherine with the kids and the cookout."

All neatly prepared. My new friends were, if anything, more efficient and better organized in taking charge of my life than were my old friends.

I lay back on the couch, a cracker in one hand and a half-empty Jameson's glass in the other. Something was wrong with the story of the near-accident in Michiana.

One of the circuits in my brain began to work again, slowly, laboriously, nonetheless effectively. I didn't know

Mary Kate's number in Grand Beach. Whom should I call? Mike Casey directly? Probably not a good idea.

I dialed the number of Holy Name Cathedral and asked for the rector. "Ryan." A mild and inoffensive voice.

"You heard about Jeannie's 'accident' in Michiana this afternoon?"

"Indeed, Brendan. A curious incident, was it not?"

"Do you think I'm wrong to be frightened about it?"

"Not in the least. I, uh, have already made certain preliminary investigations on the subject."

"Would you call Mike Casey for me and tell him it seems suspicious to me and that perhaps they might keep a close eye on Jean this weekend—not let her go out walking by herself, for example . . ."

"I believe that some protestations in that direction have already been made. I'll tell the responsible parties that your concern merely reinforces my own—not that they take the matter lightly."

"Why, Blackie?"

"I must confess that I know of no reason that anyone would wish to endanger you and your family. However, it does not at all seem unreasonable to me to suppose that you and, uh, Ms. Kelly—was that not her name?—were the real targets of the incendiary device in your yacht. There's no reason to believe that your late wife and Father Crowley used the craft often, indeed if ever before, and at a distance, at twilight, I would have thought that whoever operated the remote control mechanism could not have perceived that it was not you and, uh, Ms. Kelly on the yacht."

"That's interesting." Worn out from disuse, the active circuit in my brain ceased to function. "I suppose I'll see you there next weekend?"

"Saturday, surely, unless I want my family membership card to be revoked. I'll come back here for Masses on Sunday and then return in late afternoon. And the search for Ms. Kelly?"

"There isn't any search, I'm afraid, Monsignor Ryan."

"Ah!"

I passed the weekend in a pleasant, soothing state of nirvana in my air-conditioned apartment, away from the heat and the humidity that had settled into the city and which, punctuated occasionally by thunder showers, threatened to become the pattern for the summer. I did manage to put in half an hour in the pool, and also to sneak out of the building and watch the first two-thirds of Robert Redford's *The Natural* at the Water Tower Place. I left before the end because my soggy mind was not capable of comprehending the symbolism of the story.

However, at ten o'clock the following Monday morning, clean-shaven, dressed in somber color-coordinated gray, smelling of my expensive cologne, I presented myself at the appointed grand jury room at the Everett McKinley Dirksen Federal Building. I listened and nodded at Nick's brief instructions, asked a few intelligent questions, and then entered the hallowed chamber of the Grand Jury of the Northern District of Illinois, which was investigating the commodities market actions of John King Sullivan.

The Assistant United States Attorney for the Northern District of Illinois who was to question me was young, blonde, and very pretty. To my surprise I found myself thinking that when she was finished with her apprentice time working for the government she would certainly be welcome at Minor Gray and Blatt—and this before she had asked me a single question.

Male chauvinist, I denounced myself mentally. Eileen would be furious if she knew I was thinking such thoughts in the hallowed precincts of a grand jury room. So would Ciara.

Ciara.

Questions began about my relationship with John King Sullivan. In addition to being young, blonde, and pretty, the Assistant U.S. Attorney for the Northern District of Illinois was very feminine in her mannerisms and very, very smart. Oh, yes, we needed her at Minor Gray and Blatt.

Ciara.

I explained, in response to her question, that "taking a position" meant, in my case, a long-term estimate of whether the economy would move forward or slow down over a six-month period, an estimate I would back up with a leveraged purchase of government bond contracts.

"By leveraged, you mean, do you not, Mr. Ryan," she asked demurely, "your actual payment is only a small proportion of the market value of the contract?"

"Yes, that is correct."

"So if your guess seems to be going wrong, you will be called upon to put up additional funds in the course of the position?"

"I wouldn't use the word 'guess,' Counselor."

She blushed—very prettily, I may add. " 'Informed estimate'? Or perhaps 'calculated risk'?"

"Something of the sort. But to answer your question, Counselor, it would have been subject to margin calls if the price of a contract with the Chicago Board of Trade had increased. You see, I hold futures contracts at the market price on a given day. This means that if the price of the contract has diminished, then I abandon my position and purchase the contract at that price in order to deliver the contract, which I sold at a much higher price, and the difference is my margin of profit."

"A good deal of money was involved, was it not?"

"About a million dollars," I said mildly, noting the raised eyebrows, the shocked expressions of the good working-class and middle-class people on the grand jury.

"Your informed estimate turned out to be correct, did it not, Mr. Ryan?"

"Yes, it did."

"In fact, your informed estimates have usually been correct, have they not?"

"More often than not," I admitted.

"So if your money had been invested as you directed your broker, Mr. John King Sullivan," she glanced at the papers in front of her as if she didn't know full well that that was the name of my broker, "you would have by now realized a substantial profit?"

"Yes, ma'am," I said, "a very considerable profit."

Her eyes, gray like Ciara Kelly's, glinted with amusement. Ma'am, indeed, she seemed to be saying teasingly. How could I explain to her that I had no idea what her name was? If Nick had told me, or if she had mentioned it, I had completely forgotten.

"Can you describe to us in your own words what happened to your money?"

"I discovered, quite by accident, in a conversation with a floor trader, that Mr. Sullivan had invested very heavily in the opposite position, that is to say, he had sold government bond contracts to a bond contractor at approximately the same price at which I had purchased them, expecting a sharp increase, I presume, from the economic indicators, and perhaps a renewal of inflation.''

''At that time you questioned Mr. Sullivan about this matter?''

''That is correct.''

''And did you find his answer satisfactory?''

''No, I did not.''

''Did you report your suspicions immediately to the Commodities Future Trading Commission?''

''No, not immediately.''

''How long did you wait?''

''Several days.''

''May I ask why?''

''Mr. Sullivan and I had been lifelong friends. First of all, I wanted to be sure that the violations had indeed occurred; secondly I wanted to be sure that other investors had also been . . .''

''Victimized?''

Gray eyes like Ciara Kelly.

''I suppose so, yes.''

Ciara Kelly.

''In other words, you were willing to absorb your own enormous loss in the name of friendship, but you could not permit other investors to suffer losses?''

Ciara Kelly. Ciara Kelly. Ciara Kelly.

''Mr. Ryan?''

''Ma'am?''

She considered me curiously for a moment. ''Should I repeat the question, sir?''

There was a faint tease in the word 'sir.'

''Would you please, Counselor.''

''I asked whether your attitude at the time was that you would absorb your own financial losses but that you could not permit other investors to be defrauded of their money?''

''Yes, that is correct.''

· Ciara Kelly. Ciara Kelly. Ciara Kelly.

She was in enormous danger. Not the leggy, gray-eyed blonde who was questioning me and flirting mildly with me—perhaps in response to what she saw as my own initiation of flirtation—no, she wasn't in danger at all, but Ciara Kelly was.

"Mr. Ryan?"

"I'm sorry, Counselor." I felt my face burning. "Would you mind repeating the question?"

"We understand that you've had many serious problems on your mind recently, Mr. Ryan. Did Mr. John King Sullivan attempt to dissuade you from reporting his violations of the Commodities Future Trading Act?"

"Yes, Ms. Kelly. Only once, however."

The young woman grinned broadly. "Kennedy, sir."

"Yes. I'm sorry, Miss . . ." I saw the wedding ring on her finger. "I'm sorry, *Mrs*. Kennedy."

And so it went. The information that would constrain the grand jury to indict John King Sullivan was gently but firmly drawn from me by a very clever young woman who, understanding my own confusion, deftly adjusted her interrogation style to make me look good before the grand jury.

There was enough testimony, should the reported plea-bargaining deal break down, to send John King Sullivan, my lifelong friend, to a federal correctional institution for a good long time.

And Ciara was in danger, grave, grave danger. From whom? Where? No answers, but about the danger I had not the slightest doubt.

When I was excused at the end of my testimony from the grand jury room, Mrs. Kennedy made a charming little speech. "We're very grateful to you for your cooperation, Mr. Ryan. We understand how painful this matter must be for you. You've been very frank and forthright and helpful to us."

"Thank you, Mrs. Kennedy," I murmured, and quickly escaped from the grand jury room.

"How did it go?" Nick Curran asked breathlessly.

"We'd better hire that woman when she leaves federal service," I responded.

"Every law firm in the Loop," Nick said with a grin, "will want her."

"A job for Eileen, then."

"I agree completely."

"Well, you're enough yourself again, Brendan, to react positively to pretty and smart young women."

"How long has it been, Nick, since you've known me to react that way? Maybe I'm just the opposite of my ordinary self."

Before Nick could respond, we encountered, lounging in the corridor outside the grand jury room, Lieutenant Samuel Norton of the Chicago Police Department.

"Looking for a traffic violator, Sam?" Nick asked sharply.

"Nah." Norton jingled the coins in his pocket. "Looking for a murderer. I know you killed them, Ryan, and I'm going to get your ass in the electric chair if it's the last thing I ever do."

"You just added one more charge to our complaint to the Professional Practices Board," Nick snapped.

"I don't give a fuck about your charges," Norton sneered. "You won't dare bring them when I get the goods on this motherfucker."

"Don't say another word to him, Brendan." Nick turned on his heel and dragged me along with him. "He has no right to harass you."

"I didn't say a word, and wasn't planning to," I observed mildly.

"Eileen'll go through the ceiling when she hears about this." Nick was furious.

"Are we really going to file a complaint against him?"

"You damned well better believe we are. The asshole thinks we're afraid to risk more newspaper coverage on the murder; in fact, when we're finished with him, we'll have the truth in the papers: the police department in the person of Lieutenant Samuel Norton was so busy harassing you that it did not seriously search for the real killers."

Who were the real killers? Were they the ones who had endangered Jeannie's life last week? And were they the ones who were threatening Ciara Kelly? And how could someone be threatened who apparently did not exist?

"Have a bite of lunch?" Nick asked, as we emerged in the scathing sunlight of LaSalle Street—high noon, the only time the sun shone in the LaSalle Street ravine.

"I'm not quite up to it yet, Nick," I pleaded. "I'll take a rain check till next weekend at Grand Beach."

"You'll be staying with us, I'm told." Behind the thick glasses, Nick's eyes seemed to twinkle.

"Someone, someday, ought to do a study of how the Ryan family women arrive at their collective decisions."

"ESP!"

Ciara Kelly was in danger.

"You're looking good," Nick continued somewhat dubiously. "The Crazy Mal business in the paper didn't bother you?"

"Who's Crazy Mal?" I began to walk north on LaSalle Street, and Nick tagged along. "I'm afraid I haven't been reading the newspapers the last few days."

"Sam Norton got the word from one of his Taylor Street stoolies that a contract had been put out to a scumbag—the police term for him—named Cesare Malocha, otherwise called 'Crazy Mal.' He's a minor hit man that some of the lesser lights in the outfit occasionally hire when they need a job done that doesn't require too much finesse. He's called 'Crazy Mal,' one gathers, because his contracts tend to be a bit reckless and amateurish. Some of the top people can't understand why the police let him roam the streets." Nick smiled thinly. "They don't have a very high regard for law enforcement in this city, I guess."

"So what happened?" I was more concerned with what threatened Ciara Kelly than I was with Crazy Mal.

"Norton sweated him," Nick said with a shrug, "or tried to sweat him. Pretended that they already had a link between him and you. Mal listened to it for a while, called his lawyer, and is out walking the streets again, much to the dismay of the top brass in the outfit."

"But if he's the killer, why can't they arrest him?"

"It's one thing to know from the word on the street that he did the job, and quite another to prove it. The cops know who most of the hit men are in mob slayings, but there's never any proof that would stand up in court, so the hit men go free unless they make a mistake or somebody squeals on them and stays alive long enough to testify."

"And then he goes off and leads a new life, courtesy of the

United States government—sometimes even committing crimes that the FBI won't let local authorities prosecute.''

"When Eileen and I were working for the government," Nick said—we were standing at LaSalle and Madison, Nick's internal gyroscope tilting him back toward his offices in the Minor Gray and Blatt Annex on Jackson, mine tilting me toward my apartment and the Jameson's bottle—"we defended the Informant Protection Plan as the only way to convict someone in the outfit. Now I don't know. Anyway, Sam Norton didn't lay a glove on Mal, and I think that's the last you're going to hear of it. . . . Incidentally, the Continental Bank Building still seems to be standing there, doesn't it?"

"Why wouldn't it?"

"You really aren't reading the newspapers; the feds bailed Continental out the other day to the tune of seven billion dollars; they're looking for a merger—maybe Morgan Guarantee. . . . Banking, I guess, is too important to be left to the bankers."

The disappearance of the Continental Illinois as a separate entity would be an enormous blow to Chicago's pride and independence, far worse than losing the *Sun-Times* to Rupert Murdoch. It would also be a severe shock to Minor Gray and Blatt, which handled much of the Continental's business. I felt guilty for nurturing my own self-pity and distracting the attention of Nick and my other friends from the firm's serious problems. I was sure that he had better things to do that morning than to sit outside a Dirksen Building grand jury room waiting for me or, for that matter, standing at LaSalle and Madison trying to tempt me back into the cold waters of the rushing stream of life.

"I better let you get back to the offices. I imagine the senior partners are having fits."

"One more thing." Nick paused and jammed his fists into his pockets, a gesture that indicated he was spoiling for a fight. "The money in the trust fund you set up for the alimony is yours to do with whatever you wish. After all, the trust fund was your idea. The divorce settlement monies are another matter. Technically, the divorce wasn't final, so you have the right to the money. But the Cliffords have hired a lawyer, who has gone into court with a petition to appoint them Jean's guardians on the grounds that you're unfit to be a guardian of an innocent girl. They've also asked that, as guardians, they have control over the divorce settlement money until Jean reaches her majority. It's pure, gratuitous nastiness.''

''But Jean's nineteen years old!''

''And well able to take care of herself without Mel Clifford messing in her life like he messed in her mother's. They can't hope to win. It's a form of harassment, an opportunity for the Cliffords to attack you in public. We will beat them, but it's one more burden you don't need right now.''

''I don't suppose there's any compromise possible?''

Nick regarded me curiously, still incapable of understanding that some men were not as competitive as he was. ''We can explore that, but I don't see any. A monetary settlement wouldn't be appropriate. And in any case, the Cliffords don't want money, they want a chance to attack you.''

''You're sure I won't lose?''

''Lose?'' Nick exploded. ''You're the girl's father, a distinguished lawyer and civic leader. You have committed no crimes. You weren't the one who went to bed with the priest. . . . Sorry, Brendan.''

''Not at all. I guess I feel guilty. I feel that maybe I'm not a fit father for Jeannie. I haven't done a very good job at fatherhood, God knows.''

''That's not what Jeannie thinks,'' Nick argued hotly. ''In fact, if this thing ever gets to a court hearing, the judge will throw it out as soon as we put Jeannie on the stand.''

''I don't want Jeannie on the witness stand!'' I shouted at him.

Nick laughed at me. ''Brendan Ryan, when will you ever learn? Whether you want Jeannie on the witness stand makes not the slightest difference. She knows about the Cliffords' petition, and according to my Grand Beach sources, she's furious. She's Irish, Brendan, and like all the other women in the family, the Archangel Gabriel couldn't keep her off the witness stand.''

''My mother isn't Irish.''

''No.'' A whimsical smile spread across his lean, elegant face. ''She's Scottish. They're the worst kind of Irish.''

We shook hands and went our separate ways, Nick back into the maelstrom of trying to save the seventh largest bank in the country, with assets of over forty-two billion dollars, from its own folly, and I back to my beloved Jameson's bottle. I didn't care what happened to Continental Illinois, and I was confident that Nick could protect Jeannie from her grandparents. There was, nonetheless, one point about which Nick had not been completely honest. Cesare Malocha was a scumbag with an alibi and a high-priced outfit attorney. There was no reason for him to sing with lyrics provided by Sam Norton. Not yet. But if Crazy Mal should stumble, and even the outfit's overlords were surprised that he had not, and the police department arranged a plea-bargain deal with him, he would sing any tune that Sam Norton devised for him. Then there would surely be an indictment and a trial. Presumably Eileen Kane would tie both Norton and Malocha in knots on the witness stand, and presumably I would be acquitted. But not necessarily. Plea-bargained informants had sent innocent men and women to jail before—no one yet to the electric chair, but I did not relish the prospect, however remote, of being the first.

The murderer of my wife and friend had to be found, even if I must do it myself. But later. First to my apartment and the Jameson's bottle.

Ciara Kelly. Ciara Kelly. Ciara Kelly.

An oppressive fear pervaded my soul, weighing me down, slowing my footsteps as I trudged doggedly along Madison Street toward Michigan Avenue. Dark, somber clouds, matching the psychic energies that were bombarding me, were slipping over the city, obscuring the top half of the Sears Tower. The thunderstorm would come early today.

Some of my psychic kinks, like those of others, according to the literature, are visual: I actually see the garrison leaving Fort Dearborn, the flashes of fire over the lake, the dark shadows in the Chestnut Street ravine. Other phenomena seem to be purely intellectual, at least initially. I *knew* that Ciara Kelly was bearing my child, even before the first time I made love to her and *saw* her body blossoming with my offspring. Still other happenings are somewhere in between, emotional but not visual. I *feel* an event, neither seeing it nor comprehending it. The emotions of the event take possession of me but tell me nothing of what is happening or where it is happening or whether it is a past or a present or a future phenomenon.

My terror for Ciara, as I walked home under the glowering gray clouds, was in the last category. Ciara's emotions had become my emotions—the terror, shame, degradation, humiliation, revulsion at being used and abused. Torment, pain, a desire that death terminate suffering. Despair.

Ciara being raped by the Simbas—a recollection of the past, memory traces still lingering from the night at her apartment?

An apartment in which she had never lived.

Partly. But also partly the present, and mostly the future. Ciara was being threatened. The emotions I was experiencing were either in the present or in the immediate future. Those who wished to torture and destroy her were at hand. She needed my help and protection.

The feelings were overwhelming, the most vivid psychic vibrations I had ever experienced. At the Chicago River and Michigan Avenue I leaned against a pillar of the bridge in the shadow of the rain-drenched Wrigley Building. It was raining now. I had hardly noticed it. Beneath me one of the Wendella excursion boats bobbed on the windswept river. Ciara needed my help.

Then slowly the emotions ebbed, leaving me drained and uncertain. As I have noted previously, my psychic sensitivity is erratic, unpredictable, and mostly useless. Nor can I ever be certain that I am not producing the vibrations myself unconsciously. Had I created peril for Ciara Kelly because if she was in peril, she was real? Her danger was a confirmation that my love was not self-deception.

I was drenched from the rainstorm, which now had moved out over the lake, to be replaced by thin clouds and a sizzling sun, angry that its domination of the city had been temporarily interrupted. Thick waves of steam rose from the puddles on the Magnificent Mile.

Did I really want to go to Grand Beach? Did I want to trust myself to the enthusiastic and affectionate ambience of my new group of friends, pushy and uninvited friends?

It was too late to answer that question. I had agreed to go to the beach for the Memorial Day weekend because my daughter wanted me to. I owed poor Jeannie at least that much.

Sometimes psychic experiences linger, and other times they disappear completely. I must note very carefully here that my fear for Ciara was in the latter category. By the time I had reached the Water Tower, there was not a trace of it. Indeed, I could, with minimal effort, persuade myself that it had not happened. Moreover, and I must insist on this too, rarely do such phenomena pile on top of one another. I cannot recall an occasion when there has been more than one such event in a given day, at least not more than one intense event.

I therefore supposed that the psychic phenomena were finished for the day and perhaps, given the strength of the terror that had left me shivering on the banks of the Chicago River, finished for several days.

Exhausted, and eagerly expecting my bottle of Jameson's, I nodded to the doorman and rode the elevator up to my apartment.

If I had not been so careful about bringing Ciara into my apartment through the parking lot, the doorman could now have solved my problem.

Was I careful because I did not want the doorman to report that he had never seen a woman with me?

Because there never had been such a woman?

Or was she, like Billy Wells in Fort Dearborn, a woman from another era, another world?

I unlocked the door, walked in, and found Madonna waiting for me on the couch.

21

The woman who sat on my couch, wearing a white sports dress, relaxed, even casual, but infinitely sad, was not the praying mantis whom Ciara and I had encountered at Orchestra Hall, not the corpse burned to a cinder off Montrose Harbor. She was a young Madonna, not an adolescent, not a young bride—more like the beautiful wife to whom I had come home from Vietnam, but with none of the petulance of the woman who had welcomed me back with notable indifference.

Two comments seem appropriate here: first of all, it was an experience of considerable duration. When my Great Aunt Heather had "checked out" with me at the moment of her death, it had been a brief and phantasmagorical interlude. In the books I've read on the subject, it appears that some men and women are the ordinary "check out" points for members of their families who are dying. (No one even begins to explain the reason for this rather peculiar family role.) Such experiences, which are almost routine in their lives, are much like those with my Great Aunt Heather—brief, somewhat mystical, problematic in their content.

There are, according to the literature, other interludes of apparent contact with the dead, incidents of some duration in which the person encountered seems *physically* present, not perhaps quite the way the person was present when alive, but still not hazy or ectoplasmic. It was to this latter variety that my meeting with someone who seemed to be Madonna must be assigned.

Moreover, there was nothing uncanny or frightening about my experience of Madonna. It was not the raw material for a ghost story. She was not haunting me. Most psychic experiences, by the way, are uncanny perhaps in the telling, but not in the experience. They seem ordinary, matter-of-fact, commonplace.

So the presence of my murdered wife, reclining with mild suggestiveness, seemed neither unusual nor disturbing. It was almost as though a friend had stopped by my apartment unexpectedly and waited until I came home.

Did we talk to each other? That is a question I cannot answer. As best I can remember the interlude, words were not exchanged, but we communicated, we absorbed emotions, we understood. At the time this emotional communication seemed rich, complex, and important. When I set it down on paper, it reads like a commonplace, a cliché: we grieved over the lost opportunity of our life together, we forgave each other. We mourned our own suffering and that of our friends. We looked forward. . . .

I'm not sure what we looked forward to. Nothing explicit. But there was a very strong sensation that Madonna and I were not finished with each other. There was work yet to be done, difficult, painful, arduous work. We had no choice in the matter. That work would be done. More than that, there would be joy mixed with the pain of doing it.

My wife surely did not seem to be one of the damned. Neither did she seem to be one of the saved. She was sad, hurt, wounded, but not unhappy and certainly not without hope. She also seemed to say that I was much too hard on myself, that I blamed myself far more than I should, that—was there a hint of laughter here?—that I was far more critical of myself than she had ever been.

Then she was no longer with me and I was sobbing convulsively, like a little boy who is lost in a department store.

The reader will be skeptical, and indeed should be, for I am skeptical myself. I was troubled, anxious, guilt-ridden, devastated. I needed and wanted absolution. I yearned for a sign of hope that all was not totally lost between me and my wife. I desperately wanted an indication that, indeed, somehow, some way, the group with whom I had grown up and which had played such an important part in my life would be given one more chance. I wanted to believe that Madonna had survived. I wanted to believe that she was once again the lovely young woman for whom I had yearned so intensely, both before our marriage and while I was in Vietnam. I wanted to believe in a loving God who did provide second and third and fourth and fifth chances. The wish, as Madonna might have said herself in her fondness for clichéd proverbs, was the father of the thought. As the psychiatrist would tell me caustically a few days later, "Yah, you wanted to believe dat your wife was still alive so you hallucinated her."

I wanted to believe that she was still alive, I wanted to see her again, I wanted a promise of a new beginning, and the peculiar kinks of body and/or soul that constituted my psychic sensitivity gave me the tools to temporarily re-create her. Hardly had my weeping stopped when the rational, civilized, cautious lawyer in me took over and discounted the experience.

Later, however, Monsignor John Blackwood Ryan would peer through his thick prescription sunglasses ("Uncle Blackie won't wear contact lenses," Caitlin proclaimed, "because then he wouldn't be able to blink his eyes and pretend that he's Father Brown!") at the procession of cabin cruisers bumping along, perhaps a quarter mile offshore in the bright blue glory of Memorial Day, and murmur, "I don't understand, Brendan Herbert George Ryan, why it is necessary to determine whether the experience was 'real.' " He glared in some confusion at his empty Jameson's glass, baffled as to how the precious brew had disappeared. "Or indeed, how one can ever know whether such experiences are 'real.' Is it not more pertinent to inquire as to the validity of the message than as to the nature of the phenomenon?"

I admitted that I didn't quite understand.

"One either lives in a universe where absolution and new beginnings are possible, indeed a matter of commonplace occurrence, or one does not. The burden of your interlude was that you and Madonna could still forgive each other and still begin again despite the absurdity of death. It is surely not the first time you've heard that message. If the message is true, then all things are possible. But the issue—is it not?—is whether the message is true and not whether a particular phenomenon is possible, a phenomenon which, in the nature of things, does not admit of easy falsification or verification."

As usual, Blackie Ryan was right. However, by his own admission being utterly devoid of psychic sensitivities, he did not know the anguish, the delight, and the bafflement of such a message being communicated by someone whom you have every earthly reason to believe you have lost.

There was also a later experience for which there was at least a hint of verification.

While my mind attempted to disprove the reality of my experience of Madonna, I went to the swimming pool and swam for forty-five minutes. Then I phoned a local pizza house, very much like an adolescent, ordered a large sausage and cheese pizza. I consumed it as though it were the first food I had eaten in a week, which for all practical purposes it was, and washed it down with the last bottle of Perrier water in the icebox. I resolved that I would have a good night's sleep without the assistance of John Jameson's nectar, and that the next morning I would begin the search for Ciara Kelly.

22

The air conditioner in Dr. Otto Freihaut's office rumbled busily, but either the machine, which seemed to be at least as old as the bald, gnomelike doctor, had long since ceased to provide effective cooling or my emotional unease canceled out its effects. Sweat was pouring off my face, and my shirt clung limply to my chest and back.

"Yah, ve vill haf no talk in dis office about dat gottdam ESP," snorted the doctor, brushing cigar ashes off his soiled brown vest. "Dat is all gottdam nonsense! Ve vill acknowledge dat ve vere hallucinating, *nein*?"

I expected the doctor at some point to say to me, like the Gestapo interrogators in late-night films, "Ve haf our vays."

It was Friday morning before the Memorial Day weekend, just a few days ago, though so many things have happened since then that it now seems a couple of lifetimes ago. Jean was to pick me up at my apartment building at two o'clock so that we could escape the rush-hour traffic on our pilgrimage to Grand Beach. I had a terrible, trapped feeling that I would never escape from Dr. Otto Freihaut, that he would lock me up in an institution and throw away the key. Or perhaps sell me to a traveling carnival as a third-rate freak, a psychic equivalent of the bearded lady. The doorman at my building would tell poor Jean that her father was in the loony bin and she could only see him with Dr. Freihaut's permission, *nein*?

"Ve must admit dat ve haf a wery serious problem. Ve are haffing schizophrenic delusions mit paranoidal overtones, yah?"

"If you say so, doctor," I agreed mildly. After all, there

was a very strong possibility that the doctor's diagnosis was right.

Impulsively, late in the previous afternoon, I had asked one of my colleagues, who did considerable tax work for the psychiatric profession, if he could make a referral for me on an emergency basis. The colleague was overjoyed, doubtless convinced that I had been a sick man for a long, long time. Dr. Freihaut had a cancellation on Friday morning, and there I was in his office, trying to explain about two women whom he promptly dismissed as schizophrenic fantasies—Ciara Kelly, who had never existed, and Madonna Clifford, who did, but who was dead and could not come back from the dead.

It was necessary for me to acknowledge my sickness, to admit my systematic schizophrenic delusions, to seek admission to the appropriate psychiatric institution as soon as possible before "you do serious harm to yourself, *nein*?"

I had not intended to tell Dr. Freihaut about the interlude with Madonna, since I was very dubious myself about the reality of that incident, but he demanded that I explain to him why, after more than a week of ignoring the problem, I had suddenly begun my search for Ciara Kelly. I suppose the model in my mind was my confessor when I was a boy. If Father asked you a question in the confessional, you tried to tell him the truth, no matter how ridiculous the truth might sound. So if the psychotherapist asked you a question, you tried to respond truthfully, even if it meant saying that you began your search for a woman whose existence everyone else denies because an encounter with your dead wife gave you hope for forgiveness and renewal.

I thought the outraged little Black Forest elf would swallow his cigar. (If you objected to cigar smoking in the therapist's office, you could avail yourself of someone else. If you wanted Dr. Freihaut, you meekly accepted his cigar, *nein*?) "Iss de vorse kind of schizophrenic delusion!" he gurgled. "Iss sign werry sick man!"

I suppose so. If I were a psychoanalyst, I guess I would be driven to the edge of apoplexy by a patient who claimed to have communed with a dead wife. Such communications were, as a matter of scientific definition, impossible, and therefore the only alternative explanation was that the patient was a sick, quite possibly dangerously sick, person.

Blackie Ryan's reaction to my description, a few days later, of the conversation with Dr. Freihaut was interesting. He mercifully spared me the question why, with psychiatrists in the family, I had not sought their recommendations for a therapist. "*Herr Doktor*'s reasoning is utterly appropriate," he struggled in vain to squeeze suntan cream from an empty container, "save in one set of circumstances."

"And that is?"

He paused long enough in his struggle with the suntan cream to gaze at me in surprise. "In circumstances where the client actually has interacted with a dead spouse."

"I'm afraid the doctor believes that that is impossible."

"How does he know?" Blackie Ryan asked blandly.

My two-day search for Ciara Kelly had been brisk, efficient, businesslike. I assumed the role of a man who is trying to clear up some minor misunderstanding, just to keep the record straight. I was not desperately searching for a woman who apparently did not exist. Rather, I was trying to comprehend how this bizarre event had occurred. I resolutely refused to give up this pose, even though my respondents were embarrassed by it.

"Ah, sure," said my good friend Seamus O'Rafferty, a blond giant who looked more like a professional rugby player than the Consul General of the Republic of Ireland, "we've been friends ever since I came to Chicago, Brendan. I'd be wanting to give you every possible help, but we have no record of any Irish immigrant named Ciara Kelly. If she were here on an Irish passport, mind you, we'd know about her. And when the matter came up a few days ago, I checked with people that make it their business to be in contact with the immigrant community. No one had ever heard a word about her at all, at all."

"Perhaps she came in on a British passport," I suggested tentatively.

"Well, now, that would be a possibility, though I did call my colleague the British consul general at the time, just to be certain. Sure, he had no record of her either. Mind you, now, it's not definitive. People come in through Detroit, for example, and we have no record of them. It's a big city, and someone can be here for a long time and go unnoticed. But, sure, weren't you after saying that she worked at that Irish store down the road? Ah, it would be hard to miss someone like that.''

"She's a very well-educated woman," I said. "Trinity College, at least, and probably some sort of graduate school—literature or history or something of the sort.''

"Did your immigration service or your state department know anything about her?''

. They did not. No green card, no work permit, no tourist visa, nothing. If Ciara Kelly had come to the United States of America—under that name, at any rate—neither the Republic of Ireland nor the United States of America knew anything about her.

"That might not," I observed in the tone I normally used with the better class of IRS agents, "have been her real name.''

Everyone tried to be extremely helpful, indeed so helpful that at times I suspected a massive cover-up. The manager of Chestnut Place permitted me to interview his doorman, who had no recollections of either me or Ciara Kelly at the door of the building every night for a couple of weeks. Then the manager brought me up to apartment 960. It was empty and dusty, the walls and the carpet blue instead of beige, as they had been when I had eaten dinner and made love to Ciara in the apartment. Even the disconnected telephone was blue instead of white and a push button instead of a rotary phone, nor was the number on it the same one I had written down when Ciara had gone into the kitchen for the steaming Irish stew.

Yet, for several hours in the morning after the *Brigid* caught fire, that phone number had rung somewhere. Then, in the afternoon, a computerized voice had begun to inform me that the line had been disconnected. At one time, then, the phone number I had jotted down in my wallet was real. Had it rung in this apartment? If it had, then everything else might be fakery. The different color scheme, the new phone number, the bland assertions of the manager and the doorman that they knew nothing of Ciara Kelly. Dr. Otto Freihaut said all of this was paranoia. Perhaps it was. But what if it was not?

The staff did not remember her at the Cliff Dwellers, nor at the Hunan restaurant, nor at Jackie's, nor at Jerome's, nor at any of the other restaurants or theaters where I asked my polite questions. Gary Jensen, the nasty little gossip columnist who had been Madonna's escort at Orchestra Hall, denied that he'd even seen me there that night.

After a day and a half of determined and systematic searching, I had found not the slightest trace of Ciara Kelly.

Finally I tried Dufficy's Irish Store. Mrs. Reardon, who was in charge of the store, was huffy and uncooperative. She had been asked these questions several times by the police and by private detectives (undoubtedly hired by Nick and Eileen). Really, she had better things to do with her time than to pursue such a ridiculous subject.

I was patient and polite and deferential. Finally I was told that there were four women who worked in the store, Ms. Hurley, Ms. Creaghan, Mrs. Farrell, and Mrs. McCarthy. The former two were in their twenties, the latter in their forties, and only Ms. Creaghan was an immigrant, and there she was, herself, rearranging the Waterford on the other side of the store.

It seemed to me that the whole inside of the store had changed. When I was courting Ciara I'd paid little attention to the distribution of knits and tweeds and plaids and prints and books and crystal; yet when I had entered for my awkward conversation with Mrs. Reardon, I had had the sensation of walking into an entirely different establishment.

I asked if the book on modern Irish artists was still in stock and was assured, after an impatient search (Mrs. Reardon demonstrating the enormous virtue of her patience in seeking an answer to such a frivolous question), that the book was not in stock and never had been but that, if I wished, she would be happy to order it for me.

I turned to leave, discouraged and defeated. Then I stopped and stared in astonishment at the full-length painting that hung behind the Waterford crystal. It was Ciara, beyond any doubt, in the formal evening dress of perhaps 1840.

"What is that painting?" I asked, straining to control my fascination.

"Ah, it's lovely, isn't it? It was painted by one of the most promising Anglo-Irish artists of the first half of the nineteenth century. It was said that he was in love with the woman; Constance Keenan was her name. She died at the age of thirty, under mysterious circumstances, at her husband's manor, Castle Keenan, near Westport in County Mayo. It is said that she still haunts the house.''

I was thunderstruck. ''The woman has been dead, then, for over a century?''

''Closer to a century and a half.'' Mrs. Reardon seemed to be doing arithmetical calculations in her head. ''Her husband was never brought to trial, you know; everyone thought he killed her because she'd been unfaithful with Rory Conley, the painter. But there was no proof. Her boat tipped over on the lake, don't you see. Her husband was twenty miles away, hunting pheasants. So he couldn't have killed her, could he?''

Only after I had left the store, shaken and, to be honest about it, frightened, did it occur to me to ask whether Constance Keenan had produced any children.

Mrs. Reardon, who had warmed a bit while describing the painting, lost both interest and patience when she decided that I was not about to pay $3,000 for it.

Sometime later, perhaps, when I'd abandoned completely my search for Ciara Kelly, I might want the painting, not so much to remind me of her as to remind me of her unreality.

Again the thought flickered in the back of my head: there's something wrong with this whole picture, a piece missing, the perspective tilted at an odd, indeed impossible, angle.

I grabbed for the bat in the back rooms of my brain, but it flitted by me and away into the twilight.

Could I have seen that painting behind the Waterford crystal in Dufficy's Irish Store and in some bizarre and demented twist of my psychic kinkiness invested the woman in the painting with life?

A man who can create, from out of his psychological kinks, an image of his dead wife, smiling sadly on the couch of his living room fifty-five stories above the city of Chicago, is capable of any self-delusion.

''Yah,'' observed Dr. Freihaut, ''you created delusions. You saw de voman in der painting *und* you made her real in your imagination. Ve need no gottdam ESP to explain dat.''

I finally escaped from Dr. Freihaut, the stench of his cigars, and the inefficient rumblings of his air conditioner, by promising that I would come back "first ding" on Tuesday morning, and only after I agreed that the doctor would not be responsible for any harm I did to myself or to others over the Memorial Day weekend. He made me feel like I was an epileptic driver insisting on racing in the Indianapolis 500.

It would be a deadly weekend all right. In that respect, at any rate, *Herr Doktor* had been an excellent prophet.

I was willing to promise almost anything to be able to flee from his office before he summoned the men in white with the large syringes filled with powerful tranquilizers. I would talk to Mary Kate or Joe Murphy at Grand Beach this weekend, I told myself, with little conviction.

My first session with that psychiatrist, I knew, would be my last. I had read enough books on the subject to realize that the "gottdam ESP" was a reality in the lives of the majority of the American population. Whatever tricks my psychic kinkiness might be playing on me, I was not going to entrust myself, and certainly not at $150 an hour, to someone who rejected in principle the possibility of my experiences.

As I walked out of the office building into the rainy mists of Michigan Avenue—Jeannie had assured me it would clear up by early afternoon and be a "glorious" weekend—I wondered ruefully what Dr. Freihaut would have said if I told him about my encounters with the Fort Dearborn garrison.

"A perfectly proper decision," Monsignor Ryan agreed later, having borrowed a suntan tube from a passing unidentified niece and begun to smear the gooey white lotion on his arms and neck, with only minimal effectiveness. "Patently, *Herr Doktor* has considerable anal retentive rigidities. . . . Not that I know what that means, but I'm always impressed when my sister, the good Mary Kate, speaks that phrase trippingly on the tongue."

"Let me rub it on the back of your neck, Uncle Punk." The blonde niece removed the tube from his willing fingers. "You always forget that you can get sunburned in back as well as in front."

After the niece was appropriately thanked with a "Bless you, child" and had affectionately ruffled her uncle's hair, Blackie returned to the question at hand. "It would seem that no one, not Dr. Freihaut, nor my sister, nor the good Eileen, nor the inestimable Counselor Curran, nor the superlative sometime Police Commissioner Casey, is willing to face what I take to be obvious about Ciara Kelly.''

"That she never existed?'' I asked hopefully. If Blackie Ryan said so, then I would be dispensed forever from further questing.

"Oh, no.'' His pale, nearsighted eyes widened in surprise. "Quite the contrary. I take it as self-evident that she did and does exist.''

23

"I hope you don't mind the car, Daddy.'' Jean was sitting in the driver's seat of her mother's black Mercedes Benz 250SL convertible with white leather seats. "I kind of hesitated at first, and then I decided, gosh, it's only a car, and I don't really believe in psychic vibrations.''

Oh, don't you, my child?

"A car is a car.'' I climbed in the front seat with her. I supposed that, should I have asked her, my anti-psychic daughter would have advocated the reconstruction of the *Brigid* too.

Madonna's car had been found several days after the killings in a parking lot on Broadway and Montrose. The police speculated that Madonna and Ron had either walked from the parking lot to the harbor, or hailed a taxi on Broadway. Since they were unable to locate the taxi driver, they concluded that the couple had walked. I found this extremely unlikely. For all her pathetic addiction to exercise, Madonna did not like walking and I could not imagine her strolling for half a mile burdened with sailing gear, food, and drink. Nor, for that matter, could I imagine Ron Crowley, overweight and worn out, negotiating such a distance. Not that such speculations mattered.

"Do you mind if I drive?'' Jean was wearing a khaki

miniskirt, a red and green striped T-shirt, and expensive-looking German sunglasses. Her hair was tied back with a green ribbon that matched the green in her T-shirt. She was barefoot, as was appropriate for the official beginning of summer.

"It's all right with me. If I knew we were using the convertible, I'd have brought a ribbon for my hair too."

"Silly!" She smiled affectionately. "Hey, don't I get a kiss before we start?"

"Sure." I touched her lips affectionately with mine.

"Not bad for an old daddy." She turned on the ignition of the car and we began the trip. "I think we'll go right over to the expressway and avoid the mess your friends in city hall have made at the 'S curve' on Lake Shore Drive."

"They're no friends of mine. . . . What's new in your world?"

"Well." Jean drove skillfully and confidently in the crush of near-north traffic, hardly a reckless teenage driver. "Not all that much; my Cubs are still in first place, and the Edmonton Oilers, with that darling Wayne Gretzky, finally won the Stanley Cup."

"Did they?"

She took her eyes off the traffic for a fraction of a second to glance uneasily at me. "Don't you read the newspapers, Daddy?"

"I guess I must have missed the hockey play-offs. What do you think the Cubs' chances are? Are they going to fold in July?"

Until that moment, I had been unaware my daughter was a sports fan. Had she always been? Or was this one more dubious influence of the "other" Ryans?

She outlined for me, not without some sophistication, the sad collapses of promising Cubs teams in the heat of the summer in other years and analyzed the prospects for the present surprising Cubs. Her conclusion was that, yes, they would probably fold, but that the team was young and showed promise for the future, even though their pitching was terribly weak. "Anyway, they're exciting and they're doing *so* much better than the dopey White Sox this year. It keeps those crazy Sox fans at Grand Beach in their place."

Ah ha, the "other" Ryans were Sox fans. Somehow I had not realized that either.

I felt traces of Ciara Kelly's fear. I was unsure how I should respond to the fear. What could I possibly do to help her? Was not becoming involved in her life, if she really existed, like my involvement in the life of the Thos? I was still shaken by my interview with Dr. Freihaut. Perhaps I did belong in a mental institution. Not one where he was on the staff, however.

We drove south on the expressway, passing on the right the boundary of the royal borough of Bridgeport, with the impeccably neat old frame bungalows and streets so clean that it was, indeed, credible that housewives scrubbed the sidewalks every night. Then we slipped by the fringes of Englewood and Woodlawn, with their ravaged two-flats and apartment buildings, as devastated as any air-raid landscape.

We left the Dan Ryan, breaking, as it were, with the city of Chicago, passed briefly over Studs Lonigan's neighborhood and onto the battered Chicago Skyway, which carried us briefly through the aging steel mill community of Eddie Vrdolyak's tenth ward, and entered the Indiana Tollroad. The oil refinery haze of Hammond, the fires and chaste white smoke of Gary, the great black steel mills, seemed a surrealistic painting on the sky over Lake Michigan and under the implacable May sun, an intensely vital kaleidoscope of color, light, and energy.

Jean explained for me, with considerable enthusiasm, the arrangements at Grand Beach. The "Ryan compound" consisted of three homes: "Old House," where Ned Ryan and his second wife, Helen, and their four children—three teenagers and twelve-year-old Trish—("The last but hardly the least," Ned would say admiringly of that irresistible bundle of energy)—lived with implicit protection from the rest of the clan for their peace and privacy. Next door, in the middle of the compound, was the "New House," where Mary Kate and Joe Murphy presided over their own family and over the clan's swimming pool and recently added Nautilus equipment. Next to the Murphys' was "Cathy's Place," the new and ultra-modern home that Catherine Curran had designed and built after she'd sold her family home, some distance down the beach, to Eileen and Red Kane. The splendid garden that surrounded the Curran home was the locale for the family cookouts. Ned and Kate Collins Ryan's other children (Patrick "Packy" Ryan and Nancy Ryan O'Connor) were some distance from the central compound, for reasons of chance, personal finance, and a desire to be close but not too close to the rest of the family. We were to be assigned, for the weekend, to the Currans, because Catherine had cunningly designed her guest suites to provide a maximum of privacy. Father Blackie, who was passed from house to house, unprotestingly, would be staying with his father and stepmother.

"Nautilus?" I asked.

"Well, Nautilus and weights. Caitlin runs courses for everybody."

"Does she now?" That sounded like Ciara Kelly. "Are they obligatory?"

"The only rule the Ryan family has is that nobody has to do anything. All the women take the course, though, even Aunt Cathy and Aunt Eileen, but they do special exercises because they're pregnant."

"I've noticed. The doctors call them 'elderly' pregnancies."

Jean giggled. "They seem to love it. It's kind of nice for us younger women, because it shows us that pregnancy doesn't have to be terrible."

My little daughter thinking about pregnancy? How dare they!

"At any rate," I sighed with relief, "I won't have to do any iron-pumping."

"C'mon, Daddy, you must do a lot of exercise to keep in condition like you do. It's a good example for me."

"*You* pump iron?"

"Don't look so shocked. Everybody does nowadays. It's good for your build."

"Are you planning to be a linebacker?"

"I just want to preserve my figure."

"There's nothing wrong with your figure, at the risk of repeating myself."

"There's nothing wrong with it and I intend to keep it that way. C'mon, Daddy, you read all those books about evolution. So you know that we evolved as a creature that collected its food by hunting and gathering. So we had to be good at short-distance sprinting—not jogging, which is, like, totally bad for you. And by bending over hundreds of times every day and picking up roots and berries and plants, and then carrying them back home in big bundles. Well, we don't do that anymore, so we lift weights and work out on the Nautilus instead."

End of lecture for reactionary father who had yet to learn that neo-feminism meant "getting built"!

"Women exercising is probably the best thing that could possibly happen to the men of your generation!"

"You're an old male chauvinist, Daddy," Jeannie sputtered through her laughter as we slowed down for a tollgate. "Actually, girls my age are in much better condition than the boys. I suppose that's because the boys drink a lot more beer. Poor dears, being away from home at college is so much harder on them that I suppose they have to indulge in oral dependencies."

Not only a Cubs fan, not only an admirer of that "darling Wayne Gretzky" of the Edmonton Oilers, not only a devotee of "getting built," but the stranger who was my daughter could speak psychoanalytic jargon without dropping a syllable. What, I wondered, would she think of Dr. Otto Freihaut?

"Is Catherine Curran painting this summer," I inquired, "despite her pregnancy?"

"*Certainly*," I was informed in a tone that indicated I had asked a perfectly stupid question. Why should pregnancy interfere with painting? "Anyway," Jean said lightly, as she pushed the Benz up to the fifty-five-mile-an-hour speed limit, "I'm posing for her."

"Nude?" I sounded, even to myself, like a shocked and outraged Victorian grandfather.

"How else?" Jean snickered. "I'm not a sunburst. Are you shocked?"

"In theory, no." I rubbed the sweat from my forehead. "In practice, yes." I thought to myself that if Madonna were alive, this would never have happened. "It's up to you."

"Don't you want to know what it feels like?" She chuckled knowingly.

"Afraid to ask."

"Well . . . At first it was kind of scary and kind of silly.

Then, Aunt Catherine is so professional, it just seemed perfectly natural. You can be modest with your clothes off just as easily as you can be modest with your clothes on.''

"Uh huh."

"Then, when I saw the portrait—Aunt Catherine shows it to you and discusses it with you as she goes along because she says the model is kind of the co-painter—then it got kind of exciting. Not sexually exciting, particularly, but just exciting. I realized how beautiful the human body is, especially a woman's body, and how it was designed to be beautiful and how its beauty can be depicted in such a way that it's erotic, all right, but not obscene or exploitive. Aunt Catherine's work is feminist, just like the photographer Rena Small's. A non-exploitive painting of a woman is a judgment against all the exploitive pictures."

"Uncle Nick tells me" (was I really calling him "Uncle Nick"?) "that she was repainting *Playboy* centerfolds when she was a teenager."

"Aunt Catherine says," I was now being treated to the Aunt Catherine lecture, "that the difference between exploitation and non-exploitation is frequently a facial expression, the angle of an eye, or even a few strokes of the brush."

"A lot of people think that a portrait of a naked woman is a portrait of a naked woman."

"The kind of people who see no difference between Eve in Michelangelo's 'Creation,' " she slipped by a large semi-trailer whose driver greeted her with an admiring hoot of his horn, "and a *Playboy* centerfold: we shouldn't pay any attention to them. Any more than to that geek in the truck."

"Right!"

"And, as I look at the painting," she moved back into the right-hand lane, "I realize that I was designed by God to be attractive to men. . . ."

"She did a good job."

"So I figure that if I find a career at which I'm good and learn a few more things and acquire a touch of wisdom, *well*, I might just make some guy a pretty good woman."

"Indeed you will," I said fervently.

"You're putting me on." Her jaw tightened, hinting at anger.

"No way. Even as you are now, you'd make some guy a

hell of a fine woman. And if you work your way through that agenda, you'll be irresistible. . . . Make sure he's as strong as you are.''

"Yeah, I know. Still, I'm clinging by my fingertips, Daddy. Remember what a little bitch I was at Les Nomades? And I almost did it again, damn it.'' She pounded the leather-coated wheel of the Benz.

"When can I see the painting?''

"Oh, you can't see it!'' She was shocked, horrified, appalled. "You and Timmy and Uncle Nick can't see it until it hangs in the gallery. Then when everyone else looks at it, you can look at it too.''

The logic of that constraint escaped me, but I knew better than to argue. "Your mother's parents will be horrified.'' I tried to sound casual about it.

"Geeks.''

"Jean.'' I did my best to sound disapproving.

"Well, I don't care, Daddy, they are, like, *totally* geeks. I mean, when I was a little girl, they always brought me presents, designer dresses and things like that, and I thought they were the greatest grandparents in the world. Now I realize they were buying me off, just like they bought poor Mom off. I tried to be nice to them when they came in for the funeral because I felt so sorry for them. They were just horrid. Just horrid.''

"How so?''

"The big thing was that I had Ryan blood in me and that's dangerous blood. I had to be very careful or I'd end up like you—a warning every hour on the hour. I felt sorry for them because they were so old and so unhappy so I didn't argue. But never again.''

"You know, I suppose, about their legal petition?''

"Uncle Nick,'' she said decisively, "says we'll bury them.''

And that, I guess, settled that.

"You're a very tough young woman, Jeannie.'' I studied the sharp outline of her jaw. Was it Madonna's or Jocelyn's? "You must fit in with all the Ryan women at Grand Beach very nicely.''

"I'm a lot tougher than they are, Daddy. They're all really very vulnerable. Even Aunt Eileen, who pretends that she's such a fierce courtroom fighter, is a pussycat. I guess I've had to be tougher than they are. I'm not so sure it's a good thing, but that's the way it is.''

We then discussed her photography, and I was told to look under the jacket in the backseat for her portfolio. It was a collection of portraits of El Capitan in Yosemite National Park, imitating and sometimes making fun, with infrared lens, of the Master. The folio was kooky, comic, loving, and oddly moving.

Then we turned to her plan to work at the Board of Trade when she came back from Ireland. I discovered that her math scores were in the ninety-eighth percentile, that she received A's in computer science, and that she liked to make up her own computer games—all positive indicators for the new breed of commodities investors. I told her a little bit about the imaginary larceny I practiced on my PC XT and she listened with interest and appreciation. And a warning, "Don't ever tempt me with those games, Daddy. I might want to play them for real. Especially when I'm down on myself."

Clinging by her fingertips.

An altogether fascinating young stranger, this daughter of mine, part little girl and part perceptive, mature woman of the world. Catherine, I presumed, would capture all that in her painting. It would be a fascinating work of art.

How had Melissa Jean, now simply Jean, become who she was, more clear-headed and less self-deceptive than Madonna and more forceful and determined than I? Madonna had failed to turn her into a clone. I had been of no help to her at all. She had become who she was pretty much on her own. It would be nice to know her better.

That would not happen. She would go back to Stanford, stay in San Francisco, or move to Los Angeles or New York in pursuit of her photographic career, and perhaps never return to Chicago, or if, as seemed only a remote possibility, she should marry Tim Murphy, she would become thoroughly integrated into the Ryan clan and remain a stranger to me. Either way, this ride to Grand Beach was probably the only serious talk we would have for many years, indeed, perhaps the only serious talk ever. The moments were precious. I felt the sands of time slipping through my fingers as we turned off the expressway at the Michigan City exit.

"Hey, isn't this the wrong turn?"

"Nope. We have to stop at Karwick Plaza to do some shopping. I told Aunt Catherine she should stay home and rest."

"That's very thoughtful of you."

We crossed the thin line of scrub trees that separates the spur of the Great American Prairie reaching into northern Indiana from the several-mile-wide strip of forest and dune land that skirts Lake Michigan. The tide of duneland forest has ebbed and flowed as the character of the world's fourth largest lake, basically a melted glacier, has changed through geological eras. Soon we were on Highway 12, the sturdy concrete ribbon at the fringe of the most recent dune forest which, before the tollroads, linked the Indiana and Michigan dunes to the south side of Chicago. Even today occasional shops and houses and farms along U.S. 12 suggest the 1930s and the scraggly, deadening poverty of the Great Depression.

"Aunt Catherine is a totally remarkable woman. Awesome. She's so funny and so happy you can hardly believe that they did those terrible things to her in the concentration camp in South America."

"She was a very vivacious little kid." I was thinking of another woman who was tortured while trying to help the Third World. "We didn't realize it then, but she has enormous resiliency."

Someone else had enormous resiliency too.

Ciara Kelly. Ciara Kelly. Ciara Kelly.

The terror seeped momentarily back into my body and mind and then disappeared.

"Emily is a remarkably happy girl too."

Zap! You've been mousetrapped, Daddy.

"Emily!"

"Sure, the girl who goes to Stanford with me whose life you saved in Vietnam. I couldn't believe it at first." She laughed self-consciously. "It didn't sound like my daddy, but Emily was certain. Brendan Ryan from Chicago with a daughter named Melissa Jean."

"And that made you decide that it might just possibly be a good idea to reevaluate old Daddy?"

So that was the explanation for the transformation in Jeannie's attitude towards me.

"Were they really trying to drown her?" Jean ignored my comment.

"When I reached the edge of the pool, it was twilight. Darkness seems to come very quickly in those places. I saw one of the men pull a little bundle out of the pool. The bundle wailed, and I knew it was the Thos' baby. She was about the same size and age as you when I'd left you behind in America. Somehow you and Emily became confused with all the other babies that evil men were killing."

I was no longer on Highway 12 but back on a tributary of the Mekong River.

"Then you killed the man who was planning to drown her?"

"No, I killed the man who was holding a knife against her mother. Then the man who was threatening to drown Emily." No reason to mention the third victim.

"And the man dropped her in the water and you dived in and pulled her out?"

"Something like that. She was still breathing, thank God. The three of us redeployed ourselves—that's military terminology for running like hell—and just in time, too."

Jean nodded thoughtfully. "Emily doesn't remember any of it, but she's heard the story so often from her family that it's very vivid for her. . . . Did you love her mother, Daddy?"

"In a way."

Again Jean nodded sympathetically. "I could understand that. She's a wonderful woman."

A very clever young person, my daughter, Jean. Very clever indeed. She might make several fortunes speculating in commodities—and then taking photographs in the afternoon. Too bad it was fated that this might be the only long conversation we would ever have.

We pulled into the Karwick Shopping Plaza, a modest brick collection of supermarket and assorted smaller stores. It was only middle afternoon, but the parking lot was already half filled with cars, prudent shoppers like us getting a head start on the Friday night crunch at the beginning of the Memorial Day weekend.

A small shopping plaza in a resort area, on the eve of one of summer's two beginnings (the Fourth of July being the other) is the center of a festival of hope, like the entrance to a church before a wedding mass—cheerful conversations, happy chatter, enthusiastic greetings for old friends, eager anticipation of the summer festivities ahead.

I must state categorically that my psychic sensitivities, which had worked so furiously in the last several days, erratic as always, gave me no warning of the mortal danger in the Karwick Plaza. There were no threatening flashes of light, no feelings of danger or doom, no clairvoyant anticipation of the bloody drama that would be enacted in a little more than a quarter of an hour.

Jean took charge of the shopping expedition, just as her mother would, but gracing her domination of the event with polite requests rather than orders, and with laughter at my ineptitude rather than waspish criticism.

I was given charge of the cart, and Jean bounced around Jim's Fiesta Villa (as the rather attractive market was called) collecting materials for the hamburger and hot dog roast, which would be the Sunday night meal. "We have the big steak dinner tomorrow night after Mass, when everybody's in the mood for a huge meal to celebrate the beginning of summer. Then on Sunday night, we have a simple meal, a kind of a picnic, because folks will straggle in at different times. Monday night we'll have sandwiches and potato salad and ice cream for those who are going to stay around till Tuesday morning. Like us."

"I didn't know we were going to stay until Tuesday morning."

"Well, Daddy dear," she poked my chest playfully, "now you do!"

Four nights of Ryan enthusiasm. I was not up to it.

"What if it rains?"

"Aunt Mary Kate says that the only way to react to rain at a summer resort is to ignore it, and that anyway it's wish fulfillment to think that summer begins the last weekend in May."

Hope and wish fulfillment are almost the same thing, aren't they?

"I think her psychiatric colleagues would call that denial."

"That's what *she* calls it, and she's arguing with Uncle Joe, poor dear man.."

I was sent back to the mustard shelves twice before I produced the correct brand.

"Everybody, except nerds, uses Grey Poupon mustard, especially if they drive Mercedes cars."

She had to explain to me that it was a joke about a TV advertisement.

The shopping cart, jammed with condiments, charcoal, soft drinks, and enough hamburger meat to have required several steers, was pushed to what seemed to me to be a somewhat longer checkout lane than the others. I shared that observation with Jean.

"Sure it is, but I want to talk to Marilyn about her golf game. She's the captain of the golf team at Marquette High School. The *men's* golf team."

Marilyn and Jean chatted happily about golf. Did my daughter play golf? I did not know. I reached for my checkbook. "I hope they'll take a check."

"They will, but not your check." She tilted her nose into the air like a mock archduchess. "My treat."

She filled the check out with a flourish, presented it to Marilyn, and promised that she would see her at the dance later in the evening.

"First that I've heard of a dance."

We unloaded the cart into the backseat of the Benz, since the trunk was filled with my small duffel bag and three large garment bags belonging to Jean, who apparently was bringing enough clothes for several summers.

A battered Saab, of dubious vintage, pulled up next to us with a noisy blast of the horn and a rather vulgar squealing of tires.

"Hi, Uncle Brendan," said Caitlin Murphy, her eyes shining wickedly. "Welcome to Grand Beach!"

Caitlin emerged from the car and kissed me vigorously. Like Jean, she was wearing a miniskirt, white, with a broad red belt and a short-sleeved white blouse. Caitlin had the aloof, long-haired blonde beauty of a professional model, the self-possessed grace and balance of an athlete, and the mobile but always beautiful face of a queen of clowns. It was an understatement to call her stunning. Caitlin would bring the Indianapolis 500 to a dead halt!

She was accompanied by a little slip of a girl dressed in a seersucker blue summer uniform of the United States Coast Guard. As best I could remember the navy insignia, she was a petty officer/3d class—a corporal. She looked like she was perhaps thirteen years old.

"This is Petey's Cindasoo," Caitlin announced, rolling her wonderful blue eyes. "She's in the Yewnited States Coast Guard."

"Right proud t'make ya quaintence." Cindasoo extended a tiny, but firm hand.

"She talks real funny," Caitlin said in a noisy stage whisper. "Don't call her a hillbilly or a redneck. Them's ethnic slurs. She's an Appalachian—A-p-p-a-l-a-c-h-i-a-n—Uncle Brendan."

"I do know how to spell Appalachian, young woman," I said. And turning for a closer look at Cindasoo, "Watch out for the Chicago Irish, Cindasoo. They're strange folk."

"Ah'm Irish, too, Mistah Ryan." A glint in her brown eyes suggested Cindasoo could take care of herself. "Mah folks came over after the battle of Culloden Moor, same as the folks of that fella down in 'Ssippi who wrote all them books."

"Faulkner?"

"Yassah, old Billie Faulkner."

"And then moved out west?"

"Yassah. Beat Dan'l Boone by twenty years. Place called Stinkin Creek. Nobody never done left since. Ah joined the Yewnited States Coast Guard to see the world."

Cindasoo was a forest creature, a pretty wraith gliding noiselessly through the valleys and the hollows of the Appalachians. She was also a pixie, her thick auburn hair in a pixie cut, her solemn face barely hiding pixie laughter, and her lovely pixie body teasing you with a tiny shoulder movement. No wonder she and Caitlin seemed to be buddies. Pete Murphy had himself a handful.

"Is Michigan City, Indiana, the world?"

"Beats Stinkin Creek," she said solemnly. "Not by much though."

I suspected that her Appalachian dialect was like Ciara

Kelly's Irish brogue, a wild card to be played when and as desired.

Ciara Kelly. Ciara Kelly.

"I hear you're engaged, Caitlin." I turned to the blonde Celtic goddess, who was jiggling coins in the pocket of her miniskirt. "Congratulations."

"Not to say engaged, exactly." She rolled her eyes again. Ciara Kelly. Ciara Kelly.

"Practically engaged," Jean corrected me.

"Hasn't got him hog-tied yet," Cindasoo observed.

"The man," Caitlin said demurely, "is taking his time. He's entitled to that for maybe another week or so."

"He really is a farmer?"

"Yep." Caitlin tried to look woebegone, a virtually impossible task. "Grandfather says we're going from bog to bog in five generations."

"He teaches at Valparaiso Law School too," Jean insisted.

As we were chatting in lighthearted anticipation of the fun of a Memorial Day weekend at the Ryan compound, I noted a black car, an old Ford, I thought, which had halted between the lanes of parked cars, just a few yards away. I heard the click of an opening door, rather than saw it, was aware before I heard a sound, of a moving burst of light. Caitlin. . . .

"Brendan Ryan! Brendan Ryan!"

Not exactly a familiar voice, but demanding, surely someone I knew. I turned in the direction of the voice.

Once again, John Brodie's slow motion, the first time since the Viet Cong opened up with their automatic weapons upriver from the Tho house. The man was wearing a baseball cap, white Windbreaker, white sweatshirt and slacks, and a handkerchief with holes cut for eyes, hanging down from the cap over his face. As I watched, frames slowly unrolling one after the other, he reached under his Windbreaker and leisurely removed a small-caliber pistol, almost a toy. The .22, favorite weapon these days of outfit hit men. Cesare Malocha.

With casual patience and care, it seemed, as the frames moved slowly before my eyes, he aimed the pistol at my head. Like John Brodie "checking off" a receiver, I ducked at the moment I saw his finger tighten on the trigger. Unperturbed, he adjusted his aim and squeezed again.

This is the end of my life, I thought calmly, waiting patiently for the slow movement of the bullet from the muzzle of his gun into my head. The white burst that had swept by me was suddenly next to him. Caitlin, the flat edge of her hand slicing down on his shooting arm, hitting it just as he squeezed the trigger.

The bullet whipped by my head like an angry mosquito. An anguished cry of pain from the gunman, the black car behind him began to move. Another slash of Caitlin's hand and the gunman toppled in agony on the asphalt. My dormant psychic sensitivity suddenly began to work. I knew who the driver of the car was. I comprehended what I must do to protect Jean and myself and to exorcise the demon of Sam Norton. The black Ford slipped down the lane between the two rows of parked cars. I heard screams of fright all around, including those of two kids who, paralyzed by the sight of the gun, were in the path of the moving Ford and barely escaped it. I ran after the car, caught it before it reached the end of the lane, and yanked open the door on the driver's side. The person at the wheel was also wearing the absurd handkerchief mask. I grabbed one arm and pulled the driver away from the wheel and out of the car, a short, pudgy, squirming figure. We both fell to the asphalt and the car careened past a couple of shopping carts and smashed into a post in front of the supermarket. The driver squirmed out of my grasp, jumped up and swung an arm towards me. Only then did I realize that the right hand of the driver had grabbed a huge carving knife as I was pulling my enemy out of the car and the knife was arching toward me in implacable slow motion.

Again, a heavenly angel materializing from nowhere, the white burst of Caitlin Murphy appeared next to me. She slammed the edge of her right hand into the driver's neck. The knife spun out of my attacker's hand and before Caitlin could strike again, the driver collapsed against the rear of a BMW and toppled to the ground, knocking off both hat and mask in the fall.

I did not even have to see the twisted angry hateful face to know that it was Patsy Sullivan.

I turned around to see what had happened to Crazy Mal, a

few yards behind us. He was struggling to stand up, his right arm limp, his left hand groping under his Windbreaker.

Cindasoo had captured his pistol and, squatting in the approved pistol-fire position, was holding it extended in front of her with both hands. "Stay war you are, varmint, or I'll put a bullet plumb through your head."

She seemed a ridiculous, pathetic little figure in a make-believe sailor suit, a child with a toy gun acting the part of Calamity Jane in a school play. Cesare Malocha must have thought that she was ridiculous. He jerked his second pistol from under his Windbreaker and fumbled with his left hand as he tried to aim the gun at her.

So Cindasoo did exactly what she promised: she shot him right between his eyes.

four
THE QUEST FOR CIARA KELLY

24

Malocha lay sprawled on the pavement, a neat hole drilled in his forehead. Cindasoo was babbling incoherently. Caitlin was muttering over and over to herself words that I could not understand. Later I decided that it must be the Act of Contrition, possibly in a post-conciliar form with which I was not familiar. The crowd that had gathered was mumbling and rumbling, dangerously close to panic of its own.

I took charge of the melee with the same detached calm that I had displayed during the Viet Cong attack eighteen years before.

"Please stand back everyone, don't touch," I ordered. "Don't touch the knife or the guns or the bodies. The police will be here shortly. The man is dead. The woman is still alive."

Dutifully the crowd fell back, forming a tight circle fifteen or twenty yards from the two prone bodies. Jean was sobbing hysterically against my chest, and Caitlin, pale but dry-eyed and quiet, was consoling Cindasoo, whose shapely little body heaved with anguished vomiting.

"I'll stay with her for a few minutes, Caitlin," I whispered. "Slip over to the public phone and call your parents and the police. . . . And Caitlin," the wonderful violet eyes now devoid of their usual vitality swept across my face, "thanks a lot."

"Anytime, Uncle Brendan." A slight hint of a smile as she ran, or perhaps I should say danced, through the crowd towards the telephone. It must have been only a few minutes though it seemed like hours before the various relief expeditions arrived. God knows my own little Fort Zinderneuf needed relief. I could do nothing to revive Patsy or quiet Jean or calm the desperately sick Cindasoo, although the latter two clung to me as though I were a salvific angel.

The Coast Guard arrived first: a young, slim, black ensign with a Coast Guard Academy ring and three ratings, all very young, two men and one woman. The convulsive retching that was shaking Cindasoo's body diminished as the ensign put his arm around her and the woman rating fiercely gripped her hand. "Ah shot me lots of varmints down by the crick," Cindasoo sobbed. "Never killed me a human before. I shot him daid as four o'clock."

I made a mental note to ask later what that phrase meant. Everyone was still babbling.

Then the Ryans arrived in selective but not massive force, in an aged dark blue Volvo station wagon. How do they assemble the proper team in such a short period of time?—Ned Ryan, the white-haired patriarch and naval hero, a political lawyer with ice-blue eyes and a strong, soft voice that commanded attention; Mary Kate Murphy, a handsome, statuesque psychiatrist with gold and silver hair and enough nerve for a regiment; Mike Casey, cop and lawyer; and a red-bearded, freckled young giant, who needed only a pike in his massive arms to be an ancient Celtic pirate.

Then, last of all, the police, Indiana State and Michigan City police, lights flashing, sirens chirping. Five cars and a couple of vans roared into the shopping plaza parking lot, scattering temporarily a crowd of goggle-eyed bystanders who had been staring in grim fascination at the lifeless remains of Cesare Malocha and the pathetic little form of Patsy Sullivan.

"The damned fools could kill someone," Mike Casey murmured through clenched teeth.

At first the police characteristically made things worse instead of better, shouting orders, pushing people about, cursing vigorously. They turned my orderly crowd back into a melee, threatened to arrest almost everyone, and fought among themselves. A lieutenant of the Michigan City police and a sergeant of the Indiana State police were more interested in squabbling with each other over jurisdiction than determining what crimes had been committed. A fat, officious Michigan City sergeant, apparently informed by someone in the crowd that Cindasoo had shot the dead man, approached the small knot of Coast Guard persons and proclaimed to the accompaniment of florid obscenities that they were going to haul her little ass into jail on a murder charge. The black ensign twisted the cop's arm behind his back and forced him to his knees, as quick as an eye could blink. "Over the dead bodies of the United States Coast Guard, you fat, stupid son-of-a-bitch."

Clearly Cindasoo was the pet of the Michigan City station.

"Let 'im up son," Ned Ryan said quietly, somehow managing to sound like a retired admiral. "He'll apologize later, when the commandant gives Cindasoo a medal for bravery."

"Who the fuck is this dead motherfucker?" demanded the Michigan City lieutenant, pulling the bloody mask off Cesare Malocha's face.

"I wouldn't touch him, Lieutenant." Mike Casey moved into the confusion. "Wait till your technical people come and finish their work. His name is Cesare 'Crazy Mal' Malocha. He's a fourth-rate hit man on the fringes of the Chicago mob. He attempted to kill Mr. Ryan," he nodded his head toward me, "and his daughter. That woman," he pointed at Patsy, who was slowly reviving in response to Mary Kate Murphy's ministrations, "was driving the automobile, the black one piled up against the supermarket. Ms. Murphy, the girl in the white miniskirt, disarmed him. When he tried to draw another weapon, Petty Officer/3d Class McLeod shot him with his own gun."

McLeod? That seemed a fitting surname for Cindasoo.

"No shit!" the cop said in astonishment. "Hey, who the hell are you?"

"Casey. I used to be with the Chicago Police Department."

"*Mike* Casey?" The cop was appropriately awed.

Mike replied with a terse nod of his head.

For all practical purposes, he then took charge of the investigation. Patsy, who was now babbling hysterically, was placed in the van and, with Mary Kate in attendance, driven to St. Anthony's Hospital in Michigan City. The crowd was dispersed. A yellow rubber tarpaulin was placed temporarily over the body of the unfortunate Cesare Malocha. I was interviewed briefly by a very nervous patrol officer. Caitlin, who'd been holding hands with her red-bearded giant, Jean, and Cindasoo were excused to be interviewed later.

"It might be a good idea to impound and seal that vehicle," Mike said to the lieutenant. "Mal Malocha has been questioned about a double murder in Chicago, and I wouldn't be surprised if you found some materials related to that crime in the trunk. Lieutenant," Mike permitted himself a thin smile, "Sam Norton of Chicago Homicide would be very interested in anything you find."

Cindasoo and her Coast Guard escort, still fiercely protective enough, I thought, to fend off the entire Russian army, were entering the nondescript blue U.S. government car in which they'd come. I hurried over to them.

"Petty Officer/3d Class McLeod?" I tried to sound like the officer I had once been. "Can I say I reckon that I'm right grateful to you?"

A wan smile creased her face, which was still as white as a summer dress uniform. "Yassuh, I'm proud I could be of assistance. We Coast Guard persons are taught to be *semper paratus*, suh. That means always ready."

Incredulous laughter from her colleagues.

"*Semper parata*," I corrected her, "if the ready Coast Guard person is a woman person."

"Tell her, sir," said the ensign, "that she's not ready to go on duty tonight."

"Ensign, I am not Petty Officer/3d Class Cindasoo McLeod's commanding officer, for which I'm deeply grateful. As it is, I wouldn't try to tell her anything. She's Irish, you know."

"I'm goin on dudda," Cindasoo said flatly, in the midst of the laughter.

"I guess that settles that."

The ensign touched his forehead in a brief salute and drove off. Cindasoo, at any rate, was in very safe hands.

"Four o'clock means 4:00 A.M., Uncle Brendan." Caitlin was standing next to me, her giant in tow. "Incidentally, this is Kevin Maher. The name begins with an 'M' just like Murphy, so that's convenient, isn't it?" The red-faced barbarian blushed even more vividly. "Anyway, four o'clock in the morning is either the deadest time of the day or the time when the dead are most likely to wander, so, in Appalachian English, to kill someone like four o'clock means to kill them real dead. I thought you might want to know."

Then, and only then, as I watched the blue Coast Guard car being waved out of the parking lot and saw the first faint touches of color returning to Caitlin's magnificent face and noted the quiet and steady breathing of my daughter, who was still hanging on to me for dear life, did I comprehend fully that these two young women had certainly saved my life and probably Jean's too. Spontaneously, reflexively, they'd intervened and become involved, much the way I had in the Mekong River Valley but with even less time to think about what they were doing than I'd had. They could have easily and safely stayed on the banks and watched the river rush by. Instead, they'd plunged into the icy water, snatched Jean and me back to safety, and had terrible images burned into their memories for the rest of their lives. Would they ever wonder if they'd done the right thing?

Those two? Don't be absurd. Some kinds of generosity or courage, blessedly, never question themselves.

"I am happy to meet you, Mr. Maher." My voice broke. "I'm told you teach tax law, which happens to be my specialty." I couldn't possibly be crying. "I hope you don't mind if I hug your wonderful girlfriend. She just saved my life."

"Be my guest." The red-haired giant grinned.

So Caitlin Murphy and Jean and I wept and hugged one another in the Karwick Shopping Plaza, and I grieved, paradoxically and characteristically enough, not for what had been lost that day, but for what might still be lost in my life.

25

The Currans and I sat in reflective silence, like monks after vespers have been chanted, on the long balcony around the second floor of their house, watching the rising moon paint the waters of Lake Michigan a creamy white. "Cathy's place" was an ingenious blend of New England and prairie, of Cape Cod clapboard and Frank Lloyd Wright. Nicole, a vivacious clone of her mother, and Jackie, the family mystic, had both gone to bed, not without considerable protest. Her eyes still red, and with several assurances from me that I did not mind, Jean permitted Tim Murphy to drag her off to the young people's dance at the community center. Tim and his older brother Pete had been racing their Hobie Cat on the lake at the time of the "shoot-out at the Karwick Corral" (as it was now being called). They were experiencing powerful guilt feelings because they had not been present when their womenfolk needed them. Pete had already departed for the U.S.C.G. station in Michigan City to "kind of wait around" for Cindasoo. The whole Ryan compound seemed momentarily peaceful, a rare enough situation, I would learn in the course of the long weekend.

Mary Kate Murphy, in blouse and slacks, walked quietly onto the porch. "Mind if I sit here for a while?"

Eileen had told me once that she and her Junoesque sister had had a "classic sibling rivalry for all our lives." Her older sister was, according to my colleague, the "goddamn matriarch of the clan." She was entitled to it, Eileen supposed, by reasons of age and wisdom and psychiatric training. "The bitch is almost always right. For twenty years she's told me how to deal with Red, and finally, without much choice, I did what she suggested and I've never been so happy." A crooked grin. "Wouldn't that frost you?"

Conscious of her power, Mary Kate played the role of the low-key, laid-back precinct captain, a pose no more effectively deceptive than her brother's Father Brown mask.

"Patsy?" I asked anxiously.

"Acute, manic-depressive psychosis," she replied listlessly. "A very, very sick woman. The mania has peaked, and she's about to go into a very deep depression." Mary Kate shrugged. "I'm not sure she'll ever come out of it. If she does . . . Well, it would be a long time before that happens. Her husband has terminal cancer, you know."

"Oh, my God!" Catherine said softly.

"I don't suppose she'll ever stand trial," Nick said.

"Despite the policewoman in her hospital room taking notes, most of which probably wouldn't be admissible as evidence anyhow, I can't imagine a court ordering a trial. A preliminary psychiatric hearing ought to settle it. Will it be in La Porte or Cook County, Nick?"

"It may be one of the rare cases where both counties want the other to assume jurisdiction. All that could be charged today is attempted murder. Over in Chicago there would be a murder-one charge. I imagine her family lawyers, whoever they are, would rather a Cook County court order a psychiatric institution for her than an Indiana court."

"How long does King have?" I asked.

"A few months at the most. He's over there now, being very sweet and kind to her. A little late, if you ask me." Mary Kate stood up, hands in the pockets of her tailored jeans. "One way or another, it's all over for the two of them."

"And the kids?" I asked.

"They'll be parceled out among grandparents and in-laws, I suppose." Mary Kate shrugged glumly. "Some of them will make it, Brendan, and some of them won't, and there's not a damned thing that any of us can do about it."

We all stared quietly at the shimmering lake; for all practical purposes I was the only survivor from my grammar school and teenage group.

"Caitlin was wonderful." I tried to change the subject.

"That child will be the death of me," her mother observed proudly. "And she'll be the death of that red-bearded pirate if he doesn't work up enough nerve to give her a ring in the next couple of weeks. Isn't it ironic, Brendan? For twenty-five years of marriage I've called my poor Joe 'the pirate,' and he really doesn't look like a pirate at all, not even when he wears a beard. So my firstborn child falls in love with someone who really does look like a pirate. Joe loves it, the so-and-so. He claims it proves that there really are Jungian archetypes."

"And you say all it proves is an Electra complex." Catherine laughed.

We stared quietly at the somber waters, wishing perhaps that the tragedies of the day could be blotted out and knowing that they would always be part of our memories. We would go ahead with the festivities of the weekend, for the children and for ourselves, too, pretending that the world was normal again.

"You're staying till Tuesday morning?" Mary Kate asked. "For all the festivities down to the bitter end?"

"It has been decreed by the women in the Ryan family that that's what I must do, so that's what I will do."

We all laughed then, and continued to pretend that the tragedies of the day were wiped off the agenda. Joe Murphy appeared with martini glasses for himself and his wife, Catherine found some Jameson's for Nick and me, and a glass of orange juice for herself, and we toasted the moon and the beginning of summer.

"Caitlin says you're a modern Finn MacCool, Brendan." Joe Murphy peered at me with his kindly blue eyes. "A modern Celtic folk hero."

"I smell a Jungian lecture," his wife scoffed, and at the same time laid a hand on the thigh of his white jeans. "Take notes for the test, Brendan."

Joe was a slender man with white hair, white beard, a youthful face, and the manner and appearance of a very holy Trappist abbot.

According to family legend, he and Mary Kate Ryan began to fight the first day of her clerkship at Little Company of Mary's psych unit, in which Joe was the senior resident. They contended day and night for two months. Finally, it is said, on the last day, he said something unguarded and very un-Jungian like "It would take a lifetime in bed with you, Miss Ryan, to begin to reduce the sexual tension you generate."

And Mary Kate had replied simply, "All right."

"Was that an acceptance?" he is reputed to have asked.

"Was that a proposal?"

"I can't believe my good fortune."

Mary Kate claims that her answer was the wisest sentence she ever spoke: "I'm the lucky one."

Sometimes she adds, amid much laughter, "Fortunately the tension has not yet been reduced." So the battle, finding its origins in deep and powerful love, was not a new one.

"Well, since no one else will ask," Mary Kate continued on the porch at Grand Beach, "I'll be straight person again, Dr. Murphy. Who is Finn MacCool?"

"Finn MacCool, Dr. Murphy, was an Irish Ulysses, Agamemnon, Achilles, and Aeneas all rolled into one, with a bit of Childe Harold and Robin of Locksley thrown in. He led a group of fellow berserkers called Fenians, and they went around bashing heads of the bad guys, of whom there were more than a plentiful supply. Like all mythological heroes, he incarnates a certain dimension of the culture that creates him, in this case the wandering, invulnerable, generous, slightly demented warrior, an Irish version perhaps of a Samurai in a Kurosawa movie. Mifune perhaps."

"Brenny a Samurai?" Cathy Curran, again the imp girl of her youth, giggled. "With a broadsword or a pike like the one Mary Kate keeps in her living room?"

"The point my school would make is that your man Finn MacCool represents a model that is present deep down in the soul of most Irish males. We fantasize about playing the role. Occasionally we're given a chance, and we either blow it or don't."

"I think you might make a good Finn MacCool," Mary Kate admitted. "But you'd really have to be pushed. Same for Brenny. Pushed real hard."

"I can't imagine it," I insisted, not wanting to think of my Finn-like escapades in Vietnam.

"Did Finn have a breast fixation?" Nick Curran asked.

"He was an Irish male, wasn't he?" Mary Kate tilted the martini pitcher in my direction, then, remembering my form of weakness for the creature, replaced the pitcher on the table and lifted the bottle of Jameson's.

I begged off a second drink. "I've had a tiring day." Everyone seemed to think it was a remarkably funny comment.

"He really is Finn MacCool," Cathy commented as I slipped away. "I think he could be very dangerous."

I thought perhaps I should be offended.

The weather the next morning was perfect for a holiday weekend, warm and clear. Only an occasional fluffy cloud trailed its shadow across the calm green waters of the lake, drawing on it a fluid, inky design. A light breeze carried the Hobie Cats and the windsurfers (most of them in wet suits, because the temperature in the lake was still in the fifties) across the waters at moderate speeds. The TV minicams, probing for news about the shootout at Karwick, were kept at bay by a combination of Mike Casey's "No comment" (with a special smile reserved for mention of Sam Norton) and a bland refusal of wandering Grand Beach urchins to admit to the press that anyone named Ryan lived in the community. The swimming pool and sun deck at the Murphy House swarmed with children and adults. Uncle Brendan was very much in demand, doubtless as a result of some decision made by the collective Ryan consciousness.

"Would you like some lemonade, Uncle Brendan?"

"Come on out on the Cat, Uncle Brendan!"

"Would you put suntan oil on my back, please, Uncle Brendan?"

"Would you like a hamburger and a Coke, Uncle Brendan?"

"Please come play volleyball with us on the beach, Uncle Brendan."

"Would you tie my straps please, Uncle Brendan?"

"Come on in the pool and swim, Uncle Brendan."

"Uncle Brendan, will you come with Jean and me to water-ski at Pine Lake?"

"Want to play tennis, Uncle Brendan?"

Uncle Brendan knew he was a victim of a conspiracy but went along willingly. Why not cram into one weekend all the neglected weekends of the past?

So Uncle Brendan did go out on the Hobie Cat and did play tennis and did swim forty lengths in the pool and did eat several hamburgers and did indeed go with his daughter and his "nephew" Tim to Pine Lake, a small lake in La Porte, fifteen miles inland from Lake Michigan, which my mother would have called a "proper" Midwestern lake because it looked like it had been designed for a picture postcard or maybe as part of a set for a 1930s romantic film—weeping willow trees, tiny piers, and floating rafts in front of freshly painted cottages, roadhouses that once must have been speakeasies across the highway.

The Ryan clan kept a boat (with a 155 horsepower engine) in a marina on Pine Lake so that its water-ski enthusiasts would not be dependent on the vagaries of Lake Michigan. I had never water-skied before and was constrained to accompany Jean and Tim on the grounds that they needed a third person to be the "observer" on the boat. I was not, however, completely surprised when my daughter insisted, after she and Tim had sped skillfully (on one ski, needless to say) on the glass-smooth waters of Pine Lake, that I "totally" had to try it. I was even more astonished than she was that I got up the first try and even stayed up for a commendable period of time. Moreover, having lost all my common sense and against Jean's anxious protests that I didn't want to wear myself out, I tried it a second time and performed even more acceptably.

"Gosh, Uncle Brendan," Tim Murphy said as I climbed into the boat and tried to pretend that I was not utterly exhausted, "you're real good for a beginner. You ought to come up here every weekend during the summer. With a little practice, you'd be better than Jeannie."

"And you could keep Tim company while I'm in Ireland," said Jeannie, devastating in the most minimal of string bikinis, as she threw a towel at me. "Don't catch cold now."

"Growl." Tim revved up the boat. "The lakes are too cold to water-ski in Ireland."

Jean made an impatient face. "I'm going, Timmy, and that's final."

The slim young man shrugged. "I still think that if I asked my mother, she'd let me go with you."

"No way!" Jean exclaimed, with a touch of anger. "Absolutely no way."

"That's what I figured," Tim sighed, not altogether seriously, and steered the boat toward the narrow slip in the miniature marina at the edge of a busy two-lane highway.

So, a minor lovers' quarrel. Jean wanted to go to Ireland without the encumbrance of a knight in armor trudging along after her. She also wanted, I suspected, some freedom from Tim's obvious devotion. Tim, for his part, was being good-natured about the separation, partly because it was his character to be good-natured and partly because, like the rest of the Ryan family, he was one very clever Mick. If they had a fight over it, it would be my daughter's doing—and probably to soothe a guilty conscience about leaving him.

I prudently stayed out of the discussion and told myself that I might be much happier today if I'd had more such lovers' tiffs when I was their age.

We returned to the Ryan compound, our summer resort Camelot. Mass was scheduled for 5:30. I told my daughter and her beau that if I were to survive the hamburger roast, over which Jean was to preside, I'd better take a half-hour nap.

"A half hour?" Jean scoffed. "I'll wake you at five-fifteen. Monsignor Blackie is saying Mass at our house—Aunt Catherine and Uncle Nick's—and you'll need every minute of sleep you can get." She shook her head as one who simply cannot understand the follies of the old. "Old daddies shouldn't try to act like they're teenagers."

As I climbed the staircase from the first level to the second level—in Catherine Collins Curran's house there were levels, not floors—I reflected on how hungrily Tim Murphy's eyes devoured Jean as she lifted her arms to pull on a sweatshirt on the marina pier, a delicious offering of young womanly perfection, and I envied Tim his youth. If not Jeannie, then some other appealing and satisfying young woman, about whom he had a choice, unlike me.

I was now prepared to admit to myself that I had chosen Madonna only in the negative sense: I had not said "no" to everyone else's foregone conclusion. My fault, not theirs, but I wished I'd had it to do over again.

I did have it to do over again. Maybe. Now, however, it was all my choice. Nobody was constraining me to pursue Ciara Kelly, and she was, was she not, an improbable will-of-the-wisp?

Madonna was waiting for me again in my room, dressed this time in blue. Blessed Mother blue?

I did not believe in her, I did not want to believe in her, I willed her out of my glorious summer weekend. She was dead, as Ron was dead, as King would soon be dead, and as Patsy would be better off dead. Yet she did not disappear and did not even seem aware of my displeasure. The interlude was the same as the last one, only more intense, a kind of bittersweet sorrow, a pained nostalgia mixed with a minute quantity of hope, like a touch of triple sec in a margarita. I had no choice but to give myself over to the emotions that seemed to radiate from her and fill the room.

What was the nature of the greater intensity? I cannot say. Emotions in both interludes were unspecific, generalized, almost cosmic. Yet, when she finally was there no more and the only blue was that of Lake Michigan (also Blessed Mother blue?), I sensed that there was something she wanted me to do or that I was supposed to do or that I should do. It would go far beyond the content of the interlude to say that the woman I pictured or encountered—choose your own verb—in the Currans' guest room was urging me to seek Ciara. Yet she *was* urging me to do *something* which I did not want to do.

I glanced at my watch. Twenty-five minutes, not exactly a transient experience. A nap was now out of the question.

I found the Jameson's bottle in the Currans' liquor cabinet, poured myself what might conservatively be called a double, and found myself a deck chair on the lawn. The drink might substitute for a nap.

Ciara Kelly. Ciara Kelly. Ciara Kelly.

"Hi, Uncle Brendan." Jackie Curran, actually John Blackwood Curran, a wide-eyed, thoughtful, towheaded five-year-old. "Whatcha doing?"

"I wore myself out water-skiing with Jeannie and Tim and I'm trying to rest before Mass."

"O-h-h-h." An unfathomable mystery satisfactorily explained.

"Did you have a good time today?"

"Uh huh. It's going to rain tomorrow."

How did he know? Better not ask.

I swallowed some more Jameson's, savoring every drop.

"Uncle Brendan?"

"Yes, Jackie."

"Did that lady with the blonde hair who was looking for you find you?"

I swallowed a very large gulp of Jameson's. "The one with the blue dress?"

"Uh huh. She was real pretty."

"Yes, Jackie; she found me."

Even the unperturbable Monsignor Blackie Ryan expressed mild surprise at that part of my story. He quickly recovered. "If there is such a thing as ESP, and there's every reason to believe there is, and if my namesake has some psychic sensitivities, which wouldn't surprise me in the least, then it would not seem at all improbable that some of the energies might leap from your neo-Neanderthal vestigia to his."

Perfectly natural explanation.

"Do you want a perfectly natural explanation?"

"Not I."

Blackie was attempting to polish his sunglasses with the tail of his sports shirt (white with a green leprechaun at the pocket). "To me the theme of the message is more important than a metaphysical explanation. I was simply offering you a natural explanation if you wanted one. Do you?"

"I don't know," I said honestly.

Jean found me sitting on the lawn and reproved me for drinking when I needed a nap. I was dispatched to my room to shower and prepare for Mass.

The Ryan clan and assorted neighbors and friends assembled in Catherine's vast "living area level" for the Eucharist. Cardinal Sean Cronin himself was present, accompanied by his sister-in-law Senator Nora Cronin and her second husband, the sportscaster Bob Hurley, her youngest daughter, Noreen, and Noreen's fiancé, Steve McLean (whose mother, Maria Donlon, had recently become the first woman bank president in the Loop); the cardinal, in gray slacks and a blue sweater, shook my hand vigorously.

"You come to Blackie's Mass too?" I asked.

The hoods retracted briefly from Sean Cronin's wild brown eyes. "I have to preach in the cathedral at noon tomorrow. I thought I'd steal some of his ideas. Watch him. He'll putter around up there like a young priest who's only said Mass a couple of times, or an old priest who no longer remembers the ceremonies.''

It was a perfect description of Blackie Ryan's apparent surprise at the sight of the altar, the vestments, and the congregation. There was nothing lacking in his sermon, however.
. The gospel of the sixth Sunday after Easter depicted Jesus in his Last Supper discourse to his apostles, promising to send them the Paraclete. Blackie shuffled sermon themes like a Mississippi riverboat gambler would shuffle a deck of cards.

''The holy spirit, the Paraclete, God's spirit of variety and diversity, a kind of cosmic Tinker Bell, who flits about the universe bringing splendid new things into existence, is the spirit of courage, the spirit who gave the apostles the fortitude they needed to go forth to preach Jesus to a hostile world. Courage is also the virtue that we honor on this weekend, devoted to those who died fighting for our country in all its wars, but especially the Civil War, which was fought for many reasons but not the least among them the conviction that a nation could not survive half slave and half free. As we reconsider those wars today, it may seem to us that often, if not always, they were foolish and unnecessary, but that does not detract from the courage or the generosity of the men who fought in them, nor from the debt we owe them for their courage and generosity.

''Courage is nothing more than generosity in time of crisis and risk. It is nothing more than powerful hope translated into action when others desperately need our help. We have seen recently a remarkable display of courage from some of our young people. . . .''

One could hear a pin drop in the ''living area level.'' A few younger adolescents stole nervous, admiring glances at Caitlin and Cindasoo, the latter looking even more waiflike in Coast Guard fatigues. . . . ''We admire their bravery, but none of us is surprised because we know them both to be generous young women, generous in countless little ways to all of us every day, young women of strong and powerful hope, young women who, we might safely suggest, are in league with, indeed in conspiracy with, the Paraclete. The events in the Karwick Plaza merely demonstrate in a highly spectacular fashion patterns of generosity that are typical of their daily lives. And if, as seems unlikely, praise for their bravery the other day should cause them to suspend their generosity and their hopefulness on the grounds that, well, 'they've already done enough,' one can be certain that the good Paraclete will light a fire under them.

"Their generosity is only secondarily something for us to admire. It is primarily for us to imitate. Life is an exploration of hope, an enterprise of risk taking, a journey of ever-renewed challenge. Generosity, hopefulness, courage are not options on such a pilgrimage. If we wish to be able to respond spontaneously and heedlessly in moments of crisis, as did our two rather interestingly matched young women, then we, too, must develop habits of generosity in our daily lives. We must take out the garbage when we're asked, put gasoline in the car when we're asked, clear off the table when we're asked, help drag the Hobie Cat up on the beach when we're asked, pile up the dishes in the dishwasher when we're asked, and run to the store to buy milk, bread, and charcoal lighter when we're asked. It is of these small heroisms, and sometimes at the moment they don't seem very small, of which great human courage is created."

And as for you, Brendan Ryan, are you ready to be as generous as Caitlin and Cindasoo?

No way. Not yet, anyhow.

When Blackie had finished, the cardinal, who was standing behind me, whispered in my ear, "Well, that's my sermon for tomorrow morning."

At the bidding prayers, after the homily, Mary Kate forestalled any mention of specifics by beginning with, "For those who have died recently and those who are sick, let us pray to the Lord."

Jackie Curran followed with "that the rain not last all day tomorrow." That produced laughter from his cousins, who were confident that there would be no rain at all tomorrow. Wasn't that what the weather forecasters had said?

"For brave young women," Jean prayed fervently.

"And for brave young men who have the courage to risk their lives by giving away diamond rings!" Caitlin Murphy shouted, waving enthusiastically her left hand, on which there was now a diamond ring that would sink a battleship. Or at least a Coast Guard cutter.

The "living area level" was filled with shrieking, cheering, laughing, crying, hugging, kissing, and similar manifestations of manic Irish delight. Kevin Maher seemed even more delighted than his fiancée; since he was receiving less attention, I shook his hand first. "Lucky guy," I said.

"It'll never be a dull moment," he chuckled, shaking the rafters of the room, it seemed to me. "I hope my hospital insurance never gets canceled because of too many broken limbs."

Blackie Ryan stood behind the makeshift altar in his white alb and gold stole, smiling like a benign Irish Buddha who was perhaps not quite sure of the reason for all the merriment but certainly approving of it.

His cousin Brendan Ryan, despite himself, had become part of the celebration. I had sworn to myself, when I reluctantly yielded to Jean's decision that I must come to Grand Beach for Memorial Day, that I would not be seduced by the vitality and the enthusiasm of the "other" Ryans. It had taken them twenty-four hours to capture me—and save my life in the process. Maybe, just maybe, I would water-ski with Timmy every weekend.

Mass continued, Communion was distributed (both the wafers and the chalice, in what I suspect was a contravention of the Roman wishes—with a cardinal present at that). The little Coast Guard waif received Communion like everyone else.

After Mass, I cornered her. "You went to Communion, too, Cindasoo."

"I asked the cardinal man, and he said 'long as I was Irish, it was all right.' I dunno. My mammy done warned me 'bout you papists. She said that you're no count and you drink too much and you breed like rabbits and 'the first thing you know,' she said, 'if you give 'em the chance they'll try to make *you* a papist.' "

"Are they making any progress?"

"Monsignor Blackie, he's a powerful prayin' preacher, ain't he?—He say that you papists already have enough nocount white trash and you don't want me." She spoke with a perfectly solemn face; only a pixie twinkle in her brown eyes hinted that she was putting me on. " 'No way, Cindasoo,' he say, 'we gonna let you in.' "

"Are you all right after yesterday?"

"I reckon," she said slowly. "At least I'm fixin' to be."

Ciara Kelly. Ciara Kelly. Ciara Kelly.

Blackie's sermon, Caitlin's engagement, Cindasoo's piquant charm, the graceful courage of my new friends, the laughter, the good times, the merriment, they almost captured me, a fly yearning for honey.

The next morning, however, the rains that little Jackie had predicted did indeed come. After breakfast (which, in a Ryan house you make for and by yourself: "We put out the makings," Eileen commented, "and let them graze."), I retreated to my room to work on this diary and to acknowledge to myself, if to no one else, that I indeed am faced with a decision. The issue is inchoate and unformulated, diffuse and unspecific, as vague as it was yesterday when I imagined I saw Madonna in this very room where I am writing now, and just as yesterday, I do not want to define a decision, to give it a name, much less to make it.

26

Nicole Curran brought a large pitcher of lemonade and set it between me and Monsignor Blackie. "Mommy says there's not sand in it like there was sometimes when she made it," Nicole giggled, " 'cause I'm a good little girl and she never was. Is that right, Uncle Blackie?"

The priest's eyes blinked rapidly as he tried to switch from whatever deep thought it was that had him staring at the thundering whitecaps on the lake. "That you are a good little girl, Nicole," he said, examining the lemonade as though the possibility that it was not John Jameson's might indicate that it was poison, "is a matter that is quite beyond debate. As to your mother, I cannot recall sand ever being in *my* lemonade. It was always your daddy's. Doubtless he richly deserved it."

Nicole giggled again and fled.

"Where was I?" he sighed, resuming his contemplation of the waves. "Oh, yes, in re: Ciara Kelly."

The winds had whipped Lake Michigan into a furious boil. Even Pine Lake was turbulent, but not so turbulent that I was able to escape another try at water-skiing. After the skiing I returned, somewhat tentatively, to my room to see what if any psychic phenomenon awaited me there. The room was empty, save for this diary, and impulsively I found Nicole and sent her to seek out her Uncle Blackie and ask him if he could come over and talk to me for a few minutes. The conversation, and Eileen's revelation at the end of it, have clarified nothing for me. Spending another day at Grand Beach will only confuse me further. My daughter's plans notwithstanding, I will return to Chicago tomorrow with Jean and do my damnedest to pay no more attention to the Ryans and all they stand for.

"I should think," Blackie sighed heavily, "that the resolution of the issue is obvious."

"Oh?" In addition to being a brilliant painter and an interesting house designer, Catherine Curran made good lemonade.

"It seems to me patent, self-evident, beyond dispute, that Ciara Kelly is real and is alive somewhere, and that you must go and search for her."

I had intended to make only a few careful inquiries about what the Church thought of ESP and perhaps mention my unpleasant encounter with Dr. Freihaut (how many centuries ago was that?), but Blackie Ryan's attitude of bemused and interested sympathy accomplished precisely what it was designed to accomplish. I told him everything, the retrocognition at Fort Dearborn, the interludes with Madonna, my romance, perhaps imaginary, with Ciara.

"How can you be so sure?"

"I dismiss as ridiculous the proposition," he tasted his lemonade and seemed astonished at its flavor, as though never before had he tasted Catherine's lemonade, "the hypothesis that she is imaginary. You, Brendan Herbert George Ryan, are a sensible and reliable attorney, investor, and civic personage. You may have in your organism some vestige of Neanderthal modes of cognition and communication. These may produce some odd experiences in your life, but I reject as offensive and affronting the notion that you would have a sustained love affair with a creation of those neo-Neanderthal vestigia." He permitted himself a small smile. "Indeed, a sustained love affair in itself, you must admit, Brendan, pushes our credulousness to its outer limits. A love affair with an imaginary woman?" He shook his head decisively. "No, no, that is too much to ask us to accept!"

"But—"

He held up an admonitory hand, a timid traffic cop assuming bravely that a small wave will stop a massive truck. "Moreover, in the extremely unlikely event that you should indeed create a lover for yourself, it is most implausible, you surely will concede, that you would create such a multifaceted and interesting woman as this, ah, Ms. Ciara Kelly. Do you truly expect me to credit that as plausible a man as you could bring into being such a delightfully implausible woman?"

"I don't know whether you're flattering me or insulting me," I grumbled.

"Heaven forfend," his nearsighted eyes glinted over the lemonade glass, "that I should do either. I'm merely suggesting that the delectable Ms. Kelly is beyond imagination, that is to say, real."

"It seems to be awfully thin . . ."

"Moreover," he refilled his lemonade glass, spilling on the redwood table almost as much as he poured into the glass, "at the very beginning of this improbable criminal affair, it seemed obvious that either you or Ms. Kelly was the target of the crime and that poor Ron and your unfortunate wife were the unintended victims. . . ."

"That's not what the Chicago police thought."

"They erred. Patently. Consider: Father Crowley was a troubled and disillusioned clerical leftist who, upon being appointed pastor, shifted dramatically to the right. Unattractive, perhaps, but hardly a serious candidate for murder. And your wife, Lord have mercy on her, was a pathetic woman trying unsuccessfully to cope with the middle years of life and aging herself more rapidly than necessary. Again, sad and unfortunate, but who'd want to kill her?"

"I might want to kill her. After all, men have killed for less than three million dollars."

"Come now, Brendan." He waved the lemonade glass in dismissal of my absurd suggestion, spilling more of the lemonade. "We can reject that possibility out of hand. Anyone with the knowledge of your successful trading in the bond market would have little question about your ability to make up your losses in short order. You would match Richard Dennis's three hundred percent profit margin rather handily. Indeed, if the police had bothered to check your other brokers, I'm sure they would have discovered that, despite King Sullivan's pilferage, you have done quite nicely in this lamentable situation of failing demands for notes of government indebtedness."

"How do you know that?" I demanded hotly.

"A good guess." He stared suspiciously at the nearly empty lemonade glass, wondering apparently who had stolen the precious liquid from it. "Let us progress. Just as Madonna and Ron, God be good to them, were unlikely targets for low-quality outfit hit men, so it seems to me that you and Ms. Kelly were much more probable targets. I would have guessed Ms. Kelly, an inclination I doubtless share with her highly skillful protectors. Consider again: there is some doubt as to her actual name, we know nothing of her background save for an extremely unfortunate incident in the Congo some years ago. She is well-educated but impoverished, she gives no account of her family or of her life for the last decade and a half, a mysterious woman, a woman with a past, a woman who must disappear at the first sign of trouble—is this not the kind of person who might easily be a target for an assassination?"

"That's highly speculative . . ."

"Hear me out." Nicole reappeared and filled his lemonade glass and mine again. "Moreover, you are a well-known Chicago lawyer with unimpeachable integrity and with a strong, not to say puritanical sense of professional ethics. That you might have offended someone in the course of your career who wanted revenge is not at all improbable. Therefore, clearly you or Ms. Kelly was the target. Presumably, it seemed to me as I read the papers, Ms. Kelly. I erred, as apparently she did, and those in whose interest it was to protect her. If she and her friends had not made this error in judgment, it seems to me possible that she would not have disappeared.''

"Let me see if I understand your argument." I felt faintly dizzy. It was not the logic of the court or the law office that I was hearing. "I don't see how it follows that Ciara is real because either she or I was the target of the killers.''

"If either of you was the target," Blackie pointed a pudgy finger vaguely in my direction, "it might make perfect sense for her to disappear. Indeed, that is a reasonable assumption with which to begin, far more reasonable, it seems to me, than the rather naive notion that you created her out of a mixture of loneliness and psychic sensitivity.''

"Everyone denies her existence: the Immigration Service, the Irish consul general, the owner of the store at which she worked, the manager and doorman at her apartment building, her neighbors. Doesn't that prove that she's unreal?''

"In the possibility, the very real possibility, that she was the target of the killers, or thought to be the target, it could just as readily prove that there was a conspiracy to hide and protect her.''

"A conspiracy *that* well organized?''

"Such elaborate organization only proves," Blackie Ryan shrugged indifferently, "that those who wished to protect her are powerful, resourceful, and strongly motivated.''

"I'm still not convinced.''

"Brendan." Blackie removed his glasses and peered at me with a sympathetic and kindly face. "Their only serious mistake was the empty apartment.''

"Pardon me?''

"You could have checked easily, Brendan. That you did not do so should suggest to you that her non-existence allayed some of your fears of intimacy. In any event, I did check. Chestnut Place has a three-month waiting list for apartments. Our mysterious friends were able to remove her and her belongings from the apartment, repaint it, even change the telephone, but they did not have quite enough time to move in someone else and create the appearance of long residency for the substitutes—a more difficult task perhaps than merely covering one woman's disappearance. Still, candidly, I feel this was rather inept of them.''

There was the bat that had been flitting around the dungeons of my brain: of course, there were no empty apartments in our neighborhood.

"We should have thought of that!"

"Perhaps you lacked the perspective," Blackie shrugged indifferently, "to see it. From my roost on the third floor of the cathedral rectory it was, one might argue, easier to see the forest instead of the trees. The 'mysterious friends' probably hoped that no one would think of the waiting lists for apartment buildings." His watery eyes glinted, briefly hard and determined. "Too bad for them."

Right, they'd lost one to Blackie Ryan!

"But who could these 'mysterious friends' be?"

"Patently, men of enormous power and persuasiveness, men who could convince the cast-iron bureaucrats of the INS and your good friend the Irish consul general that it was necessary to deceive you. Men within the American government of very powerful credentials, perhaps working in cooperation with counterparts from other governments."

"Why?" Despite the chill winds off the lake I was sweating profusely.

"Ah, is that not the basic question? Does it not address itself to the heart of the mystery of Ciara Kelly? Is that not indeed what you must learn if you are to continue your quest for her?"

"I haven't even begun such a quest," I protested.

"She must be found, Brendan," Blackie Ryan insisted fiercely, now not a modern Father Brown but once more Richard, Raymond, Godfrey in the Gate. "She is, by your own admission, in jeopardy from the powers of evil and darkness. We cannot let them destroy her."

"What powers of darkness?" I began to understand the reason for Blackie's Father Brown persona. Whether he be Godfrey or Don Quixote, such a passionate contemporary crusader would scare the hell out of you.

"My Lord Cronin, as a punishment for his many sins, has been assigned to preside over the liquidation of the Vatican financial mess. It would appear that the shadow world of terrorism, secrecy, and conspiracy in reality far exceeds that presented to us by such excellent authors as Ludlum or Le Carré. Indeed, the shadow world is so incredible that no fiction writer would dare to describe it as it is, for fear that he would be dismissed as a paranoid. The CIA and the KGB and their counterparts in England, France, Germany, and Israel, for example, are a law unto themselves. But they are more legitimate than some of their occasional allies—the Masonic lodges like Propaganda Due in Italy, the Mafia, international drug traders, brokers in the arms and munitions market, fanatics who work for lunatics like Qaddafi and Khomeini, remnants of the 1968 radical groups like the Weathermen, nutcakes like the Symbionese Liberation Army that kidnapped Patty Hearst; Turkish revolutionaries, so-called, who also smuggle drugs and arms and do an occasional job for the Bulgarian secret police, like assassinating a pope, international smugglers who occasionally do a job for the Vatican, like smuggling money into Poland for Solidarity or disposing of a pope who is going to sweep them out of power, as I fear John Paul I may have been disposed of, and various other assorted psychopaths, sociopaths, mercenaries, dogs of war, and heavily armed madmen. Not to exclude the ones who started it all and will be playing the game long after the others have finished. The ones who never learn and never forget, and I don't mean the Bourbons.''

"The heirs of Michael Collins," I said thoughtfully, referring to the great Irish revolutionary leader from 1918.

"Indeed. And not as clever as Michael Collins, who understood, God be good to the poor man, that there's a time when the game must stop.''

"You think Ciara is mixed up in *that* world?"

"Is it not patent that that must be the case?" Blackie drummed on the redwood table with his folded spectacles. "After a time in the shadow world, the game becomes an end unto itself and the goals for which it is played no longer matter, if they're even remembered. Ciara Kelly, if that really be her name, has become, I suspect, a pawn in the game. And those who play it are sufficiently important to be able, very quickly, to mobilize prestigious resources from the United States government. She must be saved, snatched out of the psychotic evil of the shadow world."

"What if she doesn't want to be saved? What if searching for her would endanger her life even more? What if—''

"If she doesn't want to be saved, you should at least hear

that from her own lips.'' Blackie's sigh was almost as loud as Ciara's would have been. ''As for your quest endangering her all the more, that is perhaps a risk you have to take.''

''It all seems very thin.'' I emptied my lemonade glass and waved off his proffered refill.

Blackie sighed heavily. ''You're probably the only person in Grand Beach besides me who's read Alfred North White-head. If you want, I'll be simple: God is engaged in the business of creating beauty by drawing us forth in hope and love. Sexual attraction is but one dimension of hope, the trickiest of the games that God plays with us. It's God's best technique yet to lure us into generosity and risk taking, which are the raw materials of beauty. Bluntly, your attraction to Ciara Kelly is a trick God has played on you. 'Love Ciara Kelly, love Me' is what She is saying to you. 'Pursue Ciara Kelly, the will-of-the-wisp, the Holy Grail, and you pursue Me, the divine will-of-the-wisp . . . ''

''And thus be tricked into playing Her game of creating a beautiful universe, no matter what happens to Ciara and me.''

Blackie contemplated the ten-foot white waves for a moment. ''Will your own life be more beautiful if you search for Ciara Kelly or if you don't?''

''I'm not going to be tricked by Her sexual game!''

''She is pretty tricky.''

Eileen Kane joined us, looking tired, distraught, and angry. She poured herself a glass of lemonade and sank into the empty redwood chair between the two of us. ''God damn!'' She sipped the lemonade like it was vodka.

''You seem troubled, good sister,'' Blackie commented.

''I am angry, good brother.'' She drained the lemonade and poured herself another glass. ''I am angry at Little Redmond. He's made me awkward, ungainly, and tired, and he is currently behaving as though my insides were a soccer ball. Moreover, I am angry at Big Redmond because I have to carry the child instead of him. I have just had a monumental fight with him, which was about ninety percent my fault. In the old days I never fought with Redmond, and hence never had to apologize.'' Her sigh reminded me of Ciara Kelly. ''Now I must go apologize to him, which will only make matters worse.''

"How does Red react to an apology?"

"How does any man react to an apology from his woman?" She glared balefully at me. "It's an aphrodisiac. What else? Just what I need."

"Ah," Blackie murmured. "That is not, however, why you have joined us."

"No." Eileen strove to be her businesslike legal self. "Mary Kate thought of something this afternoon that she thinks is pertinent to the issue of the fire on the *Brigid*. Pertinent, indeed. I don't know why it took her this long to tell me. Typical of the Irish, she wants to tell you indirectly, Brendan, doubtless to escape responsibility. Anyway, one of the things that poor Patsy Sullivan said before she went into her depressed phase: she told Mary Kate, with the policewoman there taking notes, that she did not intend to kill Madonna and Ron. It was you and the woman with the long black hair and the big boobs who she thought were on the boat."

Dead silence on the porch. The wind howled, whitecaps beat against the beach, in the background one could hear shouts of children in the swimming pool next door.

"Indeed," Blackie Ryan said patiently, "Ireland is where the search must begin. I would imagine, Uncle Brendan, that a man of your influence would have no difficulty obtaining a passport immediately."

27

Jean handed me the eyeshades. "People in Ireland are going to sleep now, Daddy. Maybe we ought to do so too."

I had returned to my room in the Curran wonder house at Grand Beach, determined that neither Blackie Ryan nor God would trick me into going to Ireland on a foolish and possibly dangerous search for Ciara. I woke up the next morning, after wildly erotic dreams about her, with the same resolution. Jean and I ate breakfast together at 7:30 because I wanted to be in my office before ten o'clock. I'm not altogether sure what angel or demon invaded me. Without a precise realization of what I was saying, I remarked to her, "Would you mind if I fly over to Ireland with you? I don't belong on your photo tour, but I thought I might hang around Dublin and take a look at how law is taught and practiced in Ireland."

I could scarcely believe my own ears.

Jean swallowed half an English muffin at one gulp and embraced me enthusiastically. "Daddy, how wonderful!"

The month of June had only just begun, and here I was on an Aer Lingus 747 in first class, flying to Ireland, still not quite sure how it had happened.

The search is over now, for weal or woe, and this diary, the last previous entry of which was made on the evening of Memorial Day after my conversation with Blackie, can now be finished.

Jean took charge of my trip, purchasing the tickets, advising me on what and how to pack, rushing a passport through at record speed (activating, I believe, both the United States senators from the Prairie State), and assisting my secretary in canceling all my appointments for three weeks. No doubt about it, the young woman was an extremely able administrator, though her efficiency did not become officious. Her suggestions were careful and cautious, and never did she seem to be giving me orders. I went along with her plans, most of the time anyway, because it seemed the sensible and easy thing to do. Taking orders from Madonna, Lord have mercy on her, as the Ryans would say, was always punishment. Taking orders from Jean was pleasure. How very clever of her.

The only disagreement was whether to fly first class. She was appalled at the suggestion. All that money for a little bit of extra room and some drinks? Anyway, we're not going to drink because we're going to follow Dr. Ehret's Jet Lag Program, aren't we?

"We certainly are going to follow the program," I said, watching how neatly she folded my shirts into the lightweight flight bag she'd purchased. (The only way to travel to Europe, I was told, was with carry-on luggage. You brought a lot of clothes to Grand Beach, only a few clothes to Europe. Why did that seem so strange?) "But I, at any rate, being a tired and elderly man, value that extra bit of comfort enormously. You go coach if you want, kid, I go first class."

"Really. *Well* . . . you're paying for it. Hmmm, I guess we're going to have to take one of these shirts out."

"You expect me to have lunch with Irish lawyers in dirty shirts?"

"They *do* sell shirts in Ireland. Anybody who can afford to fly first class can afford to buy clothes in the country he visits and then give the clothes to the St. Vincent De Paul Society or something like that when he leaves. Right?"

"Right. Naturally."

So we had feasted with the Currans and the Kanes, flew out of O'Hare to New York, where we fasted and saw *Cats*, and then boarded the Aer Lingus 747 for Dublin.

A blurred image of Ciara was never far from the center of my consciousness; with the image there came constant sexual desire. Beneath the exterior image of a sedate middle-aged professional man preparing for a trip abroad with his daughter was an aborigine desperately hunting for his spring woman, lusting for her with savage appetite.

No one but Blackie Ryan was certain why I was going to Ireland, though perhaps the Kanes and the Currans might have guessed. I had no strategy, no game plan. I would go to Dublin, look around, and see what happened, perhaps contact the Irish police or the Special Branch, which was kind of their FBI. However, if Blackie was correct about the shadow world, they would be less than forthcoming. Timmy Murphy was not at O'Hare to bid us good-bye, nor was there any excuse or explanation offered for his absence. I had enough sense not to ask questions.

"Did you know," said my daughter, who was wearing a khaki jumpsuit with a pink blouse under it, "that Baileys Irish Cream, which we are not to drink on the flight over because it will violate the plan, accounts for one percent of all the exports of Ireland, that it is the most popular cordial in both West Germany and France, that it outsells all other liqueurs put together in the United States, and that such distinguished old brands as Grand Marnier have been forced to bring out their own creams to compete?"

"Remarkable," I agreed. Not only was Jean marvelously

efficient, she seemed to have acquired, in her nineteen years, a vast collection of useful and useless information.

"And you're wondering why Tim Murphy wasn't at the airport?"

"Was I?"

She nodded her head vigorously. "Yep, you were wondering. We had a big fight."

"Ah."

"You sound like Uncle Punk."

"Don't you think it would be more appropriate if you called him Uncle Blackie?"

She eyed me disdainfully. "Tim and I had a big fight. He's too intense. I can't stand the hungry way he looks at me."

"At the risk of intruding in what is none of my business, Jean, you are a very attractive, indeed sexy, young woman. Moreover, you are smart, personable, efficient at planning projects such as hasty trips to Dublin, and a storehouse of knowledge about such critically important things as Baileys Irish Cream. Any young man Timothy's age, with the standard complement of hormones, would devour you with hungry eyes."

"Hmmph."

"Moreover," I crawled far out on a limb, "you've had some rough things happen to you lately and you might be said to need some male protection. Add that to all the other factors I've just mentioned, and a young scion of the Ryan clan can't help but be intense."

"I don't need protection, I don't want protection," she pounded the armrest, "I won't accept protection."

"Oh."

"That sounds kind of silly, doesn't it, Daddy?" she asked sheepishly.

"Really."

"I can't cope with him, I'm not ready for it. It just wouldn't work."

"Was Tim making demands?"

"Making demands?" she asked scornfully. "You mean, like sex? If he was a Stanford student, he'd be trying to drag me off to bed every time he saw me. That's not how the Ryans and the Murphys act. They protect their goddamned virgins."

"He was being possessive, then."

"Not to say possessive," she said thoughtfully.

Ciara's syntax again. You are alive, my darling, but what chance do I have of finding you?

"No," Jean continued. "Tim isn't the kind of boy who, like, hangs around and gets jealous every time you look at somebody else or somebody else looks at you. He just wants to love me, like, more powerfully than I want to be loved. He doesn't mean it to be a demand, poor guy. But for me it's a demand just the same."

"I'm pretty far out on a limb now . . ."

She pounded the armrest again. "C'mon, Daddy, we've gone beyond the stage where you have to apologize for giving advice."

Indeed, as Blackie would have said. Have we now? as Ciara would have said.

"Neither your mother nor I, Jean, gave you a very good example in this respect, but don't try and do it alone."

"Do *what*?" she asked irritably.

"You know *what*. Make it, survive, grow up, get your act together, find a little wisdom as you yourself described it, whatever."

"Yeah, I know."

And then I was offered eyeshades and told that just because they were playing a movie, it didn't mean that I had to watch it.

The plan does not absolutely require that you sleep at the time that the people in the country of destination are sleeping. You must merely rest, relax, and end all conversation. But I slept like I was back in my bed in the apartment in Chicago. Jean nudged me gently. "Wake up, Daddy. Have you ever seen anything so green before in all your life?"

There was a thin layer of cloud beneath us, and then beneath the clouds the greenest fields I had ever seen, unbelievably, unbearably green, occasionally smeared with ragged gold splotches, like someone had spilled a can of paint, as the sun broke through the cloud layer.

"It must be all the rain," I murmured.

"Oh, boy," Jean said joyfully, "am I going to get the pictures here!"

"Everybody here looks Irish," she whispered in my ear as we waited in line at the Dublin airport customs.

"What else did you expect them to look like?" I asked. "It's almost like being back on the south side of Chicago."

The immigration inspectors managed to process us rapidly while projecting an image of casual unconcern. An elderly little white-haired man, who inspected our passports and stamped them, peered through his rimless glasses at Jean. "And what county would your ancestors be from, young woman?"

"Mayo, God help us," she responded, with her brightest smile.

"Ah, well," said the little fellow with the leprechaun wink, "at least you're honest about it. Take good care of your father now. Make sure he drives on the right side of the road, which is the left side here, if you take my meaning."

"I'll do most of the driving," Jean replied saucily. "Himself is one of your dreamy lawyers, sure, you can't trust 'em at the wheel of a car at all, at all."

And to me, as we walked over to the luggage carousel, "See, Daddy, I told you everybody would know you were my father and wouldn't think you were a dirty old man traveling through Europe with a nymphet. We do look a little bit alike, after all."

I wanted nothing more than to check in at the Shelbourne Hotel and go to bed, but the plan forbade that. This was, however, to be a day of feasting. I had dutifully consumed two cups of coffee before the plane landed. The Shelbourne was a rambling, untidy, and quaint old place, which if it were cleaner might have appealed to Queen Victoria, on the northern edge of Stephen's Green, which at the moment was partly obscured by what our taxi driver called "mists" and what I would have called a "driving rain."

In the mists I saw the image of Ciara. I wanted her so badly that I almost ran out into the rain to search for her. I knew that common sense dictated a day or two of acclimatization and orientation, but common sense was not so powerful in me as it used to be.

Never in my life had I experienced sexual desire so intense, so persistent, so violent.

We had to go at once to the dining room and consume a

large breakfast—bacon, eggs, melon, brown Irish bread, and several more cups of coffee. "Your body," Jean said confidently, "will now be convinced it's breakfast time instead of three or four o'clock in the morning."

"Great," I muttered, with more enthusiasm than I felt.

In order to live up to the stern discipline of the plan it was decided that we would, after breakfast, go on a tour of Georgian Dublin. First of all, however, we had to cross Stephen's Green, now wet but glowing, "like, kind of mystical" as Jean put it, in the sunlight, and pay our respects to the black marble bust of James Joyce, donated by American Express, on the south side of the green, across from Newman House, where he'd gone to college. On the front of the bust were carved the words from *Portrait of the Artist*, "Crossing Stephen's, that is my, Green."

"The poor dear man certainly had bad eyes, didn't he?" Jean scurried around the bust, Nikon in hand, trying to capture both Joyce's craggy features and the Georgian building across the street where Joyce had gone to school and where a half century before another unappreciated Dubliner, John Henry Newman, had been rector and had presented the lectures that became *The Idea of a University*. American Express had yet to erect a bust in his honor, however.

Stephen's Green was nothing more than a small park in the center of a city, a park in which Handel and Newman and Swift and Joyce and a couple of dozen other geniuses had routinely walked, across which the British army and the Irish volunteers had battled during Easter week of 1916. If you ignored the history and the literature and Newman and Joyce and the rest of them, it was not a special place. Or so I told myself as my daughter and I paused to admire every little Celtic brat being pushed through the park in a stroller.

I was then dragged to Bewley's on Grafton Street for tea and scones. It was, I was assured, the most famous tearoom in Dublin, and perhaps the best tea in Ireland. Besides, this was our day for feasting.

I was sure that a woman on the other side of the room was Ciara. I excused myself to go to the men's room so that I might see her face.

It wasn't Ciara, but my tumescent imagination wanted to undress her anyway.

I hurried back to Jean, now not only my daughter but also my link with the real world.

We stayed south of the Liffey for the rest of the day, exploring Grattan's parliament building (now the Bank of Ireland), Trinity College, Christ Church and St. Patrick's Cathedral (both Protestant, one early Norman Gothic, the other later English Gothic), Dublin Castle, Merrion Square and Fitzwilliam Square with their classic—and just barely preserved—row houses, and the Custom House and the Four Courts across from the south bank of the Liffey.

Grattan's Dublin may not have been an Irish city, but one could imagine what a smart town it must have been, men and women in expensive clothes, elegant carriages, fashionable furnishings in the homes. All of that was gone. Dublin town was crowded, dirty, and by the standards of a Chicago Irishman, still poor. The people seemed underfed, anxious, subject to premature aging, and badly in need of dental work. My daughter informed me that I sounded like an American snob and that I would probably feel better after I'd had a good night's sleep.

Moreover, she continued, as I knew very well Ireland was deep into the hardest times it had experienced in twenty years. Youth unemployment was close to fifty percent. If I was suffering as much as most Irish people were, I'd look anxious and prematurely aged.

"So would I," she added sheepishly, looking at me out of the corner of her eye as we ended our second visit to Bewley's. On this note, since it was raining again for the fourth or fifth time in the day, we withdrew to the lobby of the Shelbourne to have high tea, which, I calculated, was my fifth meal of the day. I looked around the elegantly shabby room with its canary-color walls, its plush but down-at-the-heels furniture, and its vast fireplace and wondered if I looked as overfed and as arrogantly self-satisfied as the other American tourists, who were devouring pastry like it was about to be banned by either the pope or OPEC.

"You're going to get your old daddy fat in this country," I protested as Jean shoved a cream puff into my all too willing mouth.

"That's all right." She turned to the complex task of loading her Nikon. "Eat as much as you want today because tomorrow is a fast day. Remember?"

"God forbid," I sighed.

I was permitted to return to my room and read a Dublin guidebook that had been purchased for my edification but was sternly warned not to nap. We ate supper at a restaurant in a little mews down the street from the Shelbourne, strongly and justifiably recommended by Jean's guidebook. My tour guide was uncommunicative and somber as we picked our way through the rain and the mist to the restaurant.

"Can I order some Jameson's?" I asked her.

"Two of them," she snapped. "And make them doubles."

"Is that part of the plan?"

"No, goddamn it. It isn't."

"Phone call from Tim?"

"Mind your own fucking business."

"*Jean!*"

"I'm sorry, Daddy." She grabbed my right hand with both of hers, tears welling up in her eyes. "I'm clinging by my fingernails again. *So* angry and *so* bummed."

"Angry at Tim?"

"Angry at myself. The poor boy called me from Grand Beach to apologize for the fight. Can you imagine that? His mother'll kill him when she sees the phone bill. And he didn't start the fight, Daddy. I started the fight so I was angry at him all over again. Isn't that terrible?"

Terrible it was, but I was too preoccupied with my own problem to be of much help to Jean. My problem was that every handsome woman I saw on the streets of Dublin—there turned out to be more of them than I'd realized at first—reminded me of Ciara.

I wanted to make love with all of them.

Now that I was in Ireland, what was I going to do? Wander through the streets of Dublin and accost every beautiful woman in her early thirties that I encountered?

What the hell was I doing here?

28

St. Kevin's Shrine at Glendalough did not at first seem sinister. It was a quaint and mildly interesting collection of gravestones and ungainly ruins, crude old rock buildings nestled in a valley in the Wicklow hills, which, with some exaggeration, might be called picturesque. A parking lot, or "car park," as the Irish seemed to call them, a somewhat battered and weather-beaten tourist center, where one could get a meal that might have been attractive if there were a famine, and crowds of Sunday tourists reminded me of Starved Rock State Park back in Illinois, an unspectacular tourist attraction to which you drove on a Sunday a quarter century ago when you had guests from out of town and had to be home in the evening.

It was only after I had wandered through the park in the bright afternoon sunlight while Jean joyously scampered ahead of me with her Nikon that I began to be terrified.

I'd slept well the previous night: the plan worked. I had discovered, however, that it was indeed true, as I had read in geography books in grammar school, that the days were long and the nights were short in the northern climes during late spring and early summer. There were a few hours of darkness around midnight, but by three in the morning, daylight was pouring through the holes in the shades in my room, creating patches of light on the worn blue carpet and the badly scratched mahogany-veneer furniture. I remembered Jean's eyeshades, fumbled in my traveling bag for them, and stumbled back into bed for sleep and more dreams of Ciara.

I had to wait until Monday to begin my search. Could I last another week without her? Even another day?

At breakfast Jean enthused about the cloudless blue skies and the green hills of Wicklow in the distance hovering over St. Stephen's Green and the, like, totally wonderful pictures she was going to take today in South County, Dublin. Really.

"Is that where we're going?"

"C'mon now, Daddy; you read the schedule I typed out."

So I had, and we were off to South County, Dublin. After a stop at the ugly nineteenth-century procathedral for the eight o'clock Mass (the pernicious infection of folk music at Mass, it seemed, had spread even to Ireland), we drove south on Merrion Road, crossing the Grand Canal, passing Boland's Mills, where De Valera had held out to the bitter end after the Easter rising, and circled through University College in Belfield, which Jean pronounced, in disappointment, to be "just like any American state university," and then worked our way over to Rock Road, along the edge of Dublin Bay. Jean turned up her nose at the beaches, which were, indeed, rocky, and declared that she, for one, was not going to swim in the ocean when the water was fifty degrees, no matter how many skinny, pale-skinned boys were spread out on the "strand" (which was the proper name for a beach in the British Isles, I was informed). "Yucksville!" she observed. The class passed through Blackrock and Monkstown and detoured to see James Joyce's Martello Tower, one of a series that had been built along the coast of Ireland to fend off invaders in Napoleonic times. "Why would anybody want to live in *that*?" Jean sniffed.

"So he could grow up and write *Ulysses*," I replied.

"Yucksville," she observed again.

We drove through Dun Laoghaire and watched the ferry from Liverpool chug through the harbor mouth like a supercilious elderly matron, pick its way among the yachts and sailboats that were rushing out into the bay, and slide securely into its pier with what seemed to be an enormous sigh of relief.

Several of the young women disembarking from the ferry—probably coming home for "holidays" from their English jobs—reminded me so forcefully of Ciara that only by sheer willpower did I restrain myself from running up to them.

"Maybe we should have scheduled sailing for today," Jean said. "Would you like to go sailing, Daddy?"

I had not, in fact, even thought about it. The memories of the *Brigid* were still too vivid in my imagination.

"Later on, before I leave Ireland. Today I'd be satisfied with Glendalough."

"And Powerscourt."

"Certainly Powerscourt. How could I ever forget Powerscourt?"

"Really!"

Even though we were on the fast day of the plan, I was nonetheless permitted to buy tea in a café at the head of the East Pier in Dun Laoghaire harbor. Jean took off her blue (the color, I was informed, was actually "lilac") sweater. She was wearing slacks that matched the sweater and a lilac-and-white striped blouse with white collar and white cuffs and carrying a white shoulder-strap purse as well as her camera bag. I had raised an eyebrow at such garb for a trip to the Wicklow mountains, but she replied that she wasn't going to walk into an Irish church on Sunday morning in jeans and sweatshirt and there wouldn't be time to stop at the hotel to change. It turned out that many of the local colleens had no such scruples about their Sunday morning garb. The men in the coffee shop could hardly help but notice her. She radiated fresh, young, happy sexuality. Small wonder that poor Tim Murphy had been overwhelmed.

A big brown-haired lad with broad shoulders and thick forearms held the door for us as we left. "Sure, if you don't know my cousins in the States," he said with a wink and a charming grin, "it's a grand misfortune—for them, that is."

"Is it now?" Jean cocked a speculative eye at him.

"You have to admit it's a new approach to getting acquainted." A faint tinge of color rose in his face.

"It's all of that," Jean replied curtly, swinging her rear end, I thought, a little more than usual as we walked away from the pier.

The young man caught up with us. "Am I never, never to see you again, at all, at all?" he asked. "Ah, sure, won't I be destroyed altogether if that happens?"

"I've been known to come in and out of the Shelbourne Hotel," Jean suggested.

"Should I ask for anyone by name?" The young man grinned broadly.

"Ah, you might, and then again, you might not."

"And your father wouldn't be minding?"

Jean glanced at her father. "Ah, you shouldn't let his mild manners fool you. He's a terrible dangerous man."

"You're not the kind that gets picked up?" I said, as we boarded our rented Renault.

"Not to say picked up." Jean laughed cheerfully. "He is kinda cute, Daddy. Admit it."

"Well, at least I'm happy I don't cramp your style. I bet he's more pushy than Tim Murphy."

"Tim who?"

And so we went on to Dalkey and Bray, admiring the sun-drenched blue waters of the bay, which we both agreed looked like Naples, though only Jean had seen Naples, and we were intrigued by the elegant and graceful if somewhat run-down homes of South County, Dublin.

"There are so many writers in this part of Ireland," Jean said, "that you have to push your way through them on the streets."

"You've read so much about this country that you even talk like the people."

Jean glanced at me curiously. "How many of the people have you talked to, Daddy?"

"Oh, not that many. But you certainly had that young man's dialect down."

My darling Ciara. When will I find you?

Then we turned inland and drove up the foothills to Glendalough, a mildly interesting Irish ruin on a bright, cheerful Sunday afternoon in spring, swarming with visitors, including an alarmingly large number of women with strollers equipped for two infants.

"I would say they were crazy for having two children so close together," Jean had just admired two little boy children, both of whom had flirted with her outrageously, "but both the kids and their mothers look healthy and happy."

"Maybe they don't know any better," I suggested.

"I want kids," she replied. "I want them in the worst way, but I don't know what kind of a mother I'll be."

"You're doing a fine job of mothering me on this trip."

"Daddy." A hug and a laugh that was almost tears, and despite the swarms of Irish tourists, a very nice kiss. I suspect some of them began to question their original decision that she was almost certainly my daughter.

All in all, it was a pleasant and delightful Sunday with a daughter who was rapidly becoming a friend. It was not the sort of afternoon when one would expect to be suddenly overcome by naked terror.

We were inside the ruins of what seemed to me to be a tiny stone chapel, overgrown with weeds, which the guidebook said was a "cathedral." Jean was photographing the round tower (a lookout and hideaway from Viking pirates) through the door of the ruins because, as she told me, the composition was "just right."

The terror came suddenly, without warning. Unlike my other psychic interludes, this one was uncanny, ghostly, spooky, horrifying.

I slumped into the corner of the old stone church and curled up in a knot. I felt, rather than saw, the clanging of bells, the flashing of swords, burning buildings, screams, torment, death. Death, death, death everywhere, violent, painful, humiliating death. The screams of the wounded and dying were all around, the swords of the enemy slashed through the air above me. The stench of burning timbers filled my body. I prayed for salvation and knew that there could be none. I was being swept into the agonies of hell. The fire, the noise, the smell, the anguish of death grew stronger and stronger, filled me, possessed me, overwhelmed me, dragged me toward the tomb.

"Daddy, Daddy, oh, please Daddy. . . ." A tender, frightened voice from another world. I reached for it but could not find it. This was not Fort Dearborn, not one videotape played on top of another, this was rather a world of darkness reaching up to snatch me and claim me and drag me down.

"*Please*, Daddy."

Jean. Ciara. Eileen. Catherine. Jocelyn.

I reached for the world of light and green and Sundays in spring with boys who followed pretty girls down the streets of Dun Laoghaire and little children in white First Communion dresses and suits.

"I'm okay, Ciara. I'm fine. Just," I managed a weak laugh, "a little bit too much fast on the fast day. Do you think we might go back to the restaurant and have us a wee spot of tea and a scone or two?"

I was helped to my feet by a couple of very anxious young Irishmen to whom I explained with what I hoped was a rueful laugh, "It's what happens to a Yank tourist on jet lag when he doesn't have a big enough breakfast. I'm all right, fellows, I'm fine. No heart attack."

The two young men, countrymen, I thought, perhaps up for a weekend in Dublin, looked skeptical, but a grateful smile and thank you from my lilac-clad daughter reassured them. Fast day or not, I ate two ham sandwiches and three scones and downed several cups of tea while Jean apologized, with less conviction than I might have wanted, for pushing the plan too vigorously.

"Your father is an old man out of condition," I joked.

"My father," she said grimly, "is forty-two years old, in excellent condition, and, if one is to judge from the way these hungry-eyed Irish bitches look at you, damned attractive."

"That's the comparative for cute, isn't it?" I asked.

"Superlative." She pushed my arm. "Should we go back to the hotel?"

"Nonsense," I said. "On to Powerscourt."

We visited the sad, charred ruins of that great manor house, admired the garden, flirted with the children, took pictures of a wide variety of objects, mineral, vegetable, animal, and human, and finally arrived at the Creole Restaurant in the dark, comfortable basement of a house near the harbor in Dun Laoghaire about six o'clock for supper. The psychic vibrations of St. Kevin's Shrine still lingered, but they were not powerful enough to greatly trouble me. We sat in a booth in the back of the restaurant, ordered a bottle of Niersteiner wine, and relaxed.

At any rate, I relaxed. Jean thumbed through the guidebook after she'd returned from the women's room, and found the place she was looking for. "Many people claim that the Shrine of St. Kevin at Glendalough is haunted by the ghosts of the monks who were massacred there at various times during the Danish invasions. Indeed, some psychic researchers say that it's the most haunted place in all of Ireland."

"Considering all the Irish ghost stories, that's a pretty broad claim, isn't it?" I laughed weakly.

"Let's have it, Daddy." She pointed an imperious finger at me. "I want the truth, all of it."

I comprehended clearly for the first time the essential difference between Jean's propensity to "take charge" and her mother's similar characteristic. Jean's determination and efficiency was in the service of love, still awkward and clumsy, perhaps, still searching for nuance and refinement, but not really capable of ever becoming domination. I was relieved and happy at that discovery.

"I said, let's have it, Daddy," she insisted, her voice rising dangerously.

Nonetheless, a very determined young woman. How would she and Ciara get along if she should be Ciara's stepdaughter?

"Daddy?" Dangerously close to anger.

"You told me a while back you didn't believe in ESP," I began.

"Maybe now I do. Was that what happened?"

We ordered scallops meunière and drank our seafood soup while I told her of the various strange psychic phenomena that were so much a part of my life that I took them almost as much for granted as I did winter colds or blocked sinuses in spring.

Jean became very pale and held my left hand with hers while we both manipulated soup spoons with our right hands.

"My God," she breathed softly. "How awful!"

"Not really, honey. I mean, you get used to it. This is the first time that anyone else would have noticed what was going on. I guess I should stay away from the most haunted places in Ireland, huh?"

"*Dead people*, Daddy?"

"Not very often. I'm not one of those persons with whom everybody in the family seems to check in on the way to Heaven."

"Mom?"

I hadn't told her about the two incidents with Madonna, but I suppose I knew she would ask. So I recited that part of the tale too. I even mentioned Jackie Curran's lady with the "blonde hair and the blue dress." Jean leaned back against the booth, closed her eyes, and drew a very deep breath. "Wow, like *wow*!"

"Monsignor Ryan, excuse me, Uncle Punk, says it's a neo-Neanderthal vestige, a crude means of communication that evolved before we humans had developed more elaborate forms of speech. Some of it still lingers in a few of us. Jackie

Curran and I have a common ancestor back several generations. I suppose we inherited it from him, or maybe more
likely from her. Other members of the Ryan family may have
it too. It's really no great big deal, Jean.''

"I'd die if one of my kids was that way." She sat stiff and
upright, eyes still closed.

"But you wouldn't die if your daddy was that way?"

She relaxed and laughed. "Am I ever a nerd! It might be
kind of fun to have a kid around who's even better at weather
forecasting than John Coleman."

"Jackie's luckier than me. I'm not much good at forecasting anything."

"Was it *really* Mom?"

"I don't know. Probably not. But as Uncle Punk said, the
message of forgiveness and reconciliation and beginning over
again is something I should believe even without such an experience."

"Okay, Daddy." Jean seemed to be checking that item off
her agenda. "Oh, thank you very much," to the waitress
who filled her wineglass. "Hmmm, these scallops are
yummy. Now, Daddy, one more question. You didn't call
me Jean back there in the cathedral when you had your fit, or
whatever it was. You called me another name."

"Did I?" Rapidly sinking heart.

Jean's brown eyes flashed dangerously. "You sure did.
Who is she? Who is Ciara?"

29

So in the Creole Restaurant in Dun Laoghaire, South County,
Dublin, a warm, shadowy, pleasant basement room with
marvelous scallops meúnière, I told my daughter about Ciara
Kelly.

"My God, Daddy!"

"As Uncle Punk would say, *indeed*!"

"You went to bed with her," Jean asked incredulously.

"I'm afraid so."

"Don't be afraid about it," she reproved me. "I'm impressed."

"Surprised that your father might be a lover?"

"I, like, totally won't comment on that. And you've come here to Ireland to find her?"

"I guess."

"Like wow. *Wow*!"

"I'm not sure where to begin looking." I began working on my sherry trifle, a delicacy that Jean sternly refused. For her it was still a fast day of the plan. "I'm still trying to figure out what Ireland is all about and where to start—eager and uncertain, I guess."

"You mean, you haven't any strategy at all?"

"Not yet. Maybe tomorrow."

"I'll help," she said firmly.

"No, you won't."

"The hell I won't, Daddy, and don't argue with me. That's settled."

Indeed it was settled with, as it would develop, horrible results for the two of us.

When we returned to the hotel, the young man from the morning, who was named Liam, I was informed in tones which indicated that I ought to know it, was waiting for us. I was sent off to bed while Jean and Liam went forth to explore Dublin pubs.

At breakfast the next morning, while we watched the rain pour down on Stephen's Green across the street, I asked about the pub exploration.

"It was all right," she said without too much conviction, "especially after I drew a few lines."

"Fresh?"

"They certainly move a lot more quickly over here." She daintily dug out a piece of none-too-tender grapefruit from its rind. "He made poor Tim Murphy seem slow and bashful."

"Really."

"They're smooth talkers, and you get so charmed listening to them that you almost don't notice what they're doing while they're talking. *Well*, I sorted him out, to use their term."

"And that's the end of Liam?"

"Oh, no, not at all!" she exclaimed in mock horror. "He just knows what the rules are now."

It was arranged that she would try to photograph Dublin in the rain and I would explore the Irish National Gallery, in whose highly recommended restaurant we would meet for lunch. And so we did; however, Jean had not been taking photographs.

She was wearing the jumpsuit with the pink blouse again. She dropped her trench coat and her rain scarf on the chair between us, sat down, and placed a photocopy of the *Irish Times* in front of me.

"There she is, Daddy. You weren't kidding. She really is a knockout. Her real name is Clare Keenan, and her father was a surgeon, not a lawyer. Everything else fits. The poor woman, she was so young when it happened, younger even than me."

It was the lead story in the *Irish Times* under the headline "Irish Girl Saved by Foreign Legion." The basic facts were all there just as Ciara—or Clare—had told me. Not a hint that she'd been raped so often that she'd lost count. In those days the *Irish Times* would not have reported that. Presumably everyone in Ireland could read between the lines and no one would ever mention it.

"A regular Sherlock Holmes," I remarked.

"She might not even be in Ireland . . ."

"There must be people in Ireland who know where she is."

The restaurant of the Irish National Gallery is in the basement, in a large room painted light green. Everything but the food, which was indeed excellent, reminded me of the dining room at the Art Institute in Chicago. There must be some worldwide rule about gallery eating places. We ate fresh salmon and lamb chops, and I had another sherry trifle and drank a good French wine.

"What next?" Jean demanded briskly.

"It says here that her father, Patrick Keenan, is a surgeon at St. Mary's Hospital in Castlebar in County Mayo and the family lives in Westport. Perhaps that would be the best place to start."

"That was sixteen years ago, Daddy. Maybe her parents are dead. Maybe no one there remembers her anymore."

"Maybe. But do you have any other ideas?"

"I'm going back to the *Irish Times* this afternoon to see what else I can find. See you at supper at the Shelbourne."

"What about Liam?"

"No big deal. He'll come around about half past nine to continue our pub tour. If he doesn't show, well, Daddy, there are a lot of cute boys in Dublin."

I returned to the hotel, huddling under the protection of an inexpensive umbrella I'd bought in a store on Grafton Street, went into the lobby of the Shelbourne, tossed my raincoat on the floor, put the folded umbrella on top of it, and sank into a vast easy chair near the fireplace. It was late for lunch and early for high tea, so I had the lobby to myself to think. A solicitous waiter discovered me and was only too happy to take my order of a Jameson's neat.

Despite the intensity of my love for Ciara, a love that had become an addiction only a few weeks before, she no longer seemed real to me. Ciara was now somehow a mythological figure, someone who must be pursued, indeed, but no longer a real woman whose warm, soft body would open like a flower for me again. No matter what came of the quest for Ciara Kelly—or Clare Keenan—or whatever she was called now, she would never again be my lover. That part of it was finished forever.

Nonetheless, she must be found. Why? Because I loved her and needed her and could not do without her.

Contradictory? Sure. I was in such an advanced state of sexual hunger that I could no longer think logically much of the time.

Most berserkers have suffered a long period of sexual frustration.

The absence of sex in my life had never snuffed out my intellect before.

But I'd never made love to a woman like Ciara Kelly before.

I opened a map of Ireland on one knee and unfolded Jean's photocopy of the front page of the *Irish Times* on my other knee. Clare Keenan's family were gentry, her father a surgeon, her grandfather a lawyer, descendants of the Keenan's Keep in Old Castle on the road between Westport and Newport. So she was a descendant, indeed, of the Constance

Keenan whose picture had hung in Dufficy's Irish Store in Chicago, a deliberate attempt on the part of somebody to throw me off the chase. Or maybe an accident or a coincidence. Who could say?

Somewhere the family, which had been Anglo-Irish aristocrats, turned into Irish Catholic gentry, educated professionals whose children went to private schools and then to Trinity College, not University College, Galway, or University College, Dublin. If you were West of Ireland Catholic gentry, you kept one foot in the Anglo-Irish Dublin Protestant elite. It didn't offend your Catholic clientele; and, while the Protestants never fully accepted you, there was still some social prestige in associating with them. Besides, her father probably had a fair number of Protestant cousins.

Your headstrong daughter went off to the Congo and was savagely brutalized. She came home a bit of a heroine but also a bit of a disgrace. What did you do about her? You certainly didn't seek psychiatric help. You've got to pull yourself together, young woman. You have responsibilities. You've postponed your education too long. Now that this missionary fling of yours is over, you should settle down and earn your degree. Yes, Clare, since you can no longer get yourself to a nunnery—for what nunnery would want someone like you?—and since there's enough whispers about what happened to you in the Congo that the eligible young men would tend to shy away, get yourself to a university and become . . . what? A nurse? A teacher? A sales clerk in an import shop?

A somewhat seedy-looking man in a rumpled gray suit, a battered black raincoat with missing buttons, and a gray cap, with a large umbrella in his hand, settled down in the next easy chair. What the hell? He has the whole hotel lobby available and he has to sit near me.

I drank my Jameson's cautiously. The quest was real now, largely because my daughter had made it real. I must clear the cobwebs out of my brain and start thinking again.

Even if I am never to have you again, Ciara Kelly, I am still going to find you.

Where else to pick up the trail but in Castlebar and Westport? Even if her parents were dead, surely there would be cousins or friends or other relatives who might be able to give me hints. What had happened in the life of Clare Keenan between 1969, when she was a young woman Jean's age, and 1984 to turn her into Ciara Kelly?

She was still beautiful and still haunted by what had happened in the Congo. She was also very well educated, self-possessed, desirable, witty, and, after some hesitancies, wonderful in bed. She had shaken off some of the ill effect of what the Simbas had done to her, healed most if not all of her wounds, and become learned and sophisticated in the process; university training, graduate school probably, and some other terrible secret too.

Where else to go but to Clew Bay, the stronghold of Grace O'Malley, the pirate queen? And perhaps something might be learned in Keenan's Keep, now a hotel, on the bay between Newport and Westport. If the ghost of Connie Keenan really did haunt the old castle, and if my psychic instincts were working, perhaps the ghost could tell me something.

It was an absurd notion, but the whole search was absurd. Real now, yes indeed, but not yet urgent.

"The young lass ought not to be searching the files of the *Irish Times*," said the man with the gray cap, which he had taken off. He was lean, not unhandsome, about my age. His eyes were deep brown and intelligent, his high forehead, under a brown-haired, unruly widow's peak, had a permanent bemused frown, his thin face hinted at wit and wisdom, an actor or a writer perhaps, down on his luck.

"Who the hell are you?" I demanded fiercely, an annoyed berserker.

"Finnegan," he said in a brogue so strong that I had a hard time understanding him. "I'm in the Garda, don't you see. James Finnegan." He reached across the fireplace and handed me a warrant card. He was indeed a Detective Chief Superintendent James P. Finnegan. A major more or less, or maybe a light colonel. More cops.

"Do Irish detective superintendents normally tell Americans that they ought not to read back issues of the *Irish Times*?" I demanded curtly.

"Ah, no." You might decide that he was not an actor but perhaps an undertaker, or an out-of-work bartender. Then you would notice the shrewd, hard brown eyes and you would instinctively say cop. "Only in certain rare circumstances, where the Yanks are asking questions that might cause trouble."

"We haven't asked any questions yet."

"That's a fact," he agreed mildly. Even his voice sounded like that of an undertaker or a sympathetic bartender.

"Why should we not ask the questions that you think we're going to ask, Superintendent?"

"Simple enough. They're dangerous questions to ask."

"Have you ever been in a war, Superintendent?"

"No." He raised a bushy eyebrow. "I have not."

"I have, and I don't frighten easily."

"I didn't think the United States of America gave away Distinguished Service Crosses to men who do frighten easily. But would you mind if I gave a small lecture on recent Irish history?"

"Lecture away, Detective Superintendent James P. Finnegan."

"My friends," he sighed the typical Irish sigh, "call me Jaymo."

"Indeed."

"Well," he sighed again, "as you know, there's been trouble in Ireland for the last fifteen years, particularly in the six counties of Northern Ireland."

"I do read the newspapers, Superintendent; incidentally, I presume you're from the Special Branch?"

"You might say that." He produced a pipe, stuffed it with tobacco as ineffectually as though he were Blackie Ryan, lit the pipe, which created an acrid smell that made me faintly dizzy, and continued. "What you might not know, and sure, there's no reason for you to know it, is that it did not begin with the IRA at all. In the late sixties, Captain Terrence O'Neill, the Prime Minister at Stormont—that was the seat of the Northern Ireland government—and Sean Lemass, our taoiseach, began a series of friendly conversations. Everyone was confident that we were entering a new era of peace and friendship between the two Irelands. That pleased most of us, but it didn't please much a lot of the Ulster Protestants, who voted O'Neill out of office. The trouble was that expectations of peace and equality and justice—all very great powerful attractive things—had been stirred up among the Catholics, but among some other folks, too, particularly in the universities, who thought it was time to bury the past. Do you follow me?"

"I'm not a secondary school student, Superintendent."

Yet another Irish sigh. "Well, the civil rights movement began, modeled after your own American civil rights movement. It was mostly university students, and many, but not all of them, Catholic. They were all young, all enthusiastic, and all convinced, poor daft young ones, that they could do in Northern Ireland what Martin Luther King did in the American South. Sure, it was a grand idea, but they didn't realize that the Royal Ulster Constabulary, and particularly the B Specials, a reserve force dominated by the Orange Lodgers up there, made your man Bull Connor look like a member of the American Civil Liberties Union, and that the London government was not headed by a man like John Kennedy or Lyndon Johnson or even Richard Nixon."

"Bernadette Devlin and her crowd?"

"The very same." He seemed pleased by my knowledge of recent Irish history. "At first it looked like things were going their way. They had great, powerful demonstrations, thousands of people, and your Orangemen were stupid enough to attack them and beat them, which earned them sympathy for their bravery here in the South, and in England, and I suppose all over the world."

"I remember the pictures on television."

"Well, the crowd in Stormont got nervous, and, sure, they behaved predictably. They unleashed the RUC and the B Specials, not only on the civil rights young ones, but on Catholics in Derry and in the Falls Road in Belfast. You could be a Catholic woman or child, minding your own business on the streets of either place, and find yourself banged over the head by a B Specials club. The fools seemed to enjoy especially doing it in front of television cameras, figuring that that would terrorize the Catholics back into passivity."

"Selma all over again."

"That's what the civil rights kids thought, anyway." He sighed, relit his pipe, and admitted to the hovering waiter that he would like a pint of Guinness. "Sure, I'm not exactly on duty, if you take my meaning. Anyway, there was a Labour Party in power in England, and they were half sympathetic with the civil rights kids, even if they were Irish, and it was embarrassing to them, being Leftists and all, for the whole world to see on television police in a province of the United Kingdom acting like they were American rednecks. So they sent in British troops—mind you, to protect the Catholics from the RUC and the B Specials and the Orange Lodge thugs. Paratroopers were cheered when they arrived in the streets of Derry and the Falls Road. Sure, Catholic women ran into the streets to give them cups of tea. The British army, for the first time, had intervened in Northern Ireland to protect the Teagues, as the Catholics are called, from the Prots."

"I vaguely remember that."

"Most Americans do." He considered his Guinness balefully. "Somehow they forget the details of what happened next. At the time the British troops arrived, there probably weren't more than five or six guns in any of the Catholic neighborhoods in Northern Ireland. The IRA was split into two factions: the Officials, who were Marxists, but Irish Marxists, mind you, and the Provisionals, who are anti-Marxists. Your famous Provos. They were busy arguing among themselves. No one took them seriously, and there hadn't been any violence for over a decade. Your civil rights folk were as nonviolent as Martin Luther King and his friends.

"Well, there was a British election. Your wee Bach-playing gombeen-man, Edward Heath, became prime minister, and Reggie Maulding took over responsibilities for Northern Ireland. In three months the British army, which had come to protect Catholics, had been converted into an occupying army that smashed Catholic homes and beat up Catholics in the streets of Derry. They were supposed to be searching for guns, because the Ulster Protestants were convinced that the homes and churches of the Catholics were filled with guns—there'd soon be a Catholic uprising with the connivance of the British army. Heath and Maulding wanted to reassure the Prots they would tolerate no violence from the Teagues. So, typical of everything England has ever done in Ireland, they turned a bad situation into a disaster."

"And the invisible army crawled out of the cellars and the caves."

"Ah." He knocked the ashes out of his pipe and concentrated all his attention on the Guinness. He had still not taken off his raincoat. "You are a quick man, Mr. Brendan Ryan. Jesus, the lads were the only ones who were ready to protect the Catholics. Some of our politicians here on the South shipped guns up to them, not many guns, mind you, but enough to begin the job. There were a lot of folk who thought then and think now that there wasn't much choice in the matter. It was either guns from the Republic or an army from the Republic to save the Catholics in the North, and to tell the truth, we didn't have an army then."

"Exit civil rights, enter IRA."

"Right. By ordering a search for guns that weren't there, the government in London saw to it that the guns appeared, and then once more there were gunmen in the streets. The Brits continued to do everything wrong. There was a power-sharing thing, Catholics and Prots working together on town councils and the like, even a Prot lord mayor in Derry. No decisions made unless both groups agreed. It was working very well indeed, too well for men like Ian Paisley, of whom you've doubtless heard." He cocked an eye over at me over his Guinness.

"I've heard of him."

"So there was a strike by the Protestant unions and demonstrations by Paisley's folk and hints that the British army in the North would mutiny if it was ordered to support power-sharing—that's an old game the Brits have played in Ireland before—and Harold Wilson, that fine liberal left-wing socialist, backed down. It's been the gunmen ever since."

"So what has all this to do with Clare Keenan, also known as Ciara Kelly?"

"Well, now, I'm not saying it has anything to do with her." He knocked the rest of his ashes out of his pipe and filled it once again. "Most of the civil rights kids gave it up. They left Ulster for England or the United States or even for the South. A few of them, like the wee lass—Bernadette—stayed and got themselves into a radical fringe group, Marxist mostly, if you take what they say seriously, and you probably shouldn't. By that time they'd been reading Frantz Fanon and Regis Debray—himself a fairly respectable part of Mr. Mitterrand's government in France now—and were convinced that violence would succeed where nonviolence had failed. Bernadette herself now talks a strange mixture of Marxism and Irish nationalism and violent revolution. Sure, after what they did to her and her husband and her kids, you can hardly blame her.''

"And?''

"Well, a few of them set up their own little terrorist groups, alternatives to the Provos, who didn't much like them. Sure, your Provos went to Communion every Sunday. But at first they weren't all that much worried about your atheist Marxists, not so long as they were blowing up bridges and power stations and not blowing up Provos. Well,'' he lit the pipe, ''one thing led to another, and some of these young people, without all of them hardly realizing it, began to blow up people instead of bridges and power stations and ammunition dumps. And not just British soldiers, but pubs full of Protestants. Well, for the most part they were more reckless than the Provos, and, one way or another, they got themselves caught or got killed in skirmishes with the Provos, who decided that they wanted no part of godless communism in their revolution, if you take my meaning?''

"More or less.''

"Sure, a few of the youngsters were half daft by then—if they weren't half daft to begin with. They thought that when they were let out of prison finally, they had to have themselves a wee bit of revenge on their friends who didn't go to prison, if you follow me.''

I followed him all right. Clare had returned from the Congo an angry, wounded idealist and, in defiance of her parents, went to school at Queens in Belfast, precisely so she could join the civil rights movement. Still hurting from her brutalization and angry at brutes wherever they were, she had drifted into one of the radical fringe groups of the IRA. My Ciara a terrorist killer?

"Are you telling me that the Irish government and the Special Branch can't find these men and can't protect people from them?''

"Ah, well,'' he puffed fiercely on the pipe, ''sure we find some of them, and we've done a reasonably good job of protecting the ones that need protection. Not that certain other governments haven't helped us, mind you. But there's a couple of lads, one in particular, that are powerful elusive. Imagine a handsome young fellow with some medical training, call him Rory McLafferty if you like, an actor, a comedian, a charmer, great mind and a brilliant speaker, probably a bit of a psychopath all along but not so's you'd notice it at first. Then he goes to prison and, sure, the screws—that's what they call the prison guards—don't like him at all and they make his life miserable. He goes around the bend altogether and swears he'll have revenge on everyone who betrayed him. Finally he escapes from prison, slips into the world underground, goes to Libya and Syria and Iran and God knows where else, and comes back to finish off his enemies and continue the work he'd begun. Only finishing off the enemies is what really matters, even if it means blowing up a sailboat in Chicago with the wrong people in it.''

"He didn't do that," I said. "The other governments aren't keeping you informed."

"Is that so?" he asked, now giving up completely on the pipe. "What do you mean by that?"

So I told him about the shoot-out in the Karwick Plaza a little over a week ago.

"Aye," he nodded sadly, "trust the intelligence agencies, first of all, to overreact, and then not to keep one another informed."

"So you people, or your friends, lifted Ciara out of Chicago for the wrong reason?"

"Don't blame me, Mr. Ryan," he said sadly. "I only found out about it afterward. But you take my point now, do you not? Your man Rory McLafferty is a genius and a madman. He's given the slip to police forces in five or six countries. You don't want to have anything to do with him at all, at all.''

"Why would he want to have anything to do with me?"

The Garda's eyes widened. "Wasn't I after telling you that? Well, perhaps I was being too Irish and thus too indirect. You see, he seems to think that you will lead him to Clare Keenan.''

"What?" I suddenly felt very cold. I could see where the whole conversation was pointing. Right at me.

And Jean.

"The IRA Provos are not the only ones who have friends in the United States and here in Dublin. Even a psychopath like Rory is thought to be the savior of Ireland by some people. His American friends sent him your name—never mind how we know, because I don't even know how we know. I suspect, if you push me, that the Provos, who would like to be rid of him, are feeding information to some of our fellas in hopes that we will do to him what they'd like to do.''

''I see,'' I said, feeling a deep anger rise up within me. ''And his Dublin friends have told him that I've showed up here asking questions. And your American friends have made the same reports to you?''

''He wants Clare Keenan and he thinks you're the man to find her for him, if you don't already know where she is. And he suspects the latter. He'll stop at nothing, sir; that's why we beg you to take your daughter and go home to America.''

Sage advice. But not the sort to which Finn MacCool listens.

''I'll kill him, Jaymo Finnegan. I'll kill him if he doesn't leave Ciara alone. I've killed men before for harming a woman I loved, and I'm quite capable of doing it again.''

It was not the Brendan Ryan I've known all my life who spoke those words, but a stranger, perhaps a devil, who had taken possession of my soul during the wild spring ritual dance, an ancient Celtic berserker, perhaps even the great Finn MacCool himself.

Detective Superintendent Finnegan looked at me with the astonishment he might display at a visitor from the planet Uranus. ''We have laws against murder in the Republic of Ireland,'' he stammered.

''It'll either be in self-defense,'' I said coldly, ''or you'll never catch me.''

''We can't allow you to risk your life, Mr. Ryan,'' he said, jamming his pipe and tobacco into the pocket of his raincoat. He was a good cop like Mike Casey, and a smart one too. But he lacked the mixture of brilliance and bureaucratic disrespect that made Mike one of the finest cops in the world. Not his fault, God knows.

''If you want to protect my life, then you can forget about trying to make me give up my search for Ciara—or whatever her name is—and you can forget about trying to make me leave Ireland. And many thanks for providing me with lots of information I didn't have before.''

"They said you were a reasonable man." He rose uncertainly.

"Or did they say I was a quiet man and a coward?"

"They didn't say you were a fool." He stood up, pulled his cap out of his pocket, and jammed it on his head. "For the love of God, Mr. Ryan, stay out of this."

"No, Detective Superintendent Finnegan, it is precisely for the love of God that I will not stay out of it."

What a pompous ass I was.

30

The Dublin-to-Galway train on the C.I.E. (the Irish National Railroad identified by the first letters of its Gaelic name) bounced with uncomfortable determination across the countryside, passing first through rain showers and then what British Isles weather forecasters call "sun showers." The temperature outside was certainly no more than fifty; it seemed even colder than that in the railroad car. Jean, wearing beige slacks and an Aran Island sweater, huddled within a Windbreaker but resolutely refused to complain.

"It looks like Wisconsin outside," she observed.

"The books say that the counties like Meath and Louth have some of the richest farms in Europe. It's only when you get to the Shannon River at Alone that you cross into the west of Ireland and begin to encounter poor farms and even poverty today. Those are the parts of Ireland where they raise potatoes and where people either starved or fled to America, especially in famine times in 1848 and '49. Then for the rest of the nineteenth century they were the wretched refuse of the earth who fled to America. Our people, the common folk, in other words . . ."

I could babble about the countryside now, but my craving for Ciara Kelly was stronger than ever.

"I think, Daddy," she sniggered wickedly, "if you look

again at the map you'll see the town is called Athlone, not Alone. Just above it the Shannon widens into a broad lake called Lough Ree. When we finally find your friend Ciara or Clare or whatever we're going to call her, I'm going to come back, rent a houseboat on Lough Ree, and spend a week taking pictures of the Shannon and the countryside around it."

"Fine with me."

It was madness to permit Jeannie to join my search for Ciara Kelly (and Ciara Kelly she would always be to me). She came home from the *Irish Times* with pictures of Clare Keenan marching with Bernadette Devlin and civil rights demonstrations in Derry. I repeated almost verbatim my conversation with Detective Superintendent Jaymo Finnegan of the Special Branch. "I'm going out to Castlebar and to Westport," I told her firmly. "And you are going home to the United States, where you'll be safe."

Jean tilted her chin defiantly at me. "Just try to make me."

"These are very dangerous men, Jeannie. They could hurt you or even kill you."

"Only if I don't kill them first."

"It's not like the shoot-out at the Karwick Corral. This is a different situation. I don't want to have to worry about you."

"And I don't want to have to worry about you," she fired back at me, her eyes blazing. "I'm not going to let you do this by yourself. Aren't you the one who told me that I shouldn't try to do things by myself?"

"That's different."

"*B-u-l-lshit!*"

The argument went on, though it was obvious to me after the first few moments that eventually I would lose.

Jean decided that the best way to make our trip would be to take the train from the Connolly Station across the Liffey, along the old Royal Canal north of Phoenix Park near the great seminary at Maynooth and on to Galway City. We'd spend the night at the Railway Hotel in Galway (built over the railway terminal) and then drive to Ashford Castle in County Mayo. The next morning we would go on to Castlebar and perhaps even, she conceded, spend a night at Keenan's Keep on Clew Bay—though "I'd hardly expect, Daddy, that we're going to find any clues there."

Clues? For Jeannie it was a game, a great adventure, a romantic search for a woman with whom she was already partly identifying—and also partly resenting. In the adventure movies we Americans see on television, the good guys always win. Unfortunately, there is no guarantee of that in the real world.

"Besides, if your man Jaymo is following us, which I'm sure he is, it would be easier for him if we stay in the big hotels that everyone knows."

The charming, witty young taxi driver who brought us to the railway station, the kind of devil-may-care comic who reminds you of the actor who played Florie Knox in the PBS series *The Irish R.M.*, promised us that we would have a "grand time out in the west."

"Sure," he said, "till you get to the Shannon all you meet is West Brits. The real Irish are all in the west. Few of us enough left these days. You won't see our like again."

"An endangered species?" I asked, half joking.

"Ah, endangered beyond repair," the cabbie agreed. "But, sure, we've been saying that for three thousand years. So you should not expect us to disappear tomorrow."

So it was that we passed through Athlone, now properly pronounced, in the driving rain and lumbered on to Galway city, a strange, bewitching mixture of the ugly and the picturesque, part Gypsy sorceress, part Gaelic princess, and part Aer Lingus hostess on a fully booked flight. It was celebrating its five hundredth anniversary, perhaps with a sigh of relief that it had lasted so long and still enjoyed reasonably good prospects for the future.

The sun was indeed going down on Galway Bay, and the splendid blue sky slowly turning dark when we checked into the Great Southern Railway Hotel above the railway terminal, a nineteenth-century dowager, quite conscious that she had once been among the very best of her kind and striving to remain sufficiently renewed and rejuvenated to be the most impressive lady in town without spending too much money. The corridors had been freshly carpeted and painted, the rooms were reasonably clean and newly wallpapered, and the veneer on the furniture in the room was effectively resistant to scratch and stain. Moreover, thank goodness, the central heating seemed to work.

I went upstairs to the Claddagh Grill for a late afternoon

Jameson's overlooking Galway Bay and the "Claddagh" area (it meant quay), where at one time there had been a community of densely packed thatched cottages inhabited by an impoverished people whose culture was alleged to be unique in all of Ireland. The Claddagh was urban-renewed out of existence just a few years before the threatened destruction of such an ecological/historical resource would have brought out hordes of angry demonstrators.

There was a swimming pool next to the grill. You could indeed sit at tables around the pool and sip your "jar" with the pretense that you were in a tropical resort. Where else but in Ireland would they put in a glassed-in swimming pool on the fifth floor of a hotel that was a hundred and fifty years old in a city five hundred years old next to a bay that song had made perhaps the most famous bay in all the world?

Jean appeared in the grill wrapped in an enormous towel, discarded the towel, and very quickly dived into the pool attracting, as one might expect, considerable attention from the pre-dinner drinkers who did not always see a lithe young woman in a string bikini on the fifth floor of the Great Southern Railway Hotel.

"Ow!" she screamed as she broke the surface of the water, "it's *cold*!" She kept on swimming, however.

Spring in Ireland—bikini-clad Yank colleen's swimming in an enclosed pool over Galway Bay.

Soon Ciara and I would swim in the same pool.

That was an absurd thought. Still I swore to myself it would happen.

Jean had bid Liam farewell in Dublin, promising to let him know when she returned. She also called Chicago to make her peace with Tim. "I apologized for being a bitch and starting both the fights," she confided to me as our train left Dublin behind. "I told him that if he still wanted to be friends when I came back we could talk about it. He was very nice. Daddy, what do apologies do to men?"

I thought of Eileen Kane on the balcony at Grand Beach. "Aphrodisiac."

"You're terrible." She poked my arm lightly, a means of communication that I had come to interpret as meaning I was really rather cute but I said some of the damnedest things. Nonetheless, she seem pleased by my answer.

Jean was enjoying the first phases of our search, but I was not. The conflicting emotions that rumbled inside me were hard to name or define. I was eager to find Ciara and deeply worried about her, convinced now that the terror which I had experienced in Chicago, and which intermittently returned, was terror that was still ahead for her. The pain and degradation were yet to come. They threatened but they might be averted. As much as I wanted to find her and save her, I dreaded the impending feelings of doom and death that weighed heavily on me since we'd pulled out of the Connolly Station in Dublin. I was worried about Jean, who was so much fun to be with but far too young and innocent to be permitted such risks. And I was implacably determined to kill Rory McLafferty if he threatened to harm my woman.

I killed him often in my sleep that night. He resolutely refused to stay dead.

The next morning we rented another Renault and drove across the Corrib River by the salmon weir, and around the great ugly gray pile of stones that is the new cathedral (the bishop of which was supporting communist regimes in El Salvador and Nicaragua and refused to meet President Reagan when he came to Galway. I've never voted for a Republican in my life, but I couldn't help but wonder whether his lordship would support a communist government in County Galway too).

Jean drove carefully out of Galway on the Headford road to Cong, just inside County Mayo (where the film *The Quiet Man* was made), and to Ashford Castle, one of the world's great hotels, which has been described as the kind of castle that God would create if He had as much money as a Philadelphia millionaire.

The hotel is a mixture of fourteenth-century castle, seventeenth-century hunting lodge designed like a miniature French château, nineteenth-century country home for the Guinness family, and a twentieth-century addition that expanded it to twice its size. It now looks like a Disney World medieval castle—broad, neatly trimmed lawns, thick oak beams, deep carpet, red brocaded walls, wonderful paintings of the Irish countryside (and a few nudes of an Italian peasant girl, painted by an artist whom the Guinnesses must have liked), and great windows overlooking the northern end of

Lough Corrib, sometimes glowing peacefully in the sunlight, sometimes frothing in the wind, sometimes shrouded in fog or beaten by heavily dancing raindrops. Since it was Ireland, all of these things could happen in the same day or even in the same hour.

"What's this beautiful place?" Jean peered closely at a painting of water and beach and sun and green hills. "I want to take pictures of it. Is there any place in the whole world more gorgeous?"

"Ciara and you would agree." I looked over her shoulder at the copper plaque on the frame. "It's the strand at Inch, down in County Kerry. She says she wants to die there because it's the closest place to Heaven in all the world."

"I hate the woman." Jean lingered at the canvas. "Absolutely hate her. I'll make common cause with her against you when we find her."

"Spoken like a true Irishwoman."

"What else?"

Jean wanted to check in and push on to Castlebar, a market town and the administrative center of County Mayo (and the site of the battle described so vividly in the novel *The Year of the French*), to begin our inquiries.

But I wanted time to work out more clearly my game plan: first of all the hospital administrators, then the newspaper, then the parish priest, then the pubs. The questions had to be thought through very carefully and then translated into the peculiar, indirect, answer a question with a question West-of-Ireland style. We wouldn't get a second chance. Moreover, it seemed to me that Jean and I ought to work separately, that she should find the pubs and other gathering places of young people in Castlebar and see if there were any memories in the new generation of Clare Keenan, perhaps even a relative who could tell us something about her. While I sat in my vast and elegant nineteenth-century room, whose furnishings would have deceived anyone but an antique specialist, and wrote out the questions and committed them to memory, Jean dashed down to the concrete breakwater, to hire a boat for an exploration of the northern end of Lough Corrib. I warned her to be careful, and she replied by telling me that Cong was the faerie capital of Ireland and the little people would protect her.

As it turned out, they did a poor job.

I watched her haggle with two old countrymen at the pier in front of the hotel and then bounce confidently into a small boat—little more than a canoe—with an outboard motor and chug out into the lake.

In the distance a rainstorm was gathering over the ocean and moving in our direction. I was tempted to rush down to the pier to call her back, but it was too late and I would embarrass her if I tried. At first the rain was light and the visibility unaffected.

As I turned to my work of planning our campaign, I noted a big speedboat sweep by the castle and curve away toward the far side of the lake. They were going pretty fast, I thought idly.

After I had finished the final draft of my questions, memorized them, torn them up and, with a nod to James Bond, flushed them down the toilet, I telephoned Mike Casey in Chicago. "I'll fly over," he said simply. "Collect Nick Curran and catch a plane tonight."

"Thanks much, Mike, but not yet. If I need help I'll yell."

"You need help now."

"Not yet. A small reconnaissance team before we send in the main force."

Mike was not convinced, but he finally agreed. "Call me every day at this time at this number here at the gallery. If a day goes by and we don't hear from you, the main force will move in."

"You should have been a general." I laughed as I hung up. Very clever strategy. A shame I hadn't thought of it first.

Then I did have an idea. I called Mike back, hoping that no one at the switchboard was listening. "Can you get me an Uzi?"

"What the hell is that? An Italian painter?"

"You know damn well what it is."

"Do you know how to work one of those?" Mike asked tersely.

"I won the marksmanship prize with the M16 in ROTC, and I used one in Vietnam. I'm told the Uzi is a lot simpler."

"Too damned many people with marksmanship prizes," Mike said uneasily. "You and that impish little redneck chick."

"I'm not asking for an Israeli machine pistol for Cindasoo.

Though when you bring the reserves, maybe you could bring her along.''

"Main force, not reserves. All right, you want one with a silencer, I suppose?''

"Naturally.''

"I can get it to you, as long as the Special Branch isn't inspecting the packages that are sent to you. I doubt that they're doing that yet. There'll be one waiting for you at Ashford Castle the day after tomorrow. They come in very neat little packages.''

"And enough ammunition too.''

"Enough for what? To fight off the whole Irish Republican Army?''

"Enough to hold off whoever needs to be held off until the main force arrives.''

"Fair enough.''

The Uzi automatic weapon was seen by most people for the first time when John Hinckley tried to assassinate President Reagan. If you remember the pictures on television of the incident, the Secret Service men reached inside their coats, pulled out what looked like a little boy's toy, opened the plastic folding stock, and held in their hands a weapon a little longer than an ordinary pistol but with no resemblance at all to the beloved tommy gun of Chicago crime films, or even the automatic weapons John Wayne fired so recklessly in the many different wars in which he fought. The Uzi didn't look like much of a weapon. Nonetheless, it was the best machine gun or machine pistol or automatic weapon (choose your own name) made anywhere in the world. Much better, even, than its closest rival, the Russian AK-47.

Perhaps I was out of practice. It had been eighteen years since I had fired my M16 for the last time. Maybe, if worse came to worst, the Uzi's excellence would compensate for my lack of practice.

Even now I wonder, quite literally, what possessed me to make the second phone call and ask for the weapon. It was the same hidden berserker inside me, I suppose, who decided to go into Dufficy's Irish Store after I had written Ciara Kelly out of my life, the inner demon that had sent me on this wild-goose chase to Ireland, the residual Irish lunatic who sent me into the jungle in search of Marie's bathing pond, the reckless

Celtic lover whose lips had drawn sweet milk from Marie Tho's pliant nipples and whose body had ruthlessly overcome Ciara's sexual fears. Ridiculous dissociation. Mary Kate Murphy would scoff at it. It was Brendan Ryan, not Finn MacCool, who had done all those things, Brendan Ryan who had told Superintendent Jaymo that he would kill Rory McLafferty if necessary, a Brendan Ryan whose existence I had pretended to ignore for most of my life, and now a Brendan Ryan who had crossed his Rubicon, or his Shannon, in search of an Israeli machine pistol.

I looked out the turreted window of my room. Torrents of rain were slashing into Ashford Castle. Lough Corrib had disappeared. The berth on the pier below me where Jean's little boat had been moored was empty.

I raced down the stairs and, hatless and coatless, dashed to the pier. Two old Irish countrymen in gray suits, gumshoe boots, and caps stood in the shelter of the boathouse, thoughtfully puffing on their pipes, like mourners in front of a funeral home.

"Did my daughter come back?" I shouted above the wind.

"Ah, sure, was she the wee lass in the Aran jersey?"

What a time to be answering questions with other questions. "Where the hell is she?"

"Wasn't I only after saying," said the other one, "maybe we ought to half think about taking the launch out to search for her?"

"That's the launch?" I pointed at a decrepit blue and white wooden boat that was at least a century older than the internal combustion engine.

"Ah, what else would it be but the launch?" said the first of the boat tenders.

"Are you coming with me or am I going to drive it myself?"

I jumped off the pier into the boat, which rocked in uneasy protest, shoved the hood back off the motor in the middle of the craft, pulled out what I supposed to be the choke, and turned over the key. The motor chugged reluctantly and refused to start. I jammed in the choke and tried again. With great unhappiness and infinite weariness the old six-cylinder Chrysler marine engine, which certainly had existed longer than I had, spurted into life.

"Sure," said one of the old fellows, as he awkwardly climbed down next to me, "isn't that the first time the old gal has started so quickly?"

We putt-putted slowly into the whitecaps, small by Lake Michigan standards, probably only a foot or a foot and a half, but dangerous for a shallow little fishing boat like Jean's. "Which way should I go?" I demanded.

"Well, wasn't the lass saying now that she wanted to take a picture of the island down the lake where St. Patrick's navigator is buried? Isn't that Inchagoill?"

"Which way is that?" I had to shout because the wind was howling fiercely and the rain was pounding like a hundred drumsticks on the roof of the tiny cabin.

"It wouldn't be a mistake, would it," said the younger of the two boatkeepers, a man around seventy, I should guess, "to head straight south to Inchagoill Island? It's over in that direction." He pointed vaguely to the right with his pipe, which he then quickly replaced in his mouth. It was the closest to a declarative sentence I had heard from either of them. Dear God in Heaven, please let Jeannie be alive, please, please, please.

Ten or fifteen minutes later, after fighting our way through rain that was sometimes so thick we could barely see the prow of the boat (and the windshield wiper in the front of the cabin didn't work), the downpour eased, the clouds lifted, and the mists swept away temporarily. "Ah, sure," the young fella pointed with his pipe, "wouldn't that be something floating in the water over there?"

With tight throat and sinking heart, I turned the boat toward the floating object. It looked like the prow of a fishing boat. "Isn't that the Star of the Sea?" the older fella asked, gesturing with his pipe. "And hasn't someone cut it in half?"

"Doesn't it look like your man drove a launch right through the middle?"

With Jeannie in it.

31

"Could the wee lass swim?" The old fella (about seventy-five) touched my arm respectfully as I slumped over the wheel of the boat, paralyzed by fear. "Might she have made it to the shore of the island?"

Gently he eased me away from the wheel and steered us toward the shore, throttling back to slow speed. "You wouldn't want to hit some of the rocks, would you now?"

We chugged around the island, maybe half a mile square of trees, thick underbrush, and rocky shoreline. On the far side he turned off the motor and we drifted toward a wooden plank, nailed perilously to a piling a couple of yards out into the lake. The plank was covered with three or four inches of water. The young fella tried three times to loop the boat's rope around the piling. Finally on the fourth attempt he succeeded, and the boat drifted against the plank. "You get out first, sir," said the old fella. "Aren't we a bit slower than you?"

I slipped on the plank, lost my balance, teetered towards the lake, and then steadied myself against the boat.

"Careful now," said the young fella, unnecessarily.

I stepped off the plank onto the slippery rocks of the shore and saw a patch of brown fabric, perhaps ten yards farther down the shore. Ignoring the two old men, I slipped and stumbled and finally fell towards the dead tree hanging out over the water on which the fabric was caught.

Jeannie's jumpsuit, torn almost in two. I slumped down on the rock, buried my head in my hands. I should have listened to Jaymo. Now Jeannie was dead, a victim of my own brash stupidity. The rain started again, the mist closed in, the wind howled through the trees, a banshee mourning for the dead, and I sat there mostly oblivious to the elements, grieving for my lost child. Dear God in Heaven, forgive me.

"Sure," said one of the old men standing behind me, "she

might have kicked it off to swim to shore. It wouldn't hurt to look around the island for her, would it now?''

No, it certainly wouldn't hurt.

So we searched the island, which was once the site, they told me, of a monastery founded by St. Patrick, later a nest of pirates, and still later a fishing village, now uninhabited " 'cause, sure, there's no way to earn a living on a place like this, is there?''

The two old men would only slow me down on a search of the shore, and I didn't want to risk their lives by keeping them out in the rain much longer. I told them to wait for me in the boat and that I would explore the shoreline myself. They protested, none too convincingly, and shuffled back to the boat.

There was no discernible trail along the shoreline, so I slipped on the rocks and plowed through the mud and beat my way through the underbrush, paying no attention to my chattering teeth or shivering body, or to the rain that now assaulted me through my drenched clothes. I suppose it took an hour before I circled around the little island and came back to the boat. No sign of Jean. I must not despair. There had to be something else we could do.

"The lass was a clever one, was she not?'' said the young fella, meditatively puffing his pipe.

"She's pretty smart,'' I admitted.

I slumped against the bow of the boat as it nudged against the shore and realized, for the first time, that I was panting with exhaustion.

"Would she not have known about the cathedral? And might she not have gone there to stay out of the rain? Sure, there's not much of a roof on it, but it's better than nothing, now, isn't it?''

Hope released another supply of adrenaline into my veins. "Where's the cathedral?''

"Isn't it down the path there now?'' He waved his hands at what seemed to me to be a solid mass of trees and underbrush. I plunged into it and stumbled toward the center of the island. The path was a barely distinguishable gap in the underbrush, probably created for the occasional tourist who came to the island to visit the tomb of St. Patrick's alleged navigator (why St. Patrick would have needed a navigator apparently was a question that did not arise).

I missed the cathedral entirely on my first attempt and ended up on the far side of the island. Wrong path.

I thought, irrelevantly, that I should have brought a raincoat, and turned back into the forest. I felt like I was dashing back into one of the circles of Dante's purgatory, a soggy, slippery prison, smelling of damp vegetation, in which I was condemned to run, soaking wet and haunted by guilt, with aching chest and exhausted legs, till the final judgment day.

I worked my way back along the trail with more care; my guilt-ridden panic would be of no help to Jean if she were still alive. Perhaps a third of the way across the island, I found the fork that I had, in my pell-mell rush, missed the first time. I sloshed for perhaps fifty yards in muck and slime, and emerged in a small clearing, in the center of which was a tiny ruin of a very old church, even less cathedral-like than Glendalough. No psychic vibes here, fortunately.

I was wrong. Ciara Kelly. Ciara Kelly. Ciara Kelly.

Pain, fear, humiliation, terror. Carrying my child. My child threatened with destruction.

I shook off the psychic feelings as best I could. There was a real child whose life was in jeopardy.

"Jeannie! Jeannie!" I shouted, as I blundered awkwardly into the ruin, stumbling over the rocks to the entrance and crashing into one of the walls.

"Daddy, where's your raincoat?"

She was hunched down under the bit of roof that remained of the church, a soggy, crumpled little-girl doll wearing blue underwear with a white stripe, the ridiculous analogue of men's underwear which, for some crazy reason, women were now wearing, too.

I swept the soggy doll into my arms.

"You should have gone back for your raincoat," she insisted, hugging me fiercely. "You might get pneumonia."

"That'll be two of us."

"But I'm not *old*!" she giggled.

A very tough young woman, this daughter I was still getting to know. I offered to carry her back down the trail to the boat, but she insisted she was capable of walking by herself. "I wouldn't give those bastards the satisfaction."

"What bastards?"

"It was a big speedboat. They came out of the mists, saw me, turned around, and deliberately cut the boat in half."

"It wasn't an accident?"

"No way. I think they came back to run over me too, but I stayed deep underwater as long as I could. God, Daddy, it was *cold*! When I came up finally, the mists were so thick they couldn't see me, but I heard them buzzing around looking so I guessed which way the island was and swam here. I thought it would take forever. Then I remembered this church and figured soaking wet or not, it was better to be out of the rain than in it. I know how you feel, Daddy. I want to kill those bastards too."

Tomorrow I would tell her about Grace O'Malley, the pirate who once ruled in these lands. Maybe there was O'Malley blood in us.

By the time we'd returned to the boat and the two cheering old men, whose names, Jean whispered to me impatiently, were Seamus and Dermot, the storm had swept through. Cheerful white clouds were racing across the clean windswept sky, and Lough Corrib, smelling of fresh spring life, seemed to be merrily laughing with the four of us as we wrapped a huge blanket, found in the locker in the cabin of the boat (which blanket probably had not been cleaned since before the Easter rising of 1916), around my shivering but laughing daughter and helped her on the boat.

Her adventure seemed to have neither frightened nor daunted her. (She peeled off the underwear beneath the blanket—"We wear them, Daddy, because they feel sexy as hell.") In fact, her reactions seemed merely to be anger and determination to get even. Both emotions were enhanced—like a fire on which gasoline has been thrown—when we passed Grace O'Malley's Hen's Castle and Seamus, the old fella, told us the story.

Grace's husband, Donal O'Flaherty, had various nicknames such as "the Battler" and "the Cock" because he was an ill-tempered, contentious, difficult man ("Though, sure, he didn't dare give herself any guff, not at all, at all"). "Well, he had a great terrible feud with the Joyces, and themselves no better than they had to be, who lived in the mountains south of here. One day the Joyces caught him hunting in the mountains and killed him. They always wanted this castle, called it Cock's Castle, they did, after himself, and so, with him out of the way, they swept down on it with a whoop and a holler, figuring that no woman in the world could keep the Joyces away from a castle that they wanted. Well, they reckoned without herself. Beat the livin Bejesus out of them, she did, and ever after it's been called the Hen's Castle, and mind ya, lass, that was a compliment.''

Jean's eyes were shining brightly. ''And then what happened?''

So by the time we'd got back to Ashford Castle, we'd heard many of the Grace O'Malley legends, how she'd divorced her second husband, Iron Dick Burke, a year and a day after the marriage, once she'd taken over his castle, but, sure, after she got rid of the poor man, she discovered that she loved him, so she took him back, and didn't they have themselves a son who became the first Lord Mayo and keep the O'Malleys going here in the county for another couple of hundred years. About her being a better sailor than Sir Francis Drake, about her ruling the whole of the West of Ireland coast from her stronghold on Clare Island in Clew Bay. Sure, she really wasn't a pirate at all, at all, she just charged a heavy tax on them ships that wanted to go through her part of the ocean. Mind ya, they all paid. About how the English were afraid to fight her and made peace with her, about the English governor who tried to put her son in prison, and didn't herself go all the way to Queen Elizabeth and get her son and all their rights and properties back? Whatever you say about Queen Bess, and she was no better than she had to be either, she knew a real lady when she saw one.

''Are all those stories true, Daddy?'' Jean whispered as we walked across the lobby of Ashford Castle as inconspicuously as you can when you are soaking wet and one of you is wearing a battered old blanket that trails across the floor behind you.

''They are indeed, Jean. She was one of the greatest women of her time or, indeed, of any time. Women didn't run clans in Ireland in those days. But Grace O'Malley did, according to the historians, because the men who were her followers admired and respected and liked her. She was also supposed to be gorgeous, but then, of course, aren't all Irish women?''

Jean ignored my compliment, her shining brown eyes far, far away, doubtless on Lough Corrib or on Clew Bay when Granuaile's swift, maneuverable galleys swept forth to do battle for her family and her clan and her freedom.

Later that night I was in Jean's room. She was curled up in bed, shrouded in towels, a terry cloth robe, and blankets, and sipping Jameson's, to which she was rapidly becoming as addicted as her father. "I'm still furious, Daddy," she said through clenched teeth. "They're evil, crazy men. I'm not going to let them push me around."

"It's not the sixteenth century and you're not Granuaile O'Malley, kid." I was sipping my own Jameson's.

Before she could answer, the phone rang. I had a reasonably good idea who it was. "Good evening, Superintendent Finnegan. A bit late, aren't you?"

Silence. And then: "Have you learned your lesson? Are you going home now?"

"Are you suggesting, Superintendent, that I should leave Ireland because the Gardai are incapable of protecting tourists on a boat in Lough Corrib?"

"That was a bloody stupid trick, going out on that lake."

"If Granuaile O'Malley was in the Hen's Castle, no one would get away with what happened this afternoon. Lough Corrib seems to have been safer in her day than it is now."

"Your man is unpredictable. He probably started out with the intention of frightening the wee lass and through her, you. Then he saw a chance to kill and changed his mind."

"A chance offered him by the Irish police."

"We can't be frigging everywhere," Jaymo Finnegan shouted. "We're only human and we're busy now trying to provide protection for your frigging president."

"I didn't vote for him, Superintendent," I said curtly. "My daughter and I will assume, from now on, that the Gardai are not able to protect us, and we'll take proper measures to protect ourselves. Good evening, Superintendent."

"Gee," my daughter said admiringly, "I bet you could play on Granuaile O'Malley's team too."

"He's not a bad man." I picked up my Jameson's tumbler. "He can't afford to let anything happen to us, so he's going to watch even more closely, after what happened today. And he does have some legitimate excuse. The 'Great Communicator' is on tour.''

"Did you see the woman from Cong on television the other night? No, of course you didn't. You were home in the hotel, and Liam and I were in a pub. Anyway, RTE—that's the Irish television—asked her what she thought about the president coming to Ireland and stopping at Ashford Castle. 'Ah, well,' she says, 'I suppose it's all right, but he's only an old politician. It'd be much different if it was J.R. or Sue Ellen!' ''

We both laughed and thus dismissed Rory McLafferty and his psychopathic schemes.

For Jeannie, there was an excuse. She was young, she was a romantic, she'd never experienced real danger before. For me there was no excuse at all. Yet, that day at Ashford Castle was the turning point. I had ordered an automatic weapon from Mike Casey, had rescued my daughter from a muddy, rain-drenched little island on Lough Corrib in the land of Grace O'Malley. I had warned Jeannie that it wasn't the sixteenth century but somehow, I had begun to think of myself as a pre-Christian Irish chieftain, and an invulnerable one at that. Whoever the demon was that lurked within Brendan Ryan—and he called himself Brendan Ryan, too, when he didn't think of himself as Finn MacCool—took over that day. The quiet man who didn't like competitive sports, who almost never argued with his friends, who avoided conflict whenever possible, who always offered the most cautious and conservative advice to his clients, that Brendan Ryan, who knew he was very vulnerable indeed, went into eclipse.

Granuaile O'Malley's husband Donal O'Flaherty was called Donal-on-Chogaidh, Donal of the Battles. Fair enough. Now I was Brendan-on-Chogaidh. My enemies had taken my woman and threatened my daughter. I would show them no mercy. I did not give voice to any of this foolishness, I didn't even think it explicitly. I didn't have to. The lust-crazed Celtic berserker within me was convinced of his invulnerability. It was not necessary to think at all except about ways of destroying the enemy. What had started as a search for Ciara Kelly had now become a game that was an end unto itself.

We would learn only too soon, both Jean and I, that we were by no means invulnerable.

32

We were still feeling invulnerable and mindlessly exhilarated the next day as we pushed ahead in our search for Ciara. We sang Irish and Irish American tunes, Clancy Brothers variety, on our ride from Cong to Castlebar. My pitch was better than my daughter's, but I lacked her forthright confidence that she knew all the lyrics of a song, even if that meant she had to make them up.

The thick morning fog had blown away when we arrived at Castlebar, singing of "Bold Fenian Men." Jean may have had in mind the men of 1848. I was thinking of Finn MacCool's band of followers.

Castlebar, as the name indicates, was Norman in its origin. Now, however, it was a curious mixture of typical Irish village, with attractively painted storefronts and narrow sidewalks, and Wisconsin resort town with supermarkets, filling stations, and bustling crowds. If this is what the market center of County Mayo was like during a recession, I thought, what must it be like when the country is prosperous?

On the outskirts of Cong I told Jean about the film *The Quiet Man*, which had been made just outside the town, and explained how in the original short story the protagonist was not a big fellow like John Wayne but a little man who even looked like a coward. Who could believe that John Wayne was a coward?

"Maybe I'm prejudiced in favor of little men," I concluded, watching in the sideview mirror to see if a blue VW hatchback with Dublin license plates, which seemed out of place on the main street of Cong, was following us.

"You're not little." Jean pushed the car around a lorry.

"If you are then so am I. And I'm not. So that's that. Right?"

"Right." I could not see the blue car. Perhaps it was following but at a safe distance. Where else would we be going but Castlebar?

After we arrived in the town, Jean and I split up, she with a camera over her shoulder, since the photographer's role would give her an excuse to talk to young people her own age. Eight hours later I dragged myself wearily into the lounge bar of the Breaffy House, tired and frustrated. I had learned absolutely nothing.

Yes, indeed, they had told me at St. Mary's Hospital that Dr. Keenan had been the most distinguished surgeon in the whole of County Mayo and one of the best in Ireland in the 1960s. He and his wife had been dead for some time now, however. The children? There was a surgeon in Liverpool, and the other married to a surgeon in Los Angeles. Another daughter? Clare? Oh, yes, she was the one that went to Africa, wasn't she? No, they knew nothing about her at the hospital. Nurse's training? Well, yes, that might be true, but we have no idea where.

The newspaper editor remembered the Congo incident, poor thing. Her father was a hard man, but she still would have been much better off if she'd gone to the university, wouldn't she now? Nursing school when she came back? That would be logical, wouldn't it? Bernadette Devlin and the civil rights? Young folk in Ulster? Not that I know of. She really never came back to County Mayo after what happened in the Congo. No, I haven't heard a word of her in ten to twelve years at least.

The parish priest of Castlebar was a retired professor of classics from Maynooth. "Keenan? Keenan. Let me see. Well, there's lots of Keenans around here, you know. All a part of the clan from that castle. Haunted? Ah, go along with you, Mr. Ryan, you don't believe in haunted castles now, do you? Dr. Keenan . . . I've only been here five or six years so I can't recall any Dr. Keenan. Lived in Westport, you say? Well, sure, that's another parish altogether. Involved with the civil rights movement? No, I can't recall anyone by that name. Of course, it's a long way from Derry and Belfast to Maynooth, especially if you're a professor of the classics.

Assaulted in the Congo? Sure, that was long before my time. Not at all, Mr. Ryan. Glad to be of help. Sorry I couldn't be of more help.''

Certain that Jaymo Finnegan's men were trailing us, I also suspected that they might have been ahead of us. The owner of the pub nearest St. Mary's Hospital admitted that "now and then a few doctors stopped by for the occasional pint" but could not recall a Dr. Keenan. "A surgeon, you say? Ah, well, they're the worst drinkers of all. I wouldn't want one of them cutting me open with a knife but, no, if Dr. Keenan took the occasional drink, he never took it here.''

There were still several hours before I was due to rendezvous with Jean, so I drove down to Westport, a curious fading relic of the nineteenth century with just enough picturesque Anglo-Irish elegance to suggest that whoever was responsible for historical preservation in Ireland should rush in quickly. The bartender in the lounge bar at the hotel was of no help, neither was the parish priest, who was also a new man, though he did permit me to glance at the funeral records and see that Ciara's parents had indeed been dead for almost ten years, dying only a few months apart. And sure enough, there was her own name, Clare Fiona Keenan, born August 29, 1950. So she was not quite thirty-four. Ah, to be so young that you could give away three or four months!

There was still plenty of time and the weather was still lovely, so I drove south through the Murrisk, which was Grace O'Malley's stronghold, and into County Galway, the country of her bitter enemies, the Joyces. On the road to Letterfrack and Clifden, the heart of the barren, rocky, but somehow hauntingly lovely Connemara peninsula, I stopped at Kylemore Lake, on whose smooth waters stood stately and serene Kylemore Abbey, where Ciara had gone to school, according to the article in the *Irish Times*. The young nun who spoke with me was wearing a brief veil and a modified "airplane cabin attendant" religious habit that was popular in the United States fifteen years ago. She was very polite, very cultivated—Dublin haute bourgeoisie, I guessed— underneath the modern veneer, very much a strict S'ter of the Old School.

"Yes, of course, I knew Clare Keenan. We were classmates." (Had Jaymo's crowd not anticipated me here at

Kylemore?) "What happened to her in the Congo was a terrible tragedy. We were so puritanical in Ireland in those days, it was almost impossible for a woman who had been through that kind of an ordeal to obtain any help. But her father was a doctor. He should have known better. Thank goodness women are finally obtaining their full rights in Ireland."

A stern young nun perhaps, but a feminist too. I didn't want to suggest that the problem wasn't so much women's rights as Victorian prudery enforced by Catholic obscurantism.

No, she had not seen Clare since they graduated. She'd heard that she went to nursing school in Derry. Civil rights movement? There was a rumor to that effect. S'ter was studying in Rome at the time. In recent years, nothing at all. No, wait, someone, yes, a classmate, told me several years ago that she'd seen Clare in London at the theater . . . or perhaps at a concert. In any event, she was teaching at an English university, not Oxford or Cambridge, I'm sure, but seemed quite happy. The woman felt that Clare had left most of her problems behind her."

"The Congo you mean?"

"The Congo and her parents. Dr. Keenan was a very rigid man. I'm sure Clare went to the Congo in the first place to escape from him . . . One summer, when we were still in school, perhaps fourteen or fifteen years old, my family urged me to invite her to spend several weeks of her summer holiday at our house on Achill Island. That's not too far from her home at Westport, you know. Her mother, who was a pleasant woman but not, ah, very strong, agreed. Dr. Keenan promptly refused permission. It was only when my father talked to him and assured him that we would be closely supervised that he acquiesced, I must say, reluctantly and with bad grace."

"I see."

"But she was such a lovely young woman." S'ter mellowed for a moment and smiled pleasantly. "Not only beautiful—though she was surely that—but intelligent and witty and very thoughtful of others." She sighed. "She had so much possibility. . . ."

"So many of us do, Sister." I rose and the nun rose with me, both with our own memories of failures that seemed senseless and unnecessary. And why did I have to pick women whose fathers were hotshot surgeons?

"I wonder if I have described her adequately?" We stood at the door of the abbey which was reflected perfectly in the calm waters of the lake. The serenity of the setting hinted at the wisdom of the ages. No matter what happened to Ciara and me, a nun would be standing here gazing at the waters, knowing all the answers that really mattered, a hundred, a thousand years hence. "She was what we would call today 'charismatic,' the natural leader of the rest of the class in serious work as well as in mischief. We all adored her. She was so good that I have often thought she should have been a nun instead of I. We all knew about her father, of course. He was a great County Mayo character of the old school, always worried about impressing Protestants, but she didn't seem to let him bother her—'Old Doctor,' as she called him, was usually dismissed with good-natured laughter. Is it fair to assume, Mr. Ryan, that you know her reasonably well?"

"Reasonably well, Sister."

"Is she all right?" the nun asked cautiously.

"I think she's going to be," I replied with equal caution.

"I suppose," S'ter sighed, "it was a question of the wrong time and the wrong place."

We shook hands cordially. "Until now."

For the first time I had spoken to someone who knew the same Ciara I knew. Sister Fiona had poured gasoline on the smoldering embers of my love.

Perhaps Ciara had told me her father was a lawyer because she knew I would be skeptical about another surgeon's daughter.

My own daughter was waiting for me impatiently in the lounge bar of the hotel with her now customary glass of whiskey and an open notebook. Her face was shining, her eyes glowing—Sherlock Holmes waiting for Dr. Watson. Or perhaps Cordelia Gray waiting for Adam Dalgliesh.

"It's Black Bushmills, Daddy." She pointed at the glass of whiskey. "I thought I'd try it to see how it compares with Jameson's. It's very good, tastes like cognac. I don't think Uncle Blackie would mind, even if it is Protestant whiskey. Did you have a productive day?"

"No. I see that you did."

"Right." Eager to begin, she flipped open her notebook and then paused. "She's some chick, Daddy. I suppose I'll have to hate her for a while because she'll be taking you away from me and because obviously she's not good enough for you—no one would be." She grinned mischievously. "But after a while, I'm sure I'll identify with her. Then you'll be in real trouble."

It was beyond my capacity to imagine at that moment a family made up of Ciara and Jean and me. Such a family life, perhaps with a house in Beverly, a cottage somewhere near the Ryan compound in Grand Beach, would exist in the world of ordinary reality. I was now living in the mythic world of the west of Ireland, a world peopled by such characters as Iron Dick Burke and Donal "the Battler" O'Flaherty and Rory McLafferty.

"I was certainly very much impressed by her, Jean," I said, hiding behind the formal reply.

"Okay. She did her nurse's training at the Royal Victoria Hospital in Belfast. Rory McLafferty was a medical student, a Dublin Catholic, as gifted as your man Jaymo said he is. They became caught up in the civil rights movement. Then Rory broke with Bernadette on the issue of violence. His group was never large, fifteen or twenty at the most. They weren't as careful or as professional or as well-disciplined as the Provos, who, by the way, were not sorry to see him caught by the Brits."

"By the Brits?"

"You better believe it. So they blew up bridges and power stations and munitions dumps and such like, and Rory McLafferty became a legend. In those days things were so bad for the Catholics in the North that anybody who hurt the Brits was a hero. Then he began believing his own legends, or so my friends tell me, and he turned to murder. One night after a football game, his group blew up a bus filled with Protestant fans. They boarded another bus and gunned down nineteen football players. Clare, or Ciara, had had enough. They were supposed to be an organization in which everybody agreed on everything, and he hadn't told her about the football massacre. . . . Incidentally, Daddy, they were supposed to be lovers." She poised her pencil over the notebook and avoided my eyes. "Does that bother you?"

"Sure it does." I nodded my gratitude to the waitress who brought me my Bushmills, Black Label. It was indeed "very good." I would report it to Blackie, who probably knew all about it. "But it doesn't make any difference."

"Right." She put the pencil back on the notebook. "Anyway, she said she was quitting. He said 'You can't quit.' She said 'Just watch me.' He said 'All right, you can quit, but only after we blow up this music hall filled with Prots. Once that's done, once you've got your hands bloody, then I'll let you go.' So she marched off to the British army and told them about the music hall plot. The Brits caught the whole lot of them, killed half a dozen, and put the rest behind bars."

"So she was an informer?"

"Yeah." Jeannie flipped the page of her notebook. "I guess that's something pretty bad here in Ireland. Wasn't there a movie about that once?"

"Nineteen thirty-five. Victor McLaglen."

"Who? Never mind. It doesn't matter. The kids I talked to think she was a heroine. They're not into violence around here anymore. It's like they wish Ulster could be towed out into the Atlantic somewhere near Iceland and sunk. They don't like the Brits very much, but they don't like the Provos either. The Provos, by the way, have nothing against Clare—they think she did them a favor, putting him out of circulation. The Brits wanted to give her money and a new life. She said to hell with you and went off on her own to the University of Sussex in England, where she got herself a degree in French literature, then stayed on the faculty as a reader, which is kind of like an associate professor. She was there six or seven years, until Rory escaped from prison and blew up the house in which she was living. Clare wasn't there and nobody else was killed. Then the Brits and the Special Branch and the CIA 'lifted' her."

"Lifted?"

"My friends tell me," Jean flipped another page, "that both the Brits and the Gardai are afraid that if they can't protect their informants, especially an informant that most people admire, like Clare, there won't be any more informants."

"How long ago did the house in England blow up?"

"About a year and a half ago." Jean closed her notebook and replaced it in her purse. "Nobody knows what happened to her. Maybe she was someplace else before she came to Chicago.''

"And as soon as they heard about the explosion on my boat, they lifted her again.''

"Poor dear woman.'' Jean shook her head sadly. "Anyway, I don't know where all of this gets us except that we now have most of the details. Oh, one more thing.'' She opened the notebook again. "I don't know how much this is worth, but one of my friends, she thought she saw her at a little B&B out on Achill Island a couple of summers ago, like maybe she'd come back to Ireland for a week or two, just to see what it was like.''

Achill Island again. "How did you manage to collect all this information?''

"Oh, hanging around pubs, talking to the young people.'' She shrugged indifferently, taking the keys from my hand. "I told them I went to school at Stanford with a cousin of hers named Emily. I suppose Superintendent Finnegan didn't expect I'd be asking questions.''

"He knows now that you were asking them.'' I considered ordering another Bushmills and decided against it. "And so does the other side.''

"He's a bad man, Daddy, a very bad man, and we're going to have to swat him like a mosquito.''

I was so carried along by the mythological demons I had created for myself that I didn't disagree. Yes, of course, Jean and I, a college sophomore and a tax lawyer, were going to swat a dangerous but brilliant IRA psychopath.

"You drive, Daddy.'' Jean tossed off the keys to the car, which was parked down the street from the hotel. "I had a drink while I was waiting for you. I think I'll curl up and nap.''

And so she did, looking very sweet and innocent in a plaid skirt and light brown sweater, folded up like a little girl in the seat to my left. It was only a brief nap. She awoke about fifteen minutes out of Castlebar, stretched gracefully, straightened up, and began immediately to talk. "I'm afraid I don't have a good picture of her. She sounds like she's brave and tough, but also rebellious, discontented, something of a radical—the kind of woman who would become involved in kooky movements with psychopathic leaders.''

Ah, the changing times. Stanford women wrinkling their noses at the word "movement."

"I suppose she does."

"On the other hand," she pursed her lips thoughtfully, "you describe her as sweet and funny and smart and, well, kinda cool."

"Can't she be both kinds of person?" I kept my eyes very carefully focused on the big lorry in front of us.

"I suppose." A long and thoughtful pause. "But only if she's done a lot of growing up."

"I see your point, Jeannie. Yes, I think she has done a lot of growing up."

The quest had changed: no longer *was* there a Ciara Kelly, but *who* was she?

Jeannie sighed. She'd learned the art very quickly. Her sigh sounded even more like a serious asthma attack than that of the nun at Kylemore Abbey.

"I don't know about you, Daddy." She sounded as though she were in deep, philosophical thought. "All kinds of women go ape over you, and you don't seem to be able to enjoy it."

"For example?" I tried to laugh.

"Well, for example, Grandma Ryan, Mom—poor Mom, she just didn't know how to do it—Emily's mother, Aunt Eileen, Aunt Catherine, even Caitlin and Cindasoo."

"Cindasoo? I don't even know her!"

"She sure 'nuff glowed," Jean imitated her friend, "when you were talking to her after Mass at Aunt Catherine's. Got right flustered, she did."

"Aren't you leaving somebody out?"

"You mean Ciara?"

"No, I mean my daughter."

"I hadn't forgotten about her," Jean chuckled. "She can be such a little geek that she almost doesn't count."

"I think she counts. Anyway, what's your point?"

"You don't seem to know what to do with that love. Sometimes I don't even think you notice it. If this chick is what you say she is, you'd better be able to cope with her love or you'll be in a real lot of trouble."

"I can cope with her," I said firmly.

Another West of Ireland sigh. "It sounds to me like a hell

of a roller-coaster ride, Daddy." She curled up again and, having delivered her warning, went briskly back to sleep. But not before she murmured her parting thrust: "Here in Ireland you act like you would be able to tame even Grace O'Malley. I don't know what happens when you go home to Chicago."

For the first time in the trip I was able to make explicit to myself the feeling about Jean that I'd first experienced in Dublin: I was watching a girl very quickly become a woman.

Keenan's Keep or Castle, choose your own title, was barely visible when we arrived. The fog was so thick that one could see only a few yards of water of Clew Bay. With the fog came the strong, salty smell of the Atlantic, more powerful yet cleaner than the sea smell in Dublin, suggesting a purifying detergent that would scour anything it touched.

The castle was a dark, somber, great gray-stoned pile watching us grimly as we drove up the neatly landscaped drive. "Wow!" Jeannie opened her eyes. "It's a night when Grace O'Malley would be out in her galleys."

"Or lying in wait for us in that hotel."

"That isn't a hotel." Jeannie shook her head. "That's a haunted castle. This is your idea, Daddy, not mine."

The gray, threatening sky, the stern and aloof mien of Keenan's Castle, did not have the slightest psychic impact on me. If the ghost of Constance Keenan was indeed present in that ancient pile of stone, she was keeping to herself.

Inside, however, the castle was as pleasant and friendly as it had been hostile on the outside. A warm fire was crackling cheerfully in a big fireplace "to take a bit of the chill off the air." The big overstuffed chairs and sofas, maroon in color, deep blue fabric on the walls, high oak beams, cheerful waiters circulating among the guests, clearing away the remnants of high tea and serving the first before-supper drinks. It was as though it were saying, "Look, I'm no Ashford Castle, but I can be warm and reassuring and clean. And don't believe any of the stories about ghosts. Patently, I'm too nice a place to harbor ghosts."

The rooms were small, as befits a medieval castle, but comfortable, dry, and clean. No trace of psychic clamminess.

Jean and I said we would meet in the lobby for a glass of

sherry—"in honor of the good Jocelyn"—and then supper. She was waiting for me when I arrived, in an Irish hand-crocheted light tan dress, which clung to her firm young figure in a way that would have twisted the heart of a man of any age.

"Nice dress." I kissed her cheek. "It would drive Timmy or Liam out of his mind."

"That's what it's supposed to do," she said pointedly. "It kind of replaces my jumpsuit."

Was it only yesterday that I'd found her shivering in a deserted little chapel?

"Whatever an old daddy's opinion is worth, it's a decided improvement."

"Uh huh."

Then I saw that she was looking at a picture of a painting of a beautiful woman that hung on the wall in the lobby, the same painting I had seen in Dufficy's Irish Store.

"She's the ghost that haunts this place, isn't she?" Jean asked thoughtfully. "Funny, there's not a word about it in any of the brochures."

"Maybe they think that would frighten clients away."

"I suppose," her sigh had become a ritual, "there aren't enough tourists who go in for psychic kicks." She grinned sideways at me. "Does she look like Ciara, Daddy?"

I considered the tragic Constance Keenan carefully. Somehow, the resemblance didn't seem as strong as it had in the Irish store on Michigan Avenue. Or perhaps I'd forgotten how the real Ciara looked. "Not as pretty, not nearly as pretty."

Same taunting gray eyes, however; taunting, yet somehow also thoughtful.

"Like wow!" Jean said thoughtfully. "Some dish, huh?"

"I thought of an answer to the question you asked me in the car." I told her what the nun had said at the entrance to Kylemore Abbey.

"Uh huh." Jean studied my face carefully. "Look, Daddy, I'm sure we'll get along. Maybe she is good enough for you." She turned briskly away from the painting. "Let's have that sherry and supper. I'm starved."

"Done."

The sherry was delightfully delicate, the leg of lamb was

perfectly cooked, the bottle of Bordeaux the best wine I'd had in Ireland. I returned to my room after a coffee and an Irish Cream in the lobby, safely out of sight of Constance Keenan's picture in much too mellow and relaxed a mood to seriously expect spooks. Then I remembered Mike Casey.

"Where the hell have you been?" he asked brusquely as he picked up the phone in the Reilly Gallery. "I was about to mobilize the main force."

"Drinking the best Bordeaux in Ireland," I confessed.

"The shipment will be at Ashford Castle by noon tomorrow. Be careful with it."

"I'm always careful, Michael."

"It must have been awfully good Bordeaux," he grunted. "Any developments?"

"We're finding more pieces of the puzzle," I said guardedly. "What's new on your end?"

"Some bad news, I'm afraid. John King Sullivan died last night. Apparently the tumors were worse than anyone realized. His wife is too sick to attend the funeral."

"God help us all!"

"He'd better! Or, as my wife would say, She'd better. . . . There's no chance that Patricia Sullivan will ever stand trial. Rich Daley has announced that the state's attorney's office considers the case closed. Even that idiot Sam Norton has given up."

"It's a strange world, Mike."

"You've noticed. Anyway, Annie sends her love. Be careful."

The conversation sufficiently depressed me that I now thought I was ready for Constance Keenan. I went to sleep perfectly prepared to encounter her.

And woke up the next morning, sunlight streaming through my tiny window. No psychic manifestations at all.

But one idea, a hint, perhaps, from Connie, or more likely from my own unconscious putting a few things together—a hunch, a stab in the dark.

"When fathers are later than teenage daughters," Jean glanced mischievously at her watch as I joined her at the breakfast table, "it's a bad sign."

"Senility."

"Back to Ashford Castle?" She buttered a thick slab of brown bread and poured raspberry jam on it.

"Eventually—another stop to make first."

"Oh?" She delicately bit into the bread, licking the jam off her lips with her tongue.

"A place called Achill Island." Her bread and jam looked so tasty that I prepared a slice for myself.

"A little ghost tell you?"

"Oh, c'mon now, Jeannie, no sensible, well-educated person believes in ghosts." We laughed together and departed for Achill Island.

The weather was extraordinarily friendly, the nicest day since we'd been in Ireland. What better day to meet the woman you love? And what better place than in the County Mayo, whence your ancestors escaped, it would seem, in the nick of time?

Small wonder one is required to add "God help us!" Even on a gorgeous day County Mayo is a land of rocks: rocks strewn in the fields, rocks piled neatly on fences, rocks forming bridges, and even rocks fashioned into tiny houses—in the last case, whitewashed, the old cottage attached to a newer stucco cottage and an occasional new home. In Ireland it is bad luck not to preserve at least one wall of the old home.

County Mayo, between Westport and Newport and the corner of Clew Bay toward Achill Island, is desolate and unproductive. There are almost as many abandoned old cottages as there are those from whose chimney a faint trace of smoke curls across the blue sky. At the time of the famine in 1849, this was the most densely populated section of Europe, land good for potato farming and very little else. The abandoned houses, however, do not date from famine days—the pathetic little hovels of those who died or migrated during the famine have been long since cleared away. These huts, without roofs, and often missing walls, belonged to the immigrants who left during the lesser famines at the end of the nineteenth century, when the families of most of the American Irish departed. Yet the land is green and the houses are white, and the harsh hills and rocks are somehow wildly beautiful, as though you have come upon a set for a film about Ireland. Then you realize that they shoot films in Ireland only on days when it's not raining—unless it's a film about a man on the run, like Victor McLaglen's *The Informer* or James Mason's *Odd Man Out*.

If the sun lasts until you get to Achill Island, you're in for an incredible treat. As soon as you've crossed the somewhat dubious bridge separating Achill Island from the mainland, you enter another world. For a moment you think you've left Ireland behind and have been transported to Sorrento—wide beaches, gentle breakers, dramatically sloping hills, pink, blue, and green cottages as well as white. Only the well-groomed cattle, the shaggy dogs, countrymen and -women in their gray suits and black skirts remind you that you're still in Ireland.

"Oh, boy," Jean exclaimed enthusiastically. "Why hasn't anybody done a photo book on this place?"

"Probably 'cause days like this happen here only once every fifty years."

I sensed, felt, intuited—call it what you want—that Ciara was near and that I had to find her before it was too late. Where to look for her? How to find her? Who were the lurking enemies? We stopped at a pub across the road from the beach, perhaps a mile onto the island, and ordered a pint of Guinness each and a cheese sandwich. "Isn't it a glorious day, now?" Jean asked the pub man.

" 'Tis," the man admitted, "but sure we'll be paying for it with bad weather. That's always the way. Nothing good happens but you don't have to pay for it with bad."

"A quiet time here on the island?" I asked, trying to sound casual.

"Ah, now." The man shook his head dismally. "Sure, how could it be a quiet time with all them Gardai around? Aren't they a pain in the arse now?"

"Have a Garda station here, do you?" I slipped into the routine, which I had learned very quickly, of matching question with question.

"Station is it? Isn't the nearest constable across the way in Newport? Sure doesn't he have nothing more than a bicycle to get over here?"

I sighed, hoping it sounded authentic and intending it to be a request for more information.

The man took my meaning. "Still, I wonder why all them

fellas be hanging around, particularly the men from the Special Branch.''

"The Special Branch is it?" Jeannie said, peering at the man over the top of her Guinness.

"Can't you be smelling the Branch fellas a mile away? And themselves all hanging around that pink cottage miles down the road, just beyond Joe Tim's house? Fucking piss artists.''

I would have leaped out of the booth at once, but Jeannie kept the man in conversation for a few more minutes. Then we walked casually to our car, which she backed to the road from the pub and roared down the highway at eighty miles an hour. We almost smashed into Superintendent James Finnegan's Volvo.

"I might have known you'd be here." The superintendent emerged from the rear of the car and regarded us suspiciously. "I suppose the lass is your daughter; sure she looks enough like you."

I attempted an introduction, which Jean, who did not seem to like Jaymo a bit, ignored. "Superintendent of the Special Branch or not, Superintendent Finnegan, you're driving on the wrong side of the road. In my country, even cops, even gumshoe cops, have to keep the law."

The superintendent turned beet red, perhaps because he was trying to suppress a laugh. "You're not in your country, young woman. And you've got no business to be on this road."

"I realize your civil liberties are more primitive than ours, Superintendent," I joined the argument, "but I doubt that even in Ireland you can keep us from driving down the road."

"This is all irrelevant," Finnegan replied wearily. "She's not here, she's gone, she's flown the coop altogether."

"Who?" I asked.

"Who do you think? Your woman, Clare Keenan or Ciara Kelly or whatever she's calling herself. We had her in a safe house here, herself insisting that it was only Achill Island that was good enough for her. A nice quiet place and agents to protect her. Then she ups and decides she's finished with our protection and she'd rather face your man McLafferty by herself. So she vanishes without a trace. You're late, Mr. Brendan Ryan. You're twelve hours late.''

"She was here then?''

The four uniformed Gardai who were in the car with the superintendent closed in around him, not quite sure whether they ought to be protecting him from us.

"Oh, yes, she was here. I don't suppose there's any point in asking how you knew?''

"It was obvious.'' I tried not to sound too much like Sherlock Holmes. "Achill Island was a place she loved. She came here on vacations with her school friends. She came back here at least one summer and probably several summers when she was in school in England after McLafferty was put in prison. Then you and your friends send her to the States, panic when she tells you about the explosion on my boat, and pull her out of Chicago. She reads the papers and finds out that I'm still alive, then later on that I was the target, not her. She's furious at you and your buddies and insists on returning to Ireland. She's sick of running. All right, you folks say, Ireland it'll be, but we can't risk our informers being blown up so you tell us where you want to go. Then she says Achill Island. Where else?''

No room for Constance Keenan's ghost or my own intuition. All perfectly reasonable and all made up on the spur of the moment.

"Impressive,'' Finnegan admitted grudgingly, as he removed his pipe and tobacco from his pocket.

"Elementary,'' Jean observed with a perfectly straight face.

"And I suppose,'' he puffed desperately on his pipe, shielding the lighter from the wind that swept up from the beach and along our road on its way to the top of the mountain that was the center and the core of Achill Island, "I suppose you can explain to me, too, why she's flown the coop.''

"That's easy,'' Jean said contemptuously. "She's tired of the mistakes that you gumshoes make. She realizes that if she relies on you, she'll have to run for the rest of her life and may still not get away from Rory McWhatever his name is. She figures she has a better chance of facing him alone. She's a very tough woman, Superintendent Finnegan. She's survived a lot. Now she figures she can survive a one-on-one with him.''

I suppose I would have thought of that explanation eventually. Jeannie's quickness made me wonder if she shouldn't enroll in the police academy instead of Stanford University.

''That's about it,'' Jaymo sighed, despite his pleasure with himself that he'd managed to ignite the tobacco in his pipe. ''It's like she signed her own death warrant. She won't have a chance against that lunatic.''

''Maybe she'd rather be dead than live this way.'' Jeannie dug a stone from the roadside with a dainty foot. ''You and your colleagues have not been exactly brilliant in protecting her.''

''With us she had a chance,'' he insisted, waving the hovering Gardai away. ''Now she doesn't have a chance at all. I don't suppose your Sherlock Holmes deductions tell you where she's gone?''

''You're going to keep searching?''

''That's me orders.'' The pipe went out, and with obvious disgust, he knocked the ashes into the wind. ''Some very important people in Dublin and Washington insist that we do everything we can to keep her alive.''

''Maybe she knows that.'' I removed the ignition keys from the pocket of Jean's jacket. ''Maybe she assumes that out in the open and unguarded she'll be bait for McLafferty. He'll go after her, then you can go after him.''

''Pretty reckless,'' Jaymo said disapprovingly. ''Ah, sure, she always has been a reckless woman. I don't suppose I can persuade you to go back to New York?''

''Hardly, Superintendent. And by the way, it's Chicago.''

''Aye, so 'tis.'' He paused respectfully. ''So you two are determined to remain here and become bait yourselves?''

''We're not defining ourselves as bait, Superintendent,'' I said tersely. ''C'mon, Jeannie, let's get out of here.''

''You sure looked like bait on Lough Corrib.''

''I'll drive, Daddy.'' Jean snatched the keys from my hand. ''You think.''

She started the car, turned it around, and pointed us back down towards the beach of Achill Island and the mainland. Sometime, I vowed to myself, Ciara and I would return.

''Where to?'' Jean asked.

"Back to Ashford Castle, at least for the first stop."

"And then?"

"Tomorrow is Sunday, isn't it? You lose track of the days of the week over here. Let's spend Sunday thinking about it, and then take off for somewhere else."

I was not altogether sure that Jean would approve of the "shipment" that was waiting for me at Ashford Castle. There was no reason to tell her about it.

Clouds and rain returned in midafternoon, by the time we'd gone through Cong and turned off at the gray stone gate of the castle. The same battered blue Volkswagen hatchback that had been parked at the head of the street leading to the castle when we'd left was still there. Obviously it hadn't been following us.

Jean said that she needed a nap before supper, and I said that I probably did, too, though I knew very well there were too many emotions churning inside me. Ciara was trying a desperate, perhaps self-destructive gamble. Yet I could understand why she was doing it. She didn't know yet that we were in Ireland. If she'd only waited another twenty-four hours, we might have found her on Achill. We might have stumbled into her in a pub or a grocery and let her know that she was not alone.

On the other hand, she might have thought that I would be no more help than the Irish police.

There was no reason to think that I would be. Yet I was convinced that we would find her and save her from Rory McLafferty. When you're a mythological Irish hero, any other outcome is impossible. There's no fool like a fool in love. Especially when he thinks he's Finn MacCool.

Such were my thoughts as I opened the compact, carefully wrapped package that was waiting on the coffee table in my room, a surprisingly light, almost fragile package.

Inside were five smaller packages, neatly arranged and covered with plastic bubbles. Two of them were elements of the Uzi, one a long thin silencer and the other the weapon itself, with the plastic butt neatly folded back against the stock. In another wrapper were fifteen compact magazine clips for the weapon (a couple of hundred rounds). The fourth package contained a sturdy plastic strap and a lightweight vest, marked "U.S. Government Surplus," with a number of pockets—the Secret Service's holster for presidential body-guards. Finally, in the last and smallest package, I found a .22 caliber pistol, cleaned, polished, and well oiled, which looked like a twin to the one with which Cindasoo had shot a bumbling Mafia hit man.

Why the extra gun? I wondered. For emergencies, proba-bly. Only twenty rounds of ammunition neatly wrapped in brown paper. Obviously Mike didn't think the emergencies would require much use of the small pistol. Well, I wouldn't argue with his experience.

I hid the .22 under a stack of dirty shirts in my flight bag, and put four ammo clips and the silencer in one pocket of the holster vest and the Uzi in another compartment. Then I donned my jacket and trench coat. If I put my hands in the pockets of my coat and hunched over a bit, the coat looked no more bulky on me than if I were carrying a small camera and a pocketful of film cartridges. The weapon was a bit of a weight around my arm, but not nearly as heavy as an M1 or an M16.

I strolled out of Ashford Castle and walked casually across the green lawn, by the old Protestant church (St. Mary's), past the monastery ruins that were at the entrance (including one monastic cell that had been built out over the river so the monk could fish while he prayed), along the wall of the new concrete Catholic church, and into the town of Cong, a tiny, picturesque little village (with a "Quiet Man" pub), appar-ently undaunted by the presence of the last remnants of the faeries, the Tuatha Dé Danann, who are believed to lurk in the deep limestone caves underneath and outside the village.

At the miniature crossroads—Castlebar in one direction, Headford and Galway in the other—with its little fifteenth-century stone cross, I glanced down the main street and noted that the blue VW hatchback with the Dublin license plate was still parked in front of the tobacco shop. I ducked into a side street and avoided the car.

About forty yards down the banks of the Corrib River, I came to the "rising of the waters." Lough Corrib and Lough Mask several miles to the north are connected by an under-ground river, which centuries ago had carved its path through the porous limestone of this area of Mayo. In the nineteenth century the British built a canal between the two lakes so that the waterway would be navigable to the very head of Lough Mask. Construction provided jobs for many natives who otherwise might have perished in the famine.

Unfortunately for the British engineers, however, the ground was too porous to hold the canal, and save when Lough Mask is in flood, the waters sink through the rock back to the original underground path shortly after they leave Lough Mask and then bubble once more to the surface just above Lough Corrib. Another and more plausible story is that by the time the canal was finished, the railroad had been built and the engineers decided there was no reason to seal up the limestone. Twenty-five yards or so beyond the "rising of the waters," I climbed down the bank of the dry canal and found a few yards farther up a clump of bushes that provided me with a perfect screen. The rhododendron bushes on either side of the ditch, now wet and glistening from the rain, formed a cathedral-like arch to protect my experimentation. I listened carefully for a couple of minutes. The only sound I heard was that of an occasional bee who had emerged from his shelter to ascertain whether the rain had really stopped and whether it was dry enough to return to his busy work in the rhododendrons.

I removed the two parts of the Uzi from my pocket and slipped them together easily. It was an enormous improvement over the M16, light, simple, easy to assemble and disassemble. I aimed it, moved it slowly, then quickly in my hands, an unbelievably well-balanced and responsive weapon. How easy it had become to kill other human beings.

The Uzi, named after Major Uziel Gal of the Israeli army, who developed it, looks like a slightly elongated revolver when its folding butt is not extended. Loaded with a twenty-five-round magazine (in the pistol grip), it weighs eight pounds. When the butt is unextended, it is seventeen inches long. It fires its nine-millimeter parabellum bullets at the rate of six hundred fifty rounds per minute, which means you can empty a magazine in four seconds. It is meant to be fired in bursts during quick, short combat situations. It runs out of ammo too quickly to be used in sustained combat. But modern warfare rarely requires sustained combat. In the long run everyone is too dead.

They don't, in other words, ride around the fort all night long.

On the left side of the pistol grip is a change lever. Push the lever to "E," the forward position, and the weapon will fire automatically—till you take your finger off the trigger. Set it at the middle position, marked "D," and it will fire a single shot each time you squeeze the trigger. Move it to the rear, marked "S," and the weapon is on safety: it will not fire, no matter how hard you press the trigger and squeeze the grip safety. Deadly for the target and safe for the one who holds it, the Uzi does not fire accidentally if you drop it.

I slipped the ammunition clip into the magazine chamber, attached the silencer, which looked like a slightly elongated cigar, to the muzzle, set the weapon for a single shot, pulled the cocking bolt to the rear, squeezed the grip safety, and fired cautiously at a bush ten yards away.

At first I thought there was something wrong with the weapon and that it had not fired. Then I smelled the bitter, acrid aroma of exploding ammunition and saw a branch fall off the bush. Astonishing! Almost no recoil. The Israeli gunsmiths were geniuses.

Very, very carefully I adjusted the weapon for automatic fire, squeezed the trigger lightly, and then released it. The weapon made a light *thump thump thump* sound and half the bush collapsed, as though someone had sliced through it with a giant scythe. The empty shells, exiting out of the right side of the weapon by "blowback," lined the ground at my feet.

I put the safety back on and unloaded the magazine. Good heavens! I had fired off twelve rounds without realizing it. If the bush had been a human being, he would have been torn to shreds.

I carefully collected the empty shells and leaned against the canal bank, dismayed and faintly sick. This little toy gun in my hands, no bigger and not much heavier than a machine-gun water pistol with which I had played as a little boy (much against my mother's wishes since she did not believe that little boys should play with guns—despite her use of them during the war), was a devastatingly dangerous killing machine. I was not sure I wanted to have any part of it. Certainly I could not carry the thing around casually underneath my jacket.

Then I thought of Ciara and the terror that seemed to be a psychic aura around her. So I stayed there, close to the bank of the disappearing canal, and practiced with the astonishing little weapon for another half hour. Perhaps I wouldn't win a marksmanship medal with it, and perhaps I wasn't as sharp with it as I was with the M16 eighteen years ago, but if it was necessary to fire the Uzi to protect Jean or Ciara or my child, whom Ciara carried, then I could fire the weapon with terrible effectiveness.

I wondered what some countryman might think on Sunday morning if he happened to be walking above the "rising of the waters" and saw all the decapitated bushes and perhaps even discovered some of the spent bullets. Later I carefully deposited the ejected shells in a refuse can behind a public house on the main street of Cong.

Glumly I disassembled the weapon when my practice session was over, and most of the bushes in my part of the canal had been trimmed to half their size, and tramped back to the castle.

I stopped at the gift shop on the grounds of the castle and purchased an attaché case made from Donegal tweed, a perfect container for the components of the weapon and its ammunition.

I stored the case in the bottom drawer of my dresser and covered it with my Windbreaker. It seemed to me most unlikely that an Ashford Castle maid would open a guest's briefcase.

It was four o'clock in the afternoon. Perhaps I ought to nap for an hour or two before supper. My automatic weapons practice had exhausted me.

I took off my shirt and trousers and was about to pull the spread back from my bed when the phone rang. "Brendan Ryan? Ah, who else would it be now?" said a familiar womanly voice. "No need to say who I am, is there?"

"Where are you?"

"Room three-fourteen of the Railway Hotel in Galway city. I'll be waiting for you. Sure, you're a desperate man, aren't you now?"

The line clicked dead. The search was over.

I threw on my clothes, grabbed my trench coat from the closet in case the rain should return, and hurried out of my room. Halfway down the green-carpeted corridor I paused, thought for a moment, and then decided that Mike Casey was a far more experienced detective than I was.

I returned to my room, removed the .22 caliber pistol from my flight bag, and slipped it into the trench coat pocket.

33

The forty-mile drive from Ashford Castle to Galway city required almost two anxious hours—hours of uncertainty, anticipation, and increasing sexual desire. Although it was Saturday afternoon, the roads were filled with lorries and autos streaming into Galway for Saturday night. (What do you do on Saturday night in a five-hundred-year-old city from which Grace O'Malley was excluded because she was "a bit too wild for them"?) The rain fell more heavily, the roads turned slick and dangerous, and the Irish drivers were only marginally more patient than American drivers—and on two-lane highways at that.

Finally I circled the new cathedral (as ugly as it had been a few days before), crossed the Corrib River, and crawled through the heart of the city. I drove around the main square, where there is a memorial to John F. Kennedy, God be good to him, and searched for a parking spot in front of the Great Southern Railway Hotel.

There was no vacant spot, so I circumnavigated the square again, a task that took ten minutes. In the slow movement around the corners, I noticed a dark blue VW hatchback that looked like the one from Cong a few yards behind me. It followed me around a second time. Either one of Jaymo's people or the other side.

I was pretty sure that Jaymo's men were skilled enough at ordinary police work not to be so easily found out.

The second time around, an Alfa pulled out of a slot across

the street from the hotel and I pulled in. I caught the VW's license number as it went by.

Same car.

I was glad I'd brought Mickey's .22.

He parked around the corner, facing the square. I piled out of my car and stalled for a few moments, awkwardly putting on my raincoat. The tail was a few years younger than me, short, thin, dark, with a bushy mustache and a long, lean nose. He wore a brown cap and an old-fashioned black rain slicker. Central casting's choice for an Irish gunman.

Or an Irish bachelor farmer in town for a night.

I walked quickly across the rain-soaked cobblestone street and into the lobby of the hotel, my hand firmly on the .22.

Nothing happened. I shook the rain out of my coat and off my beret and watched the tail out of the corner of my eye. He was ambling with apparent leisure toward the hotel.

Perhaps all he wanted was a drink in the lounge.

I ducked into the cranky and obsolete elevator and rode up to Ciara's floor. No point in announcing myself, especially since I didn't know what name she might have used to register.

I knocked lightly on the door.

"Yes?" No mistake about the voice.

" 'Tis the man from Jerome's," I said, feeling slightly ridiculous about the perhaps needless code.

"Brendan?" A whisper from the other side of the door.

"Who else would it be, woman?"

The door opened a tiny crack. A wary gray eye considered me briefly. The door closed again so the chain could be removed. It then opened a slightly larger crack through which a man could slip if he was slender and quick. My hand still in the pocket with the .22, I glided through the door, which shut behind me almost instantly.

The woman was not Ciara. She had short blonde hair and thick glasses; she was heavily made up and wore a somewhat tawdry maroon dress, which was a size too small and whose neckline plunged too far. A whore making a trick?

Not with those gray eyes and not with the intensity of that embrace. A clever disguise. My Ciara is good at everything.

My long-frustrated sexual hunger exploded. So did hers.

Our bodies, accustomed to and comfortable with one another, took charge.

Our love was not the sensitive, tender affection we had known the last time together in her anonymous room in the Chestnut Place. It was angry, demonic, violent love, our bodies yelling their protest against so long a separation. I stripped her quickly; dress, bra, panties were pulled away in a few glorious seconds. Then I covered her with savage kisses, assaulting her adored body with demanding affection. Finally I buried my head in the sweet-smelling darkness between her thighs, a mysterious forest where I would remain for an eternity of pleasure. The woman was mine, all mine.

Ciara's response was as violent as my attack. For a few minutes of wild passion and headlong, heedless pleasure, we existed only for each other.

In the dank little room with its musty smell and the sound of a combo somewhere in the hotel playing early Beatles, I knew that she was indeed my Holy Grail, my life, my purpose, my destiny. I might live without her, but it wouldn't be much of a life. God put me in the world for Ciara Kelly.

I must have dozed. Then I woke with a start to see her wonderful face close to mine, twisted in sadness and pain, like an Irish pietà. She looked, for the first time, not younger than thirty-three going on thirty-four, but much older, ten years at least. She was thinner than she had been. Too thin. Small wonder.

"How much have you figured out?" she asked sadly.

"Where did you do your university work?"

"Brendan, you're a desperate man." She kissed me. "Sussex. French literature." She pointed to a French novel on the minute bedstand. "Modern. I was a reader on the faculty too. Like one of your associate professors."

"You were good at what you did then?"

"They thought so."

"Should I call you Ciara or Clare?"

"Oh, Ciara, please. That's who I am to you." Tears, the first of them, in her anguished gray eyes. They were quickly dismissed.

"And you did therapy there?"

"Five years of analysis. Do you think it worked?" A faintly crooked grin.

I patted her superb ass. "You had to have a lot of guts to go through it and pull your life together. It must not have been easy."

"It wasn't. Sometimes . . . ah, damn it all." Horror-stricken face. "I'm terrible sorry about the bad word, Brendan. . . . Stop laughing at me. . . . Anyway, sometimes I think that maybe I'm a better person for it all. Then other times I tell myself that I've always been a mess and always will be."

"The first opinion gets my vote. Your nunnish classmate at Kylemore wouldn't agree that you were a mess as a girl either."

Her eyes lit up, and she enthused about dear old Fiona. I had to recount, word for word, the story of my conversation by the waters of the still lake.

"What else don't you know?" She was somber again; Fiona was good for only so much escape.

"Rory McLafferty?"

"A grand man in those days, Brendan; kind and thoughtful and full of fun and jokes and laughter. We sailed a lot on Lough Neagh; you know how much I like sailing. My father never approved of a girl doing it, so I learned in secret when he was at the hospital. Rory was a grand sailor, and he took me out as often as he could. It was never serious, like everything was with Father; always a good time and if you made a mistake you weren't lectured. I loved every second of my time with him, particularly when we were sailing. And it was like sex didn't exist beyond a hug and a kiss and a slap on the rear and a laugh at the end of the day.

"I suppose if I knew what I do now, I would have seen some psychopathic streaks. But I was lonely and scared and traumatized, and he was good to me and made no demands. I was in my first year of nursing and he in his second year at medical school, himself from Derry and an enthusiastic disciple of Bernadette Devlin. I needed a cause to believe and a man to replace my father. The cause was good and the man seemed to be good too."

"You were lovers?"

"In a manner of speaking. He . . . he didn't seem to be much interested in sex. We went to bed now and then, more because he was being good to me, I think. . . . He was terrible good to me in those days; I suppose he loved me. As best he could love anyone. There weren't any others till you, Brendan." She stroked my face gently. "After therapy was over I tried a couple of times and lost my nerve. I would have lost it with you, too, darling, if you'd have let me."

"He turned gradually to violence in response to the Brits?"

She nodded. "You have to remember the times, Brendan. Purifying violence. Wretched of the earth, that sort of stuff. We read bits of Marx and quoted Marcuse and Fanon and Lenin and Trotsky, not understanding any of them much but enjoying it all and thinking we were the hinge of history. The Provos didn't read a thing. They knew what they wanted and what had to be done."

"Let me put the latch back on the door." I remembered the man with the long nose and the cap.

"Glory be," she said, "how dumb of me!"

"You had other things to do." I climbed back under the twisted and sweat-soaked sheet, making sure that the pocket of my trench coat with the .22 in it was but an instant's reach away. "So you felt that you should begin to imitate the Provos?"

"Not to say imitate, if you take my meaning. We had a love/hate thing going with them. We hated their ideological naiveté and admired the simplicity of their dedication. Idjits that we were, we didn't realize that it was the same thing. Anyway, we took to blowing up power-line terminals and railroad tracks and even one ammo dump. All harmless as far as affecting anything, but a lot of fun for us. I'll never forget how excited I was the first night we did the power terminal. It wasn't as good as sex with you, but it was an enormous emotional release. At last I was affecting reality, I told myself."

"Poor Ciara."

"Poor, dumb Ciara. Well, Rory was becoming wilder, though so gradually you wouldn't notice it unless you looked back over the months. He was a great actor and performer. Dominated the theatricals for the hospital staff. Terrorism was like a theatrical, a stage on which to act, a play to be performed, a leading role for him in which he was the perfect hero—Robin Hood, the Count of Monte Cristo, and Billy the Kid all combined. He'd scare the daylights out of us with the tricks he'd do on his own—violation of group discipline, he'd say, if any of the rest of us did it. He'd disappear and then show up a few days later with a trunkload of plastics or a couple of crates of Russian guns."

"AK-47s?" She nodded. "Where did he find them?"

"Your man Qaddafi, I suppose. Even then he was part of the shadow world, though the rest of us were too dumb to know about that world. He loved it, every second of it. He dropped out of medical school right before graduation because he said he wanted to be a doctor only in an Ireland that was free, united, and socialist."

"The rhetoric and the violence pushed him over the line?"

"We don't know much about psychopaths." She drew my head to her breasts, pillows in which it delighted. "Maybe he was already over the line. Maybe he would have gone over it anyhow, no matter what. But we were in the Falls when the Brits smashed the heads of Catholic women who complained because their poor wee homes were torn apart. We treated the lacerations and the concussions. We ministered to the wounded and the dying in Derry on Bloody Sunday, when the paras gunned down a crowd of peaceful marchers—I was there, Brendan." The memory of that distant event made her transiently an angry revolutionary again. "I'd seen terrible things before, as you well know. This was worse. It was not drunken savages. It was not nervous draftees losing their cool, like your National Guard at Kent State. It was calm, careful murder by disciplined professional troops. It would have pushed someone stronger than Rory around the bend."

"So people became the target?"

"Aye, the soccer buses. We had a great terrible row at the meeting of our council—which was all of us, no more than a baker's dozen of kids with enough firepower to hold off half the RUC for an hour or so. We were into participative democracy in those days; all of us had to agree. If there was not a unanimous decision, we didn't do it. Mind you, the discussion was about the principle of the thing. The soccer buses didn't come up. The issue was killing people—guilty people, as he called them."

"Guilty of being Protestant soccer players."

"Sure." She sighed heavily. "He had that in mind from the beginning. Anyway, a few of us voted against it, and that was that. He laughed it off, as charming when he lost an argument as when he won it. Some of the others told me how glad they were that I fought him.''

''You were the leader of the opposition?''

''I was that, I guess. Even in those days, stupid, sick little idjit I was, I knew that killing people was wrong. So he and six others did it anyway. Four men and three women with guns killed over twenty people. Nice little toys,'' she said bitterly, ''your AK-47s.''

''Not mine,'' I said dryly. ''They were fired at me too.''

''Sure, Brendan, I'm sorry.'' She grabbed my arm apologetically. ''It hurts even to tell this again. We had a meeting afterward. They strutted around like they'd won the All Ireland championship. They were the leading edge of the Irish people. The only morality that should be heeded was the morality of the successful revolution. Morality out of the mouth of a gun. Vote taking was bourgeois revisionism. Those of us who did not want to go along were enemies of the people. We were free to leave, but we would be treated as enemies.''

''Lenin would have understood.''

''Most of them quit. They were afraid of Rory and Seamus Cagney and Deirdre Mullens, but they were afraid of the Brits and the RUC too. I stayed.''

''You did?''

She shook her head in agreement. ''Rory made love to me after they killed the soccer players. It was spectacular. The first time I had any idea what fucking could be like. The last time till you, darling.'' A brief glow of gratitude and happy remembrance. ''I was a dumb idjit, but not so dumb as to not know what he was and what would happen next. I had to stop it.''

''You felt responsible for the soccer players?''

''Not really,'' she said slowly. ''I believed Rory that there'd be no killing. But I would be responsible if he killed anyone else. The others could walk away with a nervous look over their shoulders and a pretense at a clear conscience. I didn't want to wake up some morning in my dorm at the hospital and hear that he'd killed hundreds. If that happened I was to blame as much as he.''

Of such stern principles, I thought, are heroines made.

Screwed-up little idjit that Clare Keenan was in those days, she was still made of the stuff of heroines. The kids Jean had talked to in Castlebar were right.

"Then?"

"My poor Brendan." She rubbed my cheek against a breast. "Such terrible pillow talk for you to have to be hearing. . . . Then I went down to Trinity Medical School in Dublin for a three-day course in trauma treatment—God knows I had enough firsthand experience—and took me a walk over to Dublin Castle and asked to see someone from the Special Branch. Your man Jaymo Finnegan was a sergeant then. He believed me. He put me in touch with a Brit in Belfast."

Now I understood the haggard affection I saw occasionally in his eyes when he spoke of her.

"You felt guilty about dealing with the Brits?"

"I hated their man in Belfast, one of your goddamned university graduates, like I would become later, so superior to the wee wild woman from County Mayo. And himself the grandson of Irish immigrants at that. Well, to bring an end to it, I found out about the music hall plans and tipped off the Brits. They bungled it and didn't raid our basement before we left. The plan, you see, was to set off the bombs and then gun down the people that were escaping . . . a dramatic liturgical gesture, Rory called it. Sure, he was madder than the hatter by then. The Brits were supposed to capture us as we crept out into the night and drove off in our cars to the hall. They disconnected the bombs all right, but there was a firefight when we pulled up in the car park next to the hall."

"Maybe the Brits wanted to kill most of you."

"I've thought of that often. Sure, they wouldn't have minded getting rid of me then. It was only when I survived that they began to worry about protecting an informer. It was a quick fight. In three or four minutes, everyone was dead but Seamus and Rory and me. They wanted to try them. I was useless.

" 'Get rid of the cunt,' someone said. A constable had his revolver pointed at my head before the inspector stopped him."

"The Congo again."

"I was used to it by then." She shrugged indifferently.

"Blood and corpses were part of my life. Anyway, there were a couple of hundred people alive the next morning who would have been dead if I hadn't turned informer. Most of them Prots at that."

"So the word spread around that you were an informer and the English got you out of Ireland."

"It was a disgrace then. Still is mostly. The Provos were delighted of course, because they didn't want competition from idjits. I've never felt guilty. I did what I had to do, and I don't care what people think. Well, the governments in Dublin and London were convinced that I was a heroine, so they wanted to keep me alive. They manufactured a new identity for me and sent me off to Sussex. I wouldn't take any of their money. My parents had died, and I used the little bit of legacy they left me to stay alive in the first years in school and pay for a good private psychiatrist. You know the rest."

"No, I really don't. It's a story of heroism that tops the others. I'll have to hear it someday soon."

"No, Brendan, my darling," she said sadly. "You and your fierce little daughter must return to America. It's not your fight. You'll be in the way. I don't want you to be hurt. You're innocent, like the people in the music hall."

"You come with us. We can do better than those stupid Irish cops. I have some friends. . . . ."

She pulled away from me. "They're good cops, Brendan. You don't understand how fiendishly clever Rory is. And how much money the Libyans have given him. He has bought his own gunmen, though none of them is as crazy for revenge as he and Seamus Cagney."

"Did Jaymo tell you what really happened to the *Brigid*?" I demanded fiercely, pulling her back to my arms.

"He did indeed. They overreacted. It doesn't matter. Rory would have caught up with me anyhow. I have to face him myself. It's between the two of us anyway. Maybe if he comes out in the open to hunt me down now that I'm alone, the Special Branch will get him before he gets me. I want you and the lass out of the line of fire. I have enough on my conscience."

"That's crazy," I shouted.

"Hush, darling." She touched my lips.

"How many men does he have? You'll be outnumbered."

"At the end it will be only the two of us, and maybe Seamus, who is big but dumb, too dumb to make any difference."

So, not a short man with a cap.

"It's your martyr complex, woman. Your shrink in Sussex would tell you that."

She considered thoughtfully. "Sure, maybe it is. Maybe if I rid the world of poor Rory, I'll have expiated everything."

"Expiated what? Bravery? Enthusiasm? Love? Or hate and some incestuous feelings toward your father?"

Oh dear God in Heaven, why didn't You keep my big mouth shut?

Ciara, however, was not offended. "You're terrible clever, Brendan Ryan. Maybe it is neurotic. Or maybe I still have to finish what I started ten years ago. He'll kill hundreds more if I let him."

"What are your chances of winning this soggy Irish version of *High Noon*?"

She laughed happily. "Ah, my little king, you're wonderful. Irish *High Noon* indeed."

"That doesn't answer my question."

"One in twenty . . . and don't argue. It's better dying than living with the threat of his vengeance haunting me for the rest of my life. If I win, I'll phone you. We can talk then about us."

I begged, I pleaded, I argued, I reasoned. She was a woman with an obsession. She had lived too long the life of a fugitive. She was in no position to think clearly about the subject. She had no real friends at Sussex. I would bring her back to an environment where there would be more friends than she would know what to do with (ah, my Ciara, how you would capture Grand Beach). We would protect her and love her. She would no longer be a fugitive. The spooks from Dublin, Washington, and London would have to deal with us. Cardinal Cronin's sister-in-law was a United States senator, on the Intelligence subcommittee. No more overreactions.

"You're a powerful debater," she said dubiously; but she was not totally unconvinced.

I ran for daylight. She was a mature and sophisticated woman, the girl that her classmates at Kylemore had adored, now at the fulfillment of a long and extraordinarily painful maturing process. The strain of running from Sussex and running again from Chicago had caused some old emotional wounds to be opened. She had dealt with the renewed pain very well. But now the pressures were so great that she had made an unwise decision. It was not too late to unmake it. All she needed to do was permit her intelligence to reassert itself.

"Maybe you're right, darling man." She laid her head on my shoulder. "I'm so tired from trying to think everything out that I don't know what I'm doing. Maybe I wanted to hear you say all these things."

If Mary Kate Ryan Murphy had been available, she would have told me that I had awarded myself victory too easily, that Ciara had a demonic need to seek a Götterdämmerung with Rory McLafferty. Looking back on the argument, I often wonder whether maybe Ciara was right. It may have been that she would be free from his lurking menace only when she herself obliterated it.

Anyway, I was convinced that I had saved her from disaster, one more victory for the Irish mythological hero, the Finn MacCool of the south side of Chicago.

So, to seal my triumph, I began to kiss her breasts, at first slowly, almost casually, then with a need so fierce that it frightened both of us.

"Oh, Brendan," she cried.

"Sorry." I stopped.

"I didn't say you had to stop." She gulped. "Sure, Ireland makes you one of them ravishing Irish mythical heroes."

"Like Finn MacCool?"

"For instance. Go ahead. I always wondered what it would be like to be ravished by Finn MacCool."

Our fantasies meshed. I don't know whether the result terrified Ciara. Her cries were indecipherable. It terrified me, however. I was indeed capable of becoming a wild pagan king. I discovered that there were many wonderfully violent things you could do with a woman and neither hurt nor degrade her. The rite of spring became more manic and more ecstatic.

We made love two more times, as desperately and wildly as when I first came into the room. I was once more triumphant, my child was safe and growing in her womb.

"Sure," she murmured contentedly, "you're not bad at all, at all as Finn MacCool."

Exhausted (really exhausted; I'm not as young as your man Finn MacCool in his prime, and the ravishing of women takes a lot out of you as the years go by), I fell asleep, confident that there was nothing more to worry about.

When I awoke she was gone. No message. Indeed, no sign of anyone besides me ever being in the room.

Damn stupid, stubborn Irishwoman, I thought, substituting willpower for intelligence. Off to the Congo again, asking to be a martyr.

Furious at her and at myself and grimly determined to find her and shake her back into her senses, I left the room, rode down the elevator, and stalked out of the hotel. The man in the cap was waiting in the lobby. He had fallen asleep. I studied his lean face carefully as I went by him. I would know him if I saw him again.

The ride back to Ashford was much quicker. The rain had turned into soft mist, and the roads were uncrowded. I was in my room shortly after midnight. I checked the Uzi. Safe and sound where I had left it. I was still outraged at Ciara's stupidity.

I asked the switchboard to ring Jean. I owed her an apology and an explanation.

There was no answer.

Jean was gone too.

five
THE STRAND AT INCH

34

In the 4:00 A.M. sunlight pouring through the window, Detective Superintendent Jaymo Finnegan and I stood in Jean's room amid the confusion and disarray that mark the rooms of most late adolescent young women.

"You'd be thinking that this is the way her room usually is?" he asked, unlit pipe clenched between his teeth.

"Do you have teenage daughters, Superintendent?"

"I take your point . . . So we can assume that her abductors are responsible for none of it. She was taken without a struggle. Probably put out by an injection or a whiff of something strong."

"If she were awake, she wouldn't have left quietly."

Several Gardai, some in uniform, some not, were bustling about the room taking pictures and dusting for fingerprints. Useless activity, but it kept them busy.

"Aye, I suppose not." He sighed profoundly. "It would require only two people. One to hold her and the other to stick the hypodermic in her. Bundle her up in the blanket that's apparently missing, carry her down the back steps, and put her into a car."

"While your drugged constable slept soundly."

He puffed on the empty pipe. "We'll probably find that the maid who brought him the coffee doesn't work here."

"That's hardly an excuse."

"And he'll be able to identify her, when we show him the picture, as one of the people we know is working for McLafferty."

"Much good that will do."

Jaymo sighed again and eyed me curiously. He could not understand my reaction. Nor was I about to tell him that while I was furious about the kidnapping of Jean, I was completely convinced, with the certainty of a simple addition, that I would recover her and punish those who had frightened and perhaps hurt her. I was worried about Jean, guilty, remorseful, ashamed of my stupidity. Anger and the implacable certainty of vengeance were stronger than my other emotions. Was I not invulnerable? Even Ciara thought I was another Finn MacCool.

Looking back on such idiocy, I marvel that I could have so deceived myself. Jet lag, the turbulence of the last few weeks of my life, dead bodies lying at my feet, sleep deprivation, the excitement of the chase, a few lucky guesses, and some spectacular sex had made me feel that I was an actor in a mythological saga, the good Titan in conflict with a bad Titan. The dizzying speed of spring's sacrificial dance had driven me further round the bend than McLafferty.

Was not the Special Branch officer leaning innocently against the dresser in which my Uzi was waiting for the opportunity to dispose of my enemies?

"We have roadblocks set up all over the west of Ireland," the superintendent said tentatively.

"What does he want?"

"With a shitehawk like your man McLafferty," he waved his pipe in a gesture of bafflement and frustration, his language losing its diplomatic veneer, "you can never tell. He might snatch the lass for one reason and then change his mind and use her for another purpose, like he changed his mind when he rammed her boat out on Lough Corrib. With your ordinary international terrorist, do you see, there are fairly predictable patterns of behavior. We know in general how they behave, what they want, how they'll react, even where they're likely to hide. European police forces are ahead of them now. McLafferty?'' He made a wry face. "He thinks he's an Irish Carlos. But Carlos, while he's a psychopath, is not an Irish psychopath, he's not a complete loony besides.''

"So?''

"Your man Rory wants attention, he wants to perform, he wants a chance for the absurd dramatic gesture. That makes him more dangerous and harder to hunt down.''

"And means that Jean is in greater danger?''

"Maybe. Maybe not. It all depends what kind of insane idea is in his head. Phases of the moon are more useful for predicting what he will do than any of our psychological profiles.''

I inspected pictures of McLafferty and his crowd. Seamus Cagney, the only survivor of his original band, was a big, blond, overweight linebacker type. "Loves the women, especially when they don't want it,'' Jaymo remarked dryly.

Maeve Conroy. Thick, stolid, hair tightly bound behind a square, malevolent face. Glowing eyes that reminded me of pictures of Doc Holliday when he was in the final stages of TB. "She's the killer of the crowd, the professional. Enjoys watching bodies come apart.''

Dick McBeen. Tall, skinny, bookish, with thick glasses. "Blows things up and operates radios and such like.''

Conor Murtaugh. A little man with a big mustache. "Smuggles weapons, currency, and drugs. Runs errands. Enjoys torture.'' My friend in the blue hatchback.

Kevin O'Malley. Young fellow, handsome black Irishman with thick hair hanging over his brow. "Not too bright. Up from the streets of Derry. A marvel with the automatic weapons, if you take my meaning.''

"Ireland knows how to produce terrorist kooks,'' I observed.

"Aye. We've had enough practice.''

I should have told him that Conor Murtaugh had shadowed me to Galway. I should have told him that Ciara had been in the Railway Hotel. But Jaymo Finnegan and his constables and sergeants and inspectors were now at most useful auxiliaries. I would handle this matter myself. They would provide me with occasional information and assistance.

I did not even need Mike Casey and the "main force"

from Chicago. Mike had sent me my weapons. That was enough. One Ryan was a match for half a dozen Irish gangsters. More than a match.

I would kill the lot of them and be done with this nonsense. The berserker was a Celtic innovation, wasn't it? Like the urban terrorist?

"What do you want me to do?" I asked tonelessly.

"Well," he studied me carefully, "we'll be doing all we can. Maybe, if you don't mind, you could wait in your room. Sure, your man Rory will be getting in touch with you when it suits him. We might make it easier for him to find you."

"Fine. I presume you'll monitor the calls."

"I wouldn't count on that, however. He doesn't make dumb mistakes. Rory is not as efficient as those Italian"—he pronounced it "Eyetalian"—"kids with their training in sociology. He blunders along and gets away with it because of recklessness and cunning, doesn't like to be held down to a routine or a detailed plan."

"Crazy but not stupid?"

"Aye. Here are some pictures of him in his various disguises."

The top picture was of a good-looking young man with curly hair, a thin sharp face, and an engaging smile. A big fellow whose broad shoulders and thick arms suggested athletic skill. He looked like an actor who plays minor parts in movies about Ireland—a drinking companion of John Wayne in the pub, perhaps—and whose name is on the tip of your tongue but you can't quite remember it.

Yet there was something not quite right about his face. All the parts were distinguished enough, but the fit seemed wrong, and there was a hint of exhaustion, of a man living on the edge, of a mountain climber, perhaps, who has been pushed beyond the limits of his resources.

Worst of all were his eyes. There was laughter in them, but cold, hard laughter of the sort you would hear from a prankster specializing in cruel practical jokes.

Finn MacCool or not, I shivered. Poor Jean was at the mercy of a monster. I would save her. But in the meantime she would be terrified.

It was hard to believe that he was the same person in the

other pictures—a devout old priest, a bluff seaman, a stoop-shouldered countryman, a bleary-eyed taxi driver.

The man who had driven us to the station in Dublin.

I told Jaymo.

"You see the problem. He's the very devil himself for creating disguises."

"That's fine when he's traveling alone." I handed the pictures back to a nameless inspector who seemed to lurk always at Jaymo's left elbow. "This crowd of his should be a little less easy to hide."

Again Jaymo Finnegan considered me thoughtfully. "Aye. 'Tis true. And he doesn't know yet that we are aware of whom he's hired."

"Your friends the Provos being helpful?"

"Let's say that there's lots of people in a position to know who hope that we get Rory so they won't have to do it later down the road. By the way, if you don't mind my asking, what kind of sleeping dress does the young lady wear?"

"A long T-shirt on this trip, green trimmed with gold. Notre Dame letters on the front in gold. The number fourteen on the back, also in gold."

"Patriotic," he sniffed. "I wish I could be more reassuring, Mr. Ryan. To tell the truth, Rory McLafferty is a very scary man."

"I understand."

A man who endangers my women and my children, born and unborn. A man with a very short life expectancy. We know how crazy he is. He doesn't know how crazy I am.

I waited in my room for several hours, calm, patient, and, as I fancied myself, deadly.

The phone rang. "Brendan Ryan."

"I imagine you'd be knowing who I am." An exuberantly cheerful voice.

I must be cautious. Neither panic-stricken nor threatening. Let him think of me as self-contained and straightforward.

"Indeed."

"Sure, I suppose that fucking shite Jaymo Finnegan is somewhere listening. Top of the morning to you, Jaymo. I hope you'd be after giving me credit for not telling your man Ryan to stay away from the Garda. Always thought that was a foolish instruction."

"What have you done with her, McLafferty?" I said tersely, figuring that in this round I would set him up with his lines.

"To the pretty wee girl, is it? Nothing at all, at all. Ah, sure, we wouldn't hurt her for the world. You'll have her back in a day or two, if you do what you're told."

"What am I to do?"

"At the moment, nothing at all. Go back to Dublin and wait there till you get further instructions. Jaymo and his friends will be searching for us. Sure, they might be lucky and find us. And the lass might be lucky and not be killed when they do, but if I were in your position, Mr. Ryan, I'd be hoping that they weren't lucky, if you understand my meaning?"

"I understand."

"Aren't you going to ask for proof that we have her?" He sounded a bit petulant.

"All right, prove to me that you have her."

"Well, now, if I was a proper father, I wouldn't let a daughter of mine sleep in one of them green and gold T-shirt things, even if it does have 'Notre Dame' on it. Them things rip real easy, you know."

"Oh? And how do I know she's still alive?"

"That's better now." He sounded cheerful again. "Well, for example, let's listen to the T-shirt ripping . . ."

An anguished cry of a woman in terrible pain. He had done more than tear her clothes.

"You understand, Mr. Ryan?" He laughed softly. "We have her, and at the minute she's still alive. Would you like to say a word to Daddy, love?"

"Please, Daddy, please do whatever they tell you. I'm all alone with these monsters. They'll hurt me, they'll kill me. Please, Daddy, I'm alone with them. Help me . . ." Her voice was cut short by another terrible shriek.

"I asked you if you understand, Mr. Ryan?" Pleasant but mildly impatient.

"I understand."

"Good enough then. You go to Dublin and wait for my next message. If I were you I wouldn't leave the hotel for too long."

"I won't."

"Good man," he said approvingly. "Now, as for you, Jaymo, I'm sure you'll be trying to trace this call. It won't do you any good at all, at all. But you might as well have a go at it anyhow. It'll make you feel that you're not useless altogether. And you'll keep this out of the papers, won't you? I don't want the American Marines coming in here like they did in Lebanon." He chuckled. "Not yet anyway."

"I'm sure we'll keep it out of the papers."

"Good man. Well, don't be impatient, Mr. Ryan. I'll be in touch. Good day to you."

"Good day."

When Jaymo Finnegan burst into my room a few moments later, I was sitting by the window gazing calmly at Lough Corrib.

"You understand now what we're dealing with?"

"Oh, yes."

"He's going to want to trade the lass for Clare."

"I assumed as much. Why the delay?"

Jaymo slumped in the chair across from me. "To make you frantic with worry."

"Oh."

"He doesn't seem to have done that yet." He removed his pipe and put it back in his pocket. Doesn't the man ever take off his raincoat?

"I'm worried, Superintendent," I said coolly. "Very worried. I see no point in becoming frantic."

"Well, now . . ." His big brown eyebrows shot up. " 'Twould be a bit better if you sounded frantic the next time you talk to him. Otherwise he might turn skittish on us. Your man Rory doesn't like anyone spoiling his game."

"Yes. I understand that," I said softly. "Next time I will sound properly frantic."

"He's a quare one." He shook his head dejectedly. "None of your continental terrorists would have let the lass speak to you on the phone. They'd use a tape recording to make sure there were no hints given of where she was. None of that technological stuff for him."

"He probably thought she was too frightened."

"Still, it's a risk. But then our friend Rory likes the risks."

"Yes, that's clear."

"There were no hints, were there?" he asked hopefully.

"She didn't have enough time. He didn't take much of a risk. Tell me, Jaymo, does he have sympathizers who assist him?"

"There are people in Ireland who think he's a grand man for killing Prots and Brits. They say, turn Rory loose in London and he'll kill a few thousand Brits before they get him. That's the only way to drive the Brits out of Ireland." He shuddered. "There's some method in it, Brendan. If I were a Provo I'd think the same way. Murder gets easier the more often you do it. So, yes, there are people who will help him, just as there were Yanks who protected the crazies that kidnapped the poor Hearst kid."

"Many?"

"No. But enough to provide him with some cover. And they're not your typical Provo sympathizer, either. That makes it harder for us."

"I see. Well, I suppose I'd better pack and return to Dublin."

"If it's all the same to you," he stood up, "I'd like you to drive back with us. Sure, it's a long ride in the rain."

I laughed softly. "Delighted, Jaymo. I don't like driving on your Irish highways in the rain."

I packed my things and Jean's, finding some amusement in the thought that my arsenal would ride back to Dublin in the boot, as the Irish call the trunk of a car, of a detective superintendent of the Special Branch.

Mike Casey. I had called him yesterday to thank him for the delivery of his package and assured him that matters were progressing. It was too early to call him today. Should I tell him about Jean? No, not yet. Not till it was clear that I needed the main force. Finn didn't call for the Fenians till the last minute, nor Robin for the Merry Men, nor Lancelot for the Round Table. So far, I was sure I could take care of the situation by myself. I wouldn't mention the kidnapping when I phoned him from Dublin.

The blue hatchback was no longer at the entrance to Ashford Castle. Conor Murtaugh, was it? Conor, your life expectancy isn't very great.

We drove through the Sunday afternoon rain from Cong to Dublin in silence. I was removed from the world, as immune to the passage of time as I was to terror. I would save Jean, and Ciara too.

"Would you mind if I ask a question?" Jaymo Finnegan, who had carefully refrained from lighting his pipe in the car, asked cautiously as we drove through Phoenix Park, inside the city limits of Dublin.

"By all means."

"Did you see much action in the war?"

"Some."

I wasn't going to admit that my combat experience had lasted no more than two hours.

"I see."

"Why do you ask?"

"Well," he hesitated, "begging your pardon if I'm being offensive, but you are a very cool man—as though you have had a lot of combat."

"Not that much, Jaymo. Pretty concentrated while it lasted. I'm calm because I'm confident."

"In us?" he asked dubiously as the car turned into what I guessed was the usual traffic jam on O'Connell Street.

"In myself."

"I see." He really didn't. "What will you do?" He shifted uneasily next to me in the backseat of the Volvo.

"I told you already, Superintendent. I'm going to kill the fucking piss artists."

Which wasn't exactly what I had said before but I was picking up the linguistic habits of the natives.

The woman constable who was driving the car and the silent aide-de-camp inspector who sat next to her both gasped.

"All of them?" Jaymo asked incredulously.

"Why not?"

"You're a fucking idjit," he said, not without some admiration.

I'm sure they all thought that I was more daft than Rory McLafferty.

"By the way, after I drop these bags with the hall porter at the Shelbourne, would you drive me back to the procathedral? I want to attend the five-thirty Mass."

"What if McLafferty calls?" He turned to look at me like I was a raving lunatic.

"Then he'll call again, I imagine. I'm a Catholic, and Catholics go to Mass on Sunday."

I pictured with considerable satisfaction the conversation they would have when they delivered me to the procathedral.

There was room for me in the Shelbourne. I returned to the Garda car. "All right. Now to the procathedral."

At Mass I prayed with fervor and intensity for Jean and Ciara that their hope would endure until I could free the one and find the other.

I prayed for myself too. With serene confidence that God would grant me victory. My cause was just, after all, wasn't it?

I walked back to the Shelbourne in the rain, enjoying Dublin in the mists and the smell of the sea on an early Sunday evening. The next week, I thought, would be very interesting.

I had already made one intolerable blunder, which I would not comprehend for several days.

Even Finn MacCool made an occasional mistake.

35

Monday morning I walked down Grafton Street from the Shelbourne to the Bank of Ireland in Grattan's beautiful old Georgian parliament building, across the street from Trinity College, stopping in Bewley's for tea and scones. I had picked out a number of men hanging around the lobby of the hotel who might have been Jaymo's tails. None of them came into Bewley's after me, but a young brown-haired woman, in a neatly belted dark brown raincoat, who looked like she might be a novice in a traditional religious order on a forbidden day off, did drift into the coffee shop. Hadn't I seen her in the Shelbourne too?

So, Jaymo.

I drank my two cups of tea, ate my hot scones, and returned to the chill mists. At the Bank of Ireland I demanded to see an assistant director and presented my letter of credit. The young man, who spoke like Ciara when she was affecting her Trinity College accent, glanced through his file of cables, came upon my recommendation from Continental Illinois, and agreed with a broad smile to cash my check for five thousand Irish punts (pounds to you who have never been there).

"The Continental is still open?" I asked lightly.

"Oh, yes, sir. We feel that the Fed will go first."

"Too bad they can't guarantee the Cubs."

"Yes, sir, it is," he agreed politely.

She never did go to Trinity, I thought as I left the bank; she did her graduate work in England. The woman is tricky. She is also splendid for ravishing, and there'll be more of that when I find her.

The brown-coated novice continued to trail far behind me when I left the bank and strolled across the Liffey, which smelled badly of fish, and into a shoe store on O'Connell Street. I purchased a pair of Adidas jogging shoes and a set of large galoshes of the sort that I had seen on the countrymen in County Galway.

In the next shop I obtained for myself a medium-size canvas duffel bag, which was wrapped up in a small package.

Then I walked leisurely back down the crowded streets in the heart of Dublin to my hotel. The young woman dropped out of sight at the corner of Dawson Street and Stephen's Green.

It would be reported to Superintendent Finnegan that the Yank drank tea at Bewley's, visited the Bank of Ireland, and made small purchases in two shops on O'Connell Street. He would check with the bank, lift a thick eyebrow at my five thousand punts, assume that I was planning on jogging to stay in condition, and instruct the constable to continue to watch me.

From a public phone in the lobby, I made a couple of calls to auto dealers and finally found the one I wanted on the road back to Galway.

Then I settled in my room with a book of Seamus Heaney's poetry to wait for the call from Rory McLafferty, which I did not expect that day anyway.

The next morning I scanned the lobby briefly after I had purchased my *Irish Times*. The woman constable was in a corner eating a roll and drinking a cup of coffee. I rode up to my room in the dubious cage elevator, which seemed to be required for atmosphere in all Irish hotels, grabbed my raincoat, and ducked down the stairs, out the back door of the Shelbourne, and into busy pedestrian traffic on Merrion Street. I hailed a taxi and told the driver I wanted to go to the Gresham Hotel on O'Connell Street.

A few doors down from the Gresham and around a corner on a side street, I found a secondhand clothing store, where, after more time spent on negotiating and estimating sizes than I wanted to risk, I purchased gray trousers and jacket, two shirts that would never be white again, a worn sweater vest, a rubberized rain slicker, and a battered gray cap. The jacket was a size too large for me, leaving enough room for a vest containing an Israeli machine gun.

"It's a trifle roomy, sir," said the young clerk.

"Aye," I agreed impassively.

I found a taxi at the stand down the street from the Gresham and fretted impatiently on the slow ride across the Liffey to Merrion Street. The back door of the hotel was locked, but I slipped in with a man who looked like he might be in charge of elevator repairs.

"Not working again?" I asked when he glanced dubiously at me.

"Sure, it doesn't work half the time. And the other half it's fixing not to work."

I rushed up the stairs, dumped my bundles on my bed, checked with the switchboard to see if there had been any calls for me, and then strolled with elaborate casualness back down to the lobby. My novice friend was still there, reading the *Irish Times*. Actually, with her coat off, she looked more like a postulant.

Back in my room, I packed my purchases into the canvas duffel bag, along with slacks, a sweater, shoes, and some underwear for Jean, and settled back with a copy of Maeve Binchy's *Light a Penny Candle*. Before I began to read I played over again in my mind the scenario for the conversation I planned with McLafferty. I was certain that after that conversation I would be ready to move.

No reason for that certainty other than my blind arrogance.

Late that afternoon, the hall porter called my room to say that there was a package for me in the lobby. I asked him to send a bellman up with it.

"Did you see who delivered this?" I gave the young, red-haired bellman two punts and accepted the small, oblong box, which was wrapped rather sloppily in wrinkled brown paper.

"Let me see, sir." He frowned thoughtfully. "Was it a little man in a black cap?"

"With a big mustache and a short nose?"

"Long nose, I'd say."

Conor Murtaugh. Bad risk. What if Jaymo had enough constables to watch the front of the hotel and follow the blue hatchback?

Perhaps Rory McLafferty knew that the Special Branch didn't have enough personnel to do that. Still, what if they made an exception in this case? The poor fool must have thought he was invulnerable.

After the bellman left, I opened the package and called the number that Jaymo had given me.

"Hello."

"Ryan. I have a VHS tape here. Probably from McLafferty. Can you play it for me?"

"We'll be right over."

It was the same team that had drove in from Cong—the silent inspector, the sergeant who drove the car, and the blonde woman constable. Gallantry had triumphed over feminism: the inspector rather than the constable was carrying the VCR.

He plugged it in, and I inserted the tape. We settled back in our chairs and waited for the latest entertainment from your man Rory.

Entertainment it was, of the most vicious type imaginable.

A shaky picture of a wall panel, which did not look like a room in a house. The cameraman did not know how to use his equipment.

What kind of a room was it? First clue that Finn MacCool, mythical hero and invulnerable detective, missed.

The camera zoomed back, revealing Jean tied to a chair, hands behind her back. Her green sleep shirt had been torn on one side, revealing half of her body. She looked frightened and pathetic, but her little chin was still tilted defiantly.

"She a pretty wee thing, isn't she, Brendan Ryan?" McLafferty's voice in the background. "It'd be a shame to have to disfigure her, wouldn't it now. Sure, so far we haven't hurt her much at all. Have you ever seen your daughter naked, Brendan?" A hand pulled away her torn shirt. "Lovely, isn't it? Does it give you incestuous thoughts? Ah, well, fathers and daughters are often that way. It can't be helped, can it?"

"Stop them, Daddy." Jean was hysterical. "They hurt me all the time. I'm alone. There's no one to protect me."

"The poor girl is all alone." McLafferty giggled insanely. "Isn't that a pity, Daddy? Sure, she hasn't been hurt much at all, at all. Yet. No one has even raped her yet, though there's them here that wants to."

"I'm alone, Daddy," she sobbed.

"Alone is it?" McLafferty pretended to be offended. "That's not the way to talk about your Uncle Rory, who is protecting you from all the bad men here."

"Daddy. . . ." A heartrending cry.

McLafferty chuckled as the camera jerked to her face, showing an expression of abject horror.

"I'm a patient man, Brendan Ryan," McLafferty said soothingly, as the camera zoomed back to show us Jean, slumped, perhaps unconscious, in her chair. Again a shot of the strange wood paneling, painted dark brown, in the background. "But there's a limit to my patience. You'll be hearing from me soon."

The picture ended abruptly. White electronic snow on a black background.

"Bloody bastards." Jaymo turned off the switch savagely. The young woman constable was weeping softly. The inspector, his fist clenched, was staring out the window at the fog-shrouded green.

"They're trying to frighten you, sir." Jaymo turned to me. "The lass is still alive. They've hurt her, but nothing too terrible yet. We'll find them, never fear."

"Of course, Superintendent. Of course."

I swore to myself that they would all die slowly and horribly. I didn't tell Jaymo who had delivered the package. Nor did I ask what clues, if any, they had. Soon my own plans would unfold.

"We'll take it back to the castle and analyze it." Jaymo motioned his inspector to pack up the video player.

"I'd like to see it again, if you don't mind."

The woman constable stared at me in disbelief. The poor wee man was way round the bend. Nonetheless, they played it again. A vague, as yet unfocused idea about the brown wall teased at my brain. I knew more than I was yet able to articulate. It would come. Soon.

Looking back now, I realize that I was a stupid fool to have missed it. I was too busy with the appearance of my new role as mythical berserker to see the obvious.

Jaymo and his crew left with many promises that they'd have Jean back to me "safe and sound" in short order. I hardly listened to them.

I sat there for hours, blankly watching darkness settle over the misty green. The streetlights glowing dimly beneath my window and across the street suggested Sherlock Holmes in a dangerous neighborhood in Soho.

I would kill them all, slowly, so that they would suffer terribly.

I drew the canvas attaché case from my closet and tenderly cleaned and polished the components of the Uzi. I fitted the components together carefully and squeezed the trigger to make sure that the weapon was in operating order. Then I checked, as an afterthought, Mike Casey's .22.

Finally I fell asleep and dreamed of bodies being torn apart.

McLafferty called at ten the following morning. His connection was poor, and the strong wind that was rattling my windowpanes made it even harder to hear him.

"Are we ready to do business now, Mr. Ryan?"

"I'll give you anything you want," I sobbed. "But don't hurt her anymore. Please don't hurt her."

"Ah, that's a sensible man now." He sounded pleased that my icy calm had been replaced by the reaction for which his script called. "I have nothing against the poor child and don't want to have to hurt her anymore. But there's some things, however tragic, that must be done in a nation's fight for freedom. I'm sure a Yank understands that."

Freedom ideology. I supposed he still thought he believed it some of the time.

"I'll give you all the money you want." I permitted myself to sound like I was crying. "Just give her back to me."

" 'Tis not money I want." He chuckled. "Sure, someone with more than you gives me all I need. I want something else."

Suddenly I understood where Jean was. I'd been a stupid fool. Folk heroes, however, do not permit such self-criticism to last long.

"Anything, anything." I tried desperately to concentrate on the scenario. The rest could wait. My heart, however, was thumping with eagerness for battle.

"Even Clare Keenan?"

"My God, McLafferty, I don't have her."

"Ah, sure, but you know where she is, don't you now?"

"Only that she's out there waiting to kill you."

"What?" He was astonished. "Kill me?"

"I saw her at the Railway Hotel in Galway." I stumbled as though I were in a rush to tell him everything. "She left when I was asleep. She knows you're after her. She's going to kill you when you catch up with her."

I bit my tongue to keep from telling him that his dumb friend Con Murtaugh had fallen asleep in the lobby of the hotel.

"She's against killing," he said dubiously.

"God in Heaven, Rory. You understand women. You know what they're like. A man pushes them around and pushes them around and they don't fight back. Then, one day, without any warning, they explode. A woman like that is as dangerous as a she-tiger."

"Aye," he said thoughtfully, accepting my implied flattery of his understanding of women. "That's true for a fact . . . but where is she?"

"How would I know? If she had told me, do you think I wouldn't have tipped off the Garda? Do you think I want her out there, ticking like a bomb?"

"Aye," he said again, pondering the reasonableness of my answer.

"You know her better than I do. Your guess as to where she's waiting for you would be better than mine."

I hoped I wasn't increasing the dangers for Ciara. At any rate, I would save her the same way I would now save Jean.

There was a moment of silence while Rory thought about it.

"Tell you what, Brendan, my friend; we'll work out a little compromise. We'll keep the lass while I have a look around. If I find Clare, we'll give the lass back to you. While I'm searching, we won't do anything serious to hurt her, just a bit now and then to keep up the morale of my people. If I don't find Clare, well, I'll be back in touch with you."

"Please don't hurt Jeannie," I screamed.

The phone line clicked dead, but not before he had a chance to savor my horror.

I waited a few minutes to make sure I was in full possession of myself and my plans. Then I put on my London Fog and slipped Mike's .22 into the pocket. I checked my jacket to make sure the wallet with the five thousand punts was there. Then I picked up the canvas duffel bag with my countryman's clothes and the tweed attaché case with the Uzi and opened the door to my room a crack. I looked in both directions down the corridor. No one in sight. I dashed to the stairwell and hurried down the stairs and out into the foggy alley behind the hotel. I thanked a gracious Heaven for the fog.

I boarded a taxi at the stand in Merrion Street and gave the driver the address of the place I had called on the Navan road, above Phoenix Park. He complained about the weather and the state of the economy for the whole trip. Nonetheless I tipped him generously and entered the used-car display room with a stern warning to myself that prolonged negotiations were essential if I did not want to stir up suspicions.

The negotiations were even more prolonged than I had anticipated. The car I wanted, a woebegone Morris Minor, would cost perhaps twelve hundred punts. But, sure, sir, you would not want to travel Ireland in a pile of junk, now would you?

I convinced them that I was an anthropologist from a university and it was a requirement of my work that I drive a moribund car. The salesman, who was tricky enough to be a law school dean, warned me that I could not export the car, "much as I doubt that you want to, sir, if you don't mind me saying so."

I could keep the license plates on the car while the registration was changed. Lucky accident. Finn MacCool, being a product of another age, with no understanding of modern law, had not thought of registration plates. I was covered, I assured him, by my American insurance policy. The Garda, he said, might want to see some proof of that in case of necessity but, "sure, you won't be getting into any accidents with this car, will you now, sir? It can't go fast enough to cause any trouble, can it?"

With some difficulty I got the Morris started, noticed that the roof leaked, and found a petrol station (see, I was learning the language) where, at the price of listening to doubtful comments about the car from the attendant, I had the gas tank filled. I continued west through Maynooth, where the seminary and the old castle of the Kildares (Silken Thomas and his bunch) were hidden in fog, and on towards Mullingar.

I pulled off on a side road in the country and, protected by the fog, changed into my countryman's clothes, pulling the galoshes firmly up over my Adidas running shoes. I stuffed my own clothes into the duffel bag with the clothes I'd brought for Jean and transferred Mike's .22 to the pocket of my rain slicker.

I now looked something like an Irish countryman. If I remembered to walk slowly, speak very little, and nod my head like I understood everything, I might be able to pass for a few hours—which was all I would need.

I stopped in a hardware store in Mullingar and purchased three milk cans for the backseat of the Morris. The store owner talked to me knowingly about the problems of the dairy industry and about the "super levy"—whatever that was—and the present state of the Common Market.

I nodded and mumbled "aye" and "true enough" several times, and seemed to get away with it. Nonetheless I stopped at a tobacco store and bought a tin of pipe tobacco, two old pipes, a worn leather bag, and a lighter. I hadn't smoked a pipe since college. To be an authentic Irish countryman, you need not smoke a pipe, only suck on it.

Thus arrayed I left Mullingar, bound back to the West of Ireland and my confrontation with Rory McLafferty. He would, I was confident, be dead by nightfall.

36

I sat in the corner of the shabby pub which smelled like the men's room in a broken-down railroad station, drinking my pint of Guinness as slowly as I could. Guinness, they said, was good for you. I thought it tasted even darker than it looked and longed for my Jameson's. But a countryman does not drink Jameson's in the local. Paddy's maybe, but I didn't think I was that kind of countryman. Anyway, I'd as soon drink gasoline from my Morris Minor.

I was in the town of Athlone, where I would have been Sunday night if I had listened carefully to Jean's signal that she was "alone." She was somewhere above Athlone on Lough Ree on a boat—the brown wood in the picture screamed "boat" if you knew what you were looking for.

It was possible that McLafferty and his thugs were moving the boat down the Shannon, but unlikely. There were too many locks where someone might be suspicious. Lough Ree—a ¯lake formed by a widening of the Shannon—provided plenty of room and was filled with boats. Nothing to arouse suspicion if you kept your distance from the others.

Which boat of the scores on the lake? I circled the lake as soon as I arrived in my burping and swaying Morris, looking for a dark blue VW hatchback parked between the road and the piers and marinas that lined the shore, particularly on the east shore of the lake. I could not find it.

I then scouted the town of Athlone, pausing a few moments on the bridge over the Shannon to watch that fabled water goddess (Sionna in Irish) rush under the bridge towards her Atlantic destination far away, while thick, angry sheets of rain flailed against her. I thought of Ciara, wondered where she was, hoped that I had not increased her peril, and then walked back to my invalid car.

It would not do to wander through Athlone asking questions. My countryman's disguise would not last five minutes if I did that. Moreover, if Rory had chosen to hide here, it

371

meant that he had friends and allies, perhaps sharp enough to wonder even about a new silver-haired countryman.

It was probable that he had chosen a slip or a pier or a marina on the east shore of the lake, on the Dublin side of the Shannon bridge. While there were more boats on that side, there was less likelihood that new boaters would be noticed. On a weekend the lake would swarm with people. But today was Wednesday.

So I decided to sit quietly in the public bar at the foot of the gravel road leading up the east side of the lake. The fish on the walls, the boat models, and its name—The Brass Anchor—suggested it was a place for boaters to pause for their pint or two. I knew what his crowd looked like, and they didn't know I knew. I would wait at the tiny, scratched, pockmarked table in the corner, with a bowed head that discouraged conversation, and sip stout for a couple of hours.

Perhaps one of his crowd would drop in. Maybe Con Murtaugh, returning from wherever he might have gone in the hatchback. If that didn't work, I'd have to prowl the side of the lake after dark, looking for a boat that showed lights.

While Finn MacCool does not have second thoughts, I considered again, just the same, my decision not to call in Jaymo and his troops from the Special Branch.

Doubtless they were skillful in dealing with the Provos; and they had read the confidential reports that Interpol had circulated about patterns of continental terrorist behavior. By Jaymo's own admission, however, Rory McLafferty was so mad that he didn't fit any of the profiles.

So, if they located him, they would do what all institutions do in time of crisis—not good things or wise things, but the things they do well. However much Jaymo would realize that the classic response might not work with Rory, he'd do what he would do with a Provo terrorist group because he had to do something.

They would try their Athlone informants for information, perhaps providing Rory with advance warning. Then, in the absence of information about which boat the terrorists were using, they would surround Athlone with roadblocks and close in on the lake, systematically searching every boat on the lake. When they finally found the one, whether by a tip-off or a search or luck—perhaps finding the blue hatchback

"Night," said the little knot of men at the bar. Con Murtaugh did not even look around. Which might have meant that he was very cool or that he wasn't worried about me anymore.

His blue hatchback was parked in front of the pub next to the Morris. I choked my car to life and with considerable noise chugged down the road back towards Athlone. I parked it next to a hedge perhaps a hundred yards away and slogged back to the pub. I found a tree across the road, sloshed through a drainage ditch, and took up an observation post behind the tree. It was twilight, the long twilight which, I had discovered, was typical of rainy nights in Ireland in the spring. For a couple more hours I'd be able to see the edge of the lake well enough to spot a blue hatchback.

In the meantime I had no choice but to wait in the rain and discover that not only my cap but also my slicker was no longer rainproof. Everything was soggy, branches, leaves, grass, road, me. Ireland needed two things, Frank O'Connor had once remarked, to be left alone by foreigners and one hell of a big roof. Big and thick. Until then it would not dry out till a month after Judgment Day and then only if the final act is, as predicted, fire.

Con must have consumed only one pint. He reappeared at the doorway in a panel of bright light and a burst of laughter. What a crazy way to run a terrorist operation. Only a zany Irish psychopath would permit his personnel to wander around drinking with the natives.

Nonetheless, Jaymo and the Special Branch had not found them yet.

Con glanced up and down the road, a routine inspection, entered his hatchback, backed it up, and drove north on the gravel road away from Athlone.

I gave him five minutes head start and then hurried down the road to my Morris, which now resolutely refused to start. I cursed, I pleaded, I threatened. No use. The man at the petrol station had been right: "Sure, it deserves a daycent Christian burial."

I got out of the driver's seat, kicked the engine with disgust, as I would a mule, decided to try it once more, and turned over the ignition.

It worked.

I understand you now, my friend. You've the personality of a mule.

There was no hope of following the VW's taillights now. I would have to scan the side of the road.

I drove for some time, half an hour perhaps, down the slippery road at slow speed, peering anxiously in the slowly failing light for a dark blue car.

I was convinced that I had found it next to a small marina. I parked a quarter mile down the road, jammed four ammo clips for the Uzi into my slicker pocket, and walked as slowly as I could make myself back to the marina.

I heard loud and drunken voices on an ancient cabin cruiser at the far end of the marina. Huddling in the lee of what looked like a boat house, I assembled my weapon, affixing the silencer and unfolding the plastic butt, inserted a clip into the magazine, hid it under my slicker, and eased around the corner of the boat house.

The car was blue and a VW all right, but not a hatchback. I turned to rush down the road, remembered what happened to soldiers in Vietnam whose weapons jammed, and returned to the lee of the boat house to remove the clip, disassemble my Uzi, and replace it in the Secret Service vest that Mickey had thoughtfully provided. I hoped the weapon had not been soaked by its brief exposure to the rain.

Back in the car I restrained my impatience again and dried the weapon with a handful of rags. I then reassembled and loaded it and placed it next to me on the left-hand front seat of the car. It was now growing very dark, and I might need it quickly.

I continued down the road, almost to the north end of the lough, without finding the hatchback. I must have missed it. There was no way I could retrace the search in the failing light. How much longer could Jeannie survive the horrors of her imprisonment? Time was running out for all of us.

Then I saw it, hidden behind a clump of bushes near a solitary pier jutting out into the lake from a thick growth of reeds. At the end of the pier was what looked, in the near darkness, like an old wooden houseboat.

My mouth turned dry, my stomach tightened, my fingers dug into the wheel of the car as I forced myself to drive out of sight of the boat. I was back in Nam, waiting for the VC to materialize between the rows of rubber trees.

I disassembled the Uzi and hid it in my holster vest. I debated discarding the rain slicker. It made movement more awkward, but it helped to keep my weapons and ammunition moderately dry. I checked Mike's .22, pulled off my galoshes, and in my soft running shoes walked briskly and noiselessly back to the pier.

I slipped across the road, found an opening in a thick hedge, and, stooped over in a crouch, moved directly opposite the VW. The rich, raw smell of Ireland was thick in the damp air—equal parts, I surmised, of peat, manure, and rotting underbrush.

My Neanderthal hunting instinct—if that was what it was—took over again. They must have a lookout somewhere. On a cold, rainy night, where would he be?

In the car?

I prepared my weapon, released the safety, set it at single shot, and forced my way through the hedge. As quietly as I could, I sloshed through the drainage ditch toward the car.

Con Murtaugh was inside, smoking a cigarette. I altered my course so that I would come up from the rear of the car. I could not fire through the window because the noise might bring out the rest of them. Yet I could not stand in the rain for long or my weapon might become too wet to use.

I found a rock at the side of the road, no difficult task in Ireland, and threw it into the mass of reeds. It made a dull splashing sound as it hit the water.

Murtaugh, suddenly alert, sat up straight, looked quickly out the window, and hesitated, trying to make up his mind whether to investigate.

I threw another stone.

He opened the door and stepped out of the car, peering into the darkness towards the reeds. He shrugged his shoulders, reached inside for his cap, and sauntered toward the water's edge.

In my soft shoes, I followed carefully behind him, waiting till he was almost at the edge of the water. Then I stepped clumsily on a piece of wood and made a small sound.

"What the fuck . . . ?" Con turned toward me, saw me in

a quick slow-motion frame, and began to reach for his jacket pocket.

I was perhaps five or six yards behind him. I fired twice at close range. *Thump, thump,* the sounds deadened almost completely by the silencer.

Con's voice disappeared, and so did his face.

I rushed forward to catch him so that he would not fall loudly into the water. I did not look at the remains of his face as I eased him to the ground. The end of Con Murtaugh's life was quicker in the event than in the telling. Modern violence is nightmare-fast—and leaves images that will linger for the rest of your life.

I felt no sense of vengeance accomplished. Indeed, I felt nothing at all. There was still work to be done.

I crept back to the car, planning my next move. There were still five armed thugs on the boat, four if Rory was somewhere else. Someone would have to come out eventually to replace Con. I closed the door of the car and hid in the bushes a few feet away. I had time.

I checked the magazine clip. Only two rounds expended. Twenty-three left—a few seconds of automatic fire. I put the safety catch back on.

As I waited, I remembered Ciara's diatribe about abuse of women. For most of our history men have tormented and abused other men's women as part of the routine strategy of war. It was taken for granted that they had the right to do so. How many times before in Ireland's history must it have happened? On the shores of this very lake. Women were pawns, bribes, hostages, tokens. Ron Crowley's philosophy pushed to its ultimate conclusion.

God be good to him. And teach him the truth.

A door opened on the houseboat. Laughter and light came briefly from the inside. A big man emerged, Seamus Cagney, perhaps.

He fiddled with the door as he closed it, perhaps resetting an alarm system. Or a trigger on an explosive device.

Then, singing something about "Bold Fenian Men," he weaved a dubious path down the narrow pier.

I moved the change lever on the left side of the pistol grip forward from "S" to "D" and waited.

"All right, Conor Murtaugh, you fucking little gombeen-man, it's my turn,'' he bellowed. ''Leave some of the fucking booze in the bottle for me.''

He bumped into the front of the car, hiccuped, and stumbled around to the door.

''Where the hell are you?'' he demanded.

I gently squeezed the trigger three times. *Thump, thump, thump*. Cagney straightened up, hung for a minute as though suspended in space, and then sagged against the car, moaning softly as his life breath departed him. Since I would have to change the clip anyway, I flipped the weapon to automatic and touched the trigger.

The Uzi discharged its bullets with a whooshing gasp, a single sustained *thump*.

The remains of Seamus Cagney slid quietly to the ground, the back of his jacket a mat of fresh blood. I dragged him away from the car into the bushes.

The Uzi, I thought irrelevantly, was like the blowguns the Pygmies use—swift and silent death. So easy to kill.

Two down, four or perhaps three to go. I had to move quickly now.

The rain had dwindled to a light drizzle, the classic ''soft night'' of Irish tales. I put my weapon back on ''S,'' picked up a rock from the driveway, wrapped it in a thick rag I had brought for such purposes, and walked quietly and carefully down the pier. No point in trying to hide now.

I stepped cautiously onto the boat. It swayed slightly under my weight, but no more than it would if it were pushed by an extra large wave. The name on its stern was *Mystamaid*. Not especially appropriate, I thought.

Blessing the Adidas company for their quiet shoes, I crept along the side of the big cabin.

Two men were talking.

''If your man isn't back by morning, I'm going to take her myself. Sure 'tis torture to have to look at a half-naked woman like that for four days and not be able to use her.''

''He has his plans.''

''Fuck his plans. I want her. And I want her first too. That'll be the most fun.''

''It won't do.''

''Who the fucking hell is going to stop me? You? Don't make me laugh.''

The window on the side of the cabin was at the height of my chest and reasonably large for a boat. With infinite care I peeked through one corner of it.

Two men were sitting at a table playing cards, with an almost empty unlabeled bottle of whiskey between them. Great revolutionary leader you are, McLafferty.

McBeen and O'Malley by the looks of them. No Rory or Maeve Conroy. Where's Jean?

Then I saw her, trussed up in the same chair as in the videotape, her Notre Dame shirt in tatters, her mouth gagged with dirty cloth, her face contorted in anguish, her body slumped painfully against the ropes.

"Have you never screwed an American virgin, Dick me boy? Take it from me, there's nothing like it. You have to push them around a bit to get them ready, you know what I mean? But then they get in the spirit of the thing and it's all the way home."

There was at least one more room, possibly two more forward of the main cabin. Rory was not there. Maeve?

I had no choice. It had to be now.

I moved the change bolt forward to automatic, pulled the cocking bolt back, gripped the Uzi by its stock in my left hand, and brought the big, cloth-sheathed rock against the window. It shattered with a slight tinkle.

The two card players looked up, mildly annoyed by the unexpected sound. I brought my weapon to the hole in the window and emptied the magazine into them, sweeping it across the room at waist level and then back a little higher.

Bright red spots appeared on their bellies and their chests. One of them emitted a stifled cry, half scream, half sob. The other died quietly. The short one stumbled and fell forward with a thud. The tall one merely collapsed like a sprinter at the end of a race. The room filled with smoke. Blood poured out on the floor. Tangled pieces of human insides oozed out of their bodies.

A charnel house, I thought.

I pulled the gun out of the hole in the windowpane, ejected the spent clip, and grabbed in my pocket for another. My trembling fingers let it slip away.

I hadn't noticed that my fingers and every other part of my body were quaking.

Jean was shouting into her gag, eyes filled with horror. She was trying to warn me. Of what?

I gripped another ammo clip firmly, inserted it into the magazine, and then looked through the window.

The door of the main cabin next to Jean abruptly swung open, and a squat, solid woman in sweatshirt and jeans burst through it, an AK-47 waving wildly in her right hand. She looked around the wreck of the room in wild-eyed dismay and then focused on me at the window.

She pointed the AK-47 in my direction and fired.

37

The scene passed before my eyes in second-by-second frames. The bullets left the muzzle of the AK-47 with popping noises like a string of large and rapid firecrackers. Maeve Conroy's weapon was pointed above me at the wrong angle. She had fired too quickly, a fatal mistake for her. The bullets chopped through the wall above my head as if the wall were made of tissue paper.

I squeezed the trigger of my weapon and forgot to release it. The entire clip of ordnance, exploding with a soft *whoosh*, tore into her stomach. The first woman I'd killed. New kick.

The AK-47 fell from her hands. She grabbed at her dissolving gut, expressions of surprise, disbelief, anger, and then resignation moving rapidly across her face. She saw her blood and intestines pouring out onto the floor, gave up on life, and fell slowly forward, collapsing in front of Jean, who sobbed through her gag.

I closed my eyes briefly. Five killed in a quarter hour. Not exactly Hiroshima, but a massacre nonetheless. So quickly does the thin red line around civilization disappear. A bloody, violent rite of spring.

I look back now on those moments and try to recapture my reactions. Brendan Ryan, whose colleagues won't let him go into a law court for litigation because he is too gentle and uncompetitive, had become Finn MacCool the berserker. What did I feel? Physical reactions—the terrible stench of exploding ammunition, the muffled cries of the dead and dying, the slashing explosions of AK-47, the steady thumping of Major Uziel Gal's nearly noiseless machine pistol, the swaying of the *Mystamaid* as its walls were shredded by bullets, the quavering weakness of my own body, horror at the dead bodies and bits and pieces of bodies scattered around the dimly lighted cabin. No satisfaction, no sense of vengeful triumph, vague regret that Rory was not there and that Ciara was still in danger, joy, very mild and understated, that I had saved Jean. But mostly nothing at all. I was as emotionally empty as a psychopath.

A berserker perhaps, but not one of your really first-rate berserkers. Even as Finn MacCool, not really a winner.

All this is in retrospect. At the time itself I opened my eyes and shouted, "Rory?"

Jean shook her head negatively and shrugged her frail little shoulders.

"Is the door booby-trapped?"

A vigorous affirmative nod.

"The window?"

A negative shake.

Dumb question. If it had been, the *Mystamaid* would have already been blasted into the sky.

I knocked away the rest of the windowpane with the butt of my weapon and climbed into the cabin. I stepped over Maeve Conroy's disintegrated body and pulled the gag off Jean's mouth.

"Where's Rory?"

"He left this morning," she croaked. "Said he'd be gone for a day or two. Oh, Daddy . . ." I found a knife in a drawer near the small stove and quickly cut her ropes. Then I folded my child's tormented little body into my arms. She shivered as though she had hiked through miles of Arctic cold. Gradually, in the safe protection of my arms, the shivering slowed and stopped.

"Daddy, you look so funny in those old clothes."

Mr. Dangerfield is quite right. You get no respect. "We'd better get out of here." I released her and she instinctively pulled the remnants of her sleep shirt together. I found a sweatshirt with *Mystamaid* printed on it. Not one of theirs. Awkwardly, because her body was still stiff from being cramped in the chair, she pulled it over her head. She was indeed a wonderfully lovely young specimen of womanly humankind, a compact Celtic nymph, with nerves of the same tempered steel of which the finest swords are made.

"I'm all right, Daddy," she insisted. "Hurt and humiliated and frightened and angry as hell. But I'm all right. Don't worry about me. . . . Aren't you going to take the money?"

"Money?"

"Sure. The money the Libyans gave him. It's locked up in that cabinet. He'll have a hard time without it."

There was no reason to leave the money for Rory if he should return before Jaymo Finnegan and the seventh cavalry arrived. I took an ax from its mounting on the wall and chopped through the door of the locked cabinet. The cheap veneered wood splintered easily. I pulled out of the rubble a thin attaché case, handcrafted in elegant Florentine leather. Either Rory or his patrons had expensive tastes. I flipped open the cover.

Inside were neatly wrapped packages of hundred-punt notes, it looked like a hundred in each package. Nine of the packages were unbroken, almost a hundred thousand Irish pounds. The Libyan colonel was notoriously generous to his favorites.

Rory McLafferty could kill a lot of people with this kind of money.

I snapped the lid down on the leather case and gave it to Jean, quickly disassembled my Uzi and stuffed it into my holster vest, and climbed out the empty window. Then I lifted her out onto the deck of the *Mystamaid* and helped her step from the boat to the pier. She wavered dangerously, her muscles still cramped and uncertain. I tightened my grip on her arm.

"I'm all right, Daddy," she insisted.

"Who said you weren't?"

It was now the middle of the brief spring night and dark as the inside of a cave. The soft mist had been replaced by fog. The pier was slippery and uncertain. We tottered off it and onto the soggy shore. "I'll carry you," I said.

"I can walk," she argued.

"Not a hundred yards on a gravel road with bare feet."

"All right," she conceded reluctantly.

I scooped her up, briefcase and all. She did not seem a heavy burden to Finn MacCool. What was the name of his daughter anyway?

"First time since you were a baby," I said as we lumbered through the darkness. "You were a little lighter then. Not much though."

She giggled. "I'm all right, Daddy."

"That's three times, kid. I believe you."

"They wanted to rape me," she continued. "Rory wouldn't let them. He said I would keep till the proper time. He's a strange, scary man. He gets his kicks out of humiliating and tormenting people. I bet he couldn't get it up the ordinary way. . . ."

Such candid talk from my little girl.

"Poor Ciara. Have we found her yet, Daddy? We can't let him hurt her."

"Not yet."

Maybe I've helped him to search for her. Please God I have not.

"I knew you'd come," Jean babbled on. "I knew you'd understand what I meant by 'alone.' I didn't realize that you'd come all by yourself. That was very brave, Daddy. Kind of like a man in Louis L'Amour's westerns. A quiet man, quiet and deadly. Except I never knew you were deadly."

"John Wayne's film about Ireland was called *The Quiet Man.*"

"You're not like John Wayne at all. Just quiet and terrifying. I'll be a good little girl from now on." Another giggle. She was on the edge of hysteria and fighting it every inch of the way.

"Like, totally awesome, would you say?"

"Well, not totally . . . what a funny little car."

I looked funny and so did my Rocinante. No respect at all.

In the backseat of the Morris, Jean pulled on the clothes I'd brought her. "At least I don't look totally like a *Penthouse* centerfold anymore."

"Too pretty for *Penthouse.*"

"Daddy," she said reprovingly as she jumped into the front seat with me. "Anyway," serious again, "I'm all right now."

I was prepared to believe it.

"They can hurt your body and humiliate it and violate it, but they can't get at you unless you let them."

True enough, in the short run. And as the prisoners in Korea and Vietnam had proved, true enough in the long run, too, if you were a person of exceptional stamina and courage. Perhaps Jean was indeed cut from that cloth. A tough little girl. No, not that anymore. A tough young woman.

I drove through the night toward Mullingar instead of returning through Athlone. I was not ready to risk another encounter with the publican at The Brass Anchor.

The first phone kiosk at which I stopped had no phone at all. In the second the phone didn't work. Finally we found one on the outskirts of Mullingar that accepted the emergency number Jaymo had given me.

"Hel-*lo*."

Frantically I shoved coins into the slot.

"Hel-*lo*." Louder and more upset. I had broken into his sleep.

"Push the A button, Daddy."

"Push the fucking A button," Jaymo shouted.

Ireland's favorite word. For want of the fucking A button, the war was lost.

"Brendan Ryan here, Superintendent. You folks could improve your phone system. Socialism doesn't work, you know. Sell it off to a private company."

"I'll take it up with the taoiseach."

"On the road on the east side of Lough Ree, almost at the north end, there is a boat called the *Mystamaid*. There was some shooting there tonight. A few bodies, two outside the boat, three on it. Rory is not one of them, unfortunately. You might find some clues. And, if I were you, I'd take a good, hard look at the publican in the Brass Anchor at the bottom of the road. Got it?"

"What . . . ?"

"Any news about Ciara?"

"No. What are you telling me . . . ?"

"One other thing. The boat is booby-trapped. The door to the cabin, anyway. Be careful."

"How do you know . . . ?"

"Good-bye, Superintendent. See you in the morning."

Jean babbled for the rest of the trip through the night and the fog to Dublin.

"I suppose," she said as we crossed the Liffey, ". . . hey, Daddy, your driving is not all that bad, considering."

"Quiet, deadly, and a not bad driver, considering. You suppose what?"

"Oh, I suppose that when we get home, I'll have to spend a few sessions with Aunt Mary Kate talking about all of this."

"It might not be a bad idea. I must say, though, you're a very tough young woman."

"Thank you, Daddy." She brushed my cheek with her lips. "I think I am too. It's the opposite that's the problem."

Jaymo and his usual crew were waiting in the empty lobby of the Shelbourne for us.

"Thank God the lass is all right," he said with some conviction as we walked in.

"No thanks to the Garda, Superintendent," Jean snapped at him. "My daddy had to do it all."

"Easy, kid. They're good cops, doing the best they can. They didn't create Rory McLafferty. If anyone did, it was the Brits and the RUC in the North."

"Well . . . all right, I'm sorry, Superintendent. Anyway, I brought a present for you."

There was no negotiation over what we would do with the money. Jean had made up her mind.

He opened the leather case. His crowd gathered around and peered in.

"Jaysus!" said the woman constable.

"Almost a hundred thousand punts," Jaymo said softly. "Dermot," to his assistant, the silent inspector, "make out a receipt for this."

"It belongs to either Libya or the Republic," I said. "Not to us."

"Aye." Jaymo winked. "The receipt is to make sure that no one can think any of us were tempted."

We checked Jean into the hotel, and I went with her to the room. "Do you want me to stay with you tonight, miss?" asked the woman constable.

Jean considered. "That would be wonderful, Constable Toole. Like, totally wonderful."

"Two Irishwomen together is a bad thing," Jaymo remarked philosophically as we walked back down the stairs to the lobby. "A bad thing altogether."

"Too true."

"That was quite a mess out there. The Gardai from Athlone said that it was like a slaughterhouse."

"Really?"

"Aye, they did. Your man with the machine pistol didn't take any halfway measures; butchered them into little pieces, he did."

"Nine-millimeter parabellum bullets."

"Might have been a little bit overanxious," Jaymo stared out at the green, "or a little bit out of practice."

"A fucking shitehawk," I murmured, experimenting with my newly learned Irish vocabulary.

"Your Gardai from Athlone were glad we warned them about the booby trap. The pension fund would be hard put to have supported all the widows."

"Indeed."

"It's the lot of them. Seamus Cagney won't haunt Miss Keenan anymore."

"Only McLafferty."

"Aye. We'll find him too." A long silence at the foot of the steps, next to the shuttered gift shop, while he lit his pipe. "By the way, the Gardai in Athlone say that your man with the gun must have had some experience with automatic weapons, like, for instance, one of your American M16s."

"Oh?"

"It's true." He considered me with both eyebrows lifted and keen brown eyes probing at my face and mind. "Mind you, it saved the Republic a lot of trouble."

"IRA factional violence."

"I imagine that's what the papers will say," he agreed. "The ting is," he puffed contentedly on his pipe, "the ting is that we're not sure where the automatic weapon is. This is a peaceful country, Brendan. A peaceful country."

"Sure, I wouldn't argue that at all. You can't have people wandering around with automatic weapons. Like that AK-47, which I understand was on the boat and which, I presume, was responsible for the killing."

"I suppose so. We could do ballistics tests to be certain. But then that would cost the Republic money that might well be spent on other matters, wouldn't it now?"

"You'd know that better than I."

"Indeed. Well, we'll be seeing you tomorrow, Brendan. Sleep well."

"Thanks, Jaymo. I'm sure I will."

After he left, but with several uniformed Gardai scattered about the lobby and the corridors, I went back to my "funny" Morris Minor—which I was now determined would be retired with honor at Grand Beach when we went home—removed the duffel bag with my "funny" clothes, and carried the cloth bag with the Uzi to my room while Jaymo's guards watched in total innocence.

I cleaned and oiled the weapon while I rewarded myself with two stiff shots of Jameson's. When this was over I would certainly cut down on my contribution to the distillery's income.

It was not the kingly hall to which a mythic hero is supposed to return after a victory, that he might hear the bards sing his exploits. But the market on mythic heroes is down these days, so my down-at-the-heels room at the Shelbourne would have to do. Anyway, I needed sleep, not a celebration. It would not require a third shot of Jameson's.

I went to bed and slept, if not as well as Jaymo had wished me, at least deeply. My dreams were about disintegrating human bodies.

Jean, pale but composed, told me at lunch that we were being taken to supper at one of the musical pubs by her friend Liam and that she was going to phone Tim Murphy as soon as it was late enough to place a call to America.

"Not missing a base."

"No way," she agreed brightly. "Touch 'em all."

Jaymo called that afternoon to say mysteriously that they had "one or two important leads" on Rory and that I could stop worrying about Miss Keenan. "In a day or two it will all be over."

"Will it now?"

I realized then that the body which was being dismembered by automatic weapon fire in my dream was often Ciara's. So happy was I to have my daughter back, alive and apparently well, that I had almost forgotten my woman. Finn would never do that.

Dear God, bring her back to me. Please.

That evening in the lobby, before Liam showed up, Jean whispered that Timmy had been "like, totally sweet."

At supper and while we sang Irish songs, she was gentle and affectionate with Liam. My daughter, convinced that she could be tough when she had to be, was practicing tenderness.

I wondered from whom she had inherited or from whose example she had learned such a systematic approach to emotions and behavior. You'd think her father was an estate planner.

The next morning, Jaymo woke me with an early phone call.

"We have your man McLafferty trapped in a farmhouse near Athlone. The minister wonders if you and the lass would like to fly down there in a helicopter to watch us take him."

38

The Irish government's approach to a surrounded terrorist was pretty much what I had imagined it would be. Reality after a time imitates TV clips.

The farmhouse and the thick hedge around it were isolated from the rest of the world by a circle of armored vehicles ("made right here in Ireland," the minister told me proudly) and Garda cars. Three helicopters circled overhead. Down the road a couple of light tanks were poised, their guns doubtless trained on the shabby white house. Behind the armored vehicles and police cars were Garda and army troops equipped with gas masks, flak jackets, and huge armored shields. A couple of hundred guns were aimed at the farmhouse, and a score of tear gas grenade launchers pointed hopefully at the dark gray sky. Behind one of the armored cars, a dozen or so very tough men in fatigue uniforms lolled with elaborate casualness. The stun commandos, no doubt.

Why should the Irish do it any differently from anyone else? Why send a lone berserker in with an Uzi? Finn MacCool is obsolete.

All for one terrorist and his woman. Not Ciara, Jaymo assured me repeatedly.

"I notice that your elite squad uses Israeli automatic weapons, Mr. Minister."

Jaymo rolled his eyes.

"Irish weapons, actually, Mr. Ryan. We manufacture them here in small quantities on license. They are the best automatic weapons in the world. Much better than the AK-47."

"So I'm told." I winked at Jaymo. "Ireland and Israel . . . that's a combination that's hard to beat."

"True enough," said the minister.

He was a youngish man with glasses, a baby face, and carefully crafted graying hair. A clone of Chicago's alderman Eddie Burke. I would not want him as an enemy.

We had flown down in an Irish army Sikorsky, itself a clone of the ones that had rescued my men in Vietnam: Jaymo and his Inspector Broderick (I finally learned Dermot's last name from Jean), the minister, the commissioner of the Garda, Constable Toole and Jean (who were now thick as thieves, a development that Jaymo tolerated in part because he approved of close protection of Jean and in part because, like any Irishman faced with a conspiracy between two women against all the men in the world, he had no choice), and myself.

We sped rapidly just under a glowering gray sky above the endlessly changing green fields of Ireland. Jean, her Nikon operational again, squealed in delight at the photographic possibilities. Above the clacking roar of the rotor blades, the minister urged on me the need for continued American investment in Irish industrial development.

There are no free lunches and no free rides.

We were watching from a knoll, perhaps a quarter mile away from the farmhouse. One did not risk public officials and important potential supporters of the industrial development of the Republic by permitting them to be in range of a chance terrorist shot.

Jean had slung her camera to one side and was watching the white thatched roof of the house with a very expensive pair of binoculars. When had she bought those?

The commissioner and a uniformed Garda commander seemed to be in charge of the operation. Jaymo and the Special Branch were assigned the role of watching in the background, out of the limelight. If he minded, he did not show it.

The commissioner raised his eyebrow to the minister. The minister nodded. The commissioner raised a gloved hand to the commander. The latter turned to his walkie-talkie and gave an order. The usual soft mist was filling the air.

A determined voice—Big Brother is watching—split the peaceful rural silence. "We know you're in there, Rory. We don't want to kill you. You have three minutes to come out of there with your accomplice. Hands on your heads. We have enough weapons around you to destroy you. A hundred and eighty seconds. We are counting from this moment."

There was no motion inside the farmhouse. I glanced at my watch; fifty seconds gone already.

"Two minutes," said the disembodied voice, God warning us from the heavens.

Every person with a gun seemed to lean forward expectantly, waiting for the chance to dissolve the white house in an avalanche of firepower. I watched the movement of my second digits.

"One minute, Rory. Fifty-nine seconds, fifty-eight."

A man and a woman emerged from the door of the farmhouse, hands on their heads, and staggered uncertainly toward the first line of police pickets.

"It's not him," Jean snapped.

Much later in the day, before supper, Jean and I were sipping sherry in the lobby of the Shelbourne as the remains of high tea were being cleaned away. We had sworn off Jameson's—for the day, at any rate—and returned to sherry.

"A civilized drink," I was told, "in honor of the good Jocelyn."

"Did you call her that?"

"After the first day. She asked me to."

There was no date with Liam tonight, though perhaps there would be one with him tomorrow. There had been, however, a phone call to Tim, who was described this time as "nice" rather than "sweet." In addition, there was another boy named Cormac, who was a student at Trinity College medical school who had somehow entered the picture with a suggestion for windsurfing on Dublin Bay. Jean was having her own rite of spring.

She thought it was "kind of weird" that she had also christened our Morris Minor Cormac. "Definitely a boy car, Daddy." The Minor was no longer "funny" but "cute" and "darling" and even "adorable." His retirement at Grand Beach was a matter of absolute commitment.

I thought a lot about Grand Beach. Mike Casey had told me when I made my call earlier that the next two days, Saturday and Sunday, he and Annie would be there, at Ned Ryan's. "Ned can keep a secret better than anyone in the world. Don't worry about calling."

"Are you and Annie going to buy a house up there?"

"There doesn't seem to be much choice, does there?" He laughed.

"Keep an eye open for another one. Not too far from the compound, but not too close. Something like Red Kane's location."

"Large or small?"

A good question. "Kind of large."

Yes, I would buy the old family house on Glenwood Drive, which was supposed to be for sale, and a place at Grand Beach for my growing family. The conviction that Ciara was carrying my child was as implacable as ever.

Yet I was living in two worlds: one was the world of Brendan Ryan the estate planner, in which I knew with a sinking heart that I would never see her alive again. The other world was the half-light cosmos of Finn MacCool, who was confident that he would save Ciara Kelly and carry her back to Chicago and Grand Beach as his cherished prize. Unfortunately, the real Ciara, with whom I had made love in the

Railway Hotel in Galway ages ago, existed in Brendan Ryan's world. The woman in the mythological cosmos had little more reality than did most mythological heroines; she was an object for the hero to pursue.

Perhaps my psychic propensities facilitated the movement back and forth between these two worlds. Perhaps I was slipping toward some kind of psychotic interlude as the result of exhaustion, restless sleep, emotional trauma, and fear. I will never understand it all, but I look back in astonishment and dismay at the man who calmly drank sherry with his daughter in the lounge of the Shelbourne that Friday evening as the sun once again turned the green across the street into an enchanted forest of gold (the clouds having inappropriately dispersed on our silent flight back from Athlone). He was serenely confident that he would find Ciara Kelly (though he didn't yet know how or where) and at the same time he despaired; Ciara was forever lost.

"Schizophrenic?" Mary Kate Murphy has scoffed when I have asked her about the phenomenon. "Maybe only Irish . . . besides, in their myths, if I am to believe my Joe, the women are not exactly passive objects to be pursued by the all-powerful hero."

In any event, that Friday afternoon I planned to carry Ciara back to Grand Beach and knew that I would never do so. Brendan Ryan, the conservative estate planner, did not tell his daughter that they were buying a house in Michigan.

"May I join you?"

Superintendent Finnegan had actually removed his raincoat, a sign, doubtless, of closer friendship. We made room for him and offered him a drink.

"Sherry is it? Well, I suppose it can't do me any harm."

"The Provos set you up?" I asked.

"We'll make the best out of it." He sighed profoundly. "Terry Lenihan is a nice prize, but I'm not sure we have enough on him to keep him in jail for long. We wouldn't have half bothered if we knew it was him. So that's why we were tipped off that it was McLafferty."

"Why did they want to betray him, Mr. Finnegan?" Jean asked respectfully. Even cops were the target of her campaign to be gentle.

"Who knows with them people? They have more doctrinal

disagreements than a bunch of monastic theologians. I tried to warn the commissioner and the minister that it was a thin lead." Another, even more profound sigh. "Sure, they wanted a solemn high terrorist capture, Brendan, to impress you. I think you and the girl have frightened the minister half to death."

"Have we now?"

"They've decided over in Dublin Castle that you're not just a regular run-of-the-mill rich Yank tourist. Someone looked up your mother and father's war record, and that scared them even more. Now that your man has gone home to the White House and the nuns and the punks aren't demonstrating against him anymore, they're assigning every available man to the search for Rory McLafferty. I wanted to tell you that. We'll have him soon enough now. We're watching every harbor and airport, every train station and bus terminal. He won't be on the loose for long."

Once more doing what you do well, even if it is not much good in the search for a madman like Rory McLafferty.

"Why are they afraid of us, Mr. Finnegan? . . . I think you can just leave the decanter here, waiter."

"Thank you, lass . . . Well, they know at least the outline of what might have happened that night on the *Mystamaid*. They're not sure what you're going to do, but they know whatever it is, you're quite capable of doing it, Mr. Ryan. They only hope the Irish race survives."

He grinned like a lean, middle-aged leprechaun. It occurred to me that Jaymo Finnegan admired me.

"A berserker on the loose?"

He considered the cheerful color of his sherry and then looked at me thoughtfully. "Something of the sort."

Which was all I needed to hear. Great big fucking legendary hero.

Fuckin' idjit too.

Whom his colleagues would not permit inside a law court.

It was the next day after Mass that I knew where to look. I knew not because I had figured it out but because someone smarter than me suggested it.

I had called Mike and received the weather report from Grand Beach—sunny but cool. However, the lake, according to the kids, was warming up. Eileen and Catherine were doing well, considering. Only a few more weeks now for both of them. The word was that Tim and Jean were burning up the phone lines between Dublin and Chicago.

I didn't tell him about Liam, Cormac, and Brian (a new name, which was casually mentioned to me as though I were well aware of his existence).

Then Jean and I walked across the river to the procathedral, in which the Saturday afternoon Mass, like every Saturday afternoon Mass in the Catholic world, I suspect, was a folk Mass with guitars. There was, however, some very nice music for the Ordinary, as I would have called it, in Irish. By the late Sean O'Riada, who had rediscovered Irish language religious music, Jean told me.

As we walked back to the hotel, Jean was thoughtful, preoccupied. Worrying about how to balance her large supply of swains, I assumed.

"I bet I know where she is, Daddy," she said softly.

"What?"

"She figures she's going to die, right? Didn't you tell me in Ashford Castle that she said that the strand at Inch was the most beautiful place in the world and that she wanted to go to Heaven from there because she thought it would be the shortest route? Well, if she's as much a romantic as you are—and I figure she is probably even worse—then I bet she's somewhere around the strand at Inch."

Brendan Ryan said perhaps. I have to go somewhere. Why not Inch? And Finn MacCool knew that his woman was there. So he took over and sent Brendan Ryan into exile through the next couple of days.

For weal or woe.

Jean had a dinner date with Cormac (I think). I proposed that I have a sandwich in my room and ponder the implications of her insight—which I admitted made sense. When she came home, she should stop by and we could talk more about it.

"I won't be too late," she promised. "After a certain hour, these Irish boys begin to get the wrong idea."

"What hour is that?"

"It depends."

I knew enough not to ask any more.

It was not quite one o'clock when she knocked on the door.

"Nice date?"

"Better than yucky, but not awesome." She tossed her raincoat on my bed. "What gives?"

I had not noticed before the almost transparent qualities of her Irish knit dress. I almost suggested that she should wear a bra the next time she put on the dress. Then I realized that I would be playing the role of the father stereotype. Besides, she did look most appealing in the dress. Which is the way, I told the father stereotype, that young women ought to look.

"I drive down there tomorrow in Cormac and begin to search. You stay here. I'll call you regularly twice a day. You keep in touch with Uncle Mike for me." I explained to her about the daily call to Mike Casey, and also, for good measure, about his illegal weapons shipment. She was impressed. "If I'm more than an hour and a half late, you get through to Uncle Mike immediately and tell him to come at once with the rest of the Knights of the Round Table."

"I don't like it," she said bluntly.

"Two reasons: first of all, I need someone to keep the link open to America in case there's real trouble. It's dumb to risk your communications. Second, one person can move more quickly than two. It would have been impossible for me at Athlone unless I was by myself. An older man and a young woman traveling together are too obvious. It would be like sending up smoke signals telling Rory's friends—and he probably has some in County Kerry too; it's always been pro-Republican—that we're coming."

"And third, Constable Toole will keep me out of trouble here," she said skeptically.

"That's true, Jean. But if I thought I needed your help, I wouldn't hesitate to ask you to run the risks. You've suffered more than I have in this craziness. I think this way is more effective."

She nodded in agreement, not totally convinced—when is a woman with Irish genes ever totally convinced?—but sufficiently persuaded to go along with me.

So the next day, after fierce hugs and kisses, I bid her good-bye and loaded Cormac rather ostentatiously with my duffel and weapon bag. Let Jaymo know I was leaving. I wouldn't mind his flat feet trailing behind this time; and he wouldn't try to stop me now. I set out in the sturdy Morris, now perhaps savoring the prospect of his retirement in America, at a speed which at the best didn't quite make it to forty-five miles an hour, toward Limerick.

It was the hottest day of the year in Ireland—as high as eighty-three degrees Fahrenheit—and the road through Naas, Port Laoighise, and Nenagh to the ancient city of Limerick was jammed. The crush of traffic did not bother Finn MacCool. Nothing bothered him, the dummy.

Limerick, at the head of the Shannon estuary, was shrouded in a haze of thick humidity, making it look like a faerie city in a fantasy film, a kind of down-at-the-mouth Camelot. Somehow the humidity was more burdensome than in America. Maybe because there was always a lot of rain to be soaked up, or maybe because the Irish complained more about the heat than we Yanks would at the same temperature. Limerick was sometimes shabby and sometimes picturesque and all times jammed with bumper-to-bumper traffic.

I drove along the Shannon estuary, where the traffic was thinner, and into the ancient kingdom of Cairaighe, older by a thousand years than Limerick, older even, if you were to believe Kerry authors, than Ireland itself. I cut through the town of Listowel, which produces a big crew of writers every generation (sure, 'tis something in the water supply) and then on to Tralee, the rather uncolorful city of the colorful Rose Festival, and finally to Castlemaine between Tralee and Killarney, where I left the main road and headed out toward perhaps the loveliest part of Ireland—Dingle Bay and the strand at Inch, where both *Playboy of the Western World* and *Ryan's Daughter* were filmed.

The road to Inch, clinging to the edge of Dingle on the north side of the bay, was the most crowded of the day. It was after nine when I arrived at the Inch Hotel on the spine of the peninsula, looking out on the strand, the bay, and, shimmering in the distant haze on the other side of the bay, the brooding Macgillicuddy's Reeks, the highest mountains in Ireland.

The woman at the desk of the Inch Hotel couldn't find my reservation, even though Jean had phoned it from Dublin earlier in the day.

"Not to worry." She grinned cheerfully. "We'll find it if it's here. Sure, there were more Kerrymen soaking up sun hereabouts than any time since Adam and Eve. We'll never have another day like this for the rest of the century."

She found me a room finally; it was small and not particularly comfortable, though clean enough by Irish standards. I needed no Irish whiskey to sleep that night. The dreams, however, were about disintegrating bodies, as they would be for many nights to come.

The next morning, bright and clear with the haze swept away by a brisk wind from the Atlantic, I was the American anthropologist (with a neat cloth attaché case in the left front seat of his battered old Morris Minor and a bulge in the deep right-hand pocket of the black Windbreaker he was wearing), who was searching for the sister that he had promised to meet at an unspecified time in spring in the County Kerry. She was rather tall, blonde, "quite attractive," and wore thick glasses. Had the estate agent rented anything to her lately? She had a special fondness for the beach . . . uh, strand.

I struck pay dirt the first time. Ah, sure, I remember the woman well; she'd rented the wee cottage out at the very end of the strand, another twenty yards and she'd be in Glenbeigh, across the way. She said someone might be looking for her.

If it was that easy for me to find her, it would be equally easy for Rory McLafferty. Ciara Kelly was as crazy as the rest of them. Obviously she wanted to be found. Forward Light Brigade.

Dingle Bay is almost bisected at its upper end by a series of massive sandbars formed by centuries of waves and tide. Glenbeigh on the south side of the bay is the first, and behind it, longer and larger and forming Castlemaine Harbor, is Inch, a massive reef of sand four miles long and in places a mile thick. Its spine is a continuous ridge of dunes, covered with dune grass, flowering bushes, and occasional trees. The floor of the bay in front of the strand is little more than a continuation of it, a shallow shelf of sand on which the tide rises and recedes very rapidly.

"Sure, 'tis hard on boats," the woman in the hotel told me, "if anybody is crazy enough to try to bring one in except when it's dead calm."

In front of the dunes is one of the world's most perfect beaches—hundreds of yards (at low tide) of smooth, soft, clean sand. When the sun is out (and you always have to make that qualification when discussing Ireland), the mixture of long, smooth, white breakers, blue sky, popcorn clouds, wide beach, and green dunes, with the Reeks in the distance, is indeed one of the most beautiful sights in the world, the kind of place that demands a romantic adventure story with strong knights and beautiful women and wizards and witches and mythological animals.

I was assured by the helpful estate agent that I could drive down the beach to the cottage, as long as I did not get too close to the sand which had been made soggy by last night's tide. "Sure, you have no business riding on the dark brown sand. Otherwise you'll be all right."

Cormac, my only mythological beast, had his doubts about the sand and at first refused even to start. However, properly coaxed, like any Irish male, he did as he was bidden. Nonetheless, it took almost forty-five minutes to reach the end of the strand. As the agent had said, the little old thatched cottage could not be missed.

There was no sign of life around it. I parked underneath the dune, a hundred yards short of the cottage, assembled my Uzi, put Mike's weapon in the pocket of the Windbreaker I was wearing, and, following the tactics recommended in my ROTC course long years before, crept up through a gully to approach the cottage from the rear.

I pushed the change bolt on my Uzi from "S" to "E," rushed from the gully to the rear of the house, then around to the front, and kicked open the door.

The tiny, primitive little room was empty.

There were a few clothes, including the dress she had worn in Galway, and a stack of French novels.

And a large bloodstain on the unmade bed.

39

All that day and all the next day I searched. Cleverly, ruthlessly, systematically, like a man in the grip of a divinely inspired project.

I adopted disguises, stories, excuses, spinning out tales with the glib facility of the gombeen-man of the Western world. I looked for Ciara Kelly everywhere: In the charming city of Killarney, with its statue of the mythical Kathleen Ni Houlihan, the spirit of Ireland. In the restaurant at Glenbeigh. In the Purple Mountains behind Glenbeigh, where the countryside was as quiet as an empty cathedral. In broken-down country pubs near Castlemaine and Killorglin. In the Railway Hotel lounge in Killarney, in the Europa Hotel on the side of Killarney Lake, where German was spoken more frequently than English. On the heights of Aghadoe, the ancient capital of the kingdom of Cairaighe, from which one looked down on the lakes and the town of Killarney as at a canvas of a Dutch painter, with lights and shadows racing each other across the scene. At Slea Head at the end of Dingle, where the now unoccupied Blasket Islands hovered in the distance, silently remonstrating with the world at their desertion. At the top of Connor Pass on the spine of Dingle, as the mountain sheep grazed untroubled by the fog below them, which concealed both Dingle Bay and Brandon Bay whence my namesake, the sainted navigator, is alleged to have sailed for Barbados. In Dingle town itself, on the long pier that jutted into the tight little harbor.

She had been seen everywhere and nowhere—an attractive woman with short blonde hair, how many of them wander the world? A charming man with curly brown hair and a glow in his eyes—and what else can you find in the West of Ireland?

Your sister? Your cousin? Your wife? Ah, sure, the Irish are a helpful people. Certainly, they would tell you they saw her. Maybe they had after all, and it would be a shame not to help the poor man.

It was only two days now before the solstice. The days were absurdly long and the nights hardly more than a token. Like their pagan ancestors, the Kerrymen and Kerrywomen stayed up late, reveling in the light, mostly sunlight, since the weather continued fine, against the days at the other end of the year that would be so short—storing it all up, a woman in a tobacco shop in Ventry, halfway between Dingle town and Slea Head, told me. So I searched, always under great pressure but never quite in panic, for almost twenty hours both days. On Monday night I slept no more than half an hour. I devoted the rest of the time to studying the map, oiling my weapons, pondering, analyzing, wondering, worrying.

I was pushing myself dangerously close to the breaking point. Brendan Ryan couldn't take much more stress without collapsing. Finn MacCool, however, had a limitless supply of adrenaline in his bloodstream.

I called Jean in the morning and evening of both days, filling her in on the details, rambling on needlessly about my brilliant but fruitless ideas. She sounded worried about me, as well she might have been. Her father was living very close to the edge.

I did not have a chance after the adventure ended to ask where the Special Branch was. Probably Jaymo's troops were frantically pursuing me and marveling at how fast the wee daft man was running. Then, at the end, I quite unintentionally gave them the slip.

In our second phone call on Tuesday the nineteenth of June, Jean once again proved that she was Holmes and I was Watson. Yes, she had spoken to Uncle Mike. Something about that tone of voice triggered my highly keyed sensitivities. Probably, I decided, Mike had been in touch with Jaymo Finnegan. No harm in that.

"Daddy," she said slowly. "I may be making it all up, but I think that terrible man loved boats. He said something about separating yourself from land to do your work. And he did use a boat on Lough Ree. Do you think he may have a boat somewhere down there?"

Bingo! Ciara had said that he loved to sail on Lough Neagh, outside Belfast.

You see that I was already thinking of the finale as a confrontation between myself and McLafferty, without paying much attention to the implications of such a definition, especially the possibility, indeed the certainty, once you reflected on it, that he was thinking of the finale in the same fashion. Not one of your really bright berserkers either.

"That's a hell of an idea, kid. As always. I'll be back to you tomorrow with the results."

The old-timers in countryman's dress with the smell of fish about them, who hung around the long concrete pier at Dingle, told me that yes, indeed, a man who answered the description of my brother had chartered an aging cabin cruiser, the *Kerryman*, painted blue with red trim, on Sunday evening. "Sure, it's not much of a tub, if you know what I mean. You'd not get very far in it before the engine quits on you altogether. He said he wasn't going very far, just kind of anchoring out there in the bay."

I drove up the side of the hill behind Dingle town and, with the binoculars I had borrowed from Jean, scanned the bay beyond the harbor mouth. About two miles along the shore in the direction of Inch, at a spot my ordnance map called "Bulls Head," lay the blue and red boat.

I became crafty and cunning, MacCool preparing for battle. I struggled out of my slacks and sports shirt and donned the black jeans and turtleneck I'd bought in Killarney, and my gray Adidas running shoes. Then the black Windbreaker over the Secret Service holster vest. (I did not, however, blacken my face, as commandos do in the late night films, but only because I had no black shoe polish.) I checked my weapons and ammunition, thought through again my plan of action, and drove the faithful Cormac back to the pier in Dingle town.

I avoided the fishermen who had been my previous informants and found someone who was willing to charter me an outboard fishing boat for the night, "Fifty punts for the night, and two hundred and fifty punts deposit, in case you lose it."

Why would I lose it?

Sure, there's bad weather coming up.

And you haven't got it insured against one of your clients piling it up?

Ah, sure, there's no point in taking chances, is there? Besides, if you run it up on Inch, it would break apart altogether. The storm could push you in one direction and the tide running out in the other. It would be no fun at all, at all.

I'll be back before midnight. All I want is a few hours of fishing on the bay. I hear it's good on these long spring days.

The fishing is grand all right, but it's the storm coming up about midnight that worries me. Well, two hundred punts deposit. I found out later that the boat had drifted ashore undamaged. I bet he reported it as an insurance loss anyway.

I donned the black baseball cap I'd also bought in Killarney, packed my cloth bag with the Uzi under the seat of the boat—it was a small dory with a twenty-five horsepower motor—and glided through the harbor and around a point called Beenbane. I dropped anchor fifty yards offshore and went through the motions of fishing with the rented tackle that accompanied the boat—for twenty-five more punts. The gentle rise and fall of the bay was not abrupt enough to make me any more than slightly queasy. A storm might drive me to the side of the boat for a night of vomiting. But Finn MacCool does not get seasick.

The blue cruiser, a twenty-five-footer, was about a mile and a half away, gently floating at anchor on the flat waters of the bay. There was no sign of life on her.

Not once did I ask myself whether it was not all too easy.

Rather, I calculated the process of boarding the cruiser. Obviously I couldn't run up to it with the outboard, which wasn't very fast but was very loud, going full blast. I would have to use the oars, a skill at which I was without much experience, and try to slide up to the cruiser quietly. It would be difficult enough even if the bay remained calm. But it might not remain calm. The charter boat man had warned of a storm. Already there was a haze, ugly and threatening, moving in from the mouth of the bay.

The Atlantic Ocean was out there. I did not want to have to wrestle with it. I remembered the huge waves from *Ryan's Daughter*.

If the bay turned mean, I would have to fasten onto his anchor line, climb up the rope—I hadn't done that since Fort Benning—and catch him by surprise.

I turned on the motor again and steered, still close to the rocks of Dingle, into an inlet called Trabeg. Protected from motion sickness, I could hug the shore from the mouth of that inlet without being noticed until I was only a little more than two hundred yards from the cruiser. Maybe after dark, depending on the distracting sounds of the wind and the water, I could get even closer before I had to turn to the oars.

Slowly, like a teenager who is in no rush to go home because he knows he'll be in trouble when he gets there, night slipped down the bay from Killarney and Inch. With it came the wind, at first a fresh breeze, exhilarating against your face and then stiffer and more ominous. It was blowing at an angle, across the Dingle mountains and into the bay. If it should move around a couple of points, it would be coming right up the bay from the Atlantic.

The bay itself grew more restless and uncertain, as if it were pondering a temper tantrum and had not quite made up its mind.

I rigidly forced myself not to move out of the Trabeg inlet until it was dark. The haze above me had turned into clouds. The mountains behind me were dark and somber, perhaps watching my folly disapprovingly.

I spent some of that purgatorial time of waiting examining my Uzi once again, for the final time, I told myself. I assembled it without the silencer, which didn't seem to be necessary this time, and crammed ammunition clips in all my pockets. I took Mike Casey's .22 out of my right Windbreaker pocket so that I could fill that pocket, too, with ammo clips. I thought about it for a few seconds and decided I had more than enough ammunition to rout a platoon of terrorists and returned the little gun to its resting place.

I fastened the strap, which had come with the Uzi but which I had never used before, on the holders at both ends. Plastic, but high-quality plastic. Not likely to break. Trust the Israelis to do it right.

Finally, when it was dark, or dark enough, I started the outboard, not without considerable difficulty, and moved very slowly out of the inlet toward the cruiser, a dim smudge of black against a slightly less dark sky. At low speed the motor was relatively quiet. I finally turned it off and began to row awkwardly toward McLafferty's boat, fighting against my own ineptitude and the rising swells. And against the first touches of seasickness.

What did I expect to find on the cruiser?

McLafferty, certainly. Ciara? Most likely, though there had been no mention of anyone boarding with him or being carried on board. Ciara alive?

Viewing the affair from the wisdom of hindsight, there was no reasonable probability that she was still alive. Why would she be? Rory McLafferty wanted revenge. Now he had the opportunity to take it. Why should he delay? Yet he was there, almost certainly—it seemed to me then—and he must be destroyed before he hurt others. Why he would so obviously and patiently wait for me to find him was a question that simply did not arise.

Jean probably would have asked it if she were with me.

At the very outer limit of my own sanity, however, and confusing myself with an Irish mythic hero, I had at that point only one goal—to dispose permanently of Rory McLafferty.

I lost the cruiser several times, finding it again only when a swell brought me high enough to see the light in its cabin. So there was someone on it . . . fine.

Then I seemed to lose it permanently. And the land too. The swells were turning into waves, not the quick, choppy waves of Lake Michigan, but rollers, gentle still, but menacing. I thought perhaps I should give up and return to the inlet. I would be no use to anyone drowned or disastrously seasick in Dingle Bay. I had no idea now where the inlet was.

Then Dingle Bay did me a favor. It heaved me up on an especially high swell and showed me that I was only twenty yards from the bow of the *Kerryman* and even closer to its anchor line. The rest should be easy.

It was very difficult, however. I had no choice but to tie on to the cruiser's line—which meant that with the Uzi strapped around my neck, I would have to climb up the line, hand over hand. Capturing the line turned out to be immensely difficult, even though I was only a few yards away. I stabbed at the line with my boat hook time after time, but the dory had a mind of its own, the bay was becoming rougher by the moment, and the wind was now howling in my ears.

Not so loud, however, as to drown out the scream of a woman in a terrible agony of pain.

She was still alive.

I reached desperately for the anchor line, tilted the dory precariously toward the water, straightened up, and tumbled backward, lurching towards the far side of the boat with more than enough momentum to carry me over the side.

I fell to my knees with a thud. The boat swayed dangerously, and then righted itself. I felt another twinge of seasickness, much stronger this time. A swell lifted us again and dropped the boat literally on top of the line.

Another favor from Dingle Bay, for which much thanks.

I tied the dory line securely to the anchor line with one of my best yachtsman's knots and pulled the boat up the line till I was close to the cruiser. Only a few yards of hand-over-hand climbing. I hung the Uzi around my neck, making sure the change bolt was pulled all the way back on "S," zipped up my Windbreaker, stood on the front of the dory, and gripped the cruiser's line securely with both hands.

We were hit by a mighty swell, which heaved the dory above the cruiser, so high that I was looking down at the single light in its cabin. I was thrown out of the dory and hovered for a moment over the dark, cold waters of the bay.

Then the line snapped taut and my arms and shoulders were wrenched by a vicious jerk. Pain shot through my whole body. For a moment I thought my arms had been torn out of their sockets. The bay grabbed my feet and ankles and my legs up to my thighs, then released me. My agony was so great that I wanted to drop into the water and end all foolishness. Then I heard another scream from a woman. I clung to the line, my hands aching from pressure against its coarse fibers, and slowly, hand over hand, inched my way up the bow of the *Kerryman* and onto its forward deck.

The Uzi was still there. My bloodied fingers could still press its trigger. The cabin windows were heavily curtained, which was why I had not seen the light at first from the mouth of the inlet. I eased my way around the side and slipped, I hoped lightly, into the cockpit.

This was the moment of truth. I was tense, sore, exhausted. My mouth was dry and my stomach tight again. I loved every second of it; my battle instinct was aroused for fulfillment.

I took the Uzi off my neck, shoved the safety bolt all the way forward to automatic, took a final deep breath, and kicked savagely against the door between the cockpit and the cabin.

It swung open easily. I rushed into the cabin ready to squeeze the trigger.

"Ah, good evening to you, Brendan Ryan." Rory McLafferty was holding his scalpel at Ciara's throat, his other hand covering her mouth. "I've been expecting you. It took you long enough to find us. And, to tell you the truth, like the fucking shitehawk you are, you made a godawful racket coming on board."

40

He looked older than I had expected, thinner and more haggard. His handsome face was lined with deep ruts, his hair was dirty white; his kinky smile reminded me of that of a man in a Southern prison walking from his cell to the gas chamber for the amusement of TV viewers. His eyes glowed with fire, indeed, but with a fire about to be blown out by too much draft. Inside Rory McLafferty there was a lost soul seeking release. The charming medical student who had been so kind to a young woman who had been the victim of savage rape had long since died and was now trapped in the cruel prison of his own demented flair.

His zombie, however, held a knife at the thickest part of Ciara's carotid artery. As I looked into his wild eyes I saw myself, hunched over my PC XT, enthusiastically cheating the world with demented schemes. There was not that much difference between Brendan Ryan and Rory McLafferty. We both were isolates, we both played wicked games, we both loved the same woman. I was able to distinguish still between my games and reality. But I had not been trapped in the insanity of Ulster.

The cabin was tiny, like that of all small cabin cruisers, no more than ten feet long and less than five feet wide, and crowded—two bunks, a fixed table with the leaf down, some cabinets on the wall, a floor littered with gear. Ciara, most of her clothes torn away, was tied in one of the bunks, her left hand and right foot free. Her face was bruised and swollen, her lips caked with blood, her body marked with bruises and cuts and what looked like burns.

"Get away from her," I ordered.

"Ah, no," he said with a smirk, "I won't do that. Maybe your terrible fine gun, which killed all my troops, will kill me before I can cut her throat. Maybe; then again, maybe not. But, sure, you're not all that good with your wee Uzi. They said you butchered my troops. Suppose," he crowded close to her, almost using her as a shield, "that you butcher her as well as me this time?"

I hesitated. What indeed if I did miss?

"Kill him, Brendan." She yanked her mouth free. "He'll torture us to death."

"Quiet, woman." He deftly jabbed at her breast with the scalpel, causing a thin line of blood to appear. "And herself ambushing me, would you believe it, able to kill me and losing her nerve. Sure, she doesn't believe in killing. Wanted to give me a last chance for redemption. Can you imagine that, Brendan Ryan? Me redeemed?"

It was back in slow motion now. He was a babbler. I would wait patiently until he was far away from Ciara as he was likely to be, and then shoot. As unobtrusively as I could, I moved the change bolt back to single shot.

"I see you're hesitating. Well, that's a good thing. The longer a man hesitates, the less likely he is to do something dangerous, like butchering a woman he loves, isn't that true, Brendan Ryan?"

"You leave her alone and I'll let you go free," I said calmly.

"Ah, you're the cool one, now, aren't you?" The boat swayed dangerously. "Sure it's a right fine storm you brought with you, too, isn't it?" He chuckled drunkenly.

I slipped the change bolt back to the safety position. It could be flicked off again in an instant. I did not want a swell to cause me to pressure the trigger enough to fire.

"Fair trade," I said.

"You know," he observed in a friendly, conversational

tone, "I believe you'd really keep your word. You are like all your other dull bourgeois capitalists. You don't understand the morality of a revolution at all, at all. . . . But we're talking about art, not fucking politics. I'm engaged in a work of art, don't you see?"

"Art?" Keep him talking and wait for the right second.

"Art, indeed." He adopted the tone of a senior surgeon instructing a new team of interns. "You'll note that the woman has been injured a bit, enough to hurt but no permanent damage, not yet, anyway. Note, too, by the way, how intelligently she is bound. One foot and one hand are free for resistance. The right hand is bound, needless to say. She can fight back, not effectively and at considerable expenditure of her energy resources, but it both amuses me and increases the foolish hope for rescue. Interesting concept, isn't it?"

Except that Ciara was left-handed. Had he forgotten that? Or had he never noticed?

"She knows in her head she will die a slow and horrible death. But human nature is such that our hope won't let us accept the obvious realities. Maybe it's not human nature." He waved the scalpel as though dismissing that point. "Maybe it's the capitalist system. For our purposes that doesn't matter, does it now? Anyway, the work of art is to slowly push back the frontier of hope so that it turns in the opposite direction. As I progress in my little exercise—with a professional doctor's skill, mind you—she'll continue to hope. After all, she'll say then, her wounds are not so bad that plastic surgery can't repair them. So, despite the obvious evidence, she'll hope that I'll stop. I'll encourage that hope, recall all the grand times we had together when we were kids. She'll know I'm lying, but she'll hope against hope that maybe I'm not.

"Then we'll progress a little further and she'll know that she'll be disfigured for life, an ugly and unwanted hag, but the urge to live is still strong, so she'll revise her hope again and, against all sound judgment, pray that I'll judge such a fate is a sufficient punishment for those who betray the people's cause." For a moment a tone of dedicated patriotism crept into his demented babble. "A traitor to the people of Ireland, Brendan Ryan."

I listened calmly, knowing that my silence would anger

him and make him less likely to stay dangerously close to Ciara.

"Well, to return to the issue, though I'm offended that you're not more interested, there'll come a time, postponed as long as possible, naturally, when the only hope is death. There is nothing left in the body to live for. All that remains, all that can ever remain, is pain—certain limbs permanently mangled, that sort of thing. She'll pray to God in His mercy that I've had enough revenge for the betrayed people of Ireland. She'll hope that I'll let her die. What more can she possibly suffer? You see what has happened, the direction of hope has been reversed." He giggled witlessly. "Isn't that a scientific breakthrough, a work of great art? The important question, on which we have little scientific data despite the interesting work the Germans did during the war, is how far a given person has to be pushed in pain before the hope turns towards death. And as for an ending of the work of art, well, I'm not quite sure what that will be. It makes the story more interesting doesn't it?"

"You're completely round the bend, McLafferty. A demented lunatic."

That made him angry, as it was supposed to. "Oh am I, Mr. Brendan Ryan who killed my command, stole my treasury, and destroyed my plan of battle? Well, why do you think it was so easy for you to find me? Why do you think that I have postponed everything but a mild beginning of my research on this slut? I'll tell you why." He laughed crazily. "I'll tell you why: you're part of the experiment. You're going to watch it every step of the way. And she's going to watch the same things being done to you." He was ranting incoherently now. I slipped the safety bolt to single shot. "It will be a double execution. Two war criminals at the same time."

Just as my finger touched the trigger, there was a violent lurch as the cruiser heeled over almost on its side. The Uzi jumped out of my hands, though not before I had activated the safety again. McLafferty and I crashed into each other. Desperately I brought the edge of my hand down on his wrist the way I'd seen Caitlin do at Grand Beach. I didn't break anything, but the scalpel fell to the floor next to the bunk.

We threw ourselves together in desperate hand-to-hand

combat, two jungle beasts fighting for their turf, shoving, kicking, kneeing, gouging. He was bigger than I but surprisingly weak. I was out of practice and lacked the fury of madness. I probably would have won if either of us had been able to do any damage to one another. However, we were tumbled around the cabin, crashing into the table and the bunks and the walls as the boat twisted and turned back and forth like a cork in a whirlpool.

As we struggled, I watched Ciara's free hand groping for the scalpel. It was only an inch or two away from her fingers.

I broke away from his grip, reached for the Uzi, felt it with my fingertips, and then careened across the room as the boat heeled in the opposite direction. My head smashed against the edge of the table. A current of savage pain cascaded through my body, tearing and twisting at my consciousness. I blanked out for what must have been no more than a couple of seconds. Then I was looking up at Rory McLafferty cradling my weapon lovingly in his hands.

"He who lives by the Zionist gun dies by it, Brendan Ryan. But you're not going to die yet, not for a long time."

Ciara clutched the scalpel tightly in her hand. He was too far away for her to reach him.

I struggled desperately to escape from the daze that imprisoned me like quicksand. There was something I could do, if only I could remember what it was.

"I'm going to kneecap you to begin with." He chortled wildly. "You won't be able to move. Then I'll shoot off your hands. I won't have to tie you up for the rest of the experiment, which I am hereby dedicating to the Republic of Ireland, one and indivisible!"

He pointed the weapon at my legs. At such close range he would chop them to pieces. I would fool him and bleed to death.

But what was it I was supposed to do?

He squeezed the trigger.

Nothing happened.

"Goddamn, fucking kike gun," he shouted, fiddling with the various mechanisms.

He found the firing safety on the rear of the grip and aimed again.

Again nothing happened. Vaguely I prayed that he would throw the gun away and jump on me.

"Ah, it's the wee bolt on the side, is it now?" He examined the pistol grip with idiotic interest. "The kikes are clever, aren't they? Sure, I reckon 'D' is for repeat."

He was wrong, but it did not matter. He took aim again. I waited for the searing pain in my legs,

A voice shouted at me, a woman's voice. "Mike's gun, you damn fool."

What gun?

The Uzi still would not work. "You forgot to cock it, you frigging idjit," he screamed at me as he pulled the firing bolt back.

I remembered the .22.

His face twisted with manic fury, he pointed the Uzi at me for the last time.

I fired Mike Casey's .22 through the jacket of my Windbreaker. Twice. Both bullets hit his shoulder and spun him away. The single shot from the Uzi exploded far above my head. He tried to point the gun in my direction.

I knew I should rush him, but my body was not following the orders coming down from my brain. I fired Mike's pistol again. It missed.

He ducked away from the shot as the blood soaked through his shirt, and toppled against the bunk on which Ciara was tied.

Without hesitation or a wasted movement, she slashed him neatly across the throat.

A geyser of blood erupted, spilling over his face and the front of his body. The Uzi slipped from his hand. "Cunt," he bubbled, as blood began to pour from his mouth.

"Oh, my God," Ciara was praying, "I'm heartily sorry for offending You because I dread the loss of Heaven and the pains of Hell but most of all because they offend You, my God, who are deserving of all my love . . ."

Rory McLafferty appeared to nod. He raised his hand to his forehead and dropped it to his chest—what might have been the first half of a sign of the cross—before he fell forward and died. The lost soul was free.

Perhaps not lost at all. In accordance with Blackie Ryan's

instructions, I put no limit on God's passionate love for each of us.

Who was the woman who screamed at me about Mike's gun? I don't know. It could not have been Ciara because she didn't know about the .22. It was, I think, a familiar voice, but I can't be sure. Sometimes I imagine that she sounded like Madonna, but that's perhaps the wish being the father of the thought. Maybe it was only a network of cells in my brain issuing a demand for survival.

Ciara had retched as the blood of her onetime lover and friend spilled over her body. Struggling across the swaying cabin, I picked up the scalpel from the floor, cut her bonds, and took her in my arms.

"I'm all right, Brendan." She leaned against me. "Some ice, a few patches, and some burn ointment, and I'll be as good as new."

Why do battered women have to assure me that they're all right?

"I love you, Ciara." I held her as tightly as my aching skull and disoriented brain would permit.

"You're a desperate man, Brendan Ryan," she sighed.

Then the boat heeled over again. This time it did not right itself. Instead, it spun drunkenly around and around.

"The anchor line has snapped," Ciara cried. "The poor idjit was too round the bend to use the right line."

41

I lay in a pool of blood under the rudder wheel of the cabin cruiser, vomiting desperately, not because of the blood-covered floorboard, nor because of the rictus of death, which made the remains of Rory McLafferty grin even more witlessly than he had in life, but because of violent seasickness.

Never was it written that Finn MacCool, mythic hero, was immune to motion sickness.

Above me, Ciara, wearing only torn panties, was trying desperately to start the engine and at the same time steer the tipsy craft away from the rocky shore of Dingle Bay.

I was too sick to note how beautiful she was, even bruised and burned and wounded. Now I tease my memory to recall that scene of the warrior woman taking command.

It merely makes me sick again.

We were rushing and spinning up the bay, pushed by the big rollers and pulled by the tide, which was now running in the opposite direction. The Atlantic was more powerful than the tide. We must, I thought, be plunging toward the strand at Inch. It would be rather humiliating to straggle in before God's judgment seat and vomit at the Deity's feet.

"He was totally off the wall, poor man. He would have killed me tonight. You came just in time."

I wonder even now. My arrogance and stupidity might, after all, not have made any difference.

"You don't owe me anything."

"Begging your pardon, bloody hell I don't. I should have listened to you in Galway. But no. Ciara Kelly, if you want to call her that, was going to do it all herself."

Before I was wiped out of action, I had tried desperately to fix the engine, a Chrysler marine eight-cylinder, probably older than Noah's ark. Not only could I not fix it, I couldn't even figure out why it didn't work.

The man on the pier at Dingle had said the old boat wouldn't go very far. It was going farther than he had anticipated, but hardly under its own power.

"Brendan, darling," Ciara called above the roar of the wind and the crashing of the waves. "I can see the white of the strand ahead of us. The boat will flounder and break up. We'll stand a better chance if we wait till the last minute and try to swim to shore."

"Swim in these waves?"

"We'll wear life preservers, you poor idjit. With some luck, we'll float up to the beach. Would you ever be able to get them out of the cabinet?"

"Just a minute." I was swept by another attack of nausea, vomited violently, and then between attacks staggered to the cabinet and pulled out two very ancient and decrepit-looking orange kapok life jackets.

"Don't look like much, do they? Take off your shoes and your trousers and your Windbreaker, they'll only pull you down."

"How cold is the water?"

"Warmer than Lake Michigan in May." She spun the wheel again. As if insulted, it spun her back, momentarily escaping her grip. "Bloody thing." She grabbed it and struggled with it fiercely.

Another wave of nausea. I regretted that I had eaten nothing in the last couple of days. There was little inside me for my stomach to reject.

"Put on your life jacket, Brendan," she commanded as though I were an unruly child. "Here, let me fasten it. Well, I've seen better, but I'll suppose these will have to do."

"Sorry," I mumbled, retching yet another time.

"Remember that there may be an undercurrent. When it tugs at your feet, kick them up and float with the top of the water, if you take my meaning?"

To this day, I don't know whether she laughed at that or not.

I had no sense of time. In what was both an eternity and seconds I heard a grinding crash. The boat seemed to put on its brakes and grind to a dead halt. Then it spun free and leaped violently to one side. I heard water rushing into the hull.

"I guess we've had it now. Come on, my little king, let's swim for the strand."

She guided me out the cabin door and into the cockpit, and helped me up on the gunwale. I vomited into the wind, which retaliated by slapping most of my meager contribution back into my face.

"Jump as far as you can, do you understand?"

I tried to nod.

"I love you, Brendan. I'll always love you!" She pushed me off the gunwale.

I did remember to leap far. Just as the frigid waters of Dingle Bay deprived me momentarily of my capacity to breathe, I saw her dive in after me.

A graceful dive. Ciara Kelly would not stumble awkwardly to God's judgment seat.

No way.

The cold waters of Dingle Bay are apparently a fine cure for motion sickness. At any rate, they so shatter you that you forget you're sick. As I was tossed around, pushed and pulled, tugged and beaten by the rollers and the contending currents, I tried to remember what I had read in a Dick Francis story about how long a human could survive in various temperatures of water. It didn't make much difference because I had no idea how cold Dingle Bay was. Not as bad as the Atlantic when the *Titanic* sank. Low fifties maybe. Didn't bother some of the crazy Ryan kids at Grand Beach on Memorial Day. They didn't remain in the lake as long as I would stay in the bay, however.

I thrashed and flailed and tried to swim, but without much purpose or success. The white blob that was both the beach and the rollers breaking on it was near, but no nearer, it seemed, than when I had jumped into the water. I was, I suppose, still jarred by the blow on my head from the cabin table. The final act of our drama was obviously happening to someone else.

A couple of times I thought my feet touched bottom. Then I was tugged away. Undertow or ebbing tide? Didn't matter much.

Then I was very weary and very cold. It was all too absurd. What the hell was Brendan Ryan doing bobbing around in the waters of Dingle Bay? He was a quiet, competent, conservative tax lawyer. A loser, as his best friend had once said. Was that best friend still alive? Brendan couldn't quite remember. There were a lot of dead people lately.

Brendan Ryan quit. And Finn MacCool, returned to the many-colored lands in the West, was no longer there to help.

Someone did help, however. A hand grabbed the back of my life jacket. A voice accompanied the hand. "Don't quit now, you bloody idjit, we're almost there."

No ghostly voice that.

So Brendan Ryan, good Irishman that he was, did what his woman told him to do. He didn't quit after all. His feet felt sand again; the waters tore at him, but he pushed ahead up the sand and broke out of the tug of the bay. Correction. He didn't push, he was pushed.

Then an avalanche of water hit him from behind and knocked him to his knees. Someone was pulling him farther up the beach when a second avalanche clobbered him.

Then there was nothing at all. For a long time.

I woke up slowly and promptly vomited. I was now both sick and bitterly cold. The cold-turkey cure for motion sickness was no longer operative.

One improvement, however; I now had something to vomit—salt water. One deterioration to match. Not only did my stomach feel like a tight ball of pain, my lungs hurt like hell. So, in fact, did my head. And my jaw, where that deranged Irishman had hit me. Who was it? I couldn't remember, but it didn't matter. He was dead, quite dead.

But I was alive, demonstrably alive. I hurt, therefore I am. And, no matter how cold, no longer in the water. Heaven? Not likely. Purgatory? According to common conviction, the temperature problem should be in the opposite direction, shouldn't it?

There was Dante's position to consider.

I said to hell with it and ordered my eyes to open. At first they refused to comply. Then reluctantly they went along. To my surprise it was light. Dawn. More than dawn. Pushing sunrise.

Indisputably, I was on the Strand at Inch. Hence, logically it seemed, alive.

Ciara!

I sat up and, forgetting my aches and pains, looked around desperately. No Ciara. Dear God in Heaven, please, please!

Twenty yards down the beach, a body stretched out, facedown on the sand, life jacket torn away, looking terribly blue from the distance. Womanly rump covered with a shred of fabric.

I ran, crawled, lurched, threw myself to her side.

"Ciara!" She seemed frighteningly blue and cold.

An eye opened and considered me gravely. Then its companion. They quickly inspected the environment.

"Wasn't I after telling you," she mumbled through her injured lips, "that the Strand at Inch is the most beautiful place in the world altogether?"

I turned her over and cradled her in my arms, telling her, rather unimaginatively I fear, how much I loved her.

"I'm all right, Brendan," she said again. "Nothing wrong with me at all, at all, that some ice and a few butterfly bandages and a tad of burn ointment won't cure. Then maybe a bit of food."

The thought of food, the suggestion of it, made my stomach rumble again. It had the grace, however, to do nothing more.

"Why do women always have to tell me that they're all right?" I demanded in a choked voice that sounded like someone else's. What had I done to my throat?

"So you won't fret, idjit," she said sleepily.

We clung together, shivering, I thought, in unison with one another. Or at least in harmony.

"Brendan, darling, I'm cold." A bedmate asking for another blanket.

Her short, dirty blonde hair was pasted to her head. She was not bad as a blonde, but I wanted her black hair to be straining in the wind over the beach as a pennant of victory. That could wait.

"I'll see what I can do." I struggled to my feet.

"Be careful of the boat, it's breaking up."

It was, indeed, capsized, and ground and shattered not far down the beach. We would surely be dead if we had stayed with it. But the tide was ebbing, the storm had passed through, and the waves were diminishing. I splashed through the water. My God, was I in that last night?

Then I realized that if Ciara knew that the boat was on the beach, she had been conscious before I was. She had dragged me up on the beach. Saved my life. We were even.

In a burst locker, I found two old navy blue blankets which were still reasonably dry. Rory McLafferty was still there, battered now to a shapeless pulp. So was my Uzi, caught between Rory and a smashed wall. Take it with me for a memento?

No, Cormac would suffice. The Uzi represented death. In his own cantankerous and gallant way, Cormac represented life. Maybe Ireland too. Have to think about that.

I took another blanket for good measure. Inside it, dusty

and old, was a quarter-full bottle of Jameson's Twelve Year Special Reserve—itself now nearly twenty years old.

I drank a great, powerful gulp and felt warm again.

Holy Grail indeed.

I wrapped one blanket around Ciara, who cooed, "Darling man."

"I found this, a gift from God, I think."

She accepted my dusty grail, blinked at it in astonishment, and then pressed it to her bloodstained lips.

"The Lord takes away and the Lord gives," she said with a chuckle as she gave the bottle back to me. "Don't drink it all, you idjit."

We passed the bottle back and forth till it was empty. The world felt considerably more pleasant.

The two of us together, mostly naked, on the Strand at Inch, battered, sore, sick, and slightly tipsy. We had come home, even if our promised lovemaking would not occur, today anyway.

Today? The last day of spring. Our rite of spring, Ciara's and mine, was over. Summer was still ahead. At Grand Beach it didn't really begin officially, according to the Ryans, until July 4. We'd be there in time.

"It's all over, Ciara."

She sighed. "Yes, it's all over. I wonder if I'll ever believe it." She sat up. "Come on, little king, let's walk till we find help. The woman needs some decent clothes, and we have to do something about that terrible lump on your head."

So we struggled to our feet and, shrouded in musty blankets, painfully limped along the strand toward the road to Castlemaine. I brought the Special Reserve bottle along. You shouldn't litter the strand. The bottle would spend the rest of its life in the museum, along with Cormac, the museum at our house in Grand Beach.

That reminded me of a detail to be resolved.

"Come home with me, Ciara Kelly." The words emerged spontaneously, without any thought or planning.

Pain, grief, resignation swept across her face. My heart sank. She was about to tell me that it could never be.

Then, blessedly, as she changed her mind, mischief in her wondrous gray eyes. "You want me to go home with you, do you now?"

"Would you be pregnant by any chance?" I asked stupidly.

"Well, not so you'd notice it, anyway." Her lips parted in a painful smile. "That shouldn't be hard to correct, if you've a mind to."

At a distance down the strand there were people hurrying toward us. Two tall men, one thin, one broad. Mike and Nick. The main force. The Knights of the Round Table. And between them a stubby little man. The monsignor himself. Merlin in residence. I'd need a priest in a day or two. Behind them the whirling blue lights of Garda cars.

I raised my hand in a weak wave.

A small figure emerged from the Knights, a princess in Aran sweater and brown jeans, and ran desperately toward us. At the last instant Jean made a remarkably wise and gracious decision.

She embraced Ciara first.

The blanket fell off Ciara's shoulders. The two women clung to one another, crying for joy as only women can do, especially if they are Irish. My daughter winked at me above my woman's naked shoulder. They would, as she had promised, make common cause against me. I would be outnumbered four to one.

Then I understood. My Neanderthal kink had not deceived me. In the future Ciara Kelly would give me other children. In our rite of spring she had given me back my daughter.

NOTE

The statistics on the prevalence and incidence of psychic phenomena are based on national sample research continuing at NORC under the direction of my colleague William McCready and myself. The descriptions of the experiences are drawn from interviews with those who have had them. Thus the reader may rest assured that the information contained about such phenomena in this story is accurate. Brendan Ryan is part of that three or four percent of the population, men and women perfectly normal in every other respect, for whom these phenomena are a routine part of life.

One critic of an earlier novel in which a character had similar experiences complained about "violations of the order of nature"; obviously he is the kind of man for whom some phenomena cannot happen as a matter of dogmatic a priori principle. As Blackie Ryan says, such a man would have voted against Galileo. I have no need either as a scholar or as a priest to postulate any explanation other than a natural one for psychic experiences. I am content with the position taken by Blackie—they occur too frequently to be dismissed as impossible, save by dogmatists masquerading as scientists. Perhaps Blackie is correct: psychic experiences are the result of mostly useless vestiges of communication aptitudes that were selected in the evolutionary process before we had developed the physical capabilities for elaborate speech.

Some readers may observe that the Strand at Inch was the locale for the climax of my first novel, *The Magic Cup*.

The similarity is not accidental. This story of spring, like the story of the earlier book, is a retelling of the old Irish version of the quest for the Holy Grail, a story which, in its primordial form as a liturgical cycle, was also part of a spring ritual. In the ancient story, the quest is for a cup and a woman who represent a divine power that operates not so much by creating and ordering, but, long before Alfred North Whitehead, by inviting, calling, alluring, enticing. Slavic music and Celtic story.

Like all quest stories (indeed like stories in many other genres, western, adventure, spy—in which latter this tale participates to some extent), my story contains considerable violence, which will doubtless lead to complaints from those who want no violence in fiction. There is less of it in the story than there is in life, and less than in shoot-'em-up westerns. Those who like adventure stories without danger and violence are perfectly free to pass my story by and search for something more to their tastes. Try the *Odyssey* or the *Aeneid* or the *Morte d'Arthur*. Or *King Lear*. Or the Book of Judges.

Both my stories about a quest for a sacred vessel which is also a magic princess more closely parallel the ancient liturgical cycle than does the Arthurian grail legend, which has had such a decisive and in my judgment negative impact on Western culture. Compare, for example, the wisdom of Blackie Ryan (Colum of Iona in *The Magic Cup*) to the wisdom of Merlin, his counterpart. The latter tells us that we must always seek for and never find our Ciara Kelly. The former asserts that each of us can and must find her, and that indeed she is searching for us as part of God's tricky game plan for a more beautiful cosmos.

Catholic Christians, at any rate, simply cannot accept the life-denying, flesh-denying theme of the tale of Merlin, Lancelot (poor, dear man), and that crowd. Not at all, at all.

—AMG
First Day of Summer 1983
Tucson, Chicago, and Grand Beach

Summer

Fifth Song

Lover:

There are many girls, but you're my special one,
Fierce and passionate woman, kindest friend,
Without you my hours never seem to end.
Where have you been, my sun, my moon, my dawn?
There's no escape now, I'm holding you down.
Do not pretend that you want to flee,
Tremble at my touch, you belong to me,
Be still while I slip off your frilly gown!
You were sculpted an elegant work of art,
Dark hair falling on snow white chest,
Honeydews, your high and graceful breasts,
One taste enough to break my heart.
In the curve of your wondrous thighs:
A deep valley flowing with perfumed wine
Around which wheat and blooming lilies twine
Whose sweetness invites my enchanted eyes.
I will seize the fruit, press them to my teeth.
Then, famished, impassioned, and lightly deft,
Swim in the waters of the valley's aromatic cleft
And your delicacy savor, drink, and eat!

Beloved:

I will be dry white wine to slake your thirst
And a tasty morsel to tease your mouth.
A trembling prize from the misty south,
A plundered vessel for your nightly feast,
A submissive trophy you can carry off
To a cool treasure house in your magic lands,
A most willing slave to your artful hands,
A total gift, passionate, loving, soft!

Lover:

She sleeps now, my innocent little child,
Wake her not, good winds, adore her radiant smile!

Love Song, 6:4–8:4

Prologue

Diana Lyons felt his eyes undress her. Slowly, carefully, and with lingering movements, his imagination was stripping her and reveling in her nakedness.

On the third hole of Long Beach Country Club.

It was an unexpectedly and powerfully pleasant sensation, a perfumed hot tub of admiration and desire. He was a spoiled, dishonest, overage child. His father had ruined her father's life—poor Daddy, who even at this moment was probably glued to his old radio listening to the White Sox and dreaming of the "old days," of players who were only names: Billy Pierce, Minnie Minoso, and "Little Nellie" Fox.

He belonged in jail. Her office would put him in jail. It was not her case, but still, he was a target of the United States Attorney for the Northern District of Illinois.

His delight in her body was soothing and respectful, hungry and yet somehow not lewd.

"Winner shoots first," she announced, trying to sound calm and self-possessed.

"Don't rub it in." His eyes absorbed her with tender caresses.

The gentleness of his longing was probably part of his act. You had to be pretty skillful at conning women to send out such seductive vibes. He was a phony. Definitely.

Feel vile, Diana; he's exploiting you.

"You blew a three-foot putt," she said, rubbing it in.

He relaxed on the bench, a solid, beautiful man with long blond hair and silver blue eyes, arm and thigh muscles bulging in a Notre Dame T-shirt and cut-off jeans. Cute. No, adorable.

"Mortal sin." He leaned back comfortably. "Sorry about that!"

She sensed that in his fantasy he was caressing her breasts, not harshly or lasciviously but with reverent awe. He wants me. Body and soul. The way a man in a cave wants fresh air. Don't stop.

No, do stop. You have no right to my body. Or my soul.

Damn, I can't tell him to stop without making it worse. I've never enjoyed being a sex object before. Why do I like it when a man I am supposed to hate is objectifying me?

That's not true. He's almost worshiping me, she thought, as she placed her golf bag against a tree, removed her two wood, and walked over to the tee, pretending that she was immune to his intense scrutiny.

I wish he would kiss me.

"Two wood?" He raised an eyebrow.

"Dogleg to the left. I need about two hundred yards."

Her father, incurable sports fan, even now that his health was ruined, had taught her to play golf—at a driving range where a friend let him play for nothing. Now she was betraying him and the skills he had taught her.

"If you need it," he grinned approvingly, "I'm sure you'll get it."

I want to be naked for him, she thought. I want to be spread out on the grass with him on top of me. I want to be covered by his kisses. All of me.

She dismissed the dangerous images that were racing through her mind. She should not be playing golf with a man that her office was investigating for possible indictment. She had been obsessed with him as a possible enemy, wishing that she might be assigned to his case and yet afraid, as a relative newcomer to the office, to seem too ambitious. She could not resist the impulse to spend some time with him. It was not ethically improper, not yet anyway. Know thine enemy, she had told herself.

Now her obsession had been stood on its head. I am infatuated with him. It's not love, nothing even remotely resembling love. She swallowed bravely. Only infatuation. Silly teenage crush.

The eyes of other men had appraised her critically, trying, she supposed, to decide whether someone so tall and strong would be any good in bed. She had been either indifferent or offended. Now a man she ought to despise was evaluating her womanliness, and she was wallowing in his interest.

I am in trouble, she told herself, as she teed up the ball. I must concentrate on my backswing. It's only an afternoon of golf, not a preliminary to a grand jury hearing. Or the beginning of a romance.

"Hit it hard," he urged her with a chuckle.

Straining with all her willpower, she glared fiercely at the golf ball and began her backswing. She sensed his eyes savoring her movement. No, she insisted, I will not think about him.

The ball soared off the tee, straight and true down the fairway. A hundred and ninety yards, not perfect, but adequate.

Thank God. I did not blow my cool.

Maybe he's not evil. Maybe he's just a nice boy with a few problems who needs someone to take care of him, someone to be a lover in bed and a friend out of bed. Someone like me.

Body and soul.

Lover and friend, there had never been a man before who might have been both. Fun and funny, kind and considerate. Masculine yet gentlemanly. Strong and vulnerable. Adorable boy child.

Body and soul.

If only . . . if only his father had not driven Daddy out of his job investigating the commodities racket. If Mama or Daddy knew I was playing golf with him . . .

She did not want to think about that. Mama would blow up like Mount Etna. Daddy would be silent and hurt, musing occasionally that his last child had failed him like all the rest.

"Devastating, Diana!" Conor's rich baritone laughter echoed behind her.

"Is there a comma between the two words?" she asked a fraction of a second before she wished she could bite off her tongue.

1

At the seventh hole, when she missed the three-foot putt, Conor Clarke decided with a shiver that the woman would probably become a hanging judge.

His shiver was inappropriate for a humid day when the temperature was in the high eighties and the smell of gasoline fumes permeated a hazy "inversion" over northern Indiana.

She would be the kind of judge that finally sentenced herself to the noose.

"Judge Lyons, you have been found by a jury of your peers to be guilty as charged. Therefore, I sentence you to be taken to Cook County Jail on the first day of next week and there to be hanged by your neck until you are dead."

"Yes, Your Honor."

"Since I'm your defense counsel as well as judge and jury, we won't have any of this appeal-to-the-Supreme-Court nonsense."

"What was my crime, Your Honor?"

"I forget. But it doesn't matter. You've failed. You're guilty."

"Yes, Your Honor. I deserve to be hanged by my neck until I'm dead."

"Oh yes, now I remember your crime: you missed a three-foot putt at Long Beach Country Club."

A pity to choke the life out of such a lovely neck, Conor thought. It was made for caressing, in the middle of the night preferably—tender, affectionate caressing as a prelude to more love. Not that he had any experience with such assaults on her virtue, since he'd met her for the first time only two hours ago. I need some time to make up my mind whether I am going to fall in love with her.

I think I might appeal for a stay of execution. Amicus curiae. Amator curiae, even. I would plea for a reduction of sentence: life in my bedroom. With her clothes off.

"How much time, Counselor?"

"Could I have the rest of her natural life? And maybe a few years more besides?"

In the real world, which alas interfered too often with his fantasy dialogues, Diana Marie Lyons bent over with a graceful flowing movement that reminded him of an elegant mountain lioness regally picking her way down a desert mountainside, and scooped up her golf ball. "Not too swift," she murmured, more to herself than to him.

I may have seen more lovely rear ends in my thirty years, Conor observed to himself. But never as part of such a comprehensive package.

"One over par," Conor said innocently. He pretended that the sharp stab of desire occasioned by the shifting of her trim breasts under her brown knit tank-top did not belong to him. "With my ten-stroke handicap, I'm still two strokes ahead of you."

"I should have had a bird." She tossed the offending ball into the air and caught it with a quick, angry little jab of her hand.

"Can't make them all." Conor, still entranced by the lithe and seductive grace of her bending motion, sternly lectured himself that it was chauvinistic to remove a woman's clothes in your imagination. Especially on a golf course. Actually, I didn't do it all, he insisted piously. Pick up her golf clubs and carry them off the green for her.

It could be worth his life to offer to carry her clubs to the next hole. So he picked them up without asking.

It was also, he reflected, not fair that women could do their evaluations so much more efficiently than men. In one quick glance she had taken in his long blond hair, blue eyes, and broad shoulders, filed it all for future reference, and then treated him as though he were no more important than the oak and maple trees along the edge of the Long Beach fairways.

"You should be a better golfer," she sniffed as she firmly removed her golf bag from his hand. "You have nothing else to do."

"Except sail."

Actually, he replied to his own prosecuting counsel, it is a body that is designed to be undressed. God made her beautiful so that she could attract a man who would love her and strip her and make love with her and produce children with her and live together with her to a happy old age.

Is that not so?

It sure is, said counsel for the prosecution, a benign and understanding fellow. It would be less than human if you did not find her desirable. Maybe you'd better fall in love with her.

An excellent idea, Counselor. Why did not I think of that?

Yes, it would be a very wise strategy for him to fall in love with Diana Marie Lyons, even if she did scare the hell out of him. She was the sort of woman about whom poets wrote. And he was a poet, wasn't he? Of a sort?

Then why haven't you found a metaphor to describe her? The voice belonged to the young and idealistic assistant State's Attorney who lurked behind his more experienced and tolerant leader. Why don't you stop ogling her and imagine a metaphor?

Ogling, he replied hotly, is a preliminary to a metaphor. You can't just produce them on the spur of the moment. You have to study the subject carefully, sometimes for hours, even days, before the creative powers of the soul erupt and produce, like Venus from the sea, a fully grown, if not a fully clad, metaphor. Right?

You have to concentrate.

"If you sail like you play golf, then your problem is that you don't concentrate," she interrupted his thoughts. "You're a daydreamer. You're not really paying any attention to your game."

"You've already made the argument, and I think I probably need a beer."

Diana had vetoed a golf cart. ("After all, neither of us are elderly invalids. And you look like you need exercise. Dissipation and athletics are incompatible.")

"Your defense for drinking when you sail"—her lips, full and straight, hardened into a severe line—"was that on your boat—"

"Name of *Brigid*."

"—your drink protected you from boredom. Surely an hour of golf is not so boring that you need already to ingest narcotic substances into your bloodstream."

Her lips melted into a faint, very faint, hint of a smile. I amuse her.

"There are chemicals, and then, there are chemicals, fair Diana."

"Come on." The amusement was gone. "Take your expensive golf clubs and their expensive case and let's play golf. We can discuss substance abuse later."

"Yes, Your Honor."

I think she might have actually laughed at me just then. An impatient and not altogether friendly laugh, but we have to begin somewhere.

Chemicals in the blood, is it? Glory be to God, woman, what do you expect?

There had been an instant chemical reaction between the two of them when she had climbed into his Ferrari. Hormones, of course, nothing more, he told himself in the mock Irish brogue he affected when he was feeling shy. As a man whose love life had been marked by sudden and injudicious chemically driven impulses—as often to flee as to pursue—

Con distrusted chemical reactions, especially when they were engendered by regal types like Diana Marie Lyons, regal types who could hit a golf ball, bullet straight, for a country mile.

She felt the reaction, too. When she was not bashing the small projectile the said country mile, she was covertly and judiciously considering him. Fascinated, he told himself hopefully, and repelled, he told himself sadly.

She strode ahead of him over the hill toward the next tee. Not a mountain lioness, but a mountain nanny goat, drat her. "You're not very good at sailing either." A judgment which seemed to extend to his general social uselessness. "Are you?"

The poem he was trying to compose in his head would be about double poetry in motion—her golf swing, flawless in its execution and delightful in its womanly grace; arms, back, hips, legs, all swaying in one concerted, controlled, captivating sweep of body and club. Alliteration, too.

Moreover, he could not succumb to the cliché of observing that she was well named—five feet nine inches of shapely, well-muscled nubile elegance: Diana the huntress, Diana the Assistant United States Attorney for the Northern District of Illinois.

Perhaps a symphony in brown—determined eyes with a touch of gold fleck that hinted at laughter (even if she didn't laugh much), long hair, and dark skin suggesting Mediterranean genes mixed with Celtic (armada genes perhaps?). Brown clothes, too—beige slacks, dark brown golf shoes, brown glove, and even a brown strap on her wristwatch. Nothing very expensive, but tastefully chosen and absorbing style from the slender, tough-jawed woman with delicately designed facial bones who wore them.

Not everyone would think her beautiful: too tall; too regal in bearing, too stiff maybe; too dark, perhaps even Arabian; too slender, her curves a trifle understated, or maybe it was only her height (Conor had yet to have an opportunity to evaluate her legs); a face that was perhaps too thin. Moreover, as a matter of principle, Conor tended to prefer his women shorter, fuller, fairer, more bubbly.

Or, alternatively, delicate, doll-like, exquisite.

There was nothing either fair or bubbly or doll-like about Diana Lyons.

To hell with principles.

And what's wrong with having Saudi Arabian genes?

The Saudis produced excellent race horses, didn't they? Or do they buy them from us? I can't quite remember.

He pretended again that the fantasy of slowly removing those clothes was someone else's and certainly not his—after all he had just decided definitely to fall in love with her and—and searched for a metaphor. Regal, imperial, countess, archduchess . . .

"Are you?" she persisted, definitely the United States Attorney, as they pulled up onto the eighth tee.

"Are I what?"

"Your boat was last in class in the Mackinac race this summer, wasn't it?"

"You would mention that." He heaved himself wearily to the bench behind the tee to rest while she drove. The humidity was as thick as heavy drapes; they were playing golf in a steam room. And she didn't even seem to be sweating. Just a bit inhuman. It doesn't matter. My decision to fall in love with her is final and irrevocable. My last and best offer.

Then he had his metaphor. Boats, of course.

"What are you thinking about?" She adjusted the strap on her glove, tightening it, of course.

You would have loved to lace up your corset in the old days, wouldn't you? Think of the fun I could have unlacing it. "I've been searching for a metaphor."

"You did publish a book of poetry, didn't you?" She inserted her tee into the soft, grass-covered dune—one of the many on top of which Long Beach and its country club had been constructed—with a tough brisk motion that suggested possible dissatisfaction with the glacial eras that had produced such soft turf. "And also a version of the Song of Songs from the Bible. Minor publishing house, was it not?"

"Not too minor. . . ."

"I presume the metaphor is about me?"

"Right." Conor wiped the sweat off his face. "In the sonnet I shall write tonight—a love sonnet of course—I will compare you with Grace O'Malley, the West of Ireland pirate queen of the sixteenth century."

She considered him coolly, repeatedly tossing her golf ball a few inches above her hand: everything she did was cool, even on a day when ordinary mortals like Conor were soaked in sweat. "My grandfather's name was O'Malley and he was from the Cong area in County Mayo." She arched a carefully trimmed eyebrow. "I'd be cautious about publishing such verse; even if the hint that I am piratical was not actionable—and I think most juries would vote that it was—I could still seek redress on the grounds that my privacy was being violated. . . ."

"You never would!" Conor decided that he absolutely adored her. No hurry about getting you in bed, my dearest. I just want to look at you and listen to you.

"Oh, wouldn't I?" she smiled wickedly. "You can't tell about your pirate women, can you?"

For a moment she seemed flattered, flustered, vulnerable. It was the smile, of course. The smile discarded the corset and revealed the real Diana, even more adorable, basking transiently in the warmth of his admiration.

For Conor Clarke that was too much.

"Go ahead, hit your drive, the foursome behind us is already on the green."

"I forgot I was playing with a serious golfer." She actually winked as she turned to address the ball.

She's nothing but a flirt. And if she flirts with me for long, she'll own me body and soul. And the next thing I know we'll be looking at furniture.

So what's wrong with that?

Before she could begin her backswing, Conor slipped deftly off the bench, tilted her chin back, and at the not inconsiderable risk, he thought, of having his head bashed in by her driver, brushed his lips against hers. She was startled, but neither her firm, warm lips nor her relaxed, self-possessed body offered objection or resistance.

"What was the reason for that?" A tiny, wafer-thin tremor in her words. She bent over to tee up the ball, which had fallen to the ground while he kissed her.

"Your smile demands a kiss." The Parousia now begins, Conor announced to himself. Maybe, just maybe, this is the one.

God knows, he warned himself, you're at an age at which anyone who is capable of walking down the aisle of a church and making it on her own power to the bedroom might be the one.

"Really? Excuse me now while I return to golf, which is why I thought my cousin Maryjane arranged this outing."

I bet I disconcerted her. She was pleased and frightened. She'll blow this drive. I'll have won the first round, no matter what her score.

No, it wouldn't be so bad to have to kiss that woman every day for the rest of my life.

Her drive, as always, was arrow straight, cleaving the fairway in two perfectly equal parts. Longer this time—maybe 230 yards. Her lips darted out in the tiny sign of approval that Conor had come to recognize as a stay of execution. Its opposite, an equally quick pursing of the lips, indicated that Diana was not pleased with Diana and would deny all motions for a retrial.

"You should be kissed before every drive," he said cautiously.

She grinned at him—a real live grin. "That's an interesting possibility."

"We'll try on the next hole," he said, lumbering toward the tee.

"We will NOT!" But she didn't sound too convinced.

His drive started out with all the good will in the world—like most of the efforts in Conor Clarke's life. Alas, the streets of hell are paved with well-intentioned golf balls; 150 yards down the fairway it began to wander to the right in a lazy slice that reminded him vaguely and inaccurately of a double by Ryne Sandberg off the left field wall. Into the rough and maybe the next fairway.

"Faded a little." She was smiling at him, not contemptuously, not even disdainfully. Dare he hope it—maternally?

"I amuse you?" He picked up his tee.

"You looked so frightened when I threatened suit," she said, actually smiling again, a big, warm, generous smile from a big, warm, generous woman. Conor noted that the sun, the golf course, and the rest of the cosmos went away in shame when they had to compete with her smile. "I'd be flattered to be in one of your poems."

"With your clothes off?" he blurted.

"That's the kind of poem you write, isn't it?" She pulled out a custom-made two wood—man-size, of course. "I presume you don't write from life very often, but I can't recall any part of the Grace O'Malley legend that would justify such a situation."

Had she really winked at him again? Ah, woman, you're the divil, the very divil!

"You're the divil, woman," he said aloud. "The very divil."

"Come on." She hefted her heavy bag of clubs like it was a quart of milk from the corner delicatessen. "I'll help you find your golf ball."

They found it in the rough bordering the next fairway. "Five iron," she said tersely.

"Just what I thought myself." He put the six iron back in his golf bag, removed the five iron, and with no practice swing and only symbolic aim, he hit it out of the rough and onto the fairway, only fifty yards off the green.

"Seems to help me, too—with a bit of delayed action," he murmured thoughtfully.

"Only in the short run."

She put her second wood shot three feet from the pin and earned her first birdie of the day. His best efforts produced only a double bogie. Well, they weren't really his best efforts. His rough shot had been too hurried, and he had momentarily forgotten that he was trying to lose to her.

She offered more resistance to his kiss on the par-five ninth hole, but the kiss was considerably longer in duration and involved something of an embrace. Her body was both solid and soft, light as air and as substantial as a mountain range. Her heart, he noted, was beating very slowly.

"May I drive now?" she asked coolly.

"Why not? I bet it's perfect."

It was all of that. Another long, high, straight blast that earned a faint smile of approval from the judge.

Her second wood shot was equally effective; again she had come within a few feet of the flag.

"Eagle," she said calmly as she removed the ball from the cup. "You do seem to be a good influence on me, Conor Clement Clarke. I've managed a par on the first nine."

"Abandon the law," he pleaded, "and join the professional tour. I'll be your caddy. You can also model golf clothes like that woman . . ."

"Stevens."

"Sure, you're prettier than she is. I'll be your business manager and . . ."

"Venture capital."

"Right." It was a make-believe scheme, but Conor could get as enthusiastic about jokes as he could about backing new computer chips or sophisticated but really user-friendly accounting programs. "I could learn to do the color on CBS and slip into little advertising hints for the Diana Lyons line of brown knit tank-tops that were not more concealing than they had to be and—"

"Go buy me a Coke, would you please? You can afford it better than I can."

Well, that settled that. I can't tell whether my true love—a lovely Saudi Arabian princess, *"Nigra sum, sed formosa"*— has a sense of humor or not.

"I like kissing you," he observed, as they consumed Diet Cokes under an enormous, gnarled oak tree—a powerful fertility symbol, he hoped—before starting the second nine.

"Do you?" she replied with discouraging indifference. "I

hardly imagine I am as satisfying a sex object as your models and cabin attendants and advertising executives.''

"Ah, you shouldn't believe everything you read in *INC* and Sneed and Kup's column."

"Shouldn't I?"

"Besides," he continued honestly enough, "most of those gorgeous women are pretty and nothing else. No real passion lurking behind the kiss. Not at all, at all."

"And there is in me?" She arched a skeptical eyebrow over her Coke can.

"A volcano about to erupt. Mount Etna maybe."

"Really? Isn't that a weary metaphor. Surely you can do better even on the spur of the moment."

"Well, let me see. . . . A lake ready to boil into a storm, a landslide about to unleash its first rock— No, no, strike that. An open-hearth furnace . . . what do they do? . . . Uh, lightning about to carve a slice of the night sky. . . . What about a tidal wave?"

"What about a warm fire at Christmastime with 'Greensleeves' playing in the background and marshmallows toasting on the fire and a large jug of cheap red wine and a man and a woman in heavy clothes who have just come in out of bitter cold and twenty feet of snow, wrapped up in a blanket and slowly becoming warm?"

"You're making fun of me!"

"Uh-huh. But I think the best I can do is the Christmas fire."

"You would think of Christmas when it's ninety and the humidity is ninety-nine."

"A red blanket, do you think? And had they been skiing or risking their lives on a snowmobile or trudging in from a car that broke down—a cute little red car maybe—or maybe just walking hand in hand under the naked, you should excuse the expression, trees."

"You're making fun of all my poems!"

"If it were one of your poems, they'd both already be naked in the blanket. As if people in the real world immediately take off their clothes when they come in from the cold."

"Have you ever curled up in front of the fire on a cold night with a man?" he demanded in defense of his muse.

"No. I suppose you and your pretty but sexless sex objects do it all the time. They are the kind of women who romp with you in the subzero snow, aren't they?"

"As a matter of fact, no," he admitted lamely. "They never leave the Lincoln Park bars that time of the year. Maybe you and I can experiment in these dunes come next December."

"And then again, maybe not."

"Besides, you don't expect us poets to be literal all the time do you? Aren't we permitted to use our imaginations?"

"Your imagination seems to have only one track, naked women in various compromising positions." She emptied her Coke can and considered it thoughtfully.

"Another one?"

"No, thank you."

"Sure?"

"All right." She smiled again and once more the cosmos vanished.

"Your morals are falling apart, woman. No self-control at all."

"Maybe I'm just thirsty."

The woman was smart, and clever, too, he thought on his return to the Coke machine. Well, in principle again, Conor liked women who were smart and clever. He would never marry a dummy, he had always insisted. "But, my dear," his friend Naomi Silverman, M.D., had often told him, "when your juices begin to flow, you forget about considering a woman's IQ."

Well, look at me now, Naomi Rachel Stern Silverman, I'm well aware that this woman is as smart as they come. And like I say, I don't object to smart women. So long as they are not too smart.

"Our finest wine, madam."

"Another cliché. But thank you. I'll buy the next two."

"Why are you worried so much about money?" he asked,

permitting himself to be just a little bit irritable. "We're talking about sex, not money."

"Are they that much different?"

"Money isn't nearly so enjoyable as a beautiful woman."

"So long as she remains a sex object and does not become a person. Dollars are a lot more submissive."

"In the old days, my lovely 'dark-skinned but shapely'—that's the translation . . ."

She nodded. "I studied Latin in high school, too. And I read your translation of the Song of Solomon."

"*Love Song?* What did you think of it?" He leaned forward eagerly and, honestly, without any conscious thought about it, put his arm around her.

"Less erotic than the original." She eased away from his arm. "And perhaps more lyrical, by our standards anyway. . . . Now what would happen to me in the old days?"

"Well, my Persian princess—"

"Italian. Sicilian, in fact."

"Same difference. In the old days you would have brought a high price in the slave market. A king, at least, or maybe an emperor."

"Disgusting. Besides, they wouldn't have liked a big and sturdy woman."

"Worse luck for them." Conor sighed loudly. Not sure whether he had won or lost that exchange.

Hell, he'd lost it. Going away.

"Why aren't you married?" She did not look at him as she asked the question, but concentrated on freeing a monarch butterfly that was trapped by a discarded paper cup.

"Their arrival"—Conor watched her intently; she would not step on ants, swat flies or even crush mosquitoes, he had noted on the first nine—"marks the beginning of the end of summer. They migrate to a plateau in Mexico."

"Who? Oh, the monarchs." The brown and orange-winged creature soared away. Another possible metaphor for Diana—excessively romantic, but then Conor Clarke was nothing if not an excessively romantic man. "I'd hate to be trapped like that poor thing without anyone to help," she said.

"Have you ever been to Mexico?"

"I was to Detroit once." She actually laughed. "We never had the money to travel and now I don't have the time. You didn't answer my question. You're thirty. If you were married, you wouldn't have to steal kisses from defenseless virgins on the golf course."

I'd love to take you to all the sunny places in the world and swim naked with you in all the warm bodies of water in the world. That's probably too romantic a cliché for my sonnet, but I want to do it just the same.

"There was some abetting of the felony both before and after the fact. My problem is that I don't have an office."

"Pardon?" She laughed again, genuinely amused, it seemed.

Ah, good, I begin to entertain her again, progress of a sort. I should have left out that slave-market cliché. She didn't seem to mind, though. Does she know she's beautiful? What woman does? She probably thinks she's too tall. I'll have to work on that. Reassure her that I've always liked tall women. Even if it isn't true. Not till this morning anyway. At least she resolutely refuses to stoop—a good sign.

"My cultural background is South Side Irish. Beverly Hills. St. Praxides. Right, you know the type?"

She nodded, pursed lips suggesting that she knew them and did not altogether approve, a common enough reaction by those who were not of the tribe. "You might live in Lake Forest now, if you wanted."

"It wouldn't make any difference. It's in my genes."

"Let's stipulate that you're Beverly shanty Irish."

"Thus I must seek a bride from that group. Your Lake Forest or Kenilworth nubiles of the sort I meet at the Junior Orchestra Association threaten me enormously. N'est-ce pas?"

"Not my world."

"You're lucky, believe me. In any event, consider how I appear to young women of a marriageable age and their mothers of the aforementioned Beverly Irish. And I won't accept the word 'shanty' as universally accurate: I am an unemployed lawyer who writes poetry. Would you want your daughter or sister to marry such an unpromising fellow?''

"You're a venture capitalist." Her lovely brow furrowed, doubtless she was trying to figure out whether he was serious or not.

"Indeed." Perhaps she would suspect that, as in most things, he was half fun and full earnest. "Without an office. If I had an office, the title would not be a burden in my unsuccessful pursuit of a bride. But among the South Side Irish, what is a venture capitalist? A gambler, and not a respectable gambler like your cousin or your uncle who speculates on the Board of Trade or the Merc or the CBOE. Does not the very word 'venture' suggest someone a little disreputable, possibly even piratical—which brings me back to my earlier metaphor."

"A pirate who had doubled his inheritance by his twenty-eighth birthday." She frowned, apparently disapproving of this feat.

"Without having an office or seeming to do much work and spending most of his time, as you yourself have hinted, playing golf badly, sailing boats badly, writing poetry badly, and pursuing, with notable failure, fair but passionless women."

"The poems aren't bad." The golden flecks danced in her eyes—amusement, that's indeed what they stand for. "A touch of youthful narcissism and unabashedly romantic, but not bad. Only mildly erotic. Perhaps a bit afraid of the demands of real passion."

Red lights flashed on in Conor Clarke's brain and warning klaxons wailed. "I pay my taxes."

"What . . . oh, you think that the only reason an Assistant United States Attorney would read your poems is that she's checking your tax returns." Diana turned a becoming shade of scarlet. Would she, self-proclaimed virgin (Kiss me, if you want, but no more, fellow), blush like that on their wedding night when he gently removed her elaborate and intricately fastened white finery? "I'm not, really I'm not. Your cousin told me that she had set up this match last night and gave me the book to read. . . . If you weren't afraid of marriage, you'd rent an office, wouldn't you?"

"Ah, not only a pirate and a tax lawyer, but also a woman of wisdom. Can we say, before I tee off for the second and decisive nine in this epic contest, that I'm looking for a woman who would not assign herself the lifelong task of remaking me?"

"An impossible task, I should think." The gold flecked in her eyes. A good sign, she indulges in no self-deception about the corrigibility of Conor Clement Clarke.

Nonetheless, even though she seemed to expect the attempt, he did not kiss her on the tenth tee. As a result, she merely parred the hole. On the next fairway, he opened his counterattack.

"You're not playing against me, are you?"

"Pardon?" This time her brown eyes were startled, not amused.

"I'm not a worthy opponent, but even if I were, it wouldn't matter. You play against yourself. You have a standard of play against which you measure yourself, an impossibly difficult standard if I am to judge by the ratio of these"—he made her disapproving lip movement—"to these"—he mocked her tiny smile of approbation. "It must be hard to live with a hanging judge watching your every move—kind of like what we used to think God did."

Without comment, she turned and put her first fairway shot within ten feet of the pin. Her lips did not move when she walked off the tee. "You live your way, I'll live mine."

"Sorry to pry," he apologized, contrite for the moment, then added with the old verve restored: "I'll leave your psychological clothes on for the rest of the day. Make no promises about the other clothes, though."

"You're impossible." She favored him with her amused mother's smile, waited till he had dubbed his fairway shot, and added: "It's the way I was raised. I guess we couldn't afford to doubt that what we did had to be done well."

"And I on the other hand have come to understand, in the

immortal words of G. K. Chesterton, that whatever is worth doing is worth doing badly. Thus we make an exceptionally well-balanced team. However, ought you not by your own terms be a professional golfer? You're playing this tough course even on a week's vacation from the mills of the United States Attorney for the Northern District of Illinois. If you played every day, you'd be one of the top money winners on the tournament, to say nothing of the fortune a figure like yours might earn modeling golf wear."

"A frivolous life," she snapped, distinctly displeased by his compliments. "Play that shot with your nine iron."

To display his independence, he used his eight iron and overshot the green by fifteen yards.

"I won't say I told you so," she said aloofly, then laughed in embarrassment. "Please don't stare at me that way."

"It's your fault. You made the crack about taking off psychological clothes. It put dirty ideas into my head."

"Nonsense," she snapped. "And it was your phrase, not mine. Moreover, you've been doing that since Maryjane introduced us. Like what you find?"

"Enormously. Do you mind?"

"I should. I'm not an object." She stood on the green, one hand on the red-flagged pin, the other holding her putter, now flustered and vulnerable again. Flattered by his interest, and offended—though not as much as she thought she should be—by his frank inspection.

"I can't quite control what my imagination does, Diana," he tried to speak seriously for a change. "You are a beautiful young woman and I am at a time in life when the genes of our species program a young man to react, ah, vigorously to such as you. But as lovely as you would be standing there on that green with your clothes in a heap next to you, I'd never confuse you with an object."

"Grace O'Malley, pirate queen, becomes golf course exhibitionist. Putt."

He did. Again he forgot to concentrate and putted up to his ability. The ball ran on a straight, unerring line from the edge of the green, up over a slight rise, down into a steep depres-

sion, and then, like it had eyes, turned lazily and slid contentedly into the cup, from which Diana at the last minute pulled
the pin.

"Wow!" exclaimed Diana Marie Lyons in unfeigned admiration. "Even the hanging judge approves of that one."

"See what my fantasies can accomplish."

"They make you forget that you're deliberately playing
beneath your ability." She dropped the pin with sufficient
disregard for the green as to give the relevant members of the
Long Beach Greens Committee a heart attack.

"Can't make up your mind about me, can you, Diana Marie Lyons?" He essayed his most winsome smile.

"Oh"—she bent over to putt, causing more delightfully
obscene fantasies to race through Conor's brain—"I've made
up my mind about you."

"And the verdict?"

"The old Scottish one—guilt not proven." She paused
while she tapped her golf ball into the hole. "And tell me
about translating poor old Solomon?"

"It's not exactly a translation. More of a paraphrase. I
don't know any Greek or Hebrew and only a bit of Latin. I
tried to redo the English so it sounds like poetry. I showed it
to Father Roland Murphy—you know he comes to Grand
Beach every summer—to make sure I hadn't wandered too
far from the original."

They trudged on to the next tee.

"And he said?"

"That none of the specialists in the Song needed to worry
about their jobs, but I hadn't done too much that was
wrong. . . . It's not easy." He leaned his golf bag against the
tree and, warming to the subject, began his usual lecture.
"Take for example the famous line—that I may have quoted
when I kissed a certain woman a half hour ago—in which the
Shulamite says, *'Nigra sum, sed formosa.'* Father Roland insisted that I could not render it, 'I'm black and I'm really
built.' "

"You're terrible!" She lifted his golf bag and continued
the trip to the next tee.

"It is variously translated, 'I'm black and I'm lovely,' or 'The sun has tanned my skin.' "

"And you translate it, 'Dark is my skin and slim my waist.' "

"You really read *Love Song*?" He did not bother to try to hide his pleasure.

"I told you Maryjane had a copy. I compared it with her Bible. Even the original is pretty erotic for the Scriptures. It's all allegorical, isn't it?"

"My priest, Monsignor Ryan, you know . . ."

"Judge Kane's brother."

"Right. He tells me that it's strictly secular love poetry that was included in the Jewish Scriptures because it was sung at weddings. Maybe written by a woman. . . ."

"I should think so." She dropped his golf bag against the bench and gestured for him to tee up.

"Monsignor says it's not allegorical but sacramental. Human passion, he says, gives us a hint of God's passion for us. We are most like God's love for us when we are aroused in the presence of our beloved. And we best experience a hint of God's love when our beloved pursues us."

"Really?" She searched for a tee in her pocket.

"God is a passionately aroused lover, nice, huh? And kind of scary?"

"Scary?" She considered her golf ball. "I suppose so. Beautiful, too. Now drive, three wood, I think."

Her thoughtful response so influenced Con that he did indeed use his three wood.

He sliced with it, too.

She came in with a par seventy-two. Conor, who settled down to concentrate on his golf on the last seven holes, finished with an eighty-three, giving her a one-stroke victory. If he had not deliberately hit his first putt on the eighteenth green too far, he would have won. Diana seemed about to accuse him again of deliberately losing and then thought better of it.

"Tennis? Squash?" she asked.

"A man as ancient as I am can afford only one loss a

day." He carried her clubs into the clubhouse, without protest. "Besides I can hardly wait to see you in a swimsuit."

"The next generation of children"—she sighed wearily and took her golf bag from his hands—"will be raised to understand that it is not proper to consider the body of another human being that way."

"Do you really believe that?"

"Of course."

"How much beauty will God have wasted."

"I read your poems. I know how you react to a woman's body."

"It might not be safe to be in the pool with me."

"I'd be safe enough. But I'd rather not swim." She looked around. "This place is too rich for my blood. All these wealthy idle matrons."

"They're not really wealthy, Diana." He placed his hand gently on her shoulder. "I know some of the truly wealthy ones, too. If you can stay at Maryjane's, you can swim here. Maybe even eat supper with me."

Her lower lip jutted out stubbornly. "Idle rich."

"If you say so."

"The trouble is"—she put the lower lip back in its proper place and laughed at herself—"the trouble is that having swum here every day with Maryjane, I'm hardly in a position to assert my convictions now, am I? See you at poolside, Conor Clement Clarke."

"A threat?"

"Take it as you want." She sauntered toward the women's locker room.

You could carry it off, woman, he thought, in the most exclusive country club in the world, the kind of place which wouldn't let a Beverly shanty Irishman like me by the guard dogs at the front gate.

A distinctly nasty side of her, Conor considered, as he showered before putting on his swimming trunks. Complex and interesting woman. Potentially dangerous, though I don't quite know why. Worth further exploration. Definitely.

Not that now I have the slightest choice in the matter.

Your heart will always know ...
WHEN IT'S PERFECT

When the mesmerizing Marcus Longfellow, the Earl of Renn, comes striding into Miss Mary Marsh's life, her world is set spinning. The ladies of London's *ton* clamor for the lacy confections Mary creates, but the earl is seeking something more from her. And he is very persuasive in his pursuit. Gentle, quiet Mary has always avoided romance, but her strong attraction to the adventurous nobleman is immediate and irresistible. Dare she trust the dashing lord with her secrets?

She is hiding something—Marcus is certain of it—a clue, perhaps, to explain his sister's untimely death. A sensuous seduction will surely loosen young Mary's tongue, and the determined earl is eager to oblige—for in all his world travels, Marcus has found no treasure more exquisite than she. But is his growing passion for her interfering with his search for the truth?

"Adele Ashworth has a fine future ahead of her."
Romantic Times

Other Avon Romantic Treasures by
Adele Ashworth

SOMEONE IRRESISTIBLE

*If You've Enjoyed This Book,
Be Sure to Read These Other*
AVON ROMANTIC TREASURES

AN AFFAIR TO REMEMBER *by Karen Hawkins*
AFTER THE ABDUCTION *by Sabrina Jeffries*
THE BRIDE BED *by Linda Needham*
ONE NIGHT OF PASSION *by Elizabeth Boyle*
TO MARRY AN HEIRESS *by Lorraine Heath*

Coming Soon

THE IRRESISTIBLE MACRAE: BOOK THREE OF
THE HIGHLAND LORDS *by Karen Ranney*

ADELE ASHWORTH

When It's Perfect

An Avon Romantic Treasure

AVON BOOKS
An Imprint of HarperCollinsPublishers

This is a work of fiction. Names, characters, places, and incidents are products of the author's imagination or are used fictitiously and are not to be construed as real. Any resemblance to actual events, locales, organizations, or persons, living or dead, is entirely coincidental.

AVON BOOKS
An Imprint of HarperCollins*Publishers*
10 East 53rd Street
New York, New York 10022-5299

Copyright © 2002 by Adele Ashworth
ISBN: 0-380-81807-8
www.avonromance.com

First Avon Books paperback printing: November 2002

Avon Trademark Reg. U.S. Pat. Off. and in Other Countries, Marca Registrada, Hecho en U.S.A.
HarperCollins ® is a registered trademark of HarperCollins Publishers Inc.

Printed in the U.S.A.

10 9 8 7 6 5 4 3 2 1

I'd like to offer my heartfelt thanks to the following people:

To the talented Avon Ladies,
whose work and creativity always amaze me

To Michele Albert, my wonderful friend and critique partner,
for her unfailing support and inspiration

To my marvelous agent, Denise Marcil,
for her expertise, continued support,
and hard work on my behalf

And finally to my gifted editor, Lyssa Keusch,
for letting me write the books
that are in my heart, then offering suggestions
that always seem to make them better

Prologue

"You're squeezing the breath out of me!"

Mary Marsh grinned. "If you didn't eat so much chocolate..." she admonished good-naturedly, pulling even tighter at the waist of the corset she attempted to pin into place behind the somewhat trim figure of Miss Christine Longfellow. The Countess of Renn's only daughter would be married in less than three months.

"Chocolate is a lady's prerogative," Christine retorted through a groan, lifting her arms a little higher.

"Prerogative?"

"A delicacy one shouldn't have to live without—ouch!"

"Sorry," Mary said, standing back at last. "There. How does that feel?"

Christine eyed her through the mirror. "I can't feel anything. I'm numbed from neck to legs."

1

Mary smiled, ignoring the lady's usual false pouting. "But it looks marvelous, doesn't it?"

"Ha! You're very vain," Christine replied, turning her attention back to the satin creation, rubbing her fingers along the smooth fabric covering her ribs as she rocked her hips from side to side. "But it is divine. You do such lovely work, Mary. A pity nobody will see it but me." Her lips lifted into a crooked smile. "At least till my wedding night."

Mary grinned again at that, but kept her critical attention on the corset, the seams and bits of lace that still needed trimming, noting with satisfaction that the stays were . . . staying. She refrained from mentioning that Christine had also better watch her consumption of cakes and gravies in the coming weeks if she intended to fit into her wedding gown. Christine's mother would no doubt scold her about that well enough anyway.

"Lift your arms one more time," she ordered. Christine did so without question.

Mary took scissors in hand and snipped at bits of thread and a portion of the satin that met unevenly at the top seam.

"You know, Mary," Christine continued contemplatively, "I do wish you'd stay for a time after my wedding to Exeter. I have little doubt that Marcus will return for the occasion, in which case you can actually meet him." She paused as Mary took pins to the material at the sides of her breasts, then added with conviction, "I know he'll be here."

Mary didn't reply immediately, attempting to look busy with the satin at her fingertips. Christine carried on as if she didn't expect a response.

"He's very handsome, but of course you know that from his portrait in the hall. And wealthy, of course. And he hasn't been with a lady since . . . oh, at least since he courted the Lady Stanley of Bodmin five years ago." She attempted to draw a deep breath, having trouble, naturally, from the restriction. "Funny thing she didn't want to marry him. I suppose it was his wild way that discouraged her."

Mary had caught herself thinking her own wild thoughts about the mysterious Earl of Renn these recent weeks, but would never mention that to a soul. His magnificent portrait had indeed raised her curiosity, sometimes to the level of obsession, for which she always chided herself. She supposed it was because he wasn't around to displace the rumor of him, the enigma surrounding him. He'd been gone for four years, and nobody expected his return, even for his sister's long-planned wedding to the Viscount Exeter.

"Are you listening, Mary?"

She gazed up, expression flat, pins in her mouth. Through semi-closed lips, she replied, "Yes, of course."

The lady placed her fists on her hips and looked back at her figure in the mirror. "You didn't seem to be listening. I was talking about Marcus."

Mary stood and pulled the pins from between her lips, sticking them into the black velvet cushion circling her left wrist. "Sorry. I was just wondering how you know he hasn't courted a woman since Lady Stanley. What about Egyptian ladies?"

Christine frowned at the honest question, tilting her fair head to one side.

"I never thought of that." She shrugged lightly.

"But he's never mentioned another lady in his letters to me."

Mary raised her brows as she resumed her work at the waistline of the tight ridge where satin met lace. "Well, if he has been courting, I rather doubt he'd mention it to his young sister."

"Why?"

The question was truly asked in innocence, but Mary didn't much want to expound on something she couldn't be certain of in the first place. Instead, she offered, "Gentlemen can be very secretive, and unassuming. Perhaps he didn't think you'd care."

After a slight pause, Christine said, "Oh. Maybe not. Marcus is rather unassuming, I suppose. But he's also very . . . difficult to define. As a man."

Fascinating, would be the word.

"It still needs a bit of a threading through the bustline," Mary interjected to change the subject before giving away her thoughts. Tapping her lips with her fingertips, she added, "and I'm thinking of embroidering two or three black hearts right in the center."

Christine's eyes sparkled wide. "Oh, yes. Black hearts. How marvelous!"

Mary smiled with her. "You're too easily amused."

"That's what Exeter says." Christine laughed, then grabbed her middle. "That hurts."

"I'll loosen the seam on the other side. Give me a minute."

"I'm amazed at how fast you put this one together, Mary. It's prettier than the other three you've made me. And maybe . . . daintier? Yes, daintier." She studied the corset speculatively.

"You make the most fantastic display of intimate lingerie. I'm sure all your clients in England thank you constantly."

More likely their husbands do.

Mary pressed her lips together to keep from offering that comment to virginal ears.

"And of course, as always, I'm so pleased you think so, Lady Christine."

"You're too modest."

"I'm supposed to be modest."

Christine sighed. "I suppose if I made underclothing as risqué as this, I'd appear modest as well."

Mary chuckled. "I'm just glad you appreciate my effort." Finished with the trimming at last, she began to place thread and needles back into the side pouches of her sewing basket. "I'll begin working on the hearts as soon as you're out of it. Turn around and I'll unfasten you."

Christine immediately did as she was told. "Do you wear such provocative underclothes yourself, Mary?"

She could feel the lady's gaze scrutinizing her face through the mirror at their side. Trying not to show emotion of any kind, she focused her attention on the metal fasteners, working through each one quickly. "Isn't that a rather personal question?"

Christine huffed. "From me? Certainly not."

If nothing else, Christine Longfellow was honest about herself. She remained a charming young woman, not much more than a girl, really. And so very innocent of the ways of the world.

"I wear my own creations from time to time, yes," Mary answered vaguely, as she turned back to her sewing basket, hunting for a particular scrap of black satin that might work better for hearts than embroidery threading. She had placed it at the bottom of her basket last week.

Christine eyed her for a second longer, clutching her loosened corset to her breasts. "I should think Marcus would find you utterly and charmingly whimsical."

Here we go again. "Whimsical?" She couldn't think of a word that described her less.

"And as a man, he'd surely enjoy a private showing of your work."

Mary suddenly fumbled the sewing basket, and thread, bits of fabric, and pins toppled to the floor at her feet. She stared at it, face flushing, heart skipping a beat or two at the idea of modeling risqué underclothes for the Earl of Renn, the mysteriously dark, masculine man in the portrait.

"Perhaps you should change," she managed to say as she knelt down, gathering the contents and tossing them back into the basket carelessly. "You'll not want to be late for your dinner engagement with the viscount, and it's nearly four."

Christine moved off the short stool without further urging. "And of course he's never late," she said, her brows crinkling in frown. She turned back and glanced at Mary through the mirror. "He's taking me for a ride along the cliffs after dinner. The ocean is lovely by moonlight, and there should be a full one tonight."

Mary angled her head; she stared into the younger woman's large blue eyes that conveyed such hope and trust. And daring.

Take care, Christine, she wanted to warn. But doing so was not her place. Instead, she said softly, "I'm sure you'll enjoy that. It'll be beautiful."

Christine smiled, visibly relaxing. "I have known Exeter all my life," she returned with an air of gentility, "but I have spent very little time alone with him."

Such a reply seemed to fuel Mary's unspoken concern, making her more uncomfortable than she cared to admit.

Christine whirled around and headed toward her small withdrawing room. "Help me to dress?" she asked over her shoulder. "I think I'll wear the pink chiffon. Exeter adores me in pink."

Standing again, Mary supposed she could play maidservant for now. She liked Christine very much, worried about her in a manner. And she did not at all care for the Viscount Exeter, but then that was none of her business. She would be leaving Cornwall in just a few short weeks—before the wedding of the season, and, she pondered with some elusive feeling of melancholy, without ever meeting the great Earl of Renn.

Cornwall, England
May, 1855

Chapter 1

~~~~∽◯◯∽~~~~

Baybridge House
10 June 1854

My dearest Marcus,

I was so pleased to receive your most recent letter.
The treasures you have recently discovered to the
west of Cairo sound as exquisite as ever. How ex-
citing your life must be! Someday I should enjoy
traveling to Egypt, if only to see you again.

Life in Baybridge House is as it always is, ex-
cept that I am now betrothed to Viscount Exeter.
Shall I say I am happy? I suppose so. Mother is
happy. Oh, how I wish you would visit! I have
missed you terribly, as has George. Please remem-
ber to stay out of the sun. I will be thinking of you
daily, and praying for your continued good health.

Your loving sister,
Christine

Mary Marsh would get her very first peek at Marcus Longfellow, the mysterious and seldom mentioned Earl of Renn, in only ten short minutes—less than two weeks after the tragic death of his sister, Christine, whose body she'd found in a heap of pink satin skirts on the lady's withdrawing room carpet.

She'd been living quite comfortably at Baybridge House, on the earl's estate near St. Austell, for the last four months, designing Lady Christine's bridal trousseau for two qualified seamstresses to create, never having dreamed that she'd actually *meet* the man. He'd been gone for years and wasn't expected to return anytime soon. But she supposed the abrupt and disturbing death of one's healthy eighteen-year-old sister would be enough to bring a man home, even if he didn't want to be there.

Mary had heard the commotion earlier that afternoon when every servant, it seemed to her, had erupted in panic at his surprising and rather unceremonious arrival. She, being above a mere servant in station, yet not one of the family, had remained in her room, knowing she'd have the distinct opportunity of being introduced to him at dinner—when they would all no doubt discuss his sister's untimely demise once again. And when she'd get the chance to put Christine's description of her brother to the test.

The whole affair made her more anxious than she'd felt in months. Not only did she know more than she should about England's most handsome earl, she wasn't in any way ready to return to London. She still had memories of home too crushing to contemplate, past guilt she needed to work through, which happened to be the reason she'd accepted this position in the first place. But however true that was, Mary also realized with some uneasiness that she was growing wary of the general eeriness of Baybridge House following Christine's death, and she was quite certain meeting the aloof and brooding Lord Renn would do nothing to change her feelings. She wasn't prepared to leave so quickly, and yet she knew the earl would have no reason not to release her from her duties within days, at which time she would be on her way back to London. Regardless of Lady Christine's farfetched notion of a love match between the two of them, Mary knew reality from romance. She would soon have to face her past.

Washing such uncomfortable thoughts from her mind, Mary donned her best evening gown—a full-skirted burgundy silk with cropped sleeves and scooped neckline, the most appropriate dress she had in her possession for mourning—then sat at her polished pine vanity, gazing into the mirror a final time before she made her way downstairs. Her skin was good for a lady of twenty-nine, still fresh and relatively free of wrinkles. She'd twisted her long blond hair tastefully into a chignon at her nape, allowing tendrils to curl down her cheeks and forehead, giving her an attractive yet conservative appearance. Although born of good family, she remained a spinster by choice and had no desire to be the center of anyone's attention, especially tonight.

Smoothing her palms down her skirt, Mary rose

and walked with confidence through the door of her bed chamber and out into the faintly lit hallway of the house's third floor. Not a sound could be heard upstairs, though she knew the servants below were abuzz with excitement and gossip at the earl's return. The family, of course, would be gathering in the formal dining room for this remarkable occasion, and Mary wanted to be early, so as to remain as unobtrusive as possible. At least that was her hope.

It wasn't to be. As she neared the entrance, she heard the low voices of George and Gwyneth, the earl's vivacious younger brother and his mother, the countess, as well as the clinking of dishes and silver as obedient hired help set places with family china. By all accounts the Earl of Renn had yet to appear, which to her seemed promising in some small measure. Centered in that thought, Mary pulled her shoulders back and glided gracefully into the dining room to make her presence known.

As always, elegance surrounded her, and once again she noted how everything at Baybridge House was in perfect order and of the utmost in quality and style. The Countess of Renn would never dream of eating on last year's china and table linens. But then as the widow of one of England's wealthiest owners of a productive china clay mine, she would be accountable for a luxurious table. And everybody in Cornwall knew the Countess and late Earl of Renn were of the most refined and respected members of the local peerage. For the first time since her arrival, Mary had to wonder if that distinction had anything to do with Marcus

Longfellow's departure to Africa years ago, if he was the wandering bachelor sort. But then, such speculation was none of her concern, and she would likely never know.

Mary first stepped around the long maple wood table, now set with fine white china atop lacy burgundy linens, then made her way toward the tall east windows where the countess and George stood talking in hushed voices as they gazed out to the southeastern shore of the Bay of Austell. Naturally, they were both dressed for mourning, somber faces and all, and Mary noted again how strikingly similar the two of them appeared standing side by side. Clearly mother and son.

George, rather short for a man, possessed rich, clever brown eyes that beheld another's to the point of obsession when he was engaged in conversation. At first Mary had found that boldness intimidating, until she'd grown to know George, finding him to be an intelligent, charming, and quite humorous individual. His reddish blond hair curled ever so slightly over his forehead and down to his side whiskers, and Mary imagined he had a horrendous time keeping it tidy, thick as it was. Although stunned to the point of confusion and clearly distraught these last two weeks over the death of his sister, at a glance George seemed more himself tonight. He stood confidently straight, his overall composure returned, his taut features more relaxed than they'd been in days. He wore black formal evening attire and looked every bit the distinguished and respected gentleman he was at the age of twenty-eight.

For her part, Gwyneth overpowered her son. She overpowered them all, actually, though she stood not quite five and a half feet in height, shorter than George, and even Mary, by two or three inches. An old acquaintance of Mary's mother, Gwyneth had been raised near Regent's Park, then married better than Elizabeth Marsh and thus enjoyed the luxury of living the life of a well-to-do countess, even if it meant leaving London at an impressionable age to endure the slow pace of the country and the industrial town of St. Austell.

But that hadn't seemed to matter. For as long as Mary had known her, Gwyneth had carried herself like a queen while on her estate, although exhibiting a certain gentleness, or more correctly, a certain graciousness seldom observed in a lady of so bold a personality.

She'd been a beauty in her youth, and was still, at the age of fifty-four, a lovely woman, with vivid blue eyes and the same strawberry blond hair she'd given her son. But the strain of Christine's unimaginable death had put a pallor to her skin that Mary had never seen before. Gwyneth had been unconsolable for the first few days following the discovery of her only daughter's lifeless body, taking regular heavy doses of laudanum at her physician's recommendation. This week had been better as she'd attempted to regain her dignity to some degree, and of course, hearing that her eldest son was returning seemed to put her spirits back in order. But she still looked pale, the lines and shadows on her face more pronounced even as she'd dressed to look her best. The shock had taken its toll on all of them, Mary supposed, and things at Baybridge House would never again be as they were.

Tonight the countess had chosen a traditionally formal gown, and Mary suspected it was because of her eldest son's first dinner at home in years. She wore a tight-fitting, long-sleeved, high-necked dress in black taffeta that still managed to show off her youthful figure, though she'd pulled her hair tightly into a conservative bun at her nape. She wore no jewelry, save for a pair of jet earrings made expressly for mourning. She seemed nervous as well, sipping sherry with a jerking wrist, which surprised Mary most of all. Gwyneth had never, in her presence, been nervous about anything. Tonight certainly promised to be an occasion to remember.

"Ah, Miss Marsh," George said abruptly when he noticed her walking toward them. "Join us for a sherry, won't you? My good brother will be down momentarily. I did tell him eight, but of course he's rather tired from the long journey."

"Good evening, Mr. Longfellow, Lady Renn," she replied with just the proper tone of congeniality to fit the solemn mood, taking particular note of George's rapid tongue and forced good mood.

"Mary, darling, have a sherry," Gwyneth offered rather informally, as if she hadn't heard her son. "When Renn arrives, we shall eat."

She'd said that pointedly, though without looking at her, and Mary realized the lady was more than nervous, she was agitated. They all were.

Without acknowledgment, a footman moved up beside her, dutifully holding a silver tray on which sat four crystal sherry glasses all full of the sweet red wine. Mary selected one of them and took a sip as the footman stepped back. It was delicious, naturally.

"I hope you're not thinking of leaving us soon," George remarked, fairly reading her mind.

Mary hesitated. "I'm not sure there's anything more I can do here, and I imagine my father is anxious for my return." That was probably a lie, but she followed it with, "In his last letter he implied that the Widow Brickwell is not taking care of his needs as she should."

George snickered, but squelched it with the sudden stern look his mother gave him.

"We shall miss you, Mary," the countess said succinctly, looking at her at last through eyes as clear as sharply cut glass. "You've been a tremendous help to our family during this trying time."

Mary nodded once, holding the lady's gaze, knowing that was honestly felt. "Thank you, Lady Renn. I shall miss Cornwall. I've grown fond of it these last few weeks."

"Have you?"

Mary didn't know if that was a direct and simple question, or one of the countess's attempts at taking control by demanding an explanation when she knew there wasn't one. At this point Mary didn't care.

"I have, actually. I shall miss the ocean breezes and fresh air, the quiet of village life, sunrise over the seashore—"

"Surprising you could *see* the sun with all this blasted rain," George cut in, raising his glass to his lips as they twisted in disgust. He took a short sip. "It's been a devil of a spring this year, mostly mud and clouds."

"George." His mother's grave voice reprimanded him gently, even as her thin shoulders grew noticeably rigid beneath her formal attire.

Mary had seen that reaction before.

George scoffed and glanced out the window. "I'm sorry, Mother, but there is nothing but bickering at the mine. I can never seem to keep the workers happy now that we're back at war. Some of my best men are fighting in the effort, and the nasty weather only makes the edginess and concern worse."

"Then perhaps you should offer them something that will help change their belligerent attitudes, to cheer them during this recent upheaval," was her slow, caustic response.

"And your suggestion of an offer?" George asked, unblinking, obviously not expecting an answer. "We pay them well enough as it is, and they've still had trouble following orders lately."

Gwyneth fairly jeered and leaned toward her son, lowering her voice. "Of course it hasn't helped matters that you've been away for two weeks. Our family . . . emergency has unsettled everyone at the mine. That's natural in our position. We are the family they all look to for security. We must therefore show them we are stable and that nothing has changed, even during this crisis." She pulled up to stand stiffly straight again, mouth thinned. "You must think at their level, George."

Mary raised her sherry to her lips, avoiding the debate if she could. It was probably time to change the topic of conversation to everybody's health.

Suddenly the most disturbing sensation of being watched niggled at her. Instinctively, she turned, and nearly dropped her sherry glass as she stared with her mouth opened as wide as her eyes.

In the dining room doorway, gazing at the three of them with hard, expressionless features, exuding an amazing power and vibrant strength in just his stance, stood Marcus Longfellow, fourth Earl of Renn.

At that moment, the mood in the room shifted violently and George and Gwyneth abruptly stopped bickering as they looked toward the door.

With a rustling of her skirts, Gwyneth made the first move toward her son.

"Renn, darling, we were wondering what took you."

The earl cocked his head minutely, gazing now at his mother. "Were you?"

It was exactly the reply Gwyneth would have made. But what struck Mary was the deep vibrancy of his voice.

"Of course," Gwyneth asserted with only a tinge of hurt coloring her words. "You've come home at last. You're the earl."

The man's brow raised as he folded his hands behind his back. "Thank you for that, Mother."

Mary stared, amazed, not sure if she should laugh or join in or stand in the corner and watch the family bantering unobserved. Not surprisingly, Marcus Longfellow was every bit his mother in verbal witticism and disguised meanings, but he most certainly took after his father, the late earl, in every other way.

Recovering herself, she straightened when she felt George place his fingers gently on her elbow, urging her forward for formal introductions.

As gracefully as possible she moved in the earl's direction, noting how the man had yet to wander from the doorway.

He looked nothing like she'd imagined him, and very, very much as Christine had described. He wore black dinner attire in expensive fabric, cut to fit his large stature perfectly. The man stood approximately six feet in height, she decided, with strong shoulders, a wide chest leading to a solid stomach, and long legs, from what she could decently see of them. His hair reminded her of shiny, dark mahogany, cut short and tapered around his ears. But his face completely arrested her.

He had a low forehead, with a narrow but obvious scar that sloped from his left brow to his hairline. His eyes were an uncanny shade of brilliant blue—like the Mediterranean in summer—and surrounded by long, dark lashes. His bone structure curved at hard angles, highlighting prominent cheekbones, a long, straight nose, and a rather defined, deeply clefted chin. His mouth, however, drew her attention from everything else as she at last stood before him. Surrounded by the day's dark stubble, it curved gently with the most amazing hardness—a complete contradiction in itself. Mary imagined how those lips would move in a manner that graphically expressed his shifting moods.

George lifted her hand, snapping her out of a most embarrassing stare.

"This is Miss Mary Marsh of London, dear brother."

That sounded more like a pronouncement than an introduction, and Mary felt her cheeks flush with heat when those strong blue eyes glanced down and took particular note of her for the first time.

She attempted a smile, though it was likely a poor one. "It is my pleasure to make your acquaintance, Lord Renn," she said modestly, holding his gaze.

He stood silently for a second or two, then reached for her outstretched hand. "Indeed, Miss Marsh. I've heard all about you."

Mary blinked, flustered and unnerved that he'd say such a thing in front of everyone, feeling the warmth and strength in his large fingers as they encircled hers. Then suddenly, disregarding any response she might make, Gwyneth wrapped her arm around her eldest son.

"Let's eat. I want to hear all about your return, of course."

For several uncomfortable seconds, Marcus held onto her hand. Then, with a fast glance down her person, he dropped it and turned to his mother. "And my work?"

Mary shifted from one foot to the other; George coughed then took a long swallow of his sherry.

"Of course, my dear." Gwyneth smiled flatly. "I know your work is very important to you."

An awkward moment followed, until George blurted, "This way, Miss Marsh, if you please."

The tension remained acute as they all took their places at the table. Marcus sat at the head of it; Gwyneth at the opposite end. She and George were seated across from each other at the center.

Silence ensued for a moment or two as ready footmen prepared the first course of mock turtle soup. Mary gazed down at the lovely, shining Renn porcelain china, this year's best, feeling the intensity in the air prick her skin like a physical force. She could positively feel the earl's presence, as if his mere personality swept over them all, his eyes boring into the side of her face, though she wouldn't look to him, not if she could help it. She'd certainly disgrace herself by staring if she even managed a glance in his direction. Instead she sat stiffly erect and focused on her food.

"Well, then," Gwyneth began with an exaggerated exhale, "let's hear all about your trip home."

Mary didn't look directly at the earl, but she could see from the corner of her eye that he stopped eating to sit back and assess his mother.

"It was long and tiresome," he replied. "The journey always feels longer coming from Egypt to England than the other way around."

"I wonder why that is?" Gwyneth returned lightly.

Marcus fairly grunted. "I don't know, Mother. Maybe it's because when one leaves Cairo, one is leaving warm, sunny, dry air for the dreary comforts of rain and fog and mud as the best of English weather." He paused, then added brusquely, "My bones hurt."

Gwyneth shifted her bottom in her chair, and Mary noticed how George devoured his soup with incredible speed. She sipped hers, hardly tasting it.

"No doubt from sitting in coaches for days," the countess stated, ignoring entirely the fact that her eldest son didn't appear to be in a fine mood to be home. "You certainly made it back to England quickly."

And he had, Mary considered suddenly. Nobody had mentioned it, and since it wasn't her place to do so, she had no idea whether he came home now because of his sister's death, or because he had been planning to attend her wedding next month. She didn't think it was possible for him to get news of Christine's demise and then be home from Africa in just two short weeks. Then again, she really knew nothing about how quickly a single nobleman traveled from one continent to the other when in a hurry.

Another uncomfortable moment passed in silence, save for the clinking of dishes and the movement of servants as they removed the soup bowls and prepared for the fish course. In Mary's opinion, it was altogether telling that the earl didn't attempt to conceal his aggravation at his return, nor his animosity toward his mother, from a complete stranger. She didn't know if she liked that honesty about him or not. Then again, she had no business liking anything about him, she reminded herself. As much as Christine had boasted of her brother, it hardly mattered what she thought of him.

"Tell me, Renn," George piped in at last as he reached for his wine glass, then sat back to observe them all, "what exciting things have you been doing lately? Any new, *profound* discoveries?"

Mary lifted her wine glass as well, chancing a glance at George to see the humor in his eyes that had been lacking of late. At least someone at the table attempted to lighten the somber mood.

Marcus turned his attention back to his food.

"Profound? No. Interesting, yes. The Egyptian government has been relatively helpful to our cause, and of course the history and people are fascinating—"

"For what they are," Gwyneth cut in, delicately slicing her fish.

Marcus swallowed a bite and looked at her. "What they are?"

"Heathens, dear," she finished with a satisfied smile.

"You'll be relieved to know that many are law abiding Christians, Mother, and I have yet to be seduced by the evil side."

Mary felt the urge to giggle, but suppressed it. In all the months she'd been in Cornwall, she'd never heard anyone speak to the Countess of Renn so bluntly and without fear as the lady's oldest son did.

Gwyneth sighed loudly. "Honestly, darling, I still have to wonder what you find so engaging about Africa. You've been traipsing around the desert for four years now, at risk of encountering some nasty disease or worse."

"Worse?" he asked in exaggerated shock, leaning forward. "You mean like barbarians and robbers and despoilers of women?"

His mother eyed him sharply. "I'm certain you've avoided that . . . set thus far—"

"You're right, Mother. The only robbers and barbarians I've encountered have been those who've looted the lovely treasures of the ancients." He took a swallow of his wine. "I've done what I can to stop that, along with Professor Simpson and our team of scholars and researchers, who are as concerned about preservation as I am. I should also mention that we've enjoyed relative success. Since you failed to ask."

Gwyneth ignored that and concentrated on her fish again. "Your life, your duties, are here."

"But my *work* and *interests* are there."

"And you've avoided even discussing the war in the Crimea," she carried on as if she hadn't heard him. "The estate, specifically the mines, could use your attention, now that many of the men are gone to serve."

Marcus closed his eyes briefly. "I've not avoided the issue, Mother. I saw the grisly results aboard ship on my return." He looked up again. "War is nasty and I suppose sometimes necessary, but aside from funding, I can't do anything for the effort right now. George takes care of the property perfectly well, and of course he would remain here regardless of whether I stayed." He turned his attention back to his food. "I am neither a diplomat nor a combatant. You know that. My responsibilities lie elsewhere."

Gwyneth exhaled fast and loudly through her nose. "You've always been too much of an idealist."

"I'm a realist, Mother, and practical. I must continue the work we've started in Egypt."

The ensuing silence weighted the air in the room, though Mary realized this was a family argument minced many times through.

"When are you planning to return?"

It was the first thing Mary had said since sitting at the table, and immediately she realized she shouldn't have tried to intervene pleasantly like that. Suddenly she became the dreaded center of attention. They all stopped eating to stare at her as if she'd made an incredibly gauche comment. Her mouth went dry and she clutched her napkin in her lap, fully facing the earl for the first time, refusing, if nothing else, to cower under such keen discomfiture of her own making.

Gwyneth scoffed. "We'll not discuss it—"

"As soon as I find out the truth behind my sister's death," he said very slowly, looking directly into her eyes.

Someone dropped a fork on the delicate Renn china; Mary's breath caught in her chest as her body went still. For seconds nobody moved, or did or said anything. And then she blinked quickly and turned to Gwyneth, noticing at once how the lady had gone pale, the bones of her face sticking out to create hollow spaces under her cheeks and eyes where the candlelight shone down in its obtrusive brilliance.

George rubbed his palm along his perspiring neck and sat back in his chair. Mary straightened and turned her attention once more to the earl. She had encouraged the mention of Christine, regardless of her intention, and as uncomfortable as she felt right now, she would offer her support.

"I'm very sorry, Lord Renn, for the loss of your sister," she said softly. "She was a lovely lady, and we had grown quite close these last few months. Please accept my condolences."

For a moment nothing happened. And then Marcus nodded once to her, gazing at her with shrewd eyes and wide, hard lips.

George cleared his throat. "Well, I, for one, am glad to have you home, dear brother. You'll have to find time to tell us of some of the treasures you found during your recent adventures."

Gwyneth didn't offer a word, which seemed to surprise them all as they waited for a comment. Then Marcus tapped his mouth with his napkin and stood.

"I'm exhausted, and not particularly hungry."

"Goodness, Renn, you must eat after such a journey," his mother insisted with a true hint of concern. "You need your strength."

For the first time since his arrival, Mary thought she saw a hint of a smile in those deep blue eyes. Then he drew in a long breath, which brought her attention to his wide chest.

"I'll feel more like eating after a good sleep, Mother."

Mary felt his eyes on her, and cheeks hot again, she pulled her gaze up to his face.

"Miss Marsh, I would like a word with you tomorrow morning. Say, around ten?"

She blinked, then said stupidly, "Ten?"

He pursed his lips. "If you're awake."

She couldn't tell if he was scolding or teasing her. She sat up straighter and raised her chin a fraction. "Of course, my lord."

"In my study."

She nodded. Nobody said a word in response, or asked the good question of why he wanted to speak with the hired seamstress, of all people. In that instant it occurred to her that Marcus Longfellow, Earl of Renn, had returned to his home as lord. He was once again, even after an extended absence of his choosing, in complete charge.

He turned back to George. "I could do for a

brandy, but that will have to wait until tomorrow night, brother. I'm frankly just too tired. Until then, enjoy the rest of your meal, and I shall see you all in the morning."

Before anyone could reply, the man marched from the dining room, his heavy boots leaving an eerie echo behind long after he'd gone.

Chapter 2

Baybridge House
12 July 1854

. . . Mother has begun planning for my wedding to Viscount Exeter. She's very excited about the prospect. I am resigned to it. She has hired outside help, including an old family acquaintance, Miss Mary Marsh of London, to assemble my trousseau. Oh, Marcus, I do hope you'll be able to return to see me wed! I should adore walking down the aisle on your arm . . .

Marcus stood at the glass windows in his study, gazing out to the open sea that reached far beyond the cliffs below. The day was gray, cold for May, and the ocean churned and foamed in time to the roaring wind that beat against the house, reminding him constantly of the bitterness outside and the turmoil within.

It was as if he'd never left. Many days during his childhood he'd stood in this spot, staring out to sea, wondering at the world beyond the horizon, dreaming of the time he could leave to explore it. Now, however, his heart was torn between two places, England and Africa, and, where family was concerned, possibly beyond repair.

He shoved his hands in the pockets of his frock coat and closed his eyes to the crashing tides.

His first sight of his family home yesterday had brought back so many memories, many of them good ones he'd forgotten during the years he'd been away. But the minute he'd stepped inside Baybridge House—with its unique smells and sounds and the feeling of disillusionment contained within its walls—the memories took on a freshness that filled him with a new despair, one that would certainly never fade.

Christine was dead. His healthy, cheerful, charming albeit sometimes annoying, baby sister was dead without explanation. He had loved her as the father she had never known, and he would do his duty as earl and brother to discover the truth behind that death, whatever the cost. For Marcus knew, as others seemingly did not, that the events leading up to her final weeks of life were not simply perplexing, but haunting.

God help him. If he had only left Egypt sooner—

A knock at the door jerked him from his disturbing thoughts, and Marcus quickly opened his eyes.

"Come," he bellowed a little too harshly.

The latch clicked; the tall oak door opened, and

in rushed one of his mother's frilly parlor maids, followed by his long-staying houseguest.

"Miss Mary Marsh to see you, Lord Renn."

He nodded curtly at the servant, who immediately took her leave, but his eyes boldly locked with his invited guest's as she moved forward with a swish of purple skirts that accented the paleness of her skin.

Those eyes, sharply attuned to detail, were crystal clear and bluish gray, he noted, fringed with thick, pale lashes, staring into his with only the slightest trace of curiosity.

"Miss Marsh," he said in greeting.

"My lord. You wished to see me?" She halted a foot or so away from his writing desk and stood with shoulders rigid, head angled to the side, hands behind her back.

She had the most intriguing face. Not one that might be called beautiful, but attractive nonetheless, and extremely feminine—fine curves, a touch of pink to the cheeks, full lips, high, blond brows, a small, perfectly straight nose. For a moment he studied her, then he forced himself to look away.

"Yes. Be seated." He turned back to the window and crossed his arms over his chest, listening to her skirts rustling as she did so.

The silence droned for a moment until Marcus gathered his thoughts and proceeded.

"You've been employed by my mother for how long?" he began.

She cleared her throat. "I was hired last summer, but only arrived in early January." She paused, then added, "That's when I began my duties."

That was obvious, and he almost smiled at her nervousness, or at least, at what he thought might be nervousness.

He continued to gaze out the window. "And your duties were?"

He heard a rustle of skirts again but fought the urge to watch her move in her chair.

"I more or less help the lady of a household prepare her daughter's personal items for a fashionable wedding trousseau," she stated.

To Marcus it sounded like a typical glib answer she reserved for those who had to ask but didn't care one way or another *what* she did, especially given the fact that it didn't explain what her duties at Baybridge House had been exactly.

Slowly he turned and looked at her again. The color had risen in her cheeks, and she clutched her interlocked fingers in her lap, though she remained otherwise still, watching him.

"Is that a profession?"

She quickly glanced toward his wall of hanging porcelain plates, then back again. "I have made it mine."

"And it pays well?"

"The pay is adequate for my needs."

Why the devil did he feel as if she summoned answers before he spoke the questions? With an unintended smirk at her clever evasiveness, he asked, "You assemble wedding attire for fashionable ladies, or fashionable attire for any woman who can pay what you charge?"

She blinked, and her lips parted just briefly before she spoke. "I design and correlate the necessary bedding, linens, and wedding garments for elegant *ladies* who can afford my services. I employ two seamstresses who work with me, and on occasion I assist them with the actual sewing as well."

Again, not a terribly specific answer as far as he was concerned. He kept quiet for a second or two, then pushed to clarify. "By 'wedding garments' you mean to suggest you're something of a dressmaker?"

Her lips thinned as annoyance set in. Oddly, that didn't bother him.

"No, not gowns. Ladies' . . . apparel. For *marriage*."

For a split second the answer stupefied him as her meaning dawned. Not that he hadn't seen it coming. Then he felt a warmth creep up his neck, which he ignored. "I see. Intimate . . . underthings?"

"Do you make a habit of asking questions that embarrass your employees?"

That stunned him on two fronts, first that she'd had the gall to say it, and second because it took her words to make him realize that it was he who employed her. He hadn't thought of that. He'd been away too long.

Marcus rubbed his aching eyes, which remained tired after a dreadful night's sleep, then strolled three feet to his desk. He pulled his large green leather chair out and attempted to sit comfortably, which seemed exceptionally difficult for some reason.

"I apologize, Miss Marsh," he said brusquely. "It wasn't my intention to embarrass you. Of course you had your duties, and I'm certain you performed them well."

One of her brows rose as if she questioned that response, but she muttered only a curt, "Thank you."

He quelled the urge to laugh. God, he was on edge, and she sat there primly, trying but failing to conceal both curiosity and annoyance. For some peculiar reason he admired that. Most of the women he'd been around lately were timid and unobtrusive. He'd grown rather bored with the female sex of his recent acquaintance. It was a refreshing change to sit and discuss something practically indecent with a lady who intrigued him.

Leaning forward, elbows on his cleared and polished desk, fingers interlocked in front of him, he decided it was not the time for teasing, but to get to the point.

"You see, Miss Marsh, I'm having some difficulty coming to terms with the death of my sister. I requested your presence here this morning because I would like you to help me discover what exactly happened on the day, and in the weeks, before she died."

He watched her. She frowned minutely, then shook her head.

"I'm sorry, Lord Renn, but I don't understand."

He expected that. Staring at her candidly, he inhaled deeply, and relayed his thoughts, which he knew would shock her.

"I believe," he revealed in a lowered voice, "that there was more to Christine's death than simply slipping and hitting her head on her dressing table as she fell. She was not a clumsy girl. Beyond that, I have information that suggests she was very deeply troubled by something in the weeks before she succumbed to her fate. I would like you to help me discover what it was."

The wind howled against the shutters, whistling through the windows at an eerie pitch. Mary Marsh didn't move a muscle, remaining nearly expressionless. But in her fascinating eyes he witnessed a flicker of . . . something. Marcus couldn't put his finger on it, but he suspected suddenly that she understood exactly what he was talking about.

"I'm not sure I can help you," she murmured after a long moment's hesitation. "I can relate what I know, my whereabouts on that day, and what I told the officials at the inquiry. But I don't think there's anything more of significance I can offer you."

Aside from the obvious. For the first time he truly wished Miss Marsh was old or ugly. It would make the weeks to come so much easier.

However, the fact that she didn't denounce his thoughts as nonsense was telling. Then again, social graces forbade such uncouth comments from someone of her position.

Marcus sat back in his chair as he continued to study her. A wispy curl had escaped her hairnet and floated down over her ear—a delicate ear free of jewelry. But she wore elegant, somewhat expensive clothing, spoke well for a common worker, and he realized at that moment that although Christine had gone into detail regarding appearance and disposition, both of which spoke positively toward the woman, he knew nothing of the depth of her cleverness. He did know for a fact, however, that Christine had trusted Mary Marsh, and regardless of his own ridiculous attraction to her, he needed her help.

"Miss Marsh," he said, tapping his fingertips on his desktop, "I understand your hesitancy, and that you would no doubt like to return home to London in light of recent events. If that is your choice, I'm in no position to stop you from leaving. But here is my problem." He lifted an ivory letter opener, twisting it with his fingers while his brows drew together in thought. "Toward the end, Christine's frequent correspondence with me grew increasingly strange. Her most recent letters were riddled with varying tones of despair, helplessness, frustration, and even a certain fear. That was unlike her. I've never known Christine to be afraid of anything."

That was a bit of an exaggeration, but he wanted to stress the point. It made Mary pause, too, as she glanced down at her hands.

"Did you?" he pressed in near whisper.

After a moment she shook her head. "No, though I did sense . . . I don't know, perhaps an irritation with me and certain members of her acquaintance the week before her accident, as if she were nervous, unsettled about something, and it distressed her." She looked up, directly into his eyes. "I simply assumed it had to do with her impending marriage to the Viscount Exeter, as any bride might react when her wedding date approaches."

He noted she used that word. *Accident.* He brushed over it for now, and leaned forward in his chair once more, deciding to change his tactic.

"Tell me of her mood that week."

If she noticed his altered approach to their conversation, she didn't show it. She merely lifted her delicate shoulders in a slight shrug before she spoke.

"As I said, she seemed . . . agitated, and somewhat pensive, at least around me. Frankly, Lord Renn, my relationship with Lady Christine was one of servant to employer. We were on friendly terms, yes, but she didn't confide anything that made me apprehensive of her safety, or think something in her daily life was amiss."

The perfect answer. And completely devoid of real information. He didn't know that by her words or manner of expression. He felt her evasiveness instinctively.

"So," he continued formally, "explain to me what occurred that day, if you please."

She inhaled matter-of-factly, as if preparing to tell him everything she'd already related to the authorities. It mattered none to Marcus that she obviously expected such a standard inquiry from him as well.

"Her morning began as usual at nine, I believe, with her receiving breakfast in bed. I saw her for the first time that day at eleven, and we were together for about two hours when we broke for luncheon. The next time I saw her was at approximately four, just before tea, when I . . . when I found her."

"I see."

An uncomfortable moment passed; Mary shifted her body unnecessarily in her chair.

"And why were you together?" he pressed. "What was her general mood?"

"She and I had a fitting, for which she tried on several garments. As for her mood . . ." She shook her head once, frowning. "She'd actually been rather talkative, though I assumed it to be nervous talk—"

"About what?"

Her brows rose just faintly. "I beg your pardon?"

"What did you discuss?"

"Oh. Just the usual things ladies discuss."

He reigned in his annoyance. "And that was?"

Her eyes narrowed very slightly. "If I remember precisely, Lord Renn, we discussed marriage and staying attractive for the benefit of one's husband." She gazed at him blankly again. "I'm sure you understand."

Of course he didn't, but he didn't want to touch that comment. "And yet you've never been married?"

He spoke the words without the slightest clue why, and after they were out, the sudden flush in her cheeks told him he shouldn't have been so intrusive. But he was curious about her personally, for reasons unclear to him.

She straightened; her lips thinned flatly. "No, but that is irrelevant."

He leaned farther back in his chair, which creaked against his weight, eyeing her speculatively. "But what you said to Christine, or more exactly, what she might have said to you on the day she died, could be important as I delve into the situation leading up to that death."

She studied him for a moment, almost blatantly, making him somewhat uncomfortable, even hot beneath his collar. But he didn't budge.

"I don't see how a conversation between ladies about the fact that gentlemen seldom remain passionate after the wedding vows are spoken could be in any way pertinent." She paused, then with emphasis added, "My lord."

Her abrasiveness troubled him. The pull of her eyes stirred him. And her boldness and unusual statement ushered in a charged feeling of frustration mixed with anger. It was true that like most men he didn't understand women very well, but he wanted to understand this one, if only for the short time she'd be remaining at Baybridge House. What the devil ladies discussed in private, he couldn't begin to care, but something had changed in his sister during the last few months, and he wanted answers.

"Miss Marsh," he replied at length, "I'm not trying to pry into delicate issues or conversations, or your private affairs, or even those of my sister. Your business is your own. But it might help matters and make this easier if you work *with* me instead of against me."

That seemed to confound her as her features went slack with surprise. Then, after a moment of silent awareness of the tension between them, the chilly air surrounding them, she slumped a little in her chair and backed down. It was the first indication to Marcus that the woman actually seemed troubled by recent events.

"I apologize, Lord Renn," she said quietly. "I'll start at the beginning, if it would help."

God, if only *all* women would cooperate with so little persuasion. "Please," he urged simply, not wanting to coax too hard.

She stared at her hands for a moment or two, fidgeting with them, uncertainty creasing her brow. Then she unexpectedly stood and turned, walking to the west wall to study the hanging plates.

Marcus continued to watch her, taking note of her profile, the fine angle of her jaw, her tapered neck and firm, shapely bosom, wondering for a second if her breasts were as full as they appeared or uplifted by a corset of her making—

"I think she'd grown to detest Viscount Exeter," she disclosed, her tone hesitant, "and was afraid of mentioning it to Lady Renn, to anyone."

That jerked his thoughts back to where they belonged as Marcus went cold inside. Slowly he leaned forward in his chair. "Explain that."

Mary hugged herself, grasping her upper arms with her palms, still staring at the decorative china. "I can't exactly. It's more of a feeling I had. I . . . sensed that whatever their relationship had been in the early days of their betrothal, it had changed."

"What did she say exactly?" he asked.

Mary drew a deep breath and shook her head. "It's not what she said, Lord Renn, but what she didn't say."

Marcus wanted to grind his teeth. Instead he rubbed his forehead harshly with his palm. "Miss Marsh—"

"I know, I'm being evasive and unclear."

He blinked as his hand fell to the desktop, unsure how to reply to that honest and accurate confession.

She turned to him and dropped her arms, smiling vaguely. "Please remember, Lord Renn, that your sister Christine and I were not friends in the truest sense, not equals, but we were women in spirit. I've worked with many ladies through the years and I've seen brides-to-be blush and shiver and glow with excitement at the prospect of marrying. I've also seen apprehension, nervousness, some even angry or resigned to the choice of husband made for them." She slowly began to walk toward him again, head lowered in thought. "But your sister acted differently, in a manner I can't exactly describe. She seldom talked of the viscount, to me or anyone, as far as I know, and when she did, her words were tinged with . . . something. I don't know. Resentment, maybe? A kind of fear? Disgust? It's just something I can't explain."

Marcus leaned back in his chair once more, stiffly. Of all the things he'd imagined might have troubled Christine these last few weeks, his thoughts hadn't once strayed to her betrothal to Baudwin Fife. The Viscount Exeter had been the natural choice for her to wed for years, and everybody knew it, including Christine. Exeter's land bordered theirs, and his family had been involved with the mines for generations, just as the earl's family had. In every logical respect, the match had been ideal. Baudwin was twenty-five or so, titled, intelligent, and Christine had always liked him. Marcus had liked him as well whenever he'd seen him. A marriage between the families would put a sure holding on the china mines in all of St. Austell. Everyone involved knew that, including his sister.

"Did Christine ever confide in you about her feelings?" he asked, throat tight.

Mary shook her head and interlocked her fingers in front of her. "No, not really." She briefly pressed her lips together, then added, "But the change in her appeared to be rather sudden, my lord. When I first arrived, she acted as any lady might toward her upcoming marriage. She attended parties with the viscount as his betrothed, held teas with your mother, laughed and seemed genuinely ready for the change in her life. A bit nervous, perhaps, but that's to be expected. Weeks later the laughter died in her, though she never said why."

And then she died.

Marcus swallowed and dropped his gaze to the polished black walnut beneath his arms, his body hard and immobile, his mind rushing with confusion, irritation, a surging of helplessness. But he refused to allow himself to break down and show his private emotions to anyone, especially a woman, and one he didn't even know.

Instead, he inhaled a solid breath, reached into his top desk drawer, and removed one of the letters his sister had sent him. Holding it in front of him, he stared at the expressive feminine handwriting that was Christine's, feeling her presence, as if to hold something of hers made her tangible again. In a moment's decision, he chose not to hand it to Mary to read. It was simply too personal, still too painful.

"My sister sent this letter to me shortly before she died, Miss Marsh. In it, she writes that she is afraid—*afraid*—for her future. She also says plainly that you are the only one she can trust, but that you will soon be leaving." He looked up. "And then she begged me to come home."

His voice sounded hollow to him as it seemingly echoed off the wooden walls that surrounded them.

Mary said nothing in reply, though the air between them seemed to crackle with a low-burning energy, and suddenly he could no longer remain sitting. Standing abruptly, he pivoted away from her and walked back to the window, staring at without seeing the crashing gray waves below, his hands clasped behind him, shoulders rigid.

"This is the problem," he asserted gravely. "By every account, my sister was deeply troubled weeks before she died under very strange circumstances, and yet you and I are the only ones who noticed it, though I have yet to speak with Exeter. Perhaps he did, too. My mother and brother were apparently oblivious." He clenched his jaw as he dropped his voice, but he never glanced away from the far-reaching ocean. "I don't care if her death was ruled an accident; I want to find out *why* it happened. I need your help to do that, Miss Marsh."

Mary stared at the man, her body going absolutely still after such a passionate revelation that seemed to bring Christine back to life. She couldn't speak for the moment if she wanted to. The Earl of Renn radiated a harsh power, and yet he didn't act overly authoritative or cruel, and she sensed a deep compassion in him, something she didn't often relate to men of his stature. And then, fairly knocking the breath from her, she understood his conviction with profound clarity.

"You didn't leave Cairo because of her upcoming wedding, or her death," she said with soft intensity. "You left to come and help her."

He didn't turn around, but she knew instinctively that her words had struck him deeply. Moments later, he gruffly acknowledged, "Upon docking in Plymouth, I learned I was too late."

A sense of horror washed over her—at what he must feel, the anger, the rage at being unable to help his sister that had to be burning within him. He had missed Christine by a mere two weeks. The news had to have devastated him.

"I'm so very sorry," she whispered.

The wind roared beyond the brick walls of Baybridge House; a shutter banged, and still he didn't move from the window.

Awkwardly, Mary stood where she was, facing his desk, unsure where to go, not wanting to leave his presence, though anxiously needing to retreat to the privacy of her bed chamber. She gazed again at the plates hanging on the wall—at least two dozen of the finest Renn china, in every color and style imaginable, displayed for their beauty in this dark, cold room. She shivered.

"Christine was my responsibility, and she depended on me," he disclosed at last, his resonant voice slicing the air. "She was the youngest, the delight of our family, and I cared deeply for her. I owe it to her memory to discover, if nothing else, what she'd learned that was so frightening she couldn't risk telling me in a private letter. Perhaps it had nothing whatever to do with her death, but that's what I need to find out. Because she trusted only you, I'm asking you to stay in Cornwall as my guest and help me, Miss Marsh."

She didn't want to help him. She didn't need to be here any longer, and everything inside her warned against her remaining at Baybridge House, shoulder to shoulder with the Longfellows, beside the earl's commanding bearing day after day.

But her refusal didn't come. She couldn't voice her desires because beneath it all, this surprising proposition by the Earl of Renn provided her with the much-needed reason to prolong her stay. This sudden opportunity wouldn't be her preferred reason for lingering in the country a little while longer, far from it, but it was the only one she had at the moment. In the end, selfishly, she had to work through her personal doubts and concerns, coming to terms with them before she once again faced her own family. This gave her more time, and she needed it.

For the first time in minutes, the earl turned and faced her, standing tall and stately, his vivid, revealing eyes penetrating hers. Mary felt the strain and unease emanating from him, his hard, masculine features controlled now as he waited for her to speak. In that instant, she felt something else between them that she couldn't explain or begin to put into words. Friendship? Common longing? But as uncomfortable as it was, it was there, drawing her in, forcing her to accept the inevitable.

"I'm not sure I can do anything—"

"Please."

She needed no more convincing.

"I think I would start by speaking with the vicar," she murmured through a sigh. "Your sister met with him several times in her final days."

He said nothing for a moment, just held her gaze with a fierceness that made her grow warm.

"We'll do so together, Miss Marsh," he replied with a brief nod. "I'll arrange it."

She wrapped her arms around her waist. "Is there anything else?"

His eyes narrowed. "How long can you stay?"

For some reason his question seemed remarkably intimate, though she attempted to shrug off such an absurd notion. "I'll stay as long as you think I'm needed. It shouldn't be unseemly since my late mother and yours were longtime friends and I wasn't expected back in London until July at the earliest."

His eyes opened just wide enough for her to realize he'd never thought of the propriety of her staying. But he didn't comment on it.

"Thank you," was his rather curt reply.

The awkwardness had returned and she didn't know how to respond.

"I shall speak with Lady Renn," he added. "I'm sure she'll be happy to have you remain at Baybridge House."

It was a dismissal, and she was glad for it.

"Very well, my lord."

He stood watching her, his hands still behind his back, a sudden, curious frown crossing his dark brows. And then it vanished.

"Please let me know if you think of anything else of importance, Miss Marsh."

"I will."

"Good day, then."

She curtsied slightly. "Good day, Lord Renn."

Then she turned away from him and gracefully walked to the study door, all the while feeling his eyes on her back as she tried to ignore the foreboding deep within.

Chapter 3

⌒◯◯⌒

Baybridge House
28 July 1854

> *. . . I've been feeling tired of late. I know you think
> I spend far too much effort on trivialities, but hon-
> estly, dear brother, I've been so busy! My wedding
> is still nearly a year away and already tensions are
> rising between Viscount Exeter and Mother.
> Baudwin wants one thing, Mother wants another.
> Sometimes I feel nobody ever listens to me . . .*

Baudwin Fife, Viscount Exeter dismissed his
valet, then stared at his figure in the full
length mirror beside his wardrobe. He wasn't a tall
man, but his muscled chest and arms made up for
his lack of height. Truthfully it didn't matter much
to him. He was handsome and knew it, and so did
the ladies, who tended to be shorter than he was

anyway. He'd never had trouble appealing to women and hoped it wouldn't stop now. And it shouldn't. That his betrothed had recently died made matters complicated, to say the least, but after an official period of mourning, he would find someone else. People died, life went on, and he needed a wife to bear him an heir who would carry on his good name. He was nearly twenty-six, and ready to marry. It's what his parents would have wanted, and certainly what they'd expected of him.

He missed Christine, though, and it was true her death had shocked him. She'd been so vibrant and healthy. It was hard to believe she'd died like that, so suddenly, the result of such a very bizarre and ill-timed accident. But then he'd noticed over the course of her final few days how strange and erratic her behavior had become. Naturally she chose not to discuss her concerns with him, which had probably been for the best, since he wouldn't have understood her female problems anyway.

Baudwin exhaled a long breath and reached for the freshly poured glass of his favorite expensive whiskey that sat on his dressing table, taking a long, full swallow of the strong, aromatic liquid. He was due at the Vicar Coswell's home in less than thirty minutes for dinner with the man and his wife, and he wouldn't be late. He was never late. The people of St. Austell relied on the local gentry to set the standard, and he despised untimeliness.

Unbeknownst to the vicar, this wasn't a simple dinner on Baudwin's part. He'd planned it and had invited himself when he'd first heard that the Earl of Renn had returned to Cornwall. If he considered it honestly, that news had been more of a shock

than Christine's death. He'd never expected to see
Renn again, really, even at the long-planned wedding between their families. He knew the earl's
feelings of resistance regarding his title and its responsibilities, his desire for riches—or whatever it
was that lured him to the wilds of Africa—and
Baudwin had expected these things to keep him
away for good. It hardly mattered anyway, as Exeter land was nearly as extensive as that belonging
to Renn, especially with the betrothal agreement,
which would undoubtedly remain intact. In many
ways, he and the earl were very nearly on equal
terms, now with that signing, and Renn would
never go back on his word. Not when they both
benefitted.

The saddest, most maddening part of all was
knowing that a marriage to the man's sister would
have ensured the survival of the Fife good name,
making him one of the most powerful landholders
in all of Cornwall. Now that such a marriage was
not to be, Baudwin needed to rethink his options.
His next choice for a wife would have to be well
considered, and it would no doubt be difficult to
come by a lady as perfect for the position as Christine Longfellow.

But the truly unfortunate aspect was that he
would once again have to face the only person
within three hundred miles who had ever really in-
timidated him. Baudwin hated that feeling, but
there was no escaping it. He'd always been a bit
uneasy around Renn, had actually been relieved
when the earl's selfishness had drawn him away
from England and his family years ago. Now it
would be difficult to avoid the man and the numer-

ous questions that would certainly follow. He would have to prepare.

With a final glance at his person—he wore formal black mourning attire— Baudwin tossed back the rest of his whiskey and smoothed his thick auburn mustache with his fingertips before turning and striding to the door of his bed chamber with confidence. As uncomfortable as the night would be, Vicar Coswell had known Christine's thoughts and feelings before her death, even if he, as her betrothed, had not, and just to be safe and ready for what might come his way, Baudwin wanted to discuss what he could with Coswell before the earl did. It wasn't a matter of suspicion on his part, but a matter of caution. And he had always been a cautious man.

Still, he had time for another drink to soothe his anxiousness before he left.

Chapter 4

Baybridge House
10 August 1854

*. . . I've got a terrible cold. What a bother! Mother
fears pneumonia, naturally, and I refuse to argue
with her. The dreary weather only makes matters
worse. But Exeter and I did manage to meet with
Vicar Coswell regarding our wedding next spring.
So much to do! Honestly, dear brother, I'll be glad
when the day arrives and I can finally call him my
husband . . .*

Marcus lowered his body heavily into a
winged chair of peach brocade in the small,
modestly decorated parlor occupied by Vicar Niles
Coswell and Claudette, the man's wife of thirty
years. He'd known the two of them since childhood, as they'd always been considered family

friends, and if today's welcome was any indication, they were delighted at his return. They were an affable couple, both plump, with graying hair and fair skin, still fond of one another, which his naturally cynical mind found rather amazing, and both distinctly clever. They'd apparently become acquainted with Mary Marsh during her extended stay in Cornwall, as the three of them exchanged pleasantries without much of an introduction on his part.

With their arrival for afternoon tea today, Marcus had immediately explained that he'd asked Miss Marsh to assist him in determining what his sister might have done and said in the weeks and days before her death. She was also the last person to see Christine before her fatal fall, and seemed to have known her best these past few months.

But as much as he wanted to keep his focus on the vicar and his wife and what they might know about his sister's last days of life, he felt exceptionally aware of Miss Marsh's presence at his side, in a matching chair, wearing a conservative gown with plum satin skirts that she'd attempted but failed to keep from resting against his legs. She sat so close, in fact, that their shoulders nearly touched, and he tried not to think about the enticing shape of her lovely breasts, or her exposed neck, both within arm's reach. For her part, she sat rigidly, hands folded in her lap, her cool, serene beauty and elegance possessing his concentration even when she said nothing whatever to him. He found that annoying as hell.

They'd traveled together the short distance to

town inside his private coach, but only because it had been raining steadily all day. He would rather have walked, even through a downpour, but without asking, assumed that she'd prefer his necessary closeness to the chilly outdoor damp and a chance that she'd stain her gown with mud. They hadn't spoken much during the ride, and he supposed he'd been a bit relieved that she hadn't wanted to talk since he didn't know what to say to her anyway. Women usually flustered him unless they were discussing the weather or some other such banal topic. She hadn't even bothered to address that as she'd stared out the small window for most of the ride. But he had watched her openly, studying her, wondering at her coolness.

He liked watching her, he finally admitted. Something about her intrigued him, though he'd be damned if he knew what it was, exactly. At a purely common level she had beautiful eyes and a simply gorgeous figure, or so he envisioned from what he could see of it wrapped up in a river of fabric. Now, sitting in the home of Vicar Coswell, so close to her, he felt almost uncomfortable in her company. She carried herself with so much grace and distinction, she more or less left him confounded. What he couldn't decide was if he felt that way because it had been so long since he'd been in close proximity to refined English ladies, or if it was simply because she took no apparent notice of him.

Marcus fidgeted in his chair, which was already too small for his frame, annoyed with himself for thinking of *anyone* intimately. He had no business

doing so right now, and certainly not of Mary
Marsh, the woman to last see his beloved sister
alive, and the one person he'd asked for help.

Bastard. Where the bloody hell is your mind?

With strong effort, he tried to concentrate on the
superfluous chatter between the ladies as the tea
was brought in and light conversation began. He'd
missed the first few remarks while lost in his
thoughts, but assumed that wouldn't matter.

"My, but it's been a busy week," Claudette remarked, seated next to her husband on a worn settee embroidered with large peach roses and green
leaves that matched the window dressings and
fringed lamps. She reached toward the oak tea
table and lifted the china pot, delicately inlaid with
gold leaves—likely manufactured from fine Renn
clay—and began to pour the steaming hot liquid
into four matching cups. "On Monday we entertained the Misses Grassley, such lovely women,
and then Wednesday, Viscount Exeter paid us an
unexpected visit." She shook her head and smiled.
"I don't think poor Niles and I have done quite so
much steady entertaining in recent years, though
we do enjoy it. Don't we, dear?"

"Oh, yes," the vicar agreed, amusement shading
his aging mouth.

"But of course this isn't entertaining, Lord
Renn," she added, returning the teapot to the tray
and lifting the creamer. "We were all so pleased to
hear of your return, even under such dreadful circumstances. We, too, were deeply mortified by
your sister's accident, and know how you must be
looking for answers. I'm so very sorry this grief has
come to your family."

"Thank you," he said forthrightly, tipping his head graciously.

"How is your mother faring?" Claudette continued, offering cream to her guests. "We haven't seen her since the funeral."

"She's doing as well as can be expected," was his standard reply.

"No doubt your return has helped her through this terrible time," she added.

He felt his shoulders tighten involuntarily. "She is quite relieved to have me back at Baybridge House, yes."

A moment of silence passed among them even as the rain began to strengthen to a steady pounding on the windows and roof. The parlor had grown stuffy and warm as well with the added moisture in the air, and out of the corner of his eye, he noticed Mary shift her weight in her chair.

"We are all still in shock," the vicar said at last, shaking his head as he stared at the creamy white tea in his cup. "Especially poor Viscount Exeter."

Marcus sucked in a breath as Mary placed her spoon on her saucer with a noticeable *clink*. This brought their reason for calling front and center, making it the perfect time to address it. But before he could gather the appropriate words, Mary began the queries for him.

"And is the viscount well?" she asked, lifting her cup from its saucer. "You said you saw him this week?"

They all took a sip at once—except for him. His concentration was simply too acute, too focused. But of course he would have to play his part and at least appear relaxed. Sighing inwardly, he raised his cup to his lips and took a swallow of surprisingly good Ceylon.

"The viscount is of course in poor spirits," Claudette returned after a moment, her thick gray brows furrowed. "And he seemed especially tense, I thought, but that too is to be expected after losing one's betrothed so tragically."

"Of course," Mary acknowledged as she should, lowering her teacup.

"He cared for Christine very deeply," their hostess added.

"As I'm sure she cared for him," Mary quickly added. "She spoke of him fondly."

"And frequently," the vicar echoed without looking at any of them.

The energy in the room seemed to intensify as they all quietly sipped the hot, strong brew. Then Claudette began to take great interest in passing out small china plates of cucumber sandwiches and ginger cakes.

"He was rather surprised at your return, Lord Renn," she carried on with a casual air. "He wanted to know if we'd had a chance to speak with you yet."

Marcus tried not to speculate too much about that. "Did he," he stated rather than asked.

The vicar nodded very slowly, concern etched upon his creased white brows, a gentle frown upon his lips. "I'm sure he wants to meet with you shortly to discuss . . . arrangements."

"And he'll get that chance, naturally," Marcus replied, accepting his plate of tidbits. "I'm anxious to speak with him, as well. It's been a long time since I've seen Exeter."

"The viscount said much the same on Wednesday," the vicar acknowledged after swallowing the rest of a cucumber sandwich. "Seems unfortunate, since yours have always been such close families."

Another moment passed while he took a bite of very good ginger cake. As awkward and solemn as the occasion was, he was hungry. But then he was always hungry. So was Miss Marsh, apparently, as she quickly finished off her cucumber sandwich and began on her cake. He rather liked the fact that she ate more than she played with her food, and had an appetite that nearly matched his.

Suddenly, for the first time since they'd arrived, Mary seemed to sense his presence beside her, that he was particularly aware of her and her actions. She paused in her movements and tossed him a glance, which he acknowledged with the faintest binding awareness. For merely a second their eyes locked and held—and then she blinked and quickly looked away again.

"That was delicious, Mrs. Coswell," she commended appropriately, her voice remarkably controlled as she placed what remained of her ginger cake on the tea table.

Claudette smiled as required. "I'm so glad you enjoyed it. Another sandwich, Lord Renn?"

"Thank you," he replied, reaching for what would be his third helping. He instinctively knew Mary watched him lean forward, felt her gaze on his back as his muscles flexed beneath his jacket. He took his time with the effort, enjoying the thought of possessing her total captivation.

"Mrs. Coswell," Mary said after clearing her throat, returning to the reason for their visit, "I know Miss Longfellow visited here the week before her accident, and I was wondering—without getting too personal, of course—if she seemed upset to you."

Claudette's brows drew together in frown. "Well, naturally—"

She stopped abruptly, as if unsure of her words, then tossed a swift, almost imperceptible peek toward her husband before continuing.

"Naturally," she started again, thinking carefully this time, setting her tea on the table and folding her hands in her lap, "I think Christine was nervous about her upcoming marriage, though I have no idea if it was truly a concern for her. She seemed unusually hesitant, but then, many brides are hesitant."

Marcus felt his gut tighten with annoyance. That vague explanation contained no real information whatsoever.

"Of course she had to be," Mary agreed, smiling matter-of-factly as if she'd expected such a response. "It's one of my duties, I suppose, to help settle the minds of ladies like Miss Longfellow as I prepare their trousseaus. More often than not, brides-to-be are very nervous." She took another sip of tea, then shook her head. "I only wonder because Miss Longfellow seemed to . . . change before our eyes only weeks before the event was to take place, as if something specific suddenly worried her. I simply thought that perhaps she'd shared her concerns with one of you."

The vicar sucked in a deep breath and pulled down on his cuffs, tilting his chin for emphasis. "I cannot in good conscience, reveal anything she might have told me in my professional capacity, you understand."

Mary nodded once. "Oh, certainly—"

"And yet my sister is dead, Niles."

They all looked at him sharply. Then a measured coldness enveloped the room, followed by—for the first time—the eerie suggestiveness of foul play. It was a feeling Marcus understood, knew would be forthcoming as they moved toward the truth, and despised.

The vicar blinked. "You aren't suggesting her death was somehow related to her upcoming marriage," he blurted, quite aghast. "There was a full inquiry, Renn, I assure you, and the authorities found nothing suspicious."

Marcus shifted his weight in the chair, the armrests digging into his elbows as he placed his now empty plate on the tea tray. "All I know, Niles, is that something upset her in the weeks before she died. I also know she visited you more frequently than she ever had in the past." He leaned forward, lowering his voice to a thoughtful, dark tone. "I appreciate your discretion, but I don't think that hoping to prevent bruised feelings and Christine's privacy really matter now. I am the only father figure she had, regardless of where I lived, and I would appreciate it very much if you would tell me what you know."

The stifling air became oppressive. For a long, discomfiting moment, nobody spoke as hard rain pelted the glass windows, and the parlor darkened in late afternoon shadows. Finally the vicar slumped his shoulders wearily, his face fell, and he lowered his gaze to the faded peach carpeting.

"You are right, of course," he said sedately. "You sister has moved on to Glory, and all that remains now are our memories, and her good name." He shook his head minutely. "But I cannot help you, as a man of the cloth or a longtime family friend, even if I wanted to. Christine said nothing to me of any real importance for months—"

"Except three days before she died," Claudette interrupted, voice shaky and low. "The last time she came here to visit with me."

The house creaked from rain-soaked timbers; breathing seemed to stop.

"She was . . . upset," the vicar's wife continued, "extremely disturbed about something." Claudette closed her eyes briefly, then opened them to gaze directly at him. "But all she said, Lord Renn, was that she was frightened of her future. Those were her exact words. I asked, but she did not elaborate on what it was that troubled her so. If she had, I would tell you."

Marcus could feel his frustration mount as his fists clenched of their own accord, his blood pounded in his temples. This was more of the same, not new information that would help him determine what had frightened his sister. She had said as much of nothing to him in her last letters. She'd said nothing *substantial* to anyone, it appeared. God, they were getting nowhere.

Then suddenly he caught a very slight, guarded glimpse between Claudette and Mary—meant only for the two women to see. A spark of acknowledgment that spoke of . . . what? Shared fears? Silent secrets? He didn't know.

Yet that slip of a glance told him much. They either assumed something he didn't, or Christine *hadn't* taken her secrets to her grave after all, but had revealed at least some part of her inner apprehension to one of them. Or both. But did Christine talk to them as confidantes? As friends, or just as women? The crushing weight of uncertainty and futility threatened to unleash his deep-felt anger. And regret.

"Did you tell any of this to the magistrate?" he asked pointedly to both of the Coswells, his tone expressing only a tinge of exasperation.

"Yes, of course," Claudette answered at once. "But again, we all thought her worries were related to her upcoming wedding. Nothing more."

There was more. Much, much more. As determined as he felt to discover it today, however, Marcus knew he wouldn't. But he would not let these unanswered questions rest. He would endeavor to learn the truth, and no matter how long it took, he would discover what had frightened his sister so terribly until the very day she died.

Drawing a deep breath, he yielded at last. "I thank you both, then, for speaking to us candidly."

"You are welcome any time," the vicar said, waiting for him to stand with his subtle hint of their impending departure. When he did, so did Coswell, adding, "As are you, Miss Marsh. It has been a pleasure to see you again."

Mary, who had remained silently watching the last exchange, stood lastly with grace, nodded once, and held out her hand for the vicar to grasp. "Thank you for a lovely tea, Vicar. Mrs. Coswell."

With another short discussion of the nasty weather, and murmurs of promised returns, the two of them stepped out into the damp, gloomy late afternoon.

She'd hoped to return to Baybridge House before darkness fell. That wasn't possible, however, since the rumbling thunderstorm had already blackened the sky.

The earl sat across from her, watching her speculatively, though he tried to conceal his interest beneath half-closed lids as he relaxed in his seat, his hands clasped across his stomach. Mary had been intensely aware of him all day, from the first moment they stepped into the coach this afternoon, through tea, and even now, though she tried her very best to hide her uneasiness with his close proximity. Gentlemen of all natures and passions made her nervous, and this one did especially, however unclear she was of the reason. He had the most marvelous build, and carried himself so . . . flawlessly. Marcus Longfellow, Earl of Renn, demanded attention. Even now, as she tried her best to avoid him, and conversation, she felt her palms moisten and her stomach muscles tighten with apprehension, from repressed anxiety, she supposed. And secrets tucked deep within that she never intended to reveal.

"What did you make of all that?"

She fairly jumped in her seat from even that soft intrusion. "I beg your pardon?"

He gazed at her frankly, though she couldn't be sure of his mood in the growing darkness.

"Were you satisfied?"

Her cheeks flushed hotly. "Satisfied?"

He exhaled sharply through his nostrils. "Miss

Marsh, do you so often repeat questions asked of you without offering explanation?"

Undaunted, she straightened on the cushioned seat. "Apparently so, Lord Renn."

Silence reigned. Then he chuckled and rubbed his eyes. It was a soft, deep chuckle, and she likened it instantly to someone gradually and deliberately dragging a feather down her naked spine. It made her tingle in all the most improper places and she forced her thighs together beneath layers of binding petticoats and skirts. This should not be happening. Not now.

"Lord Renn," she replied sternly, trying to gulp down her insecurities.

"You are quite a contradiction, aren't you?" he said thoughtfully, cutting into her forthcoming admonition.

"Meaning what, may I ask?" Then she realized she shouldn't have asked at all. She didn't want to know what he thought of her. Not really.

The coach hit a rut in the road and they both jerked against the sidewall, though his gaze remained focused on her.

"For all your coolness," he explained in a husky, speculative tone, "all your aloofness, your serene loveliness and quiet charm that you exhibit on the outside, I know there must be a rather warm and scintillating personality within."

Stunned, Mary sat tightly, fingers digging into her palms, wanting to look away, to escape the stuffy confines that secluded them from the outside world, but unable to do so. In a manner, he'd captivated her.

"I know this, you see," he finished in near whisper, never moving his gaze from hers, "because Christine spoke so well of you, mentioned your humor, your cleverness and warm friendship." He cocked his head to regard her even in the near blackness. "I'll bet the two of you shared frivolous stories and enticing secrets about love and romance as ladies often do. Knowing Christine, she probably even revealed a few of my own in that regard."

His voice hypnotized her, or maybe it was merely his masculine dominance so close to her feminine form. She felt like jumping out of her skin.

Your serene loveliness . . .

"I'm sure you know much about ladies and their topics of discussion in private conversation," she stated crisply, sounding, even to her ears, utterly defensive.

He chuckled again and she visibly shivered.

"Did she say you'd like me?" he asked slyly.

Her stomach flipped over. "Like you? In what manner?"

She shouldn't have asked that, for he laughed again, annoying her.

"As a person, a man," he replied after a moment, watching her closely.

She looked out the window to the dark night sky. "I'm sure you're a very intelligent, congenial gentleman, Lord Renn."

He said nothing to that for a moment, then murmured, "So she did tell you about me."

Mary swallowed, trying to breathe normally. "That's not exactly what I said."

"No, but you certainly implied it. And I knew my sister. She could talk about nothing whatsoever for thirty hours straight if she didn't need to sleep."

Mary shot him a quick glance, and although he remained in shadow, she could positively *hear* him grinning. He teased her with every word, and even in her nervousness, she had to admit she found it thoroughly enchanting. She hadn't been teased by a man in years.

With an upward twist of her lips, she remarked in turn, "She seemed to think you were nearly perfect in everything you do." Sighing heavily for emphasis, she added, "Naturally, I find that difficult to believe."

He tapped his palm on his cushioned seat as if contemplating her words.

Then he shrugged. "No, she was right. I'm very nearly perfect."

Mary almost laughed, pressing her lips together to keep from doing so. How odd, that the sullen Earl of Renn should also be witty and amusing. It was a side of his personality, she believed, that very few people saw. Christine had, and she had described him that way. Mary decided she wouldn't mention that to him, however. Let him wonder. She enjoyed his quizzical mood.

"How modest you are, Lord Renn."

He leaned back and closed his eyes. "Another of my charming attributes."

She huffed, but she noticed he still smiled.

For minutes they traveled in silence, until at last he shifted his head for a quick look out the window.

"We're almost at the house. Better to sleep on what we learned from the Coswells and perhaps discuss it tomorrow."

Indeed, she'd learned plenty at tea; plenty that she didn't ever want to discuss with Christine's brother. Still, she felt thankful at his suggestion of delay and refrained from arguing. She'd be better focused tomorrow, and not centered on her determination to get away from the alluring man who sat so close to her in a musty, dark coach that traveled slowly along a deserted cliff.

Suddenly the earl stretched out one of his long legs, and his shoe tapped against her ankle under her gown.

Mary flinched and drew back so forcefully that she bumped her knee on the coach door. Pain flared, but she held steady, unwilling to let him know the level of her distraction.

He opened his eyes once more. Surprise lingered as his mouth turned down in frown.

Mary looked away, desperately hoping he didn't witness the uneasiness welling up inside of her.

A moment later, as they stopped in front of Baybridge House, Mary practically tore herself from his presence and escaped to the safety of her room without another word between them.

Chapter 5

Baybridge House
17 August 1854

. . . I've been corresponding with Miss Marsh, the lady who will be organizing my trousseau. Did I mention her in a previous letter? I cannot now remember. She seems courteous enough, and certainly experienced with her work. Yet I can't help feeling that she is being evasive about herself. I know you would tell me not to be so inquisitive, as I am equally certain you are laughing at the thought, Marcus. I just had hoped that she would reveal more of her personality in her letters to me. I can't help but wonder if she's being deliberately vague . . .

Like an adolescent youth, he couldn't wait to get her alone again. Perhaps that was irrational on his part, especially for a man his age. He just wished he'd said something more . . . profound in the coach. Something more clever, to make their conversation linger. She'd left him fast enough when they'd arrived back at the manor.

But he had made her smile. Amazing how that had felt like a triumph. And a triumph it was. She smiled beautifully. It made her warmer in expression, made her appear quite young. When they'd met for dinner, Marcus felt certain he'd stared at her more than he should have, and only hoped his mother and George hadn't noticed his preoccupation. He didn't think Mary had, as she had notably avoided his gaze.

Now, Marcus stood next to the library door, pausing so his nerves could settle. He knew she'd gone there after finishing dessert only a few minutes ago, as she'd said she wanted a book to read before retiring this evening. He would take advantage of the private moment for a bit of conversation before heading to his own bed. What could it hurt to get to know a unique member of his staff a little better?

After one deep breath and a long exhalation, he ran his palms along his jacket front, then reached out and pushed down on the brass latch. The door clicked open and he stepped inside.

One small lamp on a side table dimly shone on row after row of filled bookcases, floor to ceiling, to his left and right. Directly in front of him, beyond a crushed velvet, tasseled settee and two matching chairs, stood the shadowed figure of Mary Marsh, her back to him as she gazed out a tall window.

Slowly she turned, when the light from the hallway cast a glow on the oak floor, and stared at him with wide eyes.

"Are you thinking about which book to read, Miss Marsh?" he asked, venturing into the library, hands clasped behind him.

She blinked as if unsure of the reason for his presence. Then she answered softly, "I was just admiring the room—the view, I mean. The garden is lovely from this window." Her shapely brows creased in a frown. "What are you doing here, Lord Renn?"

He stopped just to the side of the settee, his chin tilting a fraction. "Admiring the view."

She licked her lips, and his eyes followed the movement. Lovely lips. Full and pink.

"I beg your pardon?"

Marcus almost smiled. Clearly, she wasn't used to flirtations. Or maybe he wasn't as good at it as he used to be. He skipped over an explanation.

"The sky has cleared, I see," he said, stepping toward her once more.

She turned back to the window. "Yes, but no moon, unfortunately. I can't see the path and flowers. Or the sea in the distance."

"Ah." He stood beside her, gazing at her profile. "But the advantage of having no moon is that you can see more stars."

For a moment she stared out to the infinite beyond, her arms to her sides, the hue of the lamp behind them reflecting off the sheen of her plum-colored gown.

"And they are beautiful tonight," she offered, her voice sounding strangely detached.

"Lovely." He leaned his hand on the sill and finally peered out at them as well. "I haven't seen stars in the English sky in four long years."

"Do they look different in Africa?"

He could swear he smelled roses and forced himself to keep from leaning in closer to her. "A bit, I suppose. I'm no expert in astronomy, though, so I couldn't tell you what the differences are."

"As in where the constellations are located?"

"Precisely. But the whole universe seems to shine . . . brighter in the desert sky. Sometimes I'd stay awake for hours just staring at them, wondering at their source."

"Me, too," she returned, wistfully. "It's all so vast."

Roses mixed with fresh, clean bath water. "Mmm."

"Still, I'm rather surprised at you, Lord Renn," she murmured, absentmindedly stroking the exposed skin above her deep neckline with her long fingers.

The movement seemed highly erotic to him, especially as her breasts pushed up from the tightness of her evening gown. Everything about the moment made him uncomfortably hot.

He rubbed the back of his neck. "Surprised?"

She didn't look at him directly; she continued to gaze out the window. But he thought he might have seen the slightest lift of her lovely pink lips. "Christine seemed to think you knew everything. I would only expect you to have a superb knowledge of astronomy. I must say I'm a bit disappointed."

He flushed. *Are you teasing me, Mary Marsh?*

"Really." He drew that word out, long and quietly.

Suddenly the intimate mood lifted. She stepped back a foot, angling her body toward him and clasping her palms together in front of her, her expression turning to one of formal inquiry. "I'm sorry I'm babbling. Did you wish to speak to me about tea at the Coswells' today, my lord?"

Marcus actually felt deflated, but he didn't let it sway him. She couldn't possibly know that his heart was racing, and she waited, watching him with the expectation of a servant queuing for instruction. He didn't like that at all.

"Not tonight. I want to hear what else Christine said about me. I'm fearful."

Her brows lifted minutely, then she smiled slyly. "That's twice today you've asked me that directly."

"Twice? I see. I hadn't counted."

When he added nothing more, she sighed and relaxed a bit into her stays, leaning her hip and shoulder against the window's edge. "Let's see . . . she said you were naturally inquisitive."

"She's right. I am."

"Hmmm . . ." She eyed him thoughtfully. "She said you saved her life once."

Marcus laughed heartily at that, falling back against the window as well, facing her, the sparkle of bright stars shining on the sill between them.

"Not exactly," he replied, running his fingers through his hair. "It's more accurate to say I rescued her from her own stupidity."

Mary drew a frown, then crossed her arms over her breasts. "Explain that, if you please."

He shook his head in continued amusement, noting how the lamp at their side cast streaks of light in her uptwisted blond hair: an array of nighttime shimmer on one side, reflected gold on the other. Beauty at the center.

"She didn't tell you the story?"

Mary shook her head. "She said only that you and she had quarreled and that she'd taken a boat out into the bay and couldn't row it back in. You pulled her back to safety before she drowned."

Marcus closed his eyes and pinched the bridge of his nose, chuckling again. "That would be the way she'd tell it. Skimming the details."

"Well, you may share your interpretation of the details, if you like," Mary said impatiently. "But frankly, Lord Renn, I rather enjoyed her version of the story."

He raised his eyes to her again. "Did you?"

She didn't answer that, just lifted her brows in mock challenge.

He grinned wryly, folding his arms across his chest. "When she was about thirteen, a year or so before I left for Egypt, she and I had a row."

"About?"

He didn't expect such exactitude from her. But since she seemed to ask in genuine interest, he decided it couldn't hurt to mention it now.

"Christine wanted to go to the beachfront on the bay for a nighttime celebration, which was to include a display of fireworks set out over the water as entertainment. It was to be a true social gathering for the local gentry, including many of the eligible gentlemen from all parts of Cornwall. Naturally she wanted to be there."

"Naturally," Mary cut in, amused.

He brushed over that. "I refused her permission."

"Why?"

He furrowed his brows. "Because she was only thirteen."

"I see. Couldn't you or George have gone as chaperone?"

He rubbed his chin with his forefinger and thumb, studying her. "Yes, but that wasn't the point."

"What was the point?"

Marcus simply marveled at her audacity. "The point was that she was only thirteen. Regardless of who was to be attending that night, it wasn't a gathering for young girls."

Mary lowered her arms and clasped her hands together in front of her. "I see. So what happened?"

"She got angry enough to sneak out that evening at half past ten, climb down the trellis hanging from her bedroom window, and head toward the water." He smirked. "Of course I was waiting."

Mary grinned, then pressed her lips together. "I see. Weren't you the sneaky brother."

He leaned over toward her and lowered his voice. "Just as sneaky as my sister. I knew her well."

Mary's smile faded, and once again, from his own words, Marcus felt the raw pulling in his gut that reminded him so well of his loss.

He drew a deep breath and gazed out the window to the star-sprinkled sky. "I chased her, but she jumped into a waiting rowboat, and with one oar, began to slap the water to keep me away. It broke in two, from hitting either a rock or the side of the boat, but she had already started to drift with the outgoing tide." He remembered the scene as if it were yesterday, Christine's expression of shock when she realized she needed his help. That alone made him smile. "God, she was mad that I'd followed her."

Without uttering a word, Mary waited for him to continue, and at last he glanced back to her face.

She studied him with bright, intelligent eyes of a striking blue that radiated an intense understanding and a desire to know. It made him shiver inside, an odd sensation, to be sure.

"It was actually very funny," he murmured.

Her lips turned up slightly. "I can imagine."

Her voice was as low as his, suggesting an underlying intimacy in the moment, between just the two of them, that he hadn't felt with anyone in a very long time. Without intention, Marcus reveled in it. He only wished he could reach out and caress her hand.

"Aside from a few stars, the night was black, and it scared her," he continued. "After a few minutes of listening to her panic and call for me, I stripped off my shirt and swam out to her."

Mary pulled a face, her mouth and eyes opening in shock. "In this water? At night?"

He shrugged, smiling unabashedly. "It was cold." Bloody freezing, actually, but of course he wouldn't admit that aloud. "But Christine couldn't swim and was wearing thick skirts. She also had no oar to use. We were both lucky that the sea was calm that night and that the fireworks started overhead to give us a little light to see by."

Mary shook her head slowly. "So, you *did* save her life by keeping her from drowning."

"No, I rescued her from her own stupidity by

swimming out to her and pulling her boat to shore," he corrected, then grinned. "I'm trying to be humble, Miss Marsh."

"Ah. Humble."

She watched him, her calculated gaze skimming his face, studying every feature, which Marcus suddenly found very gratifying.

Finally, she said, "So, I suppose you punished her?"

He shook his head almost imperceptibly. "No, I never said a word. Just dragged her back to her room with a strong arm."

Her brows popped up again. "No switch to her backside?"

"Trust me, she was scared to death of it for nearly a week, which I felt was punishment enough. As it happens, I may have let a profane word or two escape me along the way. I was wet and cold and very angry, after all."

Mary laughed softly. "Rather reasonable, I should think."

He nodded once. "I'm always reasonable, Miss Marsh."

She tilted her head to one side. "And where was George in all of this?"

"At the fireworks display, of course."

She laughed again at that, harder this time, the melodic sound of it coating his ears and senses like sweet honey.

It unnerved him.

"Did your mother know?" she asked, her tone colored with amusement, and a slight trace of mischief at being part of a greater conspiracy.

He leaned forward. "Not in the least. That was

Christine's greatest fear. That I'd tell the Lady Gwyneth."

Her grin grew even wider, and the lamplight reflected off smooth white teeth. At that second, Marcus tensed his body to keep from reaching out and pressing his lips to hers.

"So this is where you ran off to, Renn."

Marcus jerked his head back as they both turned sharply at the interruption.

George stood in the doorway, his jacket and waistcoat removed, sleeves rolled up to mid-forearm, brandy in hand.

"Awfully dark in here," he added, walking toward a second lamp to the right of the settee.

"We were admiring the starlight."

George stopped short. "Indeed." He looked from one to the other, then as if drawing some conclusion, stood upright and took a short sip of his brandy. "Am I interrupting you?"

"Not at all," Mary jumped in quickly, lifting her skirts and moving away from the window. "I'd come in for a book, and your brother enlightened me on some . . . about some amusing family antics."

Some amusing family antics? She was clearly flustered, and the notion made Marcus grin solidly. "The fireworks episode," he said to his brother.

George chuckled and stepped closer. "Ah. Yes. The night Christine tried to drown herself." He shook his head in remembrance. "She kept the laughter in this house."

Silence full of remorse reigned for a moment. Then George, in an attempt to lighten the mood, asked, "Have you ever seen fireworks, Miss Marsh?"

She still held tightly to her skirts. "Yes. Twice, actually, at the openings of both of the Crystal Palaces in London."

"How spectacular," George replied.

"It was."

"How delightful," George maintained. "I'm rather envious."

"Perhaps we'll have our own fireworks display while you're in Cornwall, Miss Marsh," Marcus ventured, looking directly into her large eyes.

She blinked, glancing from one brother to the other. "That would be lovely, I'm sure," was her formal reply.

George walked to the window, peering out. "You're right about the stars; tonight would have been perfect for such a display of light."

Marcus continued to look at Mary. "I've no doubt there will be other perfect nights."

Mary took another step back, nearly tripping when her hip hit a chair. "Thank you for the delightful conversation, my Lord Renn. But if you gentlemen will excuse me, I must be off to bed."

"Without a book?" Marcus commented.

She hesitated. "A what?"

"A book?" George repeated.

Marcus looked at his brother. "She came into the library for a book."

"Oh. Would you like a recommendation, Miss Marsh?" George offered.

She fidgeted with her hands, flushing so deeply her cheeks looked dewy pink by lamplight.

"Thank you, no," she returned with a sigh. "I think I'll embroider instead. Good night, then."

"Good night, Miss Marsh," the men said in near unison.

She turned and fairly waltzed from the library.

Marcus stared at the door for a moment longer, feeling a stab of regret for missing an opportunity to do . . . something.

Chapter 6

Baybridge House
25 August 1854

 *. . . Mother and George have been bickering end-
lessly of late. We've lost workers at the mine
who've joined British forces in the Crimea. This
has caused clay production to slow, though Mother
and George seem to think I don't understand such
business. Rubbish! Sometimes I tire of being told
I'm too young and naïve to know what is going on
around me . . .*

Gwyneth, Countess of Renn, sipped her first
cup of morning tea as she peered out the decorative art glass of her drawing room window, its
diamond-shaped design cutting a pattern of sunshine on the floral carpeting from the early rays reflecting off the waters of St. Austell Bay.

Though she would always miss the excitement, the unique smells and rapid pace of the city, she adored the warmth and quiet of Cornwall, and would remain on the Renn estate till her dying breath. Of course she had prestige here, a home and fortune she had helped to build, regardless of whether others acknowledged that fact. As a woman, she had little influence on town politics, but as the wife of the former Earl of Renn, she had status, especially in the small, local community in which she'd made her home, raised her children, and now belonged.

Most who lived in or visited St. Austell referred to it as the capital of the "Cornish Alps," the lovely, shimmering white mountains that retained a vast amount of *kaolin*, an essential ingredient in the manufacture of porcelain.

In her time, Gwyneth had seen marvelous growth in the production of their mines, and the near-worship of their name because of the steady work her late husband's family had provided for nearly three thousand of the seven thousand men, women, and children who extracted, processed, transported, and exported the clay. Made of a rather rare decomposition of granite, it was, in fact, found in few places in the world, which rendered the deposits discovered in Cornwall and Devon so valuable.

Yes, china clay was Gwyneth's mainstay; china porcelain—in all its varied colors and beauty—her passion. No family in Cornall had finer displays of decorative and usable china. In her small corner of the world, the Renn name had power, and she relished it. Nothing would alter that, or jeopardize her family's livelihood while she lived. She wanted Renn home, yes; he was the earl, the rightful heir. George, however, had the keen sense of business her late husband had possessed. But Marcus would never stay if he didn't have something to *do*, and at this point she had no idea what that might be.

Gwyneth forcibly relaxed her tight facial features, breathing deeply, closing her eyes to the bright sunshine as it lingered warmly on her skin.

Marcus.

She loved him more than she could ever say or express—as she supposed all mothers loved their children. It was a fact of bearing young, she believed, a feeling lacking coherent expression. She adored all her children, naturally, through each and every triumph and tragedy, and she hurt when they didn't come home.

Christine would never come home; she was gone forever. Each time Gwyneth allowed herself to contemplate the finality of that, she wanted so badly to break down, to crumple into a mass of flesh and bone encased in bottled-up rage and battered by a flowing, tearful waterfall of uncontrolled grief. But she didn't. She wouldn't. Above all things, she had a responsibility to her family, her employees, her town folk to remain forevermore a countess and the distinguished mother of the present earl. She would always bear her grief with dignity and silent privacy. She had a life to live, if not for herself, then for her daughter's memory and good name, which would need to be protected at all costs. If he did nothing else, Marcus would understand that.

She had never expected him to come home. To

say she had been shocked would be a complete understatement. With an honesty she kept only to herself, she was in some ways leery of his return. Her elder son might not be interested in estate matters as he should be, but the renters, miners and distinguished members of St. Austell all revered him. Marcus's return could prove uncomfortable to George, whom she loved as deeply, but who had a more difficult time commanding respect, with his cheerful personality and tendency to enjoy himself a bit too much. He had only recently been able to bridge the gap between second son and distinguished land manager in the eyes of the miners. He fully deserved the distinction, too, and Gwyneth had been most proud of him. But all things considered, she wanted Marcus home for good. To her, his title demanded his presence, and ultimately, proved infinitely more important than his spending time digging up little nothings in the desert of an uncivilized land.

"Good morning, Mother."

Gwyneth's eyes popped open at the unexpected intrusion. As she turned to the door of her morning room, her gaze fell on her older son, standing tall with distinct bearing, clothed in mourning dress of charcoal gray that stood out dramatically against the lavender flower-patterned wallpaper behind him. He ordered black coffee from a waiting servant, who curtsied and remained staid of expression, as a servant should.

She sighed. "Really, Marcus, coffee?"

"What does it matter what I drink?" he grumbled, striding into the room. "Where's George?"

"It's a heathen beverage, and he's still sleeping,

I'm sure," she replied to both questions at once, her lips curling up only slightly. Marcus had always been her grumpy child upon awakening.

"Still sleeping?" he shot back in disbelief.

"It's only half past seven, dear."

She could have sworn he grunted as he moved to her side.

"The boats are out early," he remarked, studying the scattering of fishermen out for a day's work on the water.

"As always," she said, following his gaze as she took a sip of her tea. "I do enjoy watching the bay in the early morning."

He shoved his hands in his pockets and glanced around him. "This room's too purple."

She sighed again, only this time so he could hear it. "It's my room and I like lilacs. If you stayed home—"

"Don't start, Mother. I'm not staying home, and you know that." He looked down into her eyes and held her gaze. "I'll be leaving as soon as I discover why Christine died, and what frightened her so much in the weeks before. It's my duty as her brother." He turned to stare out the window again. "After that I'll be returning to my work in Egypt."

Gwyneth bit her tongue to keep from arguing. On a rational level, she understood Marcus's desire to see the world and work at something that intrigued him. But on an emotional level, she wanted him home. He belonged here, with his family, performing at least some of his duties as earl. She needed him; England needed him. But she didn't know what to do to convince him to stay this time.

It would take nothing short of a miracle, she was sure.

"I heard you saw the vicar yesterday," she noted after another sip of cool tea. "How is Mrs. Coswell?"

Marcus straightened. "She's very well, I suppose. They looked the same."

Gwyneth placed her near-empty cup and saucer on a sideboard beside a glass vase of fresh lilacs. "Is it true you traveled with Miss Marsh?"

She thought she might have heard her son inhale sharply, but she didn't look at him. Instead, she crossed her arms over her stomach, keeping her focus on the barge making its way slowly from the bay to open water.

"She went with me at my request," he answered forthrightly.

Gwyneth couldn't decide if he was annoyed at her questioning, or just annoyed in general, as he often was early in the morning. But he was altogether defensive, and she didn't like that at all.

"You know," she dared to add after a thoughtful pause, "spending time with Miss Marsh alone could be a bit . . . unseemly."

He snorted, shoving his hands in his pockets. "I like her."

"Rubbish," she shot back. "You don't even know her."

"I know her better than you think."

That reply left her speechless for a moment. Then, in what could only be described as horrible timing, his coffee arrived, its pungent odor filling the room at once.

Marcus turned from the window and walked to

the tea table where a service had been set. "Lovely china," he remarked, sounding a bit bored.

"Last year's pattern," she returned, though it wasn't much of a pattern. A simple white with gold inlaid trim. Standard but elegant.

She lowered her trim form onto a chair and spread her skirts around her legs daintily. "About Miss Marsh—"

"Nothing unseemly has occurred, Mother. She is willing to help me, and I've asked her to stay. That's all."

Gwyneth watched him move to the settee and sit, unconcerned, apparently, that his jacket wrinkled behind him. He'd obviously lost his manners in Egypt as well, but she wouldn't mention it now. There would be time for that later.

"Help you with what?" she asked hesitantly, though she was afraid she already knew the answer.

He reached for his cup, then leaned his heavy body against the settee back. "Help me to discover what happened to Christine the day she died."

Gwyneth's eyes widened negligibly. Her mouth went dry, though with all her good breeding, she managed not to show her shock. "Marcus, I don't think that's wise."

His brows rose. "Whyever not?"

"Because Miss Marsh is just an employee," she stated, relaying the obvious. "She can't possibly know what Christine's thoughts and actions were before her accident."

"God, would all of you quit calling her death an accident?" he fairly shouted. "She died, Mother, and had she been perfectly happy before that death, I could accept it. But she wasn't. She sent me numerous notes in which she sounded frightened. Something was wrong, and Miss Marsh was the closest intimate to her at the time. If she can help me discover what scared my sister so much, then I will accept that help, no matter how unseemly that might look to those who think about that kind of thing regularly."

Gwyneth sat absolutely still, watching her son's face line with anger, knowing hers paled. Her fingers felt numb and she squeezed them together in her lap. "What matters is that you keep your wits about you. I want to know the details of her fear as well, but we *must* be mindful of scandal. You cannot just expect answers from an employee. They lie—"

"Are you saying Miss Marsh has lied, Mother?"

She scoffed, her back molding rigidly to the chair. "Of course not. She's a lovely girl."

"She's not a girl," he countered prosaically, sipping his coffee at last.

Gwyneth regarded her son, tipping her head to one side. "She is not of our class, Marcus. Getting involved with her in any way would be ruinous to our good name."

"Oh, hell." Marcus placed his cup and saucer on the tea table and stood abruptly, turning his back to her as he strode to the window again. "I'm not here for that."

But he didn't deny it, she noted.

Gwyneth watched the sunlight reflect off her son's dark, shiny hair. He had always been so handsome, so reserved. It made her irritable that he'd never married, but then, she couldn't discuss it with him. He was simply not interested in marriage. At least, not now.

"What did you learn?"

He shoved his hands in his pockets again, but didn't look at her. "That she's smart; she thinks before she speaks, which I find refreshing in a woman. She's witty, I suppose, though too independent for my tastes. I also think she may know more than she's admitting about Christine's final days, but regardless of that, I still find her decent company."

Gwyneth gaped at him, too dumbfounded to speak. She hadn't been referring to Mary at all, but of what she and her son had learned from Vicar Coswell. Suddenly it occurred to her that Marcus was thinking far too much about the spinster, and yet in a moment of sheer enlightenment, she decided not to mention that to him. It would only make him think of her more, and Mary, as lovely as she was, wasn't right for him as a marriageable prize. Maybe for George, as a second son, but not Marcus, the earl who'd inherited a large, wealthy estate.

She raised her chin a fraction. "Was she able to help you at all with your inquiries, then?"

He rubbed his forehead with the fingers of one hand. "I'm not sure. She was certainly helpful in her questioning, and of course she and Claudette had things to say to each other, some of which went beyond my understanding as a man. I expect to see her this morning and we'll discuss it then, to share our combined thoughts." He pressed his lips together. "One can only hope she doesn't sleep till noon."

Mary tended to be an early riser, Gwyneth knew, so she would no doubt be here for tea soon. But she didn't think to offer that information to Marcus.

"What do you know of her?" he asked softly.

"Of Miss Marsh?" She knew that was what he meant, yet questioned him anyway.

"Yes. What of her family? Why didn't she marry?"

Gwyneth straightened her palms down her crêpe skirt, hating the color, which made her look ghastly. "I have no idea why she didn't marry, as it's none of my business."

"But you had to have asked when you hired her," he returned quickly.

"Actually, I didn't ask. I knew her mother when Mary was a child. We were fairly close friends. Miss Marsh's father is Sir Harold, the dinosaur sculptor for Richard Owen. I believe Mary has spent the last few years tending to him as a good daughter should."

She had to throw that in.

Marcus cocked his head, gazing at her from across the room. Gwyneth looked at him innocently, which made him almost smile. Almost.

"He must be very proud," he drawled.

Gwyneth held her ground, eyes opened wide. "I'm sure that he is. She's a marvelous seamstress and organizer. Christine's trousseau is lovely, and nearly complete."

She watched his smile fade at the mention of his sister. It made her heart ache, too, for all of them, but she didn't let it show. "Miss Marsh is competent, Renn, and intelligent, but I think she knows very little of the happenings that go on behind closed doors in this house or any other. If she does stay here for a time, I should take what she offers with caution. Don't dig into pasts that mean nothing to your future."

His expression clouded as his eyes narrowed. "An odd choice of words, Mother." He dropped his voice to a cool whisper. "That's nearly exactly what Christine warned me about in her last letter, the one I received in Cairo just days before I decided to come home to help her."

Gwyneth's palms began to itch, her corset poked uncomfortably into her ribs. "I'm sure it means nothing."

"It meant something to her, and I'm going to find out what it is."

That profound announcement made her bones go cold. With aching joints, she stood to meet her son eye to eye.

She murmured, "The town and mines survive in St. Austell because of our good name, Renn. I can't stop you from delving into things that are best left alone, but I beg you, as your mother and the countess of this good land, to think carefully before you act, whether that pertains to Christine *or* Miss Marsh. Digging up the past in the search for truth could bring widespread scandal to this town. Christine is dead, and there is nothing you can do to change that."

It was a dire warning, given in love, and she hoped to God he'd consider it. At least he didn't respond rashly, but then, Marcus had never been rash in his life.

A boat horn echoed in the distance, and suddenly Gwyneth wanted to get away from the ugliness of the conversation and her thoughts.

Straightening her sleeves, she said swiftly, "I'd like to freshen up before breakfast. Please keep me informed of your doings, my dear son."

Before he could reply, she strolled quickly from her morning room.

Chapter 7

Baybridge House
9 September 1854

. . . Mother has been on edge lately. Something happened at the mine last week that she refuses to discuss with me, although she did discuss it with Exeter. I wish my upcoming marriage to Baudwin wasn't so necessary to maintain family peace. It seems I'm only at the center of attention when it's convenient for bloodlines and estates. Is this how you feel about marriage, Marcus? It's no wonder you never settled down. I hope you will one day be fortunate enough to marry for love . . .

Mary sat on a stone bench built for two, situated high on a cliff overlooking the rocky coastline where it met the sea, just a few hundred yards below the front of Baybridge House. The wind had picked up to carry the cool breeze off the water, but the day had grown warm and the frequent gusts felt marvelous against her skin.

She'd been sitting here since breakfast, contemplating her thoughts of the recent days, considering her options. She could very well leave, and everyone on the Renn estate knew it, including her employer. But she hesitated to do so. She wanted to help the earl's family out of kindness, respect—without giving away too much that could hurt Christine's brother beyond repair.

And she very well knew that she might.

Sighing, Mary turned her face upward to catch the sunlight, feeling it warm her cheeks and eyelids.

She *should* leave, but something beyond her personal desire to stay away from London stopped her.

It probably had more to do with the earl, she decided. In a sense he needed her, or at least he thought he did. And she *liked* the idea of staying in Cornwall to help him. God help her. Of course this posed some risks as well. She would need to be in close proximity to a man she didn't know for an indefinite period of time. Under normal circumstances, this would mean little to her. But this wasn't a normal circumstance for any of them at Baybridge House.

Yet in some strange, inexplicable way, she liked Marcus Longfellow, which she imagined had grown out of Christine's love and trust in her brother. Mary didn't care for men in general, didn't much understand their minds, and with most of them she found little about which to converse comfortably. The Earl of Renn seemed different—different even from any man she knew. Maybe it was the way he looked at her, regarded her, as if he were trying to pry into her female thoughts, which naturally wouldn't interest even the most common of men. She didn't like that, and yet part of her wanted it to continue. The part of her that longed for ... something undefined. That small something that made her nervous when he walked into a room or sat beside her. That something that intrigued her beyond explanation.

"Do you come here often?"

Mary opened her eyes, squinting as she turned around sharply to behold the vision of her thoughts.

The earl stood beside the bench, watching her keenly, only the slightest hint of a smile playing at his mouth. He looked quite casual in pose, one hand in the pocket of his dark, thigh-hugging pants. He'd disposed of his morning jacket, and with the breeze blowing his hair up and across his face, it also pressed his white shirt into his wide and very muscled chest. In essence, he towered over her in all his masculine glory, which irritated her.

She straightened, clasping her palms together in her lap. "You startled me, Lord Renn."

His brows rose, but he didn't move any closer. "I apologize. I didn't realize you were so deep in thought."

"I was."

He did smile at that, which surprised her because her intended curtness didn't seem to bother him.

"Really," he replied, glancing up over the bay. "And may I ask what it was you were contemplating?"

"You may not," she asserted at once, though her tone had lightened of its own accord.

He actually chuckled, then without asking, moved his long legs to her side and made a great effort of seating himself comfortably next to her.

She inhaled the scent of him from the gentle breeze: pure masculinity mixed with a whiff of nearby lavender and wild flowers. It had a calming effect on her, even as he nearly touched her person.

"I have a cottage not too far from this spot," he said, leaning forward and placing his elbows on his knees, fingers interlocked in front of him as he stared out over the water. "It's farther along the cliff path, to the right and just below that group of hedges." He nodded in that direction but didn't look at her.

She inhaled deeply and tried to relax. "I suppose it's part of the estate, then."

"Yes, though it's seldom used except by me, and I'm not often here." He smirked. "It probably needs a good cleaning."

Mary had no idea why he brought up the subject of the cottage, though it was true that in all the months she'd been at Baybridge House she hadn't learned of its existence. But she had no intention of cleaning it, if that was the reason he mentioned it. And to make sure he didn't have the opportunity to ask her, and since he seemed desirous of lingering in her presence, she instead chose to discuss something a bit less intimate.

"What do you do in Egypt, sir?"

That question truly seemed to surprise him. He cocked his head to the side to regard her, his dark brows furrowed into one thick line across his handsome face.

"I work with several archaeologists and experts in Egyptian art for the preservation of Egyptian artifacts and culture."

"How remarkable," she said with genuine interest. "And what is it you do specifically?"

His mouth tilted up into a wry smile. "I'm in charge of the operation."

"Oh." Mary hoped her own surprise and utter lack of knowledge about such things didn't make her appear too idiotic. "You fund it, then?"

He nodded. "In part. But I'm also fairly well acquainted with Egyptian culture and antiquities, so my expertise comes in handy." He sighed and leaned back a little, brushing her face with his gaze. "Mostly, I just enjoy the challenge, the climate, working with scholars."

And being your own man.

Mary glanced away, knowing instinctively that to bring up his family, his mother and brother and responsibilities at home, would cool the moment. She fully understood the desire to live one's life in one's own way. It was how she'd chosen to live hers.

"Have you ever seen a real mummy?"

He laughed deeply, then admitted, "Yes, but it's not as if they're just lying around for us to find. And the few we've uncovered are not all that well preserved."

Amazed, she looked back into his bold, shining eyes. "How extraordinary."

He shrugged and leaned into her to add, "They're not nearly as frightful as they sound."

She grinned in return. "Just the same, I would abhor unwrapping one."

"Well, that I've never done. Most of what I do is research, studying the culture, transcribing hieroglyphic script."

Mary tucked a stray lock of hair behind her ear. "Is that something one can read?"

He shrugged again. "It's a language, just like any other, though an entirely written one."

"But what would be the purpose of deciphering such a language?" she asked in a complete desire to know.

He cocked his head a little to regard her. "The purpose would be to learn something new and different and unique about this great world of ours and an ancient people."

Mary watched him without moving, without adding comment. She did understand his desire to learn things that wouldn't in any way help a cause other than one's personal quest for knowledge. But she found it particularly interesting that an English earl seemed to give it more consideration than he did his own property and family.

"It all sounds very fascinating," she replied after a moment. "I should enjoy seeing Africa."

He said nothing to that, though his eyes lingered on her, and to her shame, she didn't find it all too uncomfortable, either.

"It's beautiful here, though," she stressed after a long moment of silence, breaking his gaze to peer out over the ocean again. "I suppose you miss Cornwall from time to time when you're abroad."

"Yes, sometimes. I do often miss the greenery, and sitting here by the seaside. I miss watching the fishing boats in the morning and the cool breezes off the bay that fill the air with the scent of the sea." He paused, then added, "The solitude . . ."

In the intimate atmosphere they created, Mary felt the distinct heat of him as the wind died a little and the sun closed in around them. It was as if no one else existed for miles. How very odd that right this minute, in his powerful presence, she wasn't concerned, only thoughtful.

"My mother says you're the daughter of Sir Harold Marsh."

The magic dissipated instantly as reality intruded bluntly.

"I am," she replied without hesitation.

He waited. "The only daughter?"

"No." She paused, then expounded, "My sister, Mimi, is six years younger than I. I have no brothers."

"I see." He tapped his fingers together in front of him. "And does your sister live at home with you?"

His personal questions bothered her a little, though she had to wonder if it was because of her own repressed guilt about her family that she had yet to face, or the fact that he was rather nosy where she was concerned. But she felt compelled to answer.

"My sister is now married to Professor Nathan Price, a scientist with an impeccable reputation. They reside in London, and I see them regularly."

Mary could positively *hear* him cogitating that, as she felt warmth creep up her neck.

He glanced at her face again, studying her,

though she tried not to look directly into his curious dark eyes.

"Why did you not marry? Is it because of your father?"

She had known he would ask her. It only followed his line of questioning, and for a second, Mary wondered if he'd done that on purpose. Then she inwardly scolded herself for thinking such nonsense.

"Yes, exactly, Lord Renn. His arthritis is quite pronounced and he needs me for correspondence, household matters, and of course conversation," she explained matter-of-factly.

He raised one large palm and rubbed his chin. "Then how is he managing to get along while you are in Cornwall?"

She squirmed a little on the bench, unusually self-conscious from the personal queries and the deep vibrations his low voice made as it mingled with the wind, noting inconsequentially how even this early in the day he had a shadow of a beard. She wondered how those whiskers would feel to her fingertips, and she clutched her palms together to keep from reaching for him.

"He is being provided for by the Widow Ester Thurston while I am gone, and she has written that all is well. Besides that, he has Mimi."

"I see."

He turned to study her again and didn't say anything until she looked into his eyes.

"Then I'm so glad the widow and your sister were available."

Mary caught her breath. He sat so close, and uttered words whose meanings seemed so completely foreign to her. Yet even with his proximity and marvelously staid responses, his comments *felt* intimate. Then again, maybe it was her reaction entirely. He could mean nothing whatever by delving into her personal life. And truthfully, he hadn't asked anything altogether inappropriate.

"You know," he said softly, still gazing at her, "I find it very odd that a lady of your beauty and intelligence would choose not to marry. It seems to me you'd make a nearly perfect wife."

Her insides tightened as her eyes opened wide. "I talk too much."

Suddenly he grinned—a lovely, boyish grin that made him look years younger and undeniably devious.

"You do? When?"

She had nothing to say to that, which he likely knew. "And too forwardly for my own good," she added instead.

He reached over and touched the sleeve of her gown—very quickly—rubbing fine lace between his forefinger and thumb. "That sounds like it came from your father."

"Oh," she countered with a nod, brows raised in feigned innocence. "Do you know him?"

He chuckled again, his eyes crinkled in smile. Then he dropped his hand. "Sorry, Miss Marsh. It's not often I meet women like you."

"Like what?" That was out of her mouth before she thought about it, and Mary could have kicked herself for stirring him into such frank conversation.

He briefly lowered his gaze to her lips as his own features clouded with somber thoughts. "You're outspoken yet reserved, intelligent yet restrained. You're delightful."

She wanted to squirm—or run. Instead, she scoffed as she made a great challenge of straightening her skirts over her lap. "You, my lord, do not even know me."

"I know you better than you realize," he said very softly.

She started, then rocked back to stare at him.

His entire expression had softened minutely; his fascinating eyes simply dared her to ask him how. Intuitively? Factually? Had he inquired about her professionally, or had Christine told him more than she should have? After several agonizing seconds, Mary decided that he toyed with her, and he did it very well indeed. For she, much to her disdain, completely enjoyed it.

"Well, then," she disclosed, "I suppose we know each other equally. And here I thought I would be the one to have the upper hand."

He pulled a face. "The upper hand, Miss Marsh?"

"Of course." She added nothing to explain that evasive answer, just watched him with a thoroughly engaged expression of false modesty.

"And yet," he carried on, "your hands are so . . . different from mine."

She tried not to smile. "Which *hands* are those, Lord Renn?"

He gazed to her lap. "The . . . delicate, feminine ones, with long, tapered fingers for caressing a brow softly or rubbing hard muscles after a day's labor. For exploring."

Mary just sat there, feeling the quickening pace of her heart, and having no idea at all how to reply to such a literal comment, so formally expressed even as it contained such utterly intimate meaning. They had been speaking in riddles. How quickly he had turned the conversation to one that felt improper. Suddenly, for just a very brief second, she knew he rested on the verge of taking her hand in his.

Without clear thought, she clasped her arms together protectively over her breasts.

The earl straightened, his features going slack, and he once again looked out over the bay, placing his palms on his thighs.

"Do you suppose," he asked very slowly, "that Mrs. Coswell knows more of what Christine feared than she let on?"

Mary tried to clear her muddled mind, noticing how a cloud covered the sun at exactly the same moment, just as it did her mood. If this marvelously handsome man were only a little less distracting . . .

"I'm not sure," she returned, immensely proud of how her voice remained flat as her nerves flared. "Why do you ask?"

She shouldn't have pressed him.

He looked back into her eyes, so close and candid, his brows furrowed with a combination of pain, confusion, and anger.

"I ask because she gave you—only you—a certain look that had me sensing something more."

His lips thinned grimly, then he lowered his voice to add, "Did you sense it as well?"

Mary shivered from a rush of coldness, from a sense of loneliness and despair that she felt even now for Christine.

"It's possible, my lord," she replied, rubbing her upper arms. "But I would imagine there is more to learn about Miss Longfellow than either the vicar and his wife or I can offer."

She hoped that answer would suffice. For an almost unbearable moment he did and said nothing.

Then, very quietly, almost gingerly, instead of lingering on the subject of his concern, he murmured, "I would like to call you Mary."

She nearly swooned from such a marvelous thought. But she couldn't allow such familiarity.

"I don't think that would be appropriate," she said, fearing that her hesitancy and strange desire to allow it would show through her words.

Apparently it didn't. His eyes darkened, and after a second or two, he raised his chin a fraction. "As you wish."

For an uncomfortable moment, neither said anything; they just looked at each other. Then he lowered his gaze to the wild grass beneath his feet.

"Well, I believe you're quite right about Mrs. Coswell. Which leads me to wonder about Christine's things. As far as I know they've not been touched."

Swiftly, he stood and faced her, arms at his sides. "I intend to take the afternoon and go through her personal items, Miss Marsh. I would like you to join me."

She shook her head. "I'm sorry, but—"

"You must," he interjected forcefully. "It would be . . . unseemly for me to do so as a man and her brother, but not for you as her personal"— he flicked his wrist—"trousseau . . . maker. The only other person to do it would be my mother, and she can't under the grief of the moment. I'm sure you understand."

His formality had returned again, and Mary wasn't certain whether or not she liked it better than the tiny bit of friendliness they'd shared. Yet that was irrelevant. He treated her exactly as he should—she had seen to that by denying him the right to use her given name. She could only do as he'd requested.

Mary stood then too, as elegantly as possible under the circumstances, allowing her gown to flow around her legs without adjusting it. The breeze would do that.

"I shall be as helpful as I can, Lord Renn."

He nodded once and turned toward the narrow path that led back to the house. She followed for a foot or two, and then he stopped abruptly.

"One more thing, Miss Marsh," he said, slowly pivoting to look at her again.

His eyes held a magnetic resonance as they grasped hers in silent communication. She stood too close to him, but for reasons unknown, she didn't back away.

"My lord," she replied, trying to sound helpful, yet fearing the worst.

He rubbed his jaw again. "I was wondering about last night."

Her eyes widened. "Last night?" She was hoping he'd smile to lighten the mood, but he didn't. If anything, his gaze grew grave with intent.

"In the coach, on the way home. I frightened you."

Mary felt her heart stop. He'd misunderstood her apprehension in his accidental touch. Nothing he had said to her thus far today had bothered her quite so much.

"It wasn't you, my lord," she admitted, her voice low and implicit in its conviction. "I was just . . . startled. You do not frighten me."

The wind howled around them now as they stood together high on the cliff. The clouds had rolled in to darken the sky, and somewhere in the distance a ship bell tolled, probably the noon hour. But Mary remained mesmerized by him—that hard jaw, the scar above his right eye, his intense blue eyes.

He reached out for her, and in that instant she backed away. That stopped him, his hand in mid-air. With a glance down her figure, he said almost wistfully, "Someday, I would like you to call me Marcus. Nobody calls me Marcus."

And then he dropped his arm and brushed past her.

"I'll see you this afternoon, Miss Marsh."

Mary stared after him, taking note of his broad shoulders, his hair that was a tad too long, the determination in his stride. He never looked back as he made his way now in the opposite direction of the house, toward his cottage of solitude.

Chapter 8

Baybridge House
29 September 1854

We've heard that Miss Marsh will arrive just after Christmas. I shall be thrilled for the company. She must have wonderful stories to tell having lived in the city! Did I mention that Mother heard a ghastly rumor that she also sews unmentionable risqué items for courtesans? Of course, it couldn't possibly be true. Mother says her family has always been quite respectable . . .

Marcus entered Christine's private bedroom for the first time in more than four years, painfully aware of Mary at his side. She didn't want to be here, with him in this bedroom, any bedroom, and so certain of her reluctance to engage in anything improper, he'd asked a lady's maid to accompany them. His mother wouldn't, and for that he'd been relieved. He didn't want her there anyway, forbidding him to look here, or encouraging him to look there, making erroneous conclusions and weeping or arguing. But this was his house, and everyone would do well to remember that. He had every right to enter any room he chose.

His first thought was that it was just as he'd remembered it, and the smells, color, and personality that had been distinctly Christine's hit him hard in the chest.

Decorated in various shades of pale pink and green, the four-poster canopy bed, shrouded with white lace to match the muslin coverlet and a barrage of velvet pillows, sat in the center, against the opposite wall papered floor to ceiling in a tiny red rosebud design. Thick pink curtains in linen taffeta puddled on the hardwood floor at each window on either side of the bed and at the window seat, pulled back with tassels, allowing a bit of light for nobody. Until today.

A hot staleness permeated the air, and Marcus, rigid in body and determined in mind, immediately ordered the maid to pull back the lace shades and open two windows, which she did upon command.

Mary followed him to the center of the room, then stepped to his right and toward the golden oak dressing table next to the window seat. Atop a long lace runner, his sister had placed various bottles of perfumes or lotions or whatever toilette articles ladies kept on dressing tables. He watched her pick up a small pink glass bottle, pull off the top, and sniff it.

"Roses," she commented, placing it back on the runner.

"Of course," he remarked solemnly. "Would you expect anything else in a room like this?"

If it had been any other time, she might have laughed, and he would have welcomed the feminine sound from her. But now such a release of amusement or nervous energy seemed crass.

An awkward moment passed; the maid, in formal mourning attire, stood by the doorway, looking placid yet attentively involved—which Marcus knew was a good act for a lady's maid to follow. It was her job to be available but unobtrusive.

"What are we here to look for?" Mary asked patiently, interrupting his thoughts.

He turned to the tall, painted wardrobe to his left. "I'd like to go through her clothes—pockets of gowns, primarily—to look for notes or items that may have been forgotten, or even concealed there."

"I'll help you then," she said, eyeing the wardrobe as she began to step toward him.

"Actually," he countered, crossing his arms at his chest thoughtfully, "I'd like you to go through her drawers and personal items."

She stopped short and stared at him.

"Her items of female . . . necessity," he clarified. "I don't know a thing about them, and it would be considerably more embarrassing for me to do it."

He watched her. And there it was, the slightest blush to grace her lovely fine-boned cheeks. Truthfully, he wasn't embarrassed in the least, but suspected that she'd believe that as an excuse on his part. He'd seen just about every intimate detail there was to see in his travels, but he'd rather not admit that. At least not yet, and in the presence of a dutiful servant.

Mary's features went slack and she opened her mouth just slightly as if to speak, unsure. Then she clamped it shut to do as he had bidden, whirling around in front of him in a somewhat dramatic display of exasperation, not caring that her skirts swept across his legs when there was more than enough floor space that they didn't need to.

He almost smiled.

Instead, he quashed his untimely amusement, turned, and quickly strode to the wardrobe. With one hand he carefully lifted the brass latch and pulled open the doors to reveal a wealth of fabric and an array of beautiful color that were once his sister's clothes.

The sight of them sickened him. It made Christine real again; even if he'd never seen any of these gowns before, he didn't need anyone to tell him they were his sister's.

Organized by morning, day, and evening dresses, they filled the entire space. He noted her favorite color, teal, as well as some green, sky blue, peach, and even yellow—the color he'd always favored on her, but which she hated. She'd always loathed that shade on herself, insisting it made her look sallow, but he had adored the way it made her look like sunshine. His heart ached with keenly felt emotion now as he gingerly reached out and touched a soft yellow silk that Christine had owned only because the color reminded her of him. He knew that without question.

Marcus swallowed, then bit down hard; now was not the time to pity himself with painful memories and fears of a hopeless future.

He sifted through the gowns one by one, starting with evening wear. He thought it more likely that these gowns would contain hints of her secrets, but after five minutes of careful surveying, except for two linen kerchiefs and an overwhelming scent of flowers, he found nothing substantial in his sister's outer apparel.

Mary, during this time, had turned her full attention to the dresser drawers, going through each of them meticulously, or so he imagined, since it took her nearly as long as it took him at his task.

"Why did you never marry, Lord Renn?"

The question, spoken so softly, caught him completely off guard. He jerked around, unsure at first, but realizing a maid would never ask such a thing. Mary would, and when he glanced at her to see only her backside as she knelt over a lower drawer, his insides began to churn.

"No opportunity. I've been very busy for the last few years."

"No doubt."

He grinned. She was thinking about him.

"Did you not consider that you'd need an heir?" She still hadn't looked at him.

He leaned against the bed post, eyeing her figure, nicely outlined by a trim-fitting corset. "It was not my first consideration, Miss Marsh."

After a quick peek over her shoulder, she acknowledged, "I see."

He doubted that; the idea of his not being concerned for an heir would seem considerably odd to her. But he said nothing, just crossed his arms over his chest.

"Did you find anything?" she asked a moment later, refolding a linen nightgown.

His brows rose, and he wiped the smile from his face, careful not to show too much good humor, or interest in her and what she was doing.

"Nothing much—at least nothing that would tell me of Christine's last thoughts," he answered sincerely, sobering. He had no business thinking of the female sex at such a moment, in his sister's room. God, he must be desperate.

Marcus shifted his gaze to the carved shelving next to the window seat. Christine collected delicate porcelain jars, not books, and aside from two poetry compilations, the remaining space was lined with colorful displays of Renn china. Nothing there that hadn't been there before.

Suddenly his eye caught the painted green and gilded trunk at the foot of the bed. He noticed it just as Mary did.

She made her way to it first, stopping short of it, hands on her small waist.

"The items in here are for her wedding, Lord Renn. I'm sure you don't want to intrude into what is surely a delicate issue."

Wrong. He very definitely wanted to intrude, but he hesitated. "Did you find anything of importance in Christine's under things, Miss Marsh?"

He could have sworn she gulped, and her delicate cheeks stained pink again, but she didn't budge, or move her gaze from his.

"No, nothing out of the ordinary," she replied, her voice only slightly wavering.

He inhaled deeply and slowly, ever careful of the lady's maid at the doorway and not wanting to initiate unwarranted speculation among the help.

"Miss Marsh, it seems there's nothing left but her trunk." He moved closer to her so that he could see the wisps of blond hair along her temple, feel her body heat, imagine the rise and fall of her breasts with every nervous breath she took. "I cannot conceive of a reason why I should be wary of looking at newly made sheets, blankets and nightgowns." He paused for emphasis, then added, "Should I be?"

She didn't move. "Of course not. I only mean to protect her privacy. I'm sure you understand."

"You are?"

That confused her, but she didn't back down.

After a moment's hesitation in which he was certain the maid laughed internally at the ridiculous banter between the two of them, assured now that the entire household below stairs would soon find this oddly amusing, he decided he had nothing to lose. He had a very good idea what lay inside his sister's personal trunk, and to hell with anyone seeing it.

He tipped his head to the object of contention. "Will you open it, or shall I?"

For seconds Mary did nothing; he didn't even think she drew a breath. Then, eyes flashing irritation, knowing she'd lost a significant battle, she stepped back to allow him access.

Marcus lowered himself to one knee. With great care, and infinite curiosity, he popped open the unlocked latches and lifted the lid.

It appeared full to the top with three side-by-side piles of items. On the left, he took note of what appeared to be cream and white lace tablecloths. Next to them rested an obvious set of white linen sheets and matching pillowcases embroidered with green vines and yellow roses, followed by two lace runners on top of which sat an ivory jewel case that he immediately lifted to find empty.

He supposed this would be part of the typical trousseau, and under different circumstances, he would have left well enough alone. But with Mary Marsh looming over him with a tightly reigned nervousness, he knew there had to be something more.

Without looking at her, he dug deeply into the first pile of linens and lifted it. And there it was. Red silk. He pulled it to the side to see bright pink, bold burgundy, and luscious sea green satin, royal purple lace . . .

Trying unsuccessfully to hide his wolfish grin, he instead kept his face turned from the women and sat back on his heel. "Where are the nightgowns?"

Mary let out a little squeak of a noise, and he could feel himself chuckling on the inside. God, for the last two days he had only hoped . . .

"I don't know where she kept them, Lord Renn," she admitted after a moment or two of discomfiting silence.

A non-answer. Marcus pressed his lips together to keep from laughing. This was the first enjoyment he'd had in a long, long time.

Mary Marsh made erotic underclothes, just as Christine had said she was rumored to do. He had yet to lift one from the trunk, though he recognized a lace corset when he saw one. And even though it was none of his business, and God knew it went far beyond his grasp to imagine his sister wearing such things, he now knew what lay hidden beneath a perfectly well-sewn pair of cotton sheets that Mary had wanted to keep from him.

Still, what to do with this knowledge? Did all brides wear such marvelous items? He'd never thought about it, but for the first time in ages, he truly wondered if he'd been utterly stupid not to have married long ago.

"Did you see what you expected, Lord Renn?" Mary challenged in a cool whisper from behind him.

Marcus stilled, his fingers clasping midnight blue stockings. "Yes and no, Miss Marsh," he replied after a moment's thought. Slowly, he replaced the stockings, followed by the short pile of folded, respectable tablecloths, then closed the lid of the trunk and sat back on his heels. "I do, however, find it fascinating," he added, pushing himself up with his palms on his thighs to face her again. "And I wonder . . . do all brides wear such things on their wedding nights?"

After only the slightest pause, without flinching, she cocked her head minutely and murmured, "I wouldn't know, Lord Renn."

Marcus didn't know whether to be irritated at her evasiveness, or applaud her courage at what had to be a tremendously embarrassing moment.

She stood before him, her cheeks bright, the sun from the window shining off her two golden braid loops, with her hands behind her back, ever the angelic face, eyes flashing resolve—and exposing a very clever mind.

He felt the instantaneous urge to smile, and this time he couldn't help it. His mouth lifted into a full-fledged grin of satisfaction.

She gritted her teeth. "I fail to see what's so amusing."

Very gradually, his gaze dropped down her curvy form, then back to her face, where it lingered for a moment before he answered. At last, he leaned over so that only she could hear, to whisper, "I was just thinking that you really bear no resemblance on the outside to a clandestine lingerie maker."

He heard a slight intake of breath before he'd even finished saying the words, and then he pulled back again.

She was truly blushing now, but she didn't say anything. Aside from a quick glance to his servant, who stood oblivious at the doorway, she didn't budge. For several seconds, Marcus let his imagination flow, speculating on what her tall, lovely body might look like in sea green satin or a corset of bright magenta, showcasing a curving waist and magnificent breasts. As his thoughts took wing, he felt the urging of an erection that startled him as much as it piqued his anger. His desire could not be any more inappropriate.

Clearing his throat, he clasped his hands behind his back. "I think we've seen all we need to here."

One blond brow rose in question. "I thought perhaps you'd like a viewing of my work."

Marcus's heart began to race, more at the mere thought of watching her sashay around him in provocative corsets and stockings than at her sarcastic innuendoes of solid indignation, which was surely what she meant. Then again, in a manner of speaking, he felt as if he'd invaded *her* personal belongings, which he was certain she wanted him to feel.

In a tone harsher than was intended, he said, "I'll see you at dinner, Miss Marsh."

With rigid shoulders, he strode past her and out into the hallway, knowing she burned a hole in his back with her gaze.

Mary needed to think, and the best place she'd discovered on the Renn estate for private thinking was the cliff overlooking the bay. It remained peaceful there day by day, fairly secluded as it allowed few intruders, even George and the countess, who seldom walked the cliffs. The afternoon had grown cool and windy, and she'd donned a light cloak as the darkened clouds in the distance signaled a coming rain. No matter. She adored the freshness of the coast, the smell of the sea, and the crisper air.

Marcus Longfellow troubled her. Truthfully, she wasn't so much troubled by *him* as she was by her reaction to him and all he said and did in her presence. As if he liked her more than should be appropriate for someone of her station, as if he actually enjoyed her company.

She shivered. That was impossible, especially now that he suspected she created and sewed salacious underclothes for respectable ladies. Damn it all, why had she not foreseen his reaction? Why hadn't she thought of moving the garments? Because they were Christine's, and she had no business removing any of Christine's personal belongings from the lady's room. It hadn't even occurred to her to do so.

Mary fisted her hands at her sides, confused, annoyed at herself, and wishing she could forsake her duties in Cornwall and return home. But the underlying fact was that she simply wasn't ready to face her family again. At this point, she decided with some amusement as she blindly followed the winding trail through the brush, she'd rather face the arguments between George and Gwyneth, and the entanglements at Baybridge House.

At last she spotted the open sea as the cliff line came into view—and stopped dead in her tracks.

Twenty feet away, on the stone bench that she'd shared with him only a few hours ago, sat the Earl of Renn, a single figure in black from hair to foot, outlined by the icy dark ocean as a backdrop.

Immediately, Mary took one step back, as quietly as she could, sensing a certain drama in the moment, a cold foreboding, and wanting sensibly—desperately—to avoid it.

He had most of his back to her, his head down, and in his partially outstretched hand, he held a letter he appeared to be reading.

The wind blew the corner of the yellow colored paper toward his fist, but he didn't set it right, or move at all, for that matter. He sat immobile, staring. And then he shook his head and rubbed his eyes, and Mary liquified with the knowledge that he was crying.

Christine's letter. Christine's things. The shock of it all had started to sink in, how all their lives had changed forevermore from this one inexplicable event.

Mary had no idea what to do, or if she should do anything. She'd never in her life seen a grown man cry. Not from pent up grief and a loneliness she all but felt herself.

The urge to walk to his side and put her arms around his shoulders in comfort was overwhelming. For nearly a minute, she remained standing behind him in the shadow of the brush, listening to the wind off the cliff, watching him.

Moments later, she turned and silently made her way back to Baybridge House.

Chapter 9

Baybridge House
20 October 1854

. . . Exeter will be here for our dinner party tomor-
row. I am looking forward to his company al-
though it must be said that he's been acting
different of late. He's been a bit more moody and
thoughtful. Mother thinks he's merely nervous
about our upcoming wedding and the responsibili-
ties of marriage. I love him, of course, and am sim-
ply trying to do what is expected of me as his
betrothed . . .

They were to gather for dinner at eight. The
Viscount Exeter was expected to be early,
which Mary knew was typical of him. The man,
with all his oddities, despised lateness, as she'd
heard numerous times from Christine. She had to

wonder, however, if he still grieved for his betrothed; this dinner, insisted on by the countess, could prove enlightening for all of them, and in a manner, Mary very definitely looked forward to it.

She'd decided on her burgundy evening gown with the cropped sleeves and squared neckline, made entirely of satin. As her favorite evening dress, she'd saved it only for the best occasions, and tonight's gathering would be as formal as any. She'd piled her hair high on top of her head, allowing ringlets to tumble down along her temples in front of her ears where she'd hung teardrop pearl earrings to match the single strand at her neck. She supposed it was vanity that made her want to be noticed as a woman rather than as hired help, and with a last glance in her mirror followed by a pinch to her cheeks for color, she decided she'd accomplished that.

They'd taken sherry in the drawing room at seven, though for the first fifteen minutes it had been only her and George. Gwyneth had been under the weather for the afternoon, so she took her time, and as for the earl, Mary hadn't heard a peep. Perhaps he always appeared late on principle. For some reason she wouldn't doubt it; such behavior would fit what she knew of his character.

But regardless of his reticence and disregard for social gatherings, she very much looked forward to seeing him tonight, or perhaps just addressing him while looking her best. She'd never been a conceited woman; indeed, while an attractive appearance was important to her, it had never been because she desired the attention of a man. Until Marcus Longfellow had arrived at Baybridge House, she'd not given her physical looks much thought beyond basic grooming. But as incensed as she became with herself, she wanted to look appealing for him at dinner this evening.

She sat primly next to George in matching midnight blue velveteen chairs, to the side of the now cold fireplace, sipping the expensive ruby red sherry, keenly aware of the empty doorway and who might be the next to step through it. As always, George remained in good humor under the circumstances, charming even as he spoke in great detail of trouble at the mines—lack of good help because of the war effort, the constant grumbling of the workers regarding low wages and the continuous unseasonable rain. Of course, complaint of pay was a regular irritant, but the countess's second son handled it all well. In many ways, Mary admired George and liked him as a person.

"I see my brother has taken quite a fancy to you, Miss Marsh."

Mary nearly choked on her sherry. Swallowing hard to fight a cough, she shifted her gaze to face the comment—not from George, but from the earl, who now stood in the doorway that had been vacant only seconds ago, his large frame filling out the dimensions in marvelous proportion.

He wore black evening attire in light wool, a striped gray and white silk waistcoat, and a solid white cravat, his hair combed back to allow a lovely view of his intense eyes and tanned, clean-shaven skin. He looked positively stunning, and she could actually feel her heartbeat increase with every breath.

"God, Renn, every time I see you, I'm in shock," George said with a cheerful grin.

"It's as if I never left?"

"More like seeing a ghost, brother," George replied, as he stood, drink in hand. "I've been stealing Miss Marsh's good time by offering tales of horror at the mine, though I'm probably boring her."

Marcus glanced at both of them, then began to saunter into the drawing room, hands behind his back. "You could never be boring, George." He looked directly into Mary's eyes. "Miss Marsh seemed captivated, as ladies always are in your company."

She felt that peculiar flutter in her belly as he approached. "I was, Lord Renn," she managed to respond lightheartedly. "Your brother is a delight, and has entertained me on occasion with his fascinating stories of mining and the process of making fine china. Tonight was no exception."

One corner of his hard mouth lifted in a smirk. "He's always been the charming one."

And you the mystery.

Mary pushed back that intriguing thought and raised her hand for him to take as he stood beside her at last.

The simple touch of his large palm to her fingers seemed to melt her, warm her through and through, and she felt a certain heat climb her neck when he raised her fingers to his lips. They lingered there for two or three long seconds, his bold gaze locked with hers, through every staggered breath. Odd that George had done this simple gesture a hundred times in the last few months and she'd never become breathless, or hot within.

"Exeter's not here yet," George cut in after taking a sip of his sherry.

To Mary, his ill-timed pronouncement felt like an intimate intrusion. She blinked, reality settling in once more, then gently tried to pull her hand back from the earl's grasp, which he had yet to drop.

"Unlike him," Marcus commented without adding anything by way of explanation, still looking at her.

Then he swiftly released her fingers, turning away and moving to the sideboard, where he could help himself to a drink already dutifully poured by one of the two waiting footmen. Instead of sherry, he took whiskey.

Mary felt hot all over, uncomfortable in her stays, and she decided the sherry would not do. She needed to remain focused tonight lest she embarrass herself at a formal dinner in front of the most important people in Cornwall. She placed her half-empty glass on the tea table beside her, and sat primly, her hands in her lap, noting again how even after the slight shift of her body in her chair her best corset pinched at the waist and the lace of her gown rubbed raw against her skin. How foolish she was to choose style and attractiveness over comfort. Her plain purple gown would have been a far better, not to mention a more conservative, choice.

"Have you spoken to him yet, Renn?" George asked, resting his arm across the intricately carved mantlepiece.

The earl took a long swallow of whiskey and gazed at both of them over the rim of his glass. "No," he replied after a moment, lowering the tumbler. "But after tonight, I'll make arrangements for a private meeting. I'm sure there are more things to discuss than I've taken into account."

Mary hated the thought of not being privy to the family issues and the specific gossip that was likely to take place when the viscount arrived. But she also knew it would be her place to suggest that she retire. Before she changed her mind about mentioning it, she rubbed her palms together and sat forward. "Perhaps it would be best if I took dinner elsewhere, gentlemen. I'm not sure I should be part of a discussion of family issues."

George dismissed that with a wave of his hand. "Nonsense. You're lovely company."

"I want you here, Miss Marsh," Marcus maintained.

God, she suddenly wanted to grin, though as any good guest she restrained herself and nodded negligibly. "As you wish, Lord Renn," she answered properly, shielding her delight by pinching her lips together gently.

A certain glimmer passed between them, and she noticed what seemed to be humor in his eyes as well. She could only wonder if he suspected her desire to stay and found her backhanded approach to it amusing.

"I always get what I wish for," he said, his hard mouth twitching at one corner.

Her eyes opened innocently. "Do you?"

He almost smiled. "Are you in any doubt?"

"Doubt about what, my lord?"

"Will you two stop bantering with questions?" George broke in before topping off his sherry. "It's making me dizzy."

"My God. I never thought I'd actually see you again, Renn."

Attention captured instantly, they all turned toward the doorway. Filling it impressively stood the forceful bearing of Baudwin Fife, Viscount Exeter. Tonight he looked well groomed, reserved as he should in a soft woolen suit of off-black, white shirt, and Byron tie, accenting nicely his auburn hair and fair skin.

"And Miss Marsh," he added without waiting for response, stepping into the room and toward her. "I'm enchanted, as always."

She doubted it. But she nodded gracefully as she raised her fingers for his grasp, shivering inside from some uncomfortable yet unfathomable sense she felt every time she found herself in the viscount's presence. She'd often wondered why the countess wanted her only daughter to marry the man, but then, that was none of her concern and most probably an estate issue.

"Exeter," the earl cut in at last, walking to stand beside them, "it's good to see you."

George moved closer as well and the three men shook hands in turn, all the while conscious of the somber mood and underlying tension pervading the reunion.

"Care for a drink?" George offered properly.

"God, yes," Baudwin answered in an exasperated air. "Whiskey, please."

"Whiskey it shall be."

George nodded to a servant, who had already begun pouring the amber liquid into a tumbler, then sat again in the chair beside her.

"So, Renn," Exeter remarked, pulling out his tails and making himself quite comfortable on a matching midnight blue settee across from them, "How was your return? I hope the weather was to your advantage on the trip."

Marcus moved so that he stood between Mary and George, directly across from the viscount, leaning his elbow on the cushioned back of her chair. "I didn't actually pay much attention to the weather until I returned to St. Austell," he replied.

"Right." Exeter took a long drink, then licked his lips and scowled. "It's been a nasty spring. All rain and mud." He glanced at Marcus from the corner of his eye. "I'll bet you miss the hot desert, eh, Renn?" He snickered and took another drink. "And the desert ladies. I hear they're quite . . . uh . . . different from our English ladies. Beautiful."

Mary could sense Marcus stiffening at her side, wondering at his mood, if he were as annoyed by the viscount's lack of respect as she was. But she didn't dare look up at him, or say a word as she would have loved to do at that moment.

"Beautiful, yes, in a different manner from the English, I suppose. But I am seldom in the company of Egyptian ladies." He took a sip of his own whiskey. "I generally spend my days digging and cataloguing, studying."

"That's my brother," George cut in, "all work and no play. But then there are beautiful ladies in this country, too."

"Oh, true, true," Exeter agreed. Then he chuckled again, shaking his head before finishing off his drink. "I apologize, Miss Marsh. This discussion isn't appropriate for an English lady's ears, I know, but you're older, a spinster. You've no doubt heard it all before."

For the first time in her life, Mary hated that word. The drawing room seemed to reel for a moment, grow ever hotter, until she realized it was her own sudden fury bubbling up from the inside and threatening to escape in a scathing retort. Still, because she was a lady of refined class, she did nothing but smile, albeit somewhat sarcastically, running her palms down her skirt at her thighs.

"I imagine you're correct, Viscount Exeter," she admitted prosaically, staring him in the eye. "At my age, very little shocks me."

The tension fairly crackled; George placed his sherry glass on the tea table with a loud *clack*. The earl hadn't left her side, and she hadn't felt him glance down at her at all, so with all hope, he didn't notice her cheeks flaming with supreme embarrassment.

"Frankly, Exeter," Marcus said in a dark, speculative tone, "I tend to be far more shocked by the behavior of the English than by that of the Egyptians. But then, perhaps it's because I've been away so long. Many things have surprised me upon my return, including the memory of just how naturally lovely and refined English ladies are."

Nobody said a word to that, though Mary felt the incredible urge to hug the man for his witty defense of her—which, as it happened, was one of the most surprising things she'd felt since her arrival in Cornwall.

Suddenly the viscount laughed again and raised his glass. "Right you are, Renn. Another one," he ordered the waiting footman, who quickly moved to the sideboard to do his bidding.

"Exeter, darling, I'm so glad you could make it to dinner," came Gwyneth's saturnine voice from the doorway. She glided into the room, in a wide gown made entirely of black crepe, looking perfectly preened and attractive, yet sufficiently dour that the occasion didn't appear too much like entertaining.

"And here is one of our lovely English ladies," the viscount said, arms outstretched. Gwyneth reached him first, and he grasped her shoulders, pulling her forward for a peck of his lips to her cheeks. "You're looking well, Lady Renn, especially under such dismal circumstances."

Gwyneth stood back a pace, patting the back of one hand to her cheek. "Yes, thank you ever so, my dear. It's been a trying time for all of us, and I fear the horror that has befallen our family will in no way dissipate soon."

"Oh, no, I imagine it won't," the viscount agreed, accepting a newly poured whiskey from the footman without looking at him. "I'm just so glad we're all able to be here for you."

Gwyneth smiled faintly. "Yes, as I am. Renn has returned at last. My darling son." She glanced at him, and Mary couldn't help but do the same. He stood at her side still, with fortitude, his hard face expressionless.

Then slowly, as if knowing everybody watched him with speculation, he stepped forward and kissed his mother's cheek dutifully. "I'm glad you're feeling better," he remarked.

"Thank you, dear."

Mary stood at last. "Lady Renn," she acknowledged with a tip of her head.

"Mary, dear, I'm so glad you're joining us."

Mary didn't know if that was a sincere statement, but she didn't comment, and neither did anyone else. It appeared they all felt it perfectly natural that she be included.

Gwyneth took a sherry offered her from a silver platter, and for a moment they all stood around the tea table, silently sipping their beverages for something to do, avoiding conversation and the morose atmosphere that seemed destined to plague the entire estate. Moments later, Safford, always the efficient butler, announced that dinner would now be served.

Mary followed Gwyneth into the dining room, the men behind her.

"Miss Marsh will be seated next to me," the earl fairly ordered without looking at any of them as he walked to the head of the table.

That pronouncement startled her as much as it did everybody else, but she tried not to show her surprise. Nobody objected verbally, of course, though she felt quite certain speculation ran rampant among them all. But as if it were an everyday occurrence for her to sit next to the earl, she blindly moved to his side as he reached for her chair and held it out.

"Thank you, Lord Renn," she said quietly, sitting perfectly still. He took his place to her left, Gwyneth hers at the foot of the table, George across from her, and the viscount to her right. It had been a long time since Mary had felt so exposed—for no reason—and so utterly uncomfortable at dinner.

They all remained relatively quiet during the first three courses, and Mary ate little and talked even less, though the conversation stayed casual and general, mostly about mines and clay transport. Of course the viscount had the same issues to relate to that George did, and for a time the two of them held at least part of her interest.

At last, however, between the courses of creamed white fish and roasted duck, as she knew would happen, the earl leaned back in his chair, half-filled wine glass in hand, and gazed at their guest.

"Well, Exeter," he began nonchalantly, "I'm sure the death of my sister has been extremely difficult for you."

Mary thought she might have heard Gwyneth gasp; George cleared his throat loudly.

The viscount sat back as well, his chair creaking from the weight. He lifted his wine glass and drained it, signaling the waiting footman to refill it. "It's been simply awful, Renn. Simply awful." He drew a long, full breath and shook his head. "Such a lovely girl, and I adored her. I hope you know that."

Mary stared at her uneaten duck, picking at it with a fork, acutely listening to the subtleties in inflection between the two men during such touchy conversation.

"I do, indeed, Exeter. I know she was so looking forward to marrying you."

The viscount shifted in his seat. "And I her, of

course. Her accident has been most unfortunate for everyone."

Gwyneth placed her silverware on her plate. "Please, darling, let's not talk about this now—"

"When exactly would you like to discuss it, Mother?" the earl asked matter-of-factly. "Exeter is here now, and this is a family dinner."

Mary hoped nobody would notice her.

"Um, Miss Marsh is here, too, Renn," George added hesitantly, nodding once in her direction.

She suddenly wanted to slide under the table as they all turned their attention to her.

"I'm well aware of that, George. She was also Christine's last good friend, and I enjoy her company."

What company? God, she'd hardly said two words in the last hour.

"I agree," the viscount remarked, lifting his glass. "To Miss Marsh. A lovely spinster who graces our table with beauty and smells of lavender. Thank you ever so much for sitting her next to me, Renn."

For the first time that she could recall, Mary actually felt keenly humiliated for the man—and for the Longfellows. The viscount was drunk, and it showed in his speech, voice, and actions. But as she was quickly learning he often did, the Earl of Renn saved them all embarrassment by ignoring it.

"When was the last time you saw Christine, Exeter?" he asked coolly, taking another short sip of wine.

Mary glanced up at the viscount's face. His cheeks and nose were pink, but he seemed oblivious to the importance of the question.

"Oh . . . I don't know. Perhaps a week or two before she—" he waved over a footman to refill his glass. "A week before she died, perhaps."

"And how did she seem to you?"

"Renn, really," his mother admonished.

Marcus gave her a look of cold steel, but otherwise brushed over the comment. "How did she seem?" he repeated.

"She seemed . . . the same—no, overwrought a bit." He paused. "Maybe."

Marcus leaned forward in his seat, never dropping his gaze from the man. "Overwrought in what way, specifically?"

Perspiration began to bead on the viscount's brow, and in two swallows he finished off his wine again. Mary found that amazing, as she'd never seen a person drink so much alcohol in one sitting.

"God, I don't know," he exasperated at last, waving one hand in the air then dropping it hard on the lace covered table. "The way women are from one day to the other."

A cloud of icy silence fell over the table. Mary couldn't contain her resentment any longer, though she did manage to restrain herself.

Tapping her lace napkin on the side of her mouth, she asked pleasantly, "Then you've got sisters, Viscount Exeter?"

Everyone looked at her, including the viscount, who glanced down to her person for the first time, his brows pinched.

"No. What the devil has that got to do with anything?"

She expected that. Smiling flatly, she replied, "I was just utterly amazed that you knew so much about ladies and their day-to-day behaviors." She folded her hands in her lap. "From where do you get your information?"

It seemed to Mary that everybody squirmed, including one or two of the servants, though she never dropped her pointed gaze from the viscount's pinched red face.

"Yes, Exeter," the earl urged thoughtfully, taking the cue, "Miss Marsh poses an interesting question. Do tell."

A moment passed in awkward silence. Baudwin quickly took another drink of wine from his glass, which had just been dutifully refilled without his having to ask this time, then placed it loudly back on the table.

Suddenly, losing some of his meager control, he returned his concentration to his food and began to slice what remained of his duck with fumbling hands. "Maybe she was nervous 'bout the wedding," he blurted, biting down on a large chunk, then chewing loudly. Waving his knife and fork in the air, he added, "Maybe it was her monthlies that had her confused. That happens to the lot of them, you know."

Gwyneth gasped loudly at that. Mary was mortified, and couldn't look at the earl whom she suspected had to be utterly enraged at the debasement of his sister. She did notice George fist his hands on the table across from her, however. And yet, extraordinarily, nobody said a word.

The viscount peeked around him, grumbling, "Where's a handy footman when you need him." He spotted one. "Ah. More wine, my good fellow."

The tension crackled like fire as the room fell

silent. One footman moved to do as told by the earl's guest, and Baudwin continued to eat as if nothing had occurred worth noting, while the rest of them sat otherwise silent.

Within an instant, the countess stood. "I'm feeling tired. Exeter, darling, enjoy your dessert, and do visit again, when you're ready to discuss delicate issues. Next time I should hope they'll be sobering."

It was a cold slap in the face to the man who wasn't coherent enough to understand it.

"Good night, my lady," he said without looking at her.

Marcus and George stood as well. "Mother, good night," the earl said, somewhat softer in tone than Mary expected.

George tugged at his evening jacket, then his cuffs. "I'll say good night as well. Exeter, as always, it was good of you to come." He turned to her. "Miss Marsh, I'll see you on the morrow, no doubt."

With that, he and Gwyneth left the dining room.

For a moment, she had no idea what to do or say. Awkward couldn't begin to describe how she felt, but beyond everything else, she wanted to get away from all of them and forget this horrible night.

"Gentlemen—"

The earl touched her arm gingerly as she started to rise, stopping her with the surprise of it.

"I'm hoping you'll join us for dessert, Miss Marsh," he insisted softly, his gaze implying a seriousness to his even tone.

She hesitated, until the viscount, still on her

right, jumped in, oblivious to the fact that he alone had ruined dinner for all of them.

"That's right, Miss Marsh," he agreed, snickering. "Renn and I could certainly get used to looking at a woman like you while we have our serious talk. Renn here probably hasn't laid eyes *or* fingers on a lady in ages. Looks like you'll be the one."

Mary went rigidly still. She'd had enough of this man.

"I'm not much for being a plaything, Viscount Exeter," she said coldly.

He looked up from his plate, then around the room. "So sorry," he said, wiping his napkin on his mouth, then gazing at her again. "Christine mentioned that because she knew you and her brother so well, she was hoping—"

He stopped himself, then grinned wryly, "Never mind. I'll let you guess on that."

Mary felt her skin burning, her anger rising to the surface. "If only Miss Christine had known *you* so well, Viscount."

She felt instinctively that the earl relished her boldness. But he remained silent, brooding, no doubt.

The viscount only laughed jovially as he reached to finish off his wine. "You are a clever girl."

At that moment, Mary wanted nothing more than to leave Cornwall. She'd never liked the Viscount Exeter, and many things about his relationship with Christine were coming to light this evening. Suddenly she realized why the earl continued to put up with him, why he wanted her to stay in their presence, at least for a while. Drunk as he was, the viscount evinced an inner personality and habits that were very telling. She only had to wonder if this was the man Christine knew and had known intimately; if he had been the central focus of her fears and worries; if she could have gone through with the wedding, or would have made it through the marriage.

But at that moment fate intervened and they were all saved further abasement.

The viscount pushed his chair back and stood, swaying on his apparently stiff legs, waving off the approaching footman, who carried chocolate tortes on three small ivory china plates. The footman ignored him and obediently served them anyway. Mary almost laughed at the ridiculousness of it all, and how the servants must be gossiping downstairs. It was quite absurd— and horrifying in its way.

"Let's talk tomorrow, Exeter," the earl said, dismissing his guest as he stood as well. "I'd like to have a private word with you, at your home. You'll be feeling better then, I'm sure."

Baudwin looked confused for a second or two, then shrugged and yawned. "We'll need to go over the gifts, the mine transaction."

Mary turned her attention to the earl for the first time in minutes.

He stood still as stone, enraged; she could sense it, though he remained remarkably composed.

"Naturally," he replied. He nodded stiffly. "Good night, then, Exeter. I'll contact you."

"Very well." The viscount's eyes quickly roved over her face. "Miss Marsh."

"Have a safe journey home," she said prosaically, refusing to offer her hand.

He stepped back, and with only a minor stumble, proceeded to walk from the dining room.

The atmosphere felt hot around her, moist from heavy angered breaths and salty air. The footmen still stood beside the serving table, like statues in polished livery, staring forward, probably nonplussed but hiding it as they should. Abruptly, she felt like laughing again. This was all far too strange for her. She should be in London, regardless of her worries. She should be home, where life was normal, facing what was surely easier than this.

"Would you walk with me in the garden?"

Her heart tripped in her breast, and ever so slowly, she looked back into the earl's eyes.

He gazed at her frankly, in strength, in hope and a shrewd understanding of how this all must appear and feel to her.

She shouldn't be alone with him, however. She couldn't allow herself that. Not at night, with darkness looming, in quiet solitude. It was too risky—

"Miss Marsh?"

"I'd be delighted, Lord Renn."

Chapter 10

Baybridge House
7 November 1854

. . . I've been darning old socks to give to the or-
phanage for the Christmas holiday and upcoming
winter. It's what Mother wants, though I have been
secreting chocolates away to put inside them. She
would fuss about that if she knew. "Don't let the
children hope for riches they'll never have" and all
that. Ridiculous! What do we have, if not hope? . . .

They stepped out of the dining room doors and
onto the gravel walk that wound through the
garden as it circled Baybridge House to the south.
As it was a rather balmy night, she didn't need a
wrap, though with some sense of self-preservation,
Mary kept her arms crossed over her breasts.

Marcus, at her side, didn't speak for a minute or

two as they made their way slowly around blooming rose bushes and neatly clipped hedges. The air
smelled of mist and greenery, mingled with a gentle, salty sea breeze. Mary adored the Renn garden
and found herself there frequently, though never in
such a mood as she was in now.

She couldn't have described her feelings if her
life had depended on it. She was at once appalled to
have witnessed such rudeness from a member of
the gentry, filled with heartache for the loss of
Christine, and angered that the countess, and even
the earl himself, seemed so forgiving of the viscount and his lack of culture and restraint. Frankly,
she'd met the Viscount Exeter on several occasions
and never had he been as rude as he had been tonight. For a second she actually wondered if the
cause was the full moon—but then, she'd never believed such superstitious nonsense. There appeared
to be no explanation aside from excess drink.

"He lied, you know," came the gruff whisper
from her companion.

Mary shivered from the dampness in the air,
clutching herself even tighter, staring at the gravel
at her feet. "I know."

Marcus stopped walking abruptly and turned to
face her. "You do?"

She paused, standing stiffly as they stood in
front of a marble fountain, the sound of its water
trickling in the background. By pale moonglow
and the dull, far-reaching lights of the dining room,
she could just make out the lines of wariness on his
face, his eyes encased in black shadow.

"Yes," she replied softly. "He saw Christine the
day before she died."

The earl frowned, then shoved his hands in his pockets, relaxing as he chuckled mildly. "Actually, I'd assumed as much. No, Miss Marsh," he continued, gazing out to sea, "I meant he lied about me not touching a woman recently."

Her body began to sweat. "Really, Lord Renn, that's none—"

"—None of your business, I know," he finished for her. "I just didn't want you to think I'm a failure at romance."

Mary had no idea what to say, and part of her wanted to excuse herself from his company and depart post haste. They stood alone in the darkened garden, with only the sounds of the fountain and ocean to cover their voices. It was much too intimate for her—both in atmosphere and in conversation. And yet she was also intrigued. By him, by the family. All of it.

"Don't be afraid of me," he whispered huskily, as if sensing her underlying nervousness, his eyes, now black pools of confidence, once again boring into hers.

She stilled the uncertainty welling up inside her. "I'm not afraid," she whispered in return.

For a moment he did nothing but tower over her, watching her, hands behind his back. She just continued to clutch her upper arms, refusing to move. He radiated a pull of incredible tension, like a magnet drawing her in, sizzling in its power. So difficult to ignore.

"But I will say," he continued, "that it's been ages since I've been kissed."

Oh, God . . .

She swallowed, and thought of the only thing

she could to keep from crumpling. "Why did you want a match between your sister and the Viscount Exeter, Lord Renn?"

For seconds he stared at her in darkness, but in her own determined way she refused to back down, even though they stood so close to each other she could smell his cologne.

Then he turned away from her and began pacing around the fountain, hands clasped behind his back. "Exeter's family and mine have been friends for generations. We also have clay mines that border each other's."

That didn't explain much. But then again, Mary was just thankful he'd gone along with the changes in topic and mood.

She lowered her body delicately to sit on the stone wall surrounding the fountain. "Did Christine want to marry him, or was it arranged?"

He stopped pacing and shoved his hands in his pockets, gazing down to the path. "A little of both, I suppose. It was more or less expected, and Christine had always liked Exeter—we all did, really. He was always the fun one, the jester, the one with the exuberant personality." Pausing, he drew a deep breath and lifted his head, briefly closing his eyes. "He's changed, though."

Mary heard the sadness in his voice even as she felt it in her bones. In a sense, she didn't understand her need to comfort this man, but it was there. That's what frightened her.

"I've never liked him," she admitted boldly, keeping her tone low lest someone eavesdropping near the house should hear her. "I didn't care for him when I first met him, and I dislike him intensely after tonight."

The earl seemed to hesitate for only a second, then, gazing at her once more, he walked back toward her. "I assumed as much."

She clutched her palms in her lap. "What I don't understand, Lord Renn, is why your mother—and if you'll pardon me—why *you*—would allow him to get inebriated and foul-tongued in your home without any retribution. He left here remaining a guest after insulting all of you."

It had been a forward statement, and she wasn't entirely sure she'd get an answer, or at least, one that would satisfy her curiosity. But instinctively, she realized she could say such a thing to this particular man without his thinking less of her or reminding her of her place.

With a brush of his fingers through his thick hair, he sat down hard beside her on the marble wall, his expression nearly hidden in the darkness.

"It's probably difficult for you to understand the interrelationships, as it were," he said, spreading his feet wide and leaning forward to rest his elbows on his knees. "But Exeter and his family have always been decent people, and Baudwin was never a threat to Christine. They liked each other well enough, and our families were always close, even though we were sometimes business rivals. But I suppose one reason we all wanted a match between the two had to do with land value and income. One of the most abundant of the clay mines in Cornwall is on the Renn estate, and it's producing very well. Some of the loveliest china anywhere is made from clay mined from my property. But production has always been more efficient and cheaper simply because our mined china clay has been able to be transported through Exeter land to get to the docks for shipping. If the viscount or his family were upset at us for any reason, he could bar us from crossing his property, which would cost us days of travel and pay to go around it."

He looked to the ground, shuffling his shoe back and forth along the gravel. "When arrangements were drawn up for Christine's dowry, one of the specifications made had to do with the exchange of property. For the marriage between families, Renn china clay would have unlimited access in crossing Exeter land, but more important, Exeter would gain one quarter of the riches of that one best-producing Renn mine. In other words, he, my sister, and their children would share a part of the monies earned on the sale of Renn clay, with the help of the Exeter estate in its shipping and distribution." He sighed, straightening. "Of course it's all more detailed than that, and it all seemed well and good at the time, but Exeter and I will need to discuss this issue again, I'm afraid. It's very likely he'll want to keep this particular contractual arrangement made in the betrothal agreement."

She frowned, finally understanding. "You'll lose money, won't you?"

"Yes, in a sense, because we've always had permission to cross Exeter property to ship the clay. If we fall back on giving him a percentage of the money earned from the mine simply because his betrothed has died—even if that were a reasonable option—he could very well deny us access, and use any excuse he wants." He groaned and leaned back a little, stretching one leg out in front of him. "It's very tricky, but George usually handles these business deals, as he's here and adores addressing the workings of the mines. I suppose the difficult part for him as the second son is that I'm the one who legally owns this property. It was my signature on the betrothal contract." He paused, then added solemnly, "And I'd rather be in Egypt."

Mary remained silent for a moment, letting this new information sink in. It all made sense, and of course, couples married for land and property all the time. It was nothing new, and in the course of history there were undoubtedly more difficult situations than this for families to address.

"But that still doesn't explain why you allowed him to speak as he did at table," she insisted, sitting as tensely as she felt inside. "Pardon me, Lord Renn, but he insulted you, your family, and even your sister."

He scratched the back of his neck, then glanced sideways at her again. "I was far more angry that he'd insulted you, Miss Marsh. You are my guest, a lady, and among the living."

Mary didn't move, could hardly breathe. Her mouth fell open so that she fairly gaped at him. She couldn't see his expression, but she had the idea that he smiled.

The breeze stirred around them, rustling the hedges. Still, Mary didn't look away from his shadowed face so close to her own. No, she didn't fear him like this, all alone in the garden, didn't feel anything but his inner strength, his power, his heat. It overwhelmed her. But for the first time she relished it as well.

"Tell me about your work, Lord Renn."

That startled him. He looked down at her sharply, his brows drawn together to form a solid line in the moonlight. For seconds he hesitated, as if to question whether she actually desired specific details or if she simply wanted to find another less personal topic to discuss.

"What would you like to know?" he asked quietly.

She lifted her right shoulder in a shrug. "What you enjoy about it, what you do, exactly." She glanced to her feet. "Why you left England to pursue it when you have so many obligations here."

He breathed low and evenly as he sat beside her. Mary knew he pondered her rather intimate questioning, and that he'd respond. She simply waited.

Finally, he said, "I suppose in simple terms, I'm a translator of Egyptian hieroglyphic script."

He'd told her this once before, but now it utterly fascinated her. Mary shifted her body on the fountain wall to face him squarely. "What does that mean exactly?"

"That means, Miss Marsh, that I'm well versed in the ancient form of Egyptian writing called hieroglyphics. It's an art and a science, really, and not many people in the world do what I do. The language has only been understood for thirty years or so, and of course that's relative. We're learning new concepts all the time. But for the last four years, I've been traveling with several distinguished professors of archaeology. Together, we put into context their findings, that are uncovered on sculpture, papyrus, and tombs." He pursed his lips, then added, "It's mostly tedious work, of course, a great deal of cataloging, but work I've wanted to do since I was a child."

"That's absolutely remarkable," Mary whispered wistfully after a long moment of silence, her honesty expressed without question.

He cocked his lips in a half-smile. "I enjoy it."

"More than tending to land and china clay mines?"

He breathed in very deeply. "I've never been good with practical matters on the home front, aside from getting them done with minimal effort. Too anxious to explore other lands, cultures, languages, I suppose. At my father's death, George took control of the mining and lands. I was merely in the way, with nothing keeping me in charge aside from the little circumstance of having been born first."

An extremely difficult situation for the whole family, she imagined, and not one with which Gwyneth would likely ever come to terms. She knew that as well as she knew the lady herself. It made the earl's determination all the more understandable and Mary's sympathy of the man's predicament all the more abundant.

"Did you attend school to learn what you do?" she asked, oddly treasuring the intimacy of the moment.

He nodded once. "I studied six years of language at Oxford. I speak and write Greek, Latin, and French proficiently. Later, I studied with students of Champollion, the man who first deciphered hieroglyphs correctly in eighteen twenty-two."

Mary grinned broadly, which he evidently noticed.

"How is that amusing, Miss Marsh?" he asked, with only a trace of defensiveness in his tone.

She pressed her lips together before admitting, "I think it's funny that Christine never mentioned your achievements or what exactly you *did* in Egypt. Her comments generally boasted of your personal presence, your . . . bearing as a man and an earl. She was quite proud of you and your achievements, and she spoke of you frequently, but it wasn't about language or study, it was about digging, discovering, charging into battle, as it were, the brave leader of a group of rugged scholars who found treasures of incredible worth in various tombs and pyramids." She brought her palm to her mouth to hide her grin for a moment, then lowered it again, her expression more prosaic. "Nobody ever mentioned that you were a quiet intellectual and scholar, though I find such a description much more true to what I know of your personality, Lord Renn."

His eyes roved over her face. "Christine simply found a way that she could personally accept my absence," he revealed quietly. "In her mind, as with all my family, unless I'm doing something of profound importance abroad, I should be here, at Baybridge House, doing my duty as the Earl of Renn. To my very young and impressionable sister, charging in and making discoveries of lasting human significance seemed more acceptable than my sitting in the desert, at a dry wooden table, wearing old, faded clothing, and logging words and picture-writing onto a paper tablet later to be reviewed and analyzed by various scholars." He paused then added, "There is simply no way to explain to those who care about me that doing precisely that is what makes me the man I am."

Before she thought of her words, Mary replied, "I understand."

He sat staring at her for so long, Mary began to fear she'd said too much. The fountain bubbled behind them as the only sound for miles, it seemed; nothing distracted his focus from her at that moment.

Then, thickly, he murmured, "Your interest in my work, and my desires, means more to me than you know."

She shivered, rubbing her arms with her palms as he continued to stare at her in near darkness. "I'm afraid to ask why," she whispered.

"Maybe because nobody ever seemed to listen to my wishes if they didn't correlate with their perception of what I *should* be doing."

"Like your mother?"

He nodded. "Specifically. But George, too. He's never fully understood my need to get away, to discover the unknown, as it were. He respects my decisions, but I can tell he's a bit envious that I have chosen to forsake my duties as a land manager."

"Is he envious of your title?"

Marcus frowned, glancing to the ground. "I don't think he's given it much thought because it's always been mine. I have always been the earl and he's always been the second son. We fought constantly as children, but as adults we're very much friends. He cares for me, as I do him, and worries about me when I'm gone, but he's very different in personality, as you've probably witnessed."

She smiled. "It's been rather obvious, yes."

He swiftly looked her way, then back to his shoes. "He has his own life, his own friends and ways of doing things. I sometimes get the impression from him that he'd like me either to stay and manage the land, or give him all responsibility." He dropped his voice so that it was barely audible. "I wonder if he's considered that he would have chosen a better match for Christine, but I've never asked, and he's never said as much. Though I do wonder that now."

His confessions stirred Mary to the heart. In a way, she felt privileged to be bestowed his trust, and highly flattered that he'd revealed so much of himself to her without assuming how she might respond. As if he wanted her to know the very deepest part of his inner turmoil and longings.

"Now, I want to ask you something, Miss Marsh," he said contemplatively, changing his tone as he tapped his fingertips together in front of him.

"Of course, Lord Renn," she replied politely.

He stared at his hands. "Where do you buy the material for the items you make and sell?"

That subject completely stumped her. When she didn't instantly come back with an answer, he looked into her eyes again, and Mary felt certain that he noticed her surprise since she faced the light of the distant house.

To clarify, she returned, "I beg your pardon?"

"It's a simple business question, that's all," he stated with a small lift of one wide shoulder.

Brows furrowed, she lowered her lashes as she turned to gaze out across the flowers. "Normally I purchase my materials from a Mr. Oliver Billingsly, a distributor in London; I've done business with him for several years."

"I see."

She had no idea why he should.

He twisted toward her a little more, a little closer. "So this Mr. Billingsly sells you colored satins and silks at your request?"

Her stomach began to knot and she rubbed her nose for something to do. "Lord Renn—"

"Humor me, Miss Marsh." It was a very definite insistence.

She held her ground. "Yes. He imports them and sells to a number of dressmakers."

"And trousseau . . . planners?"

Her insides truly clenched now and her palms began to perspire. "Yes." She raised her chin a little, straightened her shoulders, probably to keep herself from cowering. "He also sells me cotton and wool."

He nodded, thinking. "I'm certain he does." Suddenly he lowered his hand and rested it, palm down, on the fountain wall between their bodies, leaning on it, toward her.

"And when you get these silks and satins—"

"And cotton and wool," she added, her tone husky.

"And cotton and wool," he repeated, "what do you generally do with it?"

She didn't for a minute think he was that stupid, but she played along, wondering how they'd gone from ancient Egypt and scholars to intimate apparel. Leave it to a man to do so. "You're aware, Lord Renn, that I make nightgowns and sheets and practical accessories for the bride."

"Ah. Yes, I see. Practical accessories." He waited for a moment, then glanced into her eyes. "What do you do with the satin and silk? Can one actually *wear* a satin nightgown?"

Mary felt the heat rush to her cheeks. "I'm sure this is not a discussion we should be having, my lord."

"I'm just curious, Miss Marsh. You asked about my business, my work, now I'm asking about yours."

Oh, it was much, much more, and she was certain he knew it, too.

She inhaled deeply and looked at her skirt, rubbing her thumbs together nervously in her lap. "Very well," she said a bit too sharply. "With my business, I do occasionally make satin and silk nightclothes for ladies who request them."

"And corsets?"

She could swear her heart stopped. Her eyes no doubt appeared as round as saucers, but thank God the man couldn't see the scarlet color of her skin. Or feel it burning.

"I'm sorry, Lord Renn," she murmured hoarsely, "but I'm not sure why this is something you need to concern yourself with. A gentleman like yourself has no business—"

"That's where you're wrong, Miss Marsh," he cut in with determination. "This isn't personal, it's your business. If I choose to marry someday, I think I would like my wife to wear colorful satin corsets and silk nightgowns." He paused, leaning ever closer so that he nearly touched her, his voice a deep whisper. "Until I saw your workmanship for myself, it hadn't occurred to me that such items were for sale. You're very good. Could I call upon you for the task?"

He wanted her to make nightgowns and corsets for his future *wife*? Would he have her model them for him as well?

"My Lord Renn," she admonished in rigid form.

"Miss Marsh?" he replied innocently.

She ignored the light humor in his tone. "This type of request of my services is usually . . . is most often chosen by the bride-to-be, or her mother. Not the bridegroom. There are factors involved, a trying on and experimenting with fabrics and sizes, of showing the lady the various styles and colors. The bridegroom is the one to benefit from the surprise."

The earl sat back a little. "Ah. Benefit." He nodded. "I see your point."

"I'm glad." She smiled and quickly stood. "It's getting late. I think I shall say good night."

Immediately he stood at her side, inches away, his face looming over her shadowed form. Just as quickly, he brought his lips down to lay them softly against hers—touching, melting, burning into them.

Shock overtook her good senses, and numbly she allowed the intimate caress of his mouth as it lingered against hers. Somewhere deep inside, Mary wanted to succumb, to give in and enjoy as she hadn't in years—or to shove him away and run. Yet even as he refrained from embracing her, she couldn't bring herself to move. The feel of him was heaven. Gloriously divine. As perfect as she'd ever imagined.

He moved his lips in gentle rhythm, softly coaxing her to respond without invasion. She heard the trickle of the fountain, smelled the sea air and flowers, felt a moan well up from deep in her throat, and suddenly yearned for his total embrace.

And then, abruptly, it ended.

Slowly, he shifted his head to the side of her face, his breathing labored and warm against her cheek. She had yet to open her eyes, afraid of what she might see—or of what he might witness in hers.

"I think," he whispered, brushing his lips along her temple, "that I will call you Mary anyway, when we are alone like this."

She leaned her head back, unable to find her voice, to utter a word.

"Mary . . . the perfect name for a lady," he finished in a husky timbre. "I just wonder what fire there will be to discover beneath this outer layer of perfection."

With one last breath, he drew his thumb across her lips. "Good night, Mary Marsh."

He left her then, alone in the garden, shivering by moonlight.

Chapter 11

Baybridge House
22 November 1854

. . . The weather has been most dreary, and Exeter has made himself busy with the miners. I haven't seen him in almost two weeks. My mood has been strange of late, as well. I had the most unusual dream last night—that I was alone in a blizzard, without direction, calling to a faceless form in the distance. I thought it might be you, dear Marcus, but at the point when I needed you to show me direction, you weren't anywhere to be found . . .

With a deep frown, Marcus stared out the library window to the garden fountain—the one where just last night he had been swept away in a sweet kiss that had shocked his senses and filled him with heat to his bones.

"Where the devil is your mind today, Renn?"

He shoved his hands in the pockets of his black morning jacket and turned to his brother, who relaxed with tea on the small red brocade sofa.

Red, like silk . . .

"My mind?" he repeated gruffly.

George snickered, bringing his cup to his lips. "You haven't heard a word I've said."

That was probably true, he decided. It had been a hell of a night. "I've been thinking, George."

"Clearly."

Marcus ignored that snide comment offered with good humor. Such a contradiction in delivery was so like his brother.

He stepped away from the window, out of the beam of sunlight that had been resting on his shoulders, keeping him warm. Although it was early still—not quite nine o'clock—he'd been up and moving about the house since five, reading, catching up on paperwork, taking breakfast in the dining room. Yet he hadn't seen a sign of Mary.

"I asked you if you've made any definite plans regarding your return to Egypt. I've got issues to settle at the mines, and I can't have the villagers begin speculating on why we're both in Cornwall when one of us could be serving in the Crimea. Times are hard here as well."

Marcus hid a smile. For all his grumbling, George was no more fit for war than he was. George was a business and property manager; he was a researcher and . . . what? An adventurer, he supposed, though some people in this country didn't seem to understand that, or his desire to enrich lives and expand horizons of the mind through history. Still, his expertise with foreign dignitaries and ancient, unique civilizations and their languages could come in handy with the war effort, and there were many in the House of Lords, including him, who did nothing but contribute financially.

"Ready to get rid of me, George?" he asked wryly, sitting hard in a burgundy winged leather chair across from him.

George placed his empty teacup on a polished walnut end table beside him and grinned sheepishly. "Of course not. It's been rather pleasing to see you again, brother." He sighed with a bit of exaggeration, interlocking his fingers and resting his palms on the back of his head. "It's just that production has slowed, and certain wives and widows are wondering why we're not out there fighting to get their men home and back to work." He sank lower into the sofa. "War is beastly."

"I won't argue that," he replied somberly.

"Physically and economically," George added.

Marcus rubbed his chin. "How is Exeter managing?"

George shook his head, frowning a bit. "About as we are, I suppose. He's been able to keep his shipments moving better than we have, though he's down in production as well. But most of what I hear about Baudwin is gossip. He's been rather tight-lipped about business details lately."

"No doubt," Marcus replied, though he wondered about that. "How were he and Christine getting on?"

George's eyes clouded over as his face fell, though Marcus couldn't be certain if that was because he'd brought Christine into the conversation, or because she and Exeter had been having more negative interaction than a few pre-wedding jitters.

George gazed past him, out the window to the cloudless sky. "They got on fine, I suppose." He shook his head twice, harshly, then looked down to the extravagant floral carpeting. "Before her accident she was reluctant to visit him, though."

He'd said that so casually, and yet Marcus found it to be riveting news. He sat forward in his chair, eyes narrowing. "What do you mean by reluctant?"

George rubbed his eyes harshly with his forefinger and thumb before turning his attention back to him. "Just . . . I don't know, exactly. I suppose it was more of my impression, really." Suddenly his brows pinched in frown. "Why?"

Marcus leaned back again, regarding his brother with newfound questions— and suspicions. "I'm not sure," he said. Tapping his fingers on the thickly padded armrests, he amended, "I'm not sure, but I felt such despair from her in her letters to me. You felt it, Miss Marsh felt it—"

"What are you saying, Renn, that something was amiss between them?" George scoffed. "Christine had known Exeter all her life, more like a brother, I expect, than a lover. It's my belief that she trusted him implicitly." His voice dropped. "And besides, there was no indication that Exeter had anything to do with her death."

He'd said that so quietly, Marcus had barely heard the words. The mere idea of Exeter being involved in Christine's turn of fate was not only shocking and potentially scandalous, but pure speculation. George was right, to a point. On the surface, Christine's death had been an accident. Exeter wasn't even on the property, and nobody in this house would want to cause her real harm. But after seeing Baudwin again last night, Marcus felt even more assured that something very new and strange had played a part in his sister's growing anxiety and ultimate demise. And Exeter seemed likely to be at the center of it.

"His drinking is pronounced," Marcus said, watching his brother closely.

George waved his wrist through the air. "The strain has gotten to him, too, and he wasn't himself last night, certainly. What he said shocked even me. I couldn't respond."

"I'll take care of that."

George raised a brow. "I suppose you don't need to walk as fine a line," he said contemplatively.

Marcus understood what he meant. George had to relate to Exeter frequently, and always would, where the mines were concerned.

George blew out a long breath. "Exeter's the same man, Renn. Just . . . more like his father as the years pass. But he's just lost his betrothed, and he's taking it hard."

Marcus suspected this as well, but it had been more than a decade since Wallace Fife, Baudwin's father, had succumbed to an aging body with an unspecified heart condition. Still, he didn't remember the elder Fife ever acting as Exeter had last night.

"He drinks more than his father did," he said, feeling an irritating twinge of regret and failure seep in that perhaps this overindulgence had been noticed by Christine. But it made no sense that she wouldn't tell her brothers so, especially in private letters to him. No, whatever her fears, they were far worse than marrying a man who occasionally imbibed too much but whom she otherwise trusted.

"Maybe he does overindulge," George agreed. "He irritates me from time to time as well. But we need him; our families are connected and always will be. You know that." He paused, then asked, "Have you spoken with him yet?"

"No, but I will. He'll want to keep the provisional agreement."

George continued to stare at him. Then slowly one side of his mouth turned up in a grin. "But we've got better production than he has this year."

"Really?" Marcus hated talk of the mines. It bored him and always had.

"What is it with you and the lovely spinster?"

Marcus blinked, then felt his heart start pumping fast. "What's that got to do with mining?"

George laughed. "You always get this absurdly dour look on your face when I bring the mines up. I thought I'd change the subject to something you seem to enjoy thoroughly." He controlled himself and leaned forward a little. "The lady's a dove, isn't she?"

A dove? He wasn't quite sure how much an agreement on his part would give away his thoughts. "Indeed," was his staid yet simple reply.

George didn't accept that for a second. "Oh, come now, Renn. I've noticed how you stare long and hard at her." His brows shot up as pure delight flared from his eyes. "I'll bet Egyptian ladies are nothing like her, eh?"

Marcus snorted, then actually grinned. "Egyptian ladies are a lovely diversion in their own right," he said mildly, explaining nothing.

"But not so refined and beautiful as our seasoned guest."

Marcus didn't want to question what he meant by *seasoned*. Instead, he asked, "How did she and Christine get along?"

George's eyes opened wide in surprise. "They got on excellently, I should think. Christine adored her, talked about her frequently when they weren't together. Miss Marsh, for her part, seemed to take Christine under her wing, show her things, explain things."

"What things?"

George pulled a face. "Oh, I don't know. Miss Marsh is from the city, and I know that intrigued Christine." He glanced to a bookcase for a second or two, then back again. "She and Miss Marsh had some interesting discussions, now that I think about it. Lord, I shouldn't have overheard, but one of them was . . . rather risqué."

Marcus rubbed his chin, less shocked than he knew he should be. "Risqué?"

George chuckled again, though this time he seemed almost embarrassed.

"By risqué, I mean that it was talk for ladies, between ladies. One day they were sitting together on the bench atop the cliffs, when I came upon them. Of course, they didn't know I was there, but . . ."

"But what?" Marcus pressed, intrigued.

George shifted his weight a little on the sofa. "Oh, I don't know. I stumbled upon some discussion or another about the wedding night."

He had no idea what to say. "And?"

"And what? I left."

Marcus's hopes fell. "You just left? Without learning what they were talking about?"

"I heard a moment's talk about the color and cut of fabric, and how easy it could be to unfasten a corset with the new designs today." George's lips hardened. "When it got to more intimate details, it wasn't my place to stop and listen, although it was fairly . . . accurate, from what I *did* hear."

So Mary Marsh knew what to expect on her wedding night. He wasn't sure how to take that tiny bit of fascinating information. She might be a virginal spinster, but she wasn't young and naïve. Suddenly, for the first, time, it occurred to him that she might not even be a virgin.

She kisses like a virgin . . .

Marcus crossed one leg over the other, annoyed with himself for letting his thoughts stray to feelings. "How did Christine take it?"

"Take what?"

"Their talk."

"I've no idea." George tossed his hand up with exasperation as he sank lower into his seat. "What does all this matter anyway? It was just silly talk between ladies, and I left when I heard all I could stand."

He was right. It probably didn't matter in the least. Mary and his sister liked each other, and if Mary was in any way able to help Christine in her final months, from her concerns about her upcoming marriage, to whatever fears she kept secret, Marcus was thankful.

"Where is she, by the way?" George cut in, shifting his gaze to the wall clock above the mantel. "Usually, I see her up and taking tea before now."

Placidly, Marcus replied, "I couldn't begin to guess."

"Hmm." Slowly, George placed his palms on his thighs, stood with effort, and moved to Marcus's side. "Well, I'm off to the trenches." He hesitated, placing a hand on Marcus's shoulder, his tone subdued. "Try not to worry so much about this, Renn. It's a difficult situation for all of us. I'll never forgive myself for many of the disagreements Christine and I had before she died, but the hardest part is knowing she was closer to you than she was to me, and I lived under the same roof. That she was hurting so deeply in her final weeks, without my knowledge, will haunt me for the rest of my life."

Marcus nodded, though he never looked up.

George drew a deep breath and stepped back, clasping his hands behind him. "There are so many things in life that one cannot explain. I only wish I had been a better brother."

With that, he turned and without a backward glance, quit the room.

Marcus sat where he was for a long while, deep in thought, before rising with the conclusion that it was time to talk to Mary Marsh about the intimacies of her position and what exactly she had "taught" his sister. It was also, he supposed, time to accept the fact that he wanted to get to know her much, *much* better.

With determined effort, he walked from the

empty library, trying to calm the absurd nervousness he felt at such a challenge. It had been a long time since he'd decided with finality that he was going to pursue a woman.

Chapter 12

Baybridge House
27 December 1854

. . . Christmas dinner was the same as it always is, I suppose, although an argument in the parlor during dessert left me quite unnerved. Baudwin challenged George again about mine property and land rights, and George got angry and bopped Exeter in the nose! Oh my, what a sight! I almost laughed, but I think they were both a bit foxed. They were speaking again this morning, so I suppose all is well. I know it's not proper for me to say so, but I intend to have the upper hand in this marriage . . .

Mary walked along the cliffs, staring out to sea and down to the bay below, watching as the wind produced rather large, foaming waves, tossing the various fishing boats and their occupants about. It occurred to her how determined these fishermen were. In her very sheltered world, she had been somewhat pampered. Her life, aside from her involvement in the making of provocative lingerie for distinguished ladies, had been routine for a lady of relative wealth and means. How different life must be for simple folk who are forced make a living in such trying physical conditions. She supposed a clay miner's experience was much the same. She wondered for a moment if the earl had left his duties because of his desire to live away from such physical labor, but then decided that wouldn't have been his reasoning. It certainly had to be physically demanding to live and work in a barren land. If there was one thing Mary understood it was that one must find one's own destiny, wherever that might be.

She shivered where she stood, rubbing her bare arms with her palms. The morning had turned gray as a storm rolled in from over the deep ocean. It would rain soon, but at this point, she didn't care. The wetness would probably clear her mind as nothing else seemed to do.

Her thoughts never wavered from the events of last night. The talk with the earl, in a darkened garden, no less, should never have happened. No, the talk had been lovely; that . . . *kiss* shouldn't have happened. That marvelously horrible kiss that had made her legs weak and her stomach churn with disappointment when he had finally pulled away.

God, it had been years . . .

But it wouldn't happen again, she decided with resolve, straightening her shoulders and lifting her chin as a sign of her conviction, closing her eyes to

the wind. She was not a woman to settle on lust.
Not at her age. She got enough satisfaction wondering at the secrets of married life when she made
her underthings for ladies. And she refused to contemplate that one time years ago, when she let herself go to the brink of insanity—

"Good morning, Miss Marsh."

Mary turned sharply at the sound of his voice.
His incredible, soothing deep voice that made her
spine tingle and her mouth go dry. He stood about
ten feet from her, wearing a black morning suit that
complimented his stately build perfectly as he
stared at her person.

She swallowed with difficulty, attempting not to
cower.

"Lord Renn," she returned simply, albeit a tad
harshly.

He chuckled, and for a moment it irritated her
that he found so much irrelevant humor in a simple
acknowledgment. Then he rubbed his chin with his
fingertips and slowly began to move toward her.

"Why are you always off by yourself?"

That stumped her and she took a step back. "I
beg your pardon?"

His eyes narrowed as he halted in front of her. "I
missed you at breakfast."

Her heartbeat suddenly seemed to thud against
her chest.

Missed you . . .

She had no idea what to say.

"You look lovely today," he said softly, interrupting her thoughts.

Her mouth slowly dropped open.

"You know," he continued, getting ever closer

without actually touching her, "Christine mentioned you rather frequently in her letters to me."

Mary could have screamed. "Is that so," she said succinctly. "I hope it was all quite good and . . ."

"Useful?" he finished for her.

"Useful?" she repeated.

His gaze lingered on her lips. Then he shrugged and glanced over the bay. " 'Useful' just seemed a word you'd use, Miss Marsh. Perfectly proper, yet deep with hidden meaning."

She didn't know whether that bothered her or not, so she stood her ground. But she positively burned to ask him what accounts Christine's letters had actually contained.

God, what a nightmare.

He chuckled again and scratched the back of his neck. "Miss Marsh, you are a contradiction, on many fronts. Of course my favorite is your very proper . . . passion."

That made her fairly tingle, but she wasn't about to ask him to explain.

She drew a deep breath. "Lord Renn, I really must be—"

"Going?"

Her lips thinned as she stared him down. "Will you stop—"

"Finishing your sentences for you?"

Deflated, she wiped a palm across her face, and for the first time, felt like laughing. She sucked her cheeks in to keep from doing so, then opened her eyes wide in innocence. "Lord Renn, are you *trying* to irritate me?"

He shook his head and dropped his voice to a rough whisper barely heard above the lingering sea breeze. "Actually, I was rather hoping to kiss you again."

Mary heard the blood rushing through her ears, felt a certain prickling between her legs, knew she flushed deeply.

"That can't happen again," she insisted, though it sounded more like a croak.

Ignoring that, he sighed with mild exaggeration, stuffing his hands in his pockets. "I'm sure you'd like to know what Christine said about you."

Would you please stick to one subject? she wanted to shout. Instead, she clasped her hands behind her back and turned toward the ocean. "I'm sure it was all very superficial," she replied.

"Not really. Christine rather liked you." He stepped to the edge of the cliff and looked down. "What I find so interesting is that in several interesting ways you're nothing as she described you to be."

That thoroughly intrigued her. He seemed to anticipate this response as well, for he left the meaning open, not bothering to explain, apparently, until she asked.

Mary squeezed her fists together behind her, closing her eyes briefly until she couldn't wait any longer. "Very well, I'll ask. How did your sister describe me, Lord Renn?"

Without hesitation, he disclosed, "Well, she said you were very often of good humor."

Mary straightened, stone-faced, trying ever harder not to laugh. "Really. Is that all?"

His brows rose faintly. "Oh, no, Miss Marsh, there is quite a bit more."

She could feel her cheeks beginning to burn, but she refused to comment on that.

He stepped closer to her so that he was nearly touching. "She also said you were wonderfully witty, talented, and an engaging companion." His voice became markedly serious as he gazed down into her eyes, his a dark, crystal-clear blue. "I'm so very glad she had you for that in her final days, Mary."

He said her name with incredible intimacy, but instead of being offended, Mary felt utterly drawn to him. The wind swirled around them; somewhere on the distant wharf she heard a bell toll. But in a second's understanding of herself, she became very afraid she would lean up and kiss *him* this time.

Her legs went weak, and she lowered her lashes, stepping back and away from him to sit on the bench overlooking the water. The earl didn't seem the least bothered that she moved, and as she expected, he followed her.

"Tell me," he asked genially, "How does one go about making a corset?"

She gasped. "My lord!"

"Hm. Do you mean that as a Christian statement or do you mean me personally?"

That had her thoroughly confused. "What?"

He sighed as his mouth thinned to an aggravated line. "Do you see why I would prefer that you call me Marcus?"

She blinked quickly, and wrapped her arms around her waist. "Oh." She sat up straighter. "It isn't proper."

"Let's be improper."

Mary had the distinct notion that he was teasing her severely. And not only was she beside herself with consternation, she quite liked it, which only made her appalled at herself. But the hidden part within her that enjoyed the daring aspects of life, the part that made her the woman beneath the skin, felt a sudden passionate surge of excitement at the prospect of engaging this man. This unique man who sat beside her so . . . properly, dressed, as always, in formal attire, looking ruggedly handsome and in his own way mysterious.

"I should think," he fairly whispered, "that I would enjoy getting to know the woman beneath the facade, Mary. The woman my sister knew, the one who—for just a moment last night—lost herself to passion in my arms."

To her horror, he reached out and touched her with one coarse finger, gliding the tip of it down her hot cheek.

She swallowed, fighting the urge to scold him, to bat his arm away with hers. To lean forward six inches and mold her lips to his.

"Would you like to know a little of my work?" she said, her voice sounding husky and foreign to her ears.

For a moment she was certain he almost smiled. Then he dropped his arm and leaned back against the bench. "As much as you can properly tell me, of course."

His tone was so vibrantly smooth; Mary decided at that moment that if she remembered nothing else from her stay in Cornwall, she would never forget the sound of the Earl of Renn's magnificently deep, male voice.

She repositioned her body a little where she sat, brushing a stray lock of hair from her face that had loosened from the bun. She knew it would do no good sitting so high on the cliff in the wind, but if nothing else, fussing with her hair gave her something to do with her hands.

In a daring move, she admitted, "I prefer working with silk."

His brows rose in what she assumed was mock fascination, but she didn't comment on his apparent surprise, and neither did he.

"It's . . . soft to the touch, has such an exotic feel."

"When worn next to the skin?" he asked with a seriousness she felt certain was false.

"Yes," she replied. "And when I'm working it through my fingers."

"Do you wear your creations, Miss Marsh?"

She eyed him quickly before dropping her gaze to her very conservative honey-brown day gown. "What reason would I have to wear anyone else's, Lord Renn?"

"Touché," he said in quick response.

She smiled in spite of herself.

"I would very much like to see some of your work," he admitted after a moment of awkward silence.

Her fears had come true and she shivered. "For what purpose?" she asked bluntly, looking back into his beautiful eyes with bold innocence.

He shrugged lightly, frowning. "I'm interested

in your talent, your business," he answered flatly. "Christine had nothing but good things to say about them."

God, what *else* had Christine written him? She could only fear.

"Tell me," he asked, rubbing his clean-shaven chin, his brows furrowed in curiosity, "is it true that not all corsets need to be tied anymore?"

Her first thought was to ask him where on earth he'd heard that, but decorum restrained her. "Yes, it's true."

"Really?" He stared into her eyes. "Explain that, if you will."

She drew a deep breath, squeezing her hands together in her lap, feeling her pulse race through her veins but determined not to let him know how he, and his furiously impertinent questions, affected her.

"Actually, that's been true for some time, Lord Renn," she explained nonchalantly. "Corsets made of whalebone, which by necessity needed to be tied in back, could hardly prove efficient for the lady who had no one to help her dress."

"Or undress, I should think."

Her mouth dropped open. Then she closed it abruptly as she realized he was completely serious. "Yes," she fairly stuttered.

He waved a palm in the air. "Really, I had no idea. I assumed all corsets were alike."

This intrigued her, more so, she decided, because it gave her an opportunity to describe the speciality of her work to a typical man who probably didn't know a thing about the fusses women of their time endured simply to be presentable.

"As you'll note, Lord Renn, there are many factories today that produce a standard corset for the common woman, affordable and made of plain broadcloth or sometimes bombazine. Most are still tied, however. In more fashionable ladies of wealthier means, one will observe fasteners in back which can be immediately pulled apart for easy accessibility, some constructed of metallic stays that don't bend as whalebone does, though they do tend to rust, which can prove problematic.

"There are corsets covered with white satin for a ball; there are riding corsets that have elastic at the hips; nuptial corsets; nursing corsets with drawbridge gussets; corsets made of doeskin for summer wear; traveling corsets with stays that can easily be removed for night wear; even some made strictly for nightwear having no stays at all. There are particular corsets made for singing, dancing, bathing at the seaside; some lightly boned for morning wear as opposed to evening dress; some even constructed of silk cord netting where a lady may hang a sachet of perfume at the center." She drew back and sighed, adding dreamily, "Really, it's so complicated to be a lady these days."

As she finished her disclosure—the first such discussion ever with a man— she once more gathered the courage to look at him. Her gaze at last drifted to his face, but instead of crudeness or humor in his eyes, she saw absolute shock, and something she could only describe as awe.

After a moment, lips parted, he mumbled, "I never knew *dressing* could be so complicated."

She smiled with a splendid satisfaction. "You've never been married, my lord."

"That doesn't mean—" He stopped himself, angling his head to eye her candidly. "I've seen a corset or two in my day, Miss Marsh."

She tried not to let that faze her, though she could feel the pounding of her pulse in her temples. "No doubt in shopkeepers' windows or in pictured advertisements."

He grinned devilishly, making her insides melt. "No doubt." He waited, then leaned very close to her. "But I've never seen one made of red satin."

"Perhaps you will when you marry, Lord Renn," she whispered with bold conviction.

"One can only dream, Miss Marsh," he returned just as softly.

She suddenly became very afraid that he would touch her again, or kiss her senseless as he had last night. No, not afraid, exactly. That was the wrong word entirely. In a manner, she was desperate for it. He still sat so close to her, watching her, thinking intricately, she could tell. In that instant the world faded from her, and no longer was she on the open cliff where anyone on the shore below or in the hedges and hills surrounding them could see. She and Marcus Longfellow sat together in a world of their own. And she liked it immensely.

"I have a certain request of you, Miss Marsh," he said huskily, his gaze traveling over her face as he took in her features one by one.

She struggled for breath. "My lord?"

His lips twitched. "I think I would appreciate a showing of your expertise so that when I do marry, I know what to expect."

Oh, God.

"I'm not sure I understand you," she murmured.

He didn't move; his power enveloped her.

"I want to observe your work for myself, Miss Marsh." He paused, then added, "In the most discreet manner, of course. If you are as talented as I've been told you are, I would like to have a private look for myself."

Her heart pounded; her skin grew prickly hot. "You already employ me, sir."

He nodded once. "I do indeed."

But that's not what you meant, is it?

Suddenly Mary completely understood him. She wasn't naïve or inexperienced where gentlemen and their base reactions to females were concerned. Yet her feelings for the earl not only surprised her, they disturbed and enlightened her.

He wanted her as a man would want a woman. She could hear it in his tone, see it in his incredibly dark and passionate features. But he held back in a manner that amazed her. The most surprising thing of all was that she wasn't as repulsed as her mother and good society had raised her to be. No, she felt only pity at her own base failures because, God help her, she wanted it as much as he did.

She stood on shaky legs, her skirts billowing out in front of her from the strong ocean breeze. "I shall think on your request, Lord Renn. But for now, I must be going," she insisted, her tone shockingly smooth and relaxed-sounding to her ears.

For a second or two, she could have sworn her quick submission startled him. Then he raised his body beside her, though he kept his gaze locked with hers.

"One more thing, Miss Marsh."

She wrapped her arms around her waist. "Yes?"

"Did my sister ask you specifically to make her the more . . . exotic under things, or did you do so out of habit?"

Mary licked her lips. "I do nothing out of habit, my lord."

He nodded. Then standing stoically, his features drawn, troubled once again, he glanced out over the bay. "But did she specifically ask you to make night clothes and corsets for her that were of the more erotic variety?"

Never had Mary felt more embarrassed, and yet instinctively she knew that he'd asked her purposely, for a reason—not to humiliate her. She drew her shoulders back and lifted her chin slightly to reply. "She—" Clearing her throat, she tried again. "Miss Christine was very specific about not . . . disappointing her husband."

"I see."

She wanted to squirm in her own clothes.

He looked down at her again, his features unreadable. "Thank you for being candid, Mary."

God, she wanted him to kiss her again. Those beautiful eyes . . .

"Good afternoon, Lord Renn."

Her perfunctory farewell said, she skirted past him, refusing a final glance over her shoulder, even as she knew he followed her with eyes that exposed an intense, forbidden longing to match her own.

Chapter 13

Baybridge House
12 January 1855

. . . Miss Marsh has finally arrived. Mother put
her immediately to work, and already we have had
several fittings. She's such a lovely person, and I
have a feeling she and I will be good friends. Her
zest for life is so refreshing that sometimes we
laugh together while discussing the most outra-
geous things! I wish you could meet her, Marcus. I
am quite positive you would enjoy her company,
too . . .

He felt horribly guilty for wanting her, yet
want her he did. More than he'd wanted a
woman in a long time. She went far beyond a contradiction, he decided. She was far more intelligent
than Christine had alluded to, a listener who actu-

ally entertained interest, beautifully unique—and most certainly the only woman he'd ever known who could give him an erection by the mere discussion of corsets. Jesus, he *still* got hard when he thought about it, and it had been three hours since she'd left him. Something had to be amiss in that.

Marcus stood beside a long bay window in the drawing room at Crestmore, Baudwin's home on the Exeter estate, too restless to sit as he waited for the man. He hadn't been inside these walls in likely half a decade, but nothing had changed. The drawing room still carried frilly reminders of Baudwin's mother, who had died almost twelve years ago. The walls remained papered with the same scene of gaudy cherubs flying through pink roses that wound their way up golden trellises. The identical shade of bright pink covered the velveteen settee and winged chairs that gathered around the gold-plated mantel, on top of which sat a row of pink china cups engraved with various floral patterns. Floral oil paintings in gilded frames hung from each wall, except for a stately portrait of Baudwin that reached at least eight feet high on the far wall above a small writing desk, also covered with a pale pink lace runner.

God, so much pink. It surprised Marcus a bit that Baudwin, the only child of the late Viscount Exeter and his wife, Lady Jane, had yet to rid his home of such an utterly feminine place to entertain. Then again, maybe he'd been waiting for Christine to do it.

Christine.

Marcus closed his eyes and leaned his head back, feeling an indescribable gnawing in his stomach again. He knew it well, as he'd been enveloped with both self-pity and guilt for his maddening inability to push the form and face of Mary Marsh from his mind since he'd first seen her at dinner the night of his return to England. He wasn't here for romance; he'd returned to Baybridge House strictly to investigate, if only for his own satisfaction, Christine's unusual and untimely death. Yet the more he learned, the more Mary seemed to be in the center of all of it, especially his thoughts.

Christine had been accurate in her descriptions of Mary's serene beauty. She was indeed a lovely woman who carried herself with sophistication and ease, her cool, outward appearance disguising an inner mystery and passion all too potent to ignore. Just the memory of their discussion three hours ago made Marcus smile in deeply felt enjoyment. There was no denying it. She wanted him, too.

That probably made him a cad. He had no business contemplating a sexual affair at a time like this, and yet for the first time in ages, the idea of getting Miss Marsh into his bed seemed to chase all else from his mind. He was fairly certain he could seduce her, but then what did that make him? And what would he do with her once he took her innocence—if indeed he did take it? These questions made his skin prickle with the heat of lust and the most unusual sense of remorse. The worst part of it all was that no answers were forthcoming. He seemed deadlocked with pent-up emotions of so many kinds they made his head spin.

"Renn, good fellow, so glad you dropped in."

The jocular tone of Baudwin's introduction shook him immediately from his musings, bringing him back, with more than a trace of irritation, to the point of his visit.

"Good afternoon, Exeter," he replied formally, stepping toward his host. "You're looking well."

The viscount gave him a half-smile and a shrug as they shook hands. "As well as can be expected under the circumstances, of course."

"Of course."

"Let's sit, shall we?" Baudwin made a motion with his hand toward the pink furniture. "I've ordered sherry, and Elsie will have it momentarily."

Marcus didn't want or particularly like sherry, but didn't mention that as he sat with relative ease in an overly soft chair. He also noted for the first time that Exeter not only looked well, but rather cheerful of mood and light of manner for this occasion, one that by all accounts should prove to be reflective and serious.

Baudwin remained a handsome man, he supposed, clean-shaven except for side whiskers, his burnished red hair combed perfectly, though upon closer examination it appeared to be receding farther than Marcus had remembered. He wore a navy woollen suit, expensive and tailored to perfection, hiding an expanding belly rather well, he thought. Even with his faults, the Viscount Exeter was a good match for any lady, at least on the surface. Still, somewhere in the back of his mind, Marcus felt very uneasy that he had simply expected his sister to marry the man before examining the situation more closely.

"So, Renn," Baudwin began, pulling out his tails to sit in the opposite chair. "How is Egypt?"

Marcus hadn't expected that, though he took the comment in stride. "The same as it's been for thousands of years, I expect," he returned casually.

Baudwin laughed. "Good show. Did you enjoy it enough to want to go back?"

He felt his uneasiness spread, though he had no idea why. He'd been asked this same question a dozen times since his return to Cornwall.

"I hope to, yes." He shifted his weight in his chair and crossed one leg over the other. "I still have a great deal of work to do."

"Yes, yes, of course," Exeter agreed in dismissal. "I completely understand."

Marcus knew for a fact that the viscount didn't understand at all. Nobody in England understood his need to return to unfinished business, nor did they care about what it was he actually did in Africa. Since his return, only Mary had asked him, and that sudden realization saddened him as it hit him hard in the gut. For most of his life, not a soul on earth had ever understood him, aside from his sister. Now Mary appeared to be the only one who cared, and ironically, he hardly knew her at all.

"But really, Renn," Exeter carried on, his thick brows pinched, "how did you ever get used to the heathens?"

That got the anger brewing. He didn't come here to discuss issues that someone of Baudwin's lack of worldly expertise would never comprehend.

At that moment he was saved from an impolite retort when a woman he assumed to be Elsie stepped into the drawing room with a silver tray on which sat two crystal sherry glasses and a matching decanter filled to the rim.

"Ah, finally," Exeter said, curtly nodding to his servant. "On the tea table."

Elsie obliged without looking at Marcus. Then with a slight curtsy that gently shook her brown ringlets, she quickly left the drawing room, closing the door behind her.

Baudwin wasted no time in pouring two glasses, handing one to him as he took a sip of his own.

"So, tell me Renn," the viscount pursued after running a tongue along the rim of his glass, "why are you keeping the Marsh woman around?"

Marcus nearly choked on the high-quality drink as his heart began to pound in his chest.

He cleared his throat and sat up a little. "Keeping Miss Marsh around?" he repeated.

Baudwin snickered and took another sip. "I just would have expected her to have left by now. Are you using her services for something else?"

It occurred to Marcus that Exeter knew exactly what he asked, and he hadn't been very subtle with the question.

He refused to fall pray to utter crassness. "She's helping me to follow in Christine's last footsteps," he explained, voice low. "The two were rather close, and I've asked Miss Marsh to help me understand what might have happened to my sister in her final days."

A perfectly simple answer, and yet Marcus noticed how Baudwin seemed to pale. Or maybe it was his imagination.

The viscount dropped his gaze to his sherry and straightened. "Well then," he tipped his glass back and finished the contents, "aren't you the lucky gent?"

One brow rose faintly. "Indeed, I suppose I am. The lady is charming."

Baudwin briefly glanced at him, his expression eager for details. But something in Marcus's bearing, or frank stare, made the man hesitate.

Good humor failing him, the viscount at last reached toward the tea table and poured himself more. "I suppose you're here to discuss the betrothal agreement."

Marcus lifted one side of his mouth negligibly. "Yes, but there's something I'd like to ask first." He paused for effect, then murmured, "You mentioned at dinner that you hadn't seen Christine the week she died, and yet I heard elsewhere that you'd visited with her the day before her death." He frowned and took another quick sip from his glass. "I'm sure you forgot this when we discussed it at dinner due to the lateness of the evening, and of course all the drink. But perhaps you'll remember now."

It took only a matter of seconds for the viscount's face to go from pale to shiny red. He looked embarrassed, and even a fraction worried, though Marcus had never prided himself on reading facial expressions.

"I did see her the day before, actually," Exeter admitted, making a huge effort of shaping his neckcloth. "I had forgotten until just now."

"No doubt," Marcus assured him, noting the beads of sweat appear along his upper lip. "Was the conversation of any import?"

He knew at once that was the wrong approach, and Marcus could have kicked himself for giving Exeter the suggestion of claiming an innocent exchange, thus easily forgotten.

"Oh, it was nothing." Baudwin brushed his hair off his forehead with a jerky wrist before lifting his glass to his lips again. "Just womanly insecurities and all that."

Marcus felt his jaw tighten. "What kind of 'womanly insecurities' do you mean? Where did this conversation take place."

Exeter was plainly taken aback by that. His brows narrowed slightly as he replied, "Here. She came here." He shook his head sharply. "Something about marriage between our families. It concerned her."

That intrigued him and he sat forward again. "Why?"

Exeter snorted. "How the devil should I know? She didn't have any rational reasoning for anything that day. She was blustery and sniveling and I simply listened to her with half an ear, as men are given to do under such trying circumstances." He paused, staring down at the floor. "Seems she found a letter of some kind and was very upset about it."

"What letter?" Marcus asked, barely breathing.

Baudwin gazed at him again. "I've no idea. I never looked at it. Honestly, Renn, it didn't have any importance."

"How do you know? You didn't listen to what she had to say."

The viscount blinked, as if he wasn't sure of the

meaning behind those words. Then he shrugged and took another quick drink of his sherry. "Good God, it was female irrationality that upset her that day, nothing more. Probably had to do with a friend who lost a lover, or couldn't marry her lover, or a family who disapproved of a lover. Could have been anything." He finished off his sherry and glanced around. "Christ. I need a whiskey."

Marcus found his insensitivity appalling. "Didn't it occur to you, Exeter, that this behavior from Christine contradicted her normally rational mind, not to mention it being a trifle suspicious coming from her a day before her accidental death?"

Baudwin pulled his collar from his neck again. "No." He slumped a little. "Oh, all right. I suppose so. But I can't see how the two are related, which is obviously why I'd forgotten the entire affair."

In a world of far-fetched nuances, that was entirely possible, though Marcus doubted it to be the case here. Something burned in his gut about such strange associations—Christine's fear in her final correspondence with him, weeping and carrying on about a letter in front of Baudwin the day before she died, and especially her betrothed conveniently forgetting the circumstances around such an emotional moment. And did Mary know about the letter? It would seem odd that she'd not mentioned it, though it gave him an excuse to see her again tonight to inquire. He caught himself before he smiled at the thought.

Marcus placed his nearly full glass of sherry on the table, then folded his hands in his lap, deciding to drop the topic for now. He would get little more information from Baudwin for the time being.

"Before I leave, Exeter," he said with calm articulation, "I'd like to discuss the betrothal arrangement we signed a year ago."

Relief filled his host like a tangible thing. Baudwin visibly exhaled and breathed in again, deeply, as if his troubles were finally and forevermore over regarding such a sensitive topic as that of Christine and her untimely demise. Marcus delighted in the knowledge that *nothing* was over; he would revisit this topic again and again until he had answers.

"I'm sure you're aware," he proceeded, "that Renn china clay needs continued convenient access to and from Charleston Harbor."

Baudwin smiled flatly. "And I'm willing to continue providing it."

Marcus nodded, bubbling blood coursing through him even as he tried like hell to remain neutral in this necessary conversation. "I knew you would." He leaned forward, feet flat on the floor, elbows on his knees, palms together as he eyed the man frankly. "Let's be realistic, Exeter. We need to keep our production affordable. You'd like to keep the percentage of the mine offered you in the betrothal agreement. Regardless of the law, I propose we keep the agreement as is and between us."

Exeter frowned, gazing to the tea table and nodding briefly, just enough to suggest he was actually considering the recommendation, even as they both knew he expected nothing else.

Bastard.

Marcus stood. "I do have one small request on my end, however."

Baudwin had the good grace to look up quickly.

Marcus waited until the man stood as well, though he awkwardly rubbed his palm down his frilled shirtfront in the process.

"Of course, Renn," he yielded pleasantly.

Marcus stared down at the man, feeling a sordid satisfaction mingled with pure disgust that he truly tried to keep tempered in his tone.

Very slowly, with profound implication, he murmured, "If you ever again speak so crassly to my mother, or use your foul tongue in front of a female guest of mine as you did last night, the entire town will hear about it." He clasped his hands behind him. "You may very well become the wealthiest miner in Cornwall, but socially I will ruin you."

Without so much as a handshake, Marcus quit the frilly pink drawing room, sickened and sweating and filled with more questions than he'd had when he arrived.

Chapter 14

Baybridge House
25 January 1855

. . . Miss Marsh has taught me so much already! She's quite independent, and yet socially reserved, warm and witty, and bites her tongue when I know she'd enjoy taking Exeter on in a verbal exchange. She's from the city, as you know, and I believe she's more worldly than my betrothed, perhaps even George. Quite frankly, my darling brother, she reminds me much of you and your need to experience life. I think you and she would match wits and intelligence most excellently . . .

Mary stared at the handwritten note in her palm. He requested a meeting with her this evening, after dinner, in his study. Signed, *Marcus*. *Nobody ever calls me Marcus . . .*

God, how it frustrated her that as much as he defied social convention where she was concerned, she still couldn't think of anything but him—his sharp, penetrating eyes, his large and marvelous physique, his good humor and wit, his gentleness.

Mary crumpled the paper in her hand and closed her eyes to the ceiling of her bedroom.

Honestly, what had she thought would happen when she agreed to stay and help him? He didn't need any help. He talked to people without her, the Viscount Exeter this afternoon, his brother frequently. All without her. So for what, exactly, did he need her? In the end, there would likely be nothing of any significance to discover.

For the first time, Mary felt she'd made a certain dreaded mistake in deciding to remain in Cornwall. As time went by, it grew apparent that she needed to escape from the sorrow of remembering a lively, vivacious girl with naïve hopes, the stifling confines of Baybridge House, the final darkness of a fearful death, and most tormenting of all, the man in whose presence she grew less and less sure of her purpose.

It was time to discuss her desire to leave, which, in the end, would be best for all of them. She would do so this evening after dinner, in his study, as he'd requested.

Mary stood at his study door, breathing deeply to calm her jittery nerves. She smoothed her palms down her plum satin evening gown, then rapped gently on the door.

"Come in."

Just the sound of his deep, forceful voice made

her swallow. Then, as he bade her, she entered his study, her body erect, head held high.

"Close the door behind you, Miss Marsh," he ordered without looking at her, sitting at his desk, shuffling through paperwork.

She did so, never taking her eyes from him. She waited a moment, then said, "My Lord Renn. You wished to see me?"

He looked up, gazing at her speculatively for a moment. Then he tossed a piece of paper onto his cluttered desk and sat back in his chair, his large hands clasping the leather armrests.

"Would you mind sitting?"

She blinked. "Of course not."

She could have sworn he held back a smile, but she quickly looked away, walking to one of the chairs and sitting gracefully across from him, making a great effort of arranging her full skirts around her legs and feet. He didn't say another word until she finished, though she had the distinct feeling he took note of every move she made. Suddenly the room felt very hot and her cheeks warm. She ignored it.

"My lord," she said again.

He did smile this time—or more correctly, smirked.

She remained expressionless, hands folded properly in her lap, her back ramrod stiff by intention, though she could feel her heart pounding in her breast as he continued to stare at her unabashedly.

At last he drew a long breath and dropped his gaze to his desktop. "Miss Marsh, I'm sure you're aware that I had a visit with the Viscount Exeter this afternoon."

"Yes." *Too aware.*

His dark features turned down in a frown. "He mentioned something I found rather interesting."

She waited, not sure how, or even if, he expected her to respond.

Suddenly he stood, and after a quick tug on his frock coat to straighten it, he turned his back to her and strode stiffly to the window next to the wall of porcelain plates, gazing out to the night sky.

"It appears he now remembers seeing Christine the day before she died."

Mary inhaled deeply. So the viscount had been honest at last. How remarkable. "I believe she went to his estate to see him."

"Did she tell you why?" he asked without hesitation, pushing his hands into his pockets.

It occurred to Mary that he did that a lot, and she wondered briefly if it was a nervous gesture. Then she scolded herself for caring.

"No," she admitted, sagging a little into her corset. "But I do know she was very upset when she left. More so when she returned."

An eerie silence descended on the study and lingered. She rubbed her palms along her gown for something to do as she waited for him to absorb that information, little help as it probably was.

At last he turned around to face her, though he never moved from the window. The lines surrounding his mouth, the pronounced creases in his forehead, his dark, troubled eyes, all blatantly expressed the tension he felt within.

At last, he mumbled, "Exeter mentioned a letter of some kind that concerned her."

Mary frowned gently. "I don't recall a letter she received that upset her, but then I wasn't exactly privy to her personal affairs, Lord Renn."

His lips flattened grimly, and Mary tried to decide if it was due to an obvious sign of his irritation at her continued use of his formal name. But then she could never be informal around an earl, especially one who employed her. He should know that.

"Was she receiving correspondence from anyone regularly that you know of, Miss Marsh?"

That surprised her. "No, I was never aware of correspondence from anyone aside from you."

He waited a moment, crossing his arms over his chest, which stretched his frock coat tightly over his large shoulders. Mary tried hard to ignore that.

"And she never mentioned this letter to you?"

She shook her head minutely. "No."

He glanced at his china plates, eyes narrowed. "Did she say anything to you when she returned from seeing the viscount?"

Mary hesitated, wondering if she should disclose her feelings as well as facts. In the end, she decided to be honest. At least, without betraying Christine's dignity.

Unconsciously, she clutched her satin skirt over her thighs. "Under normal circumstances, Lord Renn, I would never betray your sister's trust. I hope you realize that."

He looked back into her eyes, his brows raised fractionally. "I do indeed."

She shifted her weight in her chair, though she never moved her gaze from his. "That afternoon, soon after returning from her visit with the Viscount Exeter, she snapped at me. Christine had never done that before." She dropped her lashes slightly, taking note of the fine fabric of his shirt. "We were rather good friends, and that afternoon, when I inquired as to her well-being, she told me to keep my business to myself as she slammed her bedroom door in front of my face." Mary squirmed again, lowering her voice as she intertwined her fingers tightly. "Actually, she screamed it. I'd never before witnessed her wrath toward anyone like I did that day. She remained in her room that night until our fitting at eleven the next morning. Even then, she never apologized, and seemed very distracted. At one we went to luncheon. I never spoke to her again."

She paused in thought, and could feel with certainty the earl's striking eyes on her person as he studied her closely, absorbing her words. In seconds, he'd know she hid something from him, would question her further, and suddenly, in the instant, Mary decided to confide what would likely be his worst nightmare.

She gazed back into his eyes. "Can I trust your confidence, Lord Renn?"

Deeply, he murmured, "I suppose it depends what you mean by confidence."

Briefly, she brought her fisted hands to her mouth, then dropped them again to her lap, clutching the fabric of her gown. "I've something to tell you but it's—delicate."

He said nothing for so long she began to feel unsure. He watched her, brows furrowed, face tight, hair slightly mussed as if he'd just run his fingers through it.

His handsome, imposing image, so close to her, made her weak inside, and yet she trusted him. Such a feeling was of indescribable significance to her, and its impact hit her hard.

"Tell me," he urged very quietly.

Moments ago she couldn't look at him; now she couldn't look away.

"I have been doing this work for several years, sir," she began, concentrating on every word. "I pride myself on creating works precisely as my clients want, including a perfect fit for every garment, for every bride-to-be."

His eyes bore into hers, but he didn't reply.

"I found that as time went by, your sister's did not."

He frowned. "Did not what? Fit?"

He didn't understand, and she felt a flush creep up her neck at the thought that she was going to have to clarify it for him. "Didn't fit from the time I began the initial fittings, to the time of her death."

He said nothing.

She continued undaunted—or trying to remain so.

"Although she never spoke of it, and this is only my conclusion, it is my belief, Lord Renn, that your sister, at her death . . ." She swallowed and lifted her chin a fraction. "At her death, I believe your sister carried the viscount's child."

As the words left her mouth, she had no visible clue from him as to how he took that news. He simply stared at her hard, unwavering.

She refused to back down, though with every breath she grew more anxious within.

Finally, after several silent seconds, his upper lip twitched. "Did she tell you that?"

The change to his voice was telling. It possessed a new hollowness that carried to her a feeling of vague disbelief coupled with fury, and something else. Something ominous and chilling.

"No," she replied honestly. "I'm not even certain she knew herself. I don't know that anyone knew, including the viscount. I am only making an educated guess because I have seen it several times before—two weeks ago the corset fit, now it's too tight in the middle, and the middle has thickened in the particular way it does during the first stages of pregnancy."

He remained steadfast, his thoughts seemingly controlled, his jaw fixed rigidly. And then at last, when she didn't think their closeness could get any more uncomfortable, he turned away from her and took several steps to stand in front of the window, his palms flat on the sill as he gazed out to the darkened sea.

"Did you mention this to the authorities when she died?" he asked.

She fidgeted. "No."

"Why?" He slammed his fist on the sill. "And so help me, God, Mary, do *not* tell me it wasn't your place to do so."

His sudden burst of anger toward her startled her. But she understood it, and even, in a very odd way, relished it because it seemed such a personal interaction between them.

Drawing a long breath, she acknowledged, "I

had no proof; this was only my conjecture, and as such, it seemed to have no bearing on her accidental death. But most significant, my lord, was the simple fact that Miss Christine was to be married to Viscount Exeter in one month. If she were carrying his child, who would care? Yes, a few eyebrows would be raised at an earlier than usual birth of a healthy child, perhaps even a few snickers—"

"At my sister's expense," he interjected.

"Yes," she agreed without hesitation. "But she is hardly the first lady to conceive a child before her wedding day, and ultimately there would be no proof of an indiscretion. It should not have even much bothered the viscount or your sister, assuming they were aware of it. Nobody knew, and I imagine it would have stayed that way had she lived. I know I'll never mention it to anyone, save you."

Motionless, he stood where he was, gazing out the window into the solid blackness of a moonless, starless night, mulling over her words.

"Claudette Coswell knows," he murmured. "That's where that look she gave you came from. It was a look of verification."

It took her a minute to decide how to answer him. Finally, she replied, "It's possible, and I had thought of this at the time. But there isn't a way for her to accurately ascertain how much of the situation I'm aware of. Christine may have spoken to Mrs. Coswell about it, even perhaps the vicar in a bit of confusion or panic, but they would never tell a soul."

The earl nodded minutely, absorbing this information as she had weeks ago. The vicar and his wife would never betray the confidence of the richest landowner in this part of the country. Nor would they dare scandalize the names of the two most important mine-owning aristocratic families in Cornwall.

Mary knew she had explained herself well, that her intentional silence about her suspicions had come from sound reasoning. Still, she had a fair idea of how shocking this would be for him as it all gradually sank in, to know his sister would not have been a virgin on her wedding day, that she'd had intimate relations with such a brash man who didn't care to wait a few more weeks for the vows to be exchanged. Unfortunately, it spoke all too well of the little value the viscount placed on Christine's reputation, which, Mary supposed, was the truth behind the earl's focused anger, whether he recognized it yet or not.

And yet, when one is in love . . .

"Thank you, Mary."

She started, confused for a moment from the softness of that simple statement. "I—I'm not sure—"

"Thank you," he repeated.

He turned to face her again, eyeing her directly, his feelings masked.

"Thank you for telling me what I certainly didn't want to know," he continued, moving slowly toward her. "Thank you for being open, and honest, and sharing your private thoughts, even as you tried not to."

Suddenly he was so close he towered over her, a vision of masculinity and grace, arms crossed over his chest in a stance of power that complemented his probing, dark eyes full of feeling he likely couldn't express.

"What are you going to do?" she fairly whispered.

He drew in a long breath. "Tonight? Nothing. Maybe nothing at all." His gaze roved over her features outlined only by lamplight from the desk. "But this won't end until I have every answer I want."

"I know." And she did know that, too. She sensed his determination, his desire for justice, his need for questions to be answered completely and without prevarication. Such was part of his personality—a hunger for fairness rarely seen.

Mary could feel herself clutching her skirt so tightly it wrinkled. With effort, she attempted to loosen her grip and smooth it.

Neither moved as seconds passed in highly discomfiting silence. At last he asked, "Did Christine ever discuss me in detail, Miss Marsh?"

His change in approach was so utterly unexpected, she jerked her head back and gaped at him. "My lord?"

He unfurled his arms and rested his hip against his desk. "In the months that you were by her side as her friend, did she mention me in depth at all?"

She had no idea why he wanted to know this. It certainly didn't pertain to their very grave topic of discussion. "I suppose so."

He spread his palms wide. "And?"

She could feel that particular heat radiating from him again. "I'm not sure what you're asking."

One side of his mouth tipped up in smile. "What did she say about me?"

She tried not to smile back. "I don't believe this pertains to the topic at hand, Lord Renn."

"It doesn't, Miss Marsh."

She pressed her lips together to stifle a grin. God, his eyes were so blue.

"She talked a little of your past, your quiet nature, your . . . care for your family. She adored you."

His smile faded to softness. "I knew that."

Mary felt her stomach tighten at his close proximity, but she didn't give in to the feeling.

He dropped his eyes to her mouth. "What else?"

She shrugged minutely. "What else?"

"Did she say," he clarified, his tone low and deeply soothing.

Mary tried to concentrate, her mind growing unnaturally fuzzy from the warmth spreading through her. "She said . . ." She took a fast breath for resolve. "She said the ladies generally adored you as well, but that you weren't interested in the lot of English ladies at your . . . disposal. That is— until you left for Africa. She worried about you, naturally."

For the first time he appeared surprised as his eyes widened. Then his brows creased in a sort of amusement that Mary found altogether melting. She wished she'd never said that.

"Really, my lord—"

"Marcus," he whispered huskily.

She ignored that. "I really must be going."

"Oh. Where?"

That stumped her. "I beg your pardon?"

"You have another pressing engagement at ten o'clock in the evening?"

Her face flushed of its own accord but she raised her brows in innocent defiance. "Only with my bed, Lord Renn."

That didn't seem to faze him. "Ah. Which room is yours, Mary?"

He didn't need to ask her that. He owned the bloody place. "Third floor, northwest corner."

He cocked his head a fraction, studying her again. "And mine is at the other end of the hallway. Northeast corner."

Burning inside, which she hoped he'd never notice, she replied, "Lovely room, I'm sure. All the private bed chambers at Baybridge House are, actually. My color scheme is a bit too pink for my taste—"

"I'd like you to be my friend, Mary," he cut in smoothly, his gaze heated with shielded meaning. "My sister would have liked that."

And wanted it.

Her heart pounded now, her cheeks reddened with embarrassment, she was sure. He stood far too close.

"Gentlemen and ladies are never friends in the conventional sense," she scolded, though refusing to look into his eyes as she turned her gaze to the wall plates, taking particular notice of them.

He chuckled and she couldn't help but be drawn to it.

"Mary, look at me," he said softly.

Quickly, she inhaled, then did as he asked, her back erect, shoulders stiff.

His eyes were telling as they melded with hers,

full of inner hurt and vivid truths. Then, very slowly but with deliberate intention, he reached out with one hand, palm up.

Mary stared at it, unsure. Her breathing quickened; her blood pounded in her temples. But without coherent thought, she lifted her hand and gently placed it in his. In an odd sense of detachment and acknowledgment, she realized she wanted to touch him, too.

Lily white skin fused with leathered brown. He had the most unusual hands for a gentleman— worker's hands exposed to years of wind and sun. Slowly he enfolded her knuckles in his large, warm fingers, and began to pull until she had no choice but to stand beside him.

Mary couldn't move, couldn't seem to catch her breath. He smelled deliciously of spice and something masculine that she couldn't identify. It emanated from him as the heat of his body did, as his goodness did.

Oh, she wanted so much to like him . . .

He rubbed her knuckle once with his thumb, and her knees went weak beneath her skirts.

"I'd like to kiss you again, Mary," he asserted in whisper softness.

"No," she breathed back, even as she closed her eyes.

Seconds passed in agonizing anticipation, and then she felt the brush of warm breath against her cheek.

He rubbed his lips along her jawline and she nearly squealed. Her balance shifted, and as quickly as he felt her lose her composure, his free arm wrapped around her waist, pulling her tightly against him. So much closer than the other time. Indecently close, and yet it felt so perfect. Scandalously perfect.

He still hadn't kissed her in the definitive sense. His lips grazed her earlobe, her neck, her jaw and chin, and Mary had the most difficult time keeping herself from embracing him and searching for his mouth with her own. She still clutched one of his hands, but the other simply had to grasp his broad shoulder where she could feel coarse wool against the heated skin of her palm.

He groaned almost inaudibly when he felt her reach for him, but she heard it most definitely, felt it in his chest that now pressed against her own, making her breasts flatten against him. Oh, he felt divine in her arms! It had been so long since she'd been held by a man—

His lips found hers, crushing down upon them as he swept her into an impassioned kiss that tore the breath from her at last. She faltered against his strength, reeling with what was surely a dream, being caressed by a man she hardly knew, feeling no remorse, not a doubt, just desire. Strong desire that she knew she shouldn't properly feel, but noting the heavy weight between her legs, the aching of her nipples to feel the touch of his fingertips. She wondered in a fleeting moment if he were erect as men get when drawn into passion, and instead of feeling repulsed at the thought as she should, she instead suddenly longed for it, wished desperately that she could feel him through thick layers of skirts . . .

His kiss grew bolder; his tongue glided along her upper lip, and without thinking clearly, she molded herself against him, kissing him back, just this once. He tasted of wine, felt hard against her own body of womanly softness, demanded more of her with each press of pleasure.

She sighed in his arms, and with that she felt the very briefest gliding of his palm up the side of her gown, against her hard corset, then barely caressing the side of her breast before he reached for her back once more, splaying his fingers between her shoulder blades.

Mary shuddered in his arms, and at long last he released her lips, briefly pressing his forehead against hers before actually hugging her tightly.

"God, Mary," he said, his warm breath caressing her hairline, his tone thick and raspy. "When I'm with you I want everything." He moaned very quietly, deliberately, then added, "It's numbing."

She couldn't say anything, wouldn't be able to find her voice if she tried. It was all too impossible, lovely, and still, in every manner, perfect.

After endless moments of holding her, he finally let go of her hand, bringing both of his forward to grasp her shoulders.

She kept her eyes closed as reality began once more to intrude. She shouldn't be here, and yet she wanted desperately to be. She shouldn't kiss him back because it would lead to nothing but heartache, yet she couldn't stop herself. Passion ruled, even when she knew passion could be the center of personal ruin.

With firm hands, she pushed against him, though she still kept her eyes closed, lest she look at him and change her mind regarding her conviction.

"I apologize, my lord," she murmured, her own voice sounding remarkably scratchy and bleak.

She expected him to laugh in light rebuke. Instead, he merely rubbed one thumb back and forth along her collarbone and whispered gravely, "We'll get through this, Mary."

Her lashes fluttered open and she couldn't help but look up at his face.

The dark, honest yearning she beheld in his eyes, on every incredible feature, told her more than words ever could. Suddenly she couldn't breathe at all.

"Tell me what you're wearing," he said huskily, "under this lovely gown that marks your figure so beautifully."

A tiny sound escaped her throat.

He pushed his fingers up into the hair at her nape. "Tell me . . ."

"I can't," she whispered.

"If you don't tell me, Mary, my dreams this night will be full of speculation."

She couldn't believe he'd said that. She knew of the despair brought on by erotic dreams, and she nearly collapsed on the spot.

A dog howled out on the cliff below the window; the wind had picked up to whistle against the shutters in the darkest night outside; servants moved about the house; somewhere Gwyneth was writing letters, commanding servants, talking with George about the day's events.

She and the earl were alone.

"It's blue," she mumbled, mouth dry, eyes locked with his.

His lips twitched. "Blue . . ."

"Blue like—like your eyes."

He inhaled sharply, unsteadily, and Mary realized how affected he was by her simple words.

"Any lace?"

"No."

"No . . ."

For a moment they didn't speak. Mary wanted desperately to run, to shelter herself away from his demanding embrace. They still clung to each other's shoulders, his grasp tighter than hers, yet gentle enough for her to move away should she choose to do so. She couldn't, and his profound self-confidence seemed to be underlined by the fact that he knew this already.

He traced his thumb along her bottom lip, unexpectedly, and she gasped. "Will you kiss me again, Mary?"

She swallowed. "No."

He almost smiled. "I want to play a game," he returned softly.

She was having a terrible time understanding his words, so she just looked at him.

He did smile now, a pulling up of his full lips to a harsh line of pure, masculine sureness. "I'm very interested in your business, Miss Marsh. I want a viewing of your best items." He paused for reaction, then added, "Can you provide it?"

She nearly fainted. Her face paled and her body now felt like lead. "I will never do anything indecent, Lord Renn." She cringed as soon as she spoke the words. She'd been nothing but indecent since she'd allowed herself to take his hand. He didn't appear to notice, however.

"Of course not," he returned without pause. "I'm merely the buyer. I want to view purchases I might make in future. For a future wife, perhaps."

Mary had no idea what he meant, or at least not much of an idea of where his mind was leading. He was a man after all. Still, that was the point, and she was fairly certain of what he wanted. That's what *she* found numbing.

He leaned in and brushed her lips with his again, and she almost melted into the carpet at her feet.

"Please . . ." he whispered against her mouth. "I could be your best buyer yet, Miss Marsh."

For one very odd second, Mary wondered why he called her Miss Marsh when his lips were ravaging hers. And then it didn't matter, for her eyes closed once more of their own accord and she embraced him again without clear thought, kissing him back while his hands rested at her hips, allowing her to enjoy him.

Seconds later, he pulled back for a final time, farther than he had before.

"I can't take any more," he said roughly.

She remained where she was, standing dreamily, eyes closed, her face and body hot and detached. "Thank you, Lord Renn," she whispered.

"You're welcome, Miss Marsh," he answered, his voice under better control and slightly tinged with humor.

For seconds they stood next to each other, then at last she lifted her lashes and focused on his marvelous eyes.

The clarity she beheld in his pointed gaze told her much. His face was as flushed as hers, his breathing as uneven. The trust she felt emanating from his entire being overwhelmed her, surrounded her in a marked contentment, though it was also true that he would never know how much.

"I—I must leave," she said, attempting to take control of her emotions, her body, at last. She licked her lips, looking around her as if to gather untold belongings.

Formally, he replied, "I understand."

With a sense of confusion, she lifted her skirts and stepped past him, toward the study door, her feet deadened as if she'd been walking uphill for days.

"Miss Marsh."

She stopped when her hand grasped the knob. "Yes."

In a gentle tone, he said, "Mary."

God, he made her name sound like a caress. She drew a deep breath and turned around to face him one last time.

His serious countenance had returned in full form. He stood erect, hands clasped behind his back, all evidence of his desire—if he shared it to the depth of hers—well hidden, though she refused to drop her gaze blatantly to check.

"Perhaps you'll join me tomorrow afternoon at my cottage, for that first business appointment. A showing of your work."

Time stopped for her. And yet he waited for her compliance, for her acceptance of a most inappropriate rendezvous. In essence he'd left it up to her. Very deep in her mind, Mary knew he wouldn't push her, at least not physically. He made it her choice.

He waited.

After a moment of watching him, hoping to grasp a sense of his nervousness, she swallowed and shakily asked, "What time?"

He blinked, and for the briefest second, she could have sworn he was utterly shocked. Then his eyes narrowed. "Two o'clock."

She wanted to laugh at the absurdity of it all. But she didn't. Instead, she glanced away, to the door again. "I shall consider it, my Lord Renn."

Then without waiting for reply or dismissal, she stepped into the darkened, empty hallway, closing the door behind her.

As she made her way back to her room, her body still aroused, feeling astonished and confused and frustrated, it occurred to her that she never did address her desire to leave Cornwall.

Chapter 15

Baybridge House
16 February 1855

. . . Miss Marsh is so interesting. She's finally al-
luded to a romance she had years ago. I think she
loved the man and he did something to hurt her
deeply. She won't tell me his name or what exactly
happened, and I haven't asked. As you know, how-
ever, I seldom give up when I want information,
and no, it's not gossip. It's talk between ladies. I
know, I know. I can hear you laughing all the way
from Egypt. I do miss you so, Marcus . . .

For the first time in his life, Marcus couldn't believe he'd acted so appallingly as to proposition a lady. And equally appalling was the fact that
it had nearly killed him to glance at the clock on the

mantel only to see that it was ten minutes after two and she hadn't yet arrived.

Christ, what next? His erotic thoughts of her and him together shocked even *his* sensibilities.

Marcus shoved his fingers through his hair then turned his attention to the field of wild flowers that swayed gently in the breeze between his cottage and the cliff overlooking the Bay of Austell. Rain showers threatened the landscape once again as the afternoon darkened from a low-lying cloud cover. The perfect summer day for secluding one-self from servants and prying eyes to partake in the luscious art of lovemaking.

Marcus felt himself getting hard again. He'd been so erect after she'd left him last night, he hadn't been able to sleep. He could only hope she hadn't noticed when they stood so close together for so many incredible minutes. Then again, maybe she had and hadn't been frightened, but aroused. He could only hope. She was such a great, beautiful mystery to him. Mary Marsh . . . such a simple name disguising the true identity of a complex woman. He had to chuckle as he realized his palms were sweating and his heart racing at the prospect of seeing her again. It had grown to an absurd nervousness he hadn't felt in years, yet very, very real.

Suddenly his eyes caught the movement of lavender skirts and blond, simply braided hair moving through the hedges. He watched her with interest and appreciation, noting her fine facial features, her graceful walk, her poise as she kept her head raised. In one hand she carried a calfskin bag of considerable size, supposedly where she kept her salable items.

Then it struck him soundly that she was here at his bidding, and his heart began to pound in his chest, his shoulders tightening with a tension he couldn't describe. Marcus wiped a palm down his face and drew a deep breath that didn't in any way actually calm him.

Mary had never been so nervous in her life. It took every ounce of strength and energy she possessed to lift her free hand and knock on the cottage door.

Seconds later, he opened it. She took one look at the earl's face and immediately wanted to run. He must have noticed her hesitation, for at that moment, without a word between them, he reached for her elbow and gently pulled her inside.

Mary swallowed hard but couldn't immediately find her voice; no matter, she had no idea what to say. The cottage was small, as English cottages were, consisting of a little round table in one corner shrouded with a red muslin tablecloth; a short, walnut writing desk; two chairs covered in faded red velvet; a small water closet in the southwest corner; and against the far wall, a bed made for one, draped loosely with a velveteen coverlet in plush burgundy.

All in all, quite functional—for an intimate rendezvous.

"Miss Marsh," he said soberly, jerking her out of needless speculation.

She whirled around to face him, her heart leaping at the sound of his richly baritone voice.

"Lord Renn," she managed to squeak out.

He smiled softly, likely certain of her discomfiture, then closed the door behind her to enclose them intimately inside.

She shouldn't be here. If anyone found out—

"Nobody knows you're here, Mary," he soothed as if reading her mind. "My mother took luncheon with the vicar, and George is at the mine."

She knew that already, of course, which made her wonder for a second or two if he were just trying to reassure her, or if he were speaking from his own anxiety. She shivered internally at the thought.

"The breeze off the bay is chilly today," he continued. "I'll pour you some sherry."

She nodded, though he'd already moved toward the writing desk without consent on her part. With concentration, he poured two crystal glasses full of the dark red liquid from a matching crystal decanter. For an absurd moment, Mary tried to decide whether he actually kept that here in the cottage or if he'd brought it here with him today. Hardly a matter worthy of her consideration, though, when she could very well fall prey to his charm this afternoon. She briefly closed her eyes. She should not be here.

"I'm so glad you came," he murmured, walking toward her, the two sherry glasses in hand. "I'm looking forward to a viewing of excellence."

She took one more deep breath, before amending, "A viewing of excellent work, I hope."

He grinned—a marvelously handsome grin—and her knees nearly buckled again. She grasped the glass he lifted to her, her hands visibly trembling which she immediately tried to hide by gripping the stem with tight fingers.

"So. What can I show you first, my lord?"

He was quiet for a moment, his smile fading fractionally. Then he cocked his head to one side and reached up with his free hand to gently stroke her cheek with one fingertip.

She jerked back instinctively, but he remained unfazed. Seconds later, he took a first sip of his sherry, then turned away from her, striding purposely toward one of the velvet chairs.

"Let's have a look, Mary."

She took a generous sip of her drink, noting how smoothly it slid down her throat, how it warmed her mouth. She needed it now.

Bravely, she walked to the round table, barely large enough for her calf-skin bag. Her nerves were fired and unsteady, her fingers shaking as she unfastened the two large buckles on top. She knew he eyed her from only three feet away, but at least he wasn't sitting on the bed.

"I could carry only a few things, Lord Renn—"

"Mary," he cut in slowly, "have you ever shown these things to a man before?"

She could positively feel her cheeks burning, but she refused to turn around and give him the satisfaction of noticing it, too. "Of course not."

"I didn't think so," he acknowledged, "in which case I fail to see why you should be so formal as you show them to me."

She gritted her teeth, making a great showing of shifting through the lingerie in her bag. "I'm sure you realize that I'm not comfortable using your given name, sir."

He didn't say anything for a moment, and she

knew instinctively that he cogitated on that one.
Then he posed, "What would make you more
comfortable?"

At last she straightened and, with her hands behind her back, spun around to stare at him, her
mouth tight. "I can't think of a situation. I am your
employee, Lord Renn."

He rubbed his jaw and relaxed in the chair,
which looked comfortable enough as it enveloped
his large frame. It was obviously made for him.

"I see," he said seconds later. Then, "Very well,
Miss Marsh, let's be formal, though I would like you
to keep in mind that it was not I who employed you.
I merely own the property on which you work."

Her eyes narrowed as she tried not to smile at
that play of words. The man was clearly a rogue at
heart. "Shall I show you the satin first?"

He nodded once and lowered his voice. "That
will be fine."

Mary turned once more to her bag of items. Although she'd chosen only those she felt were more
conservative, save perhaps one, extreme embarrassment coursed through her now for what she
was about to do. At least, thank God, he hadn't
asked her to wear them.

Before she lifted the first item, she sipped her
sherry once more, for confidence, which required a
rather large mouthful of the calming concoction.
Then, with fumbling fingers, she pulled up a plain
corset of white satin, embedded with tiny pearls
under the bustline and down the stays. With great
determination and a tightening in her belly, she
turned so he could see it.

She watched him, mesmerized as he took in her creation, studying it from afar.

"It's excellent workmanship," he said honestly after a moment or two. "Bring it closer."

She did so, ever so cautiously, doing her best to remain focused on the corset itself. "You'll notice the bodice is short, so this is made for a small woman, probably, though one of lucrative means."

"Could you wear this?" he asked softly.

Her face flushed hot again but she didn't move. "No, the—" She stopped herself from saying, *the waist is short, thus my breasts would be exposed*, as she might say to a woman. Instead, she added simply, "I'm too tall."

"I see." He shot her a quick glance, then reached out and touched the fabric.

"Lovely collection of pearls."

"Yes, isn't it." An absurd conversation and she forced herself not to roll her eyes.

"What else?"

That took her aback; she'd frankly expected more from him. But she didn't question him, thankful to move on as she was.

Quickly she retreated, sipped more sherry, and reached for a short new corset in the palest pink satin, fringed with magenta lace, and closed with the highest-quality fasteners. Rather risqué, but the sherry helped to cover her obvious hesitation.

"This is another lovely example, my lord," she said matter-of-factly as she held it up for his observation.

His eyes widened very slightly at the sight of it. Clearly he'd never seen a piece of clothing like it, and for a moment Mary wondered if she was glad for that or not.

He beckoned for her to come closer, and she did so, holding it out in front of her. When she reached him, she turned it so he could see the sleek line of the back. "Satin-covered, metal fasteners, for easy access," she pointed out as for the benefit of a buyer who had never seen such a corset before. "They're quite new in the general populace, and becoming rather fashionable."

One of his brows rose faintly. "Indeed."

He reached out and ran his fingers very slowly across the lace over the breast outline. That simple but meaningful gesture made her head swim.

"I rather prefer the tie corsets, I think," he admitted with a tone far too thoughtful for her sensibilities.

"Why?" she asked boldly, though fairly certain she knew the answer already.

He lifted one shoulder in a shrug. "Well, as far as a . . . husband is concerned, lacing the ties would be a most pleasing part of his husbandly duties."

He gave her that . . . grin again, and it annoyed her. At least a little. To counter, she looked him straight in the eye and grinned back with a charmed satisfaction.

"I'm sure," she revealed softly, "that being an unmarried man, Lord Renn, you're not aware that these metal fastener were designed so that nobody needs bother a lady when she dresses."

He stared up at her, unfazed. "What fun is that?"

She laughed outright, then quickly covered her mouth with the back of her hand before she replied, "Did you know that some men actually tied their wives corsets in a particular bow or loop or knot each morning so that in the evening they could inspect it, only to learn if someone else had retied it during the day, proving that she'd been unfaithful?"

He didn't answer at first, and that made her smile broadly once more as she stared down at him.

"Don't husbands do this still?" he returned innocently.

She shrugged. "I've no idea."

He held her gaze, and in a husky whisper, asked, "What kind do you wear, Mary?"

She felt the tightening in her belly again, and quickly she grabbed the pink corset out of his hands, turned her back to him, and walked back to her bag. "That's none of your business, Lord Renn," she asserted, raising her glass and swallowing the remainder of her sherry.

"So now wives have a way of being unfaithful without getting caught," he said blandly. "Thanks to ladies like you, who make the straying of bored wives easier."

She tried to ignore the underlying snideness in his tone, and countered, "I think, Lord Renn, that when God invents a way to keep husbands from straying, I'll stop to consider that. A chastity belt for him, perhaps?"

He laughed this time, behind her, and she felt the tension between them lift suddenly. It was a marvelous feeling, and for the first time this day, maybe ever, she felt completely at ease in the earl's presence.

For her last example, Mary pulled out a sheer black silk corset with modern fasteners, metal stays, and a shocking display of rubies sewn in at the nipples. But she paused a moment or two before revealing it. This was one of the most lascivious of all the intimate apparel she'd made, and even after a glass of wine and a deep breath, she knew this would affect him. It was, indeed, made for that purpose.

"Perhaps you'd like something like this for your future wife, my lord?" she asked, turning as she held it out from her, at a distance from her own form, for which it was made.

She noticed his mouth drop fractionally as he stared. What a perfect picture of a man mesmerized by the astounding desire to see it wrapped around a woman. Mary knew the look, and for some inexplicable reason, relished it in Marcus Longfellow.

"It's—" He cleared his throat, sitting up a bit, uncomfortable. Then he glanced up into her eyes, his gaze darkened, questioning. "That's a remarkable use of jewels."

With that he stood, and so abruptly that Mary took a step back, feeling a certain queasiness in the pit of her stomach. Suddenly it occurred to her that she might have gone too far.

He sauntered toward her, and incredibly, she held her ground.

"You made this for yourself, didn't you, Mary?" he asked in a rough, deepened whisper, moving close.

She clutched it to her, which was probably why

he guessed such a thing. It appalled her, scared her. It also stirred untempered emotions at the center of her.

"That's not something you should be asking a lady, Lord Renn."

"But it's true, isn't it?"

He stood so close he hovered over her now, and she could feel the heat from his body. She stepped back a foot or two, but her thighs touched the edge of the table. She wasn't exactly trapped, but she didn't want to run from him, either.

"May I touch it?" he asked, his words common and frank, his tone thick and intimately playful.

She had no idea how to react, what to say. She felt warm all over, her breathing stifled in the dark, oppressive cottage, and he surely had to notice her uneasiness. She never should have brought this one.

He reached up with one hand and placed his thumb on one of the rubies, caressing it softly in very slow circles as she held it against herself. She nearly fainted.

"I imagine this is absolutely beautiful on the right woman, Mary." The side of his mouth lifted dryly as his eyes grew ever more focused, penetrating hers. "These vibrant jewels are magnificent— hard and smooth at the same time, sewn to draw the attention of a man to one of the loveliest places on earth."

On earth? She licked her lips and he lowered his gaze to the action.

"My lord—"

"Marcus," he whispered.

She couldn't breathe. "Marcus . . ."

He closed his eyes as a smile of serene satisfaction lit his face. "All my dreams, right here."

Mary tried to move; his words confused her, his company unnerved her. He caught her wrist, however, just as his lids flew open.

"Don't, Mary."

She stilled. He nearly touched her, body to body, as she grasped the sheer black corset between them.

He stared frankly into her eyes, a look of emotion undefined yet so powerful it stirred the place inside of her that she'd tucked away for nearly ten years.

"What do you want from me?" she mumbled so softly she barely heard her own voice.

For a long, tense moment, nothing happened, not a sound was heard above the patter of sprinkling rain on the cottage rooftop. He didn't seem to notice any such intrusion. He never looked away.

At last, with a twitch of his cheek, he replied, "I'm not prepared to give you that answer."

She tried to pull away again, but he held her fast to add, "And I don't think you're prepared to hear it."

She simply stared into his honest eyes, feeling her vulnerability coupled with confusion, frustration, and a desire so fresh and explosive she wanted to enfold herself in his arms, to take and accept whatever happened between them as if an act of uncontrollable fate.

"I need to leave," she finally murmured, her mouth unnaturally dry.

He glanced down at last, to the corset she clutched against her breasts.

"Don't you have one more to show me?"

Her lashes fluttered. "No."

He leaned his head very close to hers. "The one you're wearing, Mary?"

"Please . . ." she breathed, closing her eyes.

He waited. "What color is it?"

"It's—it's the same one I wore yesterday."

"Blue," he said, his warm breath caressing her cheek.

"Blue . . ." she repeated.

He touched her neck with his fingertips, inciting a gasp from her lips, then drew them slowly down until they reached the edge of her gown.

"And it's evidently functional, if you've worn it two days in a row."

Mary lifted her lashes again as she tried to clear her muddled thoughts to understand him.

He smiled, his nose remaining level with hers. "Does it have laces or fasteners?"

"Wh—what?"

He ran his lips along her brow while his fingers gently penetrated the top of her gown to graze that very corset he so desired to see.

"Laces or fasteners?" he repeated in whisper, kissing her temple softly.

"Laces . . ."

He sighed. "Wonderful . . ."

In that second, Mary felt the almost imperceptible brush of his thumb along her nipple. Her nipple, not the ruby, and a low sound of pure pleasure bubbled up from deep in her throat.

"Mmmm . . ." he said against her. "I want the black one."

She had no idea what he was talking about.

"I don't care what it costs."

"It costs a good fortune," she breathed, fairly incoherently.

"I have a fortune to spend on you, Mary Marsh. But I must see you in it first." He sighed against her. "Wear it for me? Model it for me . . . ?"

Mary swayed against the table, and a moment later she sensed that he'd stepped away from her.

For seconds—maybe minutes—she didn't move. And then reality returned and she felt the pounding of her heart, the perspiration on her back under uncomfortable stays, beneath her breasts, noticed her uneven breathing. She had yet to open her eyes, couldn't look at him, so she turned awkwardly, clutching the table as she did so.

She struggled to stay standing as she gathered her items, fighting the reckless sense of abandonment that she'd experienced years ago, that had tormented her for long months and endless nights. She wanted him, too.

Damn her to hell for bringing the black silk corset.

"Mary?"

She turned around to stare at him, her eyes shining with what he surely recognized as need. And want.

"It's dangerous for me to remain here," she managed to whisper, her mouth dry, heart pounding.

His face fell to a mask of regret so obvious it nearly crushed her.

"I would never disgrace you," he maintained, his impassioned gaze locked with hers.

"I know that," she said with conviction. Straightening, she clarified, "That's the dangerous part. If I stay five more seconds, I'll give in to something that will surely do nothing but disgrace us both."

Lifting her bag of provocative undergarments, she swept past him, racing out into the rain-soaked afternoon without another glance behind her.

Chapter 16

Baybridge House
27 February 1855

. . . Miss Marsh and I have had some long talks. I finally asked her why she never married, and for the life of me, Marcus, I don't believe her reply of simply not wanting to. She is far too interesting and lovely of face. I truly enjoy her company, even if she can be rather evasive when the discussion turns to her personally. I think I shall make it my mission to discover her secrets during her few months remaining in St. Austell . . .

Mary had always despised class distinctions, but she'd lived her life by them. She respected them. She knew her place and stayed there, never attempting to stray too far above herself, while perfectly aware that those below her station had their own choices to make, their own obstacles to overcome. Life simply existed this way. To find herself now attracted to an earl presented a risk she wasn't sure she could or wanted to contend with. And yet for the first time in years, she actually enjoyed herself in the presence of a man.

If only he weren't an *earl*.

Resolutely, Mary straightened her back and stepped from St. Austell's fifteenth-century Holy Trinity Church and out into the sprinkling rain. She opened her parasol and lifted it over her tightly braided hair, squinting from the strong summer sun that shone overhead. How very odd that the sun would shine during a rain, and yet occasionally in nature the oddest things did happen. It made the water glisten brightly atop the leaves on the hedges as she made her way down the path, through the dispersing crowd, toward the street where the Earl of Renn's private coach awaited her.

The service this morning had only been about half full, likely due to the season, many of the locals either in London or abroad, she supposed. Thankfully she was here and not in the city, as she wasn't yet ready to go back. As uncomfortable as it was to remain at Baybridge House, she needed more time.

She hadn't seen the earl since yesterday at the cottage. Something else for which she remained moderately thankful. He'd evidently decided to skip coming to church this morning, though she really hoped it wasn't because he'd have to travel to and from St. Austell with her. Gwyneth had been feeling under the weather and had declined to attend as well, which left the journey into town for her and George to make alone. George, however, had left the service early to call on a friend, just as Mary knew he would probably find himself at Lady Catherine Restin's home eventually, or perhaps instead. That made her smile. George flirted with every woman he knew, including her, which she'd always found a bit amusing, since she was little more than hired help, below a lady of distinction, and, more important, someone who rarely flirted back.

"Miss Marsh, how lovely to see you at church this fine morning."

Mary froze on the sidewalk, closing her eyes to the grating voice of Viscount Exeter. She could see the Renn coach just a few yards away, at the head of the line, but to run to it now, to ignore him purposely, would be obvious and tasteless.

He touched her shoulder lightly and she tried her very best not to cringe visibly.

"Good morning, Viscount," she said pleasantly, planting a firm smile on her lips before turning around to greet him. He looked rather dashing this morning, well groomed in a suit of charcoal gray, white shirt, and gray and white striped cravat. Gone were his usually glassy brown eyes and ruddy complexion. Today he looked . . . sober. Shrewd. She shivered in the damp air.

"Yes, isn't it," he agreed, gazing up to the blue sky, spotted clouds, and sprinkling rain, holding his palm out to catch droplets. "Such strange weather, as well."

"Indeed it is." She waited, and when he didn't offer anything more, she asked bluntly, "You wanted something?"

He glanced down at her again, his gaze strangely

thoughtful. Then he grinned dryly. "How are you getting on at Baybridge House?"

Mary stood perfectly still. "Very well, thank you."

He nodded as if digesting grave information. "Will you be leaving soon?"

That took her aback, and she frowned before replying, "I'm not certain. Why?"

"Why do you remain here, Miss Marsh?"

That was certainly direct. She pulled her shoulders back, both gloved hands clutching her parasol. "There are many reasons, my lord. Why do you ask?"

He smiled again, this time with charm, forced though it might be, and scratched his neck.

"I ask, Miss Marsh, because there is nothing left for you to do." He leaned forward a little, cocking his head to the right. "Is there?"

Expose you for what you are, if that's at all possible.

"No, not really," she said pleasantly, keeping the tension she felt tightly coiled within.

He didn't at all appreciate her evasiveness. His eyes flashed with controlled anger, even as he continued to offer her a congenial expression. For a moment he said nothing, then he gazed to the sidewalk and shuffled one polished shoe along loose gravel.

"The earl seems quite taken with you."

That got her heart beating, and she did her best not to look surprised, or elated. "I'm not sure what you mean, Viscount."

He folded his hands behind his back to counter softly, "Yes you are. You're quite sure."

She felt her irritation mounting. Several yards to the left of them, Claudette stood chatting with three ladies Mary didn't know, and she wished the vicar's wife would wander in her direction. It would be a distraction well appreciated.

"Miss Marsh?"

She blinked quickly and gazed back into his probing eyes. "The earl has asked me to stay on at Baybridge House to help him in answering a few questions regarding Miss Christine's untimely death. That's all."

Exeter snickered. "That's all?"

Her body began to burn. "Yes, Viscount Exeter. That's all." She raised her chin a fraction. "And I intend on doing as he asks."

The man took a step closer and crossed his arms over his chest. "Really. How fortunate for the earl."

"Yes, I was just thinking the same thing."

His eyes widened. "You do have a rather brash tongue, don't you? Christine had mentioned that."

Mary reigned in her irritation, tossing a hurried glance to her coach. "Is there a point you're trying to make, my lord?" she asked succinctly. "My driver is waiting."

His lips turned up crookedly again. "I won't keep you, of course. I merely wanted to warn you about Earl Renn."

She noticed how the lace at her sleeves and neck of her day gown began to itch from the heat and moisture in the air. It had been a long time since she'd been so physically discomfited, and she wished she possessed the careless resolve to tell him to go away, or better, to go to hell. But in all things, propriety forbade such action.

"Warn me about what, exactly?" she asked instead, a measure of irritation, purposely placed, seeping into her tone.

"That you would do well to leave him alone. He'll be returning to Egypt soon, and will quickly forget about you. He is far above you in class, Miss Marsh, and he, like everyone else, is more than aware of that fact."

That hit her in the gut, at the center of all her fears and everything she stood for. She suddenly had trouble standing on legs of jelly. He would never know how much that hurt her. "I'm well aware of my station, Viscount Exeter."

His brows rose. "Are you? You've never, in my presence, acted with much restraint."

He took one more step toward her, close enough now to back her into a lilac bush should she move. The combination of sweet lilacs mixed with the essence of strong male cologne made her queasy.

Her displeasure quickened. "Neither have you, my lord."

His face began to redden. "You are not family, and you don't belong in Cornwall, Miss Marsh."

She pinched her parasol tightly, mostly to keep from hitting him with it. "Forgive me, Viscount," she said very smoothly, "but where I live is not for you to decide. And frankly, I wonder if you're not now relieved that you're not a member of the earl's family as well. Especially since you expect to rule your corner of the world with no encumbrances, yet more wealthy than before, once he leaves again for Africa."

The man blinked; his head shot back. "Bravo, madam." He paused for a minute, assessing her with creased brows, probably knowing full well how nervous he made her. "Christine spoke highly of your intelligence."

The change in his approach confused her a bit, though it took her only a minute to decide to use it to her advantage. "I'm very flattered," she replied easily. "Did you know Christine was with child when she died?"

That absolutely alarmed him. Very, very slowly, his mouth dropped open so that in seconds he gaped at her. She stood smugly, waiting, while she tried to decide if he were more shocked because he *didn't* know, or because she'd had the audacity to mention it to him in public.

Suddenly his features changed to express a tense repressed rage. His eyes flashed hotly, his lips thinned as his face became red from nose to ears, his fists clenched at his sides. But Mary, strangely enough, wasn't afraid. He wouldn't touch her here, where others would see, so she merely clung desperately to her parasol and waited for him to respond.

At last, he leaned very close and spat in whisper, "Are you accusing me of forcing my betrothed?"

Mary's stomach clenched; her own sense of rage swelled, despite the fact that such an argument had never occurred to her. She'd assumed a liaison, with perhaps a bit of gentle persuasion on his part, but never force. The notion that Christine might have suffered such violence in the arms of her intended made her pause in growing concern, largely because he had been the one to mention it.

"You never heard me say such a thing, my lord," she said, her voice wavering ever so slightly even as her mind churned with intruding questions.

His nostrils flared; his hard mouth curved down into a sour frown. And then he pulled himself up to an erect position, yanking down on the bottom of his cutaway coat with both hands to straighten it. But he never took his eyes off her face.

"And you never will, Miss Marsh. I hope I'm being clear."

Mary hesitated, her pulse beating rapidly. But in the end she refused to offer a word of agreement to what he wanted from her—an admission that she would, in future, keep her mouth shut. She simply stared into his hard eyes, betraying nothing, until he grew tired of waiting for a response.

Quickly, and without a formal farewell, the viscount pivoted on his heel and walked stiffly away from her along the sidewalk, ignoring Mrs. Coswell who waved her lace handkerchief as she tried to attract his attention.

It took Mary a minute or two to breathe easily again. Finally she turned in the opposite direction and picked up her pace once more, hoping nobody would stop her to engage in insignificant chatter when she had so many thoughts reeling inside her head.

It wasn't until she reached the coach that she realized the isolated rain shower had ceased and her hand had grown numb from squeezing the end of her parasol so tightly.

Chapter 17

Baybridge House
2 March 1855

*. . . So sorry to hear of your recent troubles. Did
you ever find the person who looted the dig? It's
appalling, really, that someone would purposely
steal ancient treasures. Honestly, brother, I worry
about you so . . .*

*. . . Now, to answer your questions. Miss Marsh
is tall for a lady, with a rather angelic-looking face.
She has blond hair and blue eyes. She's very beautiful, Marcus, though somewhat shy. No, not shy,
exactly. It's almost as if she has many secrets she
refuses to reveal about herself. She won't tell me
why she didn't marry, but I think it has something
to do with the man she once loved . . .*

Mary sat uncomfortably in the straight-
backed chair at the dining room table, staring down at her breakfast of fried eggs and toast
laid out conspicuously on gorgeous Renn china
plates of a blue and white floral design. Though
she hardly tasted a bit of the fare, she managed to
swallow as much as she could, listening with only
half an ear as Gwyneth and George bickered about
taxes on their property for the war effort, trying not
to steal glances toward the head of the table, where
the man of her interest ignored them all as he fairly
guzzled his food in record time.

The earl's lack of concern made her want to
laugh. She'd met many of the aristocracy in her
day, but never had she known a man so focused on
assuming a responsibility and lifestyle into which
he had not been born. And yet as she considered it
now between sips of cooling tea, it came to her attention that Marcus Longfellow's personality fit
the style of life he preferred. He had the intelligence and depth of concentration to care for an estate of Renn's magnitude, but not the desire. As
he'd told her before, he cared for history, people,
cultures, preferred the stimulating company of in-
tellectuals and worldly scholars. In many regards,
he was one of the most unusual, interesting people
Mary had ever met. She understood him, and it
had been a long, long time since she'd been able to
say that about a man of her acquaintance.

He hadn't spoken this morning except for a curt
nod and formal bidding to the three of them upon
his entrance into the dining room less than ten minutes ago, but he had looked long and hard at her.

She had to wonder what he'd been doing with his time these last three days since she'd exposed her secret works to him in his cottage—where he'd gone, who he'd seen, what he thought even now about her in the deepest corners of his very keen mind. It was entirely true that just the sight of the man made her heart race and her stomach turn, and for the first time she wondered if any man could feel these same things in the presence of a woman he desired. Maybe the bold part of her personality would encourage her one day to ask him if she affected him as strangely as he did her.

He also hadn't said much of anything to her these last three days, aside from banal discussion that had absolutely nothing whatsoever to do with his suggestion that she model her intimate apparel for him. And it was starting to drive her mad, not knowing what he thought. Still, with every thought of him, she kept coming back to an image of herself outrageously exposing her legs in silk stockings, her waist, bust, and hips barely hidden by a matching black lace corset, all for his hedonistic view in a small, dark cottage away from everything but the smell of countryside grass and the sound of crashing waves on the rocks below. The remarkable thing would be that if she went forward with the temptation he proposed, it would be the most sinfully decadent thing she had ever done. Sinful, because as wrong as she knew it would be, as disastrous as it might turn out, she wanted to do as he asked more than she'd wanted anything in a long, long time.

Mary glanced up at George, his thick auburn brows creased in frown as he nodded at something his mother said. Gwyneth, in black crepe, her hair pulled up into a tight chignon, her complexion pink and shiny, tried passionately to persuade him of her concerns. The great Earl of Renn concentrated heavily on his food while a footman scooped a second helping of eggs onto his plate.

All in all, an ordinary morning. The same as yesterday and tomorrow for the three of them. But for her, after the uneasy conflict with Viscount Exeter yesterday morning, she knew she wanted more. Nobody would tell her what to do, especially a man who held so little caring for others and so much for himself. To stay at Baybridge House was her choice, and although it was likely to be the biggest mistake of her life, she wanted to be with Marcus Longfellow during the time she remained in Cornwall. She realized all too well that the outcome would probably be messy, and painful.

She wanted him anyway.

Marcus heard the faint rustling of the wind outside slamming a shutter against the glass. Naturally, the particular annoying slamming came from the farthest window from where he slept, all the way across the blessed room. He didn't at all relish standing on the cold parquet floor and walking in bare feet and arse only to open the window to the wet, chilly air simply to fix the noise. Then again, he could hardly sleep.

Perhaps it had more to do with visions of her. Mary Marsh. A woman he dreamed about—when he actually slept. Images of her lovely shape and face kept him awake most nights, especially as he knew her bed chamber remained just down the hallway from his. That she slept even now only four doors away.

Marcus turned on his stomach and jammed his fists under his pillows.

He often wondered how she slept, in what position, what she wore. He could envision black silk, barely covering her limbs and breasts, or, more likely, simple, practical white cotton that covered just about everything. Cotton, in the right circumstances, had its appeal as well, especially when one considered the person wearing it.

Mary, Mary, Mary . . .

God, she was a beauty. Christine had certainly understated that in her letters to him. But then, women didn't look at each other in appraisal in quite the same way men did. She'd be even lovelier, he imagined, if she'd only let her guard down around him, laugh some, be herself. He wanted to know her secrets, feel her happiness, understand her sorrows, and more than anything he'd wanted in recent memory, to feel her warm body underneath his for a long, long time.

He groaned in the darkness. It had to be well after midnight, and that damn slamming of the shutter was near to driving him mad—that, and the continuous rigid state of his body.

He flipped over onto his back, staring at the ornate wooden ceiling he couldn't see at all.

"God, what you've done to me," he whispered into the darkness, envisioning her long hair loosely intertwined through his fingers, her blue eyes begging silently for love, her breasts flattening against his chest as he made her ready for intimacy. "Mary . . ."

"Marcus."

For seconds the feminine whisper went unnoticed. Then at once, as meaning dawned, he sat up straight in his bed, in blackness, his gaze sharpened for intrusion, his mind whirling with acute anxiety. Hope.

And there, as a vision in those very same dreams he cherished, she stood at the foot of his bed, beyond the sheer curtain that hung down from the posts, shadowing her curves, and her beautiful face.

Marcus blinked quickly several times, afraid this vision would vanish. It didn't. She remained there, covered with a light dressing gown, her hair hanging to her waist, waiting, it seemed, for a reaction from him.

His heart started beating hard and fast. This was real. Mary stood before him in his bed chamber at what had to be midnight.

"Why are you here?" he heard himself murmuring, his voice low and raspy.

She drew in a shaky breath, then very slowly, with extreme care, she opened her dressing gown to expose the fullness of her figure, wearing nothing but black. No, not just black. Her black corset with ruby nipples, tightly outlining her waist, lifting beautiful breasts, exposing a hint of black stockings.

"Oh, God . . ." It was his voice, he was sure, but still, he couldn't move, couldn't believe this was happening to him.

"You were right, Marcus," she said softly, "I made this one for me."

He wanted to reach for her, but in an insane instant of sanity, he also remembered he wore nothing and was only modestly covered by a sheet. It would do no good to frighten her, or raise her nervousness if she should see his swollen member, hard as it was. Instead, he held his hand out, palm up, silently asking.

For seconds she stared at it, seemingly unsure of what to do.

"Come to me, show me," he ordered in a low, intense voice that told of gentleness and trust to come.

He could see her head tilt back, and then with resolve, she stepped around the foot of the bed and toward him on bare feet, taking his large hand in hers when she could reach it.

"You're more than I dreamed," he said at last, shivering from the cold in the room, and the sight of her marvelous figure, scarcely concealed behind a shimmer of black.

"I know," she replied, lifting her free hand to touch his face.

That startled him; it had been months, maybe years, since a woman had reached for him in softness.

He let her explore as she stood before him, the room in almost total darkness, the wind howling off the cliff to shake the very foundation of the house. As his nerves felt now.

Her fingertips drifted across his temple and down his right cheek as she caressed every bump and curve, tracing a fine line along the stubble at his jaw.

"I can't stand up, Mary," he mumbled, his throat hoarse. "I'm not wearing anything."

He hoped that would be the one needed phrase to alert her that if she didn't want to continue, she'd best stop, before it went too far.

Instead, she completely ignored that and asked, "How did you get this scar, Marcus?" The scar above his right brow; she grazed her thumb along it now.

He gently grabbed her wrist and pulled it away. "How did you get so beautiful?"

She sighed in the darkness as he placed his lips on her palm, kissing it once, then again. It felt so soft and smooth, and he brushed his lips back and forth against it.

"I thought you'd be more interested in the corset, my lord," she teased, sounding almost amused.

He looked up to her face, still hidden in shadow. "I'm interested in the entire package, Miss Marsh."

"You're obviously a wealthy man."

"Wealth is a relative term, of course," he stressed, reaching up to touch the silk just above her hip.

She jerked back slightly, unexpectedly, as his fingers skimmed her stomach, them moved gradually upward until he reached the outline of her breast, the ruby shining at her nipple, but she didn't pull away. He thumbed it, feeling the hard, cool tip hiding the prize beneath. She sucked in a breath.

"Can you feel that?" he asked, though he knew she could, so pointedly, erotically.

"Yes . . ."

He placed his thumbs over the rubies, then drove his hands upward, brushing the top of the silk and lace until he felt soft, warm skin above the curve of her breasts.

Her breathing fluctuated, grew heavier, and she leaned her head back at the feel.

"This makes me crazy," he said, running his fingertips along her collarbone.

He could have sworn she smiled.

"It's supposed to make you crazy."

He smiled in return. "I'm sure your garments are produced for that desired effect, Mary, but I was talking about you."

She gazed down at him again, her features hidden in darkness, her soft hands laying timidly on his shoulders. "I couldn't tie the laces very well all by myself," she said very quietly and slowly, watching him.

Marcus felt his heart begin to race, his cold body now hot with mounting desire that refused to remain checked. "Shall I tie them for you?"

A moment of brave decision, and what impacted him as nothing else has was the lack of hesitation in her reply.

"I want you to *untie* them, Marcus."

The beauty of her voice, those carefully chosen words, would ring through him forever. The way she said his name, as if she marveled at the sound of it on her tongue, would fix itself in his memory.

Seconds of silence passed. And then he wrapped his palms tenderly around her neck, his thumbs stroking her cheeks as he rose to his knees on his bed to face her directly, the sheets and blanket falling back to expose all of him.

She never looked away; eyes remained locked, though in the dimness of his bedroom, more feelings were exchanged in touch than in observation.

As if to finally fuse the unthinkable with desire, to make it real at last, she reached forward and placed her mouth on his.

Marcus shuddered within as she begin to kiss him faintly, as she coaxed him along that marvelous brink of surrender. He followed her lead, pressing mouth to mouth, absorbing her warmth at his hands. She tasted so good, felt so perfect, and he stroked her jaw with his thumbs, her neck with his fingers, attempting to take in every wonderful second of pleasure.

At last she grew bolder, deepening the kiss, opening for him, and then flicking her tongue along his upper lip. He gave as she took, offered just as she wanted, and soon he heard the smallest of moans from deep in her throat.

He reached behind her to the ties of the garment that separated their skin to skin contact. The lace on her back felt rough, tingling his palms. She leaned forward slightly to give him better access as she sensed his need, and he responded by pursuing the kiss with vigor.

Her lips scorched his; her tongue darted into his mouth to mate with his in a show of eagerness. His hands moved quickly to the strings that bound her, and when he discovered them, tied into a loose, uneven bow, he gently pulled until he felt them give way.

Gradually her hands wandered closer, upward, boldly moving into the unknown as she began to explore him, caressing his neck and upper back, her nails tracing fine lines across his shoulders. Still, he urged her lips to respond to his, never giving in to the desire to break away to see all of her.

Her hair fell loosely over his hands as they continued to hold her corset against her back, their silky strands tickling his skin as she moved her mouth in rhythm with his.

At last she pulled away, just enough so that she gazed into his eyes while he took the first move in freeing her body from the restricting jeweled and lacy barrier that sent his heart racing.

She never faltered in her desire to give him everything.

She was beauty and desire and uniqueness all wrapped up into a package of hope for him, and he hadn't yet had the nerve to glance down at her body.

With her help, the corset slipped away, and then she reached over to lower her stockings, which drifted to a soft heap on the cold floor.

Marcus bit down hard, his emotions and nerves tingling at seeing this woman, who so often shied away from him, give him all of herself because their attraction to each other could no longer be ignored. He could only make out the slightest of female forms as she stood before him, but instinct and recent closeness told him so much more.

Gently he cupped her face in his palms, feeling the heat radiating from her flushed cheeks. Her warm breath came quickly, but still, she didn't back down or turn in fear or a rational change of mind. She reached up instead so that her hands grasped him in exactly the same way, cupping his head as her kiss became bolder.

"Mary . . ." he whispered against her lips.

She pushed her fingers though his hair. "Are we safe here?"

Her timidity was to be expected. But he reassured her as he stroked her neck with his palm. "You could never be safer. No one will dare enter."

"Except me," she noted, a soft trace of amusement coating her words.

"I left it unlocked for that purpose, dear lady."

She laughed quietly. "Beast."

He placed his forehead on hers to murmur, "You'll always be safe with me, wherever I am."

She nodded faintly as humor faded and the urgency returned. Then, pulling him closer, she brushed her lips back and forth against his, renewing the arousal, breathing heavily now so that their exhalations mingled in the cold night air.

"Lie down with me," he insisted, his voice carrying only to her ears.

She didn't comment, but she climbed onto the mattress with one knee, then the other, to face him squarely.

"God, I wish I could see you better," he said with an ache she certainly had to feel.

"Touch me, Marcus," she replied, her warm breath to his cheek.

With a groan in his throat, he grasped her around the waist and pulled her down on the bed beside him. Then, as if in dream, he slowly raised his hand, skimming her stomach until he cupped one marvelous perfectly formed breast.

A slight gasp escaped her at his warm caress. His heart raced from the exquisite feel of delicate flesh, her pert nipple that stood out already against his fingers, begging for more. She arched her back a little, and he kissed her neck, her chest, her shoulder, lowering his head until at last he kissed what she wanted him desperately to kiss.

He took her nipple into his mouth, its taste and feel electrifying him. He sucked, swirled his tongue over the rigid point while his hand moved to the other to give it equal time as she gripped his head, her fingers threading through his hair.

She moaned very quietly again, holding back in fear of being heard, and Marcus wished above all things that he could hear every loud whimper she felt as she felt it, that she had the freedom to let herself go.

One day . . .

It was all too unreal for him, so lovely to have a woman beneath him, giving and receiving, wanting him as he wanted her. Quickly the tension mounted, she held him tighter, her legs restless as they moved on the sheets. He leaned over her slightly, just enough to wrap one leg around hers as his mouth moved up to grasp hers once more.

She shuddered beneath him at his ever more demanding kiss, but he had yet to touch her fully, body to body. She yearned for it, though, just as he did. He could sense her eagerness, her abandonment, and the thought of being inside of her—only her—made his heated blood boil.

"Marcus," she whispered against his mouth, "Marcus—"

He knew what she wanted.

With his lips stealing hers, his palm still on her breast, he inched his form closer to hers so that at last, with strength of will and a surge of desire, he folded himself completely over her.

She jumped at the initial feel of him, his hard, powerful body pressed against her female softness. But as his erection brushed her hip, instead of pulling away in shock or fear, she instinctively scooted into it, craving it, satisfying every concern that lingered.

He drew his tongue across her lips, then plunged it deeply into her mouth, and she reacted in kind, grasping him behind his back, clinging to him, holding him tighter.

The wind whipped the walls from beyond the bay; the shutter banged again twice, three times. They ignored it, caught in their own surrender of wills and time.

Marcus ached to feel how wet she was. Her lust burned in her; he could feel her heart pounding beneath his, and his desire to be joined intimately with her consumed him. He yearned to feel her soft, feminine walls surrounding him, coaxing him to the edge of oblivion. His release grew imminent with each rub of her fingers on his back, each buck of her hips into his hardness, each harsh breath they shared between every brush of lips to lips, lips to skin.

As if sensing his need, she lifted herself into him, pulling him tighter against her, crossing her leg over his knee, pressing her breasts into his chest.

Marcus released her mouth and pulled his face back an inch or two to gaze down at her. He couldn't distinguish more than curves and shadows in the darkness of his room, but he sensed her need to be a part of him. He lifted his hand from her breast and drew his thumb across her lips, very slowly, and she kissed the pad of it. Her devotion and desire melted him inside. They were, in truth, the perfect gifts to him.

"I've wanted you for a long time, Mary," he whispered.

She nestled her cheek in his palm. "I know. It's not something you hid very well," she replied, her voice edged with humor.

He smiled. "I'm so relieved I was that obvious. I was beginning to fear you didn't understand."

She chuckled softly.

He stroked her jaw as seconds passed in silence. Then, in returned gravity, she breathed, "Promise not to hurt me, Marcus."

That small, hesitant plea sliced through him like a knife to his gut. Her eyes bore into his, though in blackness he only felt her defenses, couldn't mark the level of anxiety within her. She couldn't begin to understand the deepness of his response to the sight and feel and knowledge of her, or the level of his emotion he only dreamed of sharing. He couldn't express it in words if he so wanted to. At best, he could only show it.

In a tenderness that surprised even him, he leaned into her once more, and as he placed his lips on hers, he lowered his hand from her cheek to her stomach, caressing her sensitive skin as he moved, until at last his palm covered the mound of soft hair and hot flesh that drew him to bliss.

She shuddered as he pushed three fingers down between her slightly opened legs. He moaned from the magic enticing him as he discovered just how much she desire him.

God, she was wet. So wet and ready for him.

She pushed her hips into him again, begging for more, whimpering now as he deepened his kiss and began to stroke her. She held him close, kneading his back and neck, darting her tongue into his mouth.

He moaned, his breathing erratic at once, his swollen member pressed against the top of her thigh. He was ready—so ready—to make them one, and she was just as ready to feel him there. He knew that instinctively.

Marcus dropped his lips to her chin, her jaw and neck, placing soft pecks along every ridge of her he could feel but could not see. She softly sighed as his fingers grew more demanding, as he inserted one of them just marginally inside, relishing in the hot cushion enveloping it.

"Mary . . ." he murmured, his face in her neck, feeling her hair on his face as it splayed across his pillow.

"Please, Marcus," she gasped in a whisper as he continued to torment her with pleasure between her legs.

She wanted him, needed him now, and he readied her with each stroke, with each flick of his finger across the tiny nub that would bring her that exquisite ultimate satisfaction.

At last, as her restless breaths and quiet moans drew her close to the edge, Marcus lifted his body and carefully centered himself between her legs.

He kissed her neck and chest, her jaw and perfect lips as his erection pressed against her thigh. With each gentle thrust of her hips, her restless legs rubbed the outside of his, bringing a sharp sensation to his already sensitive skin. He drew in a shaky breath, his hands on both sides of her head, his fingers intertwined in her hair, his forehead on hers.

"Tell me if it's uncomfortable," he maintained huskily.

For seconds she did nothing. Then, in answer, she grasped his hips and pulled him harder against her, laying tiny kisses on his cheek and jaw, her warm breath on his neck.

Grasping her tightly, Marcus marveled in the pure, natural ecstasy that overtook him the second the tip of his engorged penis met the wet, hot entrance of the most beautiful part of her female form. The blend of delight and exquisite pleasure made his heart race, his skin tingle, his breath falter.

She stiffened just slightly beneath him, and he paused the best he could to give her time. And then with slow deliberation, he pushed his way inside, clinging to her, his lips on hers again should she feel the pain and cry out.

Nothing in Marcus's life had ever felt so perfect. Never had he wanted to share as he did now. This was no romp for physical enjoyment; this was paradise, beauty at its finest. Never had he wanted to please a woman more than he did this one.

Adjusting himself to the feel of her enveloping him, he began to move, testing her, noting how tight she was with each deepening stroke.

She sucked in a breath and tilted her head back, though she never let go of her grasp of his back. She clung to him, yearning for all of him as she found his rhythm with each gentle thrust.

Marcus lost his reasoning. She felt so damn good. She kissed his face, his jaw and neck, whispered his name as he finally pushed himself into her as deeply as he could. He wanted to make it last for her, take his time so that her orgasm came first, but he was so hard, so sensitive—

"Feel me, Marcus . . ."

He groaned and closed his eyes, allowing her to stroke him with each lift of her hips, each rotation, each pressing of her lips to his skin.

"Mary—"

"Yes," she urged through a tight moan. "Yes . . ."

Her breath came in rasps but he was beyond noticing. She sucked him in, clung to him in every way, made him crazy with need so long denied. She was close, so close, and yet so was he.

He circled his hips on hers, wanting to feel her come at the same moment he did. It would be so marvelous, so intense—

"Mary, I can't hold it."

"Don't . . ."

He heard her voice as a far-off whisper at the second he reached the point of no return.

Suddenly he lifted himself and groaned deeply; then as he took her mouth with his in one final thrust, he tried, tried to pull out of her, to save her a future disgrace.

The wondrous gratification seized him; he couldn't breathe as she clung to him tightly, rocking her body into his to make the moment last for him. Marcus pulled back as wave after wave shot through him, as his muscles tightened and his jaw clenched, as he felt himself spilling warm fluid at the entrance to her, at the crease in her thigh with each pulse of pleasure.

The power of the moment captured him, entranced him. And then he eased back to reality as the seconds ticked by, as his body surrendered to the release and the aftermath of utter fulfillment settled in.

She still lay beneath him, clutching him, breathing hard, kissing his face. He felt her response, her heat, but it took several moments for him to realize she was no longer near orgasm and that she hadn't experienced one when he did.

He didn't know exactly how to take that, or what to do. He eased off of her a bit, though he continued to hold her close with one leg crossed over hers.

Her hair stuck to his perspiring neck and body, her chest heaved with a deep inhalation as he allowed himself to shift just slightly to her side. He couldn't tell, but he sensed her eyes were closed, and she'd relaxed beside him.

Marcus kissed the side of her mouth, boldly drew his palm up to one of her nipples to feel it still tight and aroused. She responded by sighing, and with the returning desire to please, he lowered it once more to the hot spot between her legs, intent on stroking her to climax.

"Marcus . . . don't."

He ceased all movement as she covered his knuckles with her palm.

"Mary—"

"Shh . . . Lie beside me. Hold me."

For moments he didn't move as confusion abounded; then, with her gentle urging, he raised his hand from her and did as she wished, pulling her tightly against him, listening to the sound of her breathing, feeling the warmth emanating from her skin, her long blond hair tickling his neck and arms.

For a long time he stared at nothing in the blackness of his room, his mind raw with feelings he couldn't put into words should he try. Mary hadn't had an orgasm, didn't seem to want one, and most confusing of all, perhaps most troubling, she hadn't come to his bed a virgin. Never in his life had Marcus felt so helpless as a lover, and so befuddled as a man.

His last thought as he drifted off to sleep was how insane he had to be to notice at a moment like this that the wind had died and the banging of the shutter had stopped. When he awoke hours later, his room still dark before the dawn, she no longer slept beside him.

Chapter 18

Baybridge House
18 March 1855

. . . Miss Marsh has finally asked me questions about you, dear brother. She's fascinated by you and your work in Egypt. I showed her the papyrus scroll you sent me for Christmas two years ago and of course she found it unique and lovely. Sometimes I wish I found my betrothed as fascinating as she finds you, a gentleman she knows only through my description. But then life is seldom so uncomplicated . . .

As with every other morning since Mary's arrival at Baybridge House, the breakfast table had been set for the family and guests at precisely nine o'clock. Of course George, and sometimes even Gwyneth, seldom arrived in the dining room on time, or at all, though that hardly mattered. The most important element proved to be the placement of Renn china—the beauty of the breakfast area could not be complete without the year's best on display for all to see. Food, however delicious or necessary, seemed secondary.

But this morning, as Mary made her way toward the dining room at half past eight, wearing her most conservative blue morning gown, her hair wrapped in a tight chignon at her nape, her mind remained centered on the night before, on the luscious kissing, on the untamed and often risqué reflection of her seduction of the extraordinary Earl of Renn. He'd made her lose all sensibility by his very existence, and only hours ago, he had turned her to honey with every touch, every whispered word. She still felt the wave of unanswered passion within her, but as in all things, reality restrained her from acting on it.

Her stomach fluttered as she neared the dining room, but she heard no voices, only the clinking of dishes and silver as servants set the table and prepared for the arrival of the food. She hoped she'd be the first downstairs, perhaps the only one at breakfast, so she wouldn't have to face him, or anyone, until she had a good idea of how to handle what had happened.

But it was not to be. As soon as she entered, she discovered both Marcus and George standing side by side in some form of dramatic, whispered conversation near the opposite window, George's arms flailing as he tried to convince his brother of something, Marcus nodding, his arms crossed over his chest, chin resting on one fist.

Mary stopped short after stepping only a few feet inside, all nerves pulsating at the surface with the sight of him. He looked magnificent, his shiny hair combed back from his face, his large body she remembered so well dressed immaculately in a charcoal gray morning suit. He looked upon first appearance as if he'd had a bath this morning and she wondered if he'd requested one purposely to wipe away any trace of her.

She never should have left him, and yet she'd had no choice.

Suddenly he noticed her as his eyes darted in her direction.

Mary went rigidly still, unsure but standing with as much dignity as she could muster under these very odd circumstances.

His gaze drifted down her body and then up again, slowly, so that she fairly shivered from the look. But his blank expression never changed.

She tensed. Abruptly, George noticed where his brother's attention had gone and he turned, eyeing her with a grin to his handsome mouth.

"Mary, good morning," he said, pleasant as always. He rubbed his palms down his sleeves and walked toward her. "Join us for a cup, won't you? Mother will be down shortly."

She feigned a smile and nodded once. "Thank you."

"Rather tired this morning, Miss Marsh?"

That from Marcus, the devil. She broadened her smile purposely to counter, "Not at all, Lord Renn. I slept quite peacefully, but thank you ever so for asking."

She could have sworn he almost laughed.

"My dears, I'm so sorry I'm late."

The three of them turned toward the doorway once more as Gwyneth entered. She wasn't late at all, of course, but as always, needed everyone's undivided attention at her entrance.

"It's not even nine, Mother," George replied in a rather exasperated tone, closing in on her to take her arm.

"Naturally you're right. It's just so difficult to keep track of time these days." She straightened her black bombazine skirt over heavy hoops. "My dear, help me with the buffet, will you?"

Mary forced herself not to roll her eyes. Gwyneth was the only woman she'd ever known who stood so strongly against the common workers, and yet acted so ridiculously frail with her sons. No wonder the earl had chosen to leave.

Mary now stood in the middle of the room while George escorted his mother to the opposite wall, where footmen in freshly pressed uniforms arranged eggs, sausages, tomatoes, and toast for the morning fare. Before she realized it, Marcus had strolled up beside her.

"May I have a word, Miss Marsh?"

She cringed at hearing his formal use of her name after such an incredible giving of himself last night—and she feared a quiet listing of his regrets in the minutes to follow. But she remained resolute, forcing the calm within her, noting that George and Gwyneth didn't seem to acknowledge what they did, and knowing full well the earl, a gentleman by birth, would never mention their intimate encounter in any environment where he could be overheard.

She tipped her head toward him. "You may, Lord Renn."

He gently grasped her elbow and pulled her toward the window where he'd stood with his brother only moments earlier.

"My lord?" She tried to smile but flushed with embarrassment as her voice cracked.

He didn't appear to observe her discomfiture. Instead of gazing at her for a discussion about which she couldn't possibly guess, he drew in a long breath and leaned his palms on the brick sill to stare purposely out across the bay.

Mary fidgeted, rubbed her nose with her fingers, but remained silent, waiting.

"I learned something last night, Mary."

Oh, God. Her heart sank. He was going to mention it.

He didn't wait for her to reply, which was a good thing, she supposed, since she couldn't think of a word worth saying.

He pressed his lips together, then carried on, his thick brows furrowed as he appeared deep in thought, his voice low enough so that only the two of them could hear. At least, she hoped.

"I learned that in all of my thirty-four years, I've never once been given paradise. Oh, I thought I'd had paradise before, several times in fact, but I learned last night that I was wrong. Very, very wrong. Nothing in my experience has been like the paradise you gave me, Mary."

She nearly fainted.

"Lord Renn," she whispered, her mouth dry, body numb, uncertain what to add to the simple mention of his name.

He ignored her. "This afternoon," he continued, fixing his gaze on a lone fishing schooner to the north, "when the countess is resting and George is otherwise preoccupied with the mines or the ladies of the village, or with whatever happens to be his latest fancy, I'm going to walk with you to my cottage on the cliff. Inside the closed walls, as we're alone and forgotten, I'm going to undress you gently and slowly, then allow you to undress me, if that is your choice. I'm going to take your hair down and feel each strand between my fingers. I'm going to guide you to my bed and lay you down beside me while I feel the softness of your skin with my hands."

He paused for a moment, tightening his jaw. Mary couldn't move. Somewhere in the distance she heard Gwyneth order hotter tea.

"Then I'll wrap my arms around you," he maintained in a husky whisper, without a glance in her direction, "pulling your warm, soft nakedness next to mine. Later, you'll feel my urgency as I slide into you, and each thrust will take me deeper as I gaze into your eyes. Our souls will twist around one another, until we become something singular in both spirit and movement. Our bodies will tingle with pleasure while our blood surges with each moan and caress."

Mary started shaking, wanting so desperately to run, to leave him behind, to hide. But she couldn't quit the dining room without questions, and he knew that. That's why he said this to her here. Because he could, providing they were far enough away that nobody overheard.

Oh, Marcus, you are so clever, so good . . .

He turned then, to stare down into her eyes, his own revealing depths of disquiet mixed with reflection she couldn't read. She squeezed her hands together in front of her, reminding herself to stand composed, to keep from screaming for him to stop, to keep from melting into his arms in front of the family at breakfast. That absurd thought nearly made her laugh. She might have had he not leaned ever closer to her, close enough to touch should he choose to.

"As your ecstasy engulfs you, and it *will* this time," he assured her in whisper, his soft breath touching her heated face, "your cries will drive me quickly and deeply into you as the world around me blurs and my mind focuses on the intense release of emotions I want to share with you." His cheek twitched. "And at that moment, Mary, I will watch as you will find paradise with me."

Time stopped. Past experiences washed away without care as she stared into his amazing blue eyes, so real, his feelings exposed. She couldn't speak for a moment, had no idea what she would say to such an incredibly honest disclosure anyway. In essence, he had taken her breath away.

Suddenly he smirked and remarked, "Something for you to consider over breakfast, Miss Marsh?"

She blinked quickly from that slap of reality, feeling hot, flustered, ashamed of her state of arousal so obvious to herself and likely to him. It made her terribly angry that he could do this to her in so public a forum as well, and within seconds, she wanted to claw those lovely eyes out for good measure.

"I never realized what a poetic man you are, Lord Renn."

Innocent of expression, he clasped his hands behind his back. "Indeed."

"Renn, dear, the eggs are getting cold," came the far-off voice of the countess.

His brows rose faintly but he never looked away. "Shall we, Miss Marsh?"

Very slowly, facing him directly, knowing George and Gwyneth were probably watching, she smiled wickedly and said softly, "And during your breakfast, Lord Renn, I'd like you to imagine, in the most poetic term possible, where I'd like to stick those rubies."

Undaunted, he laughed outright, his head tossed back, and she couldn't help but thoroughly enjoy the sound of it. Even while furious at his gall, she delighted in him.

Straightening her shoulders, she reached for her skirts and turned her back on him as she fairly waltzed to the sideboard buffet.

More keenly aware than she let on, Gwyneth watched the exchange between her son and Mary from the corner of her eye. Of course she had no idea what he found so very important it needed to be discussed before breakfast, and without her and George's ears as well.

But she assumed it to be personal, perhaps even intimate. Mary blushed like a veritable bride, and Renn . . . God, he looked not only amused, but smitten. In all her life, Gwyneth had never seen her eldest son positively glow in the company of a woman. Yet glow he did. Or maybe that wasn't the correct word for a man absorbed in romance. Still, it was suddenly clear to her that he was.

What made her slice her sausage with force was the anger she felt at herself for allowing this inter-action between them to bother her. Certainly Mary knew her position in their household and would never intend to romance an earl, and of course Renn knew this even better than she did. Seduce, perhaps; romance, no.

But their obvious attraction to each other did bother her in many ways, some undefined. On the whole, she supposed she wanted to dismiss Mary Marsh and send her home with a smile and a pleasant good riddance, her duties completed, al-though technically speaking, that could prove dif-ficult now, with the earl in residence. However, in part, the part she couldn't quite comprehend, she began to consider that even though Mary wasn't near Renn's level in station, she had some good qualities, including being the daughter of a knighted friend of Prince Albert. That certainly couldn't hurt her status. It seemed unfortunate that she was so old, too old for a first marriage, at least, and yet Renn didn't seem to mind the com-pany of a woman near thirty.

Gwyneth chewed her sausage with care, eyeing both of them as they sat near each other at the op-posite end of the table. Her son's gaze would drift in Mary's direction, and she would ignore it, though Gwyneth knew perfectly well from experi-ence that Mary realized he fancied her, at least on some base level.

It was all so complicated. But then Renn seemed determined to leave soon again for Africa, neglecting his duties as earl, and his family. If Mary Marsh could be one way of keeping him in Cornwall, where he belonged, many of her faults could be conveniently overlooked.

Gwyneth reached for her tea. Yes, she would have to give this unusual situation some further consideration . . .

Chapter 19

Baybridge House
27 March 1855

. . . I've been telling Miss Marsh all about you, dear Marcus. She's so very curious though she tries to hide it. Honestly, if I didn't know better I'd think she fancied you, like a soldier at war, a hero one never sees but adores from afar. I've only known her for a few short weeks and already she seems like a sister to me. Baudwin is suspicious of her, though I'm not sure why. George likes her, as does mother, I suppose. But as you might assume, mother keeps her in her place . . .

Mary was scared to death. Well, perhaps that wasn't an accurate phrase. She could hardly be scared in the earl's powerful presence, but it would be quite true to say she felt just about as anxious as she ever had in her life.

He entered the cottage silently beside her, closing the door behind them. He'd obviously been there earlier, as a lamp was already lit on the table. Just like a man to plan ahead, she mused, though at this point she wasn't sure if she felt annoyed or thankful.

This afternoon he'd dressed as casually as she'd ever seen him, donning only navy slacks and a white linen shirt. It had clung to his chest as they'd walked against the wind along the cliff toward their secluded destination and it had been difficult not to stare at his handsome, purely masculine form. She supposed he dressed in easy clothing so he could get out of it quickly, and at that slightly lascivious thought, her stomach clenched involuntarily.

"Are you cold?" he asked, standing in front of the door, merely observing her, arms crossed over his chest.

She raised her chin a fraction and glanced around the room. "No."

He chuckled but didn't offer another word.

She supposed her response had sounded like she'd snapped at him, but then he had to know she wasn't cold. The wind had picked up along the cliff, brushing her skirts against her legs during the short and silent walk, but the day had been quite warm thus far, the sun shining down upon their shoulders and brightly reflecting off the sea to the east as they made their way along the grassy slope toward their private rendezvous point.

Mary knew with every breath that she should not be here now, in the tiny, dimly lit cottage, alone with him, that to follow the earl's intimate suggestion, if one could call it a suggestion, could be the largest risk she would ever take. And yet she couldn't stop herself. What made her mad was knowing he realized this as well. Smug man.

"I know you're scared."

Those softly spoken words touched the most intimate part of her. "I'm not scared," she countered softly, though she didn't imagine he believed that.

"Nobody knows you're here with me, Mary," he reassured, once again.

She relaxed a bit and turned her attention toward the table, yet never really looked at it. "Someone could have seen us leave the house together."

"True." He stepped away from the door a foot or two, stopping in front of her. "But then we could simply be walking along the cliff, talking."

"Employer to employee?" she offered wryly.

He grinned. "Man to woman."

She closed her arms over her breasts protectively. "That's probably worse."

The statement either didn't faze him, or he didn't want to respond to it. But he didn't move back.

"Why did you come to me last night, Mary?" he asked, voice low and serious.

She shifted from one foot to the other, but this time looked him straight in the eye. "I would think you'd rather want to know why I left."

He continued smiling. "That, too."

She rubbed an arm with one palm, hesitating.

He reached out and ran his fingers across her cheek. She shivered but refused to retreat.

"You're not answering me," he prodded.

Mary thought he might be on the verge of laughing, but instead managed to refrain himself for her benefit.

"My Lord Renn," she started, squaring her shoulders, not sure if she should scold him, or lie, or tell him exactly what he wanted to hear, which would be the absolute truth.

She paused long enough for him to shake his head very slowly to cut her off. "That will not do," he said pointedly. "Not privately, when we are alone like this."

He continued to appear amused, but his quiet tone expressed a desire for complete closeness and honesty between them. She understood the feeling, took note of the moment, and had never wanted it more.

Resigned at last, Mary closed her eyes so she wouldn't have to see his reaction as she fervently disclosed, "I wanted so badly to feel you, Marcus."

He inhaled a staggered breath, and just as gravely replied, "I wanted to feel you, too."

She swayed against his hand as it gently caressed the skin on her jaw and neck. "That's why I'm here now," she added in whisper. "That's the only reason. You're the reason for everything . . ."

His fingers stopped moving in mid-stroke. For seconds she heard nothing but the wind as it pounded against the sheltering walls surrounding them, felt only the heat of him through his fingertips. Then he lowered his mouth to hers.

Mary sank into him involuntarily. He captured her body against his in an embrace of both passion and tenderness, of perfection.

His lips coaxed hers softly, never pushing, just

exploring, savoring. She allowed herself to succumb with every breath, to every movement. He cradled her back in his hands, pressing her against him just enough for her to feel his chest at her breasts. She reached up and encircled his neck with her arms, pulling him closer, pushing her fingers through his soft hair.

His tongue engaged hers, and she opened for the love play. He traced her lips with the tip, then inserted it deeply, and she took him in with abandonment.

One of his hands moved lower down her back, circling, stroking, until he reached the curve above her bottom where it lingered. Mary squirmed in his arms, feeling the sudden rush of pleasure to the spot he so expertly tempted.

At last he pulled back from the kiss, brushing his lips along hers, then her cheek and jaw.

"You make me insane with need, Mary," he admitted in a husky timbre, his breath hot against her ear.

She rolled her head back and he took the hint, running his lips along her neck.

"Undress me, Marcus," she urged softly.

She'd purposely worn a light day gown in rich chocolate, with only four large buttons along the back. He had no trouble finding them.

With her fingers playing softly in his hair, she felt him unfasten her dress, one button at a time. As it opened for him, she pulled the bodice from her shoulders with his help, and it quickly dropped over her corset of rich, sea-blue satin, fringed with black lace that allowed a shimmering peek of her nipples.

He let out a small, satisfied groan as he continued to help her push her gown over petticoats, which she quickly discarded in a heap at her feet.

"Should I examine the ties," he teased, his voice deep and gruff, "so I get them exactly right when I dress you again?"

She smiled and gazed into his eyes. "I wore this one because it has fasteners. I wouldn't want you to fumble."

He grinned in return, but his fingers skimmed the lace at her breasts.

"And I didn't want to confuse you," she added as her breathing became shallow and she wavered into him again.

His face grew serious as his eyes bore into hers. "If I had my way, you'd never wear anything else in my presence."

She sighed softly, bringing her thumb around to stroke his lips.

He kissed it, then whispered, "Your beauty staggers me, Mary. It has from the first moment I saw you."

She whimpered, not just from the melting touch of his expert fingers, but from the sincerity in his eyes, the gravity in his expression, his caressing tone and utter abandonment of station, of preconceived notions. And more than all of it, to the knowledge that he knew she'd been with someone else and he still thought her beautiful, wanted her anyway.

"Marcus," she whispered, her palm to his jaw, her gaze locked with his. "Make love to me."

He sucked a breath through his teeth, and she

closed her eyes once more, to feel him, to experience his caress, to show him her absolute surrender to this time that they were about to share.

He lowered his head to her neck, leaving a fine trail of kisses across her delicate skin, upward, until he reached her mouth again. Then he took possession and she gave him all of herself.

He probed her mouth, lingered there, his hands on her shoulders, his thumbs pressed against the top of her breasts. She arched into him, wrapping her arms around his waist, feeling his hardness against her hips, joyous that he found her so arousing, so quickly.

In seconds he'd ignited the fire within her and her heart raced as she felt the heat of desire between her legs, the sudden, desperate need to welcome him there.

As if sensing the increasing hunger from her, he began to work the fasteners at her back. Mary dropped her arms from around his neck and twisted them behind her to help him. Her efforts were wasted, however, and within seconds, he pulled his mouth away from hers.

"Turn around," he said, his voice strained.

She did as he ordered, and he worked through each clasp easily enough, though seconds of waiting seemed to take hours.

Mary had yet to open her eyes, and as she felt the rush of air on her back, her stays opening to expose her, she clutched it to her breasts.

"Marcus, the light is on," she whispered.

He stuck his hands beneath the corset, skimming her waist as he pulled her against his chest, his face finding the crook of her neck and kissing it with soft pecks of his warm lips.

"I want it on. I want to see everything this time. No barriers to any curve, any look."

She groaned in semi-disapproval, but quickly forgot that as his palms brushed her ribs, her belly, one making its way up, one lowering to a shameless level at her hips.

She squirmed against his hands. "Marcus . . ."

Mary didn't know if he heard her, could hardly breathe, and yet her heart raced with every fast exhalation.

"I want to see you," he whispered in her ear.

She gave in. Leaning against him completely, she loosened her hands and released her grasp of satin and lace that hid her from his view.

His hand moved upward as the corset dropped to the floor, and gently he covered one breast with his broad, warm palm.

She moaned and leaned her head back against his shoulder.

"Tell me what you like," he murmured, his lips at her ear, then kissing her behind it.

"I like everything you do," she whispered.

He ran the tip of his tongue down her neck and she shivered.

She still wore her stockings, but her bottom rubbed up perfectly against his erection, and he seemed to like it when she pressed herself against it. She couldn't see his face, but she could hear every sharp breath he took, feel the tenseness in his arms as they embraced her.

Eyes still closed, Mary relished the feel of his

hands on her, one at her breast, stroking her aroused nipple, the other at her hip, not moving, but clinging to her, holding her pressed into him.

At last he moved to turn her, and within seconds, he had her facing him again, her exposed breasts against his chest, his mouth on hers once more as he kissed her relentlessly.

She'd loosely bound her hair, but he quickly pulled at pins and ribbon so that it flowed through his fingers and drifted down her back. In some far-off point in the recesses of her mind, Mary wondered at his skill in such a very feminine practice, but within seconds he cupped her breasts with his palms, and all reasoning eluded her.

She heard him whisper her name against her mouth as he continued his wondrous assault of his lips to hers. He ran his thumbs across her nipples expertly, and she squirmed, her legs suddenly unable to support her as they liquified and she melted into him.

He began to guide her toward the small bed, and as she felt the edge with the backs of her knees, she lowered herself. He followed, one hand still at her breast, the other splayed across her spine for support.

As if charged with heat, her body quickened. Her heart raced, her breath came as fast and harshly as his, with each kiss, each brush of fingers, each small sound of satisfaction.

With one hand he supported his weight as he lowered himself beside her; with the other he swiftly unfastened the buttons on his shirt. In only seconds he'd removed the top half of his clothing, baring his tanned and muscled chest for her view, to her touch. She didn't disappoint his obvious need for her to explore.

She sighed audibly as she placed her palms on his shoulders, then moved them downward slowly until her fingers drifted through fine, soft hair. He groaned as well, thoroughly exciting her deeply within, picking up the tempo of his kiss, his tongue in her mouth, teasing the inside of her lips then plunging deeply.

Good intentions vanished; the outside world ceased to exist—for both of them. Mary let rationality disappear as pleasure engulfed her in its raw form. She lifted her hips into his, feeling his need for her, squirming to reach it as she felt him pull back.

"Marcus—"

"You can't keep touching me like that, Mary," he said breathlessly. "I'll lose control too soon."

Those simple words from him left her intensely gratified. Her hands to his chest, she sought his lips again, but he instead lowered his head to take her breast in his mouth.

She arched against him from the contact, but he was ready for her. In seconds he reached down and unfastened his pants while he flicked her nipple with his tongue.

Through her panting, she heard the rustling of his clothes as he pushed them from his body. She raked her fingers through his hair, relishing in his delicious torment, his tongue expertly flicking one rigid nipple, his hand stroking the other.

She whimpered beneath him, wanting more,

needing to feel him as she did last night. To see his beautiful form take her from above.

His hand cupped her between her legs. She let out a soft cry of surprise, of tentative resistence, until he pressed his fingers through her folds to feel her heat, the intensity of her desire.

"God, Mary," he whispered, his face at her breasts, rubbing his cheek back and forth across her nipples as he began to gently explore her cleft.

"It feels—" She swallowed, unable to finish, to think, clenching her teeth, then gasping as his fingers found the center of her pleasure and began to slowly, deliberately stroke her intimately. "Please . . ."

"You're wet for me," he whispered, tone husky, thick with near-reverence. "You can't know what this does to me."

Emotion she couldn't begin to describe pulsed through her. Seconds later he took her nipple in his mouth again, lightly sucking as he found an easy rhythm to match that of his fingers.

Mary braced herself for the surge of pleasure to come. She knew it would, had felt it before. For the first time she wanted it from Marcus, with Marcus.

She raised her hips, begging for more. He complied, never letting it end, stroking her, flicking her nipple. She felt the tip of his erection—so hard, so hot—at her thigh, urging her toward blissful surrender.

"Marcus . . ." she pleaded. "Please—I'm going to—"

"Come for me, Mary . . ." he whispered. "I want to watch you."

At any other moment in her life she would have been mortified by such language, but not here. Not with Marcus. Sanity had escaped her and now she only wanted release from his measured, perfect torment.

"Please—"

He took her higher, concentrating on every sensitive point on her body, never yielding. Suddenly she felt herself rising to the edge.

She whimpered, panted, and clutched his head with her hands.

He sensed her closeness, fingers stroking, tongue flicking. Then he raised himself up and gazed into her eyes.

"Mary . . ."

She stared at him, intensely focused, until it happened.

Suddenly she felt the marvelous burst within. Body shaking, hips jerking, she moaned his name and squeezed her eyes shut to the exquisite pleasure as it engulfed her in lucid waves.

Before she'd relaxed, before she realized how far he'd taken her, he shifted his body so that he centered himself on top of her, between her legs. She clutched him, eyes still squeezed shut, breathing erratically, wrapping her arms around his neck to hold him close.

He groaned just as she felt him begin to slide into her. She tensed from a sudden discomfort and he paused until she eased a bit. He felt heavy above her, slick with perspiration, hot with need. Instinctively, she began kissing his jaw, running her lips across his cheek, to his ear, his temple.

In seconds he'd filled her completely, deeply,

and she drew a shaky breath as she folded her legs over his, pulling him close. He stayed still for a moment or two, threading his hands in her hair, thumbs rubbing her temples, his lips brushing hers in a tenderness she couldn't begin to fully grasp. It felt so real to her, so marvelous, to feel him all the way inside of her.

"I want this memory to last forever," she whispered in his ear, her arms tight around his back.

With his face in her neck, in a breathless whisper, he said something she couldn't hear, couldn't understand, and then he gently began to glide in and out of her.

It didn't take him long to build his passion. Mary clung to him, holding him tightly as he focused on himself this time, finding pleasure with her, from being inside of her.

I will never forget this moment, my darling Marcus . . .

His body grew rigid, his breathing fast and shaky. Suddenly he raised himself on both hands, and she clung to his muscled chest, watching him closely.

He paused again for a second, his face tight, eyes squeezed shut, the tip of him resting at her cleft.

"Mary . . ."

And then he groaned a final time as he plunged deeply into her once, then pulled himself out, thrusting his hips forward as he spilled himself into the hair between her legs, rubbing the crease at her thigh through each pulsating wave of pleasure he found in her.

Mary pulled him down on top of her again, clinging to him, her nose in his hair, inhaling the scent of him, of them together. He shuddered against her, still tense, breathing harshly until at last he began to relax.

Smiling, she held him, her mind closed to all but this room in the cottage, this hour together, content in the silence.

Chapter 20

Baybridge House
8 March 1855

. . . Miss Marsh finally confided a bit of interesting information to me. After a little coaxing she revealed that she feels horribly guilty for something she did to her sister and brother-in-law. She hasn't given me details, but I intend to discover them. I can't imagine her doing anything bad, but she asked me never to tell Mother. Of course I never would. Miss Marsh would be sent packing immediately, regardless of what it is, if Mother had even the slightest notion of scandal . . .

Mary kept her eyes closed to the feel of the soft coverlet against her naked body. Marcus lay beside her, touching her, leg to chest, his breathing slow and even, and she imagined he probably dozed.

It made her smile. It had been ages since she'd felt so content, so at peace with herself and her surroundings. As if she belonged here, in Cornwall, in his arms.

Her lids fluttered open at the thought, and she gazed to the darkened beams on the cottage ceiling, her skin cooling as her mood tempered with the notion of the world beyond these four walls.

Life at Baybridge House. So removed from this moment, and still so close and uncertain. She wouldn't be staying here much longer. She couldn't. Her father would need her; Mimi would want to see her, hug her, and tell her how wonderful her marriage had been these last few months. Perhaps, Mary wondered with a sigh, she'd been away long enough not only to receive forgiveness for the pain she'd caused her family, but to forgive herself. It's what she'd wanted more than anything from the time she'd spent in St. Austell. But most troubling, the most difficult consideration of all, was knowing that if she stayed much longer, she would, without question, fall in love with the Earl of Renn. That would be the second biggest mistake of her life, and at nearly thirty, she was far too old to make mistakes of the heart.

She shivered, unwittingly stroking his back with featherlight fingertips, as if the feel of him at her breast were perfectly natural to her, something to enjoy, perhaps for the last time, as this would likely be.

Suddenly he pulled up a bit, one hand still on her breast as if he simply loved the feel of it.

"Are you cold?" he asked, his voice resonating that particular mixture of sleepiness and sexual satisfaction.

Her lips curved up into a slight smile. "A little."

He turned and pulled the coverlet down from the pillows, then shifted his body so that he moved in between the sheets, pulling her along with him. Mary followed his lead, noting how he never let go of her as he twisted himself until they'd angled in properly and he'd given them both room beneath the covers.

As they settled between the sheets and blankets, she closed her eyes again, a bit unsure of his mood, and not particularly wanting to look at him, though she felt certain he watched her. For a few long moments he said nothing, though he did raise one hand and lightly begin to caress the hairline at her temple.

"Tell me something, Mary?" he asked in a low murmur.

She moved her face against his touch. "Hmm . . ."

"Who took your virginity?"

Her eyelids fluttered open, but she didn't speak immediately. When he refused to back away, or back down in his determination, she whispered, "Does it really matter?"

For long moments, he didn't respond, just gazed into her eyes with a burning desire to know everything within her, to reach for all of her. It made her want to cry.

"Only," he answered at last, very quietly, "if you want to tell me."

Tears filled her eyes, and when he noticed it, concern lit his brow.

"You're a good man, Marcus," she murmured,

placing the pad of her thumb on his cheek.

He didn't settle for that. "Is it that you don't trust me? Or is there a past relationship you don't want to relive or tell me about?"

She tried to smile as he brushed one lone tear from her lashes. "I do trust you. More than you know. I just—I can't talk about it yet." After a pause, she added softly, "Is it important?"

"It is to me. When, who. I want to know everything about you."

She swallowed, her insides tensing. But before she could stop herself, she asked, "Have you ever been in love?"

He physically jerked his head back from the question, his forehead creased into a frown so deep the scar above his eye turned white.

"What?"

"With a woman, Marcus," she clarified with a hint of mischief in her voice. "Have you ever been in love with one?"

After seconds of gazing at her with marked agitation, he replied, "Did you discuss this with Christine?"

She hid her smile by pursing her lips. "She mentioned the Lady Stanley of Bodmin."

His lips twitched and it took everything in her not to touch them in gentleness—or to smack the smirk right off his face.

"Oh, yes . . . Lady Elizabeth Stanley. I remember her well."

She waited, and when he added nothing, she grabbed his chin with one palm. "Do you?" Feeling suddenly racy beyond belief, she added, "Did she take your virginity, Marcus?"

He chuckled, then rubbed the tip of her nose with his own. "A gentleman never tells, my darling Mary."

"But you'll tell me, since we're telling secrets."

He pulled back a little. "We are?"

Her expression went flat and innocent. "Aren't we?"

"Hmm . . . you have yet to tell me a secret."

She didn't say anything to that, just watched him for a sign of . . . what? She wasn't sure.

Reaching up to caress his cheekbone again, she urged him on with it. "Tell me, Marcus. Have you ever been in love?"

He drew a deep, long breath, then tilted his head to kiss her palm. "I was never in love with the Lady Stanley."

"Why?" she asked in reply, though feeling a burning satisfaction deep within.

He lowered his lips to her wrist, dropping small pecks along the sensitive inner skin. "She was very much more interested in herself."

Mary giggled. "She clearly wasn't for you, Marcus."

"Clearly."

"So, was she your first?"

He nipped a bit of skin on her arm. "You are certainly tenacious."

"I am, indeed," she agreed. She leaned her head up and ran her tongue along his right earlobe, then whispered, "Tell me."

He moaned softly and said, "I never bedded her; didn't want to."

"Didn't want to?"

"I didn't want to be her first, and I never wanted

to marry her," he murmured, before dropping his mouth to hers for a long, lingering kiss that made her heart race anew and her skin grow hot with the need to touch and explore.

He drew his lips down her jawline until they met her sensitive neck where he caressed her with his moist, warm breath.

"I've only been with a small—very small—number of women," he disclosed in a gruff whisper, "and not for a long, long time. Or at least it seems that way."

She laughed softly again and pressed up against him, angling her neck for more.

"None of them was as beautiful as you, nor did they make my heart ache when they were no longer beside me, as you do."

She melted at his trust in her, from his disclosure that left all of him exposed. But she didn't interrupt. She couldn't. She wanted to hear everything.

His mouth moved lower until his lips stroked her collarbone, back and forth. "And since I always wanted to leave when the deed was done, I don't suppose I was in love with any of them."

Mary reached for his head, threading her fingers through his thick, soft hair. "Marcus—"

He leaned up enough to look into her eyes again. "The difference here, my sweet Mary, is that when *you* leave me, for any reason, I think of you, envision your smile and graceful charm, your underlying sensuality, and I long to be beside you again, even for just a moment or two." He shuddered a little, his jaw tightening as he rested his forehead against hers, eyes squeezed shut. "When I'm with you, wherever you happen to be, I'm content, and that kind of contentment is something I've never felt for another woman in my life." He pressed his lips to hers, then whispered against them, "Now that I've experienced the feeling, I don't think I want to live without it."

She clung to him tightly, afraid to let go, knowing with an array of bittersweet emotions that they were destined to part, that the loose and tender threads of what held them together were simply not enough to bind for a lifetime. Rationally, he likely knew it, too. There was too much at stake, too much she had to return to London to face. If nothing else, she had to be truthful about that.

"Marcus . . ."

"Don't say you're leaving me, Mary," he replied immediately, sensing the direction of her thoughts, his deep voice challenging her to defy him.

She stared at the ceiling of the cottage, hoping to avoid a conflict she would always regret. "You know I have to return home eventually."

"Why?" He hesitated, then in a gruff whisper, proposed, "You could start over somewhere else, explore the world. Come to Egypt with me."

For a crushing moment she thought he teased her, and it hurt her more than she could have imagined. When she didn't respond, he lifted his head to gaze down at her again.

The clarity in those deep blue eyes was very telling. He wanted her with him, and he was very, very serious.

God, my darling Marcus, how I've dreamed!

She laughed bitterly, squeezing her eyes shut to stay a new flow of tears. "It's not that simple."

"Life is never simple," he soothed, coaxing her

to succumb to his suggestion with just his tone of need.

She very nearly did, if not for remembering her purpose in coming to Cornwall in the first place. "Mine is particularly complicated right now, Marcus."

She knew, without having to look at him, that he studied her in contemplation of her words.

Finally, he murmured, "What made you want to leave home, and London, for work at Baybridge House?"

For seconds, Mary refused to answer him. He couldn't possibly want to know the gravest of her secrets, and yet she knew he brought the subject up because of their closeness, because he truly cared. In a moment of inner surprise, she realized she believed that.

Slowly she opened her eyes, her body growing tense in the fear that she'd repulse him with her revelations. But as she gazed up into his vivid eyes, she felt a perfect calm wash over her, a sense of peace brought about by Marcus Longfellow, the man.

"Why do you want to know?" she asked wistfully, placing a palm gently on his chest, feeling his slow, steady heartbeat beneath it.

She saw the slightest frown cross his brow, and then he remarked, "Christine mentioned in her letters that she thought you'd left London under . . . haunting circumstances, but she didn't elaborate. I don't think she knew the answers." He paused, then added, "I thought perhaps you would tell me."

Mary wasn't sure how to take such openness on his part. And certainly she'd never felt such honesty from a man. His desire to know everything absolutely charmed her.

"I've made mistakes in my life, Marcus. Mistakes I'm not proud of."

His eyes skimmed over her face, then he gave her a crooked smile. "How very odd."

She tried not to grin in return. "All right, I admit I'm probably not the first to do so."

He nodded once. "Probably not."

His voice had such a soothing quality it mesmerized her, and she snuggled closer against him under the covers, reveling in his warmth.

"Several years ago," she began hesitantly, looking now at his muscled arms as she grazed one with her fingertips, "I helped to ruin a man socially and professionally for personal gain."

It was all she could do not to glance into his eyes. She burned with discomfort, embarrassment. Dreadfully afraid her disclosures would cool his ardor, if not his complete fancy of her, she still felt compelled to talk to him about it. Doing so seemed right somehow with Marcus.

He waited, apparently letting her go at her own pace. That was one thing she so admired about the man. He had infinite patience.

"I thought I was doing the right thing at the time," she said in defense. "I'd wanted to help my father, preserve his career as best I could. He's a sculptor, and his arthritis was getting so bad I feared he would lose his livelihood. I had only hoped that if he didn't have to sculpt—"

"What did you do?" he whispered, sitting up a little, resting his elbow on the pillow, his cheek in his palm.

She took a deep breath and purposely stared past him, to the ceiling, as her mind drifted back to the time she would never forget.

Softly, trying very hard to put her memories into words, she replied, "One night in 'fifty-one, I hid a rare and priceless fossil from Professor Nathan Price, which not only destroyed his budding reputation, but ultimately kept him from marrying my sister. For three years they were apart because of me."

She chanced a swift glance at Marcus. Unbelievably, his features now took on an expression of pure astonishment coupled with a strange sort of delighted humor. As warm as it made her to know he didn't immediately brush her aside, or laugh at what he assumed to be an absurd fabrication, she knew she needed to explain the worst of it. And for the first time ever, Mary wanted to tell someone.

Gazing back to the ceiling, she continued. "My actions destroyed his reputation for a time, and caused Mimi to marry a man she did not love. It devastated her."

Mary felt the hopelessness and frustration returning, the gnawing in her belly. But she proceeded, her mind retracing the steps she'd taken toward her own personal shame and downfall not so long ago. "Thinking about what I did has haunted me day and night for a long time, Marcus. I never wanted to hurt Nathan; he's a good man, a smart and honest man. He'd worked so hard—"

Tears cut her off, made her swallow, choke them back, reconsider humiliating herself further by revealing such brash and harmful behavior. But she had to finish.

Closing her eyes, she lowered her voice. "In the end, my actions nearly cost several people their hopes and plans, their social and professional positions. During the last few months Nathan has worked to right the wrong, with my sister's help. He and Mimi married last summer, and I know they're happy, but he's still very angry with me. I can sense his hostility." She drew in another unsteady breath, shaking her head in self-denial. "I did help in getting them together. But I can't yet face them." She hesitated, then barely audibly, she breathed, "I hate myself for what I did, Marcus. And you're the only one I've ever told."

For moments, it seemed, she remained on the verge of crying, loath to consider the past once more, wishing he'd never brought it up. Her business in Cornwall had, in a manner, saved her from the memories, kept her busy, and with Christine's unfortunate death, transported her thoughts to something far more significant, especially since Marcus's arrival. But now, with his urging, her hurtful deeds came back to her, riding on waves of self-pity and remorse. She only wished she could convince Nathan of her sorrow, her ultimate wish that she could take back all she had done to him. Her worst nightmare was knowing she could not.

She heard a rustle of sheets, and for a slice of a second Mary feared Marcus was leaving her. He wasn't, but in fact, had moved closer so that he touched all of her naked form, enveloping her in his warmth beneath the blankets.

Then he reached up and drew a fingertip across her lashes, wiping away a lone tear. She blinked from his touch and looked back into his eyes.

His brows drew together slightly, as if he studied her with concentration. "You came here to escape."

A coldness washed over her. "No, I came here to—"

"Escape," he repeated.

She didn't know if she was irritated or not at his blind insistence. Instead of dwelling on that, she replied, "My sister was finally happy, Marcus. In a way, I'm so . . ."

"Envious."

"No," she shot back. "I was selfish."

For moments he did nothing, just stared into her eyes. Then he softly agreed, "Yes, you were. *Then*. I don't believe you are now. Now you're hurting."

She nearly started crying again. Explanation was hopeless. And yet what did she want him to say? That he understood? That it didn't matter? Marcus would never sidestep any issue. That much of his personality she knew with certainty.

He raked his fingers softly through her hair, which cascaded across the pillow. "You said they're still angry, but have your sister and her husband forgiven you?"

Now acutely uncomfortable, Mary moved a little, trying to back away, but he grabbed her shoulder to keep her close.

"Have they forgiven you?" he asked again, his tone still smooth and low, his gaze burning into hers.

At that instant she resented his honesty. "Mimi has, I think. She loves me, and she understands my actions. Nathan . . . I don't know."

He nodded slightly, as if he expected that answer. "That's what you need to find out, and staying at Baybridge House only prolongs the agony of uncertainty."

"I hate you, Marcus."

"Yes, that's extremely apparent," he murmured wryly.

Frustrated, she slammed her head against the pillow, but he never faltered in his observation of her, his gentleness.

"I'm sure you realize," he maintained mildly, "that until you confront your sister and her husband with what you just confessed to me, you'll never put this behind you. You'll live your entire life not only regretting what you did, but reliving the worst of it. Coming to Baybridge House has only put it from your mind for a spell." He softly kissed her brow, then cupped her face in his hand. "If you don't know if they forgive you, how can you forgive yourself and move on?"

He was right, of course. "I know all this, Marcus."

"I know you do, which is why I said it."

For seconds she stared at him, not understanding why he would repeat something she knew to be true. Then it struck her that saying it aloud made it real. Confronting Mimi and Nathan was something she had to *do*, physically, not something she needed to envision again and again. Marcus only put it into words.

"I'll need to go back soon, I know," she whispered, feeling not only the warmth from his body, but more specifically his inner strength. The Earl of Renn was the most compassionate person she'd known.

"Your future will unfold as it should," he said in a low murmur, running the pad of his thumb along her chin. "Don't be afraid to embrace it."

His consistent words of wisdom: *Don't be afraid* . . . just as he had not been afraid to confront his destiny to find his dreams, even over the rigorous mores of society, family, a title with which he was born but didn't want.

Suddenly Mimi felt the overpowering urge to be a part of him, connected to him, mind and body and soul. Never had she needed a man more.

In a swift action that caught him by surprise, Mary lifted her mouth to his and kissed him gently, allowing her lips to linger, running her fingers through his hair, feeling the hairs on his legs and chest tickle her skin as she held him tightly against her. She sensed his quickening passion as his breathing sped up and his growing erection teased the curls between her legs, and she pursued her interest, knowing they shared it, at least for now.

At last he broke from the kiss, slowly, allowing time for her to realize he wasn't yet ready for more love play.

She pulled back a little, but caught in her mood, she didn't open her eyes. She just wanted to feel.

"Mary . . ." he whispered, running his nose and lips softly along her cheek. "I need to know all of you. Tell me everything."

Mind clouded with passion and hope, she didn't for seconds realize what he wanted. And then, heart sinking, she understood.

Her eyes opened to his as they gazed down

upon her from inches above. She looked into the deepest part of him, sensing his acute need to know, his unsureness, his wise care. But it filled her with trepidation nonetheless because he requested an explanation she realized she would not like: *Tell me when you lost your virginity. Tell me what happened.*

She tenderly touched his face, forcing back tears again. He had to notice them breach the corners of her eyes, spill onto her lashes, but he didn't comment, just focused on her.

"There's nothing to tell," she whispered in return. "Nothing worth repeating."

The disappointment he expressed in both features and manner was palpable. He tensed beside her, let out a long, slow breath. He could never know how desolate *she* felt inside at that moment for not confiding in him. But confessing all wouldn't make one single difference. She would only mortify him, and embarrass herself. In the end, when they separated, when she left for London and he for Egypt, treasured memories behind them, she didn't want him remembering this afternoon as the time she confessed everything bad she'd ever done.

Cupping his face in her palms, she looked deeply into his eyes. "Everything good in my life, Marcus, has culminated in this cottage this afternoon, in your arms. Always remember that."

He shook his head minutely, as if in consideration—or denial; he pressed his lips together in anger or exasperation, she didn't know which. Then he did the unexpected and kissed her, warmly, fully, but in so doing, forced her to experience his irritation at her evasiveness—coupled with gentle longing, of passion shared, likely never to be vanquished.

He forced his body against her, making her feel the hardness of his need, his ultimate frustration at her refusal to reveal all. But she immersed herself in the power of him, thinking only of the moment, giving in to him completely.

Suddenly, his lips to hers—tasting, exploring—he grasped her around the waist with both hands and turned, pulling her up on top of him as he lay on his back in the center of the bed.

Mary straddled his hips, his rigid erection at her belly, her long hair draping over his shoulders, surrounding his head as she kept her lips locked with his. She tasted, directed, probed, whimpering and sitting up a fraction as his hands found her breasts and began to caress with tender care.

This was all she needed, ever wanted. She would give up everything to spend a life in simple love—no class distinction, no agonies, no broken promises.

"Marcus . . ." she whispered against his mouth.

He moaned beneath her when she moved her hips forward a little, just enough so that she covered his erection with her moist folds, snuggling it between her own warmth, expressing her own ache of desire.

He felt marvelous beneath her, hot and hard, his muscled chest flexing with every steady movement as she began to circle her hips, to stroke the tip of him intimately.

She kissed and teased; he tormented her with wisps of his thumbs against her nipples. She whimpered and threw her head back as she picked up the pace, feeling him, listening to his harsh breathing.

Quickly she neared her crest of satisfaction. He sensed it, urging her along as he found her rhythm. He wrapped one hand around her, molding her against him. She had yet to take him inside, but it felt perfect like this, and so safe, enveloped in his presence, his power and pleasure.

Mary raised her body a little and opened her eyes, staring down into his as she felt her approaching climax. She rotated her hips against his, watched him, felt all his concentration centered on her. He caressed her breast with one hand, gripped her back with the other, holding her gaze with eyes of hope and a depth of feeling far more real than she could have ever dreamed.

And then she cried out her pleasure as her arousal struck its zenith. Head tossed back, she clutched his shoulders, felt the throbbing within as her body washed over with fierce pleasure. At nearly the same moment, Marcus bucked into her and groaned as he let himself go, spilling himself onto his stomach, within her folds of wetness, created from his touch, his caress, his being.

For seconds Mary clung to him, nails digging into his skin, breathing heavily, heart racing. Then she allowed herself to fall on top of him, to mold herself against his solid, hot form, listening to his pounding heart, relishing his unique, masculine scent as she wrapped her arms around his neck and hugged him close.

Marcus pulled the covers up and over their shoulders, enclosing them in warm comfort. Silently, he kissed her forehead, then drew his fingers and palms up and down her back, soothing her as she wondered at his reflective mood.

If she'd ever feared anything in her life, nothing compared to the fear of losing him now.

Chapter 21

Baybridge House
5 April 1855

. . . Mother and I had an awful row this morning. I'm still not speaking to her. She refuses to hear my concerns about my upcoming marriage, and I am concerned, Marcus. I feel as if there's so much I don't know about Exeter. Perhaps it's only pre-wedding jitters, but sometimes the notion of living a new life away from Baybridge House scares me . . .

Mary sat across from Gwyneth, in the lady's flowery, lilac-colored drawing room, attired in an understated chocolate silk day gown, sipping a cup of tasteful Darjeeling tea, trying her best to be the pleasant guest even as her mind wandered frequently to Marcus and the wondrous hours she'd spent entwined with him in his cottage yesterday afternoon.

They had very nearly been caught by George, encountering him while returning from their intimate rendezvous at half past four. But if Marcus's brother had suspected anything untoward at the time he hadn't shown it in the slightest. His jovial nature and easy manner helped them both slip back into a presence of good mood even as doubts lingered and silence reigned between them for the remainder of the evening.

Mary hadn't seen Marcus at all today after sharing a cordial breakfast with the family, and the last she'd heard he'd gone into town. It was probably best that they'd been separated for a bit after the gentleness of love and sensual hunger they'd experienced in all of three hours yesterday. Though she inexplicably hated the idea of being away from him, this time apart allowed her thoughts to settle, her mind to come to grips with the problems facing her, namely, the main reason she still resided at Baybridge House: to find out what had happened to Christine.

Mary scolded herself each time she considered how selfish she'd become when it came to Marcus. She irrationally wanted his undivided attention, and yet she realized all too well that his attention should be focused on his sister, settling the consequences of her death, looking toward the future of his family, taking care of business. He was, after all, the Earl of Renn, the head of one of the most important families in Cornwall. He had a life that did not concern her, and here, as she sat across from Gwyneth, dressed very formally in black bombazine, her hair pulled back tightly at her nape, stoic in expression as was expected, Mary felt certain the family matriarch would remind her of that very fact.

She'd only been invited alone for tea in this room with Gwyneth twice before—at her arrival in Cornwall, for an introductory meeting, and four days after Christine's death, when her employer informed her of her delicate position and the necessity of keeping all talk and questions within the household. She'd been bluntly forewarned that gossip with the villagers would not be tolerated, though of course her actual conversation with the countess hadn't been quite so direct.

Mary now had to ponder the invitation to tea that she'd received this morning, wondering whether or not it had anything at all to do with her and Marcus. She doubted it, as Gwyneth didn't know a thing about them as a couple, clandestine or otherwise. Still, as she listened patiently to the countess rattle on about the nasty weather and the dreariness of having black curtains hanging from windows in peach and lavender rooms, Mary was anxious. Gwyneth seemed almost nervous, and that likewise, in itself, made her ill at ease.

"So, Mary. How has your lengthened stay been thus far?" the countess inquired at last, sitting on the edge of her chair and folding her hands in her lap.

Mary swallowed another sip of tea. Today the fare of petit sandwiches and raspberry-filled chocolates had been served on white china, inlaid with vines and lilacs, no doubt to accent the color of the purple room. It did match and underscore it perfectly, as Renn china always did at Baybridge House. One thing was certain: Mary had never eaten from better dishes in all of her life.

She smoothed her skirt with one hand and got to the point. "Full of surprises."

Gwyneth lifted an eyebrow negligibly, and Mary wondered with a bit of satisfaction whether the woman had been caught off guard with such an evasive answer, or had simply found it intriguing. In either case, the countess ignored it and moved on.

"I know you've been an enormous help to Renn these last few weeks, Mary, and I can't thank you enough," she said properly, one palm lying across the knuckles of her other hand, her pointer finger tapping impatiently. "You two seem to get on rather well."

A drop of tea suddenly got caught in her throat, and she coughed once, then placed her cup and saucer on the maplewood tea table between them. "We do seem to, yes," she replied with more hesitation than she intended.

Gwyneth didn't back down an inch. "He seems taken with you."

Mary felt heat suffuse her entire body, and hoped to God her face wasn't as red as it felt. "I'm not sure what you mean, madam," she said, voice low.

The countess smiled flatly. "Come now, Mary. We're both intelligent ladies. We know when a man in our company shows a particular . . . interest."

She started sweating, and within seconds, Mary wished a full-fledged wind would sweep through the room. She would never be so lucky.

Clasping her hands together in her lap, she

graced the countess with an expression of pure, wide-eyed innocence. "My Lady Renn, I'm certain your son is merely bestowing flattery where it's enjoyed and nothing more. Of course he's a charming man, as well, quiet as he is. But I rather doubt a gentleman of his station would find any interest beyond the superficial in a lady born of mine."

That was indeed bold, but directly to the point. She only hoped Gwyneth would read between the lines, as it were, and drop the subject, forever casting aside wild notions of any lustful action or thoughts from her son to an insignificant spinster in his employ.

Gwyneth drew in a long, deep breath, shifting her gaze to the window for a second or two as she gathered her thoughts. Then her brows drew together with irritation that Mary all but felt.

"It seems you don't understand," the countess said very slowly.

Oh, I'm quite, quite certain I understand.

Gwyneth's lips thinned as she leaned toward her to clarify. "So I will simply get to the point."

Here it comes . . .

"I realize it's nearly time for you to depart Baybridge House and return to London, and I'm sure your father misses you terribly. However, I've also been thinking that perhaps Cornwall is where you belong, where you might like to remain indefinitely." She smiled just enough that half-moon wrinkles creased the sides of her mouth. "You fit in very well here, and I would be most honored if you'd consider becoming my daughter-in-law and remaining on the Renn estate."

A sudden cool breeze, one that smelled of salty sea air, shot into the drawing room from the partially opened window. Gwyneth ran her palms down her sleeves, but she never dropped her shrewd, calculated gaze. Waiting.

Speechless, Mary's only coherent thought was that if she hadn't been sitting, she would have fainted for the first time in her adult life. Through every single shred of emotion that now twisted around in her brain, she never, *ever* expected Gwyneth Longfellow, Countess of Renn, to suggest a marriage between her and her son. *Either* son. Such a suggestion was not only unthinkable and impractical, it was highly suspicious. Yet sitting here in this lavender room, surrounded by papered walls and scents of freshly cut flowers, steaming tea and wild, unfettered ocean, Mary had to blink away her astonishment and force herself to come to terms with the reality of what the woman truly wanted.

As if standing in a moment suspended in time, Mary looked on as Gwyneth matter-of-factly reached for the teapot and poured them both more, then added cream and sugar to her own.

"I realize this may be difficult for you to come to terms with, Mary dear, at least initially." She stirred her tea with a silver spoon only barely held by dainty fingers, then slid it across the edge of her cup and placed it on the saucer. "And I must stress that if an arrangement can be made, you'll need to realize a new position in this household."

Mary's heart raced and, tea forgotten, she rubbed her palms along her thighs, over her gown, back and forth. "I am not *of* his class, Lady Renn," she managed to mumble seconds later.

Gwyneth continued smiling even as she lifted her cup to her lips for another sip. "We all realize that, Mary, which is precisely why it'll be so perfect for you, and so easy for your father to approve of a match. For one in your position to become a countess—"

"I will never be a countess," she said, squaring her shoulders, her wits settling once again as the absurdity of the suggestion began to take shape. Then for good measure, she added, "Aside from the fact that I am beneath him in station and too old for marriage, the earl has no intention of marrying me or anyone, at least that I am aware of."

Gwyneth tilted her head to one side, eyeing her thoughtfully. "I'm certain you understand, Mary, that a mother always knows what's best for her sons, regardless of their ages. Renn needs a wife, one that will help him to settle down and take his place at the head of this family as he should. I have been lenient with his extravagances for far too long. He enjoys your company, seems to be quite taken with you, and you'd make a perfectly decent wife. You come from a respectable family, a class above the common." Gwyneth lowered her voice, eyes sparkling with a certain underhanded excitement. "I am quite sure you'll never get another offer of this magnitude, Mary."

The warning hit home, engulfing her in a mist of unreality. Her head swam with possibilities, with a hope and feeling of contentment that could only be had wrapped in Marcus's arms, touched by his heart. Yet even as she wanted to dream and plan and hope, this request, if one could call it that, didn't come from Marcus, but from his mother. Marcus didn't want to marry her; Gwyneth wanted her son to remain in Cornwall, resuming his responsibilities as the Earl of Renn while getting an heir for her satisfaction. Whatever the outcome, the countess made this request for her own personal advantage.

But above everything else, the fact remained that she could never marry. She had no virginity as prize. Not only would she never get another offer of this magnitude, she would never get another offer, period.

Mary dropped her lashes and lifted her teacup, taking a slow sip of cooling Darjeeling that tasted now of water—lukewarm and bland, as her own existence would be when she returned to London. Even her work would no longer contain the luster and color it once did. But it was the life she had made for herself, and she would live it.

After a momentary pause that the countess no doubt assumed she used to consider such a generous proposal, Mary placed her empty cup and saucer on the tea table for a final time, then drew her fists to her lips. Seconds later, after mustering strength, she lowered them again, and looked her hostess directly in the eye, feeling her heart pounding in her temples at the quickening anxiety that pulsed through her as she readied herself to take on the Countess of Renn.

It had to be done.

"My Lady Renn," she began succinctly, "I understand your desire to have your son remain in

England. As a mother, I'm sure you miss him a great deal when he's away. But I do not fathom how you intend to force him to marry anyone. Marcus is his own man—"

"Do not propose to know my son better than I do, Mary," Gwyneth interrupted, her tone icy, her words enunciated with effort. "And do not be so foolish as to squander away this opportunity."

She highly doubted there was any opportunity at all, but nevertheless refrained from mentioning that fact. Instead, she remained undaunted, sticking to her original point. "I cannot marry a man who does not want to be married, Lady Renn."

The older woman clenched her teeth but stayed otherwise still, rigid in body as she sat straight up in her chair, her skirts billowing out to the side of her legs and those of the tea table. She looked regal, and utterly made of marble.

Mary waited, swallowing hard, refusing to back down.

Gwyneth exhaled loudly as her nostrils flared. "Your mother would not have given in so easily. She would have found a way to make him want her."

Mary blinked, then felt her own resolve crumbling under the weight of loss, self-pity, and sorrow she didn't have the nerve to face right now. She couldn't imagine that Gwyneth realized how much that hurt her. Her shoulders sagged and her throat went dry.

"I am not of his class, Lady Renn," she murmured, voice low. "Regardless of everybody's feelings in this matter—yours, mine, and the earl's—my mother would have known that, which would have been the deciding factor for her as well. She would know better than to expect to live above herself."

Gwyneth's cheeks went pink with anger she could no longer control. Still, she never moved her body.

"And if you loved him?"

Mary felt like crawling out of her skin. "That is irrelevant, and I think we both know it."

Suddenly the countess's eyes opened wide in surprise and she drew her head back. "You *are* in love with him."

Mary refused to deny it. Instead, she remained sitting in an uncomfortable chair, smelling sea air and flowers, sweating profusely beneath a suddenly tight-fitting corset, wondering what kind of humor God must have to put her in such a position at this moment. It certainly had to be punishment for her mistake of long ago.

"Scheming, Mother?"

Mary jerked her head to the doorway, taking in the broad-shouldered stance of the lady's eldest son as he leaned against the doorway, arms crossed over his chest, studying the two of them with a wry smile spread across his handsome mouth. Even now the sight of him made her heart race, her stomach clench, and she dearly wished she had the mettle, the right, to stand and walk to his side, to embrace him.

Under the circumstances, however, she wanted to crawl beneath the tea table.

God, if he'd heard—

"Renn, darling," Gwyneth said genially, reaching out for him with one pale hand void of jewelry but perfectly manicured.

Her entire mood had shifted so quickly Mary fairly gaped at her.

Marcus hesitated, then slowly entered the room, striding to his mother's side and taking her hand in his, lifting her knuckles to his lips.

"Miss Marsh," he drawled, looking into her eyes.

Mary felt her face flush crimson. "Lord Renn," she replied, her voice sounding husky to her ears.

Gwyneth eyed them both, then said, "Join us, darling."

Ignoring the implication of taking tea, he returned, "I'd like a discussion with you, Mother."

He'd intimated a private talk, and Mary wanted to kiss him for it. Or perhaps just kiss him period.

Instead, she took the hint and raised her body with grace, smoothing her skirts as she stood at his side, feeling his lingering gaze and the heat of his body, which she tried desperately to ignore. "If you'll excuse me, Lady Renn. I have a number of things to do."

Marcus lifted a dark brow, but he didn't comment. Thank God for that, because of course she had nothing whatsoever to do and they likely knew it.

Gwyneth's face looked tight enough to crack under its own pressure. "Very well, dear. I'm sure you'll take the time to ponder what we discussed."

Mary could have screamed. "Yes, of course."

"What did you discuss?" Marcus asked, not at all perplexed but rather enjoying her discomfort.

Shameful man. She wanted to stick her tongue out at him.

She smiled sweetly. "The usual things women discuss at tea, Lord Renn."

"Ah."

"Actually, we were discussing marriage," Gwyneth all but announced, gazing at her again, warning her with her eyes.

Mary cringed inside; outwardly her composure prevailed. "And how men are such very unusual creatures in that they often don't want to marry, yet are often the ones who enjoy the union most."

He stuck his hands in his pockets and looked down at the countess. "Well then, I'm glad I missed that discussion," he said mildly.

Mary pursed her lips to keep from laughing.

Gwyneth nodded to her curtly. "We'll see you at dinner."

He glanced her way. "Yes, I'll see you later."

I'm counting on it, my darling Marcus. "Of course, Lord Renn."

She curtsied once, turned, and rolled her eyes in thankfulness that she could finally get far, far away from the drilling to come.

He could still smell the scent of her skin lingering in the air for quite some time after she'd quit the room, annoying him as it cluttered his concentration. It had, in fact, taken him moments before he'd managed to drop his gaze from the doorway where he'd last watched her backside swish out the door.

He wished she hadn't left him. Then again, he'd been entirely too close to embracing her in front of his mother.

Sighing, Marcus seated himself in the chair Mary had occupied only moments before, noting that it still felt warm from the heat of her very nice bottom.

"Miss Marsh is quite taken with you," Gwyneth said, reaching for a chocolate.

He groaned inwardly and leaned heavily back into the most uncomfortable chair, his forearms lying across the armrests. "Really."

"Oh, for heaven's sake, Renn, don't treat me like a child."

That truly startled him. "A child? I didn't say anything."

She flicked her wrist, one small chocolate nestled between her forefinger and thumb. "Of course you didn't. That's precisely how men treat ladies like children."

He had nothing to say to that. In fact, he didn't even understand it.

She sat very properly, chin held high. "Frankly, I think she's in love with you."

Marcus tried not to appear stunned as he felt the most unusual stirring deep in his belly, a sensation he didn't want to acknowledge, and yet one that made him want to grin exuberantly.

"What's your point, Mother?" he asked cautiously.

She eyed him through lowered lashes as she wiped her fingers delicately on a white linen napkin, then reached for the teapot. He shook his head in negation when she offered it to him.

"My point," she stated loftily, pouring, "is that Miss Marsh is in love with you."

He didn't want to stress the fact that she'd just said this. Instead, as the whole conversation made him extremely uneasy he decided to get to his point.

"I want to ask you something, Mother."

Her lips thinned. "Do not change the topic, Renn."

"And it's delicate," he continued, softening his tone as he watched her closely.

She blinked quickly, then lowered her gaze again as she laid the teapot back on the table. "I want to discuss Miss Marsh," she maintained, though she faltered a bit in her demeanor.

His eyes narrowed. "I don't."

She grew agitated; he'd seen it before as she adjusted her skirts at the knees, then her sleeves at the wrist. One thing had never changed. He could always read his mother.

"You need a wife."

"I need to find out what happened to Christine," he answered, unswerving.

Her cheeks flared pink and she looked at him directly. "Why do you always fight me?"

That took him aback, but he understood her frustration. He'd felt it for as long as he could remember. "It's not intentional, Mother," he returned softly. "We simply view the world differently."

Her forehead creased in mild confusion. Then she brushed over that and relaxed into her chair a little. "What is it you wanted to ask me?"

Marcus leaned forward, his feet planted firmly on the Persian carpet, his elbows resting on his knees, fingers interlocked in front of him as he scrutinized her. Drawing a long breath for strength, he asked, "Did you know Christine was pregnant when she died?"

Aside from a slight twitch of one pink cheek, she didn't even respond as if she'd heard him. To Marcus, that was very telling, indeed.

And then it struck him. "You did know."

Gwyneth pulled herself up to sit rigidly again, gripping her hands in her lap so tightly her knuckles whitened. "It's not to be discussed," she said at last, teeth clenched.

That made him mad as hell. "Why?" he asked, staring her down.

Her nostrils flared. "Because it was Baudwin's child and she was to be married to him before anyone would discover it, that's why. Let your sister take that secret to her grave."

She'd given him an answer with perfectly expressed disapproval, and yet Marcus had trouble with it. Something, some part of this developing puzzle, was missing.

"Did she discuss it with you?" he continued, more curious now than he'd been when he walked in the room.

Her face grew pale; her eyes round, even clouded. "I knew. That's all that mattered. It's over, Marcus," she whispered, barely loud enough for him to hear. "Leave it alone."

Gripping his hands together, Marcus leaned against the hard chair back once more. She meant every word she said, and yet his mother, the very shrewd and intelligent Countess of Renn, told him so much more by what she didn't say. He'd never seen her scared before, not like this. But above it all, it had been years since she'd called him Marcus. In that alone, she was essentially warning him.

For minutes it seemed, they glared at each other, neither giving in, both trying to grapple with their troubled thoughts. Then, with the intruding sound of a horn blowing from a far-off fishing vessel, the spell of secrets eased.

Suddenly, she smiled, minutely, and brushed her hair back from her face with her palm.

"There is one thing I request of you, Renn."

Torn between probing her for further detail and letting the subject drop for now, it took seconds before he finally gave in.

Briefly rubbing his eyes with his fingers, he yielded. "What is it?"

Gracefully, she stood so that she could look down on him—a display of power she'd used on her children for years.

"Miss Marsh is not of our class," she began slowly, hands at her sides. "Regardless of her feelings for you, and your need of an heir, I forbid you from marrying the woman. She is too old, and quite frankly, too independent to be a suitable wife for an earl."

Dazed, Marcus simply looked at her, trying his best not to burst out laughing.

Too cool, Mother, and too convincing. You're losing your skill.

Perhaps his lack of argument made her sense that she'd gone too far, that he didn't believe her. Annoyed, the dignified Countess of Renn picked up her skirts and swept past him, head held high as she fairly waltzed from the drawing room.

Chapter 22

Baybridge House
11 April 1855

. . . I will tell you this, dear Marcus, because I love you, but I beg you please never to mention it to anyone. I had a dream last night in which you had returned to St. Austell to see me married. But Miss Marsh was the bride, not I, and you were walking down the aisle at Holy Trinity, with her as your new wife. Mother was nowhere to be found, and in the distance I saw a man without a face, staring at me, and you, and Mary. I felt such hatred from him. I don't think I've ever awakened from a dream more frightened . . .

Holding her feathered hat on her head to keep it from blowing away in the brisk wind, Mary entered the cathedral doors at the back of

Holy Trinity Church. For moments, as they slowly closed behind her, she allowed her eyes to adapt to the dimness within. Then after adjusting her skirts and brushing breeze-blown hair away from her face with her fingers, she straightened and stepped farther inside in search of Claudette Coswell.

The church, an unusual style for Cornwall, displayed finely sculpted figures on its tower. Mary found it lovely, but all too silent for the moment, damp and chilly. It wasn't exactly the appropriate place for her ensuing discussion, either, but she needed to get this done now.

She shivered, then rubbed her arms with her palms before beginning a walk down the aisle toward the altar, behind which she noticed the glow of one small lamp, the only light to be seen in the sanctuary itself.

She'd been told by the Coswells' housekeeper that the vicar's wife would be working with the organist for the remainder of the afternoon in preparation for Sunday's Mass and that she could find her here. The organ remained silent, but as Mary made her way closer to the light, she detected the unmistakable sound of muffled voices.

Claudette must have heard her approach, for she suddenly peered out from behind the wooden pulpit, the light from the music lamp illuminating her spectacles. "Miss Marsh," she said in genuine surprise, "how delightful to see you. Are you looking for Niles?"

Mary realized they weren't alone, as Claudette had to have been speaking to someone, probably Alice Mayweather, the organist, whose large bottom no doubt perched precariously on the edge of the cushioned organ bench. But she wasn't here for gossip; she needed to get to the business at hand, spending as little time as possible on needless conversation.

She smiled as she approached. "No actually, I was looking for you. Would you mind if we spoke alone for a few minutes?"

"Not at all," Claudette replied as she stepped away from the organ, seemingly relieved to escape her duties.

Alice stood as well, peeking over the rim of the organ. "Good afternoon, Miss Marsh."

She nodded once. "Good afternoon, Mrs. Mayweather. Please forgive the interruption. We won't be but a minute."

The woman stood staring, her wrinkled forehead denoting an intense interest, though she said nothing else. Mary turned as Claudette approached her, and together they began walking in the opposite direction, toward the doors she'd entered only moments before.

"Would you mind if we sat?" she asked as they neared the rear of the sanctuary.

Claudette motioned toward the last pew, squeezing her large body and wide skirts in after Mary, both of them sitting at once, angled toward each other.

It took her only seconds to gather her thoughts and begin. Folding her hands in her lap, she looked the woman squarely in the eye.

"I'd like to ask you something very personal, something about Christine Longfellow," she said softly.

Claudette's relaxed smile faded considerably as

the meaning of the request took hold. She shook her head a fraction. "I'm not certain I can discuss this—"

Mary grasped the older woman's hand with hers, effectively cutting her off. "It's very important, Mrs. Coswell. You can be assured I'll never reveal secrets to those who don't need to know them. I simply want to help the Earl of Renn discover what he can about his sister's last days, and I'm hoping you can tell me more."

Although only a trace of light surrounded them, Mary recognized a shimmer of trepidation cross Claudette's face. She quickly glanced at the altar, then behind her before gazing back into her eyes.

"This is not an appropriate place for such a discussion, Miss Marsh," she warned in a low, slightly wavering voice. "I'm sure you know that."

Mary inhaled deeply, but didn't let go of the woman's hand.

"I do know. But we're alone."

Claudette's eyes widened and she sat back minutely, swiftly understanding. They may be sitting in a building of God, but there were no men to judge, not even the vicar. No ladies to gossip. No scandal.

Claudette nodded again, this time with more conviction, then whispered, "I'm not aware of much, but I'll try to help. What would you like to know?"

Mary sensed that she needed to time this perfectly, to question the woman without demands. Her approach would be crucial.

Quietly, she said, "I know Christine visited you

only days before she died and that she was very distraught."

The older woman frowned. "Yes."

Mary had hoped for more than that, but she persisted. "She spoke to *you*, though, didn't she? Not your husband in his capacity as vicar."

Claudette sagged a little into the pew. "Yes, she wanted to speak only with me, a woman, regarding a—a delicate issue."

"I understand," Mary returned with conviction. Although she wasn't cold, the dampness inside the church, the ominous darkness made her shiver again. Still, she restrained herself from commenting on it, or glancing around. She needed to remain focused. "Did she ask for your help or advice?"

Claudette paused for only a second or two before saying, "I told her the very best thing she could do was to discuss her unfortunate situation with her mother."

Gwyneth knew . . .

Mary swallowed. "And did she?"

Claudette clutched her hand, as if needing her, or giving her strength. Her skin appeared pale and waxy in the shadow, her expression tight with consternation as she bravely gazed into her eyes.

"I don't know," she replied. "If the earl had been here, I think she may have gone to him instead, regardless of his sex. She trusted him, more than her mother, I think. Always had. But then I don't suppose he would have done anything. She still would have married the viscount. This kind of thing . . . it happens frequently and their wedding wasn't too far off."

Mary felt like crying even as her heart began to race, but she tried not to show emotion, especially her eagerness to get to the truth—and her ultimate fears. Slowly, without rousing alarm, she whispered, "Did Christine explain to you how or where this . . . incident happened?"

Claudette squeezed her hands now, clearly agitated, tossing a swift peek toward the altar and the long organ pipes, in front of which sat Mrs. Mayweather, penciling notes in her music.

Mary remained motionless, waiting with more fright than hope.

Finally, the older woman lowered her head, shaking it sharply in denial. "It happened in a coach."

Oh, God . . . "A coach?"

Claudette took a deep breath but never looked up. "One night last April, I believe. She didn't come to me until she realized she carried his child." Claudette pushed her spectacles into the bridge of her nose with two fingers, holding them there. "She seemed so angry, so scared when I talked to her," she added in a whisper. "I think—I think she had been unwilling."

And that clarified everything.

Mary made a tiny sound in the back of her throat, feeling the tingle in her nose and cheeks that signified the coming of tears. She blinked quickly as her vision blurred but didn't hold them back this time.

"There was nothing anyone could have done," Mary said softly, more to herself, she suspected. Without a witness to rape, a woman is at fault. Even if the coach driver had heard something suspicious, being employed by the viscount precluded any help he may have been to the authorities, should Christine have chosen to report the incident as a crime. Both Claudette and Christine knew this, which motivated them simply to hush it. Mary also fully understood the very narrow edge where coercion turned to force. How long had Christine denied the Viscount Exeter that night before giving in? Or did she never do so, inciting him to take her by violence?

The image of the fear and loathing such a young and sheltered woman must have felt at the hands of her betrothed made Mary want to scream. Instead, she covered her mouth with her palm, squelching a sudden wave of nausea.

After a moment of silence, and a feeling of utter helplessness that passed unspoken between them, Mrs. Coswell sat up primly again, mustering strength as she at last pulled her hands back. She lifted them to her forehead, smoothing her hair back from her pale face as she regained her composure.

"Please understand this, Miss Marsh," she muttered thoughtfully. "My main concern at the time was to support Christine Longfellow while encouraging her to inform her mother, someone she trusted, of as much as she dared. Whether she did that, I don't know, but it will forever be true that she took the breath of scandal to her grave."

Mary understood nothing better than the avoidance of family disgrace. She had lived her life with just such concerns. But she also heeded the tactful warning as the vicar's wife intended it.

"I will be very careful with this information, Mrs. Coswell, as you have been," she asserted with her own hint of caution. "But you know the earl is here, in Cornwall, to discover just such truths about his sister. He is a man who will know what to do."

Claudette almost slumped in relief. Mary saw it in the lady's bright and knowing eyes. Yet there still remained one final comment for her to make that would solidify an agreement between them of the gravest responsibility.

Mary eyed the woman directly, her gaze conveying her conviction. "I realize it isn't your place to protect the ladies of Cornwall, Mrs. Coswell. But one would hope that should the viscount again choose to marry, news of his violent nature will make its way into the drawing rooms of the socially naïve."

Claudette frowned in confusion for a second or two. Then, very slowly, she lowered her lashes, nodding negligibly, understanding that to guard against another such incident, whispered gossip would have to be spread, and spread between ladies slowly and secretly. Wild pronouncements would never do. Nobody would believe them and, insane though it might be, the Viscount Exeter would, under such circumstances, find himself exonerated.

"I only hope her brother doesn't kill him first," Claudette whispered with not a trace of humor in her tone, and not caring in the least how inappropriate that sounded in a church.

Mary melted at the thought of telling Marcus. He would be devastated, enraged, but he had to know. It would explain so many things for him.

At last she stood, touching the older woman on

the shoulder in a measure of comfort. "The confusion and hurt Christine must have felt in those final days had to have been enormous. I'm so very glad she had you to talk to."

Claudette patted her hand, offering her a fractured smile. "And I'm glad she had you as a friend, Miss Marsh."

A friend would have known. A friend should have seen it.

Choking back fresh tears, Mary squeezed the lady's shoulder once, then turned and made her way to the back of the church and out into the open air.

Chapter 23

Baybridge House
22 April 1855

. . . Something has happened. I cannot go into it now, in this letter, but I am so very worried about my future. Oh, Marcus, I wish you were here! Miss Marsh's friendship is a great comfort, but I can't tell her, or George. You're the only one who would know what to do . . .

She couldn't tell him in bed. Not when he'd sneaked into her room to make love to her, to hold her in the early hours of the morning. She'd wanted to love him one last time, before the coming of the storm.

One more day.

Mary stood on the cliff overlooking the sea, uncaring that the strong wind blew her hair loose from the ribbon at her nape, that heavy clouds gathered overhead to darken the sky to a dull charcoal gray. One lone boat drifted across the bay in the distance, tossed by the choppy ocean currents, a single lantern swaying. She stared at it, wondering at the solitude of those on board, a solitude she would soon feel again.

Although her family loved her and occupied her time, although she had satisfying and creative work to keep her busy, she would always be alone. She had seen to that, and couldn't change her past transgressions. It had been her fault that she would die a spinster, and she had accepted her fate ten years ago. But now, after weeks in Cornwall, growing to know Marcus intimately in bed and out of it, her heart ached intensely when she thought of leaving him. She wished she knew what he was feeling, but she hadn't dared ask him, and he hadn't been forthcoming about it. Sharing feelings would serve no purpose. Every factor known to man would keep them from enjoying a happiness together. The bridge was simply too great to cross.

It had been twenty-four hours or so since she'd visited with Claudette in St. Austell, and since that time a world of emotions had passed through her, lingering to agonize her until she'd finally organized her feelings. She had to tell Marcus everything, though nothing had worried her so much in recent memory.

"You've been pensive today."

She closed her eyes to the sound of his deep voice, always soothing.

He touched her then, just a gentle rub of his hand at her neck.

She turned to him, her back to the wind, her skirts billowing out in front of her to drape across his legs as he stood so close. He was magnificent of form, dressed casually in a light gray shirt and dark gray pants that matched the sky and illuminated his beautiful eyes. He watched her intently, a frown on his brow, his lips a hard determined line of concern.

She tried to smile, though the effort was weak. "I've been doing a great deal of thinking, I suppose."

He lowered his hand to her shoulder, caressing her with strong fingers. It was all she could do not to sway into it.

"Thinking about us?" he asked, his voice a near whisper.

Mary reached for his hand and pulled it down so that she could clasp it with both of hers. "I'll be leaving Cornwall soon," she breathed, afraid he might not have heard it and she would be forced to repeat her words— words that filled her with acute sorrow.

"I think that's something *we* need to discuss—"

She reached up and placed her hand gently on his mouth, silencing him. He grasped her fingers, kissing each of them one by one.

She did smile then. "You're tickling me."

He grinned, rubbing his lips against her skin. "Good. I intend to tickle you for a long, long time."

Her stomach clenched at the thought of losing everything they shared, the moods and conversation, the nuances in their looks, their tones, their intimacy. Her smile faded and he noticed it.

"What is it?" he pressed, his voice edged with concern.

Drawing a deep breath, she pulled her hand back and crossed her arms over her breasts, defensively, she supposed, though not intentionally to cut him off. She just wasn't ready to be held and caressed knowing all she had yet to say.

"I have a story to tell you, Marcus," she began, turning her body to the east again, gazing off toward the open sea. "It's not a good one."

He waited silently, with the patience she'd always admired in him even as she knew instinctively that he wanted to charge at her with questions.

At last, gathering strength, she murmured, "It's a story of a lady, well, not much more than a girl, really. How life changed for her while she didn't even notice the important things around her."

Again, he said nothing, though she did hear him inhale deeply.

A bird squawked overhead, swooping low then flying out over the choppy water, and she watched it, noting that he probably did not. She could feel his eyes boring into her, his curiosity building to the level of his concentration.

Mary rubbed her upper arms with her hands, shivering from the dampness in the air, from the roughness of cotton along her sensitive palms.

"This lady," she continued solemnly, "had been enchanted by a young gentleman, a viscount, actually, who had been a very marriageable prize for several seasons. She had fallen easily in love with him, wanting so desperately to marry him. He'd said he'd loved her, too, and that they'd make a handsome couple, that all they had left to do was to plan for their marriage and their lives together. The wedding would be festive, and beautiful, and attended by the socially elite. Her thoughts of him were so sweet, so naïve, and so bathed in the illusion of contentment and trust. Always trust."

Mary swallowed hard and closed her eyes, feeling the wind on her cheeks, in her hair, hearing it roar against the cliffs below. Marcus stood watching, waiting, no doubt confused, even troubled, but making no sound. It was time to tell him everything that should never again be spoken.

She raised her face to the cloud-darkened sky and hugged herself, squelching the cry of grief that threatened. "He was always the perfect gentleman, charming to a fault, an impeccable example of gentility," she whispered just loud enough for him to hear. "He saw to that. He wanted the lady as well, but in far more intimate terms. She was to be his, at his discretion. He was the lord, the viscount, and she so young . . ."

Marcus took a step toward her, his shoes crunching on the rocks at his feet. Mary stepped back from his approach, unwilling to let him touch her as she knew he'd attempt to do. Lifting her lashes, she faced him squarely again, gazing into eyes of intense and haunted blue. Marcus Longfellow, Earl of Renn, so large and powerful, so intelligent and caring, so perfect for her in every way but one.

She drew a shaky breath, still embracing herself against the onslaught of emotion she knew she was about to witness.

"It is so difficult for a man to understand a lady's

desires," she murmured. "They range from hope to disenchantment, from love to loathing. This lady wanted love and hope and the promise of family from the viscount of her choosing, but he instead found a way to give her only disillusionment and anger and hate."

Marcus swallowed harshly; his nostrils flared, but he didn't interrupt.

She continued relentlessly as she began to express the pent-up bitterness within. "On a beautiful spring evening, not all that long ago, this proper and illustrious viscount invited the lady he said he wanted to marry inside his beautiful coach—just the two of them—and took her out for a ride in the country. It was a bold request, and a daring move for the lady to be alone with her intended, unchaperoned. But she wanted so badly to please. And of course she trusted him, as did everyone else in the lady's family."

Mary straightened, standing rigidly against the strong wind, ignoring it, and how it blew her hair and skirts out in front of her in wild freedom.

Pressing her lips together momentarily to keep from crying openly, she finally revealed, "On that dark evening, Marcus, the young and naïve lady was not given the choice that should have been hers. The lady succumbed to her greatest fear, the greatest revulsion." She took a shaky breath, tears clouding her eyes. "It's not clear if she struggled to the end, or simply gave in out of love and hope and trust. Over time memories are lost, or sometimes destroyed by the simple unwillingness to remember."

Mary paused, loath to turn away from the shock

and pain she witnessed on Marcus's face. His eyes blinked in growing incredulity; his jaw hardened in outrage as he fisted his hands at his side. He understood, he just didn't yet know the depth of her disclosure. But she would tell him everything. There was no turning back now.

"The gracious and charming viscount ruined the lady that night, Marcus," she whispered, her tone husky and spilling over with utter desolation. "He took her innocence in mind, in spirit, and in flesh, and didn't care in the slightest that his act of power and persuasion would leave so much damage. He wanted and he took, and there was no fighting because the lady loved him. She loved and trusted him. She accepted her fate—until the viscount turned away from her."

Marcus's body clenched in rage as he stood in front of her, still as cold stone. "Who is the lady, Mary?" he asked, voice raspy and low.

Tears began to flow down her face just as a sprinkling rain broke free of the clouds above. He knew. He understood everything, but he wanted her to say it. She centered on him, on the love she felt inside for the man before her. But as much as she wanted to go to him, to walk forward three feet and take him in her arms, she couldn't. It would be too much for both of them, and Mary realized that if he pushed her away at this moment, the devastation would be unendurable.

A sob tore from her throat as she hugged herself tightly to whisper, "The lady is me, Marcus." She closed her eyes, rain patting her face, mixing with the wetness on her lashes. "And I learned yesterday, from Claudette Coswell, that nearly ten years later, it is also Christine."

He said nothing for a moment, and never had a silence been so deafening, so chilling.

Still, she couldn't look at him.

Don't hate me, Marcus.

Suddenly he stepped forward and grabbed her upper arms. "What happened?" he whispered into the wind.

She couldn't answer him.

"What *happened*?" he asked again with more force, shaking her once. "To you, to Christine?"

She didn't understand what he wanted. "I'm sorry. I'm sorry . . ."

And then, crushing every single fear she entertained within, he yanked her hard against his body, holding her tightly, his arms wrapped around her protectively, his face in her hair, whispering her name over and over.

The rainfall grew stronger, saturating their clothes that clung to their bodies, their hair to their skin; the wind blew fiercely off the cliff, and still he refused to release her.

Mary absorbed his warmth and strength, relished his hard and protective form as it molded to her own, felt the steadfast beating of his heart where she rested her cheek.

"I should have seen it, Marcus," she breathed, unsure if he even heard her. "I should have known what had happened to her."

"Shhh . . ." He squeezed her tighter, his fingers in her hair as he pressed her head to his chest.

Marcus didn't know how long he stood there, allowing the cold, pouring rain to pound down atop them from the heavens. The moment of her confession would forever be engraved in his mind, but not the time spent holding her now, feeling nothing but numbness fused with fury, and an unyielding and passionate love for the woman in his arms. If he'd not understood his feelings for Mary Marsh before, he understood them now.

Mary and Christine. Two lives crossing paths in so many ways. Oh, God, he wanted to kill someone. To rip limbs, to slice a throat, to torture slowly and without mercy until the aggressor became the victim. Instead, he soothed and held softness and beauty against him, smelled rainwater and flowers, and sensed an inner courage that he'd never imagined in a woman. He had so many questions—questions that would only bring grief, and yet he needed to know.

She didn't move, aside from a shiver or two. For minutes he held her in the wind and rain, oblivious, but she didn't push him away. She needed his strength and warmth, and that simple understanding calmed him inside, kept his mind focused and steady.

At last he whispered, "Christine told me so much about you in her letters, Mary. She had me wanting you before I ever met you."

She buried her face in his wet shirt. Softly, she replied, "She told me so very much about you as well, Marcus."

"More than I probably ever want you to know," he returned wryly.

She let out a quiet, pained laugh and leaned her

head back, eyes closed. "I wish she'd never told me anything."

That hurt him, at least a little. Then he decided he didn't understand her. "Why?"

Her lashes fluttered open and she gazed into his eyes, hers brimming with tears that spilled onto her wet cheeks. "If I didn't get to know you from her persistent and unconventional attempt at matchmaking, I would never have admired you from afar, would never have wanted to be touched by you, could have left here and never looked back." Her lips trembled as she started to cry openly. "As it is," she breathed, "I'm going to leave St. Austell with wonderful memories that will haunt me and a heart that will never heal."

Marcus released her, pulled back from the embrace, and took her hands in both of his, engulfing them, and holding them tightly against his chest. He waited until she met his gaze before he spoke. "Did you think for even a second," he demanded harshly, "that I would let you go so simply and easily after everything we've shared? That your future would exist without me?"

She blinked, unconcerned with the rain and wind that swirled around her, her features going slack with nothing short of astonishment.

"What are you talking about?" she asked, dazed.

He wanted to shake her again—or kiss her passionately until she allowed herself to comprehend the inevitable. And Marcus believed wholeheartedly that she simply didn't understand what he wanted because she had never allowed herself to consider it.

"I didn't just want you as I got to know you from my sister's letters, Mary," he said intensely, gripping her hands. "I started loving you."

Wide-eyed and incredulous, she simply stared at him.

He brought one of her hands to his lips, kissing her knuckles then rubbing them against his mouth, his gaze never straying from hers.

"Meeting you, and getting to know you at last, proved to me that *you* are the journey's end, Mary Marsh. There is no richer treasure worth discovering on earth."

"Marcus—"

He cut her off with a kiss to her mouth, so full of fire and hope, of desperation and longing.

She succumbed as she pulled her hands from his and slid her arms around his neck, clinging to him, holding him tightly as she explored him with a marvelous passion.

He threaded his fingers through her wet hair, giving her what he knew she needed, what she'd always wanted.

"I told you not to be afraid," he said fervently against her mouth. "As you've never trusted another, trust in me. Trust in me . . ."

She started trembling again in his arms, and this time Marcus was certain it had nothing to do with the damp air and wind. He tightened his grip, but just as quickly, she pulled away from him, forcefully breaking the kiss as she shook her head.

"This is not my life, Marcus," she whispered, voice pained.

He stilled within from her steadfast denial of all they felt for each other. A cold dread washed over him as he gazed down into her haunted eyes. "This is *our* life, Mary."

For a brief moment, she placed her face in her palms, shaking her head. Then she took a step back and hugged herself again, her arms crossed over her breasts. "What we have between us isn't a reality we've made together, it's a dream, a fantasy. Don't you understand? It's not real. We come from two different worlds, you and I, and they have no business combining. I learned that years ago."

The fact that she compared their relationship to that of the one she'd had with the man who stole her innocence made him incredibly angry. He stood staring at her, hands on his hips, watching a fine trail of water slide down her chest and into her cleavage. How odd that he even noticed that.

"Do not stand there and deny that you love me, too, Mary," he murmured in warning.

She remained rigid in form, refusing to back down. "Love is irrelevant."

"Your *past* is irrelevant."

"You can't love me," she insisted, dropping her arms and fisting her hands at her sides.

"And yet I do."

"That's impossible."

The rain fell in sheets now, a roaring, freezing barrier between them that neither one seemed to notice at all.

"I know what love is, my darling," he maintained, teeth clenched, taking a step closer so that he towered over her, "because I have never said those words to another woman in my life."

That revelation staggered her. Her mouth

dropped open and she stumbled back. "You're ar earl."

That put his fury over the top. "What does *that* mean? That I can't know love? I'm a *man*, Mary, who's lonely for someone to talk to in the middle o the night, for someone to hold him after a hard day's labor, for someone to understand him and love him, too."

"Yes, a man," she agreed in an attempt to be practical. "A man who must marry reasonably, choose a woman of his class. A virgin—"

"You were always a virgin to me!"

She faltered, tears streaming down her cheeks. "How can you say that? You knew you weren't my first. How can that not matter to you?"

Marcus tensed, driven by the cold, the wind, the understanding of just exactly where her worries lay. He grabbed her face, steadying her cheeks in his palms, staring into her eyes with absolute conviction as he whispered, "Because I am the *one*."

For moments it seemed she didn't hear him—or didn't want to. Then she whimpered, closing her eyes to his, shivering as she reached up to pull his hands from her face.

After seconds of clutching his fingers in her palms, she gently kissed the tips of them, her lips smooth and soft and wet from rain as they lingered against his warm skin. And then she let him go without even another glance into his eyes.

Lifting her drenched skirts, she moved away from him toward the path to Baybridge House, hesitating only briefly to glance out across the sea a final time.

Marcus stared after her until she was well out of

sight, confused, dejected, and numbed by her startling account of her past, and that of his innocent sister.

Then, with emotions locked beneath the surface, he began to walk in the other direction, toward his cottage, where he could think, plan, organize, and hope. He never expected his revelation of love to be so totally unacceptable to her that she would deny the love he knew she felt for him. But the words his sister had written him not so long ago would forever ring true: what did he have if not hope?

Chapter 24

It was well after dark when he met her at the foot of the great staircase of Baybridge House. The sight of her, on her final night in Cornwall, made his chest tighten with a mixture of complex emotions that ruffled him inside—from anger at her determination to see him as a nobleman out of reach, beyond her class, to frustration at knowing she needed to return to London to face her family and her guilt, to a sense of inner peace when he looked at her face and saw her strength of will and character.

He'd suggested she dress simply, and she had, in a gown of brown muslin that she'd covered with a black woolen pelisse, her hair pulled back into one long braid behind her.

"Right on time, I see," he said in greeting, offering her his arm.

She grinned. "You said after dark. It's dark."

"Ah, but I then said perhaps a little after ten. It's"—he glanced at the grandfather clock in the center of the foyer—" twelve minutes past." Looking back into her eyes, he added, "Are you ready, Miss Marsh?"

"For a walk to the cliffs?" She leaned toward him so only he could hear her. "I would be delighted. I'd walk anywhere with you."

His smile faded. "But would you stay?"

It was a direct question, and she fumbled with the buttons on her pelisse before replying, "I'll stay by your side all night. That I can promise."

The sweet softness in her voice nearly undid him, nearly brought him to his knees on the marble foyer floor of his very own home. In all his life, Marcus had never felt this way about a woman.

"Let's go," he murmured, linking her arm through his.

She smiled hesitantly again and followed him out the tall front doors.

"Where are we going, my lord?" she asked as they meandered along the path toward the cliffs.

He skirted the brush, angling her along behind him. "It's a surprise."

"A surprise?" She laughed faintly. "Everything about you is a surprise to me, Marcus. Every day there is something new for me to enjoy."

He didn't comment on that, just continued to move farther away from the main house, north this time, the opposite direction of the cottage. He didn't know if she'd ever ventured out this way, but getting to the coastline was a bit more difficult from here, which was why it had always remained a rather secluded area.

Bright starlight shone down from a moonless sky, bathing them in varying degrees of darkness as the lighted windows from the house grew obscure behind them. She followed him easily enough, pulling her skirts along without much difficulty, not offering a word, trusting him with every step.

Finally, Marcus cleared the last of the thick brush, leading her out into a grassy patch of wild flowers that dropped off the cliff to the sea below. He immediately smelled lavender wafting out on a gentle, warm breeze, saw flickering lights from the fishing villages on St. Austell Bay, all enveloped by a cascade of sparkling stars on every horizon.

"It's breathtaking," she whispered into the stillness, standing beside him.

He glanced down at her, her expression cast in shadow.

"Especially at night," he replied in a deep whisper. "I wanted to give you something special to remember when you leave."

She tilted her head up and gazed into his eyes. For a long, intense moment neither of them spoke or moved. Then he placed his hands on her shoulders and very gently lifted her pelisse from her body.

The night was far from chilly, and she didn't offer an argument when he placed it on the soft grass at their feet, spreading it out wide, then reaching for her hand.

She sat beside him for a long while, content with only each other, his arm wrapped around her shoulders, holding her close as she snuggled into his chest, listening to the ocean breeze and the gentle crashing of the waves on the rocky shore below.

"I'll never forget this night, Marcus," she whispered into the sweetly scented air.

"All that's missing is the fireworks," he returned, nuzzling his nose and mouth in her hair.

She chuckled softly and smacked her palm on his chest. "I thought you were an earl. Can't you do everything?"

He grinned and reached for her chin, lifting it so that he gazed into her eyes. "When the night is as perfect as this one, we make our own."

That perplexed her for a moment; her brows creased with uncertainty. Then he lowered his lips to hers. The warmth and softness of them took his breath away.

"Mary . . ."

If only. If only. If only . . .

She leaned into him, accepting him as he was without question, without doubts, pressing her lips into his as his kiss grew bolder.

He pulled her against him fully, tugging at the ribbon at the bottom of her braid until it loosened. He dropped it to the ground behind her, then reached up and unraveled each layer until he could draw his fingers through her hair.

She moaned softly, holding him tighter, opening her mouth to the faint prodding of his tongue.

He kissed her deeper, harder, concentrating on his skill, her pleasure, giving everything of himself.

At last she leaned back, swept away by the power of his persuasion, his palm to her spine as he guided her. She spread out fully on the pelisse, and he crossed one lower leg over hers, never breaking contact.

His breathing came faster, as did hers, her moan of encouragement slightly more insistent. She stretched her hands across his chest, kneading his flexed muscles through the thin linen of his shirt.

He grasped her tongue and sucked the tip of it, causing her to tilt her head back in surprise, in stark satisfaction.

Her fingers tightened as she clung to him, begging for more with her audible sighs, her short, quick breaths, her body that pulsed beneath his.

Marcus rubbed his erection against her hip to encourage her, to give him a moment of extreme gratification, knowing she could feel how hard she made him even through her gown.

He dropped one palm to her breast, grazing his knuckles across the tip, aching to feel her nipple harden to his touch. She pushed into him again, with her whole body, lifting one of her legs to grasp his.

"Marcus . . ." she whispered against his mouth.

The sound of her need only strengthened his resolve to show her everything he felt inside. He pulled away a fraction and dropped his lips to her chin, her jaw and neck, running the tip of his tongue down to her exposed collarbone, picking up the pace.

She lifted her hands to his head, running her fingers through his hair, pulling him to her breasts that remained inconveniently covered with a barrier of thin muslin.

He took both of them in his palms, rotating his

hands over them in rhythm, caressing them as he ran his thumbs along her nipples.

She arched against him when he placed his face between them, when he groaned at the feel of her. Tugging gently, he pulled at the material until he lowered it as far as possible, just to the tips of each perfect mound of flesh, enabling him to skim the dewy softness with his tongue.

She inhaled a sharp, uneven breath when he took one nipple in his mouth, sucked, tugged with precise and focused tenderness.

"Are you wet?" he asked gruffly against her. "Wet and aching for me, Mary?"

"Oh, yes," she gasped in whisper. "Oh, God, Marcus. Touch me—"

He moved lower, his hands drifting from her breasts to her ribs, marvelously satisfied to note she didn't wear a corset. Not tonight. She had known they would have one last time together.

She lifted her hips to him, urging him on. And he followed her lead, drawing her skirts up with an expertise he hadn't exercised in far too long, kissing her exposed thighs as he moved to the center of her at last.

The sweet scent of her startled him. All too quickly it pervaded his mind, his instincts as a man, striking him with a desire as primeval as time.

She whimpered and pushed against him. He traced her hot skin with his tongue until he reached the point of all his dreams, the point of his Paradise, settling himself between her legs, inhaling the beauty and essence of only her.

She jumped in surprise when he coaxed open her cleft to find the nub of her desire, tasting her, loving her. She grabbed his head and whispered something inaudible to him, to the night sky, as she leaned her head back to savor the passion.

Marcus had never been so careful, so focused, so intent on her pleasure as he was right now. Raising her knees minutely, he pushed his arms beneath her and lifted her hips to satisfy her better.

She quickly neared the edge. He knew her now, how she sounded, felt in his arms, when she climaxed, and he readied himself for her release. He turned his tongue upward so that the smooth bottom stroked her continually, back and forth, to a tempo of his making, never shifting his concentration, never pulling back.

Her hips began to dig into him as she found his rhythm and matched it. She whimpered now, lost in her world within, allowing him to help her find the magic.

"Marcus . . ."

He pressed harder, faster.

She clutched his cheeks with her thighs, her fingers digging in to his scalp.

"Oh, God, oh, God, oh, God—*Marcus!*"

She came in a sudden rush of ecstasy, crying out once, grinding into him, her wetness only pushing him nearer to the brink of his own orgasm.

It took everything in him to hold back until she calmed, until her taste, her scent, the power of her climax drove him to the point of no return.

Seconds later he eased back and yielded to his own desire, reaching down quickly to unfasten his pants. He pulled himself free and leaned over the top of her so he could look into her eyes when he entered her.

She kept them closed, face hidden in shadow, but the dampness of her tears on her lashes as they streamed down her temples reflected the light from the distant bay. Or maybe it was from the stars.

It tore at his heart.

Hot and ready, he placed the tip of him at her slick center of warmth. A Paradise of comfort and contentment that would never be his because she refused to give to him completely.

"I love you, Mary," he whispered, the ache within riding on his breath.

She took his head in her palms and pulled his forehead down to touch hers. "We will always have this moment," she murmured. "Give me all of you tonight . . ."

He knew what she meant. And recognizing that the honesty she revealed, the ache to be one with him, meant more to her than the risks, completely and utterly shattered him. His throat closed with emotion he couldn't begin to put into words. But he would give as he felt, would love her always.

Slowly, he pushed his way inside of her, feeling the intensity of their closeness as she cushioned him deeply.

He remained there for moments, holding her, closing his eyes and concentrating to temper the urge of his release so that he could savor the sublimity of being a part of her as long as he could.

She kissed his brow and lashes, caressed his cheeks with her thumbs. But with one tiny thrust of her hips, she forced him onward. He could no longer hold back.

Raising his body, he pulled out to rest his tip at the moist, soft edge of her cleft. And as he paused, she opened her eyes to gaze into his.

Starlight glistened on her tears.

"Forever, Marcus," she breathed.

He clenched his jaw. "Forever—"

Then, in one deep thrust, he lost himself. His head arched back; his muscles tensed, and with a soft groan of satisfaction, he poured himself into her, deeply, perfectly, coming hard and fast and with all the passion he felt inside. It drained him, weakened him, but simultaneously filled him with a profound sense of peace. The peace he'd sought all his life, right here, in Mary Marsh.

"Don't leave tomorrow," he whispered as he regained some control. "Stay, and I'll give you the world."

She said nothing, but her tears fell steadily as she stroked his back and neck with gentle fingertips.

Finally, he moved to her side, lowering her gown to decently cover her, holding her close, smelling lavender and sea air mixed with the essence of her, watching the stars as she did.

They held each other for a long while, neither one speaking. It didn't really matter. He knew her thoughts.

You have your world, Lord Renn, and I have mine . . .

Chapter 25

Baybridge House
30 April 1855

My dearest Marcus. Things are no longer what they seem at Baybridge House. I cannot begin to tell you of the unseemly things that have gone on in this place. I fear Miss Marsh is the only one I can trust now, but I am afraid even to talk to her, and she will be leaving soon. Please come home. Please. I desperately need your guidance and protection. Until I see you again, I will remain forever,

Your sister,
Christine

Marcus Longfellow, Earl of Renn, requested a formal meeting with his mother in his study at half past one o'clock in the afternoon, two days after Mary Marsh left Baybridge House for London.

Standing at the far window overlooking the Bay of Austell, he tried to keep his mind focused on the conversation about to take place, the information he hoped to glean from the encounter, even as his heart ached with longing for the woman he called his own.

Hands clasped behind his back, he stared down at the garden below, remembering their first shared kiss among the flowers, at night beneath the stars, the feel of her warm body next to his and the physical and emotional reaction that followed. What an insightful night that had been, and for as long as he lived, Marcus would never forget the very first feel of Mary's lips on his body.

Taking a quick deep breath, he closed his eyes, imagining her as she stood before him the night she came to him in a black corset of her making, those blood red rubies at her nipples. Nothing he'd ever experienced had been so erotic.

"Lord Renn, the Countess of Renn is here," came the timid voice of one of his mother's infinite number of maids.

Marcus tempered his mood at the ridiculous introduction of mother and son, and turned around to face the one person who remained the key to his return to England.

"Mother," he drawled, nodding once.

"Renn, darling," she replied, smiling sweetly as she glided into the study, dressed in stately black crepe, her glossy auburn hair piled high on her head, wearing not a speck of jewelry save her wedding ring. Marcus had always taken pride in his mother's appearance. She'd once been gorgeous, simply beautiful to look at, and even now, at nearly fifty-five years of age, she still had the look of sophisticated elegance that she carried oh so well, her lovely pale face void of wrinkles, her eyes crystal clear and intelligent.

Yes, Gwyneth Longfellow could be intimidating in the extreme, calculating in her pursuit of desires, and unparalleled when it came to class. She had made his father a magnificent wife and gregarious hostess, giving him two sons and a daughter before he died. And he died a contented man. Marcus thought he at least owed his mother the courtesy of knowing she'd lived the perfect life of a countess, was all that his father had asked for. Until Christine's untimely death.

Gwyneth walked to his side and leaned up to kiss his cheek.

"What is it?" she asked, her forehead creasing in that particular frown that Marcus felt certain she practiced.

His mouth curved wryly as he motioned to one of the chairs. "Please be seated, Mother."

She eyed him carefully for several seconds before turning to do as he'd requested. "My, you certainly are acting formal this afternoon."

He said nothing to that. Instead, he pivoted around to gaze back out the window, this time toward the horizon, where the pale sky faded into the distant ocean, listening to her adjust her skirts around her legs.

"Are you disappointed in Miss Marsh's decision to leave?" she asked with bold assurance that he would reply in the negative.

Instead, to unsettle her, he said, "Yes. Very disappointed." He leaned his palms on the windowsill. "I'm going to marry her, Mother. I'm sure you're relieved."

He didn't glance her way, but he could have sworn she squealed in delight from behind him. He fairly snorted.

"How do you intend to do this when she isn't even here?" she asked cautiously, trying to gauge his attitude.

He thought that was rather obvious, but he didn't remark on it. "I intend to go to London in pursuit of her."

"How romantic. Oh, Marcus, I'm so pleased!" She clapped her hands together in front of her once. "She's a lovely girl, and the two of you shall have a lovely wedding, which we can begin planning immediately—"

"I thought she was too old by your standards," he cut in, tossing a look at her over his shoulder.

She flushed, but otherwise didn't appear to be bothered by his notice of her inconsistency. "She is too old, dear, but you're taken with her and she is of good family. All I want is your happiness."

"And an heir?"

She folded her hands primly in her lap. "Of course. It's what all mothers want from their children."

Slowly, he turned back to face her fully, leaning his hip on the sill and crossing his arms over his chest. "Is that what you wanted from Christine's marriage? Her happiness?"

He watched the lines around her mouth tighten, her eyes widen slightly.

"Naturally," she replied. She tilted her head a fraction. "It's what I want for all of my children."

"And yet you wanted her to marry Baudwin."

She fidgeted in the chair. "Their marriage was arranged, Renn, you know that. They liked each other, cared for each other. It was as good of a match as any." She frowned. "Why these questions?"

Marcus inhaled deeply, knowing the time had come to get to the point, wondering how best to present it. He reached up and scratched his jaw to give him a moment or two longer to think things through. At last, he dropped his voice to a low murmur to prevent the spread of vile gossip should servants be listening where they should not.

Very carefully, he asked, "Are you aware, Mother, that the good Viscount Exeter, a family friend and gentleman of the highest culture, *forced* himself on Christine, the darling of our family, not only getting her with child, but taking her innocence without her consent?"

Gwyneth gasped; all color washed from her face.

Marcus pursued his very reckless tactic. "Were you aware that their first time intimately as a couple was inside a dark coach at his demand and her horror?"

His mother's expression suddenly waxed a brilliant rage; scarlet suffused her cheeks, but she didn't utter a sound.

Stepping away from the window and walking toward her, he continued. "Were you aware, Mother, that Christine wrote me of her foreboding and fear but was too distraught and embarrassed to give me details? That she spoke of this to

Claudette Coswell only days before she died because she couldn't mention it to anyone she loved?"

"That's quite enough!" Gwyneth blurted, rising abruptly, her hands in tight fists at her side.

He wasn't about to end it there. Standing before her, gazing down to the woman who brought him into the world, he clenched his jaw, then whispered the final blow. "Were you aware that the heir of the viscount's estate, your first grandchild, was conceived by violence?"

With a quick raise of her arm, Gwyneth slapped him hard across the mouth.

Marcus jerked back, the sting piercing him enough that his eyes watered. But the look she gave him cut deeply, hurting far worse than her hand, and filling him with more grief than he could ever possibly put into words.

She had known. It was the only explanation to her action. If she hadn't, she would have broken down, cried openly, or become hysterical in her heartache and anger. Or, if nothing else, she would have certainly grown quiet with her own sorrow and questions, attempting to place herself at fault.

But his mother had reacted in none of those logical ways. She had become enraged at him for speaking so disrespectfully, true, but most of all for mentioning such a loathsome, scandalous secret.

Secrets. The key to everything.

Marcus moved away from his mother, his features expressing a measured disgust as he strode to the wall on which hung at least forty examples of the best of Renn china.

He scrutinized those in front of him, seeing nothing.

"She was your daughter," he whispered.

Silence reigned for seconds as she refused to move from her uncompromising position. "I know that. She was also betrothed to Exeter, soon to be his wife. She wouldn't be the first—"

"Oh, Christ, Mother, you make it sound as if he forced her to take menial employment." Marcus pivoted, palms opened wide. "She trusted him and he *raped* her! The woman he was supposed to marry in just weeks!"

"Shut your mouth," she hissed, grimacing. Steadying herself with a hand on the back of her chair, she leaned toward him to enunciate thickly, "How dare you speak to me like that in my home?"

He shook his head. "You've forgotten everything, haven't you? Or perhaps it's simply that you've taken everything for granted in my absence."

She tossed a hand in the air. "You're speaking in riddles."

He pointed to his chest, his features contorted in fury. "Christine was *my* sister, *my* responsibility, and this is *my* home! And as the Earl of Renn, I will speak to you any goddamn way I like!"

Gwyneth froze. Her eyes opened wide in complete astonishment, her face drained quickly again of color as she gaped at him.

"I want the truth, Mother, now," he said, his voice conveying profound assurance. "I want to know why you're so willing to forgive Baudwin and not your daughter. I want to know why you insist on treating Exeter with so much respect when he has hurt this family so deeply. I want to know what you and Christine discussed the week she died. I want to know what secrets you're hiding, or so help me God, I will sell everything and put you out on the street."

Her eyes narrowed. "Don't threaten me with the ridiculous, my child," she warned in a low voice, thick with daring, her confidence returning as she gracefully strode toward him. "I told you once to leave things alone. Leave them alone."

She would never understand unless the rug were pulled out from under her. He knew his mother. At that moment, Marcus didn't think he'd ever felt such a keen sense of ultimate satisfaction.

Standing tall, hands behind him, he glared down at the face of a woman he adored, the face of a woman he so very much admired, the face of a calculated manipulator who was about to receive as she gave. "Your worries are over, madam," he disclosed in a deep whisper, knowing the weight of a lifetime was soon to lift from his shoulders. "I'm resigning my title to George."

She started to laugh—until she realized the gravity in that pronouncement, felt the truthfulness of his statement. Then she swayed against the desk, catching herself on the smooth edge before she collapsed.

"You can't do that," she spat vehemently.

"I most certainly can. This is not a threat. I no longer wish to be the Earl of Renn. In fact," he added with a twitch of his lips, "I never wanted to *be* the Earl of Renn."

She looked as if she might faint. "You *are* the earl."

He leaned over so that his face loomed above hers. "I was never the earl in deed, only by birth. George deserves the honor for everything he's done—"

"It's impossible."

His brows rose. "Impossible? What's impossible? He's perfect for it. I drift on and off the Continent, work at hard labor, and don't give a damn about the mines." He grabbed one of her shoulders with his hand, with the other her chin, tilting her face up to his. "It's a perfect solution."

She gazed at him for seconds, her tired eyes wide with profound trepidation. "You're serious . . ."

"I love you, Mother, but I won't be staying at Baybridge House. Let George do what he was born to do. My calling is in Egypt."

Suddenly she started shaking where she stood, swaying as she glanced around her in bewilderment, as if she didn't know precisely where she was, what was happening to her.

Marcus helped her back into the chair, observed how her skirts wrinkled at the sides and that she didn't even notice, even care. Then, for the first time in ages, he watched as her eyes filled with tears.

That stirred him deeply. He'd never wanted to hurt her.

"Everything will be all right," he soothed, leaning back on the edge of his desk.

She shook her head. "You are the earl. That's the way it should be. George manages the business;

you manage the estate. George is—" She glanced to the wall of fine china. "Oh, God . . ."

In that instant, Marcus got his first indication that she held something back, something vital. "What is it?" he asked hesitantly, without aggressively moving toward her.

For a long moment she stared silently at the porcelain plates. Then she said, "The one on the top left, that was always your father's favorite."

Marcus glanced up at the wall, unsure of her meaning until his gaze locked on the plate in question.

Of a rich, masculine flavor, the plate had a plain, cream-colored foundation surrounded by a border of brown and gold plaid, topped off in the center by a very understated but solid gold letter "R." It was the first china plate design made from Renn stock, and it symbolized the family and the title. Marcus understood how his father had taken pride in it. What he didn't understand was what that had to do with this conversation.

"All the china is lovely, Mother," he maintained, trying not to sound too impatient.

She closed her eyes and leaned her head against the padded cushion of her chair. "You'll note, however, that it's not hanging in my bed chamber or withdrawing room."

He didn't follow her thoughts, and decided not to comment on them.

After a long moment, she raised her lashes and looked him in the eye. "The one on my bedside table is blue, sky blue, with lilacs in the center."

Marcus pinched the bridge of his nose. "I can't see how this is relevant."

"No, you wouldn't."

That stung a little, so he brusquely ordered, "Explain it to me, then."

She breathed in heavily, tipping her forehead to the side as she studied him. "You know, Renn, you've got your father's look." Gwyneth almost smiled as she lowered her gaze back to her lap to add, "George has the look of his."

For a slice of a second, Marcus was confused. And then the answers to everything struck him at once—the reason for the marriage of Christine and Baudwin; the way George looked and acted only like their mother; the way she'd always been so very irritated when her oldest son would leave, especially the country, with a reluctance to perform his duties as earl.

George wasn't his father's child.

Marcus's heart began to pound hard in his chest. *But whose?*

The china on the bedside table . . . lilacs on blue . . .

He shot a look at his mother.

"I fell in love once, too, Renn," she conveyed softly in acknowledgment of his total understanding. "Your father was a good man, but not the one I loved with every part of me." She drew a shaky breath and closed her eyes. "I loved the former Viscount Exeter, Baudwin's father. George is his."

Marcus felt as if he'd fallen into a tunnel of confusion and bewilderment, of vanishing sensibilities and a world of illusions. This could not be real.

"How could you?" he murmured, his throat scratchy.

She looked into his eyes, bitterly. "You ask r that? Have you never been in love?"

He thought of Mary, of her beauty and grace ar intelligence.

His mother smiled. "She loves you as much. I' seen it. And she would do whatever it took to I with you. She just doesn't realize it yet."

Marcus was beginning to think they were all g ing mad, living in a complex nightmare. He stoc upright again, agitated, and began to pace the flo between his desk and the wall of plates.

"Does George know?" he murmured, his voi husky with anger.

She shook her head, squeezing her skirt in h fists on her lap. "Nobody ever knew"— she i haled sharply—"except Christine."

He stilled; his head jerked up. "It's why sl died. You know what happened to her . . ."

Fresh tears filled her eyes but she didn't loo away from him. "I was there."

At no other time in his life had Marcus felt suc a jumble of emotions he didn't understand. Bi numbing them all, overpowering everything, wa fear.

"What did you do?" he asked very slowly, hi body perspiring in the stuffy enclosed room, fror an oncoming feeling of dread.

The question seemed to vibrate off the wall: sounding hollow in his study filled with lovel items of display.

Gwyneth sniffed and rubbed her eyes with he fingers. "I did not kill her, Marcus."

He closed his eyes. "I know that. Tell me wha happened."

For a long minute she didn't utter a word, just fidgeted with her sleeves, her skirt, rubbed her palms together. Then at last she crumpled into her corset and slumped against the back of the chair. Marcus couldn't remember a time when his mother looked so disheveled and defeated.

"She had been with Baudwin, and he had . . . taken her intimately," Gwyneth started, her figure crumpled in her chair, her voice small and meek. "She came to me with so much anger, so much guilt. I wanted to help her. I did. But honestly, what was there to do? She was betrothed to him. He had rights."

Marcus slammed his fist into his desk. "He didn't have the right to take what she was unwilling to give."

Gwyneth gazed at him solemnly. "He had rights to her child, Renn. And in only a month or so from the incident, she would be his legally. He could take her as he pleased."

Marcus was appalled. He stood staring down at his mother, ashamed for his sister and the family that had failed her. And still, what Gwyneth had said was entirely true. Once the vows were spoken, Baudwin could have taken her against her will at any time. Any man could do so with his wife. Such a vile thought had never really occurred to him, however, and with it he felt severely sickened by the knowledge that his sister could have been subjected to such treatment by her husband. Far worse, though, was knowing that even after Christine had mentioned her fear and misgivings, her resentment and loathing, his mother had still encouraged the marriage.

Reining in his disgust, Marcus crossed his arms over his chest. "What happened that afternoon, Mother?" he asked tersely.

She shook her head, averse to relive the day her only daughter died in her reach. But he was ever patient now, standing his ground.

At last she revealed, "She came to see me, angry and determined. She—she'd gone through some of my very personal items and had found a letter I'd written to Baudwin's father years ago, disclosing my fear that I carried the viscount's child." Gwyneth swallowed with difficulty, shaking her head again, as if that small denial would make it disappear.

"She argued with me in the library for a few minutes about that, about how disgusted she was at my indiscretion. I tried to explain how I felt at the time, but she wanted to equate my feelings with her determination never to see Baudwin again after what he'd done to her. In essence . . . she tried to blackmail me. If I broke the betrothal agreement, she wouldn't tell George."

Gwyneth looked up at her son, her eyes sparkling with tears. "In spite of the fear of my child discovering the stone-cold fact that he was illegitimate, I insisted that she marry Exeter. She was with child. He was the father. I followed her to her withdrawing room that afternoon to reason with her, to get my letter back and calm her irrational notions before she reacted impulsively."

Gwyneth closed her eyes and wept openly, her palm to her mouth. Marcus stood where he was, detached.

Finally, she whispered, "I tried to take the letter from her, but she wouldn't release it. It was during that exchange that she stumbled, hitting her head on her dressing table as she fell."

Marcus felt tears sting his eyes and he closed them to the onslaught of emotion.

"You must understand," Gwyneth added fiercely, "we could not afford scandal. And we can't even now. Baudwin knows nothing. George knows nothing. All this must remain between us, Renn."

At any cost . . .

At last Marcus understood. Yet the greatest disgrace of all was a mother forcing her daughter to marry a man who pinned her against a coach door and took her innocence while she denied him verbally. That had to be a far worse sin than a sexual indiscretion twenty-five years ago.

Marcus gritted his teeth. "It doesn't change a thing, as far as I'm concerned," he said huskily. "Nobody but the two of us knows George is illegitimate, and I will never tell a soul." He leaned ever closer to the slumped figure of his mother, whose skin now looked ghostly white, eyes tired and old. "But I am leaving, under my conditions. You will then have to live your life knowing the Earl of Renn is a Fife."

She cringed, but nodded as if she'd expected this all along.

He straightened, his heart filling with sorrow for the countess who had raised her children with such self-dignity and expectation, only to be just another human being who made mistakes and now must pay for them. But she was also his mother, and that would never change. He would love her always.

"I am leaving tomorrow, and I don't know when I'll return. I will miss you, and George, and Baybridge House. But my future is elsewhere, Mother."

She reached up then and touched his cheek with the palm of her hand. It startled him for a moment, but it felt warm and comforting, an expression of goodwill. But she said nothing. Perhaps she had decided there was nothing more to say.

Marcus stood upright in the bright sunshine of late morning, feeling an immense tension coiling up inside of him as he watched Exeter's coach meander along the viscount's private drive toward the house.

Lingering next to his own coach, Marcus had been waiting for the man to return from church service for nearly half an hour, his anger growing at the thought of the pain this one man had caused his sister, the circumstances that had culminated in her death. And he felt that way without question. Baudwin Fife might not have killed Christine with his own hands, but his selfish actions had led to the discovery of the letter that had been the center of her ultimate destruction.

Never in his life had Marcus felt such hate toward another human being.

At last the viscount's coach pulled to a stop beside his. Two footmen immediately descended the stone steps from the house, intent on helping Exeter alight, but Marcus stopped them with a simple lift of his hand.

"Sir?" one of them questioned.

He smiled with a certain furious satisfaction. "I'll take care of it."

"As you wish, my lord."

Marcus lifted the latch and glanced inside. Exeter sat near the opposite wall, in the shade, but the look of surprise on his face was telling.

"What are you doing here, old friend?" Baudwin asked, recovering his composure with a shake of his head. "Where are my footmen?"

"I wanted you alone," Marcus replied, leaning over to push his large body inside, his voice raw with loathing.

Exeter frowned. "What the devil is going on?"

Marcus couldn't wait any longer; his rage consumed him. In one thrust, he shot his fist into the viscount's face with full force, shoving the man's head back so hard it hit the wooden sidewall, causing the coach to sway.

Baudwin cried out at impact, so utterly startled he couldn't immediately react in self-defense, or speak. He covered his nose with one hand, and grabbed the seat cushion with the other to regain his balance as blood began to gush down his pristine white shirt and onto his light gray, perfectly pressed morning suit.

Marcus wrapped his thick, hard hand around the man's neck. "I thought," he whispered through clenched teeth, "that since you attacked my sister in a coach, it would be fitting to show you exactly how it feels to be trapped at the hands of a madman. I only wish I could leave you with the same sense of disgrace."

Baudwin blinked quickly several times. "My

nose," he grunted, unable to speak clearly. "Get o
of me, you bloody *bastard*!"

Marcus lowered his face to within an inch of th
viscount's. Cheek twitching, he spat in whisper, "
wonder if she said as much to you."

Baudwin went still, the pain from the punc
making his eyes water. "I'll have you—"

"Arrested? I don't think so," Marcus finished fo
him. "If you tell a soul that I caused you bodil
harm in any way today, I'll tell all the mothers o
Cornwall how you raped my sister."

Fear replaced anger as Exeter fairly shook wit
it.

Satisfied, Marcus pushed against the man wit
full strength one last time, then stepped out of th
coach into bright sunshine.

He jerked at the edge of his jacket to straighte
it, then nodded once to the astonished footmer
who stood several feet away, gaping.

He was done here. No regrets.

Now to find Mary, the only person who had eve
understood him.

Chapter 26

⌒⌒◯◯⌒⌒

Mary sat beside her sister, Mimi, on a marble bench, in the younger woman's flower garden behind her London home, listening to water trickle down the center fountain that stood before them. She also noticed the sound of traffic from the streets beyond. Always traffic—and the bustling of the busy community. She hadn't realized that life at Baybridge House had also been so peaceful and quiet until she'd returned.

It had been a long journey, not so much in distance, but in the mix of emotion that still ran through her. She'd left three weeks ago, with a formal farewell both to the countess and to George, and an awkward departure from the property. She hadn't seen Marcus that day, or said good-bye as she would have liked. Their last meeting had been in bed the night before, when they'd made love at their own pace, so beautifully, relishing every precious minute in those hours before dawn to make them last in her mind forever. He had intentionally avoided her the following morning, as she'd prepared to leave, and she hadn't sought him. They had left so many words unsaid, feelings exposed. She couldn't be with him, and Mary sensed that he had at last accepted the reality of their unconventional relationship and its impending end as well. He hadn't mentioned it again.

She had cried when her coach meandered down the rocky path toward town for a final time, allowing tears to fall freely down her cheeks as she stared blindly at the calm, serene beauty of St. Austell Bay. She would miss the ocean, the people, the cry of sea birds, and the sound of crashing waves upon the cliff. Instead of dwelling on it, however, she had looked forward to new and better times. She'd missed her family a great deal in the months she'd been away, especially her father, and life would return to normal in due course. She held much faith in that.

But life, she realized, tended to be singularly amusing, even absurd. Upon her return, she discovered her father had been quite well taken care of by the Widow Ester Thurston. So well attended, in fact, that they were contemplating marriage. It was, her father had said, a rather spur-of-the-moment thing, and yet Mary could tell that her father was besotted. In a manner, she was thrilled he'd found someone else to take care of his needs, and enjoyed the company of a woman who adored him. They really were quite funny together, giggling and blushing like two in love.

Mimi, too, had changed. She'd grown large with

her first child, due in eight weeks. She and her husband adored each other as well, though they bickered frequently. It wasn't a nasty bickering, she decided, but more of an extension of their loving, intimate relationship. It was simply their way as a couple, and they had grown so close, especially with the baby on the way. Even as Mary watched her sister move uncomfortably in the summer heat, she felt a stab of jealousy for an experience she would never have.

She and Marcus hadn't bickered. They'd had so much in common being unusual individuals of society, as it were. They were two reserved people who had fulfilling work, complex thoughts, and unmatched independence, and who, for a few short weeks, had found each other. Their love story had been based on intellect, admiration, and true friendship, but it had also been one of intensity and heat and courageous love. And that, Mary mused, would be the hardest thing of all—giving up her friend and sizzling lover in Marcus Longfellow.

"You're thinking about him, aren't you?"

Mary blinked, realizing she'd been staring blankly at the fountain and hadn't heard a word of her sister's tirade about the annoyances of pregnancy. At least, that's what she thought they'd been discussing.

She patted Mimi's knee. "I'm sorry. My mind was drifting."

Her sister smiled, her clear brown eyes acknowledging a certain appreciation for the power of reflection.

"You can't hide here forever, Mary," she said soberly. "You need either to face him, or move on."

Mary sucked in a long breath of hot summer air and sat straighter, looking not at her sister, but the rose trellis beyond.

"I won't be seeing him again," she said with conviction, wishing she could doubt that. "And I'm considering some work in Bedford for Lady Larson-Cower. She'll be remarrying next spring."

Mimi nodded, giving way to another moment of silence. Mary wanted the work, but it no longer held her full attention.

"But what of him?"

Mary glanced at her sister. "Him?"

"Your earl."

Her heart raced with the thought of her and Marcus together again. "He doesn't belong to me," she corrected, though at that moment she wondered where he was, what he was doing, if he'd ever learned the truth behind his sister's demise, as he'd so hoped. She sighed and leaned back on her hands. "He's also, I'm quite sure, forgotten me."

Mimi jerked back in surprise. "I'm sure he has not."

She smiled at such naïveté. "Thank you for the confidence in my feminine charms, but he's got land to run, work in Egypt, of all places, and I—" she hesitated, then dropped her voice to murmur, "I was not for him."

For a long moment Mimi watched her; Mary could feel her gaze on the side of her face. Then her sister reached out and draped an arm across her shoulders, hugging her.

"Have you told me everything?" she asked softly.

Mary's stomach tightened a little, but she tried

o ignore the sensation. "Mostly everything," she
eplied.

Mimi grinned. "I hope the details you left out of
he adventure were merely indescribable."

She tapped her fingertips on the cool marble beneath them. "Completely indescribable."

Mimi laughed at that.

She thought for a moment, then added sedately,
'He did help me work through some difficult
houghts about you and Nathan, though. Marcus is
a good listener, and he often gives such profound
dvice."

"Good gracious, Mary, *profound* advice? You ex-
ggerate like a woman in love."

She smiled. "It's all talk."

Mimi huffed. "I doubt that."

Seconds of silence passed between them. Then
Mary glanced at her sister, taking note of her pink
heeks, the beading of perspiration on her fore-
ead.

"Would you like to go inside? You look uncom-
ortable in the heat."

Mimi shifted her weight on the bench, arching
er back so that her belly stuck out to her knees.
No," she replied, grimacing. "I'm uncomfortable
verywhere. I cannot *wait* to get this child out of my
ody."

"You're having a girl," Mary said as if she actu-
lly knew.

Mimi grinned sheepishly. "I think so, too. Poor
Nathan."

Mary laughed, then leaned forward, resting her
orearms on her thighs as she looked to her hands.
How is he, Mimi?"

"Who? Nathan?"

Mary nodded. "After everything that happened to him."

"Is that what's bothering you?" Mimi asked frowning.

"It'll always bother me," she murmured, rubbing her thumbs together purposely.

After a long moment's hesitation, Mimi said "You know, Nathan's never discussed his anger because I'm sure he doesn't want to hurt me by reliving the pain our family caused him. But please understand, Mary, that he's gotten over much of his bitterness. I think—I think forgiveness is a relative thing as well. In Nathan's mind he's been able to rationalize that the wrong our family caused him in 'fifty-one, while initially hurting him deeply, ultimately gave him his wife and child five years later, and a reputation in his field of work that's even greater than it was before." She reached over and squeezed her hand. "It *is* over, and if there are any lingering doubts in your mind, they'll fade eventually. Nathan is happy now, Mary, and that's what's important. Try and remember that."

Mary gazed at her sister, feeling a depth of appreciation unfelt before today, mixed heavily with her own longtime sorrow. It was an odd combination of thoughts that stirred her mind deeply, and yet she believed in Mimi's love and gratitude, especially when coupled with Marcus's bold pronouncement that her future would work out as it should. She needed to trust that, as she always had trusted him.

"And you?" she asked softly.

Mimi grinned slyly again. "I couldn't be more

pleased with how my life has turned out. You know that." She stretched again. "Of course I'll probably be cursing all of you when I give birth to this fifty-pound wonder."

Mary laughed with an ease in the tension, and patted her sister's bulging belly. "Fifty?"

"It feels like it, anyway. Look at my feet."

She glanced down. "Swollen again."

"And it's not even noon." Mimi sighed and awkwardly raised her body. "I think I'll go inside where it's cooler and put them up."

Mary stood as well. "I'll join you. I need to be getting home soon anyway."

Mimi placed a palm on her shoulder. "Stay here. There's something I have to show you first. A surprise."

She clasped her hands behind her, her forehead creasing in frown. "A surprise? In the garden?"

Her sister lifted one shoulder in a shrug. "It's the perfect place for this surprise, I think." She lifted her skirts. "I'll only be a moment."

With that, she turned and walked with as much grace as possible out of the fountain alcove.

Chapter 27

Mary sat again on the marble bench, arranging her yellow chiffon skirts around her legs and ankles. The day had grown quickly hot and humid, and her gown clung to her body most uncomfortably. Whatever the surprise, she hoped Mimi would bring it quickly and allow her to retire indoors. Maybe it was a new fan. One could only hope.

"Hello, Mary."

She'd never jumped so quickly in her life. At once she was standing, her back to the fountain, her hand at her chest in defense of her racing heart, staring at the spectacular figure of Marcus Longfellow standing five feet from her in a morning suit of slate gray.

She gaped at him. Stunned. "Wha—what are you . . ."

He raised his brows. "Doing here?"

She clamped down on her mouth. "You're doing that again."

He nodded, stepping closer. "Finishing your sentences for you?"

"It's a bad habit, Marcus," she said, clasping her hands behind her back.

He eyed her thoughtfully as he moved up to stand beside her, gazing down to her face. "I have many bad habits, Mary. It should give you great pleasure to discover them one by one and scold me for them. Actually, I think I'd enjoy that. Life with you should never be boring."

She shook herself, closing her eyes briefly and then opening them again in the fear that she was dreaming.

I could never dream this perfectly . . .

She started shaking as he reached out and ran the back of his finger down her cheek, but she never looked away from his brilliant blue eyes, so close she believed she could feel their heat.

"You never told me how you got your scar," she said breathlessly, avoiding conflict at all costs until she got her bearings.

His lips turned up crookedly. "Didn't I?"

She waited, and when he added nothing more, she sighed loudly for his benefit. "No."

He nodded, taking a finger and skimming it across her jaw, toward her mouth.

"I usually tell people it's a battle wound."

She laughed outright. "A battle wound?"

He smirked. "Actually, when I was about ten, George and I were playing some sort of game with tree branches. He swung at me and I forgot to jump. They stitched it, of course, but not well."

Her smile faded as he reached her lips with hi.
finger, he let the tip linger on the cushioned soft
ness, stroking it back and forth until her legs fel
like jelly and she started breathing fast.

"Marcus . . ."

His features grew serious, his gaze probing. "1
could never leave England without you," he maintained huskily. "You are meant to be with me."

Tears stung her eyes and she lowered her lashes.
He placed his palm under her chin and lifted her
face to meet his. But he didn't kiss her. Instead, he
simply stared.

"What are you doing?" she asked in whisper,
seconds later, eyes still closed.

She heard him inhale a long, raw breath.

"I'm staring at beauty," he whispered, "thinking
how much I missed it, knowing that if I never see
another lovely thing in my life, I can go to my grave
with the memory of you, right now, dressed in yellow to match the sunshine."

His lips touched hers gently, coaxing them to respond. He tasted heavenly, warm. She could never
leave this again. For anything.

"Marcus," she whispered against his mouth, "I
love you. I love you . . ."

He groaned very softly, drawing her against
him, wrapping his arms around her waist. He made
her feel as if she were the most prized of wines, the
most delicate of all porcelain. In seconds she placed
her hands on his neck and pulled him closer.

God, how she'd missed him!

"Sit with me," he urged after a second or two of
tiny kisses to her lips and cheeks, her neck.

She followed his lead as he lowered her down to

the bench, still clinging to him, still feeling him. He cupped her face in his palms, tracing her cheekbones with his thumbs, brushing his lips back and forth across hers. She threaded her fingers through his hair, feeling his hot breath against her cheek and jaw.

"There are so many things I have to tell you," he murmured, "so much has happened."

She nodded minutely and pulled back a little. He rubbed his nose on hers, then touched her forehead with his own.

"I'm going back to Egypt next week."

Her racing heart began to pound. "I knew you would."

"And you're coming with me."

She didn't even argue. "All right."

He chuckled, gave her a kiss on the bridge of the nose. "You're very easy, Miss Marsh."

She sighed against him, her eyes still closed, never wanting this dream to end. "You're very persuasive, Lord Renn."

He pulled back a little, gazing into her face. After several seconds of silence, he reached for her hands, covering them with his, so warm and strong.

She opened her eyes at last, focusing on his marvelous face, his penetrating eyes, noting how serious he was, how he studied her.

"What is it?" she asked, sitting a little straighter and caressing his cheek with her palm.

He pressed his lips together, then replied, "I'm resigning my title."

Of all the things he could have said, she had never expected to hear something so astonishing—

and yet so right, for Marcus. She noticed the concern in his voice, in his hardened, determined features.

"Are you sure?" she whispered, lowering her hand to clutch his tightly again.

He thought about that for a long moment, as if he wanted to gather a reasonable explanation. In the end, he simply said, "Yes."

Mary understood him, more than anyone, likely. Marcus Longfellow was his own man, his own person, with hopes and a work ethic unlike most. He was born to discover, roam, live life as a challenge, not as a controller. The title of earl suited George, a man who lived by convention, expected nothing more, wanted nothing less. Marcus no doubt knew this, had probably known about it for years, which he'd taken for granted on his long trips abroad. But it also could have something to do—

"This is not about you, Mary," he cut in, reading her mind accurately and observing her reaction.

She smiled slyly. "Now you're finishing my thoughts, too?"

He raised one of her hands and kissed the inside of her wrist, letting his mouth linger on the soft skin. "I knew what you'd think, yes. I knew you'd worry if I didn't set this straight in the beginning. I would have married you if I were king."

She felt her nose start to tickle, her lips tremble, and she forced a swallow. "I never thought I'd get married."

"Well," he admitted, voice firm and controlled, "I didn't know whether you'd challenge me or not, so I took the liberty of getting approval from your father last night."

Her mouth dropped open. "You asked my father for my hand?"

He shrugged. "Of course."

"That makes me mad. You saw him last night and nobody told me?"

He smiled sheepishly, rubbing her fingers with his thumb. "I wanted to surprise you."

And a more magnificent surprise she would never get. A life, a love, in Marcus Longfellow. "You're forgiven," she said matter-of-factly.

He reached into his coat pocket. "I have a ring somewhere . . ."

She started crying, trembling even in the heat, tears filling her eyes.

In a swift moment of utter sublimity, he pulled out a single gold band topped with three rows of perfectly cut rubies, holding it out for her inspection.

Sunshine illuminated it brilliantly. "It's beautiful . . ."

He gently lifted her hand and slipped it on her finger. "To Egypt."

"To Egypt," she replied, nearly choking on the words, watching the jewels sparkle in the bright rays of light. "And a world without corsets."

He laughed. "You'll have to learn to create something more efficient."

"Tablecloths?"

He pulled a face; his eyes opened wide. "For Egyptian ladies?"

"I can sew marvelous clothing, too, Marcus." Her brows rose innocently. "They do wear clothing in Egypt, I hope."

"I've never noticed," he replied, pursing his lips.

She smiled, leaning against him, staring into the water fountain as he began to caress her back and neck with his long, strong fingers.

Seconds later, she breathed, "And your mother?"

He pulled her into him tightly and kissed the top of her head. "My mother is getting what she asked for, in every way." He laid his cheek in her hair. "I know everything about Christine's death, Mary. An accident in the hands of my mother."

She stiffened, but didn't back away or look up at him, satisfied simply to be in his embrace. "Tell me."

He let out a long, slow breath. "I will. All of it. But not now. My mother is taking it very hard." Skimming the pad of his thumb along her cheekbone, he added, "There's so much. It's . . . so complicated. Baudwin Fife will never have a straight nose again, however."

She giggled, cupping her mouth. "Marcus, you didn't."

"Somebody had to," he said defensively. "I only did what Christine couldn't do the night he took advantage of her."

Mary calmed in understanding, gazing at the trickling water in the fountain. "Your sister loved you, Marcus," she whispered.

He tensed his arms around her but she held to him.

"Yes, she did, as I loved her."

"You were right, you know," she said seconds later, her eyes tearing again, her throat tight.

He ran his lips along her hairline, breathing deeply. "About what?"

"That everything will work out in the end." At

last she pulled back and gazed into his eyes once more, laying her palm on his cheek. "It has."

"I know, my darling Mary," he agreed softly. "I know."

Epilogue

Cairo, Egypt
20 December 1855

Dearest Mother,

Thank you so much for your recent letters. I'm sorry I haven't been able to respond as often as I'd like, but I've been working extremely hard of late. There have been some major hieroglyph discoveries in Alexandria recently, and Mary and I will be joining a group of American scholars after the new year as we relocate to that great city. I am looking forward to it and will write you of our progress.

I also want to share some splendid news. Mary is expecting our first child in late summer. I'm thrilled, of course, and am hoping for a girl to dote on. If we are blessed, we intend to name her Christine. I hope you'll be pleased with that decision.

Mary has been sewing for Egyptian ladies to pass the time, but quite frankly, she prefers working with me. I'm sure you wouldn't approve, but she has such an appetite for learning that I've begun to teach her to transcribe ancient texts. Of course, you needn't worry that I will take care of her and do what's best for the baby. By this time next year, you will be a grandmother.

We are enjoying each other and our marriage very much. Please have no worries that everything in our lives will work out as it should. I do miss you, and George, and was pleased to learn he plans to marry next spring. The Lady Sarah Gregory is a good choice, and God willing, there will soon be an heir.

Please keep writing. I look forward to each letter you send and enjoy hearing from you. I hope you had a lovely Christmas. Give my best to the Coswells when next you see them.

As ever,
Your loving son,
Marcus

*Chestnuts are roasting by the fire this holiday season,
so curl up with the best in romance from Avon Books*

THE IRRESISTIBLE MACRAE by Karen Ranney
An Avon Romantic Treasure

Iona McKinsey is captivated by dashing stranger James
MacRae, whose kisses ignite a burning passion deep within
her heart. But the dutiful daughter is promised in marriage
to another man—and responsibility comes before love. Or
does it?

RISKY BUSINESS by Suzanne MacPherson
An Avon Contemporary Romance

When beautiful but klutzy model Marla Meyers takes one
pill too many, it becomes Tom Riley's job to keep an eye
on her. Yet as passion flares between them, who is going to
protect Marla from a sexy heartbreaker like Tom?

THE MACKENZIES: COLE by Ana Leigh
An Avon Romance

The last time Cole MacKenzie saw Maggie O'Shea, she was
a scruffy kid with dirt on her cheeks. Now the tomboy is all
grown up, but she hasn't outgrown her teenage crush. And
she's about to prove to this cowboy how much of a woman
she's become.

HER SCANDALOUS INTENTIONS by Sari Robins
An Avon Romance

The dashing Duke of Girard believes Charlotte Hastings
holds the key to ensnaring a traitorous villain . . . so he kid-
naps the spirited miss and claims her as his betrothed!
Charlotte is willing to maintain this ruse, but succumbing to
her "fiancé's" sinful charms is another matter.

REL 1102

Avon Romantic Treasures

*Unforgettable, enthralling love stories,
sparkling with passion and adventure
from Romance's bestselling authors*

Have you ever dreamed of writing a romance?

*And have you ever wanted
to get a romance published?*

Perhaps you have always wondered how to
become an Avon romance writer?
We are now seeking the best and brightest undiscovered
voices. We invite you to send us your query letter to
avonromance@harpercollins.com

What do you need to do?

Please send no more than two pages telling us
about your book. We'd like to know its setting—is it
contemporary or historical—and a bit about the hero,
heroine, and what happens to them.

Then, if it is right for Avon we'll ask to see part of the
manuscript. Remember, it's important that you have
material to send, in case we want to see your story quickly.

Of course, there are no guarantees of publication,
but you never know unless you try!

*We know there is new talent just waiting
to be found! Don't hesitate . . . send us
your query letter today.*

*The Editors
Avon Romance*